Fluorescence

The Complete Tetralogy

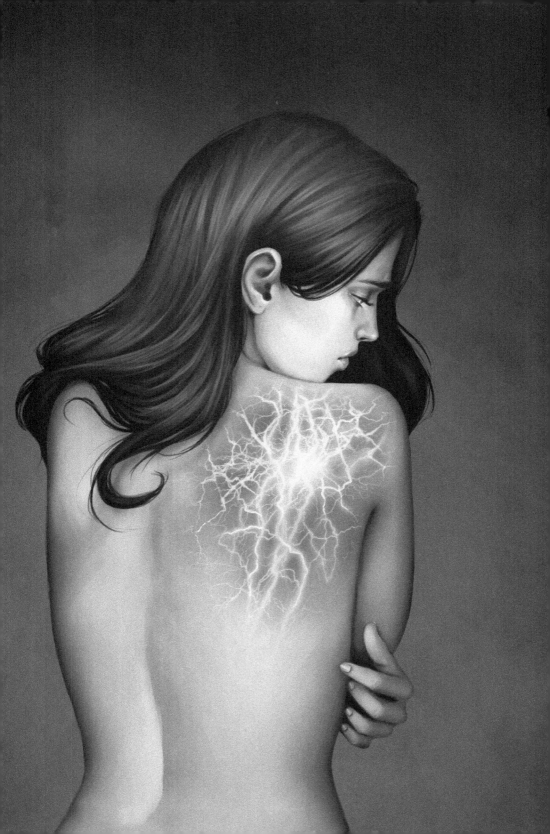

BOOK I

FIRE STARTER

·　　·　　·

My name's Alice Green. It's not my real name, but if you knew what was going on, you'd understand why I need to be careful.

Adults warn you your body will start going through "changes" when you get older. Mine did, but they weren't normal "raging hormones, mood swings, ew—periods" kind of things. Weird stuff happens, your body does gross things and then you start looking at boys differently.

Yeah. That happened—a while ago.

This is different.

I've been infected with something I can't fully explain—bioluminescence—fluorescent energy. I can't control when it appears. It's volatile, and that's what scares me the most.

I hope, for your sake, this never happens to you or to anyone you care about.

I hope you will never wake to discover this fire burning beneath your skin—this spark of living, breathing color crackling through your veins.

·　　·　　·

Chapter 1

Why me?

"Eric and his dog?" Sam asked, her brow furrowing.

Stanley—the bully's accomplice.

"Yeah. Creeps staked out the main hall this afternoon, and I was late for class because I had to take the long way around. Again." I rubbed my shoulder, recalling the brief spell of pain I'd felt following my mad dash down the hall after the bell had rung. I had never been much of an athlete.

"I'm so sorry, Alice. I wish they'd stop. I mean, really, don't they have anything better to do with their time besides make fun of *you*?" She rolled her eyes. "If they actually studied as much as they annoyed people, they'd be geniuses."

After school, I sat cross-legged, bundled up in a blanket on my best friend Sam's couch, balancing a bowl of buttery popcorn in my lap.

"I know, right?" I scooped out a greasy handful and shoveled some into my mouth. "I wish *they'd* get picked on by someone for a change."

"Enter chainsaw psycho! VROOM!" Sam lifted her arms up over her head and lumbered toward me, grinning maniacally and making sputtering sounds that drowned out the movie playing behind her.

I laughed so hard, she broke character and started giggling. No wonder she snagged the best parts in our school plays right out from under me. She *was* an amazing actress.

Really, though, I'd never wish for anyone to get hurt the way people did in horror movies—like the ones we loved to watch—but Eric and Stanley had been nipping at my heels since middle school. Using every excuse they could to make fun of me. Just because my name is Alice, doesn't mean I have anything to do with white rabbits and Cheshire cats.

Sam had been with me through it all. She was the only person I really hung out with in and out of school. We had sleepovers about once a month where we watched cheesy B horror flicks all evening and stuffed our faces with as much junk food as we could in a few hours.

Zombies. Ax murderers. This movie had both. An exaggerated death scene in the movie we were watching had me laughing so much I snorted like a pig. Gallons of bright red fake blood spewed at the camera and my bowl bounced right out of my lap.

I scrambled to catch it, but a few pieces of popcorn tumbled out onto the floor. Sam craned her neck back to look at me and chuckled, her wild curly red hair bouncing around her face.

"Popcorn overboard?" she asked with a smirk. "Uh, yeah. Sorry." I faked a dumb toothy grin and batted my lashes. We both chuckled and then I wrapped myself back up in my blanket and secured the popcorn bowl between my pretzled legs.

As we sat watching the movie, I felt a warm sensation creep up my spine, starting off mild and then blazing into day-old sunburn pain within seconds. I rolled my shoulder back and forth and rubbed it with my other hand, hiding my discomfort from Sam. It was probably leftover from my impromptu sprint this afternoon. A muscle pull or...

I doubled over. A sharp ache stabbed through me, shooting up my spine like an electrical shock.

"Oh my God. Are you okay? What is it?" Sam turned around and tilted her head to the side.

I almost cried out, but I gritted my teeth instead, trying to suck it up. "Ugh. It's... nothing." I shrugged, pulling the blanket up over my shoulders to fight the chill going through me. "I'll be back in a minute." After setting the popcorn down, I slid off the couch and trudged to the bathroom, clasping the blanket closed at my neck.

I shut the door, flipped on the bathroom light and tossed the blanket over the shower curtain rod. My arm pulsed with deep, throbbing pain and the first thing I thought was that something had stung or bitten me. A spider?

It felt like there was boiling liquid pumping beneath my skin. I gritted my teeth. A sickness swirled in my stomach. I leaned closer to the mirror and turned so I could see my back, sliding the spaghetti-strap of my sleep shirt over while twisting myself further around to look over my shoulder at my reflection. A large blotchy patch of skin blazed red. Hot to touch.

"Oh my God..." I whimpered beneath my breath.

I had to call Mom. There was something very wrong with me.

A creepy, static-charge feeling made my hair stand on end. The pain was quickly intensifying. I turned on the faucet and splashed the area with a handful of cool water. It calmed the inflammation, turning it more pink than red.

The sharp pain struck me again and I gasped. The first attack had been brief, but this one... wouldn't go away. Burning. Spreading. I forced myself up to look into the mirror, and then had to cover my mouth to muffle a shriek.

My back pulsed with an ugly neon-green glow, as if someone had cracked open and leaked instant glow stick over me. Thin bright green veins stretched up and over my shoulder toward my collar bone and down to the small of my back. It was brightest in the center—over my shoulder blade—and faded as it spread and forked out in various directions.

I pulled myself up onto the bathroom counter and scooted closer to the mirror, contorting so I was nose to nose with myself. My hot breath fogged the mirror, distorting my reflection. I rubbed it clear with my forearm.

The branching neon veins crawled beneath my skin, brightening and dimming rhythmically. A subtle dust-like aura leached out through the surface, casting off particles of glimmering light that quickly vanished.

My hands trembled uncontrollably. My pulse raced.

So bright. Such a vivid green. Disgusting. My stomach... felt sicker. Churning. I was about to throw up.

I took a squirt of hand soap from the counter and rubbed it vigorously against the skin. I scrubbed it nearly raw with a wet washcloth, but all it did was cause me to hurt more. Nothing changed. The green continued to glow, fading in and out, the tiny lines of color still spreading across my back.

Unreal.

Toxic.

I felt light-headed—dizzy. Breathing hard.

I *had* to call mom *now*. Before...

Ugh. Black and white dots speckled my vision, flashing in and out like stars.

No.

Not a panic attack. Not now.

Breathe. Just breathe!

Deep breaths. In through my nose. Out through my mouth. Slowly.

Get a grip!

I pulled my phone out of my pocket but it slipped from my shaking hands and fell onto the bathroom floor.

"No!" I bent over and scooped it up.

What if Mom thinks it's drugs? Sam and I would *never*—ever. We'd made a promise. *But...*

"Ya alright in there, Allie?" Sam knocked on the door.

I gasped.

"Uh, yeah," I replied, my voice breaking.

"Ya sure? You've been in there for, like, ever. Annnnd I heard ya squeal. Find a bug or something?" Her voice shot up an octave. She wasn't too enthusiastic about bugs either.

"Just... feeling a little sick."

"Like *period* sick? Or do you need some pink stuff?"

"I... don't know. It might be... another panic attack. I don't know. I have to call my mom." I tossed the blanket over my shoulders, hoping it would hide the glow, and cracked opened the bathroom door. "I'll be okay. I think I should go home though."

"Awww, poor baby." Sam reached toward my shoulder. I shifted, dodging her hand and her jaw dropped. "Wh-what is it?"

"I... I just don't feel good." I shuffled past. "I'm sorry, Sam." The heat diminished and I started feeling a little relief from the pain.

Her lips wrinkled into a frown and my heart tightened. Her big brown puppy-dog eyes put my stomach in even more knots. I'd known her since the second grade—my best friend in the whole world—but I couldn't bring myself to tell her what I'd just seen in the mirror.

I texted my mom.

She replied within a minute. Record speed.

MOM: Be right over...

I wiggled the phone for Sam to see.

"She's coming now. Probably be here in ten or fifteen."

"Okay." Sam sniffled, pretending that she was about to cry. "I'll miss you," she muttered, impersonating a small child.

"I know." I chuckled and tightened my blanket around my shoulders. I couldn't forget *why* I was leaving early. The pain had let up, luckily, and my stomach had calmed down. Just being near Sam made me feel better. "We'll finish our movie another night, I guess." I grabbed my purse from off the coffee table and made my way to the front door. Sam tagged close beside me and then dashed ahead to get the door.

I stepped onto the porch and shivered. My furry kitty slippers weren't much help against the brisk night air. I started bouncing on the soles of my feet to fight the chill.

"I'm sorry I messed up our night. I wanted to stay over. I really did." I turned to her and smiled as honestly as I could. "I just don't feel well." I held my belly. "It might be the new meds or something."

Sam nodded and smiled, stretching out her arms to hug me. "I know and I still love you, Alice! I hope you feel better really soon."

"I will."

She squeezed tightly and I grunted as she choked a little breath from me. Best hugger *ever*.

Mom pulled into the driveway.

"Bye!" I waved and rushed to the car. Mom had the door propped open for me. I ducked down and hopped into my seat, yanking my blanket in behind me so it wouldn't catch in the door frame as I pulled it shut. I clicked my seatbelt into place.

Sam waved frantically from the driveway, shivering and bounding up and down in place with a huge goofy grin on her face. Poor thing hadn't even grabbed a jacket on the way out.

Mom's eyes were focused on the road; she kept nibbling her lip and flexing her fingers on the steering wheel. I didn't know what to say. We'd be home in a few minutes.

"I'll be okay, Mom," I said, breaking the awkward silence.

"It's okay. I'll take you back to the doctor tomorrow. If it is that new medication, Dr. Eliza will have to get you something different. Don't take any more tonight." She veered her head toward me. "You didn't take your second dose, did you?"

"No. Not yet." I shook my head and she went back to focusing on the road. We pulled into the driveway and I tugged my blanket up again, clutching my purse with my other hand.

"You should head to bed. It's late." Mom punched a button on the keypad by the door and the garage door closed. I went upstairs to my room.

Chapter 2

Being a teenager sucks.

As a freshman in high school, I thought I was over the awkward phase. I didn't tell my mom about what had happened. She probably would have freaked out and taken me to the hospital. I didn't need to be poked and prodded.

Before bed, I did a bunch of googling and couldn't find anything useful. Glowing skin, not exactly something found in a respectable Wiki. If it's not on the internet, it doesn't exist. Right?

I texted Sam to let her know I felt better. It couldn't be the meds. I didn't see neon green skin on the list of side effects. Besides, I had *anemia,* not... cancer. I hadn't been getting chemo or even had an X-Ray that I could remember. Iron and B12 don't make you radioactive.

I stretched the collar of my t-shirt, pulled it down my shoulder and craned my neck to look back. It had stopped glowing, but I knew what I had seen, and I wouldn't forget it.

I rubbed my shoulder with my hand and sighed. *When will it happen again? Will it? What if I can't cover it up next time? Would it scare Mom if I told her about it? Or Sam?*

My internet research wasn't doing me any good. Maybe it was a fluke. Maybe it would never happen again.

·   ·   ·

I sat in the front row of the bus with one foot creeping into the aisle.

"Feeling better?" Sam smiled, nudging me in the arm with her elbow. We hit a speed bump and I clutched my bag.

"Yeah. Mom's taking me to the doctor this afternoon, though."

"That's good." She nodded. "Better safe than sorry."

"I guess." I shrugged and heaved a sigh that was probably loud enough for the kids in the back of the bus to hear. "I haaaate going to the doctor. Why can't I just be a normal kid without stupid junk wrong with me?"

"You're perfect!" Sam's curly red hair bounced on and off her shoulder as she nodded matter-of-factly.

The driver braked and pulled the lever that opened the bus door. Sam straightened up. "OMG!" She jabbed me in the arm.

"What?" I groaned beneath my breath.

"Shh!"

A tall boy dressed in dark jeans and a weathered brown-leather jacket jogged up the steps. He grabbed onto the metal hand railing in front of us and the bus driver flipped the lever, closing the doors behind him. Sam held her breath. The boy had a roguish, rough-around-the-edges look, and a confident air about him that set him apart. I tried not to stare at his pretty, light-brown feathered hair.

The bus started up and the boy stumbled forward a step. I instinctively reached out to help but he had already regained his balance, chuckling at the misstep. He then headed down the aisle, eying up the back row where Eric and Stanley sat.

"That's the new kid I heard about," Sam whispered, giggling. "Lordy, he's cuuuuute."

"Hush!" I flashed her a dirty look.

I glanced over my shoulder. Okay, so maybe he *was* cute. Definitely not pretty-boy Loki cute, though. He reminded me of a young Wolverine with longer, shaggier hair just framing his ears and the collar of his jacket perked up around his neck.

He told the two boys to pick other seats and I smiled. *Payback.* It's a good day when bullies meet their match. Maybe this one wouldn't pick on me.

"Told ya." Sam smirked, nudging me in the ribs with her elbow. She'd caught me grinning.

"Shut up."

I hunched over in my seat—a telltale sign there was an attractive boy around—and pulled my knees up to my chest, pressing my heels into the guardrail in front of me. The new boy's reflection shimmered in the wide rearview mirror hanging just above the front windshield. I couldn't help but watch him.

His hand had almost brushed mine when he'd grabbed for the railing. *Almost.* I wondered if he'd noticed me...

"Maybe he'll be in your class," Sam whispered, and then gasped. "Or mine. Maybe he'll be in mine." Her excited high-pitched voice reminded me of a cartoon squirrel.

"Sam... Please." I crossed my arms and looked away.

"Feet off the railing," the bus driver scolded.

· · ·

Of course the new boy, Brian, *was* in my class. He had been moving to sit in the very back corner where no one would bother him, but the teacher had asked him to come "make some new friends" further toward the front.

Next to who?

Me.

When he came down the aisle and walked past, I caught a faint whiff of his scent. I mean, he *looked* all rugged with that I've-been-living-in-the-woods-for-a-week kind of style, but with a nice clean smell like that, he obviously hadn't been.

Mr. Johnson told us to go to Chapter 8. I cracked open my history book and took a mechanical pencil out of my bag. The teacher started rattling off a list of things we needed to know for the next exam.

"Hey. Got a pen?"

"Huh?" I looked up.

"Pencil? Pen? You got one I can borrow?" It was Brian.

"Uh, yeah. One sec." I dug around in my bag and then pulled out a purple ink pen. It was all I could spare.

"Here ya go." I stretched my arm out to the side and handed it to him, avoiding eye contact so my dumb cheeks wouldn't get all pink or something.

"Thanks." He began scribbling something down and then suddenly pulled back, surprised. "*Purple*?"

I slouched in my seat. "It's all I have. Sorry."

"It's cool. Whatever." He wrote something in a notepad tucked beneath his book. I couldn't see exactly what it was, but it definitely wasn't schoolwork.

.   .   .

What felt like the longest class in the history of high school had finally ended. I rushed off to the parking lot to meet my mom. I tossed my bag in the back and flopped into the passenger seat.

Fifteen minutes later, we pulled into the clinic parking lot.

Before I could explain, Mom exploded into a full-on rampage about how the new medication had made me sick and how the doctor needed to be more careful with what she prescribed teen girls.

"It's only a supplement," Dr. Eliza defended, trying to stay calm amongst my mother's allegations. "It's highly uncommon it would cause any issues. Still, let's do some blood work and see if we can get her on a different dosage."

I liked Dr. Eliza. I'd had her for a doctor forever, I think. She was really kind and I never felt weird about going to see her. My mother, on the other hand, always looked for an excuse to defend her "perfect little girl." She had worked as a receptionist at an urgent care clinic way back before marrying my dad. She's seen and heard her share of medical mishaps, and because of it, doesn't trust doctors much anymore.

The thought of getting blood drawn made my stomach churn. I *hate* needles. Getting a flu shot practically had me in tears. A quick, measly little flu shot! Now I had even more to worry about. What else would the test reveal? What if the green light came back right in the middle of the doctor's office?

Dr. Eliza's nurse led me over to the lab and the technician asked me to sit down in a padded vinyl-covered chair. I laid my arm down on the oversized armrest and a lump formed in my throat.

The technician wrapped a thick rubber band around my forearm and twisted it into a knot. "Make a fist," she said, and tapped the inside of my arm a few times. The tourniquet squeezed my arm so hard, I winced.

I grunted in pain as the needle pierced the skin.

"You can relax your hand now," she said.

The pinch of the needle didn't hurt too much—the band choking my arm was the worst part. I moaned beneath my breath and the woman patted my shoulder with her gloved hand.

"Almost done, sweetie." She undid the tourniquet and changed out another tube of blood. I flinched. The faint clicking sound of her removing one tube and plugging another into the thing in my arm disturbed me. I had to look away.

Think happy thoughts. Don't think about the light. The green....

Rainbows. Unicorns. Purple bunny rabbits.

"All done." She withdrew the needle and pressed a rolled-up

piece of gauze onto the punctured spot. "Hold this a moment."

I held the gauze with two fingers and breathed a sigh of relief.

She stretched a piece of sticky bandage tape over the gauze and patted me on the back. "See? You lived."

I shrugged.

"Results will be in within a week. The doctor should call you."

"Thanks." I stood up and headed back to the lobby where Mom waited.

Mom was on her phone surfing the internet when I entered.

"How'd it go?" She sat up in the chair and tucked her phone into her purse.

"Yay. I lived." I waved a tiny imaginary victory flag in my hand.

"That's a silly thing to say, Alice."

"Hey, the technician said it. I'm just quoting her."

"Hmm." Mom put her hand on her hip. "Are you ready to go?"

Someone in the waiting room started hacking—one of those horrible phlegmy, congested coughs.

I made a beeline for the exit.

Chapter 3

We'd just gotten home from the doctor's office when my phone vibrated.

SAM: HALP!
SAM: Math homework! Study 2NITE?
ME: SURE
SAM: Yay! CU soon ^_^

She ended the conversation by uploading a meme photo of a Persian cat wearing an ugly Christmas sweater. I chuckled and shoved my phone into the side pocket of my jeans. Sam was crazy, and I loved her like a sister. She was my best friend and nothing would change that, but...

Had I known all she would do *all* night was gossip about the new boy, Brian, I would *never* have agreed to let her come over and "study."

"I mean, OMG, he's really cute! You and him should totally hook up. I bet your kids would be gorgeous!"

"Ick! Sam!" I shoved her in the arm. "Kids? Are you crazy?"

"That handsome dark hair. Those pretty... whatever color eyes he has."

Hazel...

"Bet they are dreamy. He can probably rock a skateboard. Or he owns a motorcycle. Or he's building one or... Oh! I bet he's one of those guys who will get his license as soon as he turns sixteen. Seriously. You don't think he's cute? Come on."

She hadn't taken a single breath.

"If you're so in love with him, why don't *you* ask him out?"

She pulled back. "Me?" A nervous half-laugh came out of her mouth. "Well, you know I'm totally holding out for Brent. At least until he notices me. Then, maybe. Anyway, don't change the topic! Brian! Cute?"

Brent Cole. One of the most popular boys at our school and *totally* out of our league.

"I dunno, Sam." I rolled my eyes and groaned, wanting to avoid the question altogether. It was the tenth time she'd asked. I hadn't stopped thinking about Brian since he'd borrowed my stupid purple pen—and never given it back. Sam was making things worse.

"Hah!" She tumbled backward onto some fluffy heart-shaped pillows and clutched her tablet, giggling like a hyena. "I knew it!" She rolled forward and pointed at me, flashing a maniacally toothy grin. "You like him, don't ya?"

"Shut up and let's finish this homework." I rubbed the soft flesh at the inside of my elbow. "I'm still hurting a little." The red pinprick was surrounded by a nasty purplish halo. "Sitting here all cramped up isn't making me feel better."

Sam grimaced and then resituated herself on my bed, cross-legged, her math book balancing open on one knee and her tablet teetering on the other, a social networking site left open. No doubt she had already searched for Brian on it.

I slouched over my book and tapped randomly on my graphing calculator keys.

Variable expressions. *Bleh.*

Would Brian ever return my pen? Not that the pen was valuable, but...

"Oh my god..." Sam's notebook fell onto the floor and I

jerked my head toward her.

"What? What now?"

As if she had seen a ghost, she backed herself up against the headboard, her feet digging into the bedspread and a hand covering her mouth.

"What is *that*?" She pointed at me frantically and my heart skipped a beat.

Oh no. Not here. Not in front of my (sweet, adorable, beloved) big-mouthed friend. I immediately craned my neck to look at my shoulder. Neon-green light shone through the grey fabric of my t-shirt, flaring up even brighter than it had before.

"It's okay, Sam." I covered my shoulder with my hand and used my other to reach out to her. She withdrew, cringing. "I *think* it's okay, at least. Really."

"What the heck is that?" She leaned forward and squinted. "Seriously. WTF?" Sam scooted closer, curious now that she could see I wasn't freaking out.

"Look, I don't know, okay?" I crumpled over and tried to cover it up with all of my fingers but light still shone through. I fanned my hair out and covered it that way instead. The skin radiated with heat. "I thought it was the meds but... it can't be."

"You're glowing! That is so freaky!" Her eyes widened with excitement and she reached out to touch my shoulder, but then jerked her hand back fearfully mid-motion. "Are you radioactive? Cause, that would be so not cool."

"I don't know, Sam. I already said I didn't know."

"When did this start?"

"The other night, while we were watching movies."

"When you left early? Oh my God, why didn't you tell me?" Her jaw dropped like she had never been so offended.

Because...

"Did the doctor say anything?"

I shook my head and shrugged.

"You didn't tell her? You are crazy!"

"I didn't want to scare Mom, or my doctor. This isn't normal, ya know?"

Sam's lips wrinkled to one side. "I guess not."

The burning grew more intense and I rubbed my shoulder vigorously, sucking in a breath through my teeth.

"You okay? Does it hurt?"

"It burns like crazy, actually."

"Is it a rash?" Sam tipped her head to the side.

I rolled my eyes again. *"Yeah, it's a rash*, Sam. I don't know what it is." I took a deep breath and closed my eyes, concentrating on clearing my mind.

Deep breath.

Deep breath.

The heat began to dissipate.

"Hey, it's going away," Sam said, perking up from her seat and pointing.

"Good." I looked. Both the light and color had faded. "That's what happened the other night, too. It just went away."

"Any idea what it's caused by?"

"No, not really. Last time it happened was when we were just sitting around. This time, we were... um."

I suddenly pictured the new boy and immediately my thoughts started to drift.

"Talking about Brian!" Sam beamed.

"Yeah..."

"Maybe it comes and goes when you're excited or interested or something. Like a radioactive tell. Huh? Huh?" She nudged me in the arm, thrilled with herself.

I cocked an eyebrow. "Radioactive? It's not radioactive. It... can't be. I'd probably be dead, so stop saying that, please. You're not helping."

Sam reached to the floor to scoop up her things and handed the tablet to me. "How's your Google-fu?"

"I already tried that," I replied, taking it from her. The hairs on the back of my neck perked up and a creepy-crawly, pins-and-needles sensation washed over my whole body. My fingertips tingled as I swiped over an icon on the screen and the pixels started flashing random colors.

I lost focus.

A jolt of energy surged through me like an electrical shock. I tossed the tablet onto the floor. The screen went black and a loud buzzing noise emitted from the speaker.

Sam reached for it but I stopped her with a stiff swing of my arm. "No!" I said. "It's not safe."

"You broke it?" Sam squealed.

I took a deep breath and looked her in the eye.

She stared back at me, her forehead wrinkling. "If we broke my Dad's tablet, he's gonna freak, you know?"

I trembled. The hairs on my neck perked up again and my stomach suddenly felt *really* sick. I shook my head and swallowed hard, holding onto myself tightly and rubbing my forearms. A chill swept through the air.

"I think that's the least of our worries right now, Sam."

Chapter 4

I took a seat in math class and pulled my notebook and calculator from my bag. Sam came in and sat beside me.

It had been a few days since the incident. I felt better, but we hadn't talked much about what had happened. She was pretty ruffled by the whole ordeal and jokingly suggested she'd suffered hallucinations brought on by too many sodas and potato chips.

Sam kept eying my shoulder during class. It was super awkward—like she thought an alien was about to pop out of me at any moment.

Her dad had been briefly upset about the fried tablet. We'd told him it had shorted out while we were searching the internet and he'd shrugged it off as an inconvenience, saying something about it still being under warranty. Her parents weren't exactly hard up for money, at least. I still felt bad, though.

Halfway through class, a folded up square of paper inched into view, shuttled toward me by Sam's hand. I furrowed my brow and gave her "the look." The "are you trying to get us into trouble" look. She was always passing notes in class and the teacher wasn't keen about it, even if it was less distracting than texting.

I propped up my book and slipped the note between the open pages so I could unfold it unnoticed.

"Walk home today?" it read in scribbled ink.

On days when the weather was nice, I walked home from school with Sam. Sometimes we'd do a little shopping at the strip mall on the way and then she'd stay for dinner. My mom would drive her home afterwards.

I looked at her and nodded. "Yeah," I mouthed the word. She squinted and made excited fists, pretending to squeal.

Mrs. Prather's head rose and she peered over her computer monitor to shoot us a dirty look. I put my nose into my book and went back to my work.

.   .   .

Brian sauntered into history class—a few minutes late, as usual—and plopped down in the empty chair next to me.

"Last warning, Brian." Mr. Johnson glared at him snidely and shook his head before going back to whatever he had been typing on his computer.

I tried to ignore Brian, but it was difficult. I felt him watching me and kept locking eyes with him whenever I glanced away from my book. Then, he'd go back to scribbling something in the notebook which he kept opening and closing every couple of minutes. I couldn't tell what he was doing, but he was using the pen he still hadn't given back.

Class zipped by. I closed my book bag and set it on my desk, slipping out a little stick of pink lip gloss from the outside pocket and swiping some across my lips. Only English remained before window-shopping time with Sam on the walk home. Too bad none of my friends were in English class.

"Hey... Alice, was it?"

I turned toward Brian and fumbled to snap the cap onto the lip gloss. "Yeah," I replied, trying not to let my gaze linger on his rich hazel eyes. There was a small dark brown spot in his left iris.

"You've lived around here for a while, right?"

I nodded, recalling that the teacher had mentioned something about Brian being from... Montana?

"You know somewhere close by where we could grab a burger?" He tucked my purple pen above his ear. "The school cafeteria sucks and I've only seen pizza and Chinese places around so far."

I cocked an eyebrow and stared at him blankly. New burger dives popped up almost every day in our city. He'd have to close his eyes to *not* see one.

Right as I opened my mouth to say something sarcastic, my good old brain stopped me. *Wait.* He wasn't actually asking me about a burger place. He was... asking me out... in some weird way. I had clearly heard him say *"we"* could grab a burger, not "I."

"Uh..." I stammered, trying to think of a place where we could go. "I know of a few," was all I managed to get out. Burgers weren't my favorite but, geeze, he seemed nice. Not to mention *really* cute. His messy, satiny brown hair complimented his eyes. And his modest grin.

Dang it. Mom would kill me if she caught me alone with a boy before I was old enough to drive.

"Great!" He ruffled a hand through his hair. Brian messed with his hair a lot. "Wanna hit one up after school?"

My chest tightened with excitement and I tried to make my reply not sound too eager. "I'll have to ask my mom." I felt dumb saying it.

"Oh. Okay. Whatever." He grabbed his books out of the metal basket below his desk and shoved them into his black backpack. "Let me know what she says, okay? I'll catch up with you outside after class. See ya, Al."

I meant to wave goodbye as he jogged out of the room, but all I could do was stare.

"It's Alice..."

.   .   .

The smell of frying oil and grilling burgers saturated the

building. My stomach grumbled. We were seated across from each other in a bright red booth. Someone's nearby brownie sundae caught my eye and I sighed longingly.

College students, likely from the neighboring university, were piled into the place. A family with two little kids sat behind us. The toddlers bounced around on the benches, making my seat vibrate, until their mother scolded them and they sat down. Finally, a bleach blonde waitress who looked barely out of high school herself, came by and introduced herself as Jennifer.

"Welcome to J's Grill. Is this going to be on one check or..."

"Two," I replied before she'd gotten the second part out. I grinned at Brian.

We both ordered sweet tea and Jennifer brought them to our table in a flash.

I sucked tea through a straw while grazing over the menu. Surprisingly, Mom had been quite cool about the whole "Mind if the new boy and I grab dinner before I come home tonight?" thing. Though I'd forgotten to tell Sam until Brian and I were halfway to J's. I sent her a text earlier while we were waiting for a table.

She had seemed heartbroken at first to know I wouldn't be joining her. The heartbreak had only lasted until she'd brewed up a silly motivational text about how lucky I was to be going out with Brian and how she was "missing out" on a date with the next Tom Cruise. I had to roll my eyes and stifle a laugh. She was so 80's it hurt.

Age difference aside, if I squinted and tilted my head, I could see a *slight* resemblance. Cruise was *so* last century, though.

Besides, it was in no way a "date." Still, spending time with Brian one-on-one was making me super anxious.

"So, what are you getting?" Brian asked, peeking at me from around the side of his tall menu.

My purse chirped. Another text from Sam. I quickly silenced my phone and smiled apologetically at him.

"I don't know," I replied. "Probably fish and chips. I don't like burgers much."

"Oh?" Brian lowered his menu. "Then why did you want to come here?"

"I figured I could get something different. Didn't want to be rude." I looked at him and a little smile tugged at his lips. Butterflies started twirling in my stomach.

Stop it, butterflies. Stop it.

"Aw, that was really nice of you. Tell you what. I'll get whatever you're having. If you like it, it must be okay." He slid his menu to the edge of the table and leaned back.

Jennifer swung back around and pulled a little notepad out of her apron. The back cover had a collage of sparkly rose stickers on it.

"So, what are you having, hun?" She looked at me and clicked her pen.

"Fish and chips, please. Waffle fries."

"Anything else?"

I shook my head.

"And you, sweetheart?"

"I'll have what she's having." Brian winked at me and I sunk down in my seat.

Jennifer made for the kitchen and I propped my elbows up on the table and rested my head in my hands. "You didn't just order the same stuff as me to impress me or something, right?"

Brian laughed. "Hey, if I haven't impressed you by now, I may never."

I tried to hide a chuckle. Oh my God, he was cocky, but in a charming, I'm-just-trying-to-make-you-laugh kind of way.

I liked it.

"I'm not a picky eater anyway," he added. "I'm so hungry,

fried fish is as good as grilled cow at this point." He took off his leather jacket, rolled it into a ball and shoved it into the corner of the booth. I liked the mossy-green t-shirt he had on underneath.

Movie and sports memorabilia pieces dangled in every nook and cranny of the place. Posters, jerseys, autographed celebrity photos and even some license plates from different states were hanging on the walls. Brian seemed quite entranced.

I let him take it all in for a few minutes until I finally worked up the nerve to ask him a question that had been burning in my mind for days.

"So, what is it you're always writing in that notebook of yours?"

He jerked his head toward me, stunned by the question.

"*If...* you don't mind me asking?"

"Oh... it's nothing. Just some... uh... comics I'm working on." He poked at his silverware, rearranging the fork and knife. "They're not that great, though."

I leaned closer. *An artist?*

"Can I see them? Please? I promise I won't laugh or anything. I love artwork."

He shifted in his seat and wrinkled his lips. "Well, uh..."

"Please?" I scooted closer and smiled.

"Aw, alright." He unzipped his backpack. "But you promised not to laugh," he said, pointing a finger at me.

Out came a stack of notebooks. I had no idea he owned so many. I'd only seen one at a time in class. He peeled one covered in navy blue off the top and passed it to me, first prying it open to a page somewhere near the middle. There, a burly, wolf-like humanoid had a flailing, tigerish cat in a ferocious death grip. The lines of the drawings were thick and rigid and the image really put the "graphic" in "graphic novel."

"How old are you, Brian?" I leaned down to take a closer

look at the details.

"Fifteen. Why?"

It looked as though he might pull the notebook away from me so I put down a finger and stopped him so I could take it in further.

The fur on the back of the wolf-man's neck was beautifully drawn. I'd never personally known anyone who could create such detailed original art.

"No reason. I would never have imagined a fifteen-year-old could do something like this. This looks amazing. Um... Is that a severed arm in his other hand?"

"Yeah. Do you think it's *good*?" He looked surprised.

I nodded without saying a word and carefully turned the page to find another image of the hulking wolf-man. This time, he was pictured howling up at the moon while a shadowy skull looked on from high in the sky. "These are gorgeous. Do you have more?"

A big toothy grin spread across Brian's face and he excitedly slipped another notebook from out of the pile and slid it over to me. This one had a familiar maroon cover. I recalled it from history class. My purple pen was still tucked into the spirals on the binding.

"This one is my newest," he said, opening the cover to show me the first page. It was a masked man wearing an old-style tunic with a hooded cape blowing in the wind; tribal designs adorned his costume. His hood had a pair of deer antlers protruding from it, and he was holding a long bow. A lot like Robin Hood, but with some serious modern super hero flare. I'd never seen anything like it.

"So, who is this guy?" I asked. The tribal designs alone probably could have put some well-known artists out of work.

"He's a sort of anti-hero who I've been developing for a while. This is the first full profile I've done of him but he's missing his pet raven. I need to do some research on bird anatomy before I can attempt that. Anyway, this guy can't seem to decide if his heart is set on doing good things for people or just getting by and getting what he wants out of life. I don't know if it's a good idea or not but..."

"I think he's neat." I traced one of the antlers with my fingertip, feeling the bold lines of color my purple pen had left behind.

"I still haven't quite pounded out a name. I'm somewhere between Deer Heart, or The Stag, maybe."

I laughed. "The Stag? Boy, that's not manly in *any* way, now is it? So what does this guy do for a living when he's not in costume?"

"He's an elementary school science teacher." Brian's voice lowered. "And you said you wouldn't laugh." He frowned.

My own smile melted. "Oh, I didn't mean to, Brian. I'm sorry." I closed the notebook and lifted it close to my chest. "I think these drawings are amazing. I really do." I brushed my fingers affectionately over the cover and then I handed it back to him. "Please, don't be offended. I didn't mean it. I swear."

Jennifer came over with our food and set the baskets in front of us. "Anything you need?" she asked, looking at me first and then at Brian. "How about you, hun?" We shook our heads in unison.

Brian looked over his plate and picked up a waffle fry. I grabbed the ketchup bottle from the end of the table and squirted a little red mountain into the corner of my basket. Jennifer left.

Brian raised an eyebrow. "Having any fries with your ketchup?"

"Of course." I rolled my eyes and passed the bottle to him. "Hey. Why don't you tell me about your parents?" I dunked another fry and shoved it into my mouth, then wiped my greasy fingers on a napkin.

He poked at a piece of fish with his fork.

"My mom got a job as a secretary at a law firm downtown. That's why we moved here."

"And your dad?"

He nibbled at another fry and then sighed, looking away from me.

"Military. I've grown up in different schools almost every year. My dad was a real hard-ass, always getting on me for acting out and not studying enough. I couldn't stand being tutored by strangers and I hated being left alone with babysitters."

"Sorry to hear that. Has he lightened up at all?"

"He was killed overseas three years ago. A terrorist group snuck through and bombed them in the middle of the night. Damn cowards."

My appetite waned and I dropped a piece of fish back into the basket. I didn't like it when people swore but I could only begin to imagine how much pent up anger he had bottled up over the attack. "Oh. I'm... *really* sorry."

"It doesn't bother me anymore."

"How could *not* having a father *not* bother you? Wait. I'm sorry. It's none of my business. Never mind."

He picked at his food and crumpled over in his seat.

"He was disappointed in me because I wasn't like him. While I was growing up, all he'd ever do was complain about how I'd never be cut out for the military. To him, the military was everything."

I sipped my tea, trying to quickly come up with a thoughtful reply—anything to save the conversation. If I'd known him better, now would have been the perfect time to reach across the table and take his hand—and believe me, I thought about it—but that would have been weird. Right? We didn't know each other that well. Maybe he was one of those people who hated being touched. Maybe I had no business trying.

"I think you're an amazing artist, Brian. You'll do great

things. Years from now I'll see your comics in stores and remember how I knew that boy in high school. How I sat down and had fish and chips with him."

"You think so?"

"Definitely."

He smiled. It was forced, but it made my heart feel a little less heavy.

Chapter 5

"How did it go?" Sam asked in a sing-song voice, bumping her shoulder into mine.

"Horrible." I looked down at my shoes and kicked a pile of yellow leaves off the sidewalk.

"Why?" She exaggerated a frown. "What did you do?"

"What did *I* do? What kind of friend are you?" I folded my arms, tucking my gloved hands into my elbows. The chilly air made me shiver.

"Well, what happened?"

"I brought up his parents."

"Okay. And?"

"His dad's dead."

"Oh nooo!" Sam groaned then imitated stabbing herself in the heart. She straightened back up as soon as she saw the bus turning the corner. "You'll be lucky if he ever talks to you again," she whispered out of the side of her mouth.

"Thanks for the encouragement."

Sam shrugged. "I want a shot at him, too." She giggled. "If things don't work out with Brent."

All I could do was roll my eyes while the bus pulled up. We hopped on and took our usual seats in the front. Brian wouldn't be getting on for a few more stops and my poor heart was already atwitter. I glanced across the aisle and accidentally made eye contact with Eric—one of the boys who had been picking on me. I looked away.

By now, he and Stanley—who both used to sit in the far back—had become accustomed to sitting in the front, across from us. Brian had made it very clear his first week that he wouldn't tolerate it any other way. He was a little older and a little taller—more than enough to scare them into submission. They had never been very high up in the pecking order in school, just high enough to pick on quiet girls like me.

But when Brian got on the bus that day, things went a little differently.

"You said not to sit in the back anymore," Stanley whined, looking at an equally bewildered Eric for help.

"Well, I've changed my mind. Get going." Brian motioned toward the empty row in the far back.

"This isn't the time or place, boys," the bus driver snarled, veering her head toward them. "I don't care where you sit but you had better do it now!" She spoke through clenched teeth as she reached to jerk back the lever that closed the door.

The two boys shot up from their seats and bolted across the aisle into an open row behind us. Brian plopped down in the front, across from me.

Sam's eyes were wide and wild like she might explode from excitement at any second.

Brian didn't say a thing during the entire ride. He just sat there, peacefully staring out the window beside him. Sam and I stayed quiet, glancing over at him every now and then. The same part of me that had wanted to take his hand the other day now wanted me to get up from my aisle seat and slide onto the empty seat next to him.

I didn't.

At school, Brian lagged behind us in the parking lot, showing not a sliver of fear about being late for class. I wanted to say "Hi." I *really* did. But by the time I reached and opened up my locker, and gained the courage to turn and finally say it, he was at the opposite end of the hall. We didn't have history together until the afternoon, so it would be a while before we'd see each other again. I closed the locker door, spinning the combination lock a few times for good measure.

"Alice!"

I almost leapt out of my skin. Sam let out a high-pitched squeal.

"Oh my God, what?"

She was bouncing up and down in place flapping a bright-green flyer.

"Look! Look! Look!" She waved the paper back and forth like it was on fire. I couldn't see what it was.

I put a hand on my hip, narrowed my eyes and stared at her. She stopped jumping in place long enough to show it to me.

Freshman Holiday Dance, it read. Sam pointed a finger at the line below it. *Better than a stocking full of coal! Buy one ticket, get one FREE!* Her fingers trembled with excitement.

"Can we go? Please? Pretty please?"

"*We?*" I sighed and glanced past Sam. Brian was nowhere in sight. Only a handful of students still loitered in the hall.

"Well, yeah. You and me. Unless you and your *boyfriend...*"

"He's not my boyfriend." I clenched a fist, locking my knees. "Sam, I'm fourteen years old. If my dad heard you talking like this, he'd ban me from ever seeing Brian again."

"He's one to talk." She blew a raspberry. "You haven't seen him in for*ever.*"

"Sam, please."

"Really! He left your mom years ago and you're worried about what *he's* going to say about *you* having a boyfriend? I'd be more worried about your mom than—"

"He works a lot, okay? And even Mom might... Ugh." I growled.

Years after it had happened, bringing up the divorce still made my stomach turn. I wanted to curl up into a ball under a bridge and cry my eyes out. Maybe Dad wasn't in my life as much as he could have been. Or... at all anymore for that matter. But that didn't mean he had stopped loving me or wanting to spend time with me. He was just too busy with work. And his new wife...

"Sorry." Sam hung her head and scuffed her shoe against the floor. "I didn't mean to be a jerk."

I took the paper from her hand. The dance was right before Christmas break—exactly three weeks from today. Ever since elementary school, all Sam had ever dreamed about was going to a real school dance. This was her first chance and she was psyched. I, on the other hand, could have thought of a dozen other ways to spend my time. But it wasn't about me right now. I couldn't let my best friend down.

I bent to look her in the eye. "Guess we're going to have to go dress shopping soon, huh?" I put on the best enthusiastic smile I could, eyes and all.

Chapter 6

There was Sam, smack-dab in the middle of the auditorium doing the chicken-wing like there was no tomorrow. She looked like she was about to take off any second. Zoom! Right out of the building. It's a bird. It's a plane! Nope, it's just Sam. Goofy, lovable Sam.

I'd managed to convince my mom to let me go to the dance. Sam and I had bought beautiful, glittery dresses at the mall. Mine had cap sleeves and a full-length princess style skirt in cascading gradients of pink and teal. Not Christmas-y, but I wanted something that—if growth spurts allowed—I'd want to wear again.

Elegant. Magical. Didn't fit in with all of the green and red streamers hanging from the ceiling, but that didn't matter.

Sam had paired her knee-length—even in winter—red-velvet, rhinestone accented party dress with black tights and matching flats. She'd told me she didn't want anything to get in the way of her dancing. I wasn't at all concerned with the dancing part. Sam had basically paid for my evening's worth of snacks and punch in return for tagging along and playing dress up. All I had to do was stand on the sidelines and keep an eye on her.

"Hey, Alice."

The voice startled me and I jerked my head toward the sound.

Oh my God. I should have worn nicer shoes.

Should have done my hair up.

Should have...

"Hi, Brian. I... I didn't even know you'd be here." My cheeks grew warm.

He looked nice, donning a black suit and navy-blue dress shirt. No tie, but it worked in his favor. His brown hair had been swept back out of his face and tucked behind his ears. He had been cute before, but now...

My pulse raced and a lump formed in my throat. My hands got cold. I clasped them together.

"Nice dress." He skimmed over it. "Sparkly. It's very New Years... esq."

"That's what I was going for," I stammered, lying.

He had two plastic cups of pink punch in his hands and offered me one. I went to reach for it but hesitated.

"Something wrong?" he asked, looking down at the cup. "Did you not want anything?" He glanced at my empty hands.

"No, it's just that..." The voice of reason—Mom's—reminded me not to take a drink from someone when I hadn't seen where it had come from. He *seemed* trustworthy.

"Oh, wait. I get it. I'll get you another one if you want to come with me. I just... well, it's getting kind of stuffy in here and I wanted to ask if you cared to step out for a few?"

"Don't worry about the drink." I snatched the cup from him and smiled with my eyes. Something inside kept pushing me to trust him. "I need some air myself. Of course..." I glanced at the exit. "There *is* Mrs. Prather."

She stood in front of one of the exits, arms crossed, carefully guarding the door like a Doberman. Her beady eyes locking on to anyone who passed.

"I'll take care of it," he said, and headed over to her. I couldn't hear what they said, but she looked really concerned, narrowing her eyes and nodding. A few seconds later, she darted through the crowd, whooshing right past me at record speed.

Brian jogged back over. "Come on." We scurried toward the gym exit. He propped the door open just enough for me

34

to get through. The door clicked shut behind us and the music muffled.

"Oh my God, we didn't just dodge Mrs. Prather? Did we?" The brief adrenaline rush had me shaking. I laughed. "She's gonna be soooo mad!"

"Maybe, but it was worth the risk to spend time with you alone."

"Alone?" I brushed a stray curl behind my ear and smiled shyly.

"Uh, I meant... to *talk* to you," he stuttered. "Really. I..."

"I'd love to see snow someday," I said, changing the subject. "Do you think we'll ever have snow for Christmas?" I shuddered. The temperature had gone down since we had arrived. The crisp smell of winter drifted through the air. I rubbed my forearms.

"Don't know," he replied. "But up in Montana, winter is freaking fierce." He set down his cup on the concrete and slid his arms out of his coat. "Here." He draped it over my shoulders and tried to stifle a nervous chuckle. "I know it's stereotypical, but... you don't need to freeze because of me."

"Thanks, Brian. I brought a shrug, but left it on the coat rack inside. A lot of good it did me, huh?"

"That jacket was getting a little warm anyway." He picked his punch cup up off the ground.

His body heat along with a hint of his pleasant scent lingered on the coat. Although a bit big, it helped and I'd stop shivering already.

The school baseball field was illuminated as if it were a game night, only the bleachers were empty. I'd taken for granted how pretty it could be without screaming cheerleaders and jocks running around, kicking up dust everywhere. No megaphones. No noisy billboards.

I lifted the cup up in a toast. "To..." I thought fast but nothing came. "Something awesome." I giggled, making him crack a smile.

"Yeah." He nodded. "To something awesome!"

I tried the punch and my lips pursed. "Ew. This is sour!" I coughed. "Bleh!"

He took a sip and wiped his mouth with the back of his sleeve. "Yeah. The punch is pretty terrible here, isn't it? Here, let me get that." He reached for my cup and then tossed both of our drinks into a nearby trash can.

"It's kind of pretty out here with all the seats empty," he said, staring off past the field. "Seems staged almost. Like something out of a movie."

We sat down on the concrete steps just outside the auditorium doors.

"I guess so." A bright white, almost-full moon lit up the sky. Shimmering stars flecked the deep blue nothingness. It *felt* like something out of a movie... One of those cliché boy-and-girl-at-prom scenes. I kept telling myself not to get nervous. Nothing was going to happen.

This wasn't a movie...

"What is it?" he asked.

I'd faded out. "Nothing." I cupped my hands together to stop myself from fidgeting. "You want to talk about anything?"

He shrugged.

I went back to watching my hands and we sat in silence.

Bass vibrated below our feet. The music playing inside— softer and distorted—was still audible. We'd barely escaped from the Electric Slide. Then a slow song started, the melody of a saxophone teased my ears through the concrete walls and the bass quieted below our feet.

I felt Brian's eyes on me.

"Thank you," he said.

I turned toward him. The stadium lights cast a shadow over half of his face but I could see a small smile curling his lips. "For the encouraging things you've said about my art. It's really helped me push myself to work harder. In school and... at home."

I had butterflies in my stomach and my face felt flushed.

"You're welcome," I replied. "You don't have to thank me, though."

"It was hard to make friends with all of the moving around we used to do, but I'm glad the teacher made me sit next to you." He fell quiet for a moment and looked back toward the auditorium. "Hey, the music's gotten a little better. Do you want to at least pretend we're here to dance?"

I glanced anxiously at his hands and then back into his eyes. Just thinking about touching him made my stomach knot up. Not that I didn't want to be closer to him. I did... I really did, but...

Oh, forget it.

I took a deep breath. After all, it wasn't the first time I'd *wanted* to touch him.

He stood and reached down. His warm hands cupped mine carefully. Then, he pulled me to my feet and I almost tumbled into his arms.

I swallowed hard and straightened up, smoothing down my skirt with flattened hands. Nervous, I rested one hand onto his shoulder as he entwined fingers with my other. He hesitated before placing a hand on my waist. We were both trembling, but I liked that. Brian's anxiety was genuine. Reassuring.

I didn't know a thing about dancing. I'd figured it wouldn't matter since I hadn't planned on actually dancing. Brian didn't know much about it either, but I didn't care.

We made it up as we went along and simply swayed to the music. He stayed vigilant, not stepping on my toes while I made sure I didn't smack him in the face when he let me go to twirl. We danced to a gentler, distant version of the music.

"You're really pretty, Alice," he said, gently squeezing my hand.

The bright golden glow of the stadium lights washed over his face, making his eyes sparkle. My heart thumped in my chest, fluttering like a hummingbird, drowning out the music. We stared into each other's eyes. Still as statues.

He tugged me closer and I gasped. Our bodies touched and his warm scent drew me in, stronger than before. I lost focus, captivated by his lips.

Goose bumps rippled across my arms and the hair on the back of my neck stood. A surge of warmth swept through me, making my fingertips tingle.

Brian flinched and his grip loosened.

"Brian?"

He froze, blinking. Dumbfounded. Lost.

He shuffled to the side, the lights illuminating the whites of his eyes. "Maybe... we should sit this one out," he said and then stumbled backwards and let go of me.

"You okay?" I stepped toward him and took his arm.

"Yeah." He sat down on the steps and coughed. "I..." He coughed again. "I can't... breathe well all of a sudden." He undid the top button of his shirt and stretched open his collar, clearing his throat as he did. "Probably the cold or..." He shifted as though he couldn't get comfortable.

He fell silent, staring off at nothing.

My heart plummeted.

"Shit." Brian doubled over and clutched at his chest.

"Brian!"

"I... ugh." He grimaced, gritting his teeth.

"What is it? What's wrong?" I grabbed his shoulders. "Look at me!" A faint, intermittent beeping sound came from somewhere on him. "Brian!"

"I... ah, God! Al..." He gasped for air. Short, strained choking breaths. "Alice, call 9-1-1!" His terrified eyes finally met mine. "Now."

I stopped breathing, too. So scared, I thought my heart might explode from beating so fast.

"Uh, okay." I pulled out my cell and kept watching him. My hands shook. I tried to remember three stupid numbers. Clumsy from panic, I tried twice to get it right.

"9-1-1, what is your emergency?"

"Uh, I don't know. I'm with my friend and he looks like he's in a lot of pain right now."

Brian grunted hard and looked up at me, his breathing still labored. He pulled at the collar of his shirt hard and stretched it to reveal his skin. There was a small lump in his chest just over his left pec and a thick scar line above it.

"Oh my God! You have a pacemaker!" A lump formed in my throat.

"Ma'am?" The 911 person waited for a reply.

"Uh, yes. I think he's having a heart attack. He has a pacemaker and his chest is hurting. I've never seen him like this. Please. Please help us!"

The 911 person—who said his name was James—asked me if Brian was still breathing and if he was conscious. "Yes. Yes." He was, but he looked like he might pass out any minute now. James informed me that the beeping noise was coming from the pacemaker—an alert that something had gone wrong.

I moved with Brian to help him bring his knees closer to his chest, just as James had suggested. I had to keep him alert until the ambulance came. James stayed on the line but I set my phone down beside us and put it on speaker.

"Brian?" I took his hand and held it tightly, scared I might hurt him further but more frightened of him slipping away without me there. That stuff inside me. It must have hurt him somehow. Shorted out his pacemaker. Just like Sam's tablet.

"Stay with me." I cupped the side of his face. It had become deathly pale. His skin colder than it was before.

His grasp on my hand tightened while his other hand rubbed the center of his chest. He took slow breaths, trying to steady his pulse.

"Help will be there soon," James said, and then asked me again how Brian was doing.

"Still conscious."

I wasn't much of a religious girl, but right then and there, I squeezed Brian's hand and prayed harder than I'd ever prayed in my entire life.

God, please let this not be our last dance...

Chapter 7

I awoke in the hospital lobby, my face nestled against Mom's shoulder.

"Brian?" I jumped up from my seat and my head swirled. Dizziness overwhelmed me and I plopped back down.

"Don't get up so fast," said Mom, rubbing my arm.

"Is he okay?" I held my forehead in my palm. It took me a moment to get my bearings and remember what had happened.

"He's fine"

"Thank God." I exhaled. "What time is it?" I pulled my phone out of my pocket, answering my own question. 8:32 AM.

Apparently I'd put up quite a fight last night and wouldn't let Mom take me home. I didn't remember most of it because I'd been in such a panic, but I was glad she had stayed with me.

Then I remembered.

"School!" I leapt up again.

"It's winter break, sweetheart."

"Oh..." My head was so foggy.

"They said he's stable," Mom added, while sending someone a text on her phone. I couldn't see who the recipient was. "Alice. You did the right thing. I'm proud of you for reacting the way you did."

I smiled stupidly big. Her words gave me the warm and fuzzies inside.

"You can see him if you want." She motioned toward the

receptionist's desk. "By the way, what were you doing with him last night? I thought you and Sam had gone together to the dance?"

"We did. I didn't know he was coming. We stepped outside for some air and... that's when everything happened. It was all so fast."

Her brow wrinkled as if she suspected something, but then she took a breath and let it go with a little shake of her head.

"Oh, alright."

I was glad she wasn't going to ask any more questions.

A nurse escorted me to Brian's room and let me in, then pressed her clipboard to her chest and scuttled off down the hall.

I crept inside, my heart racing, unsure of what I might see.

"Don't be scared, Alice." Brian sat up in his hospital bed when he saw me. "It was a heart attack, not a lawn mower accident."

The thought made me shudder.

There was an IV taped to the inside of his wrist and something else hooked up that tracked his heartbeat. I watched the colored line bolt up and down steadily.

"How are you doing?" I approached. My hand gravitated toward his. I stopped myself and rested it instead on the cold metal bed railing. I didn't want to risk messing up one of the nearby machines.

"So, Alice, I'm curious. Who did you tell the nurse you were?"

I looked away and bit my lip. "That... *I was a cousin.*" I said it so quietly, I barely heard myself.

"What?" He tilted his head to the side and grinned. "Really? And they believed you?"

I shrugged.

"You could have told them you were my girlfriend.

That's what I told them."

"Oh." *Girlfriend?* My cheeks got warm.

Please shoulder, don't act up now. Not here. Electrical equipment surrounded me. I clasped my hands together and pressed my arms close to my body to avoid bumping into any nearby machines. The last thing I wanted to do was hurt him by shorting something else out.

"Being my cousin makes last night kind of weird though, doesn't it?"

I chuckled nervously. "Yeah. Kind of." After everything that had happened last night, he hadn't changed a bit.

"Sorry I didn't tell you about the whole heart thing," he said. "It's not exactly a weakness I need the whole world freaking out about. Especially you. And I've got a reputation to keep up. Would *you* have been intimidated by a guy with a messed up heart?"

I stared at him with pity. "That's the real reason why you can't be in the military, isn't it? And that's the reason you had problems with your dad. He couldn't accept it."

"Yeah, well, I showed him."

"What do you mean?"

"I don't even need it anymore."

"Need what?"

He peeled down the collar of his hospital robe to reveal a fresh line of stitches and bright pink, inflamed skin. I grimaced at first, overreacting, and then forced myself to take a second look. It wasn't *that* bad.

"The pacemaker." He pointed to the place where the lump had been last night. "I don't need it anymore. Whatever happened to me last night was a miracle. It shorted out the pacemaker but the arrhythmia went with it." He smiled big and reached for my hand. I pulled away.

"No." I shook my head. "I don't want to hurt you."

"I'd been living every day in constant fear that I'd drop dead at any moment because of my heart. Whatever happened yesterday—whatever *you* did to me—saved me."

"I didn't do anything, Brian." I sat on the edge of his bed and rested one knee over the other. "Why would you say something like that?"

"Because I saw it."

I tried to act unaffected. "Saw... what exactly?"

"The light. The green—"

"Shh!" I touched my fingers to his lips. "No. Don't say it."

"Then I wasn't seeing things," he said as my fingers slid off his mouth, grazing his chin.

"You can't tell anyone!"

"I won't. Alice, I'll keep *any* secret for you. I'd die to keep your secret if I had to, but you have to promise not to keep secrets from me. Okay? Not if we're going to be friends. Or... more than that."

He reached for my hand again, cupped it between his and squeezed gently. "Last night was one of the best nights of my life. Because of you."

I playfully combed my other hand through his messy hair and grinned.

"I need to figure out what's going on with me. Promise not to say anything."

"Cross my heart and hope to die." He made a crisscross gesture over his chest and smirked.

"Don't say that, Brian."

"Yeah, don't say that, Brian," Sam chimed in.

Brian let go of my hand and I spun around to greet her, hoping she hadn't seen anything incriminating.

"It's soooo 90's." Sam knocked on the door with her knuckles. "Good morning, Alllliiice. Brian."

"When did you get here, Sam?" I asked.

"A little while ago. Your mom texted me this morning so, of course, I had to come." She held out her empty hands and frowned. "I brought you some tea but the nurse lady said I couldn't bring it in here." She pushed out her lower lip. "Meanies."

"Did they just let you in?" I cocked my head at her.

"Yeah. The lady said he's allowed visitors."

I felt really stupid. Apparently I had lied to the receptionist for no reason. *Oh well.*

"You can go with her," said Brian. "I'll be okay. Go home and get some sleep, Alice. Just do me a favor and give my mom your cell number, please? I'll text you when I'm back home."

I didn't want to leave him, but with Sam there the whole mood was spoiled. No use hanging around being sleep deprived. If the doctor said he would be okay, that was the only thing I needed to hear.

But now, despite what my brain was telling me, I felt the need to just *be there*. In his presence. It was a strong force pulling me closer. Keeping me where I was. Putting my nerves at ease.

I remembered the calming scent of his jacket. His warmth.

"Come on, girl." Sam yanked my arm.

"Ow!"

"Let's go get you some tea. Buh-bye Brian."

I waved to him as she dragged me back to the lobby.

"Here." She handed me a hot to-go cup. "Thought it would help wake you up." I cupped my fingers around it and took a slow breath of the wispy steam seeping out of the lid. English breakfast tea. Malty and warm. Creamy with a tad of sweetness.

Sam scrunched her lips up to one side and raised an eyebrow. "So, what were you and Brian doing outside last night anyway?" She leaned closer and her eyebrows bobbed up and down suspiciously.

"Nothing. We were *just* talking."

"I'm not an idiot."

"Okay, okay." My voice lowered to a whisper. Mom was

nearby. "We danced to one song and that was it. We held hands and... the next thing I knew... I was calling 9-1-1."

"Did you electrocute him?" She planted her fists on her hips. "*You* are a terrible girlfriend!"

"Shh!" I looked to see if anyone had heard her. An old woman sitting nearby had a wide-eyed stare aimed at me. I smiled, dumbly, hoping she'd stop looking.

Not that it bothered me, but was I the only person who didn't know about the whole *girlfriend* thing?

Chapter 8

I zipped my hoodie closed and flipped the hood up over my head, covering my shoulder so they wouldn't see the blazing, fiery green glow. Brighter than it had ever been. I fast-walked toward the abandoned building ahead, keeping an eye on my surroundings.

I heard a rustle in the distance and veered around.

"Alice!" Brian rushed up to me and grabbed my hand. "Come on!"

We ran as fast as we could.

Trying to escape from something. Someone.

Terrified. Confused. I didn't know who or what was chasing us. Or where we were headed, for that matter. We just had to get there... fast.

Out of breath. So tired. Muscles burned. Feet ached.

It was dark inside and the building was dirty and old—completely falling apart. Broken pieces of glass and furniture littered the floor. Wallpaper peeled. The air smelled of mold. I coughed hard, choking on dust.

I flipped a switch.

No power.

Oh, God. We were sitting ducks.

We ran up a flight of stairs. I knew that up on the fifth floor, a sky bridge connected this building to the next.

Get out before they find you. A voice lingered in my head. Whose voice? *They will kill you.*

I turned to Brian.

And yelped.

"What? What the hell, Alice?" He looked around frantically. "What is it?"

He had them—the veins. Glowing azure veins resonated beneath the skin of his left arm. The light started from just above his elbow and stretched down to his fingertips, mirroring my own in every way except in color.

"Your arm. You're..."

"What? We don't have time for this. We have to find her."

"Her?" Her who?

"What's wrong with you? We have to find her and get to the door before they find us."

Door? What door?

Something crashed behind me and I gasped.

"Let's go!" Brian grabbed my wrist. We ran, dodging debris and hopping over broken planks of wood and ceiling tiles. More dust clouded the air. I coughed, covering my mouth with my sleeve. The rooms crumbled. Every step was a hazard. The floor could give any second.

Third floor.

Fourth floor.

Fifth floor.

The sky bridge was just ahead. Only a few sliding glass doors and shattered ceiling tiles stood between us and freedom. I rushed toward the doors and started lifting and tossing aside the debris. Brian helped, digging into the piles of musty drywall and kicking pieces out of the way.

Something sliced my palm and I grunted, turning over my hand. A deep, hairline wound split open and blood oozed from my palm.

"I cut myself." I groaned. "No..."

Brian came to my side and grimaced. "It's deep." He looked around for the culprit and found it at my feet—a glimmering tin ceiling panel. "Damn it. That's no good."

He wasted no time in removing his overshirt and quickly wrapping it around my hand. He tucked a tail end into a fold and pulled it snug. I flexed my fingers. It would have to do.

"I'll get the rest," he said, making short work of what was left in our way.

The ground rumbled beneath our feet. It sounded like a floor had collapsed somewhere else in the building.

"Help!"

A female voice. Muffled.

"Help me!" Again.

Brian perked up and listened.

"This way." He motioned to the right. "I think she's over there."

I took a step and stopped. "No, Brian." I held my ground. "We have to go forward. We can't stop for anyone. They warned us."

Somehow I couldn't even remember who *they* were.

"Whoever she is, she's in trouble." He glared at me as if I were the most selfish person on the planet. "We *have* to help her."

We had almost reached the next building—and freedom from this deathtrap. There wasn't much ground left to cover. Only a glass bridge that could crumble in an instant if another tremor came through. The glass already showed stress cracks. But we couldn't get separated.

The look on his face made me feel like a villain and I couldn't stomach his disappointment if I said no again.

"Okay. But we have to hurry." I hopped over a small pile of broken paneling and followed him.

My hand ached. I flexed my fingers and squeezed the blood-soaked shirt. A few droplets of crimson fell to the floor.

Ugh. No. Now they could track us.

We *were* in trouble.

"Brian! Come on! I'm bleeding everywhere."

"Please. Help." The voice sounded weaker now but closer.

We rushed into a nearby room filled with piles of wood and broken drywall. The pungent scent of decay made my nose wrinkle.

Something moved and I backed up against a wall, afraid the floor might give way.

"There!" Brian pointed.

A dark-skinned hand reached toward us, trapped and camouflaged beneath a pile of rubble.

BUZZ

That sound. Another tremor?

BUZZ

I felt groggy and weak.

BUZZZZZZZZZZZZZZZZZZZZZZZZZ

My head hurt. I blinked and rolled over.

My cell vibrated on my dresser, jittering toward the edge.

I reached and caught it before it slipped off.

"Hey... Brian?"

"I'm sorry. I didn't mean to wake you."

"It's 2 AM. What's up?"

"I just had the weirdest dream ever."

I fell silent.

"Alice?"

"Me, too."

Chapter 9

The hospital released Brian sooner than I'd expected. They said he'd made a miraculous recovery, his body healing much faster than they had anticipated. He could go back to school after Christmas break.

Being trapped in the hospital for days after having seen my glow had made him a little crazy, though. And I couldn't have been more anxious, either. We had *a lot* to talk about.

The dream? We'd *both* had it that night. His version had varied slightly but the gist had been the same. Too much to be coincidental.

He wanted to come over and talk in person, but Mom wouldn't have it. Not while we were knee-deep in making plans for our annual family get-together—a huge dinner party she always threw the week before Christmas.

Family from out of town, a few cousins, and Sam came every year. We'd eat candy, cookies, turkey, stuffing, you name it. We broke holiday crackers and stayed up late catching up and telling stories. It was fun and I was looking forward to it, but this year, I felt kind of bad I couldn't invite Brian. I knew we hadn't been friends long but so much had happened between us. I felt really close to him. Really... really close.

．　　　．　　　．

Brian had managed to convince his mom to swing by my house on the way home from the hospital so he could "thank me." My mom wasn't happy about the idea—she hadn't even met him before the accident, so I couldn't blame her for feeling on edge.

"You'll like him, Mom. He's nice," I said, trying to re-assure her.

"It's not about *me* liking him, Alice," Mom replied, scrunch-ing her lips to the side. He'd only be stopping by for a few minutes, but the way she was acting, you'd think he was planning on staying the night.

"Mom. Mom, he's *not* my boyfriend. We're just friends, okay?"

She shook her head and sighed. "If you say so, hun. I'll take your word for it."

I went back upstairs to my room and waited.

The doorbell rang.

I heard the front door open and my mother chatting with Brian for a few moments. I tried to listen but couldn't hear a thing from the staircase.

The front door shut.

"Alice!" Mom yelled.

"Coming!" I'd already made it halfway down the stairs.

"I think you know who's here. Don't be long. His mother's waiting in the car and that cold front is really hitting hard out there." She handed me a sweater from the coat rack. It was a frumpy beige button-up I pretty much only wore when *no one* was looking.

"Thanks, but I won't be long." I declined and she hung it back up behind me, sighing.

I opened the door and Brian smiled.

"Hey, Alice." He lifted the fingers of one hand in an awkward wave. "So, how have you been?"

"I'm doing okay. You?" My words formed white puffs in the air.

"Better. A lot better."

"That's good." I nodded.

A gush of cold air blew past, and my hair tickled my

cheeks.

Brian reached out.

I held my breath.

He brushed a loose lock behind my ear.

Our eyes met and I shied away with a nervous smile.

I tucked my hands into the pockets of my fleece pullover and looked down at my feet.

Brian cleared his throat. "Thanks again, Alice," he said. "If it weren't for you, I might not be here today. I'm grateful for what you did for me."

"You already thanked me, Brian." I peeked past his shoulder to see his mom in her car, fixated on something in her lap—probably a phone. She had the radio on some country station.

"I... guess I'd better get going." He shoved his hands into his jean pockets and looked back toward his mom's car and then again at me.

I didn't want him to go.

"Alright. Take care of yourself," I said. "We'll catch up when things aren't so hectic around here. After my relatives leave." My nose tingled from the cold. It had to be bright pink by now.

"Sure." He did his awkward partial wave again and turned to leave. He took one step down off the porch and stopped.

"Oh, and Alice." He turned around, all the confidence draining from his face. "I need to ask you something before I go."

"Anything."

"Will you... be my girlfriend? I really want to get out of whatever awkward stage we're stuck in right now." I caught him glancing at my lips.

"I'm fourteen, Brian. I don't think my mom would appreciate me having a boyfriend right now."

He shrugged. "Look, don't think about it like that. We

can make it work. But, you're going to have to agree first."

"I..."

"Say yes. Please." His kind hazel eyes drew me in, pleading for me to reconsider.

I wanted to. I really did.

"Brian, I..."

He took a step up and cupped my hand, his warm fingers embracing mine.

I crumbled.

"Yes."

He was three inches from my face before I could...

He kissed me.

I closed my eyes and froze, my last breath catching in my throat.

His hands came up to cup my face, pulling me closer.

Fingers combed through my hair.

The porch disappeared beneath my feet.

If only I'd said yes sooner.

Our lips parted and my heart sank like a stone, forcing the rest of my body to acknowledge gravity again.

But then our noses touched and he lingered a moment, his warm breaths teasing my heartstrings. I'd once thought his eyes couldn't get any prettier. The soft, woodsy green encircled by hints of light amber and brown. The tiny, perfect fleck of near-black embellishing only his left iris.

"See you at the Christmas party." His lips curled and he smiled even bigger with his eyes. Brian turned away and stepped off the porch.

I traced my lips with my fingertips as he walked off, part of me leaving with him.

Okay, so maybe Mom was right to be a little concerned.

Chapter 10

"You invited Brian to the Christmas party?"

"Brian *and* his mother," Mom corrected. "I asked if they had plans and he told me they usually spend Christmas alone. It only seemed right to invite them, seeing how they've only been in town for a few months. You don't have a problem with it, do you?"

"No. Of course not. I was just surprised, that's all. You seemed really worried about him at first and now..."

"Now, I'll get to know him properly. Over dinner with family."

"Sounds good."

It then occurred to me that since Brian was coming over for the Christmas Party... it might be a nice idea to get him a small something for Christmas. Of course, I had absolutely no clue what or even where to start looking.

Nice going, Alice.

I'd been kissed by a boy who I didn't even know well enough to buy a Christmas present for. Smart move. Brilliant teenage mind at work.

"I'm excited," I added, smiling big. "Except about Uncle Teddy. He's always kind of..."

"Weird?" Mom added with a laugh. "His stories *are* pretty bad, but he's always been a good brother."

"I know."

Uncle Teddy had been the first to console her during the divorce. He'd always told her how much he had disliked my dad. Even before she had married him. I didn't know my dad before he *was* Dad, so I wasn't one to judge. I hardly saw him anymore and I missed him. I missed my dad like crazy.

. . .

"Get the door, Alice!" Mom hunched down in front of the open oven, basting a turkey with one hand and stirring a pot of sweet potatoes on top of the stove with the other. I'd heard the doorbell ring before she'd even yelled, but had to snake my way through the aftermath of the holiday explosion our home had endured to even get to it. Festively wrapped presents had been lovingly tucked in nearly every corner. Lighted artificial spruce garland spiraled down the staircase railing and above the doorframes. Our eight-foot Christmas tree twinkled with multi-colored lights in the far end of the living room. Its red velvet tree skirt—a family heirloom— had been sprinkled with holiday crackers and decorative favors.

Eleven-year-old cousin Kevin, Teddy's son, sat alongside a pile of puzzle pieces he had scattered halfway across the carpet. The contents of a 1,000 piece set he probably wouldn't finish before getting distracted by something else. *Boys.*

Aunt Stephanie was in the kitchen finishing up her homemade pumpkin pie. I'd snuck a taste early in the day as she'd stood mixing the ingredients. Spicy and sweet. The wispy scent of cinnamon and cloves would linger in the house for days after the party.

Ham. Stuffing. Turkey. Gravy. And a dash of sugar cookies to "keep the little ones appeased." So many smells melding together. The smell of Christmas. The warm fuzzy feeling of love and family. Presents and laughter.

I put on a smile and opened the front door.

"Sorry it took me so long," I said. "I apologize."

Brian's mother greeted me with a vase of lovely red and white carnations tied together with pretty gold ribbon. I invited her in and Brian followed behind, grinning sweetly as he passed me. Seeing him melted my heart.

He took his mother's coat and his own and I showed him where to hang them. My neighbor—Mom's friend, Kim—came in to greet Brian's mom. They walked off toward the kitchen together.

"Hi," Brian said, not looking me in the eye.

"Hi." I handed him a hanger.

"It was really nice of your mom to invite us. I've never been to a family dinner before."

"It's no big deal." I shuffled a foot in place. "Mom said she'd like to get to know you better."

"And now she has good reason," he said with a smirk, his eyes meeting mine as he reached up to stroke his thumb across my chin.

My knees tingled. The rapid pitter-patter of my heart made me breathless. I thought it might burst.

The floor rumbled and something scurried past.

A stout, bushy-haired little girl stopped in front of the coat closet doorway and lifted her arms up over her head, stomping back and forth like a sumo wrestler. "Blargh!" Two-year-old cousin Sandy pushed up the tip of her nose with a finger and stuck out her tongue at us. "You can't catch me!" She darted off like a jack rabbit.

"Give me a sec, Brian."

He shrugged.

I crept into the living room like a sleek hunter and listened carefully. Then I heard a snicker.

"Gotcha!" I scooped up a flailing monster-child from behind the couch. Kicking and screaming and giggling so hard she made boogery nose bubbles. I grimaced.

"Ow!" I felt the pinch of her teeth sinking into my forearm and dropped her back onto her feet. "Why, you!" I scoffed.

She scampered off into the next room before I could scold her.

"I take it you like kids?" Brian came wandering into the living room, amused.

"Not really," I replied, scrubbing kid-spit off my arm with the hem of my shirt. "That was my cousin Sandy, by the way."

He glanced at the tiny crescent of indentations in my arm and his forehead wrinkled.

"Alice!" Mom yelled from the kitchen in her "I urgently need you to grab me a can of _____ from the basement" tone.

"I'm so sorry!" I grinned, embarrassed by all of the interruptions. "Feel free to make yourself at home. There are cookies on the table in the dining room. I'll show you around when I get back." I rushed off to the kitchen.

A can of cranberry sauce, a roll of paper towels and a glass of sparkling cider later, and I'd finally been set free.

"Sorry about that, Brian."

He was standing in the living room, right where I had left him.

"Interesting," he said, drawing out the word while staring up at a bent-up metalwork star perched on top of our tree.

"My great grandpa made it back in the 20's when he worked as a metal smith. It's gotten a little beaten up over the years but it's not Christmas without it."

Brian—a good six inches taller than me—reached an arm up just high enough to trace over one of the metal points. "I think it's cool," he said with a nod. "It adds character."

"Thanks." And to think, I'd had to get onto a stepping stool to put it there.

"Not to be rude, but when's dinner? All of these smells are making my stomach want to eat itself."

"In a few hours. We're waiting on Sam."

"Are her parents not coming?"

"They can't make it. Some sort of work function going on that they had to go to. Rub noses with the big wigs, you know?" I chuckled, nervously. "They're going to drop off Sam soon."

"That kind of sucks," he replied.

"Yeah, but that's the way it's always been with them." They *never* made it to *any* of our parties. Honestly, I was glad her parents didn't come. Mom might feel out of place. Sam's parents were so uptight—not the kind of people to have a good laugh over dinner with. Their personalities differed so much, you'd almost suspect Sam had been adopted.

"She'll text me when she's on her way," I added. "Should be soon. Come on, let me introduce you to my uncle. Oh, and I saw your mom in the kitchen with my Aunt Stephanie. They really seemed to be hitting it off."

"Well, that's cool. Uh... where'd you say those cookies were again?"

"I'll show you." I walked with him down the hallway and into the dining room. We had a long, old-fashioned wood table with eight ornate chairs and a few metal pull-out chairs propped up against the wall behind it.

"Aw, now I wanna color." Brian spotted the bright blue fold-out kids table covered in coloring book pages, crayons and markers.

His comment made me laugh pretty hard.

We always had a separate table for the kids since they preferred to doodle and do their own things. Kevin had graduated to the "big table" this year. It was only Sandy by herself now, and she seemed perfectly fine with that. I worried about her eating all of the crayons, though.

"Here." I turned and presented to Brian a big plate of freshly baked cookies. "Chocolate chip. Oatmeal. Double dark chocolate. And, everyone's favorite, decorated sugar cookie stars."

He lifted his hand to take one and paused, letting it hover a moment as he contemplated his choice.

"You *can* have seconds," I said.

With that, he snatched a chocolate chip cookie from the edge and thanked me.

One bite in and he closed his eyes and sighed, a warm, content smile stretching across his lips.

"Mmmm. Oh, God. These are delicious," he said softly, savoring the taste.

"Glad you like it. I helped make them."

"Even better." He shoved the last piece of cookie into his mouth and raised an eyebrow. "I could eat them every day for the rest of my life."

Heat flushed through my cheeks.

Chapter 11

Big Uncle Teddy had fallen asleep on the couch, remote in hand, his hairy bare feet propped up on an ottoman, the TV tuned to a basketball game. Sandy, pretending to be a mole, had buried herself in a pile of clean blankets in the laundry room. I caught Kevin peeling back a piece of tape to peek at a Christmas present and shot him a dirty look. He scuttled back off to his puzzle after discovering a dress-up set meant for his sister.

All of the girls were chatting in the kitchen, so I excused myself to show Brian around the rest of the house. Oddly enough, I hadn't heard from Sam yet. She always looked forward to the Christmas party and had been raving about it since last year.

"You need to call Sam?" Brian caught me checking my phone. Pretty obvious, I guess. I'd done it three times in the past fifteen minutes.

"Yeah. I think I should. If you don't mind."

"Go right ahead." He sat down at the base of the carpeted staircase and folded his hands in his lap. "No rush."

I sent her a text.

WHERE R U?

Waited for a reply...
Checked my signal.
Five bars.
I sent another.

U OK?

Another minute...

"Anything?" Brian asked, looking at me through the handrails.

I shook my head.

"I'm sure she's fine," he said. "Her parents would have called you if something had happened. Right?"

He had a point.

"Yeah. I guess so. It's just weird." I shrugged it off for the moment and took Brian upstairs to my room.

I flipped the light switch and the shadows came to life with color. I turned my desk lamp on to make it brighter. I liked keeping it dim, though. My teenage girl version of a man cave.

"You *really* like purple, don't you?" Brian said with a tilt of his head, fixating on my purple writing desk. A matching upholstered purple chair had been pushed up to it.

A flowery skin on my laptop's lid. A string of purple Christmas lights permanently affixed around the perimeter of my ceiling. It occurred to me how girly my room looked.

"Yeah. Apparently." I chuckled, feeling really stupid about it all. I was fourteen, not six. He probably thought I...

"It's pretty," he said with a nod. "Very... calming."

"You think?" I bit my lip to stifle a sigh of relief.

"Yeah. It's different. Creative. My mom would never let me do something like this to my room. I start adding some color or get too artistic and suddenly I'm *turning gay*." He heaved a sigh and shook his head.

"That's terrible! What does being creative have to do with someone's orientation anyway?" I couldn't believe a mother would say that kind of thing. Brian was an amazing artist.

And that kiss... definitely *not* gay. I nibbled my lip, reminiscing.

"I'm sorry, Brian. Your mom really shouldn't judge you for something like that."

"I know." He pressed his lips together.

"Oh! Before I forget." I slid open a desk drawer, pulled out a flat, wrapped gift, and handed it to Brian.

"What's this?" he asked, looking unsure. "I wasn't expecting anything. I didn't get anything for you. I—"

"It's okay. Don't worry about. It's something little. I... hope you like it."

"I feel bad now." He hesitantly took the present and then spent a moment admiring the wrapping paper and shiny silver bow I'd stuck in the upper corner.

"Don't feel bad." I smiled, sitting on the edge of my desk. It seemed like he didn't want to open it. "Please. Go ahead."

He turned over the present and started carefully tearing the paper along the seam.

"Seriously?" His eyes widened.

He unlatched the buckle and flipped open the leather journal.

I couldn't tell if he liked it or not.

"This is amazing!" He fanned through the pages, closed the book and latched it shut. He took a big sniff of the cover and grinned. "Suede. Wow! Thank you, Alice. Though I kind of feel like a jerk for not thinking to get you anything."

"I'm not upset." I stood up from the desk. "Besides, being able to spend today with you makes me happy. You do like it, right?"

He set the journal down on my desk, letting his fingers drag over the cover before letting up.

"Yeah. It's one of the most thoughtful gifts I've *ever* gotten," he said, licking his lips. "And you know, I'm really glad you're with me, too." A subtle reminder I had agreed to be his girlfriend. "I've been thinking about you ever since the day I left the hospital. Since we 'talked' on the porch."

He cracked a smile.

"Me, too," I said beneath my breath.

He stepped closer and I stepped back.

"Tell me you feel it, too," he said.

It was dead quiet besides the soft whirring from the fan on my laptop. "Feel... what?"

He reached up to take a lock of my hair between his fingers.

"That tightening in your gut. Anxious nerves that won't settle. You try to fight it—tell it to go away, but it won't."

I did.

He released my hair.

"Your pulse racing," he continued. "What you felt when we were downstairs by the coat closet earlier." His thumb caressed my chin again.

Yes.

Lightheadedness. Knots in my stomach. The same whirlwind of emotions I had felt at the dance. A restless drive to be closer...

"Aren't we moving a little fast?" I shuddered, bumping into the wall behind me.

"Do you want to slow down?" he asked, his eyes glinting with anticipation.

I should have lied, but I couldn't. Excitement coursed through me, electric. Free.

My conscience warned me not to let go, but...

"I asked you a question, Alice." His voice softened and he pinned me against the wall beside my desk. A bold move. It lit me on fire.

"Brian?" I couldn't hide my eager, fluttering breaths. His warm scent clouded my mind. I wanted him so much, my whole body trembled.

One more step. His hazel eyes devouring me.

His face lowered and I tasted his breath. A hint of chocolate.

He brought his hands up to clasp my face and then kissed me.

I tangled my fingers into his belt loops and tugged him closer so our bodies touched. The back of his hand dragged down the side of my neck, making my knees weaken. He lingered, teasing my lower lip with the tip of his tongue. A quiet groan escaped me. I pushed up off my heels and kissed him back, plunging my hands through waves of his soft hair. The smell of his skin. The tension. The need to keep him near. His heat against my own feverish body.

"Alice," he whispered, pressing his lips just behind my ear and again on the side of my neck. I shuddered. He grasped my shoulder and pressed gently. "Alice."

"Wh-what is it?" I opened my eyes and gasped.

Fluorescent white-blue light tinted his left hand, glowing and spreading through his veins, skittering halfway up his arm, exactly as it had in my dream. He slid his fingers down my shoulder and watched as the green light beneath my skin chased the path of his touch, twinkling on contact and then fading away.

"You have it, too?"

His eyes narrowed and a wide, satisfied grin stretched across his lips.

"You're... you're not afraid?" I asked, shaking.

He slipped his other arm behind my waist. Our glows resonated in sync, two colors pulsing in harmony.

"Why would I be afraid? What happened at the dance wasn't the first time I'd almost died," he said. "It probably won't be the last. But whatever this is, it fixed my heart. You had the dream, too, you know. It's pretty obvious we're together for a reason, Alice."

He lifted my arm and pressed it back against the wall, dragging his glowing fingers up my wrist, circling my palm, and then taking my hand. The skin glimmered with soft turquoise light.

"With you, I feel unstoppable." He folded his fingers around mine. "As if there's nothing to fear anymore."

"But, what if my mom..."

"She won't." He leaned in and kissed me again.

Chapter 12

The doorbell rang and I pulled away from Brian. He stepped to the side so I could pass, but grasped my fingers, reluctant to let me go.

"It's probably Sam," I said, clearing my throat. "Oh, geeze." I took a deep breath and combed my fingers through my hair to smooth it down the back of my neck, trying to pull myself together quickly. My heart pounded in my chest. My palms were sweaty.

"Can you keep her busy for a sec?" I asked Brian. "I need a minute."

"So do I." He shrugged and looked away, sweeping a hand through his disheveled hair.

Oops.

I shook my head and left my room. I didn't feel like spilling our new relationship status to Sam just yet. Not while my relatives were around.

The doorbell rang again.

Oh, Sam...

I ran into the bathroom, brushed my hair and splashed cold water on my face. Deep pink colored my cheeks but faded fast. The green glow had disappeared. *Thank God.*

By the time I'd popped back out, Sam stood in the living room, bent over, shaking one of the presents under the tree, her ear pressed to the side.

"Sam?" I leaned on the railing.

"Alice! Hi!" She looked up, dropped the present and jogged toward me.

"Where were you? I was really worried, Sam."

"Oh yeah, about that." She bit her lip. "Yeah. So I accidentally sorta kinda dropped my phone in the toilet."

"Ew!"

"Well, it would have been fine, but the screen got cracked and water and stuff got in it."

"That's gross."

"Yeah. Dad took me to the mall to get it replaced and then... well, you know. I had to get a new case, too. And, you know how that goes."

I knew very well "how that goes." I'm pretty sure I know why the dinosaurs went extinct. They were waiting for Sam to pick out a cell phone case.

"Hey, Sam." Brian came out of my room, looking as cool and collected as he had when he'd arrived. *Boys had it so easy.*

"Brian?" Sam's eyes widened and her lips pursed. "What the heck are you doing here?"

"Well, you took soooooo long, Sam," I joked.

She shot me an angry glare, but then laughed it off.

"Actually," I went on, "Mom invited him and his mother since they are new in town."

"Oh. Really?" Sam raised an eyebrow. "Okay then. I'll believe that, *for now.*"

Brian walked past, trying to play it cool by not looking me in the eye. I followed behind him and we met Sam in the living room.

.　　　.　　　.

Dinner couldn't have gone better. My family really liked Brian, and that made me happy. I needed them to like him.

Afterward, Brian joined me in the kitchen to help with the dishes. Mom didn't appreciate guests doing dirty work, but he'd insisted—anything to spend another minute alone with me, I think.

"Hand me the forks, please?" I gestured toward the pile of dishes on the other side of the sink. Mom always used her best dishes for this get-together, so we had to be careful.

Brian chuckled, setting a stack of buttering knives in the sink water. "So, uh, your Uncle Teddy." He reached for the forks. "Does he offer beer to everyone or am I just special?"

"He's been doing that for years." I shook my head. "Uncle Teddy thinks we should all appreciate the wonderful nuances of beer the way he does."

"I thinks it tastes disgusting," Brian said. "If that's not weird to hear from a guy my age?"

"No." I hated the smell of the stuff anyway. One less thing to worry about and one more reason Mom could appreciate Brian.

I twisted the faucet toward hot and turned it on high. At the same time, Brian passed a dessert plate in front of me and steaming water splashed off it. I yelped, dropping a coffee mug. It hit the countertop and tumbled toward the floor. I couldn't grab it fast enough.

Brian knelt down. "Alice?"

"Don't pick it up. The pieces will be sharp." I closed my eyes and silently hated on myself. Hopefully, Mom would forgive me. It was part of her favorite set.

"Alice! You need to see this."

"What?" I turned. My jaw dropped.

The coffee cup hadn't even stopped falling.

I bent down. It hung, suspended in midair, rotating so slowly I could barely tell it was moving at all. Caught in time, floating inches from the floor.

"Hey, Mom!" I called out.

I poked my head into the dining room.

Everyone was moving in slow motion. Nearly frozen.

"Brian. What's going on?" A lump formed in my throat and I panicked.

He came to his feet and took my hand. "I don't know," he said.

The floor disappeared out from under us.

Blinding white light flashed.

I screamed and shut my eyes.

Brian's grasp on me tightened.

We fell.

Brightness all around.

I couldn't tell which way was up.

Then the floor returned. Ground beneath my feet again.

I opened my eyes.

A dozen figures dressed in matte grey surrounded us, gazes fixated on us. The room completely white—endless.

"Brian," I called, colored spots flickering in my eyes as they recovered from the trauma.

"I'm here." He pulled me closer, shielding me with his embrace.

"Where are we?"

A tall, slender figure moved closer, wearing a seamless tight-fitting uniform similar to a jump suit with raised texture.

"Don't come any closer," Brian growled. "Who are you?"

It tilted its head and stared, appearing to size us up. Then it looked to another of the figures and took a step back. A second figure, identical in appearance, came forward.

Fair, elfish and androgynous, I couldn't tell if they were male or female. Their faces appeared somewhat male. But not like adult men, more like overgrown boys. *Almost* human. Taller than either of us. Limp white hair past their shoulders, grey eyes, plaster-white skin with a sooty grey-black under-tone.

"They have chosen me to answer," the second figure said through pale, colorless lips. Its voice was gender neutral, carried no accent and no intonation. "I speak your tongue."

"Wh... where are we?" I felt safe enough in Brian's arms to ask a question.

"We are galaxies from the planet you call Earth."

I must have been dreaming. I kept shaking my head and looking at Brian, who was doing the same.

A colorless, scentless room. I struggled to breathe the incredibly thin air.

No windows. Dead silent and still.

Unnaturally still.

I even heard Brian's heart and my own, pounding like drums, but our breathing was the loudest sound in the room.

"What do you want from us?" Brian loosened his grasp on me, fatigued by his struggle to breathe.

"Unlike most other humans, the two of you carry a precise genetic code necessary to bond with our own. We have chosen you specifically for our cause."

"Your *cause?* What the hell does that mean?" Brian stepped in front of me and clenched his fists.

The figure didn't flinch.

"You will learn more about our cause as we deem it necessary."

"Brian." I couldn't stop trembling.

The figure looked to the side as if he had heard someone speaking to him, and then back at us.

"You have paired correctly," it said. "Soon, you will discover the third. She is the key to your success. You must find and start her." He—or what I thought was a he—looked at me and lifted his hand so I could see his palm. It started to glow from the inside and his long, slender fingertips sparked with fluorescent green light—exactly like mine.

"You will soon learn your role," he continued, glancing at Brian. "You, too, are essential." A second, identical figure appeared beside the speaker, fading in from nothing but more white. It lifted a hand and its fingertips lit with bright azure.

Brian took my hand again. "You freaks can't make us do anything. Who are you anyway?"

"Our kind do not have names in your tongue. However,

you may liken us to the ones your people call gods—the Shepherds. The Saviors. Those who lead and preserve their people."

Before I could disagree, blazing white light flooded the room and I closed my eyes against it. The floor disappeared and we fell into nothingness.

The ground returned beneath my feet and my senses became overwhelmed by smells and sounds. A sharp pain throbbed behind my eyes. I cupped my forehead.

The smell of warm bread, cinnamon, turkey—Christmas dinner—filled my nostrils. I opened my eyes and sucked in a breath of real air. My mouth was dry as paper.

The mug I had dropped hit the floor and shattered to pieces. I recoiled. Brian quickly reached to cup my face.

"Are you okay?"

I couldn't speak so I nodded instead.

We stared at each other, unable to say another word about what had happened. Knowing it *had,* in fact, happened.

Whatever or whoever they were, they planned on using us for something.

They had put the light inside us—had had the nerve to compare themselves to gods.

What did they really want from us?

Who were the "Saviors"?

Chapter 13

After dinner, Brian and I stayed quieter than we'd *ever* been.

I couldn't keep a clear mind. I kept fading in and out of conversations during dessert. Mom had forgiven me for breaking her cup and that was one crisis averted, but why couldn't I have been a normal girl who kissed a normal boy? That's all I should have been thinking about. A crazy-amazing second kiss.

"Pie?" Mom asked. "Alice?"

Brian nudged me in the elbow.

"Oh, sorry. Yes. Thank you." I took the plate from Mom. She'd put a slice of pumpkin pie on it with a dollop of whipped cream on the side. Aunt Stephanie glanced over at us and smiled her innocent, big-hearted smile. "You two would make such an adorable couple," she said with a sigh. "Oh, I still remember when I first laid eyes on your uncle Teddy back in college."

My mom rolled her eyes.

I hunched over. "Guys, please." I did not need my shoulder flaring up in front of everyone. Brian slid his hand under the tablecloth and clutched mine.

"I'm happy I met Alice," he said. "You seem like a great family. It's nice that I had the chance to meet all of you while you're in town." He glanced down at the kiddie table where Sandy had made a little mound out of spit and torn, chewed-up paper crayon wrappers. "Even the cute little monster over there, which I've been told is Alice's cousin."

Everyone had a good laugh.

He'd taken the focus off me. I appreciated that.

"Hey, I left my gift in your room. Can I go get it?" Brian asked. "I want to show my mom."

"Sure."

"Excuse me." Brian got up and pushed his chair in.

I sat there twiddling my thumbs. I wanted to get up and go talk to him but I couldn't think of an excuse.

"Hey, Alice!" Brian called out from the top of staircase.

I leaned back in my chair, teetering on the legs to look through the living room cutout and toward the stairs.

"Yeah?"

"Where did you put it?"

"By my desk, I think!"

"I don't see it." He leaned over the banister and shrugged. "I looked there."

"Oh, I'll help you find it. Hold on a sec. Be right back." I pushed my chair in and excused myself.

I jogged up the staircase to my room.

"We need to figure out what to do about this," he said, the journal already in his hands. "Who this other person is. What those things want from us."

"I know. But what can we do until school starts again? My mom isn't going to just let me go anywhere I want with you. Not now that she knows about *us*."

"Did you tell her?"

"Well, no. Not exactly. But you're the one who kissed me on the porch, remember? And all that flirting downstairs earlier. My mom's not an idiot."

"Of course not. I didn't say she was. She doesn't know about…"

"There aren't cameras in my room. Assuming those things aren't watching us. Ew. I feel icky now." I folded my arms and tucked my hands behind my elbows.

"Hopefully they're not. Besides, you heard them, they

said something about us 'being paired' or whatever. I don't think they care about any of that stuff. Maybe they want us to be together."

"True." I shrugged. "Though I still don't know what that means."

"Just keep in touch, okay? Even if we can't meet up again over break, we still have our phones."

"Yeah."

We were about to pass the threshold when he turned and looked me in the eye. His gaze flitted down to my lips.

"No." I shook my head. "What if *it* happens again? We can't let everyone see it."

He heaved a sigh. "You're right. Though, I don't know how I'm going to live without another kiss, or two, or a thousand from you... eventually."

I whimpered. He was joking, but still.

Pull yourself together. There had to be more to life than...

"Come on." He gestured for me to go ahead of him and then followed me down the stairs and back to the table.

•   •   •

"I can't believe you infected him!" Sam said, pointing a carrot stick at me in the school lunchroom. "Wow. You *are* a terrible girlfriend."

"Keep it down! God knows that sounds so wrong here." I face-palmed.

Most kids love a long break, but all I had been able to think about every day of Christmas vacation was Brian. I had to count the days because Mom didn't want anyone over while family was still in town. It got a little crazy with my uncle, aunt and their kids around.

"I'm not upset, Sam. Believe me," Brian protested. "Besides, we don't know for sure if that's what happened."

We had told Sam about our *condition*, since I trusted

her and she already knew about mine anyway.

"There's no way to prove I gave him the stuff," I argued. "Maybe it was just a coincidence, you know?"

Sam nodded. "I guess. But it's weird."

I heard the click of high heels approaching.

"Hey, Brian," someone said. "Are you sitting at the little girls' table now?"

I veered around. A tall, skinny girl with dark olive skin stood behind me, a hand propped on her hip as if she were on a cat walk. Thick black liner traced her eyes and metallic indigo and purple eye shadow sparkled below her shaped brows. She looked Indian—Bollywood movie Indian. I immediately envied her glossy, straight black hair. It fell down past her hips. The longest hair I'd ever seen in real life.

"Kareena, get lost." Brian shot her an angry glare and then returned his attention to me.

"Aw, what's wrong, Brian? Sad you have to babysit?" Her exaggerated valley-girl accent made me cringe.

Wow. Was this girl for real? I didn't even know her and I already wanted to tell her to get lost, too. I felt small and unattractive beside her shapely, tall, and very feminine body. She had curves in all the right places, and her black and red plaid mini skirt and black leggings accentuated those curves.

"I'm not babysitting," Brian replied gruffly, stabbing his lasagna with a plastic spork.

"Hi. I'm Alice," I said, trying to be polite. "This is my friend Sam."

Kareena scowled, cocking an eyebrow. "Sam? Isn't that a boy's name?"

"Kareena, stop!" Brian stood up from his seat and stared angrily at her. "Alice is my girlfriend. Sam is her friend. If you have anything else to say about that, then say it to someone who gives a damn."

A conniving little grin curled on her lips. "Hmph." Kareena pointed her nose up and crossed her arms. "Your loss. Let me know when you're done playing with kindergartners." She turned and sashayed away like a runway model.

"What just happened?" I slouched over, feeling inadequate all of a sudden. Unattractive and *normal*.

"Don't worry about her, Alice," Brian said, wrapping an arm around my shoulders and pulling me closer. "She's been irritating me since I started coming to this school. I'm sorry you got dragged into it now that we're sitting together. Kareena's just being... Kareena."

I never wanted to be part of *it* again.

Chapter 14

Heels clicked against the tile floor of the hallway. The sound grew louder and closer and then stopped. I held my breath.

"So, you're Brian's plaything, huh?"

Again with the obnoxious valley-girl accent.

I didn't reply and, instead, pretended not to hear her. I had misplaced my fourth period notebook somewhere in my locker and needed to find it.

"What's wrong?" she asked, raising her voice. "Hearing problems?"

She was only a few inches from my face.

"I don't know who you are, but I don't want any trouble with you." I shut my locker door and looked down at my sneakers. "Leave me alone. Please."

"I've got news for you, missy. You see this?" She held out her phone, and I reluctantly looked up to see the screen glowing with a social networking app. "I have over 2,000 friends. I'll bet that's 2,000 more than *you* have."

"Those sites are stupid." I shook my head and looked down the hall. Why did Brian's and Sam's afternoon classes have to be so far from mine?

"Oh yeah?" She tucked her phone back into her sparkly pink handbag. I could imagine a tiny shivering dog shoved in there on weekends. "Well, you know what? I get whatever I want." She pointed a bright red fingernail at me. "And I'm going to get your little Brian, too. You just watch."

"No!" I grabbed her by the wrist and squeezed harder

than I thought I could.

"Shit!" Her eyes widened, the whites outshining her bright green pupils. She dropped her bag and lip-gloss rolled out.

"I asked you nicely," I spoke through gritted teeth. "Leave. Us. Alone."

A sudden pulse of energy jolted through me and into her. Kareena shrieked and jerked away, shielding her hand close to her chest. Her jaw dropped.

"Oh. My. God. You little bitch! You freaking shocked me. How the...?" She shook her hand and then reached down and scooped up her things from the floor. "Ugh! Forget it!"

I had?

"I... I didn't mean to." The adrenaline dissolved and my voice softened. "I'm sorry." I twirled the combination on my locker and then quickly backed away, wanting to get out of there as fast as possible.

"I am sooo done with you," Kareena sneered. "Brian made a big mistake. He has no idea what he's missing." She turned and stomped off, her heels clacking on the tile floor.

My throat tightened. My stomach mangled itself up. Heavy and sick.

Who was she to judge?

She'd had some nerve saying what she had to me.

And how big of a chip did she have on her perfect little shoulder?

·   ·   ·

"You are going to have to do something about that girl. I can't stand her." I plopped down beside Brian on the bench outside by the bus stop.

"Eh, she's all bark and no bite. Don't worry so much."

"How long has this been going on?" I pulled my book bag up into my lap and nestled my hands on top of it.

"Since last year. Since I started here, I think. Before the

break—before *everything* changed—I never sat with you at lunch so you never had to put up with her, but she's been at this for a while, believe me. I don't know why she can't just hit up a guy in her own nasty attitude league. There are plenty of horny sophomores here."

"Brian, don't talk like that, please."

"Sorry. But I don't like her either. She seems to think if she pushes enough, I'll go for her. I won't. She doesn't have any self-respect. You'd think she spends nights hanging out on street corners."

"Yeah. She kind of does have tramp written all over her."

"Exactly. I like to think I have better taste than that." He tapped the tip of my nose playfully with his finger and I blushed.

Sam came up beside us and sat. "Hey, guys."

I scooted closer to Brian to give her more space on the end of the stubby bench.

"I'll talk with her about it later," replied Brian. "Trust me, Alice, I'll put an end to this stupid game of hers."

"Thanks." I smiled. "Oh, and... the reason I brought it up is because she confronted me between classes today."

"What the hell?" His voice rose.

"But something else happened, too." I lowered my voice.

"Yeah?" He perked up.

Sam leaned in closer.

"I got upset and grabbed her hand. Squeezed it pretty hard."

"She probably deserved it." A cocky grin curled in his lips.

"Then... I shocked her."

"What?" The smile vanished and his eyes widened. "You shocked her? Like..."

"Yeah. Exactly the same. She seemed okay, though. Just angrier."

"Don't worry about it." Sam pressed her shoulder into mine. "No biggie, right?"

"Maybe, but I didn't think I could hurt people." I slumped over. "Electronics, maybe, and you," I motioned toward Brian, "because of your pacemaker, but a normal person? What if I'm becoming a danger to people? What if this stuff..."

"Touch me," Sam said, excitedly. "Come on. Just do it." She held out her open palm and wiggled her fingers.

"No. I don't want to take a chance of hurting you."

"I'll be fine. I don't have a pacemaker." She beamed playfully at Brian. "Now come on. Do it."

I looked at Brian. He shrugged. "Worth a shot," he said. "You apparently didn't hurt Kareena too much, anyway."

"Okay. Okay." I stretched out a hand toward hers and she grabbed me.

I closed my eyes and sucked in a breath though my teeth.

"Hah! Nothing!" Sam shook my arm wildly, shaking my whole body with it. I almost toppled off the bench. "I'm fine!"

"Yeah. I guess. But what does that mean?" I slouched and wrapped my arms around myself. Then I glanced at Brian. "I wonder why I've only shocked you and Kareena?" Sam pried my arm loose so she could snake her own around it.

"Shit!" Brian pulled back. He swallowed hard, widened eyes staring off at nothing.

"What! What is it?" I grabbed his knee.

"You. Me. Kareena..." he said quietly, his voice breaking. "What if..."

"What if what?" I looked into his eyes. "What if what, Brian?"

"What if she's the third one?"

I gasped.

No. No.

Not... Kareena.

. . .

"I think it's something we need to consider," said Brian.

"You heard them. They said there was one more. Maybe... as horrible as it may be... she's it."

I flopped onto the couch in the living room and put my phone on speaker. "With an attitude like that, I hope to God she's not."

"Me, too. But think about that dream we had. The one where we were trapped in the abandoned building. Whoever that was we found, they had dark skin. And it sounded like a girl from what I remember."

"I don't remember that much. All I know is we were in trouble and I was hurt. And there was someone else *you* were trying to save. I didn't want anything to do with whoever it was."

"Alice. You heard the... Wait. Am I on speaker?"

"Yeah, but Mom's not here. She went to grab groceries." I kicked my shoes off and propped my feet up on the arm rest.

"Oh. Anyway, you heard what the Saviors said. Something about finding the third one and how you were needed for that. Don't you think it's just a little weird how Kareena is so interested in you? In us? Maybe she's more than just jealous. Maybe she senses something different about us?"

"I think that's crazy. I think she's just being a brat. That's what I think. Besides, you said she's been after you for a while now."

"Can I come over?"

"I don't know. I'm sort of embarrassed to ask my Mom."

"You can come see me, you know."

I laughed out loud by accident. "Yeah, right. I'm sort of at the mercy of my mom and her car."

"Yeah, well, you won't have to worry about that for too much longer. I'm totally getting my license next summer."

"That doesn't mean we can go out driving wherever we want." I heard a car pull into the driveway.

"No, but we can see each other more often than this. I can't stand being stuck on the other side of town every night

and not being able to come see you."

The garage door opened. I didn't have much more time to speak uncensored.

"So... if this Kareena girl is one of us? Then what? How do we know for sure?"

"I'll think of something..."

I heard Mom jiggling the key in the front door so I sat up and took Brian off speaker phone. "Mom's home. I need to go. I'll talk to you later. Bye."

"Bye."

"Was that Brian?" Mom asked, setting an armload of stuffed brown paper grocery bags on the kitchen countertop.

"Yeah."

"When was the last time you talked to Sam?" She took a carton of eggs out and tucked them into the fridge door.

"Uh, today. At lunch. Why?"

"Okay. Just wondering." Mom shrugged.

I knew that shrug. It was the "Okay, whatever you say but I hope you're telling me the truth" shrug.

Chapter 15

The doorbell rang.

We weren't expecting anyone.

I crept down the stairs and listened as Mom opened the door.

"Brian?" she exclaimed.

I tiptoed down to the first floor and into the living room so I could hear the conversation.

"I need to see Alice," he said.

Hearing those words made me sigh.

Yeah. I had it bad.

"You weren't invited. Nor have I given you permission to come over. How did you get here anyway? Where's your mother?"

"I walked. My mom's at work... and... really..." I couldn't hear everything. "I have to see Alice. Please."

"You walked all the way here from Jefferson?"

"I hopped a bus for a few blocks, but yeah."

"To see Alice?"

I couldn't hear his reply.

Mom said something else, but I couldn't make that out either.

Brian went quiet.

She shut the door.

I would have told him not to come, if he'd asked *before* trying.

I flipped on the TV, hoping Mom wouldn't suspect I had been eavesdropping.

"Alice!" she yelled.

"On the couch!"

Mom came into the living room a moment later. "Someone's here for you," she said flatly, and then walked past me and into the kitchen, shaking her head.

I leapt off the couch so fast, I stumbled over the throw rug in front of it. Then I took a deep breath and tried to calm down. I couldn't act too excited. I wasn't supposed to know it was him and... he wasn't supposed to be here at all.

I cracked open the front door.

"Brian?"

He greeted me with a subtle smile.

"Hi, Alice."

My heart beat a little faster. I looked up at him through my lashes.

"Hi..."

.   .   .

He hadn't been to our house since the Christmas party and now I was bristling with emotions.

Excited. Happy. Worried. Scared.

It thrilled me to finally be alone with him again. Well, as alone as we could be with my mom around, of course. And scared because of all of the crazy feelings swirling around inside. Part of me honestly knew we needed to study for the next history test or do something productive. But some stupid part of me just wanted to spend the evening cuddling.

As if that could happen with Mom around.

I'd convinced him we needed to do something important with our time, so my mom wouldn't get upset about the unwelcome visit. If I wanted to spend more time with him, I needed Mom to trust him. Trust began with us being responsible.

We sat on the couch in the living room with our history books open. Studying.

Trying to study.

"What did Mom say to you earlier?" I toned my voice down to a whisper.

Brian leaned over and picked up a notebook from the coffee table. "She said I had to be good to you. Or that I wouldn't be welcome here ever again."

"Ah." I nodded. That sounded like something she'd say. "What did you say back?"

"You really want to know?" he smirked.

"Yeeeah."

Brian scooted closer to me and our hips touched. "I told her... I would never do anything to hurt you." His lips came close to my ear and he lowered his voice. "And that I had it bad for her gorgeous daughter." He snuck a peck on my cheek before I could push him away.

"Gah! You're crazy!"

He shrugged. "Okay, so maybe I didn't tell her the second part. But I did tell her the first."

"You're a piece of work. You know that?"

He liked to make me laugh. I liked it, too.

As we sat there studying, my shoulder pressed against his, our books in our laps and two cups of hot tea steaming on the coffee table, I caught him glancing at me and my heart skipped a beat.

He'd been trying harder than ever now to do well in school. He'd started slacking years ago when his father died because he felt like no one cared. Ever since we'd met, he'd been trying really hard to do better. It showed. He wasn't even late for class anymore.

"So, about Kareena," Brian started, setting his book down onto the coffee table.

"What about her?"

"I have an idea." He folded his hands together in his lap, twiddling his thumbs nervously.

"Okay..."

"Well, I thought about what you told me about getting her off your back and I went to talk to her about it." He paused again.

"And?"

"Then she... sort of invited me over."

"What? You told her to get lost, right?"

"Yeeeah... no, I didn't." He ran a hand through his hair and wouldn't keep eye contact with me.

My jaw dropped. "No way! Why? Why would you do that? She's a creep! And what about me? I thought I was..."

"You are. This has nothing to do with that. I didn't agree to see her because I like her. I swear. Only the three of us know what's going on, and Kareena's not exactly willing to talk to you. I need to see if I can get close enough to her to find out if she's the one we're looking for. Maybe if I can get her alone she'll..."

"Alone?" I crossed my arms and leaned back against the couch cushion. "Hmph. This is a bad idea, Brian."

"Maybe if we're away from other distractions, I can convince her to open up to me. What? You don't trust me?"

"Whatever. All I'm trying to say is I've only known you for a few months. I'm supposed to trust you completely?"

"I want you to, yes."

"Don't do anything stupid, okay?"

"I know. I know."

Beautiful Kareena. Long sleek hair. Brilliant green eyes. The body of a tall, shapely lingerie model.

Did I mention *shapely*?

And me, a scrawny 5'2" fourteen-year-old.

It scared me to imagine him alone with her.

If I were a boy his age... A hormonally driven teenage boy...

I didn't feel like studying anymore.

•   •   •

"Seems like you've been spending an awful lot of time with Brian," Mom said, hanging her coat up in the closet by the front door. She'd felt bad about letting Brian walk home alone in the dark, so she'd driven him back herself. "On the phone. On your computer. In class. At lunch, too, I'm assuming. Right? Maybe you should hang out with more *girls* your age, like Sam and some of her friends."

"Mom, he's my friend, too."

"You mean your *boyfriend? Friends* don't act the way you two do."

I shrugged. "Either way, don't I have the right to spend time with him?"

"Yes. You do. But as your mother, I have the right to decide which people I think are good influences and which aren't."

"And you think Brian is a bad influence?" I slid my feet off the coffee table. "He's never done *anything* to hurt me."

"It's not about him hurting you." She came into the living room, peeled off her black gloves, and tossed them onto the couch. "I've seen the way he looks at you. He *really* likes you, Alice. No doubt he more than just *likes* you."

"Ew, Mom. I know he *likes me*, but you don't have to go all birds and bees. I'm not stupid."

"I'm not calling you stupid, sweetheart." She sat down, her weight sinking into the cushion beside me. "I'm concerned. Stuff can go wrong even when you believe you're doing the right thing. I'm asking you to think about how much time you've been spending with him. That's all. You're not even halfway through high school. There are so many more people out there to meet."

"Are you trying to tell me he's not good enough for me? What has he done to make you feel that way?" I put my hands on my hips and tilted my head. "Mom?"

She took a deep breath. "It's not that I don't like him, Alice. He seems like a nice boy. If you say he treats you well, then I'll believe you. It's important we trust each other. Now more than ever. But you two seem to be moving so quickly. Kids your age don't act like kids nowadays. You're my little girl, but, when you're with him..."

"We're not sleeping together if that's what you're worried about." I leaned back and pulled my knees up to my chest. "I'll make that crystal clear to him if I need to. I'm not ready to handle the consequences of *that*." I shook off the icky feeling crawling all over me. Sex? No. *I really liked him, but...*

"When do you think you will be ready?" She crossed her arms and stared at me. The look on her face was not so much one of skepticism as it was of honest curiosity.

I shrugged, uncomfortable. "Geeze. I don't know. When I'm eighteen. Once I graduate. Maybe. I don't know, Mom. Is that what you wanted to hear?"

She rolled her eyes and sighed. "Until you were married would have been better, but at least this gives me a few years before I really need to start worrying. Things are different for you guys than it was for my generation. You're growing up so quickly. I just want you to know you can talk to me about anything at all. Okay?"

"I wouldn't hide things from you, Mom."

Things that didn't involve aliens.

She smiled as though the weight of the world had been lifted from her shoulders. "I love you, Alice. I only want what's best for you." She squeezed my hand.

"I have that now." I wrapped my arms around her and hugged tightly. "I have loyal friends and the greatest mom in the world."

Chapter 16

*B*rian and Kareena...

I couldn't stop thinking about them. Horrible images of her hanging off him, talking with him, making out with him, or whatever she wanted to do, kept flashing through my head. It made my stomach turn. I trusted Brian. I did, but...

I grabbed my phone and called Sam.

"Hi."

"What's up?"

"Would you mind if I came over for a bit? I'm *really* bored."

"Sure. I'll ask my mom to come get you. It's getting dark already. Stupid winter. Let me ask. One sec."

She went quiet for a moment but left her phone un-muted. I heard her in the background talking to her parents.

"Okay. We'll come get you in a bit."

"Thanks, Sam. Bye!"

"Hey, Mom." I'd come downstairs to find her sitting on the couch watching the evening news. "I'm going to Sam's for a bit, okay? Her mom's going to pick me up."

"That's fine. Be back by 9:30. Got that? It's a school night."

"Yes, Mom. I'll make sure."

Mom never had a problem with me going to see Sam. She lived a few blocks away, unlike Brian, who lived near the end of the bus route. It would have been nice to live closer to my boyfriend.

It had taken a lot of guts on his part, but Brian had made

me proud when he'd worked up the nerve to talk to my mom. Knowing he had smoothed things over with her made me happy. He was a nice guy—responsible and determined— and I knew she'd like him if she gave him a chance. Just like I had. Still, the whole Kareena business had me ruffled and uncomfortable. She was just so pretty. It wasn't fair.

Sam and her mom showed up shortly after I called and they took me back to their house. We spent the next few hours channel surfing and streaming random internet videos to kill our boredom. No homework and nothing else to keep me busy with Brian being gone at Kareena's.

"You seem distracted." Sam waved a hand in front of my eyes. "You okay?"

"Yeah. I'm fine. Why?"

"You look like you're somewhere in space right now. It's Brian, isn't it? I just can't catch a break with the boy taking up every second of your brain. Can you spare a minute, Alice? Please?"

"Sorry, Sam. I'm just preoccupied."

"Ya think?" She cocked her head to the side and shrugged at me. "You can't even focus on the TV right now. You've got it real bad."

"Brian's hanging out with Kareena tonight."

"WTF! You're kidding me! But I thought you two were..."

"We are. Apparently she invited him over and he humored her so he could 'get to know her better' or something." I stuck out my tongue and made gagging sounds.

"Ew! I wouldn't want *my* boyfriend getting to know that skank at all."

"He'll be fine. Whatever. I trust him." I didn't want to tell her the real reason why Brian was hanging out with Kareena in case we were wrong.

"If you say so. You do know she lives, like, down the block, right? At the end of the cul-de-sac?"

"No way! Why have you never told me this before?"

"Uh... Because she's a jerk and we hate her."

"Why don't we ever see her on the bus?"

"She drives to school."

I threw my hands up. "Seriously?" What did she NOT have?

"Daddy and Mommy bought her a car when she turned sixteen last year. She's been driving it to school ever since. She's too good for the bus, apparently."

I huffed. "Brat."

"Yup." Sam nodded, popping the 'p.'

"And now she wants my Brian." I grumbled beneath my breath. "Tramp."

"Well, we could do some reconnaissance and check in on them." Sam smiled a deviously toothy grin. "No one has to know." She pulled a nearby blanket up over her head, wrapped it around her face and peered at me through a gap between the wrinkles. "Sneaky. Sneaky!"

"Won't *your* parents freak?"

Sam shook her head, still covered in the green mink blanket. "They won't care. We'll just step out for a minute."

A minute? That could work. A little peek here. Some spying there.

I took out my cell phone and swiped it on. I silenced the ringtone. If we were going to stake out Kareena's house, we had to be quiet about it.

•   •   •

Sam was right. Kareena lived at the end of the block and her house was even bigger than Sam's.

"Wow," I said quietly, taking in the stupid-large house she lived in. I imagined it having a heated indoor pool. Sauna. Marble hot tubs. Elevator. Gold-plated sinks. I couldn't see anything beyond the short, white picket fence out front or through the window blinds, which were closed tight at this hour.

"This was a stupid idea," I said, looking back at her. She had a black scarf wrapped around her face like a ninja. She'd taken this mission thing way too seriously. "We can't see inside the house anyway."

"You're right. Sorry, Allie. Let's go back."

We turned and started walking back up the sidewalk toward her house when I heard a familiar voice.

Brian!?

It was faint, but I heard him talking. Then I heard a girl's voice. Kareena. Definitely. No mistaking that diva accent of hers. I turned and caught the two of them walking through the grass of the front yard. They were heading our way!

I shoved Sam ahead of me and we ducked down behind a line of hedges in the neighbor's yard. A stick poked the top of my ear and I grunted.

Please don't come this way. Please.

I couldn't begin to imagine explaining myself to either of them if they spotted us. Kareena would have a cow for sure, and Brian... well... I could only hope he'd understand.

They took a few steps across the driveway and Brian sat down on the curb. Kareena sat beside him. The streetlamp overhead provided enough ambient light to watch.

I held my breath. Sam scooted behind me.

"What are they saying?" she whispered.

"I don't know." I put a finger to my lips. "Shh." Then I pushed her away from my face.

I listened hard. Harder than I'd ever listened in my life.

"I just needed some air, alright?" said Brian, shrugging.

Kareena pushed him playfully on the shoulder and added a fake girly giggle. I scoffed.

"Are you sure you didn't want to take me out here because it's dark... and private?" She tipped her head and batted her lashes.

"Why would that matter? Your parents aren't even home."

My eyes widened. *Her parents weren't home!?*

Kareena shook her head and looked off toward the distance. "Wishful thinking."

"Sorry. By the way, I should really be going."

"Aw, so soon? But we hardly had time to do anything."

"We've been talking for the past two hours."

"Oh, I know. But..." She reached up and combed her fingers through his hair.

Sam gasped.

I clenched my fists. Hell if I'd I let her touch my boyfriend like that. I moved a step forward and Sam grabbed my arm. I gave her a dirty look but she shook her head and yanked me back.

I took a deep breath and tried to cool down. Focus. Listen.

"Kareena." He moved her hand away from his face.

"I love the way you say my name." She grinned.

I tried not to gag.

Brian came to his feet. "Kareena, please, I really need to go. Can't you just take me back home?" He walked over to a red sports car parked in front of the driveway.

Kareena stood and heaved a sigh. "You could have anything you want from me, Brian. Anything at all." She marched over to join him near her car. "My parents are out of town and I have practically thrown myself at you. But no, you have to be all noble. Worrying about your little—"

"Is that what you want, Kareena? For guys to treat you like crap? Because I can do that if you really want it, but I don't think that's what you need."

"What would you know about my needs!?"

"Enough to know you've never been touched by another guy who didn't want to sleep with you."

"Ugh!" She huffed, stamping her shoe on the ground. The stick-thin heel snapped off and she tumbled forward. Brian lunged to catch her.

"Let go of me!" She shoved him away and stumbled over

the curb.

"I'm sorry, Kareena," he said. "But it's the truth and you know it. You can't keep living like this. Letting people use you. Filling some kind of void with meaningless sex."

"What kind of guy are you, really? Are you gay?"

"You know exactly the kind of guy I am. Who do *you* want to be? Do you want to be seen as a whore for the rest of your life? Or do you want people to respect you and actually care about you? How many people do you know would be there for you if you needed them? I mean really, actually *needed* them to help you for nothing in return?"

She leaned against the hood of her car and crossed her arms, pouting. "I'm not getting used. I chose this life. It's always been this way."

"No one *wants* to be used, Kareena. Stop fooling yourself."

"Well, maybe I don't like being alone. How do I make friends if everyone hates me?"

What a joke. I almost laughed.

"Everyone doesn't hate you." Brian sat beside her on the car hood.

"Yeah, right. Even in my stupid-ass dreams, I'm alone. Trapped and freaking alone. I was so damn scared. I..." She crumpled over. "I called out for help and no one could hear me." Her voice trembled. "It's not fair." She covered her face with her hands. "Please, just don't look at me like this. Jesus..."

I leaned forward, holding a clump of hedge branches down to keep them from obstructing my view.

"So you had it, too, Kareena?" Brian moved closer and gently pried her hands from her face. "That was you buried beneath all that rubble?"

Her eyes widened. "How do you know about that?"

"That's what I needed to talk to you about, but you didn't..."

Sam's phone chirped—e-mail. I swerved around. My jaw dropped. "Sam!" I mouthed angrily. She shrugged and pulled her phone out of her pocket.

"I thought I silenced the ringer," she whispered frantically, scrambling to change some settings.

"What the hell was that?" Kareena turned, raising her voice. I swallowed hard and ducked down behind the hedges, backing up a few feet. Her heel clicked against the pavement. She staggered closer and closer.

"Probably nothing," said Brian. "What I was trying to say was—"

"Oh, hell no!"

Kareena had spotted us. I froze in place, holding my breath.

"I see you. Come out of there right now!" she roared.

Sam and I crept out from behind the bushes.

The appalled look on Brian's face made me feel like an idiot.

Kareena turned toward him and propped a hand on her hip. "Oh, don't act like you didn't know about this, Brian. You had to bring along your little lame parade, didn't you?"

"I didn't know about them, I swear," he defended.

She pointed at him accusingly. "You know what? You can walk your lying ass home. In fact, why don't you take your little sisters with you? I am done here." She threw her hands up and turned away.

"Maybe if *you* weren't such a bitch all of the time, people would actually like you," he retorted. "I hope you're happy with yourself."

"I am." She stuck up her nose and marched back up her driveway, tripping once on her broken heel.

Brian looked at me, disappointed, and my heart sank.

"I'm sorry," I said, looking down. "I really am."

"I asked you to trust me, Alice. What were you so worried about that you had to stalk me?"

Sam came out from behind me and held up her hand. "It was sort of my idea. I'm sorry, too."

He shook his head. "Jesus, Alice. I was kind of hoping you trusted me just a little bit more than—"

Kareena shrieked.

We veered our heads toward the sound but she had already disappeared from the driveway. Brian darted up the brick walkway toward the front door of her house and vanished into the shadows.

"Guys!" he called out.

I ran to meet him and my heart plummeted into my stomach. Brian was kneeling on the ground at the base of the porch, Kareena sprawled lifelessly across his lap.

"What happened?" I fell to my knees beside them and tried to find someplace to put my hands. I touched something warm and damp. Blood on the concrete. I gasped and frantically wiped my fingers off on my jeans.

Brian swept her long tangled hair away from her face, his blood-covered hands shaking.

"I-I think she tripped on the steps," he said, a shudder in his voice, cradling her head in his lap. An open wound on her forehead oozed blood. A streak of crimson trickled down her face. "She's unconscious. Those damn high heels of hers."

"What do we do? What do we do?" Sam whimpered.

A splash of red darkened Brian's jeans and I winced.

"We should call 9-1-1," I said. "Definitely."

Sam scrambled with her cell phone. "On it!"

"Wait!" Brian held up his hand.

"What?" Sam paused and loomed over us, panicking. "What?"

A rosy pink color radiated up the right side of Kareena's face, followed by tiny sparks of hot pink light forking both up toward her brow and down toward her collar bone.

"We were right!" Brian took Kareena's hand.

I untangled the stringy scarf from around her neck and

bundled it up into my hand to press against her forehead, hoping it might stop the bleeding.

"We need to call an ambulance!" Sam paced behind me.

"We can't let anyone see her like this," Brian replied.

"She could DIE!" Sam cried.

The pink grew brighter and brighter, coloring the entire side of Kareena's face with a fuchsia glow.

"Alice!" Brian brought his other hand out from behind her back. His fingers resonated with fiery white-blue light. The veins snaked up his arms, burning much more intensely than before. An aura of color came to the surface of his skin and blue vapor wafted from his fingertips, like dust in a sunny window. He touched her face, tinting the pink of her cheek a rich purple with his light.

"Kareena, come back to us, please," I said, holding tightly to her frigid hand. Her body temperature was dropping fast, her grip weakening. "I might hate you, but I don't want you to die!"

"It's doing something. I can feel it," Brian said, readjusting his grasp on Kareena and propping her up against his leg. "The heat. The light. Something's changing. Take that away." He pointed at the scarf.

I carefully peeled it back and watched as a violet glow webbed around the torn flesh, lighting and blurring the edges of the wound.

The bleeding stopped.

Kareena opened her eyes and cried out in pain. She choked on a drizzle of blood streaming down her face and Brian wiped it from her cheek.

"It hurts!" she muttered, the agony in her words making my stomach sick.

Brian cupped her face in his glowing hand.

Beneath the dingy yellow cast of the porch light, I saw the wound closing—healing. It softened and smoothed over, the new skin forming like a fresh coat of paint overlaying the gash. It was as if nothing had ever happened to her perfect olive skin.

"Are you doing that?" I asked Brian. He looked me in the eye.

"I... think so. I can feel the energy moving through me."

"Leave me alone!" Kareena growled, pushing me off her and struggling feebly to shove Brian away, too. "What the hell is going on?" She came to her feet and took another step up the porch steps, wobbling and mumbling to herself furiously. Brian followed.

She stopped cold in her tracks, looked down at her hands and screamed. There was blood on everything. The ground. Her shoes. Her clothes. She took a clumsy step closer toward the door and reached for the handle, her hand shaking. Then she let out another piercing shriek.

The reflection in the glass front door revealed her pink face glinting back at her.

Brian held up his glowing blue hand. "You're one of us now," he said.

Chapter 17

The police officer opened the car door for me and I stepped out, nauseated. Mom stood in the driveway, fuming.

"Your daughter and some friends were loitering in the street past curfew. Neighbors heard some bickering and called it in. Thankfully, it was only an accident."

"An accident?" Mom shot me an angry glare. "What happened?"

"The older girl they were with apparently had a fall on the pavement. A paramedic checked her out and said she should be fine."

"Paramedic?" Mom's angry look transformed into a death stare. Her eyes narrowed. "Alice?" Her voice turned really gruff. "What the hell were you doing out in the street in the dark? I thought you were with Sam."

"I was. I really was. But..."

"I don't want excuses right now. Get in the house." She pointed sternly at the door. "Now!"

"Yes, Mom." I slunk past her and rushed into the house.

She stayed outside with the officer for a while longer. I had no idea what they were discussing. It was just a lot of nodding on the officer's behalf and some angry shaking of Mom's head in response. It scared me to death imagining what she'd say to me when she came back inside. She looked furious.

The door slammed behind her.

"Alice!" Mom yelled hoarsely. "Get down here right this second!"

"I'm coming." My voice broke. I tiptoed down the staircase.

"Alice! What the hell do you think you were doing outside this late? With Brian? And that... older girl. Whoever the hell she is. Really, Alice?"

"I didn't mean for anything to happen. I just... wanted to check on Brian." I couldn't tell her the whole truth.

"Oh yeah? Well, I'll tell you what. How about we make this little escapade the last time you see him? How's that sound?"

"Mom, no! He didn't do anything wrong."

"But *you* did. I can't tell them what to do. If their parents are idiots, that's their problem. What I say to my own daughter is what matters to me. You need to listen to *me*, Alice."

"Mom, please! This is crazy!"

"No. You being brought home by a police officer past 10:00 at night is crazy! Seeing that car pull up into the driveway scared the crap out of me. I tried to call you three times, Alice. Three times and you didn't pick up."

Oh, God. I pulled out my cell and turned on the ringer. "I didn't mean to."

"Then I called Sam's parents to check on you, thinking maybe you were just in the basement watching movies and weren't getting a signal, but no, they told me they didn't know where you two had gone. Do you know how goddamn scared I got when I heard that?"

"I'm sorry..."

"Sorry is not good enough right now."

"Mom."

"I don't know what to do about Sam, but... I don't want you talking to Brian anymore. Do you understand?"

"You can't make me—"

"Don't talk back. And yes, I can. He's not allowed over. You're not allowed to call him. No texting—and believe me, I can get those records if I need to. If I catch you emailing him or anything else, I will take your computer away. I swear."

"No! I need it!"

"Apparently not as much as you need to keep secrets from

me. I trusted you, Alice, and you lied."

"I didn't lie."

"You told me you were going to see Sam and somehow... somehow the night ends with you, Brian, and the police. I gave you two a chance but apparently that was a mistake. You're not mature enough to be in a relationship. This stupid little game is over."

"Please listen."

"You didn't listen to me." Her lips thinned. She crossed her arms and looked away. "Go to your room!"

.   .   .

Sam had been smart enough to grab the garden hose and wash down the steps of the patio, but the police showed up literally minutes later, asking questions. Nosey neighbors... We had such little time to clear things up with Kareena before everything went south. To make things worse, our stupid city had an early curfew for teens under seventeen. Kareena was exempt—lucky her. Brian, Sam and I didn't get off so easily.

I hadn't heard from Brian since last night but found him at lunch time, resting on a table, his head nestled in his folded arms. Sleeping? His wrinkled clothes made him look like he'd stayed in the woods overnight.

"Hi," I said quietly.

He looked up at me almost mechanically, exhausted. Dark circles shadowed under his eyes. He didn't even acknowledge Sam, who was standing right beside me.

I brushed a hand through his hair and frowned. "Oh, Brian. You look so worn out. Are you okay?"

"Yeah," he groaned beneath his breath and cupped his face with his hand. "Three sodas and I still feel like shit. Sorry, Alice. I mean..."

I'd told him before I didn't like him swearing. He was so

tired, though, I had to let it go.

"It's alright." I nudged him in the shoulder and sat down on the bench, scooting closer. Sam sat down across from us.

I leaned over to kiss his cheek, playfully tickling the back of his neck with my fingernails. He forced a smile. It faded with his next heaving sigh. It was tough seeing him like this.

"When did your mom pick you up from the police station?" I pulled a little compact brush out of my bag and brushed his messy hair, straightening it as best I could. He scowled at me.

He dropped his head onto the edge of the table with a thud. "She didn't," he grumbled.

"I'm sorry." I put my brush back in my bag.

"She told them to keep me there because I deserved it. I was at the freaking police department all... freaking... night. They hauled me back to school this morning."

"That's why you weren't on the bus. I'm so sorry, Brian. You should have called me. Maybe..."

"Your mom was pissed, right?"

"Yeah. She was upset. Scared me a little, even. I've never seen her so angry in my life."

"She's been looking for an excuse to hate me since we met. Now she has one." He turned his face toward me. "What did she say?"

I didn't want to tell him the truth, but hiding it wouldn't make things better either.

"I'm even not supposed to be talking to you right now, technically."

"What?" He groaned again.

I imagined Brian being the kind of guy to bound up onto the lunchroom table, kick off food trays, toss yogurt cups into the air and shout at the top of his lungs something about discrimination and teen oppression.

"She can't do that." He sighed, too worn out to even raise his voice.

I put my arm around his shoulders and squeezed him

closer. "Well, she's my mom. She can do whatever she wants with me for the next four years."

"That sucks." He sat up and looked at me, his eyelids barely able to stay open. "And it's not fair to me at all."

"She says I'm not mature enough for a relationship." I scoffed, rolling my eyes. "She has no idea what's really going on between us, or about the... you-know-what. All she knows is she doesn't want you over ever again."

"What the hell does that mean? Ever?" Hearing those words had jarred him awake.

"No texting. No calls. No emails."

He sneered and his eyes narrowed. "I'll be damned if she can keep me away from you forever."

I cupped a hand over his. "You *have* to respect my mom, Brian. Please."

"I know and I'm sorry. It just pisses me off. And I can't do anything about it."

"We'll work something out. Somehow." I smiled, trying to be optimistic.

He stared at me for a moment, scanning my face, and I thought he might try to kiss me—right in the middle of the lunchroom.

He didn't. He only sighed, looking defeated, and then laid his head back down on his arms and closed his eyes.

The familiar sound of the clicking of heels on linoleum drew close.

I looked up at Kareena and wrinkled my lips, judgingly. "Yes?" I rested a hand on Brian's forearm protectively. I knew she was done with him for now, but I still felt the need to take ownership.

Sam screwed up her face and crossed her arms.

"Uh... can I sit with you guys?" Kareena looked around the room, clearly hoping no one else had heard her, as if it had been the most difficult thing she'd ever had to say to anyone.

Sam pointed her nose up and scoffed. "Nope."

Kareena slumped over, fighting back a scowl.

I wasn't going to make her beg.

"Yes. It's fine." I pulled my book bag off the table to make room for her tray. Sam got a quick raspberry off at her.

"Sam, stop."

"Hmph." She looked away. "Make me."

"Please? We've been through enough."

She shrugged, conceding. "Fine."

Kareena set her tray of food down and sat directly across from me. She glanced at Brian, still resting, and took a deep breath. I was surprised to see a genuine fondness and admiration for him in her gaze. It had me almost feeling sorry for her. For a moment, she appeared to show concern for someone other than herself. Maybe she really did like Brian but didn't know how to approach a nice guy. Regardless, of course, he was with me now and I liked it that way, even if she didn't.

"I don't feel like talking about last night," said Kareena. "But, I know we need to."

"Yeah. We do," I answered, nodding.

"I tried to tell myself nothing happened, but I know some serious shit went down. I have a blood-stained blouse in the wash that proves it." She picked at her fruit cup with a plastic fork, moving things around and sneaking a peek at Brian every few minutes.

I brushed a lock of his hair behind his ear and nudged him again.

"Brian? Lunch will be over soon. You've got to get up."

He growled, not moving.

"Please? Just two more classes and you can go home."

"I don't want to..."

I pushed him firmly in the arm with my hands. "You have to."

He lifted his face from his arms and yawned. His eyes were bloodshot and watery. I brushed my fingers over his cheek and smiled. He took my hand, squeezing it in thanks, smiling a tired smile.

Kareena shook her head and looked away.

Chapter 18

Sunday afternoon.

Mom had gone shopping, leaving me alone in the house. I sat on my computer chair with my knees pulled up to my chest. Thinking. Regretting. Hating myself for being so nosy. Contemplating how I might find a way to spend time with Brian again.

I wanted to see Brian. I wanted to see Sam, too, but mom wouldn't let her over for another three weeks. It was part of my punishment. Basically grounded from life for a month, grounded from Brian for "forever," and not allowed to walk home from school until Mom deemed it okay. With such little time between classes to be with my friends, it was starting to wear me thin. And to think, I had another four months of it to endure before summer break. That's when things would get really tough.

Life sucked.

My phone chimed—text message.

UNKNOWN: Hey! We need to talk.
ME: Who is this?
UNKNOWN: OMFG. Kareena.

Even her texts had attitude.

ME: Mom won't let me out of the house.
UNKNOWN: Sneak out grl!!
ME: No way! :O Mom would freak!

I added her number to my contact list while waiting for a reply.

KAREENA: @ the cafe on the corner of Forth and Birch. Brian's here.
ME: . . .
KAREENA: No, really. Can send a pic.
ME: I hate you.
KAREENA: U coming?
ME: Mom will KILL me.
KAREENA: Have it UR way. L8R

She made me so angry. As if it wasn't bad enough I couldn't see Brian outside of class; now he and Kareena were hanging out. Sure, Mom would be gone for a little while longer but not long enough for me to sneak out and sneak back in without her knowing. The last thing I needed was her banning me from the world and... who knows... pulling me out of school or something crazy.

I snatched a pillow off my bed and jammed my face into it, screaming and kicking my feet until I ran out of breath.

That took a while.

I could *try* to leave, but if I didn't get back in time, it'd be the end of it. Right there.

The End.

I groaned and tossed my pillow at the door. I walked over to look out my bedroom window, pulled up the blinds, and then pried the window open. Cool air gushed through and I shivered, slamming the window back down.

Forget that.

I wanted to text Brian something... anything. But she'd find out. I couldn't let this be the end of us. I liked Brian way too much to let it end now. Things would never progress if my mom kept stifling us, though.

"Most high school romances don't last," she'd said to me

the other night, hoping I'd give up my incessant brooding.

If that really was the case, then I wouldn't let it be just a "romance."

. . .

I shoved my notebook into my locker and sighed, puffing out my cheeks. My four-week complete social banishment had finally ended and I could hang out with Sam again. That didn't fix everything, though.

Someone's arms circled around me, ensnaring me by the waist. I squealed.

"Hi, Alice," chuckled Brian, embracing me and craning his neck to kiss the side of mine. I melted, closing my eyes as he nuzzled the back of my head.

He let go and I spun around to face him.

We'd had zero private time together since the *accident*, and I had somehow convinced myself that *not* kissing him would make our time apart easier to tolerate.

I was wrong. Every time I saw him it was all I could think about. All. Day. Long.

Teen separation anxiety at its max.

Brian got a mischievous look in his eyes. He raised an eyebrow at me and a grin curled across his lips. He reached past my head to pull my locker door open further and took a step closer. I backed up, bumping against the other lockers. He leaned in to steal a kiss, our faces partially hidden from the public.

I exhaled a sigh as he brushed my hair behind my ear.

"Why did that take me so long to try?" He chuckled.

"Not here," I said, embarrassed, wriggling away from my locker door, hoping my shoulder wouldn't flare. "You know better!"

He shrugged and rolled his eyes. "Okay. Then find somewhere else we can go and I will gladly kiss you there. I'm tired of this." He exaggerated a frown and made sad, puppy-dog eyes. "I need you, Alice."

"I don't want to take any chances here, you know?"

"Yeah," he said, stroking his fingers through my hair, giving me goose bumps. "Sucks you can hardly get out of the house anymore. I want to be with you. More."

"I know, but that's life for now. Until we can find a way to change things."

"I think you should tell your mom the truth."

"Are you crazy?" My eyes widened. I shut my locker and spun the combination lock. "Why?"

"You can trust her, right? You trust your mom, don't you?"

"Well, yeah, but... what if she freaks out? This isn't something that happens to normal teenagers."

"If you trust her, then tell her. We could use her help." He shrugged again. "I'm just saying, it's an option. Maybe?" He took my book bag from me and shouldered it.

We walked together toward history class.

"Anything new with Kareena?" She kept giving me the silent treatment during lunch.

"Don't know. I don't talk to her much more than you do. But no, I don't think so. Ask her yourself when she's done with... whoever that is." Brian gestured toward the lockers on the other side of the hall.

"Ew!" I gagged.

Some senior jock had Kareena plastered up against her locker, his hands in all the wrong places while they made out. This was a school...

Gross.

"Aw, now I'm jealous." Brian smirked at me.

I stopped dead in my tracks and shot him a dirty look. "Excuse me!?"

"No. No. Not of *him* being with her. I meant of me not being able to do that with you." He stared longingly at me. "Oh, Alice, if only you'd let me..."

I whimpered. I couldn't even imagine Brian's hands all over me like that... Or maybe I had already. My face felt flushed.

Brian beamed a toothy grin at me and then took my hand. "But I respect you *so* much more than that," he added. "Besides, I wouldn't want to embarrass you in public. Especially not doing what he's doing."

I sighed in relief and we laughed it off together.

"What the hell?" Kareena shouted with a stomp of her heel against the tile floor.

Something was wrong.

The crowd of passing students had become frozen in time, their silent mid-sentence expressions captured in slow-motion. The jock she'd been swapping spit with was also freeze-framed, propped up against the lockers in front of her.

"Oh, no." I closed my eyes and recoiled, knowing what came next. Brian grabbed me, pulled me closer, and shielded his eyes with his arm.

The floor disappeared. White hot light burned through my eyelids, stinging my retinas.

Weightless. Spinning. Falling.

Kareena screamed, wasting her breath. I was clutching onto Brian's shirt, so I couldn't cover my ears. I wanted to tell her to shut up—that it would be okay, that it would all be over soon.

But I couldn't breathe.

Chapter 19

The sour smell of vomit made me retch.

Kareena fell to her knees and arched over, hands flattened on the once immaculate white floor. She coughed hard, her face drained of color. I looked away and dry heaved, trying to occupy my mind with thoughts of butterflies and kittens. Anything to keep my own stomach from erupting.

She wiped her face with the back of her arm and gagged again, keeping it down this time. A putrid stench wafted through the air, stinging my nostrils. I grimaced, holding my breath as I tiptoed over the mess.

"Don't freak." I touched her shoulder and then offered her a hand.

She staggered to her feet, putting so much weight against me, I nearly toppled over. Brian grabbed onto my other arm. He tried hard to keep his cool, even as Kareena clenched her fingers onto his jacket sleeve and hung off him, staring into his hazel eyes like a miserable puppy.

You threw up. Get over it. That's what I had wanted to say out loud, but there were too many other eyes watching us now.

The room flooded with bright light a second time and I gasped. Kareena screeched. I let go of Brian to cover my ears and squeezed my eyes shut until she stopped.

"It's okay." He pressed his fingers against the small of my back. I eased open my eyes. Kareena had let go of him. The floor was immaculate. Not a trace of her mess.

Lightning-fast room service.

"We have brought you to the council once more for the purpose of discussion," the one we thought was the translator said. He stepped in front of several others there and their outlines blurred and faded into the white of the room, going out of focus. I squinted, trying to readjust my eyes, but it was no use. They were purposely camouflaging themselves to keep our focus on the one that mattered.

"Brian?" The Savior's grey eyes focused on him.

Brian flinched.

"What?" He straightened up. I wrapped my fingers around his hand.

"You and... Alice..." The figure stopped to study me as my name caught on his tongue. "You do not spend adequate time together. This is of great concern to us."

"We have parents, that's why," I butted in. "We can't just run around doing whatever we want, you know?"

The translator tilted his head and stared, blinking at me as if *I* were the idiot.

"In an era of freedom and advanced rights, why does this prove to be an issue? Historically, humans have chosen mates at much younger ages. Do your parents not wish for you to become independent?"

"Sure they do," Brian added. "But legally, we aren't allowed to. Not until we're older. It's the law."

The translator's eyes narrowed. "The law? Excuses," he said without inflection, and then directed his attention to Kareena who stood embracing herself, shaking. "You. You are not authorized to choose a mate."

"What?" Her voice cracked. "What does that mean? Who the hell are you guys anyway?"

Brian shrugged. "I think it means you can't go around hooking up with everyone," he said out of the side of his mouth. "Just shut up and listen."

"Hey!" Kareena pursed her lips and took a step closer, analyzing the Savior's chalky-white skin. "Listen, you—who could totally use a tan—I can do *whatever* I want with *whoever* I want." She squared her shoulders and jiggled her head like a diva, brushing her hands down her skirt. "I'm a free bitch, baby."

The translator stared. Silent. Unmoved. Deathly still. His ashen eyes glazed over with apathy. Raising her voice to him was like arguing with a robot. An ultra-realistic robot with human features and the sallow skin of a fresh corpse.

Kareena backed away, whimpering beneath her breath and softening her posture.

"You cannot allow others to interfere or discover what you are." Though the inflections were subtle, he meant business. "Unauthorized interaction with others will jeopardize this. You *will* stop."

Her jaw dropped. Telling Kareena to stop hanging out with boys was like telling a normal person to stop breathing.

She would have scoffed if the air hadn't been so thin, but she was struggling to breathe already. Her chest was probably tightening, like ours. I could see it on her face. Each subsequent breath became heavier—harder to suck in.

The translator approached and looked down his small, sharply-curved nose at us. He stood well over a foot taller than Brian.

"You possess it now," he said to Kareena.

"Possess what?" Her lips quivered.

Brian fake-coughed. "An STD," he muttered.

I shot him a dirty look, but he stared at me with widened eyes like he was totally in the right. Maybe he was. But still.

"The bioluminescence implanted inside you lives now, started—activated—by Alice not too long ago." He lifted a flattened hand and drifted his palm over Kareena's face, a few inches above her skin. The hot pink light flared up on the right side of her face. Thin jagged lines of color forked and spread from her cheek to her forehead, as if her veins had suddenly been illuminated from the inside. She gasped, likely seeing the pink tint in her eyes.

He moved and hovered his hand near my shoulder. Green sparkled through my sleeve. Then he stepped over to Brian who stiffened considerably, his left hand and forearm already beaming with hot azure light.

"Due to your differing genetic makeup, the fluorescent proteins have bonded with each of you differently."

Brian rolled his shoulders back. "Why have you done this to us?" The question had been burning in my own mind for a while. "We deserve to know."

"The answer to that is not a simple one," the Savior said, lowering his hand back down to his side. "A virus has long plagued our race, taking us one by one until we are few more than those you have seen here. We are working to create a cure but it is taking longer than expected. The virus grows stronger every day we fail to annihilate it. Humans are closely compatible with fluorescence in terms of genetic makeup. We are using you to preserve a portion of our own DNA while we search for a cure." His gaze went back to Kareena. "However, to keep the strain pure, you must abide by our requests to segregate yourselves from those who are not part of the preservation process. We cannot risk the proteins being tainted."

"B-but," stammered Brian, pointing at me and then himself. "Alice and I are okay together, right?"

The translator tipped his head, something he must have picked up from watching us because he'd never used a gesture before. He had been observing us intently today.

"Guess you're on your own, Kareena." Brian shrugged.

She sneered.

"Will it hurt us?" I asked.

The translator's head turned. "No. It will reside peacefully, cohabiting with your own DNA until we are in need of it. All you must know is how vital you three are to our cause."

Again with the *cause.*

The other Saviors abruptly came back into focus. It startled us, like disconnected headphones suddenly being plugged in at full volume. The translator looked back at them and then at us.

"The fluorescence requires more time to manifest in you before we can carry forth with the next step of our study. As you may have noticed, time here flows differently than on earth, so we cannot be sure of when you will be ready. We can assure you we *will* summon you again. But, remember what we have told you. If your elders continue to hinder your interactions, we will not hesitate to stop them."

"Don't touch my mom!" I yelped, louder than I had meant to. "Please."

The Saviors gazed at me in unison and my whole body started shaking, my stomach twisting into knots. So many pale grey eyes judging me with their stares.

"We'll make it work," Brian defended, taking my hand. "Don't do anything to hurt our families, please."

"Yeah," Kareena murmured, looking down at her feet. "I need mine, too." She scuffed the ball of her foot against the floor.

I winced, closing my eyes tightly to the flare of burning white light.

Kareena let out a high-pitched squeal.

Brian grunted. He hadn't inhaled fully before the fall.

Chapter 20

The room flashed and a hoard of students surrounded us once more. Everyone inched forward a few frames in slow-motion before time returned to normal speed.

Jarred from the journey, Kareena dodged her boyfriend's half-puckered lips, sending him to smooch the cold locker door beside her. He smacked into the metal and then pulled back, grunting and shaking his head. "Hey!" He scooped his arm around her waist, pulling her toward him. "The hell?"

"Not right now." She batted his hands from her midriff. "My head hurts."

"Since when?" The jock pinned her, his hands flattened on the locker doors on both sides of her head. His lips wrinkled with disgust. "And why do you smell nasty?"

"Leave me alone, Chris." She wriggled down and slipped out from under him. Chris grabbed her hand and jerked her back.

"Let her go, jackass." Brian confronted the senior, who was much bigger and more muscular than he. I was scared he'd get punched. Kareena was so not worth a black eye. Especially not on *my* boyfriend.

"Butt out, freshie." Chris snickered. "Why don't you go back to your little girl? Leave the women to me."

"I mean it." Brian clenched both fists and puffed out his chest. "She asked you to leave her alone."

The jock glanced at Kareena and then back at Brian, unsettled, confused.

"Please, go away," she murmured, tugging her hand out

of his.

Chris scoffed. "Screw this." He turned and walked away.

Brian lifted his chin and exhaled proudly. I sighed in relief and came up beside him to tuck my fingers into one of his belt loops and scoot closer.

"You're really brave. You know that?" I smiled.

"Only when I have to be." He shrugged. "I didn't *want* to get beat up."

"Thanks, Brian," Kareena whispered, lowering her head.

"When I said you were one of us, I meant it, Kareena," Brian added. "Even if you were a jerk back then, there's always time to change. We need to stick together from now on. We need to learn to get along."

Kareena cupped her hand against her forehead and groaned.

"My head is killing me," she said, squeezing her eyelids shut.

"Maybe you don't tolerate intergalactic travel well." I laughed, trying to lighten the mood. It worked on Brian.

Kareena cringed. "No. My head is really hurting. I've never had a..."

"Come with me." Brian took her by the wrist and gestured for me to follow him outside school.

Me and the hot girl both tagging along with him must have appeared interesting to the other boys in the hall. I caught a few awkward—jealous—stares.

We walked out into the parking lot where Brian stopped, turned toward Kareena and lifted his hand up to her forehead.

I gasped. "No! Not here. Someone could see us."

By now, Kareena had all but doubled over, grimacing and moaning beneath her breath.

"She's in a lot of pain, Alice," he replied, his eyes pleading with me. "I have to at least try to help."

"Just be quick." I scanned our surroundings for anyone

who might tattle on us. I'd never played hooky before in my life. Call me a prude, but I don't like getting into trouble or skipping class.

Brian's fingers trembled. He pressed them against her forehead and closed his eyes. The blue immediately sparked to life in his arm, veins of color forking up through his hand and into his fingertips, growing brighter along the way.

Kareena took a deep breath and exhaled slowly, her eyes closing. Freckles of white and blue light dotted her hairline, glittering like fiber optic tips over her skin.

I looked around. No one had seen us.

"Is it working?" I asked anxiously, standing up on my tiptoes to look over Brian's shoulder at her.

"Yes." Kareena nodded, sighing in relief and opening her eyes to look into Brian's. Seeing such thankfulness in her gaze made me incredibly uncomfortable. I plopped back onto my heels and shuffled in place.

She admired him so much; I couldn't even begin to imagine how hard it must have been for her to feel his soft touch and then have to move on, knowing he would never be hers.

"Let me know if it comes back." Brian dropped his arm down to his side. The blue extinguished instantly.

"You're a miracle worker, Brian." I nudged him in the shoulder.

"I doubt that. But apparently, I *am* a healer of some sort."

So far, we had established that I was some kind of alien DNA jump-starter, and Brian was a healer. Only time would tell what Kareena's role in all of this would be.

•   •   •

The headaches didn't stop.

A few weeks later, Brian and I found Kareena sitting

outside on the lawn, knees pulled up to her chest, back pressed up against the brick wall of the school. Her skirt was dotted with darkened blotches—tears. Smudges of black eyeliner stained her cheeks.

"I'm sorry they did this to you," said Brian, kneeling down to put a hand onto her shoulder.

She looked up through her lashes and sniffled. "How can I have a boyfriend ever again? It's not fair. You and Alice get to be together but I can't get within inches of any guy *besides* you without feeling like my damn head is going to burst."

When the Saviors said her "mingling" had to stop, they meant it. Migraines: the torture of the future.

"I'm sorry, Kareena," I said. "We have no control over this. So we just have to muster up the courage to pull through until they're done with us." I rummaged around in my book bag for a tissue and then bent over and handed it to her. "Here. And think about it. Brian and I aren't even allowed to see each other outside of school. We're not that well off, either, you know?"

"I guess." She sniffed hard and tried to clear her congested throat. "I don't like people telling me how to live my life."

"Neither do we," Brian added, looking up at me.

Chapter 21

Friday was my birthday.

I'd technically caught up with Brian age-wise, but in a few weeks, he'd be sixteen and I'd be a year younger again. Not that it mattered, anyway.

He'd slipped me a sweet card at school with a purple sketch of a knight holding a bouquet of flowers and a little IOU for an "upcoming, much greater, belated gift."

I hid the card under my mattress so Mom wouldn't find it. A shame, but I couldn't take a chance. I wanted the world to know how awesome my boyfriend was. His art deserved respect. It didn't deserve to be smothered between metal coils, cotton and polyester.

For my birthday, I had dinner with Sam and Mom. We ate at an Italian place and then came home to have mint chocolate chip ice-cream. Mom had bought me a round dark chocolate ice-cream cake with a cartoonish purple dolphin—my favorite animal—piped on top. It made me smile.

Fifteen.

One year closer to freedom. One year closer to a future with *him* and whatever it would take to get us there.

I blew out the candles and I made my wish.

I wanted Brian with me. For my birthday. For an evening. Just some time—any time—away from school. Like a normal boyfriend and girlfriend. I wanted to stare into his hazel eyes and know I would be safe wherever we were.

I hated how he had been punished for my mistake. It wasn't fair to either of us. We weren't being stupid teenagers.

Mom had no idea what we were dealing with. This was about more than rebelling. More than hiding petty secrets.

One month until summer break.

What then?

I'd been lucky enough to sneak a few texts off to Brian from Sam's phone while I was with her, but hiding everything from Mom was driving me to my last nerve. I had a right to be with him.

"Brian says happy birthday," Sam whispered.

"What?" I looked up from the slice of cake I'd been pushing around my plate for the past several minutes. Mom had left the room to get my gift.

"You heard me." Sam elbowed me and grinned. "Don't be such a downer. At least he's thinking about you."

I hunched over my plate, twirling a blob of purple frosting into a lumpy mound with my fork. The purple and white started blending together into violet with cake crumbs mixed in. "It sucks he can't be here. You're only fifteen once."

"I know, Allie." She tossed an arm over my shoulders and hugged me. "I support you and I'll do whatever I can to make sure you're happy."

"Thanks."

"Even if that means me keeping your hot boyfriend a secret while wallowing in eternal loneliness without one."

I laughed, but then my heart sank.

Loneliness.

• • •

Brian's birthday fell on the Saturday before summer vacation. I couldn't see my boyfriend—who also happened to be part of a crazy, alien-race-saving conspiracy—on his sixteenth birthday. This would only get worse. Soon, the stress caused by my mother's hysteria would officially ruin our lives.

We almost played hooky from class on our last day of

school, just to get some alone time, but I decided against it. We hadn't come this far to screw up and get into more trouble.

Today, we sat in the back of the bus. Sam guarded one of the rows in front of us so other kids couldn't sit there and disturb us.

"I'll keep in touch... somehow." Brian tried to hide his feelings behind a smile, but couldn't shake the worry from his eyes. "It's only a few months."

"Yeah."

"Really, Alice, I will." He tipped my chin up and caressed my face with the back of his fingers, wiping a fresh tear from the apple of my cheek with his thumb. "Things are bad now, but they'll get better. I promise."

I believed him.

My chest tightened. Tears were inevitable, though I tried to keep them in. Any minute now, Brian would step off the bus and out of my life and I wouldn't see him again for months.

A lot can happen to someone in a few months. I wanted to be there for all of it. Every laugh. Every smile. Every screw-up and every success.

He leaned over and kissed my cheek. His lips lingered a moment. I closed my eyes, telling myself things would be okay. He was worth waiting for and it was worth it for us to struggle now to make things right for our future.

People (and Mom) say high school romances can't last, but what we had *wasn't* a run-of-the-mill fling. Sharing the same type of alien DNA did—in a way—reinforce my belief that what we had was unique, but our relationship hadn't been built on that alone. We felt a connection in the pits our stomachs—the cores of our hearts—a strong desire to trust each other.

His fingers entwined with mine and our palms pressed together. I shuddered, sucking in a salty breath from my tears. He pulled me close to his chest with his other arm and embraced me tightly. I nuzzled him, soothed by the warmth of his body heat and the softness of his t-shirt.

He kissed the back of my hair and then nestled his head against mine. The light, familiar scent of his skin calmed me. The nervous pitter-patter of my heart settled. I took in a deep breath of him and exhaled, my entire being softening in his arms.

The bus slowed down and came to a hissing stop. The driver pulled back a lever and the double-doors swung open.

Brian tightened his arm around me before letting go. Then his fingers slipped from between mine and he stood, reaching for his backpack at the end of the row, and shouldered one strap. His forehead creased and he looked down at me, a frown weighing down the corners of his lips.

"Let's go, Brian," the bus driver called, glaring at us impatiently.

I mouthed the word "bye" and he turned and shimmied his way down the aisle toward the door.

Halfway down, he stopped, looked over his shoulder at me, and smiled.

It wasn't the usual flirty kind of smile.

It was more confident. Reassuring. Hopeful.

Brian's way of saying things would be okay.

·　　·　　·

They weren't.

Weeks passed without my seeing him. Weeks filled with window shopping at the mall and mindless derping on the internet for cat videos. Weeks spent catching up on TV shows and reading books I'd bought last summer while sitting alone in the café down the street. I patched the wound in my heart with things that were once fun. Happiness now became shallow and short-lived. Unimportant. I couldn't be happy without him anymore.

Boring. Quiet. Lonely. Weeks.

Keeping in touch with Brian had become more and more difficult. He'd gotten a job at some restaurant downtown and was hardly ever around when Sam and I were together. Most of my texts went unanswered and, frankly, I got tired of playing blind ping pong with messaging him on Sam's phone. I kept throwing out lines, hoping he'd reply when I was with her but he never did.

I knew he wanted to work to earn the money to get a motorcycle and get out of the house, but I couldn't even text him anymore. I'd been losing sleep, too, spending so much time worrying about him. Maybe I didn't need to, but I did.

The Saviors had told us we *needed* to spend more time together. The way things were going, it wouldn't even be possible.

Summer vacation sucked so far.

So I made a decision. To be strong. To be brave. To follow my heart.

Mom couldn't stop me from telling him the truth.

Only the truth.

I grabbed my phone off my dresser and opened text messaging.

I typed a single line knowing I could delete it after it sent.

The phone chirped.

Sent.

I need you…

Chapter 22

Someone knocked on the back door.

I panicked, my heart nearly leaping into my throat.

No one came to the back door. Not without hopping the fence first.

Mom wouldn't be home for another hour or two.

I pried open the blinds and peeked out the kitchen window.

Brian!?

My heart almost stopped.

I opened the door a crack, my pulse quickening.

"I'm not allowed to let you in, Brian," I whispered, knowing right then and there that I shouldn't have locked eyes with him.

"Then don't." He flattened a hand against the door and pushed.

I backed away, giving up too easily.

He passed the threshold, turned, and shut the door quietly.

I swallowed hard.

"How did you know my mom was gone?" I asked.

"I've been sitting across the street for the past hour."

"So, you were stalking me, then?" I let out a nervous chuckle. "What if she'd never left?"

"But she did," he replied flatly. "You've told me before that she always goes shopping without you on Sundays." He looked down at me, his pupils enlarged and fixated on mine. "It's been weeks since we've seen each other, Alice. Don't act like you don't want me here." He lifted a hand to stroke my arm with the back of his fingers. A faint glimmer of blue light faded into my skin, sending a rush of warm energy through me. "Alice." He exhaled slowly. "Did you mean what you said in that text last night?"

"I... guess." Chills swept over my body. He cornered me against the wall behind the door and reached a hand up toward my face.

He leaned down and kissed me.

My mind emptied. The room faded away.

"You guess?" His lips inched up my jaw line, dragging toward my ear. "I need an answer."

I sucked in a breath. The fingers of his other hand cradled the back of my head. Brian had a way of asking questions that left me with few ways to answer.

"Yes. Yes, I did. I did mean it." I buried my hands in his hair and licked my lips. "I need you, Brian," I replied, eagerly pulling him into another kiss. Tasting him. Breathing him in.

He bent down, grabbed me by the back of the thighs and lifted me up. I shrieked at first, scared he'd drop me. Then I kicked off my sandals and wrapped my legs around his waist. My heart pounded like a drum.

Feet above the floor and my back pressed to the wall, my face was level with his—for once. I threw my arms around his neck and stared into his colorful eyes. Beautiful and captivating, like his...

I kissed him. Deeply. Savoring him. The heat of his breath. The shape of his mouth. His lips enveloped mine. Taking me in. Stealing me away with each subtle pause. Each exhale softening my body. Freeing me. Every inhale making me stronger. Fearless. As if I'd just come up for air. Just begun to breathe real life.

Our breaths grew heavier. My heart beat faster and faster. Our bodies pressed together. My legs clasped around him, holding him close. Fingers lightly scratching the nape of his neck. Through his hair.

Restless.

Unsatisfied.

He tightened his grip on me, stepped back from behind the door, and set me on the nearby kitchen counter. It freed his hands to take the hem of my shirt and wrinkle it up my ribs. I lifted my arms and he peeled the shirt over my head. The collar caught on one of my earrings and I worked to untangle it, embarrassed, my hands shaking.

The fabric slid over my skin and down to the floor.

"You're beautiful." Brian scanned my face at first and then let his gaze wander. Across my shoulders. Down my sides. His fingers caressed my skin, tracing the curves of my waist, the passion in his touch stripping me of my insecurities. Stoking a fire. Raising my body heat.

He kissed me again and I shuddered, his tongue teasing mine, seducing my lips. I couldn't bring him close enough. My legs straddled his hips, squeezing tight. Hands grasping fabric. Energy flitted through me. Electricity. Every inch of my skin tingling. Stimulated by his touch.

I tugged at his t-shirt, un-tucking it from his jeans. He tore it up over his head and tossed it onto the floor.

My hand slid across his bare chest.

Puberty had done him right. A lean, strong body. Perfect skin. A low, velvety voice. An alluring gaze. Intoxicating scent. My fingertips drifted over the scar above his heart and stayed there a moment, tracing the raised line. My gaze softened.

Not too long ago, I'd felt childish. Clumsy. Unsure of myself.

Today, he knew exactly where I wanted his hands and where I *needed* them. That excited me. I wasn't a little girl anymore. Not in his arms.

He bit his lower lip and grinned, taking my chin in his fingers and pulling me into another kiss. More intense than the last. His soft hands gravitated to the milky-white skin beneath the hem of my shorts. My breath trembled. Every nerve in my body quaked with urgency. Yearning. Weakness.

"I want you, Brian," I exhaled.

"I want you, too, Alice," he strained, sucking air in through gritted teeth.

The fluorescence in us sparked to life. Brighter than ever. Green and blue melding together in a web of neon light, tinting our skin with molten turquoise.

He kissed my throat, a smooth shaven cheek sliding across hypersensitive skin. A strap of my bra slipped off my shoulder. A hot breath against bare flesh. My head fell back and I gasped.

My conscience told me no.

Tell him the truth.

You told Mom you wouldn't until...

Stop now. Don't...

"We can't," I groaned, halfheartedly. "I'm... worried."

"Don't be." His breath tickled my skin. "I won't hurt you." He pressed his blue fingers against my skin again and a wave of heat flushed through my body.

Coaxed by his words, I slid to the very edge of the counter. Our bodies touched and his grasp tightened on my outer thighs. The friction blurred my sanity. I wanted him so much closer. I tasted the salt on his naked skin and imagined us coiled together beneath freshly wrinkled sheets.

Safe.

But it wasn't reality.

"We should wait," I uttered in a labored exhale.

"They say waiting is overrated." The sensual lilt of his voice had me forgetting where I was again. The warmth of his fluorescence kept pulsing through my veins, destroying the will to say no. Enticing me to surrender.

I had to resist. I had to try.

"But, my mom..." I stressed, breathless.

"Don't worry so much." His fingertips massaged my back.

"No," I strained. My head was spinning. "I have to tell you something. Brian, please."

"What?" He huffed and pulled away, glaring at me. "What is *so* important?" His voice was gruffer—frustrated.

"My mom and dad..." I wiped sweat from my forehead with the back of my hand. "They were *really* young."

"And?" His expression softened.

"She was sixteen."

Brian shrugged.

"When... she got pregnant, I mean."

He exhaled a scoff, like he was suppressing a laugh. "Is that what this is about?" He rested his hands on the outside of my thighs. "I care about you, Alice, and I wouldn't want that to happen, either. We don't have to be stupid." He leaned in to kiss me again but I stopped him.

"She's not stupid!"

"Look. I'm sorry that happened to them, but it won't happen to us. We'll be more careful. I'll be more careful."

"It's not always that simple, Brian. It wasn't meant to happen to her either. They used protection, too, but I was an accident. Don't you understand? Having me ruined her life. She dropped out of school and couldn't even get a job. My dad married her because she needed help and because of me. Now they're divorced because of me. I'm not ready for that kind of mistake. I don't think we're ready for that." I looked down at my lap and sighed. "I've changed my mind, okay?"

He cupped my face in his hands and looked into my eyes. "It's not your fault your parents messed up. We won't let that happen. I'm not going anywhere. I love you, Alice."

"Don't say that to me, Brian." I mustered up the strength to shove him back. I hopped off the countertop and stumbled, my legs wobbly. "That's exactly what my Dad said to me. I haven't seen him in almost three years."

I picked my shirt up from the floor.

"I. Am. Not. Your father, Alice," he hissed through gritted

teeth. The sound of his seething voice made my skin crawl. An ugly sneer wrinkled on his lips. His eyes narrowed. "Don't compare me to him, damn it."

"I think you should go." I crossed my arms and looked away. "Before my mom gets back."

"I am sick and tired of running from this! From *your* mother. From *us*. Alice, please."

I fondled my shirt, twisting it around my fingers and kneading the ball of fabric anxiously. "I told her we'd wait. Okay?" Tears welled in my eyes. "I'm sorry I didn't tell you." A lump swelled in my throat and I swallowed hard, fighting back the tightness choking my vocal cords.

"Did you tell yourself that, too? Because you weren't objecting to this earlier. Giving me all the wrong signals. Telling me all the wrong things. Touching me..."

"I'm sorry, Brian." I wiped my eyes with both palms. "I'm sorry. I was stupid, okay?"

"Forget it. If you want to let your mother and her mistakes control how you live, fine. But she's not going to change me." He bent over, snatched his shirt up from the floor and put it back on.

He slammed the back door behind him.

I shuddered.

It had been months since we'd been alone. Truly alone without distractions.

I wanted Brian so much it ached. That pain had blinded me and had almost led me to let go without even thinking. A few weeks apart and already we'd gone mad from separation. How could we possibly wait three more years when I'd almost given in already? We were volatile, full of longing, and this insanely voracious need to consummate that passion.

I fell to my knees and crumpled over onto the kitchen floor, my face in my hands. My chest tightened and every breath squeezed my lungs harder. My face hurt. My heart throbbed. I couldn't stop crying.

How damn stupid had I been to send him away like that?
I hadn't meant to lead him on.

Maybe we were young—impulsive—but I knew we were
meant to be together.

Even the Saviors knew it.

But, Mom... didn't.

. . .

Mom pulled into the driveway. I'd had some time to cool
down and get myself together, but the scent of Brian's skin still
lingered. Taunting me. I wanted him back already; I couldn't
stop debating whether I had made the right decision. An
overwhelming sick feeling convinced me I hadn't.

Mom came inside and put an armload of brown paper bags
onto the counter. I swallowed hard, the guilty truth on the tip
of my tongue.

The doorbell rang.

She glanced at me to see if I knew who it was. I shrugged.

I followed her as she went to answer it.

It was Brian, again.

"We need to talk," he said, sternly.

I held my breath.

"There's nothing to talk about. Go home." Mom tried to
shut the door but he held it back with his hand.

Her eyes went wide.

"Ugh! Don't you dare," she bellowed, her enraged glare
burning at him. "I'll call the police. I'm not afraid of you."
The hoarseness in her voice gave me goose bumps.

"Mom!"

"Alice. Go back up to your room right now. Brian, go
home."

"No. I..." He stuttered at first but regained composure.
"No. I'm in love with your daughter and I will not let you
keep us apart because of a stupid misunderstanding. I think

it's time you found out the truth about us, because there's a hell of a lot more to it than this."

"Brian, no." I stood a few feet behind my mom.

He looked past her at me. "She needs to know, Alice."

"Needs to know what, exactly?" Mom glared at me accusingly.

I whimpered beneath my breath.

She squinted, studying Brian. Then turned to me again. "Alice?"

I backed away.

"You have five minutes, Brian." She held open the door and stared him down as he walked past. She was hesitant to shut it behind him but finally did.

"We have something to show you," said Brian. He approached me and gestured for me to follow him into the living room. He closed the blinds behind the couch first and then the blinds beside the television.

"What are you doing?" Mom asked, tilting her head.

"Give me a sec, please. Alice?" Brian motioned for me to come to him. "You need to... show her."

I looked down and wrinkled the hem of my shirt in my hands. "I don't know if she can really see it through my..."

"Then..." He shrugged. "Take it off."

"How dare you!" Mom freaked.

Brian shot her an "I know what I'm doing" look but she thinned her lips and glared back at him.

"It's okay, Mom. You'll understand." I rolled my eyes and avoided looking at her again.

I took a deep breath. In my nose. Out of my mouth. Just like I'd learned from yoga in middle school. Then I reached down and peeled my shirt up and over my head, careful to avoid my earrings this time. The air had just kicked on. It was cold. I shivered and rubbed my arms.

Mom cocked an eyebrow. I could tell she was biting her tongue and trying hard not to go on a full-out rampage.

Brian reached out and grasped my bare shoulder, his fingers abnormally hot. I took another deep breath.

The temperature rose within me and my pulse throbbed. It started on me first with the green emitting from the skin on top of my shoulder and then it showed on Brian, igniting his fingers with bright azure. It spread up his arm to just above his elbow. The colors resonated, glowing and fading in unison.

"Jesus!" Mom gasped and stumbled backwards, her knees locking when she hit the couch. Horrified, she fell onto the seat and shook her head violently. "No. This isn't possible."

"It's okay, Mom."

Brian released me, still gleaming a bright, electric blue.

"But... my baby!" Mom buried her face in her hands.

My shoulder cooled and the color died down.

"Mom, please. It's okay. Don't be upset."

Brian knelt at her feet and put his right hand onto her knee. "This is why we need to be together. Alice and I."

My mom peeked over her hands at Brian and sucked in a sobbing breath. I grabbed a tissue from the table beside the couch and patted her damp cheeks.

"Mom? I need you. *We* need you now more than ever."

"I know," she mumbled into her hands. "I know." She gasped short, strained breaths, fighting back more tears. "I can't believe it. I just can't believe it."

"I know it's weird, but you have to listen to us."

"Those bastards!" Mom moaned.

"What?" Brian perked up. "Who?"

My heart skipped a beat.

"They lied to me. Those damn things lied to me."

"Mom?" I sat beside her and put a hand on her quaking shoulder. "Mom, you're scaring me. What are you talking about?"

She looked up, tears glistening on her cheeks, eyes staring blankly across the room. "They lied. The Saviors lied!"

Chapter 23

"You know about them?" Brian asked, looking at my mom but glancing at me every few seconds with frightened eyes.

She nodded, choking on a congested breath. "Yes." She sniffed hard and reached for a tissue from the box on the coffee table. "I was one of the chosen ones. Like you two. But mine was... umm..." she stammered, overwhelmed.

"It's okay, Mom. Take it easy." I massaged her shoulder.

"On my leg," she continued. "I was able to hide it from your father back when we were dating, but it was always going off at the most inopportune times."

"I know the feeling," I said with a little chuckle. "This stuff knows how to embarrass you."

Brian leaned closer. "What happened to yours? Do you still have it?"

I braced myself against the deafening honk of her blowing her nose.

"No," she replied, shaking her head. "They took it away. Or at least, they said they would. They told me I wasn't good enough anymore. That I'd *tainted* it or something. I wasn't supposed to have a baby with your father. So they told me they were going to take the stuff out of me. But..."

She doubled over, sobbing into her hands.

Brian's forehead wrinkled. Sadness loomed in his eyes. I felt horrible. All this time we had kept it a secret. Brian had been right to want to tell her. Too right.

"They lied to me," she murmured, her words muffled by

her damp fingers. "They said they would take it out of me but they only gave it to you instead. They used me. Those bastards used me!"

"They never told us any of this, Mom."

"Just like them," Brian grumbled. "They seem like they're only telling us exactly what we have to know, and only when we need to know it. I'm starting to wonder if the little bit of truth they claim about that disease is even true?"

"The one killing them?" my mom asked, patting her cheeks with a third tissue. "Are they still fighting that?"

"I guess." I shrugged. "It's the story they gave us."

"Are there others? What about Sam?" Mom straightened up. She had stopped crying.

"Yes, but not Sam," Brian answered. "That older girl we were with the night we got in trouble—one of Sam's neighbors. She's one of us, too. She has it on her face. It's pink, though."

"So, that's why you guys were out so late? Huh?" She heaved a sigh. "I'm so sorry, you two. I had no idea this was still going on. I had no idea they were going to give it to my baby." Her eyes shimmered with new tears. "I wish you would have told me sooner. You must have been terrified."

"It's okay. Brian's been helping me deal with it. The Saviors told us we were meant to be together and I really believe he's different from other guys in school. Maybe it wasn't right to sneak off to spy on him, but I was worried because I care about him. That's what I've been trying to tell you all along, but couldn't."

Brian reached over my mom's lap to caress my hand.

"I'm doing the best I can for her," he said, looking my mom in the eye. "I meant what I said to you that day I walked here uninvited. I care about her and I'd never do anything to hurt her. I swear."

"I know, sweetie." Mom patted the seat next to her. Brian came up from his knees and sat beside her. She forked her fingers through his hair, ruffling it and smiling at him.

"You're a *really* nice boy. I wanted to believe that the first day I saw you and the first time I saw you look at my little girl. But, that's just it, she's not a little girl anymore." She heaved a sigh. "She's growing up and she's going to want someone else to love her." She stretched out an arm behind him and hugged him to her side.

"Aw, Mom." I couldn't stop a huge smile from lighting up my face. Heat flushed through my cheeks. It was seriously the best thing I could have ever heard from her right then.

She reached her other arm around me and pulled me in. "I know it's hard when you're young, and sometimes you don't make the right decisions. Sometimes you rush into things. Sometimes the people you think you love, don't really love you."

I frowned, knowing she referred to Dad. I loved my dad so much, even if he didn't love me. I wanted to believe he did. That he would come back someday with open arms and tell me how much he needed his daughter in his life.

Nearly three years had passed since the last remnants of the marriage had dissolved and I hadn't seen him since. I wanted to involve him in my life. I really did. I wanted him to meet Brian. I wanted him to warn me about *boys* and tell me I was stupid to be in love so young, but I was naive to think that could happen.

"We can get through this without Dad. Brian's been a big help in school for me."

"And Alice has made me work a lot harder, too," Brian added.

Mom let us both go and pressed a tissue to her eyes.

"So, can we see each other again, now?" Brian asked.

"Brian!?" I shook my head at him.

"No. No. He's right to ask, Alice." My mom stood and gathered the pile of wet tissues from her seat. She inhaled deeply and looked down at us. "You're perfectly in the right to ask, Brian. Now I know the truth and I'm sorry I had to punish you for what happened that night, but I didn't know what was really going on at the time."

I held my breath.

"Yes. You two can keep seeing each other. In fact, if your mother doesn't mind, Brian, I'd love to have you over for dinner once in a while." Mom tilted her head and smiled at him with her eyes.

"Sure. That'd be great," he replied, excited. "I'm pretty busy with the new job and all, but I'll definitely find the time."

"I am going to have to add a little bit of motherly advice, though. When you go out together, I want you both home before curfew. I don't want any more late night police visits. Do you understand?"

"And I don't want to spend any more nights at the police department either." Brian shook his head. "Seriously. Not gonna happen again."

"Good. Then we're done for now. You've probably stressed yourselves out enough just trying to tell me all of this. We can talk about it more later on." She headed toward the kitchen and looked over her shoulder at us. "In the meantime, if the Saviors say anything else, you have to keep me in the loop. I'm part of this, too, even if they're going to pretend I'm not."

"Of course," we replied in tandem.

Mom disappeared into the kitchen and I sighed in relief, the knots in my stomach finally uncoiling.

"Oh my God. I thought she was going to throw you out."

"Me, too." Brian flinched. "But your mom's cool. She took it really well. Surprisingly. Probably because she doesn't know about what we almost..."

"Shh." I shook my head.

"Speaking of which." He looked down. "I'm... sorry for assuming something I shouldn't have." He raised his head and looked me in the eye. "You have the right to say no. I just..."

"It's okay, Brian."

"You sure?"

"Yes. I should have told you earlier. I was afraid you'd be angry."

"No. I wouldn't have been. I just overreacted because I didn't know what you wanted and thought..." He sighed.

"Forget it. If you're not upset, I'm not upset. Alright?"

"Yeah." He nodded and smiled a little. "Okay."

We stood there for a moment, not saying anything, our eyes meeting briefly again and then glancing away.

"Geeze." I grumbled. "I can't believe they took my mom, too, and didn't even bother to tell us. Did they not think it was important? I mean, really? How stupid did they think we were?"

He shrugged. "I don't know, but I'm glad I don't have to creep around like a stalker anymore."

"And I can text you from *my* phone."

"Speaking of stalking... what you wore to bed last night was..." He bit his lip and raised his eyebrows at me.

"Ugh!" I pretend-punched him in the arm, a little harder than I'd meant to.

"I'm kidding. I'm kidding." He laughed and rubbed his shoulder. "Ow. Geeze."

I knew that...

Chapter 24

The doorbell rang.

"I'll get it!" Mom yelled from the kitchen. Delivery people usually came in the afternoon.

I went back to derping on my computer. Sam messaged me the link to another internet meme video. I clicked it and laughed out loud. Stupid dance crazes.

The front door shut.

My phone chirped.

BRIAN: You have 20 minutes to get ready, or I'm leaving without you

"What?" I was still in my frumpy day clothes. *Not* dressed to impress.

ME: That is so unfair
BRIAN: So is having to wait on your GF to get ready
ME: :(
BRIAN: Wear something "nice".
BRIAN: Don't come downstairs until you are ready ;)
ME: @_@ KK..... I may need more than 20
BRIAN: . . . ?
ME: NM I can do it
BRIAN: You're such a grl . . . :P
ME: Aren't U glad?

He didn't respond to the last one. I felt triumphant.

I dug through my closet for something nice and not wrinkled. It was cloudy and in the low 80's outside, so I reached for one of my skirts. A deep blue velvet one with the hemline just above the knee. I found a pretty coordinating lacy tank top. Deep violet purple with little rhinestones along the sweetheart neckline. Filigree up the sides and a ruffle on the hemline. It was pretty. He would like it.

BRIAN: Oh, and jeans ;) Sorry

I rolled my eyes. A little late.

I changed out of the skirt and into a pair of dark blue jeans. Popped on a pair of black flats and then ran into the bathroom to comb my hair. I twisted it up into a ponytail and flipped it in front of my shoulder. Some quick, light make-up. Lip gloss.

Why couldn't I move any faster?

I took a deep breath and looked myself over in the mirror. Everything looked okay.

I ran downstairs, assuming I'd find him in the living room.

"Mom? Where's Brian?"

"He's outside. In the driveway."

The driveway? It was over 80 degrees out. Ick.

"Okay. Thanks."

"Hey, wait a minute." Mom came out of her room. "You two be careful, alright?"

"Yeah, sure." I shrugged, cocking an eyebrow. "Why wouldn't we be?"

"Well..." She bit her lip. "Never mind." Then she forced a smile and gave me a quick hug. "Love you."

"Love you, too, Mom."

I opened the front door, strolled down the walkway and then froze in the driveway.

I gasped and my eyes widened. "Oh my God!" I squealed excitedly, hopping up and down like a cheerleader.

Brian was dressed in light jeans and a black leather jacket, standing beside a sleek, electric blue motorcycle.

"You finally got one?" I clapped.

"Yeah."

"Was it... expensive?" I felt bad asking, but I was curious.

"Depends on what you consider expensive. For me, yes." He polished the gas tank with his sleeve. "But that's why I've been working so much. It's used, though, so I've got it partially paid off already. Not the latest or greatest, but it's nice and it will work for what we need it for."

"We?"

"Yeah. *We.* I'd have bought something much smaller, and *cheaper,* if I hadn't been so worried about taking my girlfriend with me everywhere."

I grinned shyly.

"I didn't know you liked blue so much," I said, running a finger over the metallic blue gas tank.

"What can I say? It's been growing on me." He did spirit fingers with his left hand and laughed. I smiled. "Besides, it reminds me of your eyes. Not quite as pretty, though."

I probably blushed. Thank God I wasn't diabetic. Brian was sweeter than sugar.

Seriously.

My phone chirped again.

SAM: Still alive? You stopped messaging me
ME: YES!!! Sorry!!! Brian came over. Will TTYL about it!

I snapped a picture of his bike and texted it to her.

SAM: OMG Lucky!
ME: ;) Yes! TTYL! Weeeee!

I couldn't contain myself even in a text. It was like Christmas all over again. I think every girl's secret fantasy is to have a motorcycle-riding boyfriend. Apparently it was one of mine.

"So you got your license?" I brushed off the seat and gave him a cute little "can I?" look, batting my lashes for effect. He nodded and lent me a hand to help steady myself as I lifted a leg up over the bike to sit on the seat. It was warm from the sun, but firm.

"Hell, yeah. Like the week after my birthday. You have to apply for a motorcycle one separately, so I wanted to make sure I had everything I needed."

"Drive it much yet?" I curled my fingers around the handlebars, squeezing the rubber grips.

"A friend of mine back in Montana used to have a sweet dirt bike he let me ride on the weekends. But I've had this one for a few weeks, actually. Been riding it every single night for as long as I can." He drove a hand through his hair and shrugged. "I wanted to make sure I felt comfortable with it before I asked you to join me."

I grinned like a Cheshire cat, shaking with excitement.

"I'm sorry it took so long for me to tell you. The best news is, you won't have to take the bus to school anymore if you don't want to."

My jaw dropped. "That would be so cool!" I clapped. Being able to go to school with Brian would be a-maaaazing. Other girls would be so jealous.

"I know I asked you to dress nice and I understand it's hot out, but you're going to have to wear this." He handed me a brown leather jacket. "I don't want anything to happen to you."

I slid my arms into the sleeves and shrugged it over my shoulders. It fit snugly but wasn't tight.

"Here." He tossed me a helmet. Metallic dark purple with a pair of black leather gloves inside.

"Yay! Purple! Thank you!" I beamed, polishing the top. "Aw. This is not as sexy as it is in the movies."

"Neither is being dead," he said, and flipped down the

clear visor on my helmet, then adjusted it a bit.

"True." I shoved the gloves onto my hands and tugged the fingers taut.

He flicked his head back to get his hair out of his face and then shoved his black helmet on.

"Can you get up for a minute?" He gestured for me to move back. Then he sat on the leather seat in front of me and motioned for me to sit back down. "Now I'm going to walk you through this, because it's going to be something you'll need to adjust to."

"Okay."

"And if you don't mind, I want to ride a couple of blocks here in the subdivision so I can get used to the weight difference, too."

"Are you calling me fat?" I chuckled, the sound muffled by my helmet.

He looked over his shoulder at me, his face darkened by the tinted visor on his helmet. "No. But this bike is going to handle differently with two of us on it. I want to make sure I get a feel for it before we head onto the main road. I'll explain it as we go, okay? You can hold on to the sides of my jacket, or whatever you can. Just make sure you don't make any sudden movements. This thing's going to lean into the turns and it's something you're going to have get used to."

"Right." I nodded, reaching to clutch onto the sides of his jacket. "Talk me through it."

He was serious. I had always thought riding a motorcycle would be fun and carefree, but there's a learning curve. It's definitely not something they tell you in the movies. Hop on, hold on and let the wind blow through your hair. IRL, hit the ground and end up in pieces. Road rash, bikers called it, as Brian had politely informed me.

I had no idea steering a motorcycle was such an art. Who was I kidding, though? I hadn't even gotten my learner's permit or set foot on a gas pedal yet. He had much more experience under his belt thanks to his dirt bike riding friend in Montana.

Brian handled his bike like a pro. Not that I had anything to compare it to, but he seemed like a natural. Turns were gentle. Stops were smooth. You'd think he'd been riding for years.

I listened and I learned.

He was careful. Confident.

It was easy to trust him with my life.

Chapter 25

Brian took my jacket and pulled out a chair for me.

"I hope you don't mind me bringing you here," he said. "I thought it'd be nice for you to see where I work."

I sat. "It's fine. Really." I sniffed the air. It smelled of fresh-baked bread and burning firewood. There was a brick oven across the room in an open area of the kitchen. Flames were licking up through the metal grate inside.

He draped his jacket over the back of his chair and sat across from me.

"You look great, by the way." He smiled. "Sorry I didn't say anything earlier."

I looked around. We weren't the only people wearing jeans, but I felt underdressed. White linen tablecloths. Fabric napkins. A real tea light candle burning on the table—not one of those LED ones. I lifted the burgundy leather-backed menu and cracked it open. The fancy parchment-style pages even had raised text.

"Do you need a suggestion?" Brian asked, peering over his menu at me.

"Maybe?" They had a lot of seafood. Not my thing.

"I'll order you something then. How's that?"

"Oh, a surprise. Sure."

Our server, James, returned with a serving tray. He set a tall glass of iced tea in front of each of us and pulled two straws out of his black apron. He placed a set of cutlery to the side of our plates, followed by a basket of steaming-hot rolls in the center of the table.

"I'm guessing you don't have any questions about any-thing," James said. "Have you decided what you'd like?"

"Yeah." Brian put down his menu and reached to take mine. "We'll both get the house specialty."

"Alright, then." James scribbled down something in his notepad and tucked it into his apron. "I'll get that out to you shortly."

"So, what did you order me?" I reached across my plate to grab a roll from the basket. I broke it in half. Piping hot with a delicious smell.

"A burger."

"What?" I stared at him, doubtful.

"Just kidding. I know you don't like burgers. I got you the house chicken special. It's chicken roulade with mango chutney and brie."

"Um, you lost me after chicken." I nibbled on my bread. Buttery with a hint of sweetness I couldn't place. Honey, perhaps.

"All you need to know is that I think brie is the best cheese in the world."

"I see." I licked my lips.

.   .   .

After dinner, our server cleared the plates from our table and brought us a sharable slice of French chocolate cake. Dark chocolate sprinkled with a dash of powdered sugar and served with a dollop of whipped cream and fresh raspberries on top.

"That looks really good." I nibbled my lip in anticipation. Mmm, chocolate. "I would eat the whole thing if I hadn't eaten too much already." I laughed.

"That's why I ordered one and not two. I'm not going to eat the whole thing, either."

I fished around my plate for the dessert fork.

That's when Brian's hand came across the table, sliding something toward me.

"Happy birthday, Alice," he said, lifting his hand from a small white jewelry box.

"Oh!" I gasped. "But you've done so much already."

He smiled and shrugged. "I'm behind a couple of holidays."

What a gorgeous box! White brocade with a silver ribbon tied on the lid. Just looking at it made me nervous. And excited and...

"I hope you like it. Go ahead. Open it."

I cupped the box in both hands and stared, admiring it. Imagining what might be inside. Then I lifted the lid and squealed out loud. Someone nearby cut a glance at me and I ducked down, bashfully.

"I love it!" I untangled the silver chain from the indentions in the box and lifted out the pendant—a silver dolphin curved in a crescent shape with a purple amethyst faceted between its fin and tail. "It is *perrrfect*. I love it." I couldn't keep my voice down.

"I showed your mom and she agreed it was something you might like."

"She *was* right! It even matches my top." I pried open the lobster clasp with my thumbnail and put the necklace around my neck. "Thank you. It's wonderful." My eyes watered a little. Brian smiled, looking quite pleased with himself.

"I'm glad you like it. I'm sorry I had to miss your actual birthday, though."

"I'm sorry I had to miss yours, too. Sixteen is a big one. I would have liked to have been there. I..." I looked down at my dessert plate. "I want to do something nice for you, but I don't know what."

"I can think of a few things," he said with a smirk, raising an eyebrow.

"Excuse me?" I squinted.

"No, not *that*." He rolled his eyes and chuckled. "That's

out of the equation for now. I'm totally aware. But, seriously. You spending time with me means a lot. If you wanna go out riding with me once in a while, that'd be cool, too. I just want to spend time with you."

I exhaled, my gaze softening, my lips settling into a contented smile.

I picked up my helmet from the chair beside me and swapped seats with it so I could sit closer to Brian.

"It looks nice on you," he said, glancing down at the necklace.

Our eyes met, then I brushed my fingers over his ear and kissed him.

"Thanks, Brian," I whispered, cutting it short because we were in public.

His eyes opened slowly and he sighed. "You're welcome, Alice."

•   •   •

"Enjoy your evening?" Brian asked.

We were sitting on the top step of my porch.

"Yes." I fiddled with the dolphin pendant, tangling the chain around my fingers. "I lost a shoe on the way back, but otherwise, it was really nice."

"Sorry about that. Lace-up shoes next time."

I nodded. "For sure."

Our fingers intertwined and he stretched his other arm behind me, resting his hand on my waist.

"I just had the best night of my life," I said.

"Really?" He gazed at me.

"You're a wonderful boyfriend, Brian. I only hope I can repay your kindness somehow."

He held my hand, massaging his thumb over my knuckles. "You don't owe me anything."

"Sometimes I feel like I'm not doing enough. Like, I'm not

good enough or..."

He let go and pressed two fingers onto my lips. "Don't even finish that. If you want to know what you can do to make me happy, then learn to love me. Okay?"

I stifled the urge to laugh. "What does that mean?"

"You heard me. I love you, Alice. I've said it before, and I'm not afraid to say it as many times as I need to. But, I expect to hear it from you, too. Someday. When you're ready. Then I'll be happy. Then every second I've spent with you will make that day all the more rewarding."

I batted my lashes, glancing into his eyes. "Will you wait?"

His forehead wrinkled. "For?"

"For me to say it? When I feel it's right?"

"Yes. I'm not rushing you. I'm just saying, I would really like to hear it from you eventually. You know?" He weaved his fingers through my hair and kissed my cheek.

"Yeah."

I rested my head against his chest and exhaled, relieved.

Chapter 26

A summer thunderstorm hit late Friday night. Water droplets splattered against the glass of my bedroom window, distorting my view. Lightning skittered across the sky and thunder crashed. Every few minutes, the room would flash white, rattling my bones, reminding me of the horrible drop we'd endured each time the Saviors called for us.

It was barely past midnight and I had just lain down to go to sleep, when the doorbell rang. My heart almost jumped out of my chest. I threw on my robe, jogged downstairs and met my mom in the living room.

"Who is it at this hour?" she asked, a frightened look glistening in her eyes.

I shook my head and crept over to the living room window. Peeling back the blinds, I peeked out at the porch. The curtain of torrential rain made it difficult to see anything but I recognized a distinct glimmer of blue metal in the driveway.

"It's Brian!" I ran back over to the front door and double-checked through the peephole. "Yeah. It is."

Mom came up behind me, tightening the belt on her green terrycloth robe and folding her arms.

I flung open the door. "Brian? Are you okay?" He stood hunched over, hands tucked into his elbows, bracing himself against the rain blowing down through the overhang. Soaking wet locks of his hair lay plastered against his face.

"Can I come in, p-please?" He shuddered.

"Yes. Of course!" I backed away from the door, shielding my face from the gust of rain that blew in behind him. "Do you need us to put your bike in the garage?"

"It's not a big deal, but if you can…" He looked at me through flattened spires of dark brown, his face a shade lighter than usual. My heart sank.

"I'll get it for him," Mom said, snatching her keys off a hook on the wall in the kitchen.

"Let me grab you something." I ran into the laundry room and pulled open the dryer door.

"Here." I handed him a fresh towel and helped him out of his drenched leather jacket. "I'll hang this in the bathroom for you." His shirt and jeans were drenched, too, but we didn't have extra clothes he could wear.

"Thanks." He plopped onto a chair at the kitchen table, the vinyl seat squelching beneath him, and then ruffled his hair with the towel.

Mom came back in, her clothes dripping wet. "Okay. I got your bike put in the garage."

"Thanks." Brian forced a smile.

"It's late. What on earth happened, Brian?" Mom sat in the chair across from him. "Why are you…" Her brow furrowed. "Wait, give me your shoes. They're soaking wet."

He kicked off his black sneakers and she scooped them up and took them into the kitchen. There, she laid out a stack of paper towels and set his shoes on top. She flipped on the nearby electric kettle and sat back down at the table. "Anyway," she said, tightening the belt on her robe again, "Why were you out driving in this weather? And at this hour?"

Brian rubbed the towel against the back of his head. "I came home from work and ended up getting into a fight with my mom. She told me to get out. I didn't know where else to go."

"She can't do that!" Mom scowled. "What on earth were you fighting about?" Her jaw tightened. "Never mind. Regardless of what you two were fighting about, she's not allowed to throw you out like this. You're still a juvenile. It's against the law. I'll call the police." She was halfway up from her seat already.

"Please, don't!" Brian dropped the towel into his lap. "I don't want to go back right now. Not with her acting like this. You don't know how crazy she can get."

"What did she do to you, Brian?" My mother stood and walked over to him. She lifted her fingers to his face and swept his damp hair away from his forehead. "What did she say to you?" Her eyes narrowed with concern and she cupped his cheek in her hand. "You can tell me, you know. Really. You can."

Brian fidgeted in his seat.

"She didn't do anything to me," he replied, driving my mom's hand away as gently as he could. "And I... don't really want to talk about it. It's stupid shit, really. Look, I can pay for a hotel room, but I can't check myself in because I'm not old enough. I swear to God I won't cause any trouble. I just need someplace to crash for a day or two. That's it. She'll cool down after that and I'll go back."

Mom crossed her arms, screwing her mouth up to one side. "What kind of mother throws out her son in the middle of the night during a thunderstorm and then tells him to fend for himself? I'd like to give her a piece of my mind."

"The same kind of mom that thinks her son is gay because he likes to draw," I said, rolling my eyes and sticking out my tongue.

Mom stared in shock, her mouth hanging open. "You're kidding me?"

"Nope. He told me that waaaay back when I first met him."

She covered her mouth with her hand and looked at Brian sympathetically. "Oh, goodness, Brian. I'm so sorry. I can't imagine how anyone could make such an assumption simply because you're an artist."

The hot water kettle clicked off and she got up and went

to grab a mug from out of the cupboard. "Why didn't you tell me about this earlier?" She dunked a sachet of chamomile tea into the hot water and brought the cup over to the table, tossing a little glass coaster underneath it. The rising steam drifted toward me, teasing my nostrils with a subtle grassy scent.

"I... I didn't want anyone else worrying." He wrapped himself up in the towel and held it closed at his neck. "I also never thought it'd get this bad." He arched over the teacup and closed his eyes, inhaling a deep breath of steam.

"We'll take care of you. Don't worry. Alice, go get him one of my old robes to wear so he can change out of his clothes and we can dry them. Oh, and grab some fresh sheets for the downstairs guest room."

"On it." I rushed off into the laundry room to gather everything.

I'd just finished making up the bed when Brian came down the basement stairs and into the room, still wearing his wet clothes.

"Hey," he said, carrying the towel I'd given him earlier. "I really appreciate this."

"How was the tea?"

"Good. I think it helped, actually."

"Chamomile can do a lot. Mom's quite the expert with tea."

"I believe you." He smiled and then glanced at my necklace. "You really do like it, don't you?" He cracked a smile, his teeth showing a little.

I clasped my hand over the silver dolphin and polished it lovingly with my fingers. "Yes. Mom said you can change out of your clothes and we'll put them in the dryer upstairs." I took the wet towel from him. "It's late. Grab them in the morning if you want or I can bring them down for you. Do you think you'll need anything else tonight?"

"Just you," he said, his eyes narrowing gratefully. "But that will always be the case." He reached out to trace his cold fingers across my cheek. "I'm not going to overstay my welcome here, that's for sure. Your mom's amazing. Thank her for me, please."

"I will. Leave your clothes at the top of the stairs and I'll take care of them."

"Thank you, Alice." He sat on the edge of the guest bed. "I know we need to get to sleep, but... can I tell you a secret? Before you go? I just... need to get this off my chest."

"You can tell me anything." I sat beside him and put a hand on his thigh. His jeans were damp.

"After my dad was killed overseas, my mom became really depressed. She started drinking... a lot. And mixing up her medications. Then she..." He took a deep breath and exhaled, puffing out his cheeks. "She... tried to commit suicide."

"Oh, God." I covered my mouth. I'd *heard* about people attempting suicide, but I'd never personally known anyone who had come close to trying.

"Luckily, I was able to stop her before it was too late. Threw out the rest of the damn pills before she could..." He paused again and cleared his throat. "I've never told anyone else about it."

"Why didn't you call the police?"

"I was barely twelve at the time. Child services would have snatched me up in a freaking minute. I didn't want to be taken away from home, so I had to do what I could to make things better."

"What did you do?" I leaned closer, my fingers unconsciously pressing into his leg.

"I convinced her to see a doctor. She got put on a different antidepressant for a while. It helped, but only so much. Then she started having mood swings and acting like a completely different person. Eventually, she stopped taking the medication. Ever since, I've had to tiptoe everywhere to keep her from flipping out on me. Now it seems like every damn thing I do sets her off."

"She seemed okay, at the Christmas party."

"She was back on them then, too."

"Oh..."

"Now she's off again. Threatening to quit her job and move back to Montana. Asking me what I've been doing with my money and where I go every day, even after I've told her a hundred times. Talking crazy stuff. I don't know what to do. I'm worried about her, but I'm more worried about myself."

He clutched my hand tightly and stared at me with tired, fearful eyes. "I have way too much to lose now, Alice." His eyes shimmered with tears, but he resisted them.

"I'll take care of you, Brian, as best I can. You can stay with us for a little while, like my mom said. That will give your mom time to clear her head."

"That's fine and all and I appreciate your mom letting me stay, but it won't make things better forever. I've been struggling with my mom on and off for years. One minute she's fine and then the next..."

"Alice!" Mom called from the top of the stairs.

"I'm coming! Just a sec!" I looked at Brian and shrugged. "I have to go. I'm sorry."

"I know." He swallowed hard. "Thank you for listening anyway. You're a great girlfriend, and an even greater friend."

"You're welcome." I stood and he walked me to the base of the stairs where he hesitated to release my hand.

I pushed up off my toes and kissed him on the cheek, half-expecting him to veer his head and catch me on the lips, but he didn't. I dropped back down to my heels.

"Goodnight, Brian," I said, and headed upstairs. Halfway to the top, I looked over my shoulder, took one last glance at him, and blew him a kiss.

His brows twitched, fighting back a frown, but he mustered the strength to put on a smile for me.

"Goodnight, Alice."

Chapter 27

"Sleep okay?" I fluffed the back of Brian's hair with my fingertips and bent down to nuzzle his ear, smelling a hint of fabric softener. He sat at the kitchen table, hunched over a stack of printer paper, drawing.

"Well enough. Yes." His attention didn't break from his work.

"Do you need anything?"

"No." He squinted, tilted his head, and then darkened a line of ink with several strokes of his pen.

I sat beside him, peering over his arm.

"What's that?" I asked.

"Something I thought of last night. I needed to get it out."

"Oh?" I cocked my head and leaned closer. It looked like a comic book page. He was on the last part. The top panel showed his deer-antlered superhero climbing up the side of a building, his cape whipping in the wind. The middle panel looked as though the man were slipping off his hood and mask. The bottom panel was white—unfinished.

"Is this for your comic?"

"Yeah."

"Have you come up with a name yet?"

Brian reached under the stack of paper for another page. He flipped it over and passed it to me.

Staggered Hart, it read, in stylized rough-edged script, fitted inside a jagged heart outline.

"Oh, this is awesome! Great wordplay, by the way. I think

it fits him well."

"Thanks." He continued sketching, fixated on the page. Like magic, an image took shape before my eyes. It was almost machine-like, how diligent and precise his strokes were. Each stroke carefully calculated and placed on top of faint, sketchy pencil lines. I watched him quietly, mesmerized by his craft, until Mom came out of her room.

"Good morning, Alice."

"Morning, Mom."

"You get anything to eat yet, Brian?" Mom opened up the pantry above the sink and rummaged through the cereal boxes.

He shook his head.

"Alice. Why don't you get him something?" She switched on the tea kettle.

Me? I didn't know how to make anything that required more than pouring milk or stirring in chocolate chips.

"Like what?"

"Don't worry about it." Brian looked up at me from his page, a fleeting grin swept across his lips. "I'll make something."

"You're our guest, Brian," Mom replied. "We can make you breakfast."

"No, really," he insisted, standing up from his chair. "I can scramble eggs, or cook toast, or whatever you want. I've been making my own meals for years now."

My heart sunk. Really? So his mom didn't even cook for him? I felt privileged all of a sudden.

Mom frowned.

"I'm finished with this page." He slid it to me and I glanced over it.

In the bottom panel, the Hart could only be seen from the neck down, grasping his headdress in his arms, one of the antlers broken, dangling by a shred.

"Looks kind of sad," I said.

"It is. He's debating whether or not he wants to keep doing what he's doing or go back to what he thinks is easier. A life of crime."

"That's terrible. I hope he makes the right decision."

"Me, too," said Brian, aligning all of his pages together between his hands and then tapping them against the table to straighten the stack. "Anyway, what do you want to eat?"

"I don't know."

Mom pulled a tray of eggs from out of the refrigerator and set them on the counter.

"French toast?" Mom asked, twirling off the metal tie on a loaf of Texas toast.

I shrugged. "Sure."

"Brian, do you know how to make French toast?" Mom reached for a mixing bowl from on top of the refrigerator.

"Can't say I do."

"Want to learn?" She offered him a whisk. "Might get your mind off things for a while."

"Sure."

The tired look in his eyes faded. He seemed excited about the idea. I was happy for him, and at the idea of Brian cooking for me.

I sat quietly at the kitchen table, watching them work. Mom pointed at the griddle, turned a knob, told him how to avoid overcooking and how to mix the egg batter her special way. Brian paid close attention, working alongside her.

Mom set a bowl of cinnamon sugar on the table and asked Brian to take the butter from the fridge. He stood in front of the open refrigerator for a moment, trying to locate it.

"On the top shelf on the left," she said, pointing from the other side of the kitchen.

"Got it." He pulled out the stick and brought it to the table.

We had breakfast together, as a sort of extended family. A perfect Saturday morning.

"Are you working today?" Mom asked, taking up our empty plates from the table.

"Yeah. But not until 2:00." He stood up and started a mini tug-of-war with Mom over dish-duty.

"I will not have you doing the dishes for us," she said, staring him down until he relinquished his plate. "You're a guest right now, and I won't have you acting like you're at work. Relax, Brian. Just sit down and enjoy the off time while you can."

He shrugged, defeated, and flopped back down in the chair beside me, crossing his arms.

"Where do you work anyway?" Mom set the stack of plates in the sink and twisted on the faucet. The water gurgled.

"The French-American grill downtown."

"Jacques'?"

"Yeah."

"One of my friends has been there. She told me it was a pretty fancy place."

"It's nice, yeah."

Mom looked at me and tipped her head to the side. "That's where he took you when he brought his bike over, wasn't it?"

I nodded.

"How was it?"

"Good."

Mom redirected her attention to Brian. "So, do you make good tips there? You're very likable. Oh, sorry if that's too personal to ask. I'm just wondering."

"Some nights I make quite a bit. And sometimes I even doodle little drawings on people's checks. They seem to get a kick out of it. It's been a good place to work so far. The manager is nice and he doesn't treat me like a kid, either."

"The drawing on the checks thing is adorable," I piped in.

He grinned.

"Speaking of which." Mom switched off the faucet and turned toward us. "If you have to work tonight, maybe you should call in. You've had a rough night and people can usually sense when you're stressed. We don't want you getting fired or anything. I'm sure your boss will understand."

"I doubt it," Brian replied, shaking his head. "Getting into a fight with your mom seems like a lame excuse to cut work. I need the money. I'll suck it up and deal."

"Only a suggestion. I thought you could use the break with school starting up Monday and all."

"The restaurant is closed tomorrow. I'll survive."

"Well, then why don't you two take a walk or something? The fresh air could do you some good. It's nice and sunny today." She motioned to the open kitchen window.

The clear sky gleamed as blue as the ocean. According to the weather report, it would be a nice day. Maybe even a great day for...

"You wanna take a ride somewhere?" Brian looked at me.

"Sure." I'd never turn down the chance. "Though..." I rubbed my belly. "I'm just a little sick to my stomach today. It's not a big deal, though," I assured him.

He tipped his head to the side. "Are you okay?"

"Um..." I stammered. "Yeah. Girl stuff. That's all. No biggie. I'll take something before we leave." I shrugged. Mom heard me and started digging around in the medicine cabinet. Period cramps never were my friend.

"Ah. I see." He nodded and looked off to the side, a little jarred and unsure of how to respond. "Well, okay, I don't *actually* know exactly, but... I get it. I get it. Gross stuff happens, girls get cranky and things hurt. I've heard guys complaining about their girlfriends going all PMS on them. You never seem to change though and that's cool."

I chuckled at his odd compliment. "Yeah. It can get a little overwhelming sometimes, but I'll be fine. All of the stress from last night has got my stomach in more knots than usual.

One thing after another."

"Hey, I'm not in a hurry as long as I get back in time to get changed and—aw, damn it." He whacked his hand against the table and scowled. "I don't have my work clothes. I am not going back home right now to get anything. Not while she's there."

"We can swing by the mall and grab something," I suggested, taking a glass of water and some ibuprofen from my mom.

"That would work. I could use another pair anyway. Hey, thanks for breakfast Mrs.—"

"Call me Jane. Jane is fine."

"Are you sure? I don't mind..."

"Yes, Brian. Just Jane will do."

"Well then, thanks, Jane. Alice is lucky to have a mom like you." He shoved his hand into a pocket in his jeans. "Shit! Where's my key?" He leapt up from his seat and patted frantically at his pants pockets.

"Oh! Just a sec!" Mom grabbed something from the table near the entryway and jogged back over to us. She set the key to his motorcycle on the table and slid it toward him. "It was in the dryer this morning. I meant to give it to you. Didn't mean to scare you."

He exhaled a huge sigh of relief. "Thanks. I was worried I'd dropped it outside or something." He looked back at me and frowned. "Sorry, Alice. I'm trying. I really am."

He'd been swearing less than he used to, but I knew I couldn't change who he was. I didn't really want to. I just wanted him to act better than the other boys at school. The ones who couldn't say a sentence without enhancing it with something crude.

"I know. Don't worry about it." I tugged playfully on his t-shirt. "Let's go so you'll have time to come back and get ready for work."

If I was remembering correctly, the servers at Jacques'

wore classy white button-up shirts, black slacks, and a black vest. I imagined how it might look on Brian. Black worked well for him. And so did button-up shirts. I loved to tease him by playing with the top few buttons near his collar.

I sighed.

"Alice?"

"Sorry. Just thinking."

"I noticed. About?"

"You."

He smiled with his eyes.

Chapter 28

I didn't tell my mom what Brian had told me last night. I probably should have, but I thought doing so might jeopardize the trust he'd put in me. He had asked me to keep it a secret, after all.

I'd never seen Brian so worried. So vulnerable. When your mother is the only family you have, you can't afford to be on thin ice with her.

"You look nice," I said.

He tugged at the cuffs of his white shirt and brushed down the edges of his collar. The classic black and white combination gave him a gorgeous air of nostalgia. The crisp black vest. The smooth white sateen shirt. They made him look refined and even a little older. Mature and polished.

"Besides the fact that parking and traffic are hell on weekends, it was nice having lunch with you at the mall," he said, bent over, tying his black shoe laces. Mom had dug out a polish stick this morning and cleaned them off while we were out.

He adjusted his belt by a notch and looked up at me. "Well?"

I nodded, grinning in approval, utterly smitten.

"I'm starting to think girls might go to Jacques' for more than food." I snickered. Something caught my eye and I reached for it. "Oops," I said, peeling a small white branding sticker from his sleeve. "Missed this." The label dangled from my fingertip.

"Thanks." He laughed. "Oh, and tell your mom I appreciate

her doing my clothes for me."

"It's not a problem. Are you sure things will be better Monday?"

"Yeah," he replied, buttoning the top button on his shirt. "She's... done this before, actually."

"No way."

"Before we moved here. That friend with the dirt bike I told you about earlier? Well, I crashed at his place a few times." He adjusted his bowtie.

"I'm so sorry."

"It's okay. I just can't wait to get the hell out of my mom's house." His lips thinned. "All of this legal stuff is ridiculous. I can have a job and a motorcycle, and I know guys my age who even manage to buy and smoke cigarettes, but I can't get away from my mother without the government butting in and trying to drag me off to some stranger's house. Talk about a load of bull." He heaved a sigh.

"You have me and my mom now." I wrapped my arm around his and brushed up against him. "We'll do whatever we can to help you."

"Thanks. Being able to trust your mother means a lot to me, and finding you was the best thing that's happened in my whole life." He leaned down toward me.

"Alright down there?" Mom called from the top of the basement stairs.

"Yes," we replied in unison.

"Just like in the movies." I rolled my eyes. "*Moms.*"

I walked up the stairs behind Brian and suddenly felt a sharp pain in my belly. I cupped my hands over my stomach and grunted, freezing in place.

"You okay?" Brian looked over his shoulder at me.

"Uh, yeah." I resisted a second grunt of pain and swallowed hard. The pain killers weren't working so well today and the cramps were getting worse. I really needed to lie down.

But not before seeing him off. I took a few breaths, re-

166

gained my composure and jogged up the remaining steps.

Brian shut the basement door behind me and looked at me, concerned. "Are you sure? I've never seen you *this* sick before. Can I do anything? Maybe..." He lifted his left hand toward me.

"No. I'll be fine. It comes and goes. The anemia doesn't make it any easier either."

"I wish I could help."

"Thanks. But it will pass." The spasms made my jaw clench.

"Okay. Let me know how you're doing."

"Yeah. Okay." I nodded and we went into the kitchen together.

"Oh, wow." Mom looked at him and her gaze softened. "Now don't you look handsome? Oh my gosh, Brian."

Brian looked at his feet, hiding a shy smile. I slid my hand down his arm and took his hand.

"That's what I've been trying to tell him," I added.

I think I embarrassed him, and I kind of liked that. It was cute. Considering how he'd looked last night, dragging himself through the door like a drowned rat... well, I'd take his sweet bashfulness over his traumatized vagabond any day.

· · ·

Sunday afternoon, Brian walked his motorcycle out of the garage and stopped in the driveway, propping it up with the kickstand. He tucked his work clothes into a compartment under the seat and then I handed him his helmet and gloves. He lifted one leg up and over the bike and sat down.

"Thank your mom again, would you?" He pulled one glove on and then the other.

"I will. Don't worry. Just let us know how it goes, okay? If she keeps it up..."

"I'll let you know, Alice."

"Thanks." I looked at my feet. I didn't want to let him go. Not today. Not ever again.

Mom had convinced him to go home earlier than he'd planned. He'd originally hoped to sneak back in while his mom was still at work and then talk it over when she got home, but Mom believed the extra day wouldn't change things. That, and school started back up tomorrow. He needed to get his things together and wouldn't have time if he stayed another night.

He flicked his hair back and shoved his black helmet on. A moment later, he pulled it back off and set it behind his seat. He reached out and wrapped his arms around my waist, reeling me in. I stumbled forward, straddling his knee. His fingers crept under the edge of my tank top and caressed my side.

"I'll see you tomorrow," he said, and then tugged me down into a kiss.

I closed my eyes and savored it.

Kissing on a motorcycle, checked off my bucket list.

"Don't take this the wrong way Alice, but I doubt this will be the last time we spend a night together." His fingers drifted down my neck. "I only hope the circumstances will be different next time."

I bit my lip.

"Be safe," I said.

"I will." He scooped up his helmet from the seat behind him and put it on. "Alice, I..." He hesitated, catching himself before he could finish the sentiment. I knew what was on the tip of his tongue. Today, he fought the urge to say it. "Never mind." He grinned and put down his visor.

I backed away. He turned a switch on, pulled the clutch, and flipped the starter button. The engine growled and he flicked a partial wave at me with his hand before buzzing out of the driveway.

Every second away from him made my heart ache. A void

of emptiness consumed me when our hands parted and my whole being felt a little less... complete.

I was kidding myself to think I wasn't in love with him.

He needed to hear it from me.

And the words were right there, rising from my heart, but still I choked... every time. I'd only ever told one man that I loved him—my dad—and he had turned his back on me.

Chapter 29

"That tissue isn't going to get any smaller, Alice," said Sam, cocking an eyebrow at me.

I'd been fiddling with it since I'd gotten on the bus, coiling it around my fingers absentmindedly. Brian had never gotten on this morning, and neither had my head, apparently.

"I'm worried about him, that's all," I replied, shoving the crumpled-up mess of linty white fluff into my book bag. "He told me everything was okay, but I thought he'd be on the bus at least today. First day of school and all."

"Maybe he took his bike?"

"Without me?" I shuffled in my seat. "Maybe."

I stepped off the bus at school and walked across the parking lot. Brian stood waiting for me at the opposite end.

"Good morning, beautiful," he said, presenting me with a small pink daisy. I plucked it from his fingers and thanked him with a smile. A weight lifted off my heart.

The journal I'd given him for Christmas last year was tucked under one of his arms and the top of my purple pen peeked out over his ear.

"Have you been drawing?" I asked.

"Yeah. I want to show you later."

Sam jogged up beside us. "Well, I'll just be heading off to homeroom, okay? You two have fun. Nice to see you, Brian. Bye Allie!" She waved and rushed off.

"Did everything go okay with your mom?" I took his hand.

"Yeah. She'd cooled off a lot. I told her I spent the night

at a friend's house and she didn't even care. Guess she never did. Go figure."

"No apology, though, huh?" We strolled toward the school entrance.

"Nope. None expected."

I shook my head and sighed. "That just sucks."

"Yeah."

"Guys!" Kareena's high-pitched squeal was unmistakable.

We veered around. She came flouncing toward us, her heels clacking on the pavement and her plaid skirt rippling in the breeze. A wide-eyed look of panic was painted across her face.

"You're glowing!" she said, pointing a trembling finger at us. "Your shoulder, Alice. Your arm, Brian! Crap, you two! We have to get out of here! People are going to see you!"

I looked over at Brian and saw nothing blue besides his jeans. He studied my shoulder in return and then shrugged.

"I don't see anything," he said, staring skeptically at her. "I think you've inhaled too much hairspray."

"Jesus, guys!" She stamped her heel on the ground. "Why won't you listen to me? You're freaking glowing. I can see it clear as freaking day."

I really thought she was screwing with us. We couldn't have been glowing right then and there; a few other students straggling in the parking lot didn't seem interested at all.

"We aren't, Kareena," I replied, craning my neck to take a second look at my shoulder to reconfirm. "Nope. Nothing there."

She crossed her arms. "Ugh! Forget it. When somebody else sees it, you'll know I'm not talking shit."

Kareena shoved her books into her locker, rustling things around loudly on purpose, muttering to herself. Her locker was beside ours this year because she'd sweet-talked a junior boy into switching with her.

"I think she's losing it," I whispered to Brian, who silently mouthed his agreement.

"Look, I know you guys don't, like, value my opinion," she started, slamming her locker door shut and turning toward us with a huff. "But I'm not joking. I can see it." She folded her arms and leaned her back up against her locker.

First day of the tenth grade. Kareena had lost it.

·　　·　　·

"You guys kinda suck as friends," Kareena said, picking at her macaroni and cheese and exhaling loudly. She'd kept up her rant all through lunch.

"Don't say something stupid like that." Brian snatched the plastic fork out of her hand. "And stop playing with your food. It's annoying."

She put her elbows on the table and propped her head in her hands, groaning and looking away from him.

"Sorry, but if you can see it, why can't everyone else?" Brian looked at Sam to make his point.

"I don't know. Maybe you guys just can't... Shit!" She pushed her tray forward.

"What?" I looked up from my brownie. Kareena's eyes were locked onto someone sitting at another table. I couldn't pinpoint who.

"What is it?" Brian stared in the same direction. "Who are you looking at?"

"That guy with the blonde hair and the red t-shirt. The one with the energy drink in his hand."

"Haven't seen him before," Brian said. "I think he's a freshman. I don't know. A little young for you, don't you think?"

"Damn it, Brian! Listen!" Kareena's eyes widened and she shot up from the bench. "There's something in him. He's... glowing."

I stood up, too, freaked out by her allegations. "Lower your voice, Kareena," I hissed. The entire lunchroom didn't need to hear us. "What do you mean you can see something in him?"

She stared, holding her breath, fixated like a cat stalking prey. He was talking to another student and hadn't noticed the four of us gawking at him.

"It's faint, but it's, like, alive," she continued, her voice cracking. "It's a small ball of white light with some kind of black dust coiling around it. I think it's sleeping. The glow keeps fading in and out like a heartbeat."

"That got poetic real fast." Brian exhaled. "Come on. This is all a little crazy, don't you think?"

"No!" She swerved around. "Do you think I'm joking, Brian? I'm not." She lunged at him, grabbing him by the sides of his face and pulling him closer. "Do I look like I'm joking?" Her nostrils flared.

"Ah!" Brian grimaced and forced her off him, blinking and shaking his head like he'd been blinded by a camera flash. "What did you do to me?" He grunted, holding his head in his hands, doubling over. "Damn it, Kareena! What did you..."

"Brian! Brian, are you okay?" He wouldn't look at me.

His face came back up and his gaze shot across the room at the boy in the red shirt. "Jesus. She's right," he said. "I can see it. And that girl behind him, too."

"You're right," Kareena replied with a nod, her gaze locking onto someone else I couldn't pick out.

Brian looked at me, his eyes skimming over my shoulder and then across Kareena's face. "I can see ours, too." He bent over, groaning and rubbing his temples. "Ugh, my head."

"Now you know how I feel," Kareena sneered. "Migraines are shit, aren't they?"

"Brian?" I put a hand on his shoulder. "Are you okay?" I rubbed his arm.

"Yeah." He shook his head again and blinked several more times. "It's going away. She's telling the truth, Alice. Those other kids have it, too—whatever it is. It's some kind of energy. I couldn't tell much else. The vision faded too quickly."

A few nearby students stared at us and I turned to confront them. "We're fine," I said, forcing a toothy grin at them. "Thanks for your concern. Feel free to go back to whatever it was you were doing." They shrugged and looked away. One of them had the nerve to roll their eyes at me.

"I can still see it," said Kareena. "Alice. You should go talk to them. See if you can figure anything out. Touch him, maybe. Do whatever it is you do."

"What? No." I shook my head. "I'm not going to just go up to some stranger and grab him."

"Just say hi. Introduce yourself or something," Kareena added with a shrug. "You're a cute girl, that guy will be okay with it."

Had Kareena just called me cute? How badly did she want me to do this?

"Don't tell her what to do." Brian tugged my hand, motioning for me to sit back down.

"I'm not." Kareena scoffed. "I just think we need to figure out if he's one of us or not. We could use more friends, you know?"

"I think you just want a new boyfriend," Brian grumbled.

"No. I'm serious. I thought the pasty crazies up there said Alice was supposed to be the 'Starter' or whatever. She apparently activated it in both of us. So... maybe she needs to go over there and touch him, too. Maybe that's what they want us to do. The Sav—"

"Shh!" I gave her a dirty look. "Quiet." I got up and stepped over the bench, careful not to get a leg tangled in my book bag strap. "I'll do it."

"You don't have to." Brian snagged the edge of my shirt.

"It's okay. I'll be fine." I looked at Kareena, whose eyes were still locked on the guy. "The boy in the red shirt, right?"

"With the sports logo on the pocket. Yes," she confirmed.

I took a deep breath and exhaled, puffing out my cheeks. "Okay." I put on my best friendly smile and meandered over to the table a few rows across from ours.

"Hi. My name's Alice," I said, my voice shaking. "I'm... um..." I froze up. "Um."

Think! Think!

"Yes?" The guy's eyebrows furrowed. He set down his drink and screwed the plastic cap on top. "Can I help you, Alice?"

I felt like an idiot.

I offered my hand and smiled even bigger, forcing it so much it probably looked creepy. "I'm with the student government. I just wanted to say hello and welcome you to our school."

"Uh... Thanks? But, I've been here for a year."

"Oh? I'm sorry." Even more of an idiot, now. "I didn't know. They just told me..."

"It's okay." He grinned. "Don't worry about it." He leaned over to glance back at my table and then looked me in the eye again. "Weren't you just sitting with him?"

"Yeah, she was." Brian came up behind me.

"Hey! You're the guy with the motorcycle, right? I saw you this morning. It's real nice, man. It's no wonder girls like to hang out with you."

Okay. I raised an eyebrow. Guess he thought Kareena, Sam and I were all...

Brian laughed. "Not really, but thanks. Name's Brian."

"Hi. This your girlfriend?"

I hated being the focus of a conversation.

"Yeah," Brian replied, proudly.

"Alice." I eagerly stretched out my hand toward the stranger again, holding my breath this time. He hesitated, his eyes darting from Brian's to mine, contemplating if being friendly with the motorcycle guy's girlfriend was a good idea. Brian sensed his misplaced concern and took a step back.

"I'll go grab your stuff," he said, heading back to our table.

"Adam." The guy grinned, reaching up from the table to shake my hand.

Our palms touched and my heartbeat quickened. The hairs on the back of my neck perked up, my fingertips flushed with heat, and my skin prickled with goose bumps. Static flitted through my body.

I gasped.

Adam snapped back.

"Whoa!" His eyes widened and he stared at me, blinking. "What have you been doing, girl? You are electric." He shook his hand. "Ow. You shocked the hell out of me."

"I'm... sorry," I said, backing away slowly.

"Wait. Where are you going?"

"I'm so sorry, Adam."

Chapter 30

"I was right! There *are* others!" Kareena jabbed me in the shoulder and I recoiled from the prick of her sharp fingernail. "I told you I knew what I was seeing."

"I'm sorry, Kareena," I said, switching out one of my textbooks in my locker. "We didn't know."

"Did you feel anything?" she asked. "After you touched him, I mean?"

"It was about the same as when I touched you. A pulse of energy and then he got shocked. I feel bad about it, really."

"The light totally changed, though." She flipped open a makeup compact and started reapplying her bright red lipstick.

"It did?"

"Yeah." She snapped the lipstick closed and smacked her lips together. "It got super bright. It didn't change color or anything but as soon as you touched him it exploded into this, like, little ball of white fiery stuff. Kind of creepy almost, but whatever." She shrugged and tucked her makeup back into her purse.

The bell rang.

"We gotta get to class." Brian reached for my book bag and slid it off my arm, shouldering it himself. "See you, Kareena. We can talk about it later."

"Okay. Whatever." She rolled her eyes and clicked off down the hall in the opposite direction.

"So what exactly did she do to you?" I asked, walking beside him. "It sounded like you were seeing things, too."

"I was. It was like putting on a pair of really dark sunglasses. Everything got blurry. That's why I started blinking like crazy. When things came back into focus, they seemed washed out, like the colors weren't all there. That's when I saw it—the light."

I leaned in closer.

"It resonated in Adam's chest, flickering like a dying flame. Weak, but moving—alive, I think. Sleeping. That was the first thing I thought of when I saw it. Doesn't that sound crazy to you?" He paused and looked down at me.

"Yeah. Weird."

"Definitely weird. But at the same time, wouldn't it be good to have more people we could trust? More people who knew about..." his voice came down to a whisper, "the fluorescence?"

"Yes."

"You have to admit, some little part of you got excited after you thought about it, right?"

I nodded.

"Then maybe... this is what you're supposed to do. What we're supposed to do. Find others like us and..."

"It felt wrong, though," I interrupted, tangling my hands together nervously. "Touching him."

"Hey, I'm not upset or jealous," he added with a smirk. "Besides, did you see the look on his face when I told him you were my girlfriend?" He chuckled.

This wasn't funny.

"Not about that, Brian." I tugged on his belt. "I mean, what if he didn't want this? What if what I did to Adam was wrong? They've hardly told us anything about it. How do we know it's safe?"

Brian stopped and turned toward me. He cupped his hands around my shoulders and pressed them gently. "All I know is, it made my heart better and it helped save Kareena's life. I've got no complaints."

"Maybe you're right. Maybe we can do some good with this. Maybe we're meant to."

.   .   .

I tossed my book bag onto the couch and went into the kitchen. Brian had dropped me off after school. He would have stayed but had to be at work in an hour.

"How was your first day of tenth grade?" Mom asked, bent over the open oven door, checking on a pizza she was cooking. Cheese bubbled and the room smelled like garlic and oregano.

"It went fine, thanks."

"That's good. And how's Brian doing?"

"He's okay. His mom never apologized for anything, but he's alright."

"I'm sorry to hear that, Alice. Guess not all kids are as privileged as you are, huh?" She grinned and closed the oven door. "Pizza will be done in about ten minutes."

"Got it." I took two clean plates out of the dishwasher and set them on the counter behind Mom. "Oh, I almost forgot."

"Yes?"

"We may have found another few students like us."

"With fluorescence in them?" She plucked several paper towels from the roll on the counter and started folding them in half.

"Yeah. Not like ours, but a variation of it. We just learned Kareena can see it in other people and she can see ours, too, even when it seems inactive to us. Boy, did she freak out at school today. I hope she'll get used to it eventually. Her voice is sooooo..."

"Oh, great. So they're messing with more kids?" Mom shook her head and huffed an angry sigh. "Just in time to ruin dinner."

"I'm sorry." I sat on a kitchen chair and clasped my hands together on the table.

"No, it's okay. I asked you to let me know. I wish they would find a cure and get it over with or die trying and leave us alone. One of the two."

"Mom. That's just mean. No one wants their *entire* civilization to disappear. What if there weren't many of *us* left and someone was willing to help keep *us* alive? Would it be right if the entire human race just died?"

"When you put it that way. No... But I wish the Saviors would have considered getting some kind of consent before they started." She laid the folded paper towels beside our plates at the table and set two coasters down. "We didn't ask to be part of this. And I didn't want you to be part of it, either. It's hard enough being a teenager in love, but you and Brian can never have a normal relationship because of them. It's not right. You're only young once."

"We've been okay so far." I got up from the table and pushed in my chair. "We're happy and we'll get through this." I pulled open a cupboard door and reached up, feeling a slight twinge inside, but ignoring it. My fingers wrapped around a tall glass and then I cringed, clenching my teeth.

Searing pain erupted in my stomach and I cried out, doubling over. Crumbling to my knees. The glass came crashing down, shattering on the linoleum. Pain ripped through me, squeezing, twisting my stomach. I held my belly, trying to avoid shards of broken glass on the floor even as my vision began to blur. Tears welled in my eyes.

"Alice!" Mom knelt by my side.

I gasped for air but it was like sucking in water. The room dissolved in and out of focus. My head felt heavy, and it was weaving from side to side. I couldn't keep my chin up.

I swallowed hard, on the brink of throwing up. The sharp, stabbing pains spread up my abdomen. Into my ribs. The room swirled. My chest burned.

"Alice! Alice, say something!"

I felt my mom holding me, but couldn't respond. My lips

wouldn't move. Everything inside me tightened and I tipped over onto the floor, my eyelids closing, my mind blanketed by darkness.

.   .   .

Soft amber light burned my eyes.

I awoke on the couch; the lamp in the living room had been dimmed.

I squeezed with my fingers. Someone squeezed back.

Mom sat by my side, clutching my hand tightly in hers.

"Thank God you're awake!" She brushed her fingers over my forehead and cupped my cheek.

I struggled to sit up, blinking, fighting to open my eyes fully. My body felt so heavy. My eyelids were tugging closed again. I held my head in my hands, sickness roiling in my gut.

"How do you feel?"

Weak.

I looked up at her, drowsily. "The... Saviors..." My voice echoed in my head. My ears were ringing.

"What? When?"

"When I fainted." I groaned. I felt disconnected—out of body. Drifting. Like I was dreaming. "They told me the anemia made me lose consciousness. That they would fix it before..." I dropped my head again and grumbled. "They said something about suppressing the symptoms of... I don't remember everything." I sighed.

"I'm glad you're okay, Alice. You had me scared to death. I didn't know what to do. If you had been out any longer, I would have had to take you to the hospital."

"It's okay. I'm okay, Mom." I swallowed hard; a strange metallic taste tainted my mouth. "Ugh. Can I have some water, please?"

"Of course!" Mom rushed off into the kitchen and came back a moment later with a glass filled to the brim. She helped me hold it.

"Thanks." I took a sip, my hands trembling. Water splashing up over the rim of the glass. I fought to steady myself.

"Do you remember anything else?" She supported the glass between sips.

I wiped a drip of water from my lower lip. "I don't think so. All I really remember was this light. This bright, colorful light that..."

I stopped breathing.

Chills swept over me.

The room went out of focus.

My hands tingled. Cold. Numb.

"What?" Mom set the water on the coffee table. "What is it?"

My face tightened. Mom said something. Drowned out by mental static.

"Brian." I mouthed his name. My eyes fixated on nothingness.

"Brian."

•   •   •

"She's been like this since I called you," my mom said, leading Brian into the living room. "Please do something. I don't know what's wrong, but she won't talk to me."

He sat beside me on the couch and the cushion sunk in with his weight. He wrapped his arm around my shoulders. I stiffened, resisting unintentionally.

"What's wrong, Alice?" he asked, his voice shaky. Out of breath. "What happened?"

"I... remember now," I muttered, focused on nothing. "Bright light scorching my eyelids. Grey eyes staring at me, judging me. Disappointed in me. In... us."

I looked toward the kitchen and saw Mom leaning against the door jamb, watching us.

She couldn't know the truth.

"Ask Mom to leave us alone," I whispered.

Before Brian could even stand, Mom backed away and disappeared into the other room.

"I'm fifteen, Brian. Why did they have to pick us for this?" I rubbed my arms. The hairs bristled on end. Every inch of my skin was hypersensitive. "Why couldn't it have been someone else? Anyone else?"

"You're sounding a little crazy, Alice." He swallowed hard. "What did they say to you?"

I fidgeted with the hem of my shirt, twisting it around my fingers and untwisting it again.

Over and over.

And over.

"Alice?" Brian pressed his palm against my knee. "Answer me."

"They told me you were supposed to heal my anemia but didn't. That they would have to correct it, instead."

"How? I didn't know I could."

"And they told me what Kareena did was the right thing. That she is supposed to help us seek out others with dormant DNA. I am supposed to start them the same way I started Adam." I filled my lungs with air and exhaled slowly, a sick feeling creeping around the pit of my stomach. "How do we know he wanted to be part of this? We never asked him. I was stupid to just touch him like that."

"Alice, please stop talking like this. You're not making any sense." He shook me gently.

"I'm making perfect sense, Brian," I said, raising my voice, looking him in the eye. The soft colors were snuffed out by frightened, enlarged black pupils. "Those creatures up there, they want us to do things for them. Things I don't want to do."

"Like what? Like what, Alice?"

"One of the Saviors came up to me and took my wrist.

Its fingers felt lukewarm—room temperature. It was terrible. Corpse-like." I swallowed and gasped for air. "It turned my hand over and pressed a thumb against my vein. I felt a sharp prick." I shuddered.

Brian took my hand and immediately checked my wrist for marks. There were none.

"Then I felt this heat come over me—a calm, comforting warmth. Almost like yours. Familiar. They released me and a tiny light appeared in the palm of my hand. Flickering. Alive. But fragile and scared.

I stood there staring at it as it rested within my grasp, glowing, breathing. Soothed by my touch. Smiling, even though it had no face. Invisible—weightless. But... I could feel it inside me. Part of me."

"Part of you?" Brian's voice wavered. He shifted in his seat and moved a little closer. "What do you mean by that?"

I flattened my fingers against his hand until our palms touched. The fluorescence ignited beneath our skin, escaping through the surface as wafts of dusty vapor. His hand burned hot blue—mine no longer green, but bright turquoise. His heartbeat quickened, his pulse throbbing against my fingertips.

"Part of us," I said, looking up at him.

He sucked in a breath.

"The Saviors think we might be the answer to saving their race, but we need to do more than just store their DNA. All that stuff they kept saying about us spending time together? It was their way of skirting around the truth of what they really wanted from us."

He pushed up off his seat. "This isn't a goddamn sci-fi movie, Alice. Spit it out!"

I squeezed my eyelids shut. "I'm pregnant."

He just stood there staring at me.

"Jesus. You're... you're kidding me, right?" His voice broke. "Alice?"

"No! I'm not."

He scowled.

"This is real, Brian!"

"Like hell it is! So, you're trying to tell me the Saviors knocked you up with some bastard alien baby?"

"No, it's not like that. You don't understand." I stretched a hand up toward him but he stepped back, out of reach.

"I understand enough!" he said. "You were right, weren't you? They're using us for their own sick games. I'll be damned if I'll let them use me for anything."

"Brian, please listen! Please." I reached out to him again but he was still too far away. Too weak to stand, I slipped from the couch and down onto the floor, scuffing my knees on the carpet.

"How am I supposed to react to this? That..." He grimaced, pointing at me. "That... thing in you. Whatever the hell it is."

"She's ours."

His jaw dropped. "What?" His eyes narrowed.

"She's yours and mine. I know she is."

"She? How the hell do you know that?"

"I felt it in the glow. I felt you in her, too. I know she's ours, Brian. It's what they wanted from us from the beginning but..."

"They got antsy and did it themselves?!" He clenched his fists. "Those bastards! I can't even..." His knuckles turned white. "This is all wrong."

"I know you must feel..."

"Like shit. Yeah. I do." He forked his hands through his hair and tugged it flat against his head. "I'm going outside. I need some air." He stormed out of the living room.

The front door slammed and the floor shook beneath me.

My shoulder ached and the pain rippled through my torso, tightening my chest and straining my heart. I fought for every breath, just to get air in and out. My emotions were drained, my entire body overwhelmed with fear and... even hate. I dragged myself back up onto the couch and sunk into the cushions.

Why was he freaking out on *me*? Did he think I wasn't hurt by this? Did he think I wasn't shaken enough by the thought of having a baby I never even wanted?

A baby we *never conceived on our own.*

Afraid of screwing up, I had tried to make the right decision, but the wrong one had been made for me. Forced on me.

He'd had reason to be upset, but not to walk out on me like that.

I was too tired to cry, my eyes drained of every tear already.

Sharp pricks riddled my temples. I closed my eyes in response to the budding headache.

I heard Mom scuffling around the kitchen, debating whether or not to check on me.

I couldn't deal with her right now.

The front door opened and shut again, more quietly this time.

"Alice?" Brian staggered in.

He fell to his knees at my feet. "I'm sorry," he said, his lower lip quivering. "Please forgive me."

I was wrong about the tears. A fresh stream drizzled down my cheek. I tasted the salt on my lips.

"I'm scared, Brian." I wheezed. "I don't want you to leave me."

"Don't say that." He came to his feet and sat on the edge of the coffee table across from me, bending over and cupping his hands onto my shoulders.

"But..." I lowered my head, choking on a congested breath. "I can't lose you."

"Hush. I'm not going to leave you. Look at me. Look at me, Alice." He reached a hand toward my chin, tipping my face up toward his. His eyes shimmered with tears. "I've told you before, I am not your father. I will never be anything like him. I swear to God, I won't leave you. Not like this, and if I can help it, not ever." He brushed my hair behind my ear and used his other hand to wipe the shine from his own reddening cheek.

"I meant what I said and I'll stand by it no matter what happens." He tried to smile. "I love you. We'll get through this together." He reached for my hands and enveloped them in his.

I gasped. His fingers were cold as ice.

"Alice, the truth is... I'm scared, too."

BOOK II
CONTAGIOUS

Chapter 1

I eased the door closed behind me and tossed my helmet onto the couch.

Horrible tips. Got off late. Another slow, crappy day at work.

"Hey!" Mom stepped out of her bedroom and into the hallway, blocking the only path to my room. "Where are you going?"

"I'm going to lay down," I replied, avoiding eye contact. I loosened the black satin tie around my neck and unbuttoned the top button of my shirt. "I'm tired. Okay?"

"Where have you been?" She crossed her arms.

I pressed my lips together.

"Brian?" She sneered. The ugliness of her expression made me scowl.

"Really, Mom? Are we gonna do this again? You want to know where I go all of the time?" I took a few steps back, without breaking eye contact with her, and scooped my motorcycle helmet up off the couch. "First of all, I've got a job at Jacques' downtown. I got the job a few months ago, which you were clearly aware of because I told you. I wasn't lying about that, you know. I've got the pay stubs to prove it."

She rolled her eyes.

"Secondly, I hang out with my girlfriend."

Mom came closer and pointed a stiff index finger at me. "You never even came home last night."

"It's not like you give a damn whether or not I'm here. Anyway, I was with her." I polished the top of my helmet with my sleeve and looked away.

"The little... brown-haired girl?"

Oh my God, Mom. She had really lost it this week.

"Alice," I corrected, offended. "Her name's Alice, Mom. And if you haven't already forgotten, we went to her mother's Christmas party last year."

"Oh, yes." She huffed and muttered something beneath her breath. "I remember. I didn't like her mother much. All her family and friends over like she was some kind of little goody-two-shoes. Janet. June. Whatever her name—"

"Jane," I interrupted, tucking my helmet under my arm. "Her name's Jane. And, unlike you, she actually cares about her kid. She cares about me, too, for that matter."

"Quit being a smartass." She raised her arm, threatening to swipe the back of her hand across my face. I didn't flinch. "Just because you've got a job and a motorcycle, doesn't make you king of anything."

You don't scare me.

"Mom, please." I bit my tongue and took a deep breath to keep from saying something I'd regret.

She lowered her hand and pushed past me. "Actually, I don't care where you go, or what you and your girlfriend do," she said. "But I know you've been spending a lot of time with her—way too much for a boy your age, so you'd better watch yourself. If she ends up pregnant, I'll disown your ass."

Great timing...

"Thanks for the advice." I clenched my fists. She was treading on thin ice. "Because I'm an idiot, right? You just have to tell me every little damn thing. You know what, why *don't* you disown me? You and Dad never wanted me anyway." I shimmied past her and into my room. I threw my helmet onto my bed and turned to close my door. "I know I'm not your perfect goddamn poster child. I'm sorry I was born with a heart defect, but at least I was born with a heart."

"Don't you dare!" She raised her eyebrows.

I slammed the door shut and locked it. "Shut up." I lowered my voice. "Just, shut up." My demands were safely distorted by the door.

There was my mother, teetering on the ledge of sanity. Every day a gamble and every tomorrow threatening to send me spiraling into hell.

I wouldn't let her drag me down into her misery. She'd been slipping for a while, and it had gotten progressively worse over the past few weeks. She acted as though her life was so hard.

Ever since Jane had lifted her ban on my seeing Alice, things had gotten better. Alice and I had been able to spend more time together. I felt responsible now that I'd gotten a job and started paying off my motorcycle.

Growing up would be a lot of work, but I was ready to face reality. To step up and be the man Alice needed me to be.

I thought about her all the time, and there were nights I desperately wanted her by my side, curled up safely in my arms beneath the bed sheets. But in the eyes of the law, we were kids. We couldn't make all of the choices we wanted to. All the decisions we *needed* to.

The damn Saviors couldn't wait. They'd slammed Alice and me with the consequences of a decision we'd never made— the decision to bring a child into the world.

As if having fluorescence inside us wasn't enough to worry about.

And if my mother used the "little brown-haired girl" line one more time, I'd snap. I'd known Alice for no less than a year, yet she pretended to not even remember her name. Sometimes I thought it was the medication talking. Other days, I *knew* she purposely tuned me out.

The boy with the running mouth. The stranger who lived in her home.

She and Dad had always hated me for things I had no control over. I wasn't good enough for the military. Because of my arrhythmia, I wasn't strong enough to run and play like other boys my age.

They couldn't push me to the limits.

They couldn't break me.

"Damn it!"

I slammed a fist into the wall, sending a cloud of drywall dust scattering across the floor, then recoiled from the hole, my hand trembling. Ivory knucklebones protruded, glossy and raw. Bloodied patches of torn skin wrinkled backward like wet paper mâché.

I grunted through gritted teeth, slurring and hissing as pain bolted through my arm.

Jesus.

Light brown showed through the indention in the wall.

A stud. A freaking stud.

Blood drizzled down my fingers, soaking the carpet near my dresser with a soggy patch of bright crimson. I cupped my wrist and lifted my arm above my head to try to slow the bleeding. Knuckles fractured, I couldn't move my fingers. Sticky pink flesh peeled up around them. I bit my tongue. I couldn't let Mom hear me. I wouldn't give her the satisfaction of finding me in pain.

Hot white and blue sparked from the tips of my fingers and skittered up my arm, igniting the skin with electric blue light. Warmth washed over me and I exhaled a sigh of relief. The pain quieted. Frayed edges of skin relaxed and sunk down over the bones, stretching and smoothing across the wound like liquid flesh pouring over my hand.

The azure glow dimmed and faded completely into my skin. I turned over my hand, wiggling the fingers and rotating at the wrist to judge the range of motion. Normal.

I'd never broken a bone before, but I had twisted an ankle taking a fall from my skateboard years ago.

That was back when I was younger—a *normal* kid.

Being a teenager blows.

Chapter 2

My name is Brian. No last name, but Azure will do. If you insist.

I'm a Healer.

The blue light in me—the one that saved my fractured knuckles a trip to the ER—is alive. It's a type of DNA known as fluorescence, and it was implanted in me not long ago by an alien race called the Saviors.

My girlfriend, Alice—also implanted with fluorescence—is the reason I'm still breathing. The reason I haven't become a runaway and chosen to face the world on my own, struggling to keep police off my back. Life at home with my psychotic mother is hell and every day a nightmare to live through.

Frightening? Maybe. Not half as scary as being called away from work by my girlfriend's mother because her daughter had had a nervous breakdown and wouldn't talk to her. Why? Because she'd just found out she was carrying *my* child. This despite the fact that we'd never actually slept together.

Okay, so it wasn't like we were saintly kids who'd never thought about sex, but Alice had insisted against it mostly out of fear of, well, *this* happening. I respected her decision but it's hard being in a serious relationship at an age when your body is still working things out.

Age of consent. What a joke. Mother nature doesn't give a damn about laws. All she cares about is keeping the species alive. Raging hormones and all of the crazed internal shit wants us to slip up and do what nature intended.

We didn't and we still got screwed over.

The Saviors put it there, and now we're the ones who have to deal with it. I couldn't imagine what went through Alice's head after she found out. I was petrified when she first told me. So furious, I had to step out and let off some steam. It wasn't her fault.

It wasn't my fault, either.

No matter who did this to her, I had to take on responsibility for it. Her father may have walked out on her, but I sure as hell wouldn't. I needed to be there for her no matter what.

·　　·　　·

"Emancipation. Transfer of Guardianship." Kareena— another fluorescent one—slid a stack of papers across the lunch table to me. "You've got a few options."

Alice leaned in to share a look, sweeping her long brown hair back and out of the way of her food tray.

"Marriage?" I furrowed my brow. "Seriously?"

Sam—Alice's best friend—stuck out her tongue and wrinkled her nose in response. She sat across from us in the cafeteria.

"Well, if your mom wants to get rid of you *that* badly." Kareena shrugged.

She'd really done her homework. The only homework I'd ever seen her do, actually. It'd be a miracle if she graduated this year. Kareena acted like a bitch most of the time, but apparently she cared. A little.

Alice sunk down. I reached over and took her hand.

"Don't worry, Alice. I think getting married is our *last* option."

"I know." She nodded.

"Besides, would it be *that* bad?" I looked into her bright blue eyes and smiled, brushing her hair behind her ear. "I mean, really?"

She looked down. "Well, no, but…"

Who was I kidding? Alice was fifteen, for God's sake.

I understood why she was hesitant. It wasn't that I couldn't see myself marrying her, but the thought of making that commitment in binding legalese in the middle of our sophomore year of high school jarred me. Someday. Just not today.

That, and Mom would never do me the favor of signing anything. The law states that each minor is required to have one parent present for a marriage like that to go through. Count my mom out.

Luckily, Kareena's bigwig lawyer of a father had exposed her to law despite her efforts to avoid it. I recalled seeing their massive library of law books when I'd perused her house, just before we'd found out she was one of us. It had filled an entire room to the ceiling. I remember because I couldn't help but imagine what it must be like having the money to fill spare rooms with books alone.

"Emancipation then?" Kareena sifted a stapled packet out of the pile and plopped it on top. "It's an option if you can prove you're better off on your own."

I didn't think I was that well-off yet, but…

"However," Kareena continued, "if there's cause to believe your mother is negligent—which we all know she is—then it will be thrown out and picked up by social services first."

Damn.

"This is ridiculous!" I groaned and covered my face with my hands. "I can't keep dealing with her like this. She's making me crazy. And I can't keep expecting your mom to take me in when things go south." I looked at Alice and took a sip of my soda. "She's done so much already."

The first time had been out of necessity, but I'd stayed over the other night, too, when Alice had told me the news. We'd slept on the couch—or at least tried. Leaving Alice alone then had felt wrong and, luckily, her mother hadn't argued with me.

"I'll look this stuff over later. Alice? Can you hang on to it for me?" I slid the stack over to her.

"Sure." She gathered up the pile and shoved it into her book bag.

"Thanks."

Kareena and Sam each went their own way, and we headed off to chemistry class.

"Are you feeling any better?" I asked Alice, reaching to take her hand. We hadn't told the others about the pregnancy yet.

"Yeah." She looked up at me and her gaze softened. "Thanks to you. Having you there the other night calmed me down a lot. I'm still scared... but at least I have you."

"You certainly do." I squeezed her hand gently and smiled.

I love Alice so much, it sometimes makes my heart hurt.

•　　•　　•

I pulled my motorcycle up into the driveway and squeezed the brake. Alice hopped off and I flicked down the kickstand. We slipped off our helmets and tucked them under our arms.

"It will be okay," I said, taking her arm. "We'll be okay, Alice."

She swallowed hard and fumbled through her book bag for her house key, clearly preoccupied with the fear of telling her mother about the pregnancy.

We strolled up the driveway together and her mother, Jane, came to the door before Alice could find her key.

Jane smiled, a generous, toothy grin that was a little forced but still friendly. I tried my best to act natural and grin back. We walked past her and into the living room.

"Staying for dinner, Brian?" Jane asked.

"Sure. If it's not too much trouble." I flopped down onto

the couch and Alice dropped down beside me, leaning back into my embrace.

"Don't worry, okay?" I said, holding her close.

"I know." She rested a hand on her belly and sighed. "But, I'm still scared. I can't even believe it. I don't want to believe it."

"Believe what, Alice?" her mom asked, standing in the archway between the rooms.

"Oh. I-I, uh," Alice stuttered.

"Tell her," I said, nudging her gently, rubbing her arm with my hand. Goose bumps rose across her skin. "It will be okay. I promise."

Alice gulped and her body trembled against mine.

"It's okay, Alice," I assured her again.

"Mom... I'm..."

"I know," her mother interrupted softly.

Alice gasped. "You do?"

"Yes." She looked at me and nodded. "Brian told me after you'd fallen asleep."

"Oh." Alice sunk down, reaching a hand up to fidget with her dolphin pendant.

"You don't need to stress out about me and what I think." Her mother came over and sat on the coffee table in front of us. "Alice, honey, you're all I've got. If those monsters up there are going to mess with my little girl against her will, then with God as my witness, I will do everything I can to protect you and make you comfortable."

"I don't want this," Alice said. "Brian and I..."

"I know," her mom interrupted again. "He already told me. You two never..." She cleared her throat. "Slept together. And unlike most parents of teens, I trust you and have reason to believe you two have told me the truth."

"I'm so scared, Mom." Alice leaned forward to hug her mother.

I was scared, too. Scared of what was growing inside the

girl I loved. Scared of how much or... how little of it was really ours.

Chapter 3

We tried to discuss options, but not knowing exactly what kind of baby it would be or whether or not it would have fluorescence inside it, too, made deciding on anything difficult. Abortion was something we had discussed, but it didn't seem like a possibility worth pursuing. Odds were, if the Saviors had put it in her once, they wouldn't hesitate to do it again. Alice didn't need any more pain. Physical or psychological.

Her mother had offered to help in any way she could, but high school would get in the way regardless. Homeschool wasn't even an option with her mother having a full-time job. Online classes maybe, but again, it would require some cooperation from my own mom.

Not going to happen.

We'd have to face this one way or another.

So much to consider and so little time. Seven, eight months tops?

Thinking about it made my stomach turn.

I wanted to go on living—pretending it had never happened—but that'd be lying to myself. For now, we were doing what we could to keep our minds off it. We tried to find peace amidst the chaos. Even if only for a little while.

. . .

Students bustled up the stairway to the school entrance. Alice and I hung back, ducking out of sight and into an empty corner. A cutaway between buildings where we were able to find some quiet time between classes. I leaned up against the brick wall.

"You know..." I smirked, reaching out to take her by the waist and pull her closer. Her body pressed into me. "I swear you're a little taller than you used to be."

"Yeah. Maybe." She shrugged.

"I like it."

We spent so much time together, changes were subtle, but once in a while, I'd stop and suddenly notice something different. Day by day, her distinct and beautiful curves became more beautiful.

I tucked my hands into the back pockets of her jeans. "It makes you easier to kiss," I said, raising an eyebrow and brushing my nose against hers. She giggled, shying away and combing a wave of her hair away from her face. "Jesus, I love your smile."

I kissed her and slid my hands out of her pockets to clasp her waist, my thumbs massaging the rounded jut of her hipbones through her snug jeans. I kissed her until her knees went weak and her body pulsed against mine, slender fingers wrinkling my shirt. Tasting her. Our breaths mingling.

I inhaled her sweet, honey-like scent. Subtle and fleeting like the final days of spring. She enchanted me. The flowing lines of her petite waist. Her amazing silhouette.

But none of it satisfied the selfish, carnal desire to make her mine. Hungering. Haunting me. Ever since I'd found out about the pregnancy, my physical attraction toward Alice had intensified. Maybe they were sick, misguided feelings over what the Saviors had done, but I couldn't shut them out. They clawed at my sanity day and night. I needed to regain the strength to keep myself in check—to stop ruminating about the one thing she wasn't ready to do.

For now, I had to push it aside and worry about *her* needs.

She trembled in my arms, letting out a stifled groan as I

released a warm breath onto the sensitive flesh behind her ear. Her body softened against mine, our breaths growing shallower. She dragged her hands up my chest and then wrapped her fingers around the back of my neck, interlacing them through my hair.

"Brian, I..."

I held my breath.

Damn. The words were right on the tip of her tongue.

"I... want you in my life." She exhaled and nuzzled her face against my shirt.

It wasn't exactly what I'd needed to hear, but I couldn't force it out of her if she wasn't ready.

"I love you, Alice." I kissed her forehead and she looked up at me with starry eyes. I lost myself in their soothing blue shimmer.

"Alice!" Kareena shrieked, jogging toward us.

Alice pulled away from me and turned. "What?" she asked, flustered, hastily straightening her wrinkled shirt.

I rested my weight against the wall, unsettled by her sudden withdrawal.

"What the hell is going on with you, Alice?" Kareena looked her up and down frantically. "Can you not see it?" She scoffed. "You're glowing, like, two different colors. Green and a weird turquoise kind of shade. It's..." Her eyes went wide as she focused on Alice's abdomen. "Brian? You have to see this!" She came at me with outstretched arms, her hands targeting my face.

"No!" I ducked, shimmying to the side. "Don't! I don't want to feel that again."

Last time she'd touched my face, I'd started seeing things in other people—dormant lights—and then got a *killer* migraine right after.

No thanks.

She sneered. "How else do I show you?"

"We already know," Alice said, frowning.

"You do? Well, why didn't you tell me? What does it mean?"

"I'm..." Alice's voice lowered to a barely audible whisper and she motioned for Kareena to come closer.

"You're pregnant!?" Kareena repeated, louder than she should have.

"Shh!" Alice pinched the edge of Kareena's blouse and tugged. "Keep it down."

"Yeah. Please," I added, furrowing my brow at her and then glancing around nervously. The few passing stragglers didn't seem to have noticed. Thank God.

Kareena's forehead creased and a weird, excited-confused grin flashed on her face. "Oh my God. So... you two actually had sex?"

"No!" Alice raised her voice, defensively. "We... we didn't."

"Well, now's your chance." Kareena snickered.

"Kareena!" I shot her a dirty look. "This is serious."

"Sorry!" She shrugged, backing up a step. "Well, whose is it, then?"

"Mine." I took Alice's hand. "But the Saviors put it in her. We weren't going to tell you yet. But I guess you can see it inside her?"

"Yes." Kareena's lips wrinkled. "Um... Ugh. I'm sorry guys, but I'm so glad it's not me. I hope they don't try to knock me up. Ew." She held her belly and shuddered, sticking out her tongue. "I don't even want to think about being pregnant."

Alice whimpered, twisting the hem of her shirt around the fingers of one hand while squeezing my hand tighter with her other.

"Can't you show a little sympathy?" I glared, tipping my head to the side. "You're emotionally dead, aren't you, Kareena?"

"No. I just don't know what to say, okay?" She rolled up her sleeve and pressed three fingers into her bicep, revealing a match-stick like object embedded beneath her skin.

"I've never had to worry about it before. My parents hooked me up a long time ago."

An implant?

"That's not the type of thing you need to be showing off." I scowled. I'd heard about girls getting them, but didn't know exactly what they were and had no idea how they worked. I wasn't a girl, but the thought of having something stuck in me like that made my skin crawl.

"Well. For those of us who actually do stuff, it beats getting pregnant." She crossed her arms and looked away from us.

A frown tarnished Alice's lips.

"Hey, we need to stop focusing on the pregnancy and start focusing on Alice," I said.

"I haven't told Sam yet," Alice added beneath her breath.

"Oh." Kareena's eyes widened. "Well, good luck with that."

Sam—Alice's best friend—had been the first person to witness her fluorescence. She wasn't one of *us,* though.

The school bell rang and Kareena started off toward her class. "See ya," she said over her shoulder.

"I'm a horrible friend, aren't I?" Alice sighed.

"Don't ever say that." I brushed my fingertips across her cheek. "Sam will understand."

.   .   .

Alice and I sat in the shade on the front porch of her house after school, watching the sprinklers twirl water across the lawn like silver confetti.

"What do you think they want the baby for?" she asked, staring off at nothing, twisting a blade of grass between her fingers.

"No idea." I shrugged. "We must have something awfully special in us for them to get this desperate. Maybe this will be the end of whatever it is that's killing the Saviors."

"Do you think they'll leave us alone after this?"

"Don't know."

She fell silent.

We sat there for several minutes, quietly watching people walk down the sidewalk and cars pass by in the street. I plucked a piece of tall grass from beside the porch and started tangling it between my fingers, then tossed it back onto the lawn.

"Do you... want her?" Alice looked up at me through her lashes, her cheeks red and her eyes glistening.

My heart skipped a beat.

Did I want our baby?

Me? A sixteen-year-old sophomore, with an evening job, an almost-paid-off motorcycle, and alien DNA in my blood. Did I want a baby right now?

Hell no.

But did I want to be with Alice? Hell yes.

And if being with her meant being a father to our child, I would do it. At least, I would give it a damn good try. Maybe it was the fluorescence talking, but a little version of Alice and me might be cute. A shit-load of responsibility, but cute. Juggling that with high school and work? All hell was going to break loose. It was definitely a loaded question.

"I want what's best for *you*," I answered. "That's all I want. I'd never want to put you through any pain or in danger." It seemed like I was more worried than she was at this point, and I didn't have a test-tube baby growing in my belly.

Pregnancy and childbirth weren't walks in the park from what I'd learned recently. I'd been spending hours researching online. It was kind of scary to me, actually—the things that could go wrong.

"I don't know if I can handle this," she murmured. "All I wanted was to be a normal girl. I don't even know if I want kids *ever*. I hadn't really thought about it that hard. I just want to graduate from high school." She sniffled.

"Me, too." I wrapped an arm around her shoulders and hugged her close.

Chapter 4

It was a Friday afternoon and we were curled up on the couch in her living room in front of the TV.

"Everything okay with your mom?" I asked, pulling a blanket up over Alice's knees. It wasn't quite cold enough to switch the heat on, but the changing autumn temperatures made her a little uncomfortable.

"I guess," she replied and nestled against me. "She's been acting weird for a few days. Work stuff's got her on edge, I think. She won't really talk to me about it."

"Oh. Okay." I didn't know what else to say. If Alice wasn't concerned, I didn't feel the need to be either.

I wrapped an arm around her shoulders and leaned in to kiss the side of her neck. She exhaled, content.

A clicking noise sounded from the hall, followed by a patter of footsteps. I pulled back from Alice just as Jane came into the room wheeling a carry-on suitcase behind her.

"What's going on, Mom?" Alice sat up and leaned forward in her seat.

I took the remote and paused the movie.

Jane propped her bag against the doorframe and walked over to us, a stack of printouts and a manila folder tucked under her arm.

"I didn't want it to work out this way," she said and heaved a breath. "But... damn it, I couldn't get them to let me off this time."

"What?" Alice untangled the blanket from her lap and stood. I gathered it up from the floor and away from her feet.

"What do you mean? What happened?"

"I wasn't even going to say anything to you because I thought I could get out of it." Jane massaged her forehead and sighed again. "I was on the phone for an hour last night. I just got off the phone with her again a few minutes ago. My supervisor won't budge. She just doesn't understand what it's like to be a parent."

"Wait. Is this about that seminar in Seattle? The one you didn't go to last year?"

"Yes," Jane replied, pressing her lips together. "The organizational leadership crap they keep pushing on us. Donna let me off last year, but now it's company policy that all staff attend it at least once within a year of being hired. I've been there for almost seven and the new supervisor won't let me skip it again." She riffled through the folder and took out a few pages.

"Here are copies of my flight and hotel reservations so you'll know where I'll be." She stretched an arm out and Alice took the papers. "I did everything I could to try to get out of this conference, but Donna put my job on the line and I can't sacrifice that."

"I understand, Mom." Alice glanced at the flight plans. "Why didn't you tell me sooner?"

"I didn't want you worrying," Jane replied. She unzipped the top pocket of her carry-on and shoved the folder inside, zipping it closed afterward. "I know I can trust you, but I've never had to leave you alone for more than a few hours. You'll be okay, right?"

"Yes, Mom. I can survive a few days by myself."

Jane turned toward me.

"I should go," I said.

"Thanks, Brian. I know you're worried about her, but she can take care of herself. She's a big girl now. Alice, there's a notebook on the table in the kitchen with everything you need to know in it. Phone numbers. Addresses. Emergency information." Jane flashed a grin that seemed uneasy and forced. "I should be back Monday afternoon. *If* my flights don't get canceled." She flexed her fingers around the handle of her carry-on bag and groaned.

Alice's shoulder glinted anxiously with wild neon green light.

"Be careful, Mom."

"I will." Jane released the suitcase and hugged Alice. "Make sure he leaves soon," I overheard her whisper.

Alice nodded.

I scooped my riding jacket up off the back of the couch and followed the two of them into the garage. I shrugged on my coat and lifted my helmet from the seat of my motorcycle.

Jane started her car and backed out, stopping in the driveway to wave briefly. She pointed at me and gave me a quick tilt of her head as if to reiterate the fact that she wanted me to go. *Soon.*

The tail lights faded into the distance as the car disappeared down the street, swallowed up by the night.

I turned back toward Alice and my heartbeat quickened.

I didn't want to go. I didn't want her to be alone. Not for even a minute.

"No," she said, cupping my hand in hers. As if she knew what I was thinking. "You have to go home, Brian. I'm sorry. Mom said so."

"Do you want me to go?"

"Well, no, but..."

"It's okay. I know. I'm sorry. Just being difficult. You know my mom drives me nuts."

"Yeah. I know. Sorry."

I shrugged. "Can I see you tomorrow? After work?"

"Sure." She bit her lip and looked down. "I'll be thinking of you."

"I know." I smiled and tipped her face up toward mine so I could kiss her.

"Goodnight, Brian," she murmured, as our lips parted.

"Bye, Alice. Have a good night."

My mouth was barely able to say goodbye.

My eyes simply couldn't.

Chapter 5

I punched a code into the number pad and then headed back down the driveway. The automatic garage door opened and I walked my motorcycle up to park it inside. I set my helmet onto the seat and slid my black satin work vest off, draping it over my arm.

"Alice?" I entered through the door that led from the garage to the house and passed through the empty kitchen. My pulse quickened when she didn't respond.

Stepping into the family room, I peered up to find her sitting in the middle of the staircase, staring off at nothing.

"Hey." I stopped at the foot of the stairs. "What's going on?"

She jerked her head toward me. "Oh, hey! I'm so sorry." She stood, took a few steps down and leaned on the banister. "I was... thinking. I didn't even hear you come in."

"I noticed. Good thing it was only me, huh?" I jogged up the steps and reached out to embrace her. She hugged me tightly. "You look really beautiful tonight," I said, admiring the way her sapphire tank top made her eyes appear even bluer than usual. "Is this new?" The silky smooth fabric was cool to the touch and clung to her curves like satin. My fingers drifted up her waist; the softness of her shirt reminded me of the softness of her skin.

"Yes. I've never had a chance to wear it." She looped her fingers around my belt and nuzzled against me. "I missed you so much today."

"I missed you, too." I leaned down and kissed her.

She pulled away, sooner than usual, with an anxious shudder.

"Are you okay?"

"Yeah." She looked down at her feet. "I'm fine. I just..."

The staircase wasn't the best place to stand and talk.

I took her hand and walked with her up to the second floor. We sat on the top step and I wrapped my arm around her. "Are you *sure* you're okay?"

She nodded, her smiling eyes gazing into mine.

"Good." My thumb drifted over the strap of her tank, across the milky-white flesh of her bare shoulder. Then I pulled her in and gave her a little peck on the forehead.

She giggled quietly and entwined her fingers with mine.

"I love you, Brian," she said, resting her head against me.

"Wh-what?"

"I said, I love you." She squeezed my hand and looked up, the subtle sheen of her lip-gloss captivating me. "I'm sorry it took me so long to say but..."

I cupped her face in my hands and kissed her again.

She melted into me.

Fingertips coiled in my hair.

I dragged a hand down her back, holding her firmly but gently. Savoring the sweetness of her mouth. Hesitant to let her lips abandon mine. The warm scent of her skin drew me in and kept me close until a groan welled in her throat.

"I love you, too," I replied, barely breaking away to say it. I combed a hand through her hair and stared into her eyes. She stared back, piercing my heart with her eager, consenting gaze.

A faint whimper escaped her lips and she shrunk back.

"What is it?"

"My heart," she said, reaching up to touch her chest. "It's beating so fast. Like it's gonna burst right out of me."

"Mine, too." I took her hand and flattened it over my heart, slipping her fingers in between the shirt buttons so they made contact with my skin.

"I need you, Alice," I whispered, tracing my thumb over her blushing cheek. "Only you."

"I know." The breathy words poured from her mouth as her hands rose toward my collar. She started to unbutton my shirt.

My throat tightened and I swallowed hard.

The second button came free. Then the third. The final button came undone and I shrugged the shirt down off my shoulders, dropping it onto a step below.

I stood and helped pull her to her feet. We took a step back from the stairs and she stumbled into me, an anxious grin stretching across her lips.

"Come with me." Hearing her wanton request made a breath catch in my throat. She pulled me past the threshold of her room, a devious look in her eyes.

A sudden, dizzying rush of nerves hit me. My whole body trembled in anticipation.

Alice shut the door and pressed her weight against me, slamming my back against the wall beside her desk. She slung her arms around my neck and pulled me down into another kiss.

The heat of her body overwhelmed me, evoking primal desires. I wrinkled the hem of her shirt and slipped my fingers beneath it.

Her lips parted from mine, but our eyes remained locked, those pale blue irises casting their spell.

I clung to her hand.

She led me toward her bed.

Our breaths quickened.

Fluorescence sparked to life in our veins, the vibrant colors glinting brighter than ever. Ethereal green swept up over her shoulder toward her collar bone, enchanting me with its intense glow.

Coils of wild dark locks framed her face. I weaved my

fingers through her hair and kissed her again, our weight sinking into the softness around us.

A kiss to the side of her neck. Tasting the salt on her skin. Then my lips slid to the hollow of her throat, her head fell back and she gasped.

A rush of heat washed over me. Vivid blue light flickered in the darkness and tiny bursts of color danced through the veins in my hand.

Every nerve felt electrified. Alive.

Restless fingernails pressed into my back and she whispered my name.

The word was tangled up in a heated exhalation.

And—for a fleeting moment—all of the fear and all of the uncertainty complicating my life faded away.

.   .   .

A soothing buzz settled my body and I closed my eyes, inhaling a deep breath. The comforting warmth of her bare skin pressed against mine calmed every anxious thought flitting through me. I felt at peace—invincible. It was a thrilling sensation of insecurities being stripped away, just like our clothing had been. Exposing vulnerabilities in an ultimate exchange of trust.

She came up onto her elbows over me and stared into my eyes, a smile twisting her lips. Splashes of blush colored her skin. Moonlight filtered through the window blinds, accentuating the sweat on her body, making her shimmer.

"You're amazing, Alice. You know that?" I brushed her hair behind her ear and cupped her warm, glistening cheek.

"Really?" She laughed. "*Amazing?*" Her eyes closed and she nuzzled my hand. "Then, why do guys make so much fun of girls like me? Girls who haven't..."

"First of all, I'm not one of those guys. And secondly, don't believe what anybody else says." I smirked. "Besides, it seemed like you enjoyed that." I tangled my fingers into the disheveled coils of her hair.

"I... did." She bit her lip.

"Good. That's what matters to me."

She cuddled up close.

Maybe things hadn't gone exactly as we might have imagined they would, but it didn't make it any less meaningful. Anyone who claims their first time wasn't a little clumsy is probably either lying or had been with someone with far too much experience. I liked the awkwardness of it all. Every second of it was ours and ours alone. Unforgettable. Real.

A mess alright.

A *perfect* mess.

I wouldn't have wanted it any other way.

"Do you... think we should have waited?" Alice said, breaking the silence. She threaded her fingers through my hair, absentmindedly.

Hearing those words made my heart sink.

"Are you regretting it? Already?"

She exhaled. Slowly. Fingernails dragged lightly down the side of my neck.

"No." She nudged her cheek against my chest. I felt her lips stretch into a smile. "No. Not at all."

"Good." I embraced her tightly. "I don't want you to regret anything that happens between us."

She closed her eyes, her fingers settling near the scar above my heart. I kissed her forehead and inhaled a deep breath. Her warmth on my chest made me feel complete. It was as if I lived only for her, and she for me, and we were meant to be together despite decisions the Saviors had forced upon us.

"I want to marry you someday, Alice. You know? When all of this crazy stuff is said and done, I want you in my life. I want to wake up to you every day and... make love to you every night." I massaged the back of her neck and a sigh of pleasure slid from her mouth.

A warm tingle started in my fingertips and flushed through my arm. I lifted my hand and watched the neon veins twinkle and fade, pulsing and moving through me. Soft indigo-teal burning with flecks of white and neon green. The same glow tinted the fair skin of Alice's shoulder.

I smiled, the sight of our blended colors further satisfying the visceral need I'd had to make her mine. But now it would be even harder for us. Tonight, we'd had a taste of each other and there could be no going back.

Chapter 6

"I'm just glad the whole ordeal is over with and I won't have to worry about it next year. It's nice to see the house still intact, too," Jane said with a smirk, getting up to take our plates off the table. She had returned home Monday while we'd been in school. I'd dropped Alice off earlier in the afternoon and had been invited to stay for dinner. We'd been sitting at the table for a while, listening to her talk about all the craziness she'd endured during her short trip.

"You're sure your mom's okay with you being over this much? I don't want her getting upset with me."

I tried not to scoff. "She doesn't have a problem with it at all."

Truth was, Mom didn't give a shit where I was. She was probably glad I'd up and left. Probably hoping someday I'd leave and never come home. "Thank you, Jane, for being so nice to me. Alice is lucky to have you."

Jane came up and gave me a hug. A big, tight bear hug like I was one of her own. It caught me by surprise. Awkward and nice at the same time. My mom never hugged me any-more. I couldn't even remember the last time she had.

Out of the corner of my eye, I caught Alice beaming.

Jane released me. "I'll be in the kitchen cleaning up. Take care, Brian. Be safe going home."

"Thanks, Jane."

She headed back over to the sink and Alice and I went into the garage.

I didn't want to say goodbye, though I had to. I'd fallen

asleep beside Alice and woken up with her still there, within arm's reach. It had been a perfect weekend. Exactly how I wished every day of the rest of my life could be.

"I don't know how I'm going to sleep now," I said, looping my arms around Alice and resting them at her waist.

"You will," she said with a smile. "But it's definitely going to be a little harder now. You just... felt so right, and for once I wasn't worrying about anything else. Not school. Not the future. Not..." She looked down at her belly.

"Don't. Don't ruin a good thing, Alice." I lifted her chin with my fingertips. "We'll be fine. You'll be okay. I'll see you every day. Somehow. I don't care if I have to break some rules to do it, I'll be here for you no matter what happens."

"Thank you." She lifted herself up to kiss me. "I love you. Thanks for caring about me so much. For giving me the time I needed to make up my mind. Although..."

"Alice, I want our relationship to last," I said, sweeping a stray lock of her hair back over her ear. "I know things started off a little bumpy, but I feel like we understand each other better now. I'd never want to do anything to hurt you or push you away."

"Be careful going home." She took my hand and heaved a sigh. Her eyes started to glisten. A hint of turquoise light shone through her shirt at her shoulder, the color appearing slightly greener than it had been last night. "I know it's stupid to say this, but I feel like I'm letting a part of me go. It's only for a little while, but—"

I kissed her mid-sentence.

"No," I whispered, our lips almost touching. "No, Alice, it's not a stupid thing to say. But you know I can't leave if you don't want me to." I gazed sternly into her eyes.

"I know." She sucked in a breath and nodded. "I'll be alright. I'm okay now."

It was hard on me, too, but I finally managed to get onto my bike and back on the street. I didn't want to leave. I didn't want to let her fingers slip from mine.

A few seconds.

Minutes.

Hours.

Any amount of time we spent apart felt like too much.

· · ·

I left my bike in the garage beside my mom's car and rummaged through my pocket for the house key. No point knocking. She wouldn't come to let me in anyway. I went inside and headed for my room.

No TV. No music playing. No clanking and clanging from her fumbling around in the kitchen because of her obsessive need to clean and rearrange. The silence unnerved me.

Whatever.

I wouldn't let her get to me anymore. Not as long as I had something so much better to live for. Someone who *actually* loved me.

I popped into my room, shut the door behind me and hopped onto my bed. I texted Alice to let her know I'd gotten back okay, then I flipped open my laptop and streamed a rerun of a late night comedy talk show I'd missed over the weekend.

The quiet time was nice. While it lasted.

Afterward, I crept out of my room and wandered into the kitchen to grab a glass of water. There were dirty dishes everywhere. I pulled open the cupboard door below the sink. The trash hadn't been emptied recently either.

It wasn't like Mom to leave it for more than a day. I turned toward the kitchen table. Used utensils still scattered on top of wrinkled paper towels.

What the hell?

"Mom?"

Silence.

I checked the living room. Empty.

"Hey, Mom?" I raised my voice.

My stomach tightened.

I'd seen her car in the garage.

I knocked on her bedroom door.

No answer.

Shit.

I turned the doorknob and held my breath, easing the door open.

An empty room.

My eyes scanned down.

She was sprawled out on the floor beside her bed. Pale bare feet sticking out from beneath folds of her terry cloth robe. Her body motionless.

"Mom!" My heart skipped a beat. "Mom!" I fell to my knees beside her and lifted her up. Saliva oozed from the side of her mouth. She let out a long, drowsy groan, barely conscious.

"Jesus Christ, Mom! What did you do?"

"Where's your father?" she mumbled. Her face was drained of color, her hands freakishly cold.

How long had she been like this?

"Dad's dead. Mom? What the hell happened?"

Her eyes rolled back in her head and she slurred something I couldn't understand.

"Mom! Stay with me." My heart was thumping so hard I thought I was going to have another heart attack. I scooted back, resituating myself on the carpet, and felt a hard crunch below my knee. I looked down.

Pills.

I saw the open bottle on the nearby dresser and reached for it.

Alprazolam, an anti-anxiety drug. Part of her anti-depressant regimen.

"Shit. How many of these did you take?" The bottle was

empty and only a handful surrounded me on the floor. I'd picked them up from the pharmacy recently. There had to have been a few dozen left when I'd gone away.

"Damn it, Mom." I shook her gently, but she still didn't respond. "I leave for a few days and... Shit!"

I propped her up on my knee and held her with one arm while I scrambled for my phone.

My hands trembled. I kept hoping my fluorescence would spark to life again, that it might do *something—anything* to help her.

But it didn't.

Jesus, Mom...

.   .   .

I texted Alice during the ambulance ride to the hospital. Every other word coming out incorrectly. My nerves shot.

It was just past 8:00 PM. Sunset. I hadn't finished my homework for school tomorrow, but...

Damn it.

My mother may have been on the brink of death from a drug overdose and all I could think about was homework? What the hell was wrong with me!?

The ambulance pulled up to the hospital and one of the EMTs flung open the back doors and hopped out to help his partner.

I've seen scenes in movies with people bustling around the hospital ER, pushing, telling people to stay out of their way. Keep clear. Blood gushing everywhere from some tragedy or another.

This was different. They wheeled my mom in on a gurney, corralled me into the empty white-walled waiting room, shoved a clipboard into my hands, and turned away, leaving me alone with a crummy pen and a long form demanding a bunch of medical history. I sort of wished there were other people in the room, but it was just me and the receptionist.

My mouth was paper dry. My stomach wouldn't stop churning, threatening to erupt. I swallowed hard and flopped down onto a waiting room chair. An uncomfortable, vinyl-covered metal chair. Hard. Cold. Barely large enough for an average person.

I turned to the forms. Medical history. Prescriptions. Allergies. Primary physician. Emergency contact. Most teenagers don't know shit about their parents' medical histories.

I knew more than I wanted to. More than I should have.

I finished filling out the last page and clipped our insurance card on top of the stack.

"Thank you, hun." The receptionist beamed a fake smile at me.

I asked her what they were doing to Mom, but she shook her head and shrugged, telling me she wasn't sure and wasn't able to speculate.

I lowered my head and scuffled back to my chair.

Bull. My mom wasn't the first person to ever OD on something. But I was at the mercy of the hospital staff, and there wasn't anything I could do.

Mom had been on the edge before but she'd never gone over it. Last time, I'd stopped her. This time? I had disappeared for a few days and...

Damn it!

I wasn't supposed to be responsible for this kind of shit at my age. I was supposed to be a kid. A rebellious teenager doing stupid crap, living life. Getting into trouble with friends. Not taking my mom to the ER because she couldn't keep her own life in check. Not worrying about glowing alien shit coursing through my body. Not worrying about a pregnant girlfriend whose baby wasn't our fault even though the baby was supposedly *ours*.

I kept busy in the waiting room by searching online for information about the drug Mom had taken. Overdosing on it could be fatal. They'd probably have to pump her stomach. There were other things they could do, but it was all dependent upon how much she'd taken and how quickly. The fact that she was conscious was a good sign at least.

My chest tightened. I felt sick to my stomach. Couldn't tell if I needed to throw up or just get out of that damn overlit waiting room. I wanted to get on my motorcycle and ride somewhere. Anywhere. Just get out. Get some air. Get away from the sickening smell of disinfectants.

But I needed to know if she was going to be okay or not first.

I dragged my hands through my hair and growled, letting off some steam. The receptionist peeked over her monitor at me, raising her eyebrows. I didn't care. My shoulders ached already from hunching over all the paperwork. Even breathing felt like a chore now. I buried my face in my hands. How was I supposed to...

"Brian!"

I looked up. Alice was jogging down the hall toward me.

"Alice?"

She sat in the chair next to me and grabbed my hand, squeezing it tightly.

"We came as fast as we could," she said, wide-eyed. "Is she okay? Is your mom—"

"I don't know." I shrugged. "They aren't telling me shit."

"I'm sorry. I'm so sorry, Brian."

Alice's mom came in shortly after and headed straight over to question the receptionist. She came over toward us a few moments later.

"They won't tell me anything either, Brian. I'm sorry," Jane said, taking a seat in a chair across from me.

Alice leaned over the armrest and wrapped her arms around me. I rested my head on her shoulder and my throat started to hurt, twisting up, making it difficult to swallow.

"I'm here for you," Alice said in a soft, calming voice. "I

know you're upset and that's okay. Let it out if you need to. There's no one else here. No one's gonna judge you."

I didn't want to, but my eyes were already swelling with tears.

"I just want us to be normal, Alice," I said, my words muffled by her shirt. "I just want to have a normal life with you." She tightened her arms around me and brushed her fingers through my hair, resting her cheek against the back of my head.

"I know, Brian. I know." She kissed my head.

I sucked in a congested breath and coughed. Jane stretched out an arm toward me, offering a stack of tissues she'd just pulled from a nearby box. I took one and plastered it onto my quivering face.

I didn't want to look weak in front of Alice. I sure as hell didn't want to cry.

But... everything hit me and I couldn't hold back the tears anymore.

It had scared the hell out of me to find my mother like that. Lying on the floor like she was...

Was it my fault because I'd left?

What if she had died before I'd found her? What then?

What now?

"Brian?" A man in a long white coat came into the waiting room. S. Alexis, MD, his ID badge read.

"Yes?" I wiped my face on my sleeve and scrambled to get up from my chair. "How... how is she?"

Alice stood and clutched my hand.

"We've stabilized her for now and are performing a gastric lavage—pumping out the contents of her stomach— to clear out the medication. When that's complete, we'll administer flumazenil, an antagonist to the sedative effects of the alprazolam. We'll also give her some fluids and observe her."

"So... is she going to be okay?"

"She should be, yes. You got her here before too much of

the medication was absorbed into her bloodstream. Any longer and..." He stopped mid-sentence and his lips thinned. "Well... let's just be thankful you got her here when you did. You're a responsible young man."

"Thank you, Doctor," I said, reaching out my hand to shake his. "Thank you for taking care of her."

"She'll need to stay here for a few days. We'll review her medical history and contact her primary care physician in the morning. Considering the nature of the overdose, your mother may need further psychiatric review or treatment for her condition."

Exactly what I was afraid of hearing.

I'd known for a while now she needed help but just didn't know who to go to or when. Sometimes her mistakes just didn't feel like *my* responsibility.

The doctor left and I stumbled back down into my chair and hunched over. Alice put her hand on my arm and leaned down to look me in the eye.

"Hey." She smiled. "Things will be okay. I'll stay here with you as long as I can. Okay?"

"Yeah." I tried to smile but couldn't get my face to comply. I was mentally exhausted. "Thanks."

"Here." Jane came over and set a foam cup on the glass table beside me. Steam wafted from it. "I know it's not the good stuff we have at home, but even hospital tea is better than nothing." She set a few sugar packets and a coffee stirrer beside it.

"Thanks." I picked up the cup and held it in my hands.

"It's very hot, Brian. Be careful," Jane added, sitting down across from us again.

It *was* hot. Uncomfortable to hold, even.

Frankly, I didn't care.

Chapter 7

"Brian? Brian? Wake up."

Someone nudged me in the arm. I dragged my eyelids opened.

"Alice? You're still here?" I sat up in my chair and yawned, my whole body drained and aching. "What time is it?" My eyes began to water. I wiped my palms across my cheeks and then stretched my arms up above my head. Jane was sitting across from us.

"It's about 8:45," she replied.

"Oh? Wait! You're going to miss class. Alice, you don't have to do that because of me."

She smiled and shrugged, sweeping some hair away from my eyes with a flick of her fingers. "My mom said it's okay. Besides, I think this is more important than math class. Don't stress out."

"Thanks."

What had I done so right to deserve Alice?

"The nurse said you could go see your mom now if you'd like," Jane said. She was nibbling on a breakfast sandwich of some kind and had a paper cup of coffee-shop coffee wedged between her legs. "I brought you something, too." She grinned, handing me a paper bag from a local fast-food place.

"Thanks, Jane." I set it on the seat beside me and got up. "I'm going to go check on my mom first, if that's okay."

"Sure."

I spoke with the receptionist first, who called the nurse over to take me to my mother's room. The nurse told me they were going to move Mom to a different wing of the hospital shortly since she no longer required intensive care.

The nurse, Patty, held open the door to Mom's room and I entered cautiously. The distinct smell of disinfectant made my nose wrinkle as I walked in. I was all too familiar with hospitals; I had come to stay frequently before the fluorescence had healed me. Electrical wires dangled from different kinds of equipment. Ugly off-white walls surrounded me.

Mom was hooked up to a heart rate monitor and had an IV drip taped to her wrist. Some of the color had come back to her face but she still looked like shit. Sallow skin. Dark circles under her eyes. She looked up at me and shook her head, squinting.

Was I supposed to feel pity for her?

I didn't.

"Why'd you do it?" I asked, stepping closer to her bed. "Why'd you do it, Mom? What the hell is so wrong with your life that you have to keep doing this to yourself? To me? I don't deserve it."

"You wouldn't understand," she replied, looking away.

"Bullshit. I understand you don't give a damn about your life or mine anymore. I told you to get help, Mom. I tried to stop you, but apparently things got so bad you couldn't help yourself, could you? I leave for a few days and you go to hell. Why? Tell me why, Mom." I set a hand on the metal railing beside her and watched the pulse monitor bounce up and down a few times before returning my attention to her.

She wrinkled her lips to the side. "You're a kid, Brian. What the hell do you know about anything?"

Her attitude sickened me.

"Enough to know life is valuable and worth living," I replied. "Something you still haven't learned, apparently. No thanks to you, I now understand what it feels like to love and be loved by someone. There are so many people out there who fight every day just to stay alive—just to get by. And here you are with everything you need and you throw it away to some damn pills because life's getting too hard. Because you're too goddamn cowardly to suck it up and move on. You keep making up excuses about how life seems so hard, instead of trying to make it better. Dad died and he's not coming back. Killing yourself isn't going to change that. Treating me like crap won't either. I don't deserve this. Not after everything I've done to keep your head above water."

My lip quivered. I clenched my teeth, tightening my grip on the cold bed railing. "You keep treating me the way you have and I might not be there at all next time. Think about that." I turned my back on her and headed for the door.

"Brian, wait. Brian!"

I ignored her and walked back to the lobby.

"Well?" Alice asked, standing up from her seat and staring anxiously at me, her hands entwined. "How is she?"

"She's well enough to act like a smartass, so apparently she's fine."

"Oh." Alice sat down and frowned. "I'm sorry." Her voice lowered.

"Don't be. She's never going to change." I flopped back onto my seat and reached over to take the bag from the table beside me. "Thanks again, Jane," I said with a grateful smile. Alice handed me her to-go cup and I took a sip of the five dollar, so-much-better-than-hospital-tea tea.

There were more people in the ER now than there had been last night when I'd arrived, but I didn't care. I had the only people I needed with me and didn't feel lonely anymore. Alice and I sat there talking for a little while until a police officer and a woman sauntered in and caught our attention. I couldn't help but eavesdrop on their conversation with the receptionist. I heard my name and my mom's being thrown around and I perked up in my seat, wishing I had superhuman hearing.

The receptionist pointed at me and then the two came

strolling over to where I sat. I shifted in my chair. Alice sat up.

"Brian?" the tall, dark-skinned woman asked. She had her hair pulled back into a tight bun and wore a grey pant suit and bright red lipstick. The officer stood behind her and crossed his arms, glaring at me like he was expecting me to do something stupid. Or like maybe he was hoping I would?

"Yes?" I got out of my seat.

"Let me introduce myself." She took an ID card out of her pocket and showed it to me. Government-issued of some kind. "My name is Angelica Barnes. I'm with the Department of Social Services. We're here because your mother is scheduled for a mental health evaluation later this week and, in the meantime, we need to place you somewhere you will be safe."

"I can take care of myself," I sneered. "I don't need anyone's help."

"Well, you may believe that, but according to the law, you are a minor, and as long as your mother is in the custody of the hospital for psychiatric care, you are without a legal guardian."

"We can take him in." Jane came to my side.

"And you are?" Angelica looked down her nose at Alice's mother.

"I'm Jane... um... Alice's mother. She's... well, we're friends of the family," she stammered.

"Do you have a letter or note from the child's mother stating your responsibility for guardianship in her absence?"

"No, but..."

"Well then, I'm sorry, Ma'am, but you'll have to file a petition with the court for custody."

"How long will that take?" I asked, my pulse racing.

"A few weeks or more usually. It depends on how quickly the paperwork is turned in and how soon we can have someone come and evaluate the petitioner's living arrangements for suitability."

"Weeks? But..." My voice broke. "How will I go to work and school and—"

"We'll arrange for that," Angelica interrupted. "You'll be able to continue working and attending school, but we'll have to place you in an emergency foster home until either your mother's health improves or," she looked at Jane, "your petition is approved by a judge."

"Alice?" I looked desperately to her. It was a gut reaction; I knew she couldn't help me.

"You'll have to come with us, Brian," Angelica said.

"I... No."

"Please. Don't make this difficult for us."

The officer stepped up and firmly took me by the arm. I gasped.

Shit.

"Jane?" She shook her head and frowned. "Alice?" I looked at her and she shrugged, fear and uncertainty glistening in her eyes.

Is this really happening?

"Come on, son." The police officer tugged on the sleeve of my jacket.

"Brian!" Alice went for my hand. I held back just long enough for her to wrap her fingers around mine and reach up and kiss me goodbye. "Be safe! Please!"

"He'll be just fine, young lady," Angelica said, and then rolled her eyes after she turned away from Alice. She'd done this before, apparently. Pulled kids away from their significant others. Just another lovesick teenager.

What would the Saviors do now? What would Alice do?

Sitting in the back of the police car during the drive, all I kept thinking about was losing my job. Losing the one chance I had at freedom. Yeah, I could get another job, but I liked the one I had. I made decent money. I'd made enough to almost pay off my bike completely. That job was my first step toward being a responsible adult.

The officer drove me downtown to the social services building where he let me out and clutched me by my sleeve like he thought I was going to make a dash for it. Couldn't blame him, as I'd thought about it already. But resisting the authorities is never a good idea. Especially when your future is in their hands.

I was invited into a small office where Angelica and another woman were seated behind a long desk.

"We pulled your mother's medical history. She's got quite a background, Brian," Angelica said, shuffling through a manila folder with a bunch of papers inside.

I sat down in a chair, crossed my arms and looked away. "And?"

"We're concerned about your home environment," the other woman chimed in. Her name was Barbara, if the business cards on the desk were, in fact, hers.

"Look, I'm fine, okay? What do you want from me? I've never had any trouble with her. I don't get into fights at school or anything. Not anymore. I just want to go home. I can take care of myself."

"The law does not classify you as an adult until you are eighteen," Angelica said. "You know this, Brian."

"Yeah, whatever. So what does all this mean for me?"

"According to your mother's medical history, she's been on and off antidepressants for several years now. Any previous suicide attempts?"

Yes.

I swallowed hard.

"No."

"Are you sure? You don't have to lie to us, Brian." Barbara leaned over the desk and stared at me with concern. I felt like they were playing good social worker, bad social worker with me.

"Yes. I'm sure. She's had some problems, but this hasn't happened before."

I wasn't lying, technically. She hadn't gone this far before, since before this I'd always stopped her.

"So, no previous suicide attempts then?"

"No." I fixated on a plaque in the back of the room. An award certificate of some kind.

Angelica scribbled something down.

"Any abuse in the home? Verbal or physical?"

I furrowed my brow. "Seriously? Do I look like I've been abused?"

"Most people who are in abusive relationships don't look the part, Brian," Barbara added.

I was already tired of talking to them.

"I'm fine. My mom has her job. I have mine. We live in the same house, but we don't get in each other's way. There's no law against just keeping to yourself. I'm not starving. I'm not homeless. I'm fine. Okay? Can I go?"

I wanted the nightmare to end.

"I'm sorry, Brian. No." Barbara stood up and handed me a stack of papers. "Here's some information on the process you're going to go through. You're going to be placed into an emergency foster home for now until either someone steps up to claim guardianship or—"

"Jesus! You're kidding me. A foster home? I'm sixteen, for God's sake, not five." I clenched my teeth.

"It's the law, Brian. We're just doing what we have to until we receive the full psychiatric evaluation back from your mother's physician. We'll have Officer Parston take you to your temporary foster home shortly. We're just waiting for confirmation from the family."

A lump formed in my throat and I could hardly swallow.

I felt like I was going to throw up.

Chapter 8

The temp family lived halfway across town.

The Jamesons—Thomas and Sue—were an older couple with an adopted ten-year-old son from China they'd named Peter.

They allowed me to pick up my motorcycle and keep it in their garage, even though the mother—Sue—had told me to my face how adamantly she was against boys my age having a license. My brain wasn't mature enough to handle the dangers of driving, she said. But I had a job to keep and a girlfriend to see, so she'd have to deal.

"I'm sorry to hear about your mother, Brian," said Thomas, carrying a large, steaming cup of coffee over to the kitchen table and sitting in a chair across from me. With his thinning brown hair, peppered with grey, his wrinkled temples and the bifocals he used to read his newspaper, he had a friendly, grandfatherly air about him. His deep-set golden hazel eyes looked at me with genuine concern, something I wasn't accustomed to at home.

"I'll be okay. I just, no offense, need to get back to my normal life." I sipped from my mug of hot tea and kept my head down. Peter was sitting at the other end of the table on the edge of his seat, gawking at me like I was some kind of rock star. To him, having another "boy" in the house was a dream come true, and he hadn't hesitated to tell me this within twenty minutes of our introduction.

The Jameson's home was larger than mine, roomy but cozy. Reminiscent of something from the older days. Beige stucco walls. Crown molding. Furniture upholstered with floral patterns. Old paintings and photos hanging in various places. The rustic smell of cinnamon and orange potpourri reminded me of Thanksgiving.

Over a dinner of homemade lasagna and garlic bread, Sue told me the story of their daughter, Grace, who had died several years back while serving with the police task force. At only twenty-two, she had suffered a fatal shot to the chest during an armed robbery. She'd been trying to assist a hostage.

"She probably would have had a thing for you when she was your age," Sue said, looking past me at a photograph on the kitchen wall. "She liked the rough-around-the-edges type. Always being adventurous. Backpacking. Swimming. Biking. Anything to get out of the house and keep moving. She was stubborn sometimes, but she always worried about others more than herself."

She did sound a bit like me. I'd do anything to get out of the house, but probably for a very different reason than Grace had had. I felt bad for their loss. They seemed like a really sweet couple. No one should have to deal with the pain of outliving their child.

Thomas and Sue also told me they had gotten married right out of high school—over thirty years ago. It reaffirmed my belief that Alice and I really had a chance.

If any good came out of this foster home business, it would be the inspiration to keep my head up and believe in *us*.

Even though my own life had just been thrust into chaos, I started worrying about my Mom's. Social services had warned me not to contact her directly until they had finished their investigation. Still, I thought about her.

I also thought about how long I might be stuck with this family. How long Peter would have a "foster brother," as he was already excitedly calling me. How long before I could see Alice on my time and not someone else's.

These thoughts rattled me. I didn't sleep much at all the

first few nights. Instead, I stayed up texting Alice until just past midnight, when Thomas would come in to ask if I needed anything. He was a night owl, too.

"No, but thanks," I'd reply, forcing a grin.

I just wanted to go back to school.

I wanted to see Alice.

I wanted normalcy.

.　　.　　.

Peter eagerly awaited my presence at the breakfast table.

"Good morning, Brian!" he said with a huge, toothy grin. He was kneeling on his chair. "Can you show me your motorcycle after school today? Pleeeeeease?" He teetered on his seat.

"Knees off the chair, Peter," Sue scolded.

He plopped down onto his butt and slumped over. "Sorry, Mom."

"Did you get any sleep, Brian?" she asked, pulling some cereal boxes out of the cupboard.

I shrugged. "Not really."

"I'm sorry to hear that. I know it's hard, but maybe you'll feel better after you get a little more adjusted here."

"Maybe." I sat at the table across from Peter and fidgeted with the place setting. Fabric napkins, ruffled and tucked into napkin rings. Ceramic bowls—not flimsy plastic ones. The robust, undeniable scent of freshly brewed coffee infusing the air.

"Is cereal okay or would you like something else? We have granola. Waffles. I could make you some scrambled eggs if—"

"Cereal's fine, thanks," I interrupted.

Peter beamed. "I love cereal, too!" he blurted, grabbing the half-gallon of milk from the middle of the table and dousing his corn flakes. "It's my favorite!"

I couldn't *not* smile. Such a cute kid. So full of life and innocence.

"So, what do you want to be when you get older?" I asked Peter, shoving a scoop of soggy cereal into my mouth while casually glancing at my cell to check for texts from Alice. I'd gotten one from Kareena last night. She'd said she'd try to get her dad to help with the petition stuff. Speed up the process, if that was even possible. He knew quite a few people in the local court system.

"I want to be a news reporter!" Peter held his spoon up like a microphone, pursed his lips together, and pressed his fingers to his ear, pretending to listen to an earpiece. "This is Peter Jameson reporting live from New York City."

He really had the deep reporter voice down.

"We're not moving to New York, Peter," Sue said, picking up the milk and carrying it over to the refrigerator.

"I can when I'm older, though," he replied, screwing up his face. "You can't stop me." He crossed his arms and looked away.

"No, I suppose I can't once you turn eighteen. But until then..." Sue sighed. "How about you, Brian? Do you know what you..."

She paused, mouth open. Everything around me slowed. Peter froze, mid-blink.

No.

I cringed and shut my eyes tightly against the blaring white light flooding the room. The floor disappeared out from under me and the falling sensation made my stomach spasm. Milk. Cereal. Intergalactic travel.

Not a good combination.

I locked eyes with Alice, and then with Kareena, who wasn't throwing up this time. Thank God. My stomach had been shaken up enough by the traumatic teleportation.

"Brian?" Alice brushed up against me and wrapped her

hands around mine. "Are you okay?"

"Yeah. Are you?" I glanced down at her belly, fearing the trauma might have harmed the baby. The jarring travel had to be hard on her body. It was on mine.

She was hardly showing yet, but...

"Yes. I'm fine."

"Kareena?" I looked over at her.

"Yeah. Fine. Whatever."

The usual crowd of Saviors surrounded us, their blank expressions, chalky complexions and grey eyes set on us.

"Why are you with a foreign family? We assumed you were staying with Alice." The translator stared down his nose at me and even cocked his head to the side for emphasis— something he must have learned recently.

"I was," I replied. "But I can't live with them permanently right now. As for the other family, my mother freaked out and that's what happens to *kids* in our country—the government takes us away when things go south. We've been trying to tell you we don't have any rights until we're older. It sucks, but it's the truth."

"We do not understand these laws of yours." His eyes narrowed. "They are ridiculous."

"That aside, what the hell kind of business do you guys have forcing Alice to have this baby for you? Do you even know how this is going to affect our lives? How this is going to affect Alice?"

"You two have obviously consummated your relationship," the translator said. "We do not see a problem."

Kareena raised an eyebrow at us. Alice looked down at her feet.

I pushed aside my discomfort and clenched a fist. "That doesn't make what you did to her right."

"Many your age bear children. Years ago, it was quite normal for a woman even younger than Alice to carry."

"We're not in the dark ages anymore," I sneered. "Do

your homework. You'll learn something. We're supposed to go to high school and then to college."

"Do not, if it interferes."

"You don't understand. In this country—the United States of America—we aren't free to make our own choices until we are eighteen years old. *Eighteen.* I don't know how good you are with math but that's—"

"Approximately one point seven earth years from now for you," he finished my sentence. "Two point six for Alice."

"Yes. And until then, Alice doesn't have a say in what happens. We're scared the baby could be taken away and given to someone else."

"Brian?" Alice glared at me. I hadn't told her these fears before now.

"I'm telling them the truth, Alice." I returned my attention to the Saviors. "Is that what you want? To put your race in jeopardy at the hands of people who don't know who you are? Who don't care if you live or die? We could have this child taken away and we would have no say in it. That's how our society works."

"It is required that you two raise the child." Then the translator looked at Kareena suspiciously. "You are eighteen. Correct?"

"I can't take care of it. My parents would freak. And I can't have kids," she whined, backing away and shaking her head violently. "I just don't... Ew. No."

"You will not have to worry about that," he said. "Their child is the only one that matters to us." He looked back at Alice. "We will consider your opinions and come to a conclusion at a later time. We do have other work for you to do in the future. Work that is too dangerous for her in her current state. It could harm the fetus."

"I'll do it," Alice said, stepping closer to the Savior. "I'll do whatever you want if you take it out of me."

"Alice?" I grabbed her hand.

"Think about it, please. I could have the baby later and things would be better for both sides. No adults getting in the way. No laws endangering her." Her lip quivered.

The room flashed with white hot light. My eyes burned as we fell and my ears ached from Kareena's high-pitched shriek.

The screaming dissipated, then I felt Alice's hand slip from mine. I wheezed, unable to suck another breath from the empty atmosphere.

Alone again. Weightless. Falling.

"Brian?"

Fingers pressed into my shoulder and I jumped, slamming my back against the wooden dining chair. I grunted in pain.

"Brian? Are you alright?" Sue asked, stepping to my side and leaning down to look me in the eye.

"Uh. I..." I coughed, the raspy reply catching in my dry throat. "I'm sorry. What?"

"I asked what you'd like to do with your life after you graduate. I'm sure Peter would love to hear about your aspirations. Well?" She smiled.

Peter's eyes widened with anticipation.

I took in a deep breath and sighed.

"For now, I just want to survive high school."

Chapter 9

"Can I? Can I? Please?" Peter grinned and rocked back and forth on his feet, his eyes glittering with excitement. I lifted him up onto my bike, steadying him as he eagerly grasped the handlebars.

"This is the coolest bike ever!" he shouted, hunching over as if he were catching air while speeding down a make-believe highway. I saw Sue watching us from the living room window. She'd told me earlier I wasn't allowed to take him riding anywhere.

"Yeah. They are cool," I replied. "But they cost a lot, too. I've been working hard to make the money to pay for it."

"I get an allowance. Maybe I can start saving, too," he said hopefully.

I chuckled. If only things were so simple. "Maybe. But it's going to take an awful lot of allowance to pay for something like this."

"Hmm." He shrugged and went back into racing position, leaning a little to the side and then weaving to the other side as if he'd made a sharp turn. He mimicked the sounds of a sputtering exhaust pipe and I kept my arm near him in case he toppled off in his excitement.

"Mom says they're dangerous." He pretended to rev the engine.

"They are. You need to wear a helmet so you don't get too hurt if you get into an accident. Have you thought about starting with something less expensive? Like a bicycle or a skateboard?"

"One of my friends has a skateboard! But..." He dropped his head down and sighed. "Mom says he's going to grow up to be a troublemaker because of it. I don't think Matt's a troublemaker."

"Aw. I'm sorry to hear that." I patted him on the shoulder. I wouldn't have bothered to argue with Peter's mother, although her views were too conservative for my taste. Over-protective, even. Assuming a boy was a troublemaker because he had a skateboard was a little extreme, but it was none of my business how she raised her son.

She probably would have hated me at Peter's age.

Spending time with him helped keep my mind off other things, like the super early curfew the Jamesons had set for me. The curfew that had me confined to the house between school and work, with very little time for Alice.

Peter looked up to me. He made me feel like an older brother—a mentor. Like I mattered. He also couldn't stop talking about my motorcycle at dinner. Sue rolled her eyes at least twice during the conversation, even glaring at me a few times as if asking why I'd turned her son into such a monster.

A boy his age could learn *anything* he wanted to on the internet, at school, or from friends with smart phones. Motorcycles were the *least* of her worries.

.   .   .

My mother's mental evaluation had finally come back. She had been diagnosed with PTSD, drug dependence, depression and social anxiety to top it all off. The physicians also determined that her condition made her unfit to care for me while in rehabilitation, which could take several months, or even years. I would have to be transferred to another foster home if one of my few relatives didn't step up soon, or if Jane's petition was declined.

My court hearing would be in six weeks—at the beginning of December. It was supposed to have been in late January, but Kareena's dad had pulled a few strings and gotten us a hearing sooner. He'd mentioned how things sometimes got crazy after Christmas break and New Year's, and how people looking forward to the holidays were often much more lenient in their rulings. We'd have to wait and see.

The law stated we *had to* inform all living grandparents on both sides and any direct siblings. As far as I knew, no one in my small extended family wanted me, so I wasn't concerned about someone intercepting the petition.

Alice told me family services had already done the house check and approved them. Now I had to plead my case to the judge. Normally, they didn't let minors have much of a say, but since I was over fourteen, they asked me to give a testimony. According to Kareena's father, I'd have to fess up about my mother's past behavior to give Jane a fair chance at winning guardianship. I didn't want to do it, but if it was the only way, then I had to.

Who knew what the Saviors would do if I ended up moving away with some other family? I didn't want to think about it.

·　　　·　　　·

My day in court was fast approaching. Kareena texted me to set up a meeting to discuss my testimony and what I needed to remember. Although her father was confident that the odds were in my favor, he agreed to show up court day pro-bono just in case the judge needed extra convincing. I couldn't help but wonder how much whining she'd done to get him to help some random "boyfriend" of hers. No doubt it was what she'd told him I was.

He explained that custody cases and guardianship transfers weren't a big deal for kids my age, and outcomes were fairly predictable. I still worried. Worried about telling the court the truth about my mother. Seeming ungrateful, maybe. Worried about what would happen to me if we lost the petition. Worried about Alice and the baby that was now several weeks closer to being a real flesh and blood part of our lives. Wondering if the Saviors were still deliberating over our request or if they had already tossed the idea behind them.

Kareena texted me after she'd pulled up into the Jameson's driveway. I grabbed a notebook and went outside to meet her. The autumn sun reflected off the freshly waxed lipstick-red sports car, blinding me for a moment. I covered my eyes to avoid the glare as I approached. The passenger door opened and I staggered back, startled.

"Hi Brian!" It was Alice.

I smiled.

"Hey!" I walked up to the car door and waited for her to step out before closing it.

"Thanks, Brian," Kareena said sarcastically, slamming her door. "Oh, and you're welcome, by the way."

"Sorry." I shrugged. "There's only one of me."

"Yeah. Unfortunately."

Seriously? She was still jealous of us?

Kareena popped open her trunk and grabbed a satchel out.

"Where can we go to talk?" she asked, shouldering the strap of the bag.

"They have a picnic table in the backyard," I replied. "Is that okay?"

"Sure. Better not be any bugs. I hate bugs. I hate mosquitoes. I hate ants." She brushed at her arms as if she were already being assailed by insects. "Ugh."

"Kareena, quit being a diva. Come on."

Thomas came to the door to greet Alice and Kareena, and then Sue came out of the living room to meet us before we could head to the backyard.

"Would you kids like anything to drink while you're here?" she asked as the three of us passed the threshold. "Tea?

Coffee? Juice?"

Kareena shook her head. "No, thanks." Thomas ushered her and Alice to the back door.

Alice was too polite to ask, so I clicked the hot water kettle on myself instead, apologizing to Sue for her shy behavior.

"She's quiet," I said.

Sue seemed to understand.

"She's a lovely girl," she added, just as Thomas showed them to the back door.

"Alice?"

"Your girlfriend, yes. Her mother must really like you to go through all of this trouble."

"Yes. Well, her mom has a reason to fight for me. She knows how hard it is and how few people I have in my life, and she doesn't want me to end up with strangers. No offense to you guys. You've been more than good to me."

Sue smiled. "Oh, I know you're appreciative, Brian, and I understand you're under a lot of stress right now. That's very kind of her mother. I hope you and Alice last."

"You and Thomas did. And we will, too," I said, with a confident grin. "We definitely will."

I poured two cups of English breakfast tea, added a spoonful of sugar and a splash of milk to each cup and then brought them outside.

Kareena pulled a stack of papers out of her bag and set them in front of me on the table.

"Look over these when you have time," she said. "It will give you a better understanding of how exactly the process will work and what considerations the judge will take into account. My dad also highlighted some things you should be aware of. You'll be under oath, too, so be careful about what you say."

Alice sipped her tea and smiled at me with her eyes. I reached under the table to take her free hand, contemplating what I would give to spend another night with her.

"Heeeeeeey, Brian!" Peter shouted, jogging across the

lawn toward us, his backpack bouncing up and down on his back. "Hey! Are these your friends?" He waved at Kareena and then Alice.

"Yeah."

"Wow. Your girlfriend's real pretty, Brian," he whispered out of the side of his mouth while leaning toward me. No filter at all. *Cute.*

"Yeah. She is." I laughed.

Alice blushed. "I've heard a lot of good things about you, Peter. It's nice to meet you," she said, offering him a hand to shake.

"No!" Kareena shrieked, lunging across the table to slap Alice's hand away. She stared at Peter with widened eyes and her face went pale. "Don't touch him!"

Alice and I stared.

We knew that face. The wild-eyed, holy expletive, I-just-saw-something-crazy-that-you-can't face.

Peter was infected.

"Wh-what's wrong?" Peter asked, frowning.

Alice tucked her hand away into her sweater pocket.

"Nothing," I intercepted. "Alice is... a little sick, that's all. Yeah. She's got a cold. A *really* bad cold and we don't want you catching it."

Alice faked a sneeze.

"Oh. She looks okay." He shrugged.

"Well, that's how this cold is. You look fine and then all of a sudden..." I gagged, pretending I was dying of something horrible and then dropped my head down onto the picnic table with a thump. He got the message and backed away from Alice, moseying over to stand beside Kareena instead.

"Hi. I'm Peter," he said, beaming.

"Hi," Kareena muttered, rolling her eyes and shifting in her seat.

"Be nice to him, please." I glared at her. And I meant it. Now more than ever.

If Kareena was right, things were starting to happen around us.

I wasn't going to let Peter become part of this.

Chapter 10

I stopped to look around, sinking back from the crowd of bustling students rushing off the bus. Alice wasn't waiting for me in the parking lot.

I texted her.

No response.

I headed up the entryway stairs into the school. Down the hall. Toward our lockers. There I found her, crumpled over on the floor, her back against the lockers, knees pulled up to her chest and her face down in her folded arms. Sam sat beside her with an arm slung over her shoulders. My heart plummeted into my stomach.

"Alice!?" I knelt and tried to pry one of her hands out of her lap. She wouldn't budge. "Alice? What's wrong?" Patches of tear-soaked denim darkened her knees. I looked frantically at Sam.

"She's been like this all morning," she said. "Do something, Brian. Maybe she'll listen to you." Sam stood and backed away to give us some space.

"Come on. You have to talk to me." I nudged Alice's shoulder gently. "Alice? Please?"

Alice brought her face up, cheeks and nose flushed bright red. Her eyes shimmered with tears. Her lips were wet and quivering.

"I can't do this anymore," she murmured, then dropped her face back down onto her knees and continued sobbing.

"Do what? What's wrong, Alice? You're not telling me anything." I tried to force her hands off her knees again, but she jerked away and snapped back into her closed-off position. I flopped down beside her and thrust my back against the locker doors. "I can't help you if you won't talk to me!" I crossed my arms.

I sat with her, silently watching students rush to class. Anticipating the ring of the bell. Expecting someone to come and scold us for being late.

"What's going on?" Kareena approached and bent over slightly, looking down at Alice and tipping her head. "Wait. Oh my God!" She gasped and covered her mouth.

"What? What is it?" I straightened up. "Kareena?"

"I want to go home," Alice muttered, turning her face toward me. "Brian, I just want to go home."

"Please, tell me what's wrong first," I tried again, pressing my hand into her shoulder and scooting closer.

"They think they can do whatever they want to me," she grumbled. "That I'm just a body. A shell. I'm not supposed to be a science experiment."

"What did they do to you, Alice? What did they do to..." I lowered my voice. "The baby?" I came to my knees and flicked my hair out of my face. "Alice. Talk to me. I know it's your body, but the baby—she's *ours*. I *need* to know what's happening."

"There isn't one," Kareena said grimly.

"What?" I craned my neck back to look at her. "What do you mean?"

"The baby," Kareena continued. "It's gone. I don't see the second light inside her. I think it's gone, Brian. I think they..."

"Shit! No. Just like that? Without telling us?" I stood and reached down to help Alice to her feet. "Is this true, Alice? Did they..."

She jerked away from me.

"I don't know. Maybe. I think." She wrapped her arms around herself and hunched over. "I just... I feel... horrible right now. Empty. My stomach hurts. I want to go home. I want to be left alone." Her shuddering breaths made my heart ache. Tears kept pouring from her eyes.

"Allie?" Sam stepped closer to us and reached a hand up to grasp Alice's shoulder. "Please tell me what's going on. Please. You guys are scaring me with all of this... *baby* stuff."

"Kareena?" I looked at her. "Explain to Sam what happened, okay? Take her somewhere you can talk quietly. I need to take care of Alice right now."

Jane wouldn't be back from work for several more hours—a staff training session had kept her from responding to any of my calls—so I had to take things into my own hands.

"Come on, Alice. I'll take you home, okay?"

She finally looked up into my eyes.

"Thank you," she murmured, and then sniffled loudly, her throat and nose congested.

"But I'm *not* leaving you alone," I added firmly.

"I'll tell the nurse she got sick so they know where you guys went," said Sam, reaching to brush her fingers over Alice's hand. "Take care of yourself, okay? Take care of her, Brian."

"I will."

Kareena looked at me, pity filling her eyes and making them go red. A frown tugging at her lips. Her eyeliner a little smudged.

"I'm sorry," she whispered, her voice cracking.

•　　　•　　　•

As soon as we got back to the house, I had Alice sit on the couch and then texted Jane to let her know what had happened. I also called the Jamesons. Sue picked up and then proceeded to threaten me with warnings about playing hooky from school with my court day so close at hand. I wanted to be honest with her—which is why I had called in the first place. But I didn't need the third degree.

Eventually, she drove me over the edge.

"*Tell me the truth, Brian,*" she'd said, in a stern tone.

I glanced over at Alice, who had collapsed into a blubbering mess on the couch, and I decided to take the conversation into another room so it wouldn't upset her further.

Then I told Sue the truth about Alice—the pregnancy, at least. Well, *half* of the truth. Getting pregnant against her will. Losing the baby after she'd come to terms with wanting to keep it. I didn't tell Sue the baby was actually *mine*.

"*Does her mother know?*" Sue asked.

"Yes. Of course. We told her a while back. As soon as we found out."

Then she asked me why we didn't go to the police about what had happened.

"It's complicated. We've already done *everything* we can. Trust me."

"*Oh...*" I heard her sigh. "*I hope she'll be okay. It's... hard losing a baby. Especially in the second trimester. She'll need a little time to recover. But, you know, Brian, maybe it's best for you both. God's way of helping her move forward. Of helping you both start fresh.*"

Sue—a devout Christian—thought *everything* was God's will, even the death of her beloved daughter Grace, as tragic as it had been. Grace had died in the line of duty. She'd sacrificed herself for others, just like Christ had. That's what Sue had told me, at least.

By this point, she'd concluded that Alice had been raped—not completely untrue, considering how the pregnancy had, in fact, been forced on her—and that I was stepping up to take responsibility because I loved her—also not completely untrue. She could think that if she wanted to. Anything to take the blame off Alice. Off me. It had never been our fault to begin with.

The (partial) truth put things into perspective for her,

and she backed off after that, realizing how very important the guardianship issue really was for me—for us. I had to get away from my mother. I *had* to protect Alice.

"I need to go. I'll be back as soon as I can, I swear. Please don't tell anyone else about this. Tell Peter I got caught up at work so he doesn't worry about me."

"*I understand,*" Sue replied, and hung up.

I went back into the living room. Alice had nestled her face against the arm of the couch and fallen asleep. I touched her cold hand and then left the room briefly to grab a blanket for her.

I sat on the nearby ottoman for a while, watching her stir in her sleep, whimpering lightly. Digging her fingers into the couch periodically. She must have been in the middle of some horrible nightmares. Or memories...

It hurt me to see her in pain, but there was nothing I could do. Even I had grown fond of the whole baby idea, and now they'd snatched her away from us. Even if Alice had suggested they take the baby back, they didn't have to do it without warning.

Poor Alice got the worst of it—the physiological effects of losing a baby. The Saviors likely had it locked up safe in some sort of cryogenic freezer. A little timer on the case set for Alice's eighteenth birthday. Thinking about it made me sick to my stomach.

I wish they'd told us first. She'd had no chance to mentally prepare—not that it was something we could have prepared for—but they'd waited longer than I'd expected them to. We thought they'd forgotten the request by now.

The Saviors had a way of doing that—making us forget about them and then stepping back into our lives right when our guard was down.

I leaned down to kiss her cheek.

She groaned and wriggled under her blanket, pulling it up to her nose.

As if the mental anguish hadn't been enough, she was probably suffering from a sort of postpartum depression—something usually caused by giving birth, but also known to occur after miscarriages and even abortions. With the Saviors involved, neither had likely happened, but that wouldn't stop the pain she felt over the loss.

KAREENA: How's Alice?
ME: She's… OK I guess

There wasn't much to say.

KAREENA: Let me know how she's doing
ME: I will
KAREENA: THX
KAREENA: Sorry :(Glad she has U

I tucked my phone into my pocket.

Alice went back to sleep. I stayed there, trying to come up with a way to make her feel better. I felt so damn helpless.

Jane left work an hour early. I heard the car pull into the driveway. She came in and tossed her keys onto the kitchen counter.

"How is she?" she asked, looking at me first and then at her daughter. "Oh, my baby." She knelt down beside Alice and caressed her cheek. "I'm so sorry."

"I'm sure the baby's fine," I said, trying to be optimistic. "They're probably just keeping her temporarily."

"Leave me alone," Alice said, stirring.

"Alice?" I reached out to touch her. "Is there anything I can do at all? Tell me."

"No."

Jane looked at me and shrugged. "I think she needs time, Brian. This is hard on her body. It's trying to cope with the sudden changes."

Grief takes time, but she needed time I didn't have. I

couldn't stay with her all day. Or all week for that matter. Not until the petition had been honored.

"I want to be here for her, though," I replied. "I feel so useless otherwise."

"It's okay. I'll take tomorrow off and stay home with her so you won't have to worry." She forced a smile. "Will that make you feel better?"

"I guess." I shrugged. Nothing could really make me feel better. Nothing but knowing Alice would be okay.

"I promise you I'll keep a close eye on her. I won't let her be alone. You can even come see her after school if the Jamesons are okay with it."

"They will be. I... sort of told them what was going on."

Jane's eyes widened. "What? You told them about—"

"No. No. I just told them enough to keep them off my back. Enough to keep them from asking too many questions. Enough to make them understand how much I needed to leave school today."

"Thanks, Brian, for doing that. Telling the truth helps, even if it is a little distorted. To be honest, I'm dreading our court date. It will be here before I know it. Less than two weeks. I just hope everything goes well."

"Don't be so worried, Jane." I put my hand onto her shoulder and smiled genuinely. "I am more than thankful for what you've done for me. I can't imagine any other kid my age being so lucky. I know you're a good mother. Be yourself and the judge will see that, too."

Chapter 11

Waves of dark hair danced around Alice's face, roused by a gust of brisk autumn wind. She swept the stray locks behind her ears. Her toes curled into the sand and she gazed off into the distance. A quiet sigh slipped from her lips, and she closed her eyes and leaned her head against my shoulder.

We sat barefoot on the beach, watching waves crash against the shoreline. I inhaled deeply, the breeze teasing my nostrils with a salty sweetness.

People walked their dogs along the water, some tossing flying discs for them to catch, others enjoying a jog. Children bounced beach balls at the water's edge. Others built sandcastles in the fading light of dusk.

I took Alice's hand into mine and cupped it tightly in my lap. Taking her to the beach was my attempt at helping her to focus on other things. Fresh air. New sounds and sights. Anything to get her out of the house—out of the downward spiral of depression. Anything to keep her mind occupied.

She had wanted to shut me out, and that had hurt. Depression is a difficult beast. It causes a biological change in the brain and has to be dealt with carefully, and in our case, *without* medical attention. We had to make sure Alice was eating properly and keeping up her strength. I had to get her out of the house and keep her moving, looking forward, forgetting what had happened.

The Jamesons knew I needed to spend extra time with Alice and adjusted their strict curfew for that reason. But then work got tough. Things added up and my ability to pay attention to anything other than my two biggest worries quickly dwindled. I worried about Alice and the court day constantly.

If it took an hour every day of just sitting silently beside her on the ocean shore, holding her hand, and providing a shoulder for her to cry on when she needed it, I'd do it. I'd do it for as long as I had to. Whatever was necessary to bring my Alice back.

·　　·　　·

I took a deep breath and exhaled, brushing my hair back with a comb, checking the mirror to make sure my tie looked straight. I'd outgrown the suit I'd worn at last year's dance, but thankfully Thomas had one I could borrow that fit. With a few adjustments.

Court day fell on a Monday, two weeks before Christmas break. I was nervous as hell. Nervous about what I might say... or *forget* to say. Nervous the fluorescence would flare up and send the judge into a frenzy. Nervous the idiot Saviors would yank me out of the courtroom and then plop me back down, making *me* look like the crazy one.

Alice texted me first thing in the morning a genuine (non-depressed) text. The first in almost two weeks. It lifted a weight off my shoulders. It gave me confidence.

She'd finally come around.

ALICE: I hope everything goes well. I'll be thinking about you
ME: Thanks. I'll be thinking of you, too
ALICE: Thank you for everything...
ALICE: I love you :)
ME: I love you, too!

Maybe she'd have me back tomorrow. *Permanently.*
Maybe.
If everything went well.

Kareena's father arrived early, before the Jamesons and me. We met outside the courthouse where he gave me a quick briefing and told me not to worry about anything. In the courtroom, he reviewed my case with the judge and then asked me a few questions about my mom's history. I told the judge how she had attempted suicide once before—when I was younger—and how I had stopped her then, but had been too afraid to go to the police. The judge sympathized with me.

I told him I'd gotten a job as soon as I'd been able to in order to get out of the house and take responsibility for myself. Make money. Afford transportation. He also asked me about my motorcycle, whose property it was and how I'd acquired the money to pay for it, considering a kid my age could not legally be bound by a loan. So I told him the truth—something I hadn't even told Alice. Jane had sponsored me and I had paid her back for it in full already.

I'd mentioned it to my mother a while back, but she'd wanted no part of it. I had no choice but to go to Jane; she knew where I was coming from and how badly I needed the help.

"You're very responsible for a young man your age," the judge said with a tilt of his head. "It's a shame more teenagers don't take life quite as seriously as you seem to be doing."

The compliment caught me off guard and I couldn't help but crack a smile.

"Though I regret finding you in court under such unfortunate circumstances. Children need to grow up in reliable and safe environments. This doesn't seem to be the case for you with the severity of your mother's mental condition escalating." He adjusted his glasses, propped an elbow on the desk in front of him and rested his chin in his hand. "Let me ask you something, Brian."

"Yes, Your Honor?" I tangled my hands together to stop myself from fidgeting.

"From what I have been told about this case, you and the petitioner's daughter are... how do I put this plainly? Involved?"

I swallowed hard and glanced at Kareena's father, who had an unemotional look on his face. He shrugged, gesturing for me to hurry up and answer.

"Um... yes."

"And if you and the daughter have a fallout, how do you think that may affect your home situation, should I choose to honor this petition today?"

I straightened up in my seat. "Well, if you'll forgive my presumptuousness, Your Honor, I don't believe that will happen."

"Nothing is set in stone, son."

"True, but I'm doing the best I can. I don't have to be a scientist to know most high school relationships don't last all that long, but we've already been together for over a year. Since the beginning of our relationship, I've set out to put more effort toward graduating, studying for my classes, showing up on time. Giving a damn about my education even though I never had before. I work a real job as hard and as long as I'm allowed, just to save money to pay off my motorcycle. Things were getting bad back home and I never had much of a reason to try before I met Alice."

The judge's eyebrows rose and his jaw eased open. "I see," he replied with a nod. "Quite a thoughtful response. Thank you for answering with honesty. It has put your case in perspective for me."

I held my breath while the judge leaned back in his chair and rubbed his chin.

"Very well. I have decided to honor the petition and award full guardianship and its responsibilities to the petitioner."

Yes! I heaved a sigh of relief.

"That girl's mother," he said, pointing at Jane, "truly believes in you. I hope for both her and her daughter's sakes that things work out."

"Me, too. Thank you, Your Honor."

"Thank *you,* Brian, for upholding a respectable image for young people today. I've heard good things about you from the Jamesons. It seems you've been an influential role model for their son."

Hearing that made me feel so much better about myself. I'd never thought I was being a role model by any means. I was just living—being me—and trying to keep Alice in my life the only way I knew how.

. . .

"I'll miss you, Brian," Peter murmured, staring at his feet and scuffing his shoes against the driveway pavement.

"I'll miss you, too." I offered up a hand and we fist bump-ed.

"Before I forget... let me get something from the house." I ran back inside and grabbed a box off the couch.

"I got this for you," I said, handing Peter the large cardboard box.

"Wow! A present! What is it!?" He set it down onto the driveway and dropped onto his knees.

"Merry early Christmas, Peter."

He ripped the long strip of tape off the top of the box and pulled open the flaps. His eyes widened.

"YES!"

Half the street probably heard his excitement.

He plunged his hands into the box and lifted out a shiny metallic blue skateboard with a red bow attached.

"My very own skateboard!? And it's the same awesome color as your bike, too!" He hugged it tightly and beamed. "Thanks, Brian! You're the best brother ever!"

He got up and reached his arms out to hug me, still holding

tightly to the skateboard and bopping me in the kneecap with it.

"Hey. There's more." I motioned for him to check the box again.

He dug down inside and pulled out a helmet, and then elbow and knee pads. All part of the deal I'd made with Sue and Thomas. He could have a skateboard if I got the protective gear to go with it. Peter was more than mature enough to handle something I'd had even before I was his age. I'd never even had any of that protective stuff when I'd hit the concrete. Talk about growing pains.

"Can you help me put these on before you go?" Peter held up the elbow pads.

"Sure. I'll even show you a little bit of what I used to do. I'll make sure you get off to a good start."

"Yessss!" Peter jumped up into the air and ran around in a half circle, flailing his arms excitedly. "I can't wait to show Matt!" His huge toothy grin was contagious.

I helped strap the elbow and knee pads onto him and then hopped onto the skateboard deck to show him a few tricks. He squealed and shouted as I did a grind on the street curb and then a few ollies—little hops that brought the board off the ground. Neither was a big deal really, but it impressed him. I didn't want to screw up and faceplant in front of his parents. It had been a while since I'd been on a skateboard.

I surrendered the board back to him and let him try. He stepped up onto the deck and I explained how to balance and center his weight properly so he wouldn't fall. I walked beside him as he kicked forward to gain speed, and then I had to jog after him. The kid was a natural.

He hit a small pothole and toppled forward. I lunged and snagged him by the shirt, catching him before he hit the ground.

"You gotta watch for those," I said.

"Yeah. Thanks for saving me."

He chased after the board as it rolled down the street.

"Stay on the curb while you're learning, okay? Don't play in the street when there's cars. Keep an eye out."

"You sound like my mom," Peter said, walking back toward me. He set his board down on the grass at my feet and polished the deck with the side of his hand.

"Sorry, but I care about you." I chuckled. "We care about you. I want you to be in one piece when I come back to say hi someday."

"Yes!" His arms shot up and he bounced in place. "I can't wait until you come back to see me! Can you bring Alice if she's not sick? She seemed really nice."

"Sure. I'll try."

Peter shrugged and kicked a rock down the driveway. "So, are you gonna marry her?" he asked.

"Alice?"

"Yeah."

"I hope so."

"Cool. Maybe I can come over and play with *your* kids."

His words made me laugh out loud. "I think it's going to be a while before any of that happens. Hopefully." I meandered over to my motorcycle and picked up my helmet off the seat. "Well, I gotta go, Peter. I'm sorry. I hope you like your board. Be careful."

"I will!" He came over to me and stood by my bike. "I'm going to miss you, Brian," he said softly, frowning. "You're the coolest guy I've ever known."

My heart sank, but I forced a smile so I wouldn't bring him down. "I'll miss you, too. You're a good kid. Don't let *anyone* tell you otherwise. Got that?"

"Yeah." Then he shuffled closer and fidgeted.

"Go ahead. Give your bro a hug." I bent over and wrapped my arms around him. He hugged me tight and I ruffled his hair with my fingers. "Take care of yourself. If you ever need anything, your mom knows how to reach me."

In only two months, the kid had grown on me. So much so, in fact, that if someone bullied him in school, they'd have a much bigger kid to deal with now.

Peter wanted to meet Alice again. It made me feel terrible, but it wasn't possible. I couldn't even tell him the real reason why. We couldn't risk starting him until we knew the truth behind the fluorescence and what the Saviors wanted out of those who had been implanted with it. Peter was too important to me.

Chapter 12

"Hi," said Alice, standing up from the grass as I pulled into the driveway.

"Hi." I slid my helmet off and tucked it beneath my arm. A twinge of emotion made my throat tighten.

She opened the garage door and I walked my motorcycle inside.

"So... this is different, huh?" I said, dragging a hand through my hair. "I guess I don't have to go home now."

"This is home," she replied softly, almost smiling.

I flipped down the kickstand and parked my bike near the wall. My stomach twisted into a knot of anxiety and excitement. I wanted to take Alice into my arms. Embrace her tightly. Kiss her deeply. But the thrill became stifled by awkwardness. Maybe it wasn't right or I was overstepping my boundaries now.

Maybe she didn't even want it. She'd been through a lot. Who knew what new fears and concerns were brewing in her mind now that so much had changed?

"So, how was class today? Did I miss anything?" I asked.

"Good. And no, you didn't miss anything important." She opened the door that led from the garage to the house and we stepped inside.

"Are you doing okay?"

"I'm feeling better, yes."

Finally.

"Good."

"Mom's going to pick up Chinese food after work tonight

to celebrate."

"Cool. I know this has been hard on everyone. I wish I hadn't been such a burden to you guys."

"You weren't," said Alice, clasping my hand. "I felt confident it would work out. I trust my mom and she trusts you."

"I'm glad it did work out." I squeezed her hand. "We need each other... now more than ever."

She sighed.

"Alice?"

She looked up at me with tired eyes.

"Besides... losing *her*... what else is bothering you? You seem... drained." I closed the door behind us.

"Anything can happen," she said, exhaling loudly as she flopped onto a kitchen chair. "It's hard to plan life around something you can't plan for at all. I'm scared."

"I know what you mean." I pulled out the chair beside her and sat. "And I'm sorry about this whole mess. Especially what they've put *you* through. At least you have me now. That's definitely something you *can* rely on."

A little half-crescent tugged at her lips. She cocked an eyebrow.

"This doesn't make you some kind of adopted brother, does it? Because that would be *really* weird."

I laughed hard and she cracked an honest, toothy smile. It was a smile I hadn't seen in a while. "No. It doesn't," I assured her. "And yes, that would be weird. I wouldn't want to make out with my sister."

Alice burst out laughing and brought a hand up to shyly cover her mouth.

Anything to make her laugh.

Anything to get the old Alice back.

"It's nice outside. Do you want to go for a ride before dinner?"

She shrugged.

I took it as a yes.

.   .   .

Traffic was sparse at sundown. We'd narrowly avoided Monday evening rush hour. I took a back road to get to downtown. We flipped open the visors on our helmets and enjoyed the cool air. Winter wasn't much of a winter on the coast. Not like in Montana. High 60s doesn't exactly scream "Christmas" to me.

Strands of shimmering white lights and coils of spruce and holly garland decorated streetlamps along the narrow downtown streets. Bright red banners swayed in the wind and speakers blared tired instrumental Christmas carols all around town. The same worn-out classics I'd been subjected to every day at work since Thanksgiving.

We stopped at a red light and Alice leaned against my shoulder.

"It's pretty downtown," she said.

"Yeah. It is."

"My mom and I used to come every year and walk around after Black Friday. Do some shopping. Get a waffle at Stan's over there." She pointed past my arm to a little cubby-hole of a bakery across the way.

The light changed to green and I squeezed the gas.

"Maybe we can come back after dinner," I replied, raising my voice to combat the growl of the engine.

"Maybe."

We rode down several other streets and then circled back toward the main square where a huge Christmas tree stood, glowing with thousands of colorful lights and decorated with hundreds of oversized ornaments. I parked nearby and we strolled down the block and past a string of brightly decorated shop windows toward the tree. It must have been a few stories high. We had to crane our necks back to see the bright gold star perched—slightly crooked—on top of the tree.

"Now there's no way I could straighten *that* star," I said, pointing a finger and tipping my head to the side. "I'm not *that* tall."

Alice chuckled, recalling how I could touch the star on her tall Christmas tree back home without straining.

I hooked an arm around her waist and pulled her in to an embrace. She exhaled a sigh and nuzzled her face against my shirt. After a few moments, I took her hand and walked with her to a nearby bench. We sat beside each other near the foot of the tree and I wrapped an arm around her shoulders. She settled her weight against me and we sat there for a while, watching the colored lights twinkle.

The smell of pine saturated the air. Evening shoppers strolled by with bag handles draped over both arms. Many had steaming drinks balanced precariously in their free hands. I could almost taste the hot chocolate just thinking about it.

I looked down at Alice as she rested her eyes, her head pressed against me. A gentle breeze whipped through the locks of her dark brown hair. The thought of her surrendering, trusting me, made my heart ache. This was so right, it hurt. But it was a good hurt. A pure, wholehearted, all-sacrificing kind of hurt.

We'd been together for a year. I remembered asking her to be my girlfriend just after the holiday dance last year around this time. Then came our first real kiss the night of the Christmas party at her mom's house. The kiss that brought my fluorescence to life. The kiss that changed *everything*.

"Would you mind getting me a drink?" she murmured, nudging me gently and looking up at me with a smile on her face. The violet light of dusk reflected in her gaze, tinting the blue purple.

"It won't spoil dinner, will it?" I asked jokingly.

"Nothing spoils Chinese," she said with a smirk.

"True. It's so greasy and sweet. Alright then." I reluctantly slid my arm from around her shoulders. "What would you like?" While we'd been sitting there, people had been popping in and out of the café just down the street.

"No, wait," I interrupted her just as she separated her lips to reply. "Let me pick out something, okay?" I stood from the bench and took a few steps before turning around to look at her. "Are you going to be alright by yourself?"

"For ten minutes? I think so, yeah. Besides, I've got pepper spray," she whispered, gesturing toward her bag and raising her eyebrows in exaggeration.

She did have pepper spray. A little girly-pink can of it, too. But there's absolutely nothing girly about pepper spray in the eyes. Besides, our neighborhood had a low crime rate and I wasn't that worried about leaving her in the middle of a bustling town square.

I shrugged and walked off toward the café.

I propped open the door for an exiting woman and little girl. They thanked me and then I entered behind them, the glass door closing behind me. A brass bell jingled above the doorframe.

A sweet menagerie of smells assailed my nostrils. Waffles. Freshly brewed coffee. Caramel. Cinnamon.

My mouth started to water.

"Hello." The young woman behind the counter smiled and straightened her apron. "Welcome to Stan's. What can I get you?"

Alice and I both loved tea, but I had a taste for something else.

"Uh... can I get a large hot chocolate and medium black tea latte, please?"

"Sure thing." She poked a few buttons on the cash register. "That's eight dollars even."

I handed her a ten. She gave me back the change and then slid the receipt over to me. I tossed a buck into the tip jar.

"I'll get those right out to you," she said in a cheerful voice as she reached under the counter to grab two Christmas-themed paper cups. I took a seat at a little table a few feet away and waited.

A young couple came in—a girl latched onto the guy's arm. The two snickered quietly. I smirked. *Cute.* Is that how Alice and I looked to others? They seemed barely past the first kiss phase, if I was reading them correctly. All bright-eyed and smitten with each other. A little too oozy for my taste—in public, at least.

"Here you are, Brian." The barista set two drinks on the counter.

"How did you know my name?" I asked, getting up to retrieve them.

"It's me, Christy. I used to work at Jacques', too, but I quit a few months ago. You don't remember me, I take it?"

Her round face and curly black hair did look vaguely familiar.

"I think I do. Yeah. Sorry, I've been going through a lot lately and life's been hitting hard. Sorry I didn't recognize you."

"Don't worry about it, Brian." She smiled with her eyes. "We all have tough times. Merry early Christmas. Oh, and I hope she likes her drink," she added.

She'd read between the lines. And she was right; I had a girl to get back to.

"Thanks, Christy." I took up both steaming hot to-go cups and headed back out into the streets toward the main square.

Alice was waiting patiently on the bench, her hands folded neatly in her lap and her gaze lovingly fixed on the Christmas tree.

"Hey."

"Yay! You're back." She straightened up and reached to take the drink from my hand. She sniffed the steam wafting from the slot in the lid. "Smells good. What did you get?" She leaned over as I sat beside her and I held my cup under her nose. "Hot chocolate? Mmm..." She closed her eyes and took a second sniff. "Delicious!"

I felt stupid. I'd only gotten one hot chocolate, and by the look on her face, I could tell she wanted it.

"Oh. Oops. I mixed them up. The hot chocolate was for you." I took the cup from her and offered her mine. "They must have mixed up the sizes," I added, thinking fast.

"Yay!" She cupped her hands around it and nudged me with her arm. "Thanks, Brian. I love you so much."

I smiled and tried to act cool about the screw up. "You're welcome."

"Gonna have to let it sit a while, though. It's super hot." She pried the lid off the top and scooped a dollop of whipped cream off with her tongue. Then she popped the lid back on and set the cup by her feet.

"Yeah. Mine, too." I set mine down beside hers. "Oh well. We've got some time before your mom gets home."

She leaned her head against my shoulder.

"So, what do you want for Christmas, Alice?" I had to ask, seeing how I'd already screwed up the drink order.

"Having you is more than enough," she replied, tightening her arm around mine.

Nice answer, but not helpful.

"No, really. I don't even know where to start this year. Any ideas at all would be great considering how short on time I already am. Sorry."

"A kitten!" She squealed and bit her lip.

My eyes widened and my smile went flat.

"Just kidding! But I would like a cat someday, so I hope you're okay with that."

"Sure." I shrugged. Cats. Kids. Dogs. Whatever. I didn't care one way or another as long as it made her happy.

"Yes!" She rubbed her hands together excitedly.

"But really, Alice. Something I can *actually* get you this year?"

"Oh, right." She screwed her face up and squinted. "Hmm.

Trying to think of something I haven't already told Mom or Sam. Oh, I don't know, Brian. I don't need anything else." She tangled her fingers around her dolphin pendant and shrugged. "I still love this, though. I can't think of anything. Really."

Apparently, I'd never top the necklace I'd given her for her birthday...

"Wait! I've got an idea! How about... oh, God."

I shuddered, feeling it, too.

Emptiness. Silence. A tingling on my skin.

The earth stopped.

And then we fell.

Chapter 13

We landed with a thud on rough, hard ground. I scrambled to my feet and brushed dust from my jeans. Alice knelt beside me with her hand on her forearm, groaning in pain.

"Are you alright?" I helped her to her feet. She had bashed her arm against the concrete when we'd hit down and a bloody smudge decorated her skin.

"Yeah. Everything hurts." She rubbed the back of her leg with her hand. "They didn't have to drop us in the middle of..."

"Goddamn it!" someone shrieked behind us.

We both veered our heads.

Kareena clenched her fists and pushed her lower lip out. "Where the hell are we?" she growled, stamping a high-heel on the pavement.

A flash of light caught my attention and I looked away. An unmistakable landmark loomed in the distance.

"Shit." I released Alice's hand unintentionally.

Towering above a series of other buildings, the tip of the Eiffel Tower shimmered in white and gold lights. Behind that, a huge black glass pyramid beamed with a blazing spotlight shooting straight from its peak toward the stars.

"We're in Las Vegas," I said, shaking my head. "Las-freaking-Vegas."

I pulled Alice closer and tangled my arm around hers.

"Don't take a step without me, please," I whispered. "We can't get separated here."

Kareena came up beside us. "How the hell did we get here?"

"I don't know, but... ugh." I shivered, shocked by a brisk gust of wind that blew past, and pulled the collar of my shirt up around my throat. I reached into my pocket and took out my phone. It wouldn't turn on.

"Damn it!" I shoved it back into my pocket. "Alice, can you check yours?" She and Kareena had already taken theirs out.

"Nothing," Alice confirmed. "It's like the battery's dead."

"Piece of shit!" Kareena whacked her phone against her palm.

"That's not going to help," I said, rolling my eyes. "The Saviors must have done something to them. Who knows? We need to get out of here. So let's figure out what we're here for so we can get it over with and hopefully be sent home. Fast. It's late, and I sure as hell don't want to be trapped in Las Vegas for the rest of the night. Or week, for that matter."

"Where is everyone? I'd pictured Vegas as a really busy place," said Alice, peering down the empty street. "There's no one here."

"The city that never sleeps, right?" I added.

"That's New York City, genius," Kareena sneered, propping her hand on her hip. "This is Sin City."

"Oh, right. Well, excuse me."

A creepy crawly sensation swept over me. My stomach tightened and Alice squeezed my arm. I sucked a quick breath through my teeth just before the earth disappeared from beneath my feet again.

We touched down on solid ground a second later and I shielded my eyes with the back of my hand. A million lights glistened. I eased my eyes open and looked around. Vivid colors. LEDs. Giant overhead speakers blasting music. Animated screens bombarding us with advertisements. Sights and sounds came from every corner.

I took a deep breath and smelled nothing. Surreal, eerie emptiness. Like a dream.

A glowing green sign hung above the entrance of the strip.

Fremont Street.

The wide, covered, street-like strip mall of windows and storefronts went on for as far as I could see on both sides. Even the curved ceiling brandished an enormous fitted screen that made it into a massive moving advertisement. Casinos and bars everywhere. An oversized block of red and yellow lights electrified the word *Mermaids!*. Something I didn't even attempt to fathom.

"Hey!" Kareena stumbled forward and let out an angry huff, swerving around as if someone had shoved her from behind. "Who the…"

"What happened?" I asked.

"I don't know. It felt like someone pushed me."

I held my breath.

Smoky, faded silhouettes began to materialize. Hundreds of them. Surrounding us. Moving. Pushing past each other. I dodged the nearest one I saw and quickly jerked Alice out of the way of another.

The silhouettes manifested into definable human shapes but remained a little boxy and blurred, like video streamed at low bandwidth. Identifiable if you looked hard enough, but distorted from a distance.

"Well, that answers your question about the people," I said. "Come on, Alice. Kareena. Let's be careful not to bump into anyone. Seeing how you got slammed by someone earlier, it's safe to assume they can feel us even if they can't see us. Watch where you're going, okay?" I clutched Alice's arm tightly and we walked through the street, avoiding the crowd and dodging street performers and vendors who were scurrying around like frenzied ants.

A buzzing noise sounded overhead and we cut glances toward the ceiling. Someone zoomed by, dangling from an indoor zip line. Then a massive LED screen flashed just off to our side above an entryway. The ad featured a blond in a bikini pretending to strip behind a huge censor box. A gentlemen's club.

"Ew." Alice huddled closer. "I hope we don't have to go in there."

"I doubt it," I reassured her, looking into her eyes. Her pupils were so big and anxious, they nearly blocked out the blue. "Why would we need to?" I hooked an arm around her back and cupped her shoulder. "I doubt the Saviors have a sense of humor." I tried to laugh, but it came out as an awkward chuckle. "Anyway. Don't worry about that right now."

"What are we supposed to do here?" she asked, fixating on a giant cowboy-shaped sign in the distance. "This place is soooo crowded and... loud." She slumped over and cupped her face in her hands. "Ohhhh, my ears hurt."

Kareena stared off into the distance, her eyes wide and her focus darting from side to side.

"Kareena?" I reached to touch her arm and she jolted. "Do you see something?"

She whispered her response so quietly that I was forced to read her lips: "Yes."

"Well?"

A high-pitched whine reverberated in her throat. "There are so many of them. Oh my God." She turned and looked me in the eye. "There are so many infected people here."

Infected people?

She meant people with white light inside them—sleepers, she called them—people who had dormant Savior DNA. Like the boy at school Alice had shocked a while back. And Peter. These people had a passive form—*uncolored* fluorescence— as Kareena described it to us.

"So, Alice is supposed to start these people?" I asked. "How many are there, really?" I gasped. "Hey, Alice!" I yanked her out of the way of another street performer she hadn't even noticed dancing toward her—a woman dressed as Marilyn Monroe. Quite a pretty one at that. So many beautiful girls strutting around.

Stay focused.

"There are dozens," Kareena replied, shaking her head. "Like... a hundred or more. I don't know. I just see white lights everywhere. Bouncing around the street. Going in and out of buildings. They're everywhere. And I mean freaking *everywhere.*"

"So, I assume they want Alice to deal with *all* of them?"

"I'm guessing yes." Kareena shrugged. "Why else would we have been dropped right in the middle of a place with so many sleepers?"

I heaved a sigh. "Fine! Come on. Let's get this over with so we can get home. Kareena, can you tell her who she needs to touch?"

"I'm on it. Just give me a sec. Crap. There are a lot of them."

We set out walking.

"Him." Kareena pointed at a blurry man with a bright yellow shirt. "The one wearing the ugly shirt."

Alice clammed up.

"Alice, touch him." I nudged her. "Please? It won't hurt you."

"It's not me I'm worried about," she muttered. "We have no idea what we're doing to these people."

The man pushed by and passed us.

"I'm more concerned with what the Saviors will do to *us* if we don't go through with this." I tugged her arm gently. "Alice. Just do it. Go on!" I followed him and pulled her alongside me.

Finally, she reached out a shaky hand and squeezed her eyes shut. Her fingers brushed against his and he slowed on contact, his movement seemingly missing frames as his walk turned sluggish and jerky, like a sloppy flipbook animation.

Then, as if he had just been rendered into HD, his outline

sharpened and he became crystal clear. Now we could easily differentiate him from all the other infected and non-infected who remained out of focus.

"So that worked?" I asked, watching Alice nervously clutch her hand close to her chest.

"Yeah." Kareena nodded. "It's definitely active. The light is a lot brighter inside him now."

"Then let's keep moving," I said. "The sooner we get this done, the sooner we can go home. Don't be so frightened, Alice." I took her hands into mine. "I'm here with you. I won't let... watch it!" I stepped to the side and pulled her with me, narrowly avoiding a collision with a trio of '20s style gangsters marching by. Black and white suits, fake Tommy guns and all. "I won't let anything happen to you. Okay?"

"I don't want to be here." She hunched over. "It's so bright. Loud. I don't like being around so many people. It's like the place is closing in on me and..."

"I don't want to be here either. But I don't think we can leave until we finish what they put us here for. Alice, please. You don't have to feel like you're alone. You have me, and I'll protect you any way I can."

"Oh my God, you guys!" Kareena groaned. "Alice, stop being a little bitch and let's get this over with."

I glared at Kareena, a nasty threat on the tip of my tongue, wrinkling my lips.

She rolled her eyes at me.

"Sorry, Brian. But seriously, who knows how long we'll be stuck here if we don't get moving?"

I couldn't deny her rationale.

"She's kind of right, Alice. Let's get through this so we can go home. Together."

Kareena gagged.

"Quit it," I snapped, shooting her another dirty look.

"How many people do they need?" Alice asked. "This place is packed."

"I don't know. But we can't think about that right now. Let's just do whatever the hell it is they want and hopefully they'll get us out of here."

Along the street, contortionists folded themselves up, squeezing into tiny boxes. Girls did tricks with hula hoops. Drag queens paraded around in six-inch glittering heels between Elvis impersonators big and small. Camera flashes went off left and right. An oversized LED-encrusted Aladdin's lamp sparkled in the distance.

Scantily clad women danced on top of a long bar along the side of the street, pushing some type of alcoholic slush drinks. Music thumped from speakers perched overhead. I couldn't hear myself think anymore.

We made our way through the crowds, single file, as swiftly as we could, dodging people who hadn't been infected and honing in on those who had. Couples, singles, groups of college-age girls and guys. Party-goers. A never-ending stream of people.

"I don't like this at all," Alice said, folding her arms. "I don't know any of these people. I hate touching strangers."

"It might be the only choice we have right now," I replied, shrugging. "If I could take the responsibility from you I would, but I—"

"Watch out!" Kareena shouted.

I veered around just in time to sidestep a man stumbling toward me.

"Him, too, by the way." Kareena pointed. "He's *totally* smashed, though. Sorry, Alice."

"Really? Ugh." Alice growled. "Fine. Whatever." She went marching after him. He weaved through the crowd, clumsily bumping into others.

Alice crept up from behind and shimmied her way between people. I kept my eyes on her the entire time. Just as she came within a few feet of him, the man suddenly changed direction, veering around so quickly he lost his footing and toppled toward her.

She lifted both hands into an offensive stance and slammed him in the chest with her palms, pushing him away. He fell back in creepy slow-motion, jittery and staggered like all the others she'd started before him. Then his image burst to life in crisp, vivid color.

"That... worked?" Alice shuddered, her hands shaking.

"Sure did," Kareena confirmed, watching with a smirk as the disoriented man righted himself just in time to be escorted off by a pair of security guards. "Hey, at least now you know you don't have to get all touchy-feely with them all."

"Great." Alice exhaled. "That makes things a *little* easier."

A few dozen sleepers later, I started to feel pretty useless. There I was, following two girls around some parallel plane on the Vegas strip, watching *them* do some kind of job, while I dragged behind like baggage. I had healed Alice when she'd hit down, but now I felt like a third wheel. There was nothing for me to do. No way for me to help make this easier.

"Hey!" Kareena stopped cold in her tracks and pointed. "You guys can't see that, can you?"

I looked, but only saw more of the same—out-of-focus people coming and going in all directions.

"No," I answered. "Unless you mean people. Lots of them, obviously."

"Come with me." She gestured for Alice to follow. I tagged along behind them. "See that chick there? She has, like, black stuff in her and her outline is all dark and jagged. It's totally not like the others. I mean, I think she definitely needs to be started, but it just looks different."

Alice jogged over to the woman and brushed her fingers against her forearm.

Nothing happened. No clarity. No color change.

She looked back at me and shook her head.

"Try again?" I mouthed the words. The noise level would have drowned them out anyway.

She briefly tapped the woman's hand.

Still, nothing.

"You didn't start her," Kareena said, narrowing her eyes at the woman as she came walking past.

"What do I do?" Alice began to panic. "What if we have to get all of them? What if they don't let us go home? What if—"

"Alice, calm down!" I held up my hands. "You're sure about that one, Kareena?"

"Totally." She nodded.

I returned my attention to Alice.

"Just take a breath," I said. "Let's try it again." I walked beside her toward the woman with the strange aura neither of us could see.

As we approached, heat flushed through my fingertips and the hairs on the back of my neck perked up.

"Brian!" Alice's eyes widened. "You're glowing!"

I looked down.

My left hand sparkled with hot blue light. A strange twinging sensation flushed through me and the heat in my arm intensified. The warmth flowed in my veins, pulsing and throbbing deeper and stronger.

I reached a hand out and touched the woman's shoulder.

She froze in place.

Blue light flickered through her, flashing like an explosion of tiny fireworks and then dissipating without a trace. She became a blur again.

"That's it!" Kareena rushed up beside me with a triumphant grin on her face. "That's totally freaking it! Try again, Alice! I think it will work this time."

Alice stretched her fingers out and lifted her arm toward the woman. A quick tap and she recoiled.

"It worked! I felt it." She shook out her hand. "It shocked me a little more than usual, but it worked."

"It did," Kareena confirmed.

So, the Saviors had a plan for me, after all.

There weren't many sick ones in Vegas, but there were a good dozen or so, which made me feel useful enough.

Of course, a few stragglers had popped into the strip clubs—where Alice refused to go—so we had no choice but to wait for them to leave before we could finish our job. They all wandered back out eventually, and within a few hours, Alice had been able to start them all.

Hunger pains were making me sick to my stomach. Far past midnight and the three of us remained trapped in the middle of a busy Las Vegas strip. Starting sleepers had taken a lot of energy out of Alice and the fatigue was starting to slow her down.

Kareena started to get grouchy.

We'd all had enough.

"I think we got everyone. Right?" Alice grumbled, doubling over.

"As far as I can tell. Yeah." Kareena shrugged. "I don't see anyone else." She spun around a few times and scanned our surroundings. "I don't see... wait." Her eyes narrowed. "That chick behind the bar in the back there. In front of the Casino. By the orange palm tree."

Alice stood on her tip toes to look over the crowd. Many of them were fully visible now—all the ones we'd started.

"The dark tan girl in the black bikini?" Alice asked. "The one holding the drink tray?"

"Yeah. That one." Kareena confirmed.

"Okay. I'll be right back."

Alice pushed through the crowd and I lost sight of her.

"Alice!" I shuffled past a group of opaque people and then darted past a few out-of-focus women who weren't infected.

"Alice!" I still couldn't see her.

Just as I approached the bar, the waitress in black materialized in front of me. I gasped as she came within an inch of my face, almost swiping me with her drink tray as she spun around and gyrated her hips to a song blaring overhead.

I ducked.

"Damn it! Alice! Where are you?" I looked back at Kareena, who shrugged.

"Alice?"

A breath caught in my throat and my skin tingled. The ground below me disappeared.

I couldn't breathe.

My feet hit the ground and my surroundings went pitch black. I was blinded by darkness. In a few moments, my eyes adjusted and I realized where I was.

"Brian?" Alice came up next to me.

We were back in the middle of town square in front of the Christmas tree. The smell of pine filled my nostrils again. The lights had been turned off and all of the music had stopped. Darkness. Quiet. The shops had closed. The streets had emptied long ago. Our drinks still sat beneath the bench where we'd left them. Cold.

I felt a chill up my spine and took Alice by the arm. I pulled out my cell, which was conveniently functioning now.

Six missed calls. 2:00 AM. Unlike the previous times when the Saviors had taken us, time hadn't stopped while we had been gone.

Great.

We walked down the block to the parking lot. There were a few cars still in the reserved spots, but my motorcycle was gone.

"Shit!" I looked around. Someone had either stolen it or...

"I'm guessing it was towed," said Alice, pointing to the sign at the end of the lot. It read: No parking after-hours without a permit. All unauthorized vehicles will be towed.

Jesus. Another expense I didn't need, and more to explain. Things couldn't get any worse.

"Mom's going to be really upset," Alice said, swiping the lock screen off her phone. She had eleven missed calls. Most from Jane. Three from Sam.

The buses weren't even running, so I called a taxi. I should have called Jane, but I was too afraid of the assumptions she was probably already making. It'd be easier to explain things to her at the house.

·　　·　　·

We hopped out of the cab and paid the driver.

"Where the hell have you two been?" Jane crossed her arms and glared at me as we meandered up the driveway.

"Mom, we're sorry but—" Alice started.

"I didn't go through all of this trouble to help you, Brian, only to have you disappear half the night with my daughter and not even tell me where the hell you were going!"

"We didn't disappear, Jane. I swear. My bike got impounded and we had to get a cab home."

"And how did *that* happen!?" She narrowed her eyes at Alice.

"Can we come inside first, please?" I asked.

Jane stepped to the side and let us in, then closed and locked the door behind us.

"Explanation. *Now*," she growled.

I took a deep breath. "The three of us—Kareena, Alice and I—we were in Las Vegas."

"What? That's impossible. You weren't gone that long." Alternating looks of horror and confusion passed across Jane's face. "How?"

"Apparently, it isn't impossible," I said, taking out my phone. "We couldn't make any calls. We tried. I swear, we tried."

Alice nodded in agreement. "Our phones weren't working."

We laid both phones out on the table so she could see our message logs.

"With the help of the Saviors," I said, "we apparently can make it to Vegas in seconds. And we did. They teleported us there and it was like we were stuck in some kind of alternate dimension where others couldn't see us or hear us. We were sent there to start others with fluorescence in them—those infected with Savior DNA. There were dozens of them there. We don't know how many more there could be around the country or when they'll move us again. It was unreal, Jane. You have no idea how frightened we were. I thought we were trapped."

Stunned, Jane took a seat at the kitchen table. Her eyes were wide and she was lost in thought—staring off at nothing. Shaking her head.

"It never ends, does it?" she murmured.

I took a seat across from her. "I think it's just begun. The plan they've had for us all along... starts now."

Chapter 14

Four o'clock in the morning. Wide awake. Exhausted yet unable to sleep. Anxious. Frustrated. I couldn't stop thinking about what had happened. Everything we'd seen. All of the lights. Sounds. People. So many infected sleepers. How many more were out there?

I had always taken for granted how much atmosphere a sense of smell conveyed. Without it, surroundings become creepy. Dreamlike. The air tastes thin. Hard to breathe. Bland and stale, like the air in a museum.

Unsettling.

In Vegas, I'd expected the smell of beer and cigarettes to be wafting through the air, to get a whiff of someone's bad cologne or a woman with way too much perfume. Food. Plastic. Sweat. Life. *Anything.* Yet there had been nothing but haunting emptiness. The sensory deprivation had made the entire thing seem like an out-of-body experience.

Alice had been so shaken by it all that she'd refused to be left alone. She'd curled up on the couch next to me and drifted off, her head nestled against a pillow in my lap.

It didn't drain me to heal people the way it did for her to start them. Every touch sucked a little more energy from her and she needed time to recover from the fatigue.

The red scuff mark still colored her forearm. I traced my fingers over it and allowed my azure light time to sink into her skin. The scratch softened and the redness faded.

My first day legally allowed to stay with Jane and Alice and already things had gone to hell. One more week left of school before Christmas break. All I could do was hope the Saviors would keep their hands off us until then—until we could be safe from public places where people might see us vanish.

What if it had happened in school? During class? In the lunchroom? What then? How would we have explained it?

Kareena had been in her room at the time, so it hadn't been a crisis for her. She usually hung out with friends at all hours of the night, so her parents hadn't been overly concerned about her disappearance. But what if she had been out and about like we had? What if she had been... driving?

What if I'd been riding with Alice?

Jesus...

I had to sleep. Even if only for a few hours. I had to put my mind to rest. Worrying wasn't doing anything but making me agitated.

I closed my eyes and leaned back against the couch, placing a hand on Alice's shoulder. My head pulsed, thumping to the rhythm of all the bass music we'd been subjected to. Squeezing my eyes shut couldn't snuff out the blinking fire of millions of lights. The huge spotlight blasting out of the center of that glass pyramid. Animated signs all around.

.   .   .

"So, Alice. You never told me what you wanted for Christmas. It's gonna be here before you know it."

We were standing at her locker between classes. Jane had driven us to school. Neither of us felt comfortable taking the bus after what had happened yesterday. Hopefully, Jane would get my motorcycle out of the impound lot soon. Though I wouldn't have felt comfortable riding it again just yet, either.

"Oh, I don't know, Brian." Alice shoved her English book into her locker and took out Chemistry. "How about a normal life?"

I took her book from her and she shut her locker door and spun the lock.

"I don't think that's an option right now," I said with a shrug. "But I'd make it happen if I could."

"I know. Sorry." She dropped her head down and heaved a sigh. "I'm just tired of this. It's something new every time."

We started walking toward our class.

"Kareena's lucky she's graduating in the summer," I added. "We're stuck here for a few more years. It sucks."

"Yeah."

"Not to mention I'm a little worried about social services coming to check on me in a few months. If I'm not there... *awkward*. You know? We can't even predict this stuff. They just do it whenever."

Alice nodded.

Before we entered our classroom, she stopped and turned toward me. A group of students pushed by and we took a step back from the doorway.

"Thanks," she said.

"For what?"

"Fixing my arm." She brushed her fingertips over where the bloodied scuff had been last night.

"So you noticed?"

"Yes. I went to wash it off this morning and it was gone. Thank you, Brian."

"You don't have to thank me. It's what I'm here for."

She looked up into my eyes, contemplating my words. A tiny smile curled at the corner of her lips and she reached up to run a hand through the hair at the back of my head. The sensation of her warm, slender fingers sliding over my scalp made me sigh.

"I'm glad I have you," she said, and then lifted up off her heels to kiss me. I closed my eyes and lost myself for a brief moment.

"I couldn't do this without you," she whispered.

"And I couldn't do *this* without you, Alice."

She grinned, her eyes narrowing.

"High school, I meant." I motioned toward the classroom.

She laughed and it made me smile.

Chapter 15

New Year's Eve. The party and the countdown to the ball drop had already begun in New York City, with only two hours to go before midnight on the east coast.

Jane hadn't thrown a Christmas party this year. With the whole guardianship thing going on and me staying in the guest room downstairs, she didn't want the hassle. She also didn't want to deal with all of the questions her brother would have about me staying in the same house as the girl I was dating.

Alice sat beside me on the couch, leaning against me while fiddling with the silver dolphin earrings I'd gotten her for Christmas. I had bought them at a local art fair. Little curled dolphins set on posts with a small flower perched on the tips of each of their tails. Elegant, but cute. I would run out of dolphin-themed ideas eventually.

"You guys can stay up until a little past midnight if you want," Jane said, "but then I want you to get to bed." She carried a tray of cookies, crackers, and cheese over to the coffee table. "Okay?" She sat in the recliner next to us and twisted open the bottle of cream soda she'd brought with her. A low hiss sounded from beneath the cap.

I reached out, snagged one of Alice's amazing chocolate chip cookies from the tray, and then sunk my teeth into the warm chocolaty goodness. They were as sweet and delicious as they had been last Christmas.

Junk food and music—a great way to send off our first official year "together." An accomplishment most couples are usually psyched about. We were relieved to know we'd *survived* that long.

Literally.

Sam came out of the kitchen carrying a plate of chips and salsa and I quickly slid my arm off Alice's shoulders. I didn't want to make Sam uncomfortable, seeing how she hadn't been dating anyone recently. No one likes gushy couples. With Jane and Sam there, we didn't have much time to ourselves anyway.

"Who's playing tonight? Anyone I like?" Sam flopped down on the end of the couch and shoved a nacho chip into her mouth. She passed the bowl to Alice, who took a handful of chips and then offered some to me from her cupped hands.

"Some super secret surprise guest. Oh, and they said the Backstreet Boys are getting together for a one-night-only reunion song."

"They never quit, do they?" I laughed. I hadn't even been born yet when they had started hitting it big. I wasn't a fan of their stuff, but Sam had some of their songs on her phone. She had a bunch of '80s songs on there, too. If she'd been born a few decades earlier, she would have fit right in amidst the boom boxes, the outrageous hair and the neon colors.

"Wonder who the special guest will be," Sam said, kicking off her shoes and pulling her feet up onto the couch. She hoarded the chip bowl.

I grabbed another cookie from off the coffee table, took a bite, and winked at Alice. She averted her eyes for a second and shyly smiled back.

The announcer on TV introduced another band—an all-girl group doing a punked-up rock version of a Lady Gaga song. It wasn't bad—had a nice hard rock edge to it—but I didn't like gothy girls with black lipstick and thick eyeliner. Torn skintight jeans and studded silver and black leather vests with frayed collars.

Sam bobbed in her seat and chomped on a mouthful of chips. While everyone was looking away, Alice reached to take my hand and moved in to kiss me. Just as my eyelids squeezed shut, the volume of the music cranked up and the couch disappeared out from under me. My stomach churned and Alice's grasp on me tightened. I sucked in a breath and opened my eyes.

"Alice?" I stumbled forward as a phantom shape shoved into me. Alice's face filled with fear and her eyes darted around.

A heavy bass-thumping version of "Paparazzi" rattled my head, making my ears hurt as the lyrics blasted in stereo. Whiney, breathy vocals saturated the air and electric guitar riffs and drums reverberated beneath my feet.

Alice huddled close to me. I looked up. Huge skyscrapers surrounded us. Bright signs and storefronts glistened in the darkness.

I shivered. White puffs of breath escaped my lips. On the TV, we'd seen people bundled up in heavy jackets with hats. Gloves. Scarves. They'd known what they were doing. It was freaking cold in Times Square.

We weren't dressed for this...

Chapter 16

Shadowy human forms materialized all around us. We could hardly breathe amongst the crowd as we were jostled back and forth.

The punk band finished their performance and everyone went crazy, screaming and cheering, jumping up and down, waving posters and colorful flags. I veered around and saw Kareena, squeezing her way through the crowd to get to us. No one could see her, either.

"I'm freezing!" she squealed, hopping up and down in place while pressing her short plaid skirt down against her thighs. "It's so freaking cold here. What the hell?"

"We're all cold, Kareena," I growled, raising my voice so she could hear me. Alice shivered and I shielded her as best as I could with my arms, pulling her in close. "I don't know what to do right now, but we've got to stay warm. Let's head toward the stores."

"Okay!" Kareena nodded and hugged herself, rubbing her hands up and down her arms briskly and hunching over.

We shuffled through the crowd until we reached an entrance with tall, rotating glass doors. A quick push and they started to move. We darted inside.

The department store had four different floors, glass walkways overhead, and escalators near the entrance. It was nearly empty inside because everyone had crowded into the streets to watch the performances.

It felt comfortable—warmer—and we were able to gather our thoughts for a few minutes. You'd think with all those people shoved together like sardines, body heat would accumulate. It didn't.

"We have to do something," said Alice, groaning and holding herself. "I'm freezing."

"You're freezing?" Kareena sneered. "I'm wearing a freaking skirt. Jesus."

"That's not my fault," Alice grumbled. "You shouldn't be wearing a skirt in winter anyway."

"I was in my house, you little brat! Besides, I can wear whatever the hell I want. It's a lot warmer in—"

"Guys! Please!" I lifted my hands between them. "Stop it! I'll figure something out. Just give me a damn minute. Okay?" I drove my hands through my hair and leaned up against a store display.

"Can we just... take something?" Kareena reached a hand out to stroke her fingers down a black wool jacket hanging nearby.

"No! Don't touch anything!" I pushed her hand away from the rack. "You don't know how it will be affected by us."

"Maybe we should try?" Alice said, shuddering. "We're going to freeze to death out there if we don't at least try to get something to keep warm."

"That's... stealing, though," I stammered. "I don't... I don't want to steal anything. How do we know we won't get caught? Or... I don't know. Damn it!" I shoved my hands into the pockets of my jeans and shook my head. "Just give me a minute. Okay?"

"I've got an idea." Kareena glanced up at a monitor showing feed from a nearby security camera. "Let me try something. I'll be right back."

"Kareena, please." If she'd just give me a freaking minute...

"Guys!"

"What?"

She had slipped a shirt off a nearby rack and was holding it in her hands. Alice and I watched as the security camera reflected the movement of the object.

I panicked, thinking people might see the shirt hanging in midair and freak out. "Put it back before someone..."

"Look!" Kareena shrieked excitedly.

I gazed back up at the camera feed and saw that the shirt had disappeared. But... it was still in her hands.

"We can take things," she said, turning toward me. "It crosses over to where we are and people won't even know we took it."

"That's still stealing."

"Can we maybe pay for it?" Alice asked, rummaging through her pocket. "Shoot. I don't have my wallet."

"Pay for it with what? Invisible credit cards?" I scoffed.

Kareena tossed the shirt onto the floor and we watched the camera footage for a few moments. I held my breath as the shirt materialized on the screen again and a store employee came over to grab the garment from up off the floor. We stepped back a few feet as the woman looked around, puzzled. She shrugged and went back over to her register.

"I want to go home, Brian." Alice huddled close to me and took my arm. "Please? Can't we just grab a few things so we don't freeze out there? They probably won't let us go home until we get this over with. Just like in Vegas." She dropped her head down.

I groaned. "Yeah... I guess. Whatever we need to do. Let's just get out of here as quickly as we can. All of these people are making me nervous. I don't want any of us to get hurt."

By the time I'd gotten the words out, Kareena had already yanked a red leather jacket and a beaded scarf from a nearby display. My eyes darted toward the security monitor. Both items dissolved off screen within seconds. What we were doing was definitely going to weird out the security people later on, but we didn't have a lot of options.

"Just don't take the most expensive stuff, okay? Take what

we need, but nothing else. Kareena!" I stopped her from plucking a rhinestone-studded purse from a counter top and shot her a dirty look. "Only what we need."

Alice took a heavy wool coat from behind a display and shrugged it on. It fit well enough. I grabbed a black one from nearby and did the same.

I checked on Kareena again, who was now thoughtfully deliberating between a knee-length leather car coat, and an ankle-length one. Her mouth was screwed up to the side as she compared them to some gloves she'd grabbed.

"Come on, Kareena. This isn't Fashion 101. Get something that fits and let's get out of here."

"Okay, fine!" She huffed and tugged the knee-length coat off the hanger.

Of course. Too busy worrying about fashion to worry about comfort. It was probably below thirty degrees out and she'd picked out a knee-length coat to wear over a mini skirt.

I shook my head.

"Let's go." I gestured for the two of them to follow. As we approached the rotating doors, I glanced at the security camera video once more. We still weren't visible.

The doors swirled around and popped us back out onto the sidewalk. A narrow walking path wrapped around the shops with large "no stopping" signs posted every few feet. I took Alice's hand and followed the pathway up toward the concert area. Another band started to play. I couldn't distinguish my own heartbeat from the pulsing bass vibrating through the soles of my shoes.

"Alright, Kareena!"

"Yeah?" She raised her voice, too. The crowd had become boisterous again and the music was blaring at us from an insane 360 degrees.

"Let's do this." I motioned for Alice to start taking Kareena's cues and focused on helping her navigate through the crowd without getting crushed.

A person's face when something they can't see shoves them back several feet is something you don't forget. Shock. Surprise. Confusion. They don't know what to do with themselves. Some of them fell back even further and started retreating while others brushed it off and went right back to their excited, inebriated dancing.

.   .   .

Twenty minutes left until the ball dropped.

"Is that everyone?" I asked.

Kareena took a long look around us and then pointed.

"No," she said. "There's someone else over there. I think it's the last person, though. I don't see any others."

Alice followed her lead and we came across a family bundled up in matching bright yellow puffy jackets.

"Which one is it?" Alice asked.

Kareena looked down and a grimace tugged at the side of her mouth. "It's... him." She pointed briefly at the smallest member of the family—a child—and then dropped her hand back to her side.

"The little boy?" Alice's brow furrowed. "You're kidding?"

Kareena shook her head and looked at her feet. "No," she mouthed.

Shit... more kids?

I knew they'd infected Peter, but at the time I had hoped he was an anomaly.

Apparently not. This kid couldn't have been more than three or four years old, tops. Just a little thing all wrapped up in a brightly colored scarf, waving a metallic streamer like his life depended on it.

"I... don't want to touch a kid," Alice whined, backing up and bumping into me.

"Well, just do it quickly and we'll get out of here," Kareena shouted, toppling forward as someone else shoved past.

"No." Alice shook her head and looked up at me with wide, worried eyes.

"Then forget it," I said, shaking my head and moving away. "If we don't start him, what's the worst thing they could do?"

"Leave us here," Kareena yelled over the noise. She was a few feet away now. "I don't want to get stuck here!"

"They won't leave us!" I shouted back. *Hopefully.* "That would be stupid! Screw it. Come on! Let's get out of here." We filed our way back out of the crowd.

An announcement boomed and a series of brightly lit numbers sparked to life on the One Times Square building.

Fifteen minutes to go.

Alice had started well over a hundred people tonight. More than we had in Las Vegas. I'd lost count after the first several dozen.

Our heads hurt from all the noise and I felt sick to my stomach. The ground wouldn't stop shaking. The noises just kept coming, blasting at us. The screaming. The bass. The announcers. Advertisements. Colored lights.

I wanted to leave, but...

"Alice! Let's stay here and watch the ball drop." I tugged on the sleeve of her coat. "Come on, I have an idea. We'll never get the chance again."

We stopped right at the edge of an announcer's platform, a few feet from the large stage where the bands had performed earlier.

"Come on." I climbed onto the platform and helped pull Alice up. I reached out a hand toward Kareena, but she ignored me and climbed up on her own, slipping a few times as she struggled to get a grip through her gloves.

We sat and dangled our feet over the edge of the platform. The announcer sat behind us, oblivious to our presence. Looking up, we had a perfect view of the building and the ball.

"From this point on, there will be no more commercial

breaks," the announcer said after the ten minute mark had passed.

I reached an arm around Alice and pulled her closer. She shivered and rubbed her hands together. She couldn't start people through gloves for some reason, so she had to keep pulling them off every few minutes and putting them back on.

She cupped her hands close to her face and blew hot breaths into them. Kareena pulled her coat tightly closed around herself and brought her knees up to her chest so she could tuck them closer to her body. Flimsy shin-height boots weren't much good against the cold, but they were better than sandals or six-inch heels—her usual preferences.

We sat there for the next few minutes, watching our surroundings. I tried to take in as much of the scenery as possible. We would never be here again. Not like this.

All of the moving I'd done as a kid had made me hate traveling, but I had to admit, getting this close to something so outrageously popular was pretty cool.

Kareena pointed out a nearby cameraman who was infected. Alice reached out and caught his ankle as he made a quick pass by us. The announcer ecstatically notified the crowd of the five minute mark. People went wild. My heart started to beat faster and I didn't even know why. The overwhelming excitement was getting to me.

I held one of Alice's hands in my lap and squeezed her shoulder in closer with my other arm.

I took a deep breath and exhaled a puff of white. I watched the people around us as we sat there and waited. So much energy. So much life.

Then the glowing white-blue ball perched on top of the building began its slow descent. The TV screens plastered atop every surrounding store projected the countdown in sync.

Five.

Four.

Three.

Two.

One.

Loud horns and whistles rang out and rainbow-colored confetti rained down around us. Colored sparkles clouded the air. I could barely see the people anymore. Cheers bellowed from the crowd. People, including the host who stood behind us, hooted and hollered from every direction.

I'd planned on stealing a kiss from Alice when midnight struck, but things had changed. She was pressed up against me, quaking from the cold, and Kareena was hunched over, trying to keep her bare legs from freezing off.

The excitement had ended in what had seemed like the blink of an eye.

I wanted to go home.

We all did.

Chapter 17

Alice never touched the final sleeper in Times Square—the little boy. He and his family left several minutes after midnight. He'd been perched on his father's shoulders, waving his streamer as he was carried through the crowd.

We sat for a while longer, until a group of people began dismantling the stage and announcement platform. People scattered. Some stragglers were still burning their way through miraculous stores of energy. I grew tired watching them bounce around, cheering and kicking at the piles of confetti littering the streets. A large clean-up crew rushed in once the majority of the crowd had cleared.

I hopped off the platform and took Alice by the waist to help her down. Kareena plopped onto the ground beside us and gave me a dirty look. I would have helped her, too... if she had waited.

I knelt down, scooped up a handful of metallic confetti and shoved it into my pocket. Alice and Kareena tugged pieces from their hair.

"What now?" Alice asked, wrapping her arm around mine.

"I don't know. We should get inside. Warm up in case we're stuck here for much longer."

"Yeah. Good idea."

Kareena made a dash toward an open restaurant across the street. We followed her, purposely lagging behind several feet so we could talk.

"Been a crazy night, huh?" I said.

"Yeah."

"I'm glad you're with me, Alice. No matter how crazy things get, I'll be okay if I have you."

We paused in the middle of the street and side-stepped a man sweeping with a wide industrial broom. Alice looked up at me. I flicked a flake of silver paper from above her ear.

"I'm so tired," she said with a groan. "Starting people makes me exhausted. I need to go home."

"I know. And we will. As soon as they—"

"Are you coming or what?" Kareena shouted at us from the doorway of the restaurant.

Alice opened her mouth to respond and then froze, her eyes widening. The pavement beneath me vanished and I covered my ears against Alice's high-pitched scream.

The sudden return of my sense of smell overwhelmed me.

It took a moment to acclimate.

"Alice!" Jane grabbed her daughter's hands and shook her gently. "Alice! You're home."

Sam stood in the hallway, jaw dropped, eyes huge.

"Oh my God!" she shrieked and rushed over. "Are you okay, Alice? Ohmigod! Ohmigod! Ohmigod!"

"She's fine, Sam," I said, putting a hand on Alice's shoulder. "Aren't you?"

Alice looked up. "Yeah."

Being moved between places on earth was jarring as hell. Bright white light didn't blind us and we didn't lose our breath like we did when we were taken to see the Saviors, but the change in atmosphere was always sickening.

"Where were you two?" asked Jane. "You've been gone for hours!"

"You missed the ball drop in Times Square and everything!" Sam shook her head and pointed at the TV.

I reached into my pocket and pulled out some confetti. "No, we didn't," I replied, lifting my hand up in front of Sam and releasing rainbow fragments into the air. They drifted down to the floor.

Jane gasped. "Oh my God! You were in..." She covered her mouth.

"Times Square. Yeah."

Sam perked up. "You were there with—"

"You know the platform he broadcasts from? The one with the big logo on the floor?"

Sam's eyes widened even more.

"We were sitting there, right behind him, watching the ball drop," Alice said.

"Holy cow! You guys were in Times Square on New Year's! Wow!"

"It's not as fun as it sounds, Sam," Alice said with a long face and a tired glance at her friend. "Really. It wasn't. These jackets..."

"I was just about to ask about them," said Jane.

"We... kind of stole them."

"What? No." Jane pulled back. "You didn't! Alice!?"

"Yeah." I flipped over the sleeve of my coat and revealed the magnetic security tab attached at the cuff. "We had to or we would have frozen out there."

"Don't worry, Mom, no one saw us," said Alice.

"But what if they had?" Jane continued. "Then what?"

Alice hunched over, put her head down and tangled her hands together.

"You weren't there, Jane," I raised my voice in Alice's defense. "You don't understand the circumstances."

Jane crossed her arms. "I know, but..."

"No. You don't know!" I shook my head. "You don't know how it feels when we get pulled out of one place and dropped into another. You don't know what it feels like to be trapped in a foreign place where no one can see or hear you but the two people you're trapped with. We wouldn't have done it if we didn't have to."

Jane remained silent for a few moments and then shrugged. "I'm sorry." She frowned. "You're right, Brian. I don't understand, but I'm trying to do the best I can. I'm sorry you have to go through all of this, but please don't get so upset with me. I'm sorry I can't stop all of this from happening to you."

"I need to go to bed, Mom." Alice reached out to touch Jane's arm. "I'm so exhausted I can't stay up any longer."

"What? But there's still a few hours until midnight here," Sam whined. "You're not going to wait up with me?"

Alice had told me how she and Sam spent every New Year's Eve together. How they stayed up until midnight every year and stuffed their faces with junk food, played charades, and acted like goof balls.

That was, until the Saviors changed everything.

"I'm sorry, Sam," Alice said, looking away guiltily. "I *really* need sleep now. I'm burned out. New York City was really cold and crowded. I just want to go to bed, okay?"

"Alright. I'm sorry." Sam reached out to give Alice a hug. "I'll be on the couch if you need anything tonight."

"The couch?" I cocked an eyebrow. "Why the couch?"

"Because you're hogging the guest room, stupid." Sam propped a hand on her hip and shot me a dirty look. "Duh."

True. If I'd only taken a second to actually think about the situation. It seemed kind of wrong to make Sam sleep on the couch, though. It wasn't that comfortable, really. I'd done it before and ended up with aches in places I hadn't realized could hurt. It also felt wrong of me to ask to switch beds with Sam, seeing how I wasn't *her* boyfriend.

"Alice," I said. "Why don't you sleep in my bed downstairs? Then Sam can have yours. I'll sleep on the couch."

Alice shrugged. "Oh, um, okay. Is that okay with you, Sam?"

Sam nodded. "Sure. Whatever."

"Well, I'll see you guys in the morning," said Alice. "I'm going to grab some things from my room and then head to the basement. Goodnight, Mom." She hugged Jane and kissed her on the cheek. Sam hugged her once again for good measure and this time wouldn't let go without a fight.

Then Alice came up to me.

"Goodnight, Brian," she said with a tired, caring little grin. "I love you."

I leaned over and kissed her briefly.

"I love you, too. Sleep well, okay? I'll be here if you need anything." I watched her leave the living room.

Sam heaved a sigh and groaned beneath her breath. "Well, this is no fun anymore. I guess I'll get ready for bed, too. Goodnight, guys. I'll see you all in the morning." She slouched over and meandered toward the staircase.

I felt guilty about the whole thing, even though it wasn't my fault at all.

No one had known this would happen.

No one could have stopped it.

Jane and I remained downstairs.

After several minutes of New Year's Eve coverage from a local station, she picked up the remote, clicked off the TV, and leaned back in her chair.

"Well, now I don't feel like staying up anymore either," she said and then inhaled a deep breath and puffed out her cheeks. "Worrying about you guys wiped me out. I need some rest, too."

"I'm sorry, Jane. And I'm sorry we had to resort to stealing."

"Don't be, Brian. It's not your fault. I realize that." She shook her head. "I wish you guys didn't have to go through this."

"I hope we won't have to deal with it for too much longer," I said, trying to be optimistic.

"Do you need anything else, Brian? I can get you some extra pillows or whatever you want. I know it's not as nice as the bed downstairs, but after everything that's happened... I want to be sure you get some sleep."

She knew I didn't sleep well when things got weird. Last time—after we'd come back from Vegas—I'd hardly slept at all for days. The most I had gotten in one night was the few hours with Alice on the couch, and even that had been near to nothing.

Maybe it wasn't right to ask, but I certainly wasn't about to start sneaking around behind Jane's back. The truth was, everything was easier with Alice beside me.

"What are you afraid of, Jane?" I blurted, as a sudden urge to stop stifling my real feelings won control of my mouth.

"What? What do you mean?"

Alice slipped through the hallway across from the living room and then disappeared down into the basement. I knew she wouldn't be able to hear our conversation from there.

"If... Alice and I... If we stayed in a room together instead of—"

"No." She shook her head violently. "Absolutely not. No. I won't have it. It's wrong."

"What makes you think she and I haven't—"

"Shut up, Brian. Please. Just shut up." She squeezed her eyes closed and turned away from me, biting her lower lip angrily.

"Alice needs someone to protect her. Someone who knows what it's like to have this freaking curse."

"And sleeping with her is going to change that?"

"We're beyond that, Jane. Besides, I'm not asking for your permission..."

"Brian. No! You two aren't married. I'm her mother and I don't have to listen to anything you say. This has nothing to do with keeping Alice safe."

"It has everything to do with keeping Alice safe!" I stood up from the couch and clenched a fist unconsciously. Her eyes went wide at the gesture, and she gasped, offended. "Listen to me, Jane." I lowered my voice and flexed open my fingers. "I know you're worried. I know you're scared for your daughter, but I need to be there. I need to be with her—close."

"Or what?" She shot out of her chair and glared.

I knew I was on thin ice, but I didn't care anymore. Jane couldn't just throw me out. That might expose my fluorescence and, in turn, put her own daughter in danger. Either that, or social services would come asking questions.

I couldn't stop thinking about Alice—about how anxious I became when she wasn't there—when I couldn't grasp her hand. Always on edge. Always alert. It was wearing me thin.

"After we returned from Vegas," I started, "I barely slept at all for days. Every time I tried, I ended up waking in a cold sweat, fearing for Alice—scared to death she might disappear or be hurt in the middle of the night and no one would even notice. I know there's nothing I can do to stop the Saviors, but I need to be able to reach out and know she's still there—that she's safe. She needs me, too. To feel protected."

"I can protect her just fine, Brian!"

"Really? Were you there when she hit the pavement in Las Vegas?"

"What's happened to you?" Jane scowled, narrowing her eyes at me. "Who are you?"

"I'm the exact same person I've been since you met me, Jane. But I'm living a very different life. And so is your daughter."

There was a long awkward silence. Jane took a step back and the look on her face changed into something between confusion and fear. She fell back into her recliner, shaking her head. Her expression softened and her eyes started to water.

"I... I don't want to betray your trust in me, Jane. I'm only trying to be honest."

She remained quiet.

I started to wonder if the next words out of her mouth would be a request for me to go. Somewhere. Anywhere.

Just to get the hell out of her house. To leave her and her daughter alone.

But this was Alice's mother. Not mine.

"I've never had to deal with a situation like this before," she said, looking down at her hands in her lap. "The only thing I have to go on is what I learned from the mistakes I made when I was her age. I never thought I'd be arguing with a sixteen-year-old about how to care for my own daughter."

"I'm not trying to argue. You're a good mother and you've done all you can for her. It's time you trusted someone else with that responsibility for a change."

She fell silent again.

I swallowed hard and watched her consider my words. She looked worried, defeated even. I hadn't been trying to push her to the edge, but I had. I'd only wanted her to understand how I felt.

"And you are absolutely right, Brian." She looked me in the eye. "I can't protect her like this. Not from them. You're the only one she has when they take her. You and that girl, Kareena, who I don't really trust." Tears glistened on her cheeks and she sucked in a muffled breath. "I didn't want to admit it, but I can't protect my own daughter anymore."

"I will."

"I know you will, Brian," she said, sniffling. "And that's what hurts the most. Knowing you'll probably do a better job of keeping her safe than I will." She grabbed a tissue from the box on the coffee table and blew her nose.

I felt a little relief in hearing her finally admit it.

·   ·   ·

Five minutes until midnight.

Jane had gone to sleep a while ago. I lay stretched out on the couch, my head on a stack of pillows that weren't nearly as comfortable as my own, staring at the textured ceiling.

Silence filled the room, until the heater kicked on and the vent in the living room began to rattle.

I pushed up from the couch and headed toward the basement door. My fingers grasped the knob and turned it slowly, so it wouldn't squeak. The stairwell was dimly lit by soft yellow lights along the guardrail. At the base of the stairs, I entered the guest room just off to the side. The door had been left open. Alice was fast asleep on the bed, her fingers wrinkling up the edge of my pillow.

I crept onto the bed and lay down on my side, facing her. She stirred for a moment and then nestled her head against the pillow. I brushed my fingertips over her cheek and her eyes eased open.

"Happy New Year, Alice," I whispered, and leaned over to kiss her. She exhaled a sigh and reached her hand out to stroke the side of my neck.

"Happy New Year, Brian."

A single breath of her scent made my heart flutter. Her warm touch soothed my nerves. There beside her, I felt whole again.

"You should probably go before Mom finds out," Alice added, tickling the back of my neck with her nails. "I wish you could stay."

"Don't worry about that, Alice. Just get some sleep," I said, tugging the blanket up so it would cover her bare shoulder. I brushed her hair to the side and kissed her forehead. "I'll be here."

Chapter 18

First awake. First into the kitchen in the morning. I flipped the switch on the electric kettle and removed a few mugs from the cupboard, careful not to clink them together.

Sam came wandering in shortly after, her fluffy teal slippers scuffing against the linoleum.

"Hey. Good morning, Sam." I opened up the refrigerator and took out a carton of eggs. I slid a loaf of bread off the counter and reached for a mixing bowl.

"Any special requests before I start anything?" I asked and gestured toward the cupboard behind her. "Can you grab me the cooking oil out of there, please?"

She shuffled through the cupboard and passed the jug of canola oil to me.

"No," she replied with a shrug. "Not really. Mind if I hang out and watch?"

"No. Though, actually, I'll need you to go knock on Jane's door in a bit and see if she's up. I'll wake Alice in a little while if she doesn't come up here on her own. That girl hibernates like a bear." A wonderfully cuddly soft teddy bear. I grinned to myself as I cracked an egg on the side of the bowl. From the corner of my eye, I saw Sam anxiously twisting the hem of her shirt around her fingers. I dropped the eggshell into the trash and reached for another egg from the carton.

"What is it?" I asked.

"I wasn't really *trying* to pry," she replied in a hushed tone, "but I sort of heard you guys arguing last night. You and Jane."

"Oh? Well, please don't tell Alice, okay? It was nothing and—"

"I won't." She shook her head. "Besides, she's right. I mean... you're right." She leaned against the counter. "Only you can protect Allie now. None of us can. Not if those freaks up there keep jerking you guys away from us. We're kinda helpless, but I'm glad she's not alone."

"Thanks, Sam. Thanks for understanding, too." I tugged open a drawer, pulled out a fork and started whisking the eggs.

"Just... don't hurt her, okay?" Sam added.

I paused and turned to look her in the eye.

"She loves you a lot," she continued. "I don't want her to get a broken heart. I may not be there to comfort her."

"She won't. Trust me, Sam." I went back to stirring the eggs. They melded into a bright yellow-orange color. "I've never been so sure about anything in my entire life. I'll do everything I can to make sure she doesn't get hurt by anyone or anything—including myself."

"Thanks, Brian." Sam came over and pressed her fingers gently against my forearm. "You *are* a good guy. I get what she sees in you."

I chuckled lightly and smirked. "I sort of recall you having some kind of thing for me, too, when I first started going to your school."

Sam's eyes widened and her cheeks flushed pink. "Um... back then? Well, that was a while ago. Like, ages ago. I... don't really..."

"It's alright, Sam. I'm just being stupid. Trying to lighten the mood, that's all. Apparently I suck at that."

She cracked a smile and I kind of felt like an ass for embarrassing her.

I pulled a stick of butter from the fridge.

"Grab me the large frying pan from out of the cupboard below the counter, please. And then would you mind going to see if Jane's up yet?"

Sam rummaged around for the pan, making more noise than an elephant in a china shop. Pans banged and clanged against each other, making me grimace. If Jane and Alice hadn't been awake before...

Finally, Sam stretched out an arm and offered the pan to me. I heard Jane's bedroom door creak open and took that as my cue to go wake Alice.

.   .   .

I shoveled the last piece of French toast into my mouth, the room so quiet I could hear myself chewing. Silverware clinking. Tea being sipped.

Last night had shaken all of us.

I wanted to have a word with the Saviors, but it wasn't like we could pick and choose when to talk to them. They only brought us up there when *they* had something to say. We hadn't seen them for months. Not since the baby had been taken away.

They just worked their sick magic on us and forced us to do their dirty work. I was tired of it. Tired of how they were treating Alice, especially. The excursions left her burned out and depressed. How many more would there be?

"I think we should stop," I said, breaking the silence.

Alice looked up at me from her plate. Sam shoveled another forkful of scrambled eggs into her mouth. Jane took a sip of her tea and focused on me.

"Stop what?" Alice asked, laying her fork down on the napkin beside her plate. She'd eaten most of her food—more than she'd eaten in a while.

"Whatever it is they want us to do—the Saviors. I think we should stop. Then they'll have no choice but to talk to us again. Right?"

Alice shrugged.

"You don't want to upset them," said Jane. "We don't

know what they're capable of."

"I'd like to think they aren't violent," I said. "We don't know for sure yet, but it's worth a shot to tell them no. We don't want to be their guinea pigs anymore. They've gotta have more than enough people by now. We must have touched a few hundred. I say next time we get sent somewhere, let's not start anyone, and we'll see if that doesn't provoke them into making some kind of move. If they're as docile as I'm hoping they are, maybe it will do us some good to stand up to them."

I looked at Alice for a response, but she stared down at her empty plate.

"Alice?"

"Whatever it takes to get them to leave us alone," she muttered. "I don't care either way. I just want to get this over with. Maybe if we help them, they'll eventually stop bothering us and we can get back to our normal lives."

"What about the baby? Is that going to be our *normal life* in a few years? If we have to raise that child, that's eighteen years at least—not that our kid wouldn't be worth living for, but no matter what we do, we're going to be plagued by this for the rest of our lives."

"I get what you're saying, Brian." Alice looked up. "But I don't want to start trouble."

"They're the ones who started trouble," I growled. "First with your mom and who knows how many others by now. And then with us. Having the audacity to force us into having a child. Now we have to steal things to get by because they don't even give us any warning before they whisk us away to these random places. As far as I'm concerned, the Saviors have crossed the line, and I'm not going to deal with it anymore."

"Maybe Brian's right," Sam said, putting down her fork and looking over at Alice. "Maybe if you stop doing what they want you to do, they won't want you anymore."

"Maybe." Alice heaved a sigh. "But what if they choose

others instead—maybe kids even younger than us—and the cycle continues? I don't want to be responsible for that."

"You already are, Alice," I said. "You've been starting people you don't even know. Who knows the consequences of widespread infection? We don't even know what this fluorescence is going to do to *us* in the long run, let alone hundreds of people and their descendants."

"Guys." Jane lifted her hand. "Please. Do whatever you have to to get home in one piece, okay? I can't lose my daughter. And I don't want to lose you either, Brian. We need to be cautious of the decisions we make from this point on. Even so, we obviously don't have the technological capabilities to compete with what the Saviors have, and there's a possibility you could get hurt if you disobey."

"I told you before, Jane, that I'll protect Alice at any cost, and I meant it."

· · ·

Sam went home after lunch.

"Any plans for the rest of the day?" Jane asked, sliding our plates into the dishwasher rack. She washed her hands in the sink and dried them on a kitchen towel.

"Not really." I shrugged.

"Alright. I'll be in the living room if you need me." She left the kitchen.

I'd wanted to focus on my comic during Christmas break, but the stress from recent events had given me major artist's block. Drawing usually helped me focus and kept me centered. *Usually*. It had been several weeks, but I hadn't been able to finish my most recent panels from Staggered Hart.

"Be right back," I said to Alice, and excused myself to dart downstairs and grab the leather journal she'd given me last Christmas. This year, she and Jane had teamed up to buy me a set of inking pens—a graphic novelist's best friend.

Learning how to feather and cross-hatch properly with the inks would take time, but I had to start at some point.

I jogged back upstairs and took a seat at the kitchen table. Alice sat beside me and rested her head on my shoulder as I riffled back and forth between unfinished sketches and full penciled panels.

If it hadn't been for Alice, I would never have pushed myself to improve throughout the year. Since we'd become friends, she's been my muse. I'd finished the first comic in the series because she'd convinced me to believe in my dream of becoming a graphic novelist. Before her, I'd only had a messy book of half-sketches and an incoherent storyline.

Now, I had *something*. Something great. Something tangible.

"Are you going to ink and color these once you learn how? And then maybe... try to get it published?" Alice stared at me, admiration shimmering in her eyes.

"Maybe. But I'm probably not good enough. I've got a long way to go. I should probably be learning other, more valuable life skills, but I just can't stop drawing. It's who I am."

Stress and fatigue had left me weak—susceptible to the debilitating disease that is self-doubt—an artist's worst enemy. An art killer. But how do you make good art when you've got alien DNA pumping through your veins, changing the way you live?

"Don't you want to do more with your life, Brian? Really go places?"

"Yeah, but I don't know anything. I'm an artist. I just draw shit."

"You don't draw shit." Alice stopped, realizing what she'd said, and then let out a nervous chuckle. I laughed, too. "What I meant to say was, your art is amazing. I saw that even before we had started dating, and you've improved so much since then. You've completed your first comic. You're talented and I know you've got potential. You just have to keep your chin up. Keep trying and keep pushing forward no matter what."

"Even if aliens keep screwing with my life?"

"Yes. Even if aliens keep screwing with *our* life, Brian."

Chapter 19

New Year's Eve replayed in my mind each night as I tried to sleep, clear as day—nearly touchable—like a vivid dream. Keeping me awake. Impossible. Unbelievable. But real. I almost didn't believe it had happened, but four other people could vouch for my sanity.

We returned to school Monday, more fatigued and less motivated than we had been before the holiday break. Classes seemed longer and teachers' monologues drier than before. Plus, the ongoing threat of being abruptly sucked from this safe familiarity and thrown into a loud, foreign city was a total buzz kill.

I tucked my drawing pad into the crease of my English book and pretended to read along with the teacher and take notes. In reality, I was plotting the next installment of my graphic novel.

Marcus Velour—AKA the Hart—had decided to remain within the grey area between crime fighting and crime. He helped those in need, stopped assaults on innocents, and intercepted robberies, but all the while pocketing a few rewards for himself here and there. He justified the thievery by calling it "payment" for all of the good he'd done in the city. A sort of Robin Hood vigilante.

There were moments I had while creating art when I'd see myself bleeding through the lines as I drew—my own experience breathing life into Marcus. The curse of being an artist is that your art is often a reflection of yourself.

Jane had made us anonymously mail everything we'd taken on New Year's Eve back to the store. It took a weight off my shoulders, though I could have used the new coat and the store wouldn't have missed it. But it made Jane and Alice feel better.

Hell, my own mother wouldn't have even noticed the new jacket. Always in her own little world—the one without me in it. Still, as much as I hated what she'd done to me, I couldn't help but think of her once in a while. Mostly while having dinner with Alice and her mother. Dinner as a family— something I hadn't had in years.

After the holiday, I'd tried to check in on my mother at the mental institution, but hit nothing but road blocks. I called several people, including social services, but everyone shut me out.

By law, they weren't able to disclose her health information to me. Ever since the guardianship transfer had gone through, she was not legally allowed to contact me either. Child services had deemed her unfit to care for me, and therefore she'd been slapped with a restraining order on top of being put away for rehab.

It sucked, but she'd earned it.

Half of me wanted to know she was getting better—that she would recover and move on with her life without me. That someday, she would drag herself out of the mud and find a true purpose in life.

The other half of me didn't give a shit.

·   ·   ·

A bicyclist buzzed past us on the sidewalk as we walked home from school. I reached out and pulled Alice toward me and out of the way of the next bike zooming up from behind. *College kids.* In too much of a hurry to use the bike lane like they were supposed to.

We passed the little coffee shop she and Sam used to frequent and paused to look in. Leftover specks of artificial snow freckled the corners of the glass.

We stood there and contemplated going in for a drink. I eyed the entrance, memories of sugary indulgences past pressuring me to give in. The phantom taste of sweet hot cocoa and whipped cream made my mouth water.

I took a step toward the door, lifting my arm to push the handle. It opened a crack, but wouldn't budge any farther, as if someone was forcing it closed. Keeping me back. The bell hanging on the inside of the glass began to jingle. A slow, drawn-out hum hung in the air, as if the sound had been paused mid-ring, the clatter of metal bouncing against glass softened by the sudden halt of time.

Then we fell into a chasm of blinding white light.

We touched down on solid ground, and the stale, thin air made my lungs feel like they were being squeezed. Alice was still beside me, but Kareena was nowhere to be seen.

Only us?

"It has been some time since we have spoken," said the translator, looking down at me with emotionless eyes. "There are things we need to discuss. It seems not all of those you were meant to start have been activated."

"I don't know what you're talking about," I replied before Alice could speak.

"The little boy you were housed with—Peter, we believe his name is. Alice did not start him. There was another incident recorded on the thirty-first of December. Another child overlooked. This is unacceptable. We must have all of the marked ones started."

"It was an accident," I lied as well as I could. "But even so, it shouldn't matter. You asked us to help you and we have. But we don't have to do everything you tell us."

"Yes, you must," the translator said with a faint sneer rising in his voice. An expression he'd probably learned from

Kareena. "We require them all. Every one of them."

"But I don't want to." Alice looked up into his grey eyes. "I don't want to start children, please. We don't know how it will affect them. I'm scared it might—"

"It is none of your concern." The Savior tilted his head at her. "We did not ask you to choose for us. We have already made our selections. We have confirmed that your Seeker located each of the sleeping ones, but you two collectively conspired against us and refused to start them. There is no excuse for this behavior."

"It's not right!" I said, pulling Alice behind me. "Why should we trust you with children? Why should we trust you at all? We don't know how it will affect them and you haven't even told us a thing about your 'cause'—whatever the hell it is. We don't want to be responsible for—"

"Give her back," Alice said quietly, taking a step out from behind me.

"What?" The translator stared, unmoved. "Repeat your words."

Alice cleared her throat. "Give her—our baby—back." She swallowed hard.

"Alice, what are you saying?" I grabbed her by the wrist. "Alice?"

"We'll make it work." She shot a desperate glare my way. "We can. Mom will help us. We can make it work. I know we can."

The translator drew nearer and looked down his nose at Alice. "You previously complained of age restrictions. You are not yet eighteen. Why do you want the responsibility back now?"

"Yeah, Alice, why now?" I tried not to hold her wrist too tightly, but I was trembling with budding fears. We didn't need the baby. *Not right now.*

"You mentioned before something about it being danger-ous to travel while carrying her. What if I take her back...

and you let us stop doing this for a while? Then I won't have to start anyone else. You said you needed her, too—that our child could be the key to finding a cure. Now you won't have to wait as long. Please consider it."

"It is a tempting offer, yes," the Savior said, nodding slightly. He turned and looked at the lineup of other Saviors observing us from behind him. They were easier than usual for us to see. The unusually thin grey haze made them appear only slightly out of focus today.

He turned back toward us and avoided eye contact. "It cannot be done," he said flatly.

"Why not?" Alice asked.

"It is complicated," he replied. "We will require more time and…" He stopped.

"And… what?" I prodded, suspicion tainting my voice.

"And we would require another fetus."

Alice gasped.

"What? What do you mean?" I took a step closer. "Why would you need a second one?"

"We underestimated the capabilities of the disease that plagues our kind. Exposure was inevitable, but we were certain it would not be a problem. However, the disease was very strong and the fetus too weak to resist. It perished."

"No," Alice murmured beneath her breath.

"No!" I clenched my fists. "You son-of-a-bitch," I hissed. "How long have you known about this!? When were you going to tell us?"

"She's dead?" Alice whispered, tugging on my sleeve, her bright blue irises shimmering with fear. "Our baby is…?"

"An unintentional casualty," the translator interrupted. "That is all."

"You bastards!" I lunged at him.

White hot light burned my retinas and a jolt of pain shot through me. I slammed into the sidewalk in front of the café and let out a howl. A humming noise rattled my brain. My hand stung with the bloody scuff across my knuckles.

"Brian!" Alice helped me up off the ground and sheltered my arm with her body so no one would see the glow. A little girl with huge eyes plastered her face against the café window and stared out at me.

"I was right, Alice. They're nothing but goddamn liars." I tucked my arm beneath the flap of my overshirt and quivered as the fiery pain tore through me. Hitting the concrete had skinned nearly my entire forearm raw.

"I'm not giving in to them anymore. We aren't doing anything for them." My blue light began working its magic. The skin started to stretch and reform over the wound. "Let's get out of here." I wiped the residual blood onto my jeans and we fast-walked away from the scene. Didn't need people freaking out about the bloody stain I'd left on the pavement.

"If they send us somewhere again," I said through gritted teeth, "we won't do anything. Okay? We'll stay still and wait it out. They can't keep us there forever."

"But, what if they do?" Alice sighed. "What then?"

"They won't." I tried to make a fist but it hurt.

Hopefully... They won't.

Chapter 20

"Brian!?" Jane turned off the kitchen faucet and came rushing toward us. She took hold of my arm and her widened eyes scanned it, up and down, taking in the dried blood.

"It's nothing," I replied, tugging away from her. "I'll be fine. It healed."

"Oh, thank God. What happened?"

"We had a little talk with the Saviors," I said. "And I didn't like what I heard." I went over to the sink and twisted on the faucet, leaving rusty red fingerprints on the chrome. Warm water poured over my hands and I lowered my forearm beneath the spout. "They told us we weren't doing our job—that we had to start every single 'marked' person. Even children." Crimson water swirled down the drain. I turned off the water and then grabbed some paper towels to dry my hands.

"Jesus, I wish they'd just leave you two alone!" Jane quickly checked Alice's hands for blood.

"I'm fine, Mom." Alice pulled away and took a seat at the kitchen table. She dropped her head down. "There's more," she muttered.

I took a deep breath and came up beside Alice. "Yeah," I said, putting a hand onto her shoulder. She was quaking. The green light ignited beneath my hand. Warm, faint jolts of static energy pulsed through my fingertips. "They..." I cleared my throat, but a lump formed. I choked on the words. "The bastards killed our baby."

Jane gasped, staggering back against the kitchen counter.

She bumped into a glass and it toppled over, splashing water everywhere. I lunged for the nearby hand towel and passed it to her before too much dripped onto the floor.

"She caught whatever disease is killing them and..." The skin of my face felt taut and warm. I cleared my throat again. "She... died. They weren't even going to tell us." I swallowed hard and fought back against the sadness creeping through me, tightening my throat. The next few breaths were difficult, as if an iron weight was pressing against my chest.

Be strong for Alice, I kept telling myself.

"They killed her? Why would they let that happen? How? I thought they were more competent than that... that they knew what they were doing. I mean..." Jane's voice broke. "I understand you didn't really want a baby right now but... for them to just let her die. Oh, dear God." She covered her mouth and shook her head. "They're monsters."

"I know." I pulled a seat out beside Alice and sat down. "And we're not doing another damn thing for them ever again. They don't give a damn about us. They don't care at all about how we feel about any of this."

Alice took my hand and stared up into my eyes, her lower lip quivering.

"If they want their dirty work done, they can get someone else to do it," I said. "Screw them. All of this crap we've been through for them, and they've not done a single thing for us in return."

"They fixed you," Alice said, placing her trembling palm on my chest. "Your heart, I mean."

"Surely we've paid them back enough for that by now. The baby. All of those people we started. Damn. I'll take the pacemaker back if I have to."

"Don't say that. You don't mean it!"

She was right.

I didn't want it back.

I'd never felt so free and alive as I had since the night

my fluorescence healed my heart. My body worked the way it was meant to and I didn't have to fear for my life every time I got hyped up about something. But then, I had other things to be grateful for. I wouldn't have Jane without the Saviors. I wouldn't have had the freedom or the ability to stay with Alice.

I'd still have my mother and all the close-minded skepticism she brought with her.

I wouldn't have shit worth living for.

"Do you wanna go somewhere, Alice?" I stood up and reached out a hand for hers. "For a ride. We can go to the beach or whatever. Anywhere. Just to get some air?"

"I-I guess. Sure."

"Jane? Is it okay?"

"I suppose." She shrugged. "But don't you have to work tonight?"

"I've got a few hours before I need to be in. It will be okay." I intertwined my fingers with Alice's and we headed toward the garage.

I shrugged on my jacket and got on my motorcycle.

"Your helmet, Brian?" Alice held it out to me.

I'd deliberately left it on the nearby shelf.

I shook my head. "I don't need it. I'll be fine."

I'd heal if...

"What? But..."

"I'll be alright, Alice. Don't worry."

She came around to the front of the bike and set the helmet on the handlebars.

"No. It's not okay, Brian," she said, her stern gaze cutting a hole straight through me. "I love you and I won't let you get hurt because you're being a jerk about what happened earlier. I know you're angry and upset, but so am I. It's no reason to be self-destructive." She crossed her arms and looked away. "Take it. Or I won't go with you."

"Okay. Okay." I shoved my helmet on, feeling like a total

ass. The one time I try to rebel...

"Thanks." She straddled the bike behind me. "I can't lose you, Brian," she said, leaning forward to hug me. "I just can't."

"I know, Alice." I flipped the starter button and the engine rumbled beneath us. "I know."

. . .

"What do you think they'll do if we quit starting people?" she asked, holding tightly to my hand as we walked along the shoreline. Rolling waves of sea foam tumbled toward us, narrowly missing our shoes.

"I don't know. But I'm not afraid of them. Someone needs to stand up to them so they'll learn not to mess with us."

"I'm scared." She stopped and tugged on my arm. Bright tangerine-colored sunlight reflected off her eyes.

"Don't be." I smiled and kissed her. "You have me."

She closed her eyes and sighed.

We walked further down along the shoreline until we found a quiet place to stop. I lay back against the sand and filled my lungs with cool salty air. Alice rested her head against my outstretched arm, nestling close to me.

It was harder than ever to clear my head. So many things I couldn't change even though I wanted to. We were teenagers, but we had to act like adults now. We had to think that way, or we'd never find our way through this mess. We'd never make the right decisions.

So much static. So much anger bubbling up inside.

The thought of them killing our child made my heart hurt. I tried to not let it eat at me, but I was crumbling inside. They had destroyed a part of us, and that I couldn't ignore.

"Did you want her?" I asked, my fingers slipping beneath the hem of Alice's shirt to caress the soft skin of her abdomen.

She closed her eyes.

"I don't know," she said softly. "I didn't—when all this first began and I wasn't mentally prepared—but then I started to accept the possibility of it all and... now that she's gone, I feel kind of, well..."

"Me too."

I pulled Alice a little closer. She wrinkled my shirt with her fingers.

"Maybe when all of this over with and things are better..."

"When will things be better?" she asked, lifting her head abruptly. "What if they never get better?" She sat up and pulled her knees to her chest, a stifled whimper sounding from her throat.

"I don't know," I replied, coming up beside her. "Maybe they will or, damn it, maybe they won't." I tucked a hand into one of my jean pockets and rummaged around. I felt the cool touch of metal and closed my fingers around it. "But that won't stop us from living—from being who we were meant to be. We have to move forward with our lives, Alice. We can't let the Saviors hold us back."

I took her hand and turned it over, palm up.

"We work well together." I pressed my closed hand gently into hers. "We'll make our own choices."

My fingers unfolded and the ring released into her hand.

"I was going to wait to give this to you, but why bother? There's no difference between one day and another anymore. They blur together. They come and go. Like dreams."

She cupped her hand and examined the ring. Light glistened off the delicate s-shaped swirls of gold embracing the silver band. In the center, the curls came together to cradle a small sparkling white diamond.

"Consider it a promise," I said. "A promise to someday ask you the question that already burns in me every night."

"It's beautiful." She grinned.

My heartbeat quickened as she slid it onto her left ring

finger. It fit perfectly, thanks to Jane's help.

Alice reached her arms out and hugged me more tightly than ever. "Don't ever break your promise," she uttered, her face nuzzling my chest.

Such warmth against me. Her sweet scent mingling with the ocean breeze was perfect—unforgettable. I ran a hand through her satiny hair.

But our happiness was bittersweet, and the weight of reality quickly dragged me back down. Fear. Uncertainty. Things could change at *any* moment.

"I love you, Alice," I said, taking her hand into mine and brushing my thumb across the ring. "I'd do anything for you. Anything at all. You know that, right?" The subtle shade of pink in her cheeks looked stunning beneath the warm hues of sunset.

"Yes. I do, Brian." She averted her eyes. "And sometimes knowing that scares me."

"Why?"

"I worry about you getting hurt. I mean... you didn't even want to take your helmet with you today."

"Maybe that was a naive thing to do, but I'm not stupid, Alice. Still, I'd be lying if I said I wouldn't take a bullet for you."

She fell silent.

"Alice?" I pressed my fingers to her chin and tipped her face up toward mine. "Don't feel bad. And don't feel sorry for me, either. Remember, I'm the one who heals. I *could* take that bullet if I had to."

Chapter 21

I had to be at work in an hour. Hardly enough time to change and head back out, but now wasn't the time to worry. I squeezed the rubber grips and focused on the road. Car engines rumbled all around us. Alice tucked her hands into my jacket pockets.

Someday, I'd buy her an even better ring.

One that was more...

Our surroundings blurred.

Shit!

My wheels locked and I went flying headfirst over the handlebars, straight toward the rear window of a white SUV.

Street signs softened out of focus. Speeding cars slowed to a crawl. Alice drifted behind me, caught in mid-air over the asphalt. We tried to reach out to each other, but just seconds later we came slamming back down onto the ground. The thud of my helmet hitting asphalt made my ears ring. I came to my knees and shook my head, disoriented.

Alice cried out in pain. I scrambled to my feet.

"My hands!" she shrieked, holding out her arms.

"I'm here." I slid off my helmet, tossed it aside, and then carefully removed hers. It was dark as hell and I could barely see. Only faint moonlight and a few buzzing, flickering street-lamps loomed overhead. Alice's palms had been scuffed raw, muscle tissue showing through in patches of shiny, open skin. I tugged off my gloves and then took her hands into my own, her warm blood seeping through my fingers.

"It hurts," she whined, squirming and tugging for me to

release her. "Let me go, Brian!"

"I know it hurts, but you have to calm down," I said. "Just breathe in and out. Slowly. I'll heal you, but you have to give me a minute. I'm trying."

She gritted her teeth and groaned, stifling a moan with each shallow exhale.

"Just breathe." I cupped her trembling hands and concentrated on the wounds—on the peels of supple white flesh curling up around them. Fresh blood drizzled down my palms. Alice sobbed and sucked in a congested breath.

Blue fluorescence started to appear, radiating from deep beneath my skin at first and then quickly rising up and skittering across veins near the surface. The open patches on her palms began to smooth over with fresh skin. The wounds eased closed.

"Better?" I asked, examining her hands as well as I could in the darkness. They felt smooth and intact again.

"Yes. Thank you."

Water dripped into my ear and I shook my head. Cold droplets of rain fell on the back of my neck.

"Damn it! Rain?" I couldn't recognize where we were, but as usual, the air tasted stale and bland. I looked around. Empty streets, abandoned storefronts. Dim alleyways. I couldn't see much in the distance. It was lit only by beat-up streetlamps shuddering on and off. "We need to find shelter."

A clap of thunder rumbled and, seconds later, a white line of lightning bolted across the sky, highlighting our surroundings for an instant.

"Where are we?" Alice asked. She rubbed her arms briskly. Her teeth chattered and she took short breaths through her mouth.

"I don't know, but we need to find Kareena and get the hell out of here before we get hypothermia from this goddamn rain. Let's get moving."

We pushed forward down the street until we came to a

crossing with signs posted. Brent Street. Briar Lane.

Where in hell?

We kept walking, sticking close to the sidewalk and the meager overhang that stretched out over the doors along the strip of abandoned shop buildings. Graffiti. Broken windows. I took a step and heard a crunch beneath my shoe. Glass. The crackling sound sent a shiver up my spine.

Maybe it was the rain. The damn cold rain. It kept coming, pouring down, making it hard to see.

Never-ending.

No sign of Kareena.

"Do you think she's here?" Alice asked with a shudder, holding the collar of her jacket tightly closed at her throat.

"Maybe. I don't know. I don't even know where we are." The rain clattered against the rooftops and down the gutters, sputtering out toward our feet. I stepped over a rush from a downspout and turned to make sure Alice got across okay, too.

We fast-walked another two blocks in the shadows before the rain slowed and we could finally get our bearings... or at least try. Very little had been marked in this whole place. The broken shop windows were old. What signage we had found had most of the lettering worn off. Wherever we were, it hadn't been inhabited for years.

We found a broken-down pick-up truck with rusted out sides and checked the license plate. Michigan. Just on the other side of the street was another torn up convertible with what looked like... gunshot holes riddling the door. The leather seats had been destroyed. Steering wheel removed. No license plate.

My shoes squelched with every step. I brushed a hand through my hair to slick it back. My jeans dripped. My soaked shirt stuck to me beneath my jacket. I felt disgusting. I tried my cell phone in vain. It wouldn't turn on.

Of course.

"Where in the hell are we?" I thought out loud. "What kind of ghetto is this? There's no one here. Why would they send us here? What could they possibly—"

"Brian!"

An unmistakable high-pitched voice sounded from the distance.

"Kareena!" Alice and I said in unison, glancing at each other.

"Kareena!" I called back again.

We heard voices. People arguing.

Thunder rumbled and the sounds were muffled.

Then Kareena called out again.

I took Alice's hand and we ran toward the sound.

Down another street corner. Past an abandoned garage. Past a mountain of busted up car parts. Lightning struck again and the sky lit up white. A tall chain-link fence blocked our way.

"Damn it!" I shoved my hands against the cold metal and pulled back. Further down, curls of broken wires sagged toward the ground. Places where links had been cut or rusted.

I searched along the fence until I finally came across an opening large enough for us to squeeze through.

"Be careful, Alice," I said, carefully prying back a section of wire. She ducked down through the tear and came out the other side. I followed.

"Help!" Kareena shrieked. Her voice was closer now.

We hurried toward the sound. Down a dark alleyway. A sharp turn around a corner. There she was—beneath a bright blue-white streetlight—being restrained by someone. Hot pink fluorescence flowed beneath the skin of her face.

"Get... your hands... off me!" Kareena screamed, straining her voice. She struggled and tried to wriggle free. One of her arms had been pulled tightly behind her back and the stranger had his other arm hooked around her neck.

"Let her go!" I yelled, shielding my eyes from more drizzle

while trying to make out the face of whoever held Kareena.

"Let go, you bastard!" she moaned, grunting and jerking her body around. He twisted her arm further back behind her and she yelped in pain.

"Who are you?" I took a step closer to them and was able to make him out a little more. Dark skinned. Black hair, maybe. Tall. A little muscular, but not enough to intimidate me. I couldn't tell much else.

"You're here," he said, and then shoved Kareena to the ground. She coughed hard and held her throat. "Took your sweet-ass time. Didn't you?"

"What do you want from us?" I asked, raising my voice against the booming thunder.

"I'm here to make sure you do your job," he replied, his voice low and gritty. "And I'll break you one at a time if I have to."

He shot a glare toward Alice.

"Don't you dare touch her!" I roared, stepping in front of her.

"He's one of us!" Kareena said, struggling to catch her breath. "I... saw it... inside him."

"What? What do you mean he's one of *us*?" I locked eyes with the man and took another step toward him. I could see now he was older than me, but not by much. Probably in his late twenties.

"Who are you?" I asked again, wiping the rain from my brow.

"We have to help her!" Alice pushed past me and ran to Kareena's side. The man lunged for Alice and caught her by the wrist. He twisted her arm back behind her and she wailed in pain.

"Alice!" I bolted at him, fist first.

Contact! He reeled backward. My knuckles ached from the impact, but the sight of that bastard tumbling to the ground and holding his face made it worth it. I rotated my wrist. Shook it out.

"Are you okay, Alice?"

She quickly helped Kareena to her feet and then came running to me. We huddled together and backed away.

"Yes. Thank you," she replied, and then gasped. "He's up!"

"You little son-of-a-bitch!" The man came to his feet, his lips curled into a nasty sneer. His eyes were hidden in shadow. Lighting struck and a glimmer of light reflected off the blood drizzling down his cheek. He swiped his fingers across his face and huffed.

"You'll pay for that." He clenched his fists and rolled his shoulders back.

"You don't scare me," I growled, gesturing for the girls to back up.

He chuckled. "I don't have to take shit from you kids. I told you, I'm here to make sure you do your job."

Amber light sparked across his chest, emanating through his shirt, beginning around his sternum and then forking up across his collar bone toward his shoulders.

Jesus. He *was* one of us.

I froze in place and locked on to him.

He stretched an arm toward me and flattened his hand, spreading out his fingers and pointing his open palm at me. The gold light skittered through his body, illuminating his arms and hands all the way down to his fingertips. Veins of fluorescence flickered beneath his skin.

I took a step back and swallowed hard. His fluorescence appeared brighter than any of ours.

"What did the Saviors say to get you to come after us?" I asked. "Did they make you some kind of promise? Well, they won't keep it! They're lying bastards. They'll never—" An invisible jolt of energy shot through me like a punch to the gut. I lost my breath. My knees hit the ground. I hunched over, digging my hands into gravel and earth. Straining to suck in air.

Nothing came in. I wheezed. Tightness closing my throat. *Shit...*

The energy pulse shook me to the bone, squeezing my chest tight and crushing my lungs and heart. I couldn't breathe.

Alice came to my side, shouting things I couldn't make out. Pressure built in my ears. Ringing. Then a dull buzz deafened me.

My head ached.

I doubled over. Unable to comprehend the muffled words I was hearing.

Finally, my blue light sparked to life. The color grew bright and hot, leeching through my skin like plumes of dry ice fog. The pain subsided. Slightly.

"You're a freaking coward!" I shouted as soon as I gained the strength to lift my head. "That's all you are. You can't trust the Saviors. They're liars."

"Enough!" His light grew even brighter, jagged veins blazing like yellow fire within his chest. It hadn't even physically touched me, and yet, I could feel its energy, sucking the strength right out of me.

A tingling sensation washed over me and my vision blurred.

I felt lightheaded.

I gritted my teeth hard. Bright splashes of color flashed across my field of vision, distorting my surroundings. Blackness. In and out. Fading spirals of light.

"Brian!" Alice put her hand on my shoulder. "Brian. Please. Come back to me."

I strained to pull myself upright, but I couldn't focus. My head felt heavy. Everything around me was spinning. Light flashed through my arm, the color a more potent blue than I'd ever seen before.

I wiped my face with the back of my hand.

Warm. Crimson.

A nose bleed!?

I hadn't even taken a damn hit.

"Are you okay?" Alice brushed my wet hair out of my face and wiped the rain from my forehead.

"Yeah," I said, wiping my mouth again. Tasting iron.

Lightning flashed. The back of my hand glistened red. I took a deep breath and sat back on my ankles.

"So," the stranger said, looking down at me, "are we gonna play nice now? Or would you prefer to keep bleeding?"

I bit my tongue. If only I hadn't been too weak to fight back. My body was so drained.

"I don't know what they said to you up there," I wheezed, laboring just to breathe, "but you've lost your mind. There's no one here. Who the hell are we supposed to start? This place is abandoned."

"Oh, there are people here," he said with a chuckle. "You just have to look for them." He pointed at Kareena. "Seeker! Why don't you make yourself useful and start seeking?"

"I'm not your bitch." She clenched her fists. "I don't have to do anything."

The amber light sparked in his chest again and Kareena gasped, stumbling backwards a few feet.

"Okay. Okay," she yelped, before he could use his fluorescence against her. "Whatever. Just please don't hurt me again." She bent down at my side. "I'm sorry, Brian." She wrapped her arm around mine and Alice took my other hand. They helped me to my feet.

"Thanks."

Alice stuck close by me and helped to steady my steps as we followed Kareena through the streets. The stranger lingered close beside her, threatening her with a nasty glare every time she stopped to look back at us. His golden light—though faded considerably—lingered. A dim, haunting glow.

I wanted him dead.

We didn't even know his name, but he was a turncoat. Forcing us to do the Saviors' dirty work even though he had no idea who we were or what we'd been through.

"There!" Kareena called out, pointing down an alley in the distance. "I see someone."

We followed her down the alley until we came to a pair of blurred outlines huddling together. Children. Orphans, or homeless. Or both.

I felt a flush of warmth in my arm. Blue light flickered through my fingertips.

"You need to heal them, Brian," said Kareena, motioning for me to go ahead of her. "They're ill."

"What the..." I coughed hard. The trauma to my body had made my lungs tight. "The hell do the Saviors want them for? They're probably homeless. Sick. They need help, not this! Not this curse!"

"It's none of your concern." The man crossed his arms. "Let's call it a social experiment, shall we?"

Chapter 22

"Do it!" He jabbed me in the arm and I swerved toward him, clenching my teeth and tightening my fists. The smug look on his face had me one second away from decking him again.

But, on second thought, I couldn't risk it. Not after what he had just done to me. I couldn't deal with the feeling of my organs hemorrhaging again. Pressure choking me. Crushing my insides. Jesus, I'd thought I was going to die.

"Alright!" I replied. "Stop pushing us around."

There were more homeless people. Young ones. I healed them and Alice did the rest. Most of the adults weren't infected. One very old infected lady had made a shelter of moldy cardboard boxes and plastic tarps. Being forced to start such devastated people was like some kind of sick torture. Payback for the rebellion we'd staged earlier, perhaps.

"Do you even know what they want them for?" I asked. The stranger sneered and turned away from me. "Have you even thought about it? About what they want with us? Why all of these people?"

"Shut up." He shot me a penetrating glare. Golden light sparked beneath the open flaps of his jacket. "Shut up and do your job." He zipped up his coat and propped the collar up around his neck, shaking his head and grumbling to himself. The cold was probably getting to him, too.

Alice and Kareena had gone up ahead to start someone else. I had stayed where I was, keeping a close eye on him.

My drenched leather jacket did little to keep out the

rain. It kept coming and going in short bursts. Thunder rumbled beneath our feet, and white streaks of lightning shot across the black sky every so often. I wanted to go home. I wanted to take a shower and go to bed early. I didn't even care about...

Work.

Damn it. I was going to be late, if I even made it in at all.

"What's your name?" I asked, trying to break the silence while also keeping an eye on Alice up ahead.

He looked at me and furrowed his brow. I still couldn't make out his face clearly, but he had facial hair—a goatee, what looked like a trimmed mustache and some narrow sideburns. Dark skinned. Hispanic?

"David," he replied flatly. "Now stop asking questions."

"Brian."

Maybe telling him our names would humanize us—make us real to him. "The tall girl is Kareena and the shorter one—"

"Alice. I heard you earlier. She your girlfriend or some-thing?"

I didn't know how much I wanted him to know.

"You could say that."

"Oh?"

"It's complicated."

"So is life."

I shrugged. David seemed like a normal guy. Now that he'd stopped barking out orders and tearing up my internal organs.

"Do you have family back home? Wherever that is."

"That's enough!" His nostrils flared. "I told you to shut up."

I pressed my lips together and heaved a sigh, exhaling through my nose, mustering every bit of patience inside just to keep from snapping at him.

Up ahead, faint green and pink light marked the girls in the darkness as they headed back toward us, their fluorescent glows growing brighter as they drew nearer.

"I think that's everyone," Kareena said, quickly looking at David for approval. "Right?"

"Yeah. I started them all," added Alice, her voice trembling. "Even the kids. Even... a really little one." She looked exhausted. Broken.

David crossed his arms and looked down at them. "Are you sure? You got everyone?"

"Yeah," Kareena confirmed. "I'm sure. Now... can we go home? Please?"

"They will choose when we can leave," David said. "Once we've finished the job and only once we've finished the job."

"They said they were done," I added, moving in to take Alice by the hand. She was cold as ice. Shaking. I wanted to give her my jacket, but it wouldn't have done any good. We were both soaked. "We need rest."

"What do I have to do to get you to stop talking?" David said, gritting his teeth at me. "Seriously. Shut up, kid."

"I'm not a kid!" I growled.

Alice squeezed my hand.

"Shh," she whispered. "We'll get home soon. Don't worry." She shook her head and swept her wet hair out of her face. "Let's get out of the rain."

"Alright," David said.

Finally, something we could agree on.

We made our way toward an overhang on the other side of the street. An abandoned pizza shop.

The thought of food reminded me how hungry I'd gotten since we'd arrived.

Kareena hunched over, wringing the water out of her hair. Her skimpy little midriff-baring jacket was dripping with water. I felt sorry for her, but Alice and I weren't doing much better. We were all drenched.

I took another look at David—his profile outlined by a brief flash of lightning.

What was his story? He was cocky, pushing us around like we were dogs. Maybe he was just like us. Scared. Confused. Tormented by them.

Maybe they had threatened him or...

"What are you looking at?" David asked, his voice rising above the clattering rain on the overhang.

"Nothing. Sorry." I looked away. *Awkward.*

Then again, maybe he was just a creep.

Standing there with him, I didn't have a clock to tell time, but it felt like at least a half hour or more passed. Maybe it did. Maybe it just felt like an eternity because of the darkness. The rain. Drenched like drowned rats and starting to feel like we were, in fact, carrying a plague.

Kareena stood beside me, leaning against the door of the pizza shop, biting her fingernails. She kept glancing over at David, as if she thought he might attack her again. I wish I could have assured her otherwise, but I couldn't. I'd try to stop it, at least. Jesus, I'd try.

Alice huddled close to me, her heavy locks of wet hair clinging to my jacket. Her cold hands tucked between the flaps of my coat for warmth. I closed my eyes and took a deep breath. We couldn't be out in this all night. We just couldn't. We'd get hypothermia.

I opened my eyes and turned around to look at the storefront window. The glass was intact. I tugged the handle of the door. Locked. Through scum and dirt, I saw the push bar had been chained to the walls with a padlock from the inside. No one could get in or out.

I cupped my hands on the glass and pressed my face into them to peer inside. No lights, but the place looked dry. I took a few steps over and flattened my hand against the larger section of the glass storefront window. Ice cold. Solid glass. A bolt of lightning lit up our surroundings and a few hairline cracks gleamed in the glass.

"Move back," I said to Alice, perking up the collar of my

jacket and taking a deep breath. I braced myself as I drew back and then rammed my shoulder into the window. Glass shattered to pieces. I grunted, rolling my arm to shake out the pain. Subtle blue light tinted my fingertips and then faded away.

"Shit!" David staggered back. "What the hell?"

"We're not staying out here all night, damn it!" I replied. "Not on my watch."

I stepped over the window pane and tried to avoid a huge piece of glass on the tile floor. Remnants crunched beneath my sneakers and I swiped my foot across the debris to shove most of the fragments to the side. I spotted a broom nearby and used the handle on the inner edge of the window to break off remaining shards. "Careful, Alice." I lent her my arm for balance and helped her step over the window pane.

"What do you think you're doing?" David asked, raising his voice again.

"Getting out of the rain. We can't take this. The damn Saviors are taking their sweet time tonight and we can't wait for them anymore."

"We can... break stuff?" Kareena asked, creeping through the window behind Alice.

"Don't touch anything else," David said, standing outside the store looking in. "Where are you going? Get back here!"

"Come inside," I replied. "It's a little warmer here. No draft."

"Probably rats," said Kareena with a shudder. "Or roaches. Ew."

"Shut up, Kareena," I said. "Seriously? Your intuition is just—"

"Brian, please." Alice took my hand again. "Don't yell at her. She's scared, too. We're all cold. We all want to go home. Even you, right?" She looked over at David, still standing outside.

"Yes," he said. He ducked down and stepped in through

the window pane.

"What the hell is taking them so long?" I sat down on a barstool and spun around once. It let out a rusty, ear-piercing screech and I flinched. I shrugged off my jacket, draped it over my shoulder and slid off the stool.

The place had been ransacked a long time ago. Broken dishes on the floor. Cash register stuck open. I walked behind the bar and dug around beneath the counter, moving carefully in case there was more broken glass. All I wanted was a flashlight.

The streetlamps outside projected a dim glow on our surroundings, but the shadows were difficult to maneuver through. Any amount of light would help. My phone would work... if it would turn on.

"These might help." Alice came over with a stack of grungy dishtowels. I took one from the top of the stack. It smelled old and musty, but looked clean. I wiped the rain from the back of my neck and shook my head.

Kareena's lips wrinkled at the sight of the dingy towels.

"Wait," she called as Alice turned away. "I'll take one, too. Sorry." She wrapped it around her hair and twisted it tightly.

Alice nervously offered one to David. I rolled my eyes.

Let him freeze.

"Th-thanks," he replied, caught off guard.

Alice always thought about others, even when things got tough. Even when they didn't deserve her kindness.

"Thanks, Alice." I held onto her towel while she shrugged off her coat. Then she handed the dripping wet, heavy-as-hell thing to me and I draped it over my arm so I wouldn't lose it. She dried her hair with the towel as best she could and we sat down at the only table we could find that hadn't fallen apart.

My muscles hurt. The humidity didn't help the heavy feeling in my chest. I could feel my fatigue wearing on me.

Kareena sat on a barstool, etching something into the bar with the tine of a fork. The scratching sound made my skin crawl.

David sat a few seats over, watching us with tiring eyes.

Alice rested her head on my wet shoulder and I wrapped an arm around her.

Thunder rumbled quietly in the distance. The patter of raindrops on the roof ceased and I looked toward the front window. The rain had stopped.

My body tingled and I sucked in a breath.

Everything blurred.

I hit the ground hard. My wet jacket squelched as it landed on the asphalt. Bright street lights blinded me. I shielded my eyes with the back of my hand and scrambled to my feet.

"Brian!" Alice screamed.

Two blazing white suns were coming straight at me.

I dodged the car and tumbled into the grass on the side of the road, the blare of a horn piercing my ears.

"Are you okay?" Alice helped me up and handed me my jacket. A fresh tire mark ran across the sleeve.

"Yeah. I'm fine." My heart had jumped into my throat, and it was still beating like a drum as I stumbled through the grass. I stepped on something hard and lifted my foot to see what it was.

"Oh, God," I groaned.

Scattered pieces of metallic blue fiberglass shimmered beneath the moonlight.

Chapter 23

White light stung my eyes. I squeezed them shut. My chest tightened and I wheezed, barely able to breathe. The sensation of weightlessness engulfed me, lifting me off my feet. Then I fell.

I awoke with a gasp, winded. Panting hard. Jarred from sleep by an awful nightmare—rain and never-ending darkness surrounding me. Pain shooting through my core, boring into my bones.

Crushing pain.

I sat up in my bed and held my face in my hands. Sweat beaded on my forehead. My stomach coiled into knots.

Alice shifted in her sleep and rolled over to face me. Her eyes eased open.

"Brian? Are you okay?" she murmured, reaching a hand up to caress my back.

"Yeah," I lied. "I'll be fine. Go back to sleep."

"Okay. Just checking." She groggily rolled back over and nestled into her pillow.

I wasn't okay.

I could barely stay awake during the day anymore, my nights had become so hellish.

Ever since the night David had hurt me, Jane had given up telling us what to do. No more advice about the Saviors. No more objections to Alice and me staying together at night. She couldn't change things.

Still, I hadn't slept worth a damn in almost a week, even with Alice within arm's reach.

For the second time in my life, I had been on the brink of death. The sickening ache had rippled through my veins, tainting my mouth with the metallic taste of iron. Blood.

I'd started to believe the fluorescence made me stronger—invincible almost.

I'd been wrong.

David could have killed me if he had wanted to, and I couldn't have raised a fist to fight back. He had paralyzed me—crushed me with a force I couldn't even see.

What if he had killed me? What if he had hurt Alice? How far were the Saviors willing to let him push us to get the job done?

The Saviors didn't give a damn. Their lack of sympathy was appalling. It seemed like each time we were transported someplace, they did it less delicately. And they were never apologetic. *Never.*

Cowards.

What if we disappeared in the middle of class? What then?

Social services would be coming back to check on me soon, too. What if I wasn't there? Would Jane get into trouble? Would it put her custody in jeopardy? My future? Again?

I'd turn seventeen in a few months, but I'd never wanted to be eighteen so badly in my entire life. I needed the independence—the space.

What little precious freedom I had gained—in the form of my bike—had been totaled just weeks after I'd finished paying it off. Days later, the memory of shattered motorcycle parts strewn across the street still angered me. Because of the Saviors, I'd almost lost my job, which was now hanging on by a thread.

Life's a real bitch.

·   ·   ·

"You have to pass this year," said Alice, putting her hand on my shoulder as she sat down beside me at our lunch table. "You just have to. We can't be separated next year."

I put down my pen and clapped my sketchbook closed.

My grades were suffering again. I'd never given a damn about grades until Alice had come into my life. She'd made me change my mind. Convinced me to try harder. For a little while, at least.

Now I couldn't care less about classes or homework. None of it mattered, not as long as *they* were screwing with our lives. We were toys to them—pawns in some ridiculous game we couldn't win. A game with no rules. No limitations.

I had the weight of the world pushing my head underwater—drowning me in fear and uncertainty. Good grades weren't going to stop the Saviors from hurting us—from playing God with us.

"I've been accepted into the college I applied to," said Kareena, swirling her mashed potatoes around on her plate with a plastic fork. "I hope you guys graduate on time. Maybe we can meet up again after college."

"Does college really matter anymore?" I glared at her.

"Well, yeah. We can't stop living because of this," she replied, laying down her fork beside her tray. "We don't know when it will stop."

"And what if it doesn't?" I asked.

Kareena shrugged and lowered her head. "I dunno. I... hope it does."

"Hope hasn't gotten us anywhere so far." I pushed my lunch tray away, sat back and crossed my arms. "Hope didn't stop them from turning us into freaks." I gritted my teeth. "It didn't stop that coward, David, from almost killing me!"

"Shh." Alice looked around nervously. "Keep it down, please."

"See? You're already worried about people hearing us. I'm being honest, Alice. Lying doesn't change things and neither does hiding from the truth. Face it. We can't keep doing this. They've already taken us right off the street. Someday, they're going to pull us out of class and people are going to see it. We can't take chances. We shouldn't even come to school anymore."

"I know. I know." Alice looked down, fidgeting with the bendy straw sticking out of her chocolate milk carton. "But I think we should do our best with what little time is left this school year. It's only a few weeks. We can't give up. I want to do well, Brian. I want you to do well, too." She reached her left hand out and cupped it over mine. The gold and silver band glistened on her finger. I glanced at it and then back at her. She smiled. "Please. Keep trying. Please do it for me? For us?"

I wanted to give up. Hide myself in a dark secluded place far away from school and work. Away from people. Away from responsibility.

I wanted it all to stop.

"Please?" Alice's fingers entwined with mine.

I took a deep breath and sighed.

"Okay." I placed my other hand on top of hers. "For now, I'll try."

"And keep working on your comic," she added. "Don't let go of your dreams, Brian. You're so gifted."

My drawing had become sporadic lately. The few sketches I had managed to squeeze out had been dark and angry, full of blood and gore—not the sort of subject matter that Staggered Hart was originally meant to focus on. It was supposed to be about a hero—a man trying to find himself—but it was turning into a story about struggling with identity and morality. Something too close to home now.

"You of all people have been through so much," I said to Alice. "What they did to you was inexcusable. Doesn't it get beneath your skin? Everything that's happened? Doesn't it make you angry? Make you want to..."

"Yeah." She frowned. "Of course it does. But when I sleep at night knowing you're close, cared for, and in a stable family—that makes it bearable. That makes every morning worth waking up to."

She was right. We were luckier than most people our age. Lucky we had someone like Jane who understood our problems.

"I've put it behind me for now, but I won't forget that guy. That... David," said Kareena, scooting closer and leaning toward us. "I've never been so frightened—so violated—in my entire life. And I never want to be again."

"We won't give him that chance next time," I said. "We'll fight back." I glanced reassuringly at Kareena. "He needs to be put in his place. But we have to be prepared to take action next time. There has to be a way to stop him."

The thought alone of a "next time" made my heartbeat quicken. A sickness twisted up my stomach and the memory of the gut-wrenching pain he'd inflicted on me made my entire body tense.

Chapter 24

Kareena's early summer graduation ceremony was hell. The boisterous crowd reeked of soda, body spray and sweat. People surrounded us in every direction. I was on the edge of my seat with a horrible throbbing in my stomach, certain *something* would happen—that we would be pulled right out of the middle of the crowd and dropped somewhere with that bastard, David, again.

We should have stayed home. We shouldn't have come.

"Brian? Are you okay?" Alice wrapped her arm around mine and looked into my eyes, a concerned wrinkle in her brow.

"Yeah. I just... I'm worried."

"We can't live every moment in fear," she said. "If they want to take us somewhere again, we can't stop them."

"No. But we can try to not be in public so much," I whispered, shifting in my hard, uncomfortable seat on the bleachers. I'd been on pins and needles since the opening speech. "This was a bad idea, Alice. We should have stayed home."

"This is the last day of school, Brian. We'll be fine. Then we have all of summer break to figure something out."

"What about my job? I won't be able to afford another motorcycle for a while, but they'll want me to work longer hours soon. I need the money. We need the money."

"You'll be okay. Mom will drive you when she can, and you can hop the bus the rest of the time."

"I guess." I hated the bus. The fear of vanishing in public ate at me every time I stepped foot on one. "I'm just tired of having to rely on your mom all of the time."

"Shh." Alice shushed me with a flattened hand and her gaze fixated on the podium in the center of the auditorium. Kareena had just been called and was sashaying across the stage in a navy blue cap and gown. The top of her cap had a rhinestone letter K glittering on it. She'd pretty much gotten over the whole David incident by now and moved on. *Lucky.*

"Wow. That blue is not her color," I said, shocked she'd be caught wearing something so horrible. I was honestly surprised she hadn't stayed home instead.

Alice snickered. "That's not nice, Brian."

"Well?" I shrugged.

Kareena had tied a sparkly beaded sash around her waist so she would stand out, but it made her look like a frumpy wizard instead of a runway model.

"Okay. Maybe it isn't the best, but it's not like she picked the color."

Kareena looked up at us and waved, grinning like a thirteen-year-old girl at a boy-band concert.

At *me*, not Alice.

Alice hopped up out of her seat to wave back, flaunting a big toothy grin as if she'd thought Kareena had been waving at her. I felt bad, but shouldn't have. It was Kareena, after all. The girl with the emotional depth of a mannequin.

Alice sat down.

"Wow. Really, Alice?"

"I'm happy for her. Aren't you?"

"I'll be happy when we're both over eighteen. That's all I want right now. I couldn't care less about this."

She screwed up her face and narrowed her eyes at me.

"Sorry." In my defense, no amount of homework would get the Saviors off our backs. "Yes. I'm proud of her. To be honest, I'm surprised she graduated at all, considering how little she seemed to care about studying."

We met Kareena outside on the school lawn after the ceremony. She'd already taken off the hideous robe and had it draped over her arm. Her cap and crumpled up fake diploma were in her hands. Like everyone else who'd graduated that day, she'd get the real one in the mail in a few weeks.

"So, you want to come over to my place and celebrate?" Kareena asked, raising an eyebrow at me.

"Um. No. Not really." I shook my head and tried not to grimace so obviously.

"Aw, but Daddy said I could have whoever I wanted over." She grinned at me again. I caught a glimpse of something glittering on her nose. A diamond stud in her left nostril.

"Oh, you noticed?" she said, tilting her head to the side so the sun made the gem sparkle. "Graduation slash eighteenth birthday gift from me." She giggled.

I rolled my eyes.

"Did it hurt?" asked Alice, standing up on her toes to get a better look.

"No," Kareena replied matter-of-factly. "Well, yeah. It hurt like hell, actually, but it was tooootally worth it. It's hot, right?" She bit her lip and looked to me for a reply.

I shrugged. "Whatever."

Her lips thinned. "Fine," she said, crossing her arms. "Be that way. Look, what's your problem lately anyway, Brian? You barely dragged your ass out of the tenth grade and now you're mad at the world!"

"My problem? Really?" I raised my voice and clenched a fist unconsciously. "My problem is—"

"Brian, no. Just drop it, please," Alice said, stepping in front of me. "Please? Just let her have fun today."

Kareena scowled and turned away. "You guys suck. I can't believe I got stuck with you two as friends because of this alien crap inside me. This is so unfair."

"How do you do it, Kareena?" I asked, my blood boiling. "How do you go about every day acting like nothing has happened? You pretend you're not a part of something bigger, that you aren't as susceptible to the risks as we are. How do you know they don't have other plans for you, too?"

She turned back and her expression melted into a frown.

"You can't let anyone have fun, can you?" she said. "Who made you king, anyway? You're so goddamn selfish and you think everything is about you. Poor Brian. He's got a bad heart. His motorcycle got trashed. Oh, poor Brian, his mom went mental."

"Shut up, Kareena!" I took a step closer. "Don't you dare bring my mother into this. She's got nothing to do with it."

"Yeah, right. You're so sorry for yourself it makes me sick. All you do is complain and moan and groan about how rough your life is. Ever since that guy hurt you, you haven't shut up about it. You're just a whiney little brat. Well, you know what? He hurt me, too. And my life isn't exactly going the way I'd like it to, either. I haven't been able to have a boyfriend since this shit started and you... you at least have *her*. Hell, you get to live with your damn girlfriend. I can't get close to another guy without feeling like my head's gonna freaking explode." She looked away, trying to hide the redness flushing her face.

"You're a real buzz kill, you know that?" she added with a huff. "Some of us want to move on. Some of us want to believe this shit's temporary." Kareena turned her back on me again and started walking away. "I'm not letting you ruin a good day for me, Brian. I've got friends waiting."

"Kareena, wait!" I called after her, but she flipped me a middle finger and then jogged off, disappearing into a crowd of other graduates.

I hadn't been trying to upset her. I had only wanted her to come to terms with reality. Was I wrong to be so worried?

We weren't normal teenagers anymore. If Alice and Kareena thought we were, they were lying to themselves.

Chapter 25

My surroundings began to materialize.

Midday sky. Faded blue, muddled with puffs of white and grey. Long stretches of city sidewalk on both sides of an asphalt road, and industrial buildings as far as the eye could see. Transparent, blurry outlines of people appeared all around me.

No blinding neon signs or blaring music, but the hellish, sticky heat overwhelmed me. I took in a deep breath of thick humidity and dirty air.

"Alice?"

I started off toward a nearby building made of huge grey cinderblocks. A large decorative brass emblem of a caduceus—a winged staff entwined with two snakes—loomed above the glass doors. A pharmaceutical industry building.

I craned my neck back. Reaching up what looked like a hundred floors, mirrored glass windows reflected the sooty-blue sky. The skyscraper loomed over the rest of the street, taller than anything I'd ever seen.

I bent over to rest my hands on my knees and groaned, exasperated by the scorching heat. I loosened my tie and rolled the sleeves of my dress shirt up to my elbows.

They'd taken me straight from work this time, the Saviors.

"Alice!" I called out. "Where are you!?"

Sweat drizzled off my brow, stinging my eyes. I grimaced and wiped my forehead with the back of my hand. The roar of city traffic and disgruntled drivers honking at each other made it almost impossible to hear anything else. People at a nearby crosswalk raised their voices to combat the noise.

The heat bore down on me, making it hard to breathe. I unbuttoned the top few buttons of my shirt and shrugged off my satin vest. It slid to the ground, and within seconds it materialized on the other plane. The small cursive embroidery that read "Jacques'" glittered in the light, catching the attention of a passerby. A woman stopped dead in her tracks just a foot away from me, looked down and tilted her head to the side. Then, she glanced back up—straight through me—and her eyes almost made contact with my own. Oblivious.

"Brian!"

I jerked my head toward the sound of the voice.

"Alice?"

She came running full speed around the block. I hurried to meet her.

"I was worried about you," she said, panting. "I yelled... but I didn't hear anything." She doubled over to catch her breath. "Then I heard you call my name and... I didn't stop running until I found you."

"Thank God you're okay. Any sign of Kareena or...?"

"David?" She shook her head. "No. I was hoping we wouldn't find him, actually."

"I kind of hoped we would." I cupped my fist with my other hand.

"What?" Her eyes widened and she straightened up. "Why?"

"I already told you. He needs to be stopped."

"Yeah, but... I didn't think you were serious."

"I don't talk shit, Alice. You know that."

She swallowed hard. "Yeah. I know."

We walked along the sidewalk, avoiding people as much as we could. A group of kids came bounding toward us on skateboards. They blurred by and we narrowly avoided them by pressing ourselves flat up against the wall of the nearest building.

Alice sighed. "I hate this," she said.

"Me, too. And this heat!" I plunged two fingers into my collar and pried it away from my neck. "We should get out of it." I wiped my forehead again.

"But we need to find Kareena."

"She'll find us. Hopefully."

"Kareena!" Alice had cupped her hands to her face and shouted at the top of her lungs. The sharp pitch pierced my ears.

"Keep it down! What if he hears you?"

"We need to find her! Karee—"

I grabbed Alice and covered her mouth with my hand. She grunted, struggling to push me away. I released her and she stumbled forward several steps.

"Brian!?" She swerved around and glared. "What's your problem!?"

"Shh. We'll find her, okay? I just don't want *him* to find us first."

She huffed. "Don't treat me like I'm useless."

"I *never* said you were useless."

She marched off in the direction I had come from and I bolted after her.

We walked a few blocks and then circled back around toward where I had been dropped off originally. We turned a corner and Alice gasped. Kareena stood leaning against the wall of a building, her arms folded together.

"Kareena!" Alice rushed ahead of me.

Kareena cracked a weak, fatigued smile and took a step toward us. Her head dropped and she toppled over. I darted after her and barely caught her in my arms.

"Hi," she muttered, hardly able to lift her face.

Heat exhaustion?

"How long have you been waiting for us?" I asked. "Never mind. Let's get inside." I motioned toward the doors of the pharmaceutical company.

"Wh-what about all of the infected?" Kareena murmured, resting a lot of weight on me as I helped her back to her feet.

"Screw it for now. We need to rest." I swept Kareena's thick, disheveled hair back. "You need rest."

Alice pried her fingers between the sliding glass doors and forced them open.

A burst of ice cold air shocked us. Goose bumps rose all over my skin and I shivered.

Inside, we found a quiet, low-traffic corner and I helped Kareena down to the floor so she could sit.

"How'd you know we would come here?" Alice asked, sitting down beside her and leaning against the glass curtain wall that ran around the entire perimeter of the ground floor.

"I found Brian's vest on the ground there." She twisted around and pointed out the window. It was still there. Trampled on and kicked off to the side, but there.

If only I'd been smart enough to have left it on purpose.

"Smart girl," I said, putting a hand onto her bare shoulder. Her skin felt hot and moist with sweat. "I'm glad we found you. I was... worried."

She smiled a genuine smile at me. My heart sank.

I cared about her. But I didn't care about her the way she hoped I would. It really got under my skin some days—how badly she wanted something more from me. Other times, it just made me feel terrible—like I was betraying her somehow—leading her on.

But I wasn't; my intentions to keep up a relationship with Alice were obvious, and they nearly always had been. Kareena needed to accept the truth.

"Are you feeling better?" I asked.

"Yeah. Thanks," Kareena replied.

"Good." I glanced around the office building, watching out-of-focus men and women in dress suits hustling in all directions, briefcases in hand. Headset pieces slung over their ears—speaking to phantoms.

A slender woman wearing a dress jacket and skirt came rushing past us; her hair had been pinned up into a tight bun and an earpiece was clasped over her ear. "What do you mean, one of the subjects had a seizure?" she said, furrowing her eyebrows and coming to a sudden halt right in front of us.

Alice shrunk back against the wall. Kareena came to her feet.

"That wasn't even a side effect in the original trials!" she continued. "I'll have President Greenmire get back to you." The woman pressed the side of her earpiece and shook her head. "Liars. Seizures. He's full of it." She rolled her shoulders back and closed her eyes a moment while she tried to regain her composure.

We waited quietly for her to move on, but she just stood there a while, staring out the window—through me—at the street. I swallowed hard when she took a step closer.

"Damn." The woman brought a hand up to her ear again and pressed the receiver. "This is Davis." She turned away and rushed off down the hallway.

I exhaled. Alice stood up beside me and wrapped her hands around mine.

"I wonder what she was talking about," she whispered.

"I don't know, but it's none of our business."

Alice nodded. She turned to the side and gasped.

"Brian!" Her grip on my hand tightened. "It's him."

I veered around to look out the window behind us.

"Shit! It is!"

The three of us ducked. David had been walking down the sidewalk on the other side of the street.

"He's coming this way," Kareena said, backing away from the window. "We have to go."

Yeah.

We *should* have run as fast as we could in the other direction.

I'd even felt it once.
Once would last me a lifetime.

Chapter 26

A pounding migraine thumped between my temples. I came to my feet, leaning some of my weight against Alice's shoulders. My knees trembled. Pins and needles all over.

Blue light surged through my body, healing me. Slowly. So slowly.

I swallowed, my throat dry as paper. The taste of iron still tainted my tongue, and a deep, shuddering inhale made my lungs ache.

David screamed, wrenching in pain while Kareena held on tight, possessed by some newfound bravery. Her hands were locked around his head like a vice, her fingers driving hot-pink light through his body.

The power horrified me. It was something I hadn't even known she could do.

I coughed and wiped my mouth again. Blood smeared across the back of my hand. God knew how much blood had spilled into places it didn't belong inside me.

"Brian, we should go." Alice tugged my arm. "While he's still down."

"But, what about..." I wheezed and shot a glance at Kareena while taking a step in the opposite direction. My foot came down onto nothing.

I fell.

My eyes adjusted to the darkness after a few moments. A long steel counter stretched out before me. Clattering dishes sounded all around me. A sudden surge of scents hit me—warm, freshly baked bread. Italian spices. Roasting meats and open flame.

"Hey!" Jacob stumbled into me, nearly dropping an entire tray of drinks over my head. A wine glass teetered on its foot, white wine splashing up over the rim.

I toppled forward, slamming into the condiment table, and latched onto the side to stop from falling. I caught my balance, swerved around and tucked my glowing left arm behind me. The fluorescence hadn't faded yet.

"Jesus, man. What happened to you?" He wrinkled his lips with disgust and looked me up and down quickly. "You look... sick."

Stains from the blood I had coughed up earlier flecked my white shirt.

"It's nothing... I..."

Fell? No. Ugh.

"Spilled a drink. It's nothing."

"You look like shit, man. You really should..."

"Brian?"

Damn it.

"Yes, sir?" I veered toward the voice. Jacob ducked his head down and scuttled off in a hurry.

The restaurant owner, Jacques himself, approached. He took one look at me and grimaced.

"Pardon my French," he said, "but what in the hell happened to you? And where have you been for the past hour and a half?"

"I..." My chest burned.

Think.

"I was... um..."

"And what are you hiding behind your back? Brian?"

I froze.

"You were a really good server when I first hired you. I liked you. A lot."

"I can explain. Please give me another chance!" I pulled my arm out from behind me, hoping the color had faded. It had.

"I can't keep letting you off the hook when you come in late... or not at all, for that matter. You've been slipping for a while now, Brian. This is a real job and I'm trying to treat you like a real adult, but you can't be having your mother call in sick for you when something happens."

"She's not my mother, she's... Never mind. Please, just—"

"I can't. I'm sorry, Brian." He looked away from me and sighed. "There are people who value their jobs so much more than you seem to these days."

"Sir, I..."

"Please take your things and go."

"No," I hissed, dropping my head down. Hating myself for something I couldn't have prevented. "Shit!"

"Watch your language around our customers, Brian." Jacques shook his head with disdain and walked past me, avoiding eye contact.

"Well, damn. He didn't look happy," muttered Jacob, lumbering back into the kitchen with a stack of dirty plates piled up to his chin. "Sorry, man."

"Life sucks, you know that?" I rested my hands on the edge of a nearby counter and hung my head low. "Things start getting better and then you get punched with some shit you can't begin to understand, let alone handle."

"Uh... yeah. I guess." Jacob dropped the pile of dishes onto a tray and swerved around to grab a stack of to-go containers from a shelf to the right. "You take care of yourself, okay? Good luck out there with whatever's been eating you."

"Thanks."

I dragged myself to the back room and took out my cell phone to call Jane.

Two missed a calls and a text. Alice and Jane were already on their way to pick me up.

I crossed my arms and closed my eyes, dropping my head

back against the seat of the car. Alice took my hand and pulled it into her lap.

"I'm sorry, Brian," she said, pressing her shoulder into mine in the back of Jane's car. "I'm really sorry."

I heaved a sigh.

Alice leaned over and kissed me on the cheek.

"I love you," she whispered, close to my ear, and then nuzzled my neck with her nose.

I tried to smile.

I really tried.

·   ·   ·

I ruffled a towel through my wet hair, relieved to not be festering in my own blood and sweat anymore.

The long, hot shower had me thinking about a lot of things—mostly about how we weren't safe.

We just weren't. No excuses or arguments would change that fact.

I tugged on a clean pair of jeans, pulled a fresh-smelling t-shirt over my head and grabbed my phone and wallet. I'd have to take a walk after dinner. I needed the air—the space. My mind buzzed with fears and I knew restlessness and insomnia were creeping up on me again.

"Jane?" I quietly closed the basement door behind me.

She stood in front of the oven, stirring a pot of soup.

"Yes? How are you feeling?" She set the long wooden spoon down onto the spoon rest and looked me over sympathetically. "Alice told me about everything. God, I'm so sorry. I wish I could do something. I'm sick of feeling powerless."

"It's okay. We got out of there alive, at least." I pulled up a seat and sat down on the other side of the kitchen island.

"Who is this David guy? And why is he so determined to hurt you?" Jane pulled a box of pasta out of the cupboard behind her and set it beside the pot.

"I don't know." I shrugged. "I tried to ask, but he didn't want to talk about it. I think he's following orders because he's scared like the rest of us. At least, that's what I'm hoping his case is—that he's not being a murderous ass for the fun of it."

"Me, too." She cut a glance at the soup. It was bubbling up to the sides of the pot and she snatched up the spoon to stir it back into submission. "Maybe this isn't the best suggestion, but, do you think the police can help at all? Since you know what this guy looks like?"

I scoffed and rolled my eyes.

"What?" Jane asked, looking away from me and at the roiling soup as she dumped half a box of dry egg noodles in. "Do you have any better ideas at this point? What do you want me to say?" She gave it a quick stir.

"Really, Jane? The police? You really think they'll be able to do something?" I got off my seat and leaned on the counter. "We get ripped out of thin air and dropped into different cities in the blink of an eye. Our cell phones never work when we do, and this bastard, David, can pretty much explode our insides by giving us a dirty look. And the police are going to help us how?"

She shook her head and shrugged. "I-I don't know."

"Exactly!" I raised my voice more than I'd meant to. "You *don't* know. They can't help us and neither can you at this point. Not anymore."

"Brian!" She stared at me threateningly. "How dare you speak to me like that after everything I've done for you!"

"And I'm grateful." I lowered my voice. "I really am."

"Then act like it!"

"Is... everything okay in here?" Alice asked, creeping into the kitchen with her hands nervously tangled together. She bit her lip and glanced at me, then at her mother.

"I have it under control," Jane replied, speaking through gritted teeth. "This isn't something you need to worry about,

Alice."

"Oh, okay." She slouched a little and turned to leave.

"No! Wait, Alice. You should be involved with this." I motioned for her to come over to me. "It matters to us both."

"Brian!" Jane's lips pressed thin together. "You're getting on my last nerve with this. Drop it already, please!"

"I mean it, Jane. No one can protect us at this point. No one. And you need to start facing the truth. Alice and I are in danger as long as we keep living life like nothing has changed. We can't go to school and just pray and hope we aren't jerked out of class. I lost my job because of this. It's only a matter of time before people start asking questions."

Jane shrunk back and heaved a breath. "Well, maybe... I," she stammered. "I can get you two out of school. Home-school you or—"

"You can't quit your job to baby-sit us." I shook my head. "Besides, that won't be enough and you know it."

Alice slunk behind me, her fingers still clinging to my hand.

"Alice. Come here." Jane flashed a demanding glare. "Alice!" She slammed the wooden spoon down onto the stove and pointed a finger to the floor beside her. "You come over here right now."

Alice stepped to my side. "I-I think he's right, Mom," she murmured beneath her breath.

"What? Like hell, he is! You go to your room while we settle this."

Alice's grasp on my hand tightened. I squeezed back reassuringly.

"No," she said, looking up from her feet, rolling her shoulders back. "No, Mom. I can't. I won't. He's right."

"Jesus, Alice. What has he done to you? You used to listen to me and now—"

"He almost died today, Mom!" Alice slammed her hands onto the counter, rattling the dish rack.

My eyes widened. I'd never seen her this angry before.

"He... almost... died. It's not about what he's done to me. It's about what they've done to us."

Jane's mouth hung open. Speechless. Appalled. Her eyes huge, frightened, and brimming with disbelief.

I backed away.

"Wh-where are you going?" Jane flipped off the stove and stared at us, horrified. "Brian! I've done everything I possibly could for you. I fought for you in court, gave you a home. I... for some idiotic reason, let you sleep with my daughter, for God's sake, and now... What are you thinking?"

I snaked my arm around Alice's and adjusted my grip on her hand. She trembled in my grasp.

"Please, listen to me!" Jane stepped closer. "I care about you, Brian. I do. But if you don't listen to me, I'll... I'll..." She stamped her foot. "I'll call the police, damn it! Then you'll have your own explaining to do."

"Go ahead." I turned away and left the kitchen. Alice followed.

"Come back!" Jane shouted as we approached the front door. "You can't run away from this!"

I swerved back around and stared Jane in the face at the threshold.

She gasped and held her breath.

"I'm not running away from *anyone* anymore," I said and pulled the door shut behind us.

"Where are we going, Brian?" Alice asked, stopping in the middle of the sidewalk to look up at me. Trusting me. Hoping I had an answer that could stifle her building fears.

"I don't know, Alice. I'm sorry. I just had to get out of there and I wasn't leaving you behind. I'm glad you followed me."

"Mom's gonna kill us if we don't go back right now." Her worried eyes glistened in the amber light of dusk.

"*They're* going to kill us if we do, Alice," I said, gazing down at her. "The Saviors are going to kill us if we don't find a way to fight them—to stop them from playing with us. We can't keep pretending we have normal lives. We don't!"

"But I'm scared, Brian! I don't want to run away from home!" She tightened her grasp on my arm.

"I don't either. And I didn't mean for the conversation to get so heated. I just... freaked the hell out and..." I let go of her and drove my fingers through my hair, groaning out loud to let off steam. "Damn it!" I took in a deep breath of hot, salty summer air.

What the hell was I thinking?

We couldn't survive a night on our own.

Not without help.

"I have an idea." I pulled my phone out of my pocket and started typing a text.

While awaiting a reply, I eyed the bus stop in the distance.

"Let's catch a bus to Central and then I'll come up with something."

"Central? That's like a half-hour ride." Alice held her stomach. "I'm really hungry."

"Me, too, Alice. We'll get something to eat when we get there. I promise."

.   .   .

"Happy Birthday, Brian," said Kareena with a fake grin as she slid a shiny hotel key card across the table.

I scoffed.

"There's nothing happy about it," I grumbled, snatching up the card and shoving it into my jeans pocket before anyone noticed. "And you know it, Kareena."

The twenty-four hour diner was relatively empty.

"Yeah. Okay." She shrugged. "Sorry."

Alice cupped her hands together on the tabletop and

twiddled her thumbs.

The waitress swung back around to bring our drinks. Hot teas for us. Diet soda for Kareena.

"Thanks," I said beneath my breath. The waitress tipped her head.

"You're welcome, dear." She smiled. "I'll get your food out to you in just a few."

I ripped open a little foil package and tossed the tea bag into the cup of steaming hot water. A few tugs of the string had dark brown liquid spiraling in the cup.

Alice poured a sugar packet into hers and stirred it with a spoon. The dinking sound of metal against porcelain made my head twinge.

"Thanks," I said to Kareena, looking briefly into her eyes. "For everything and... for what you did for me earlier. I... never thought..."

"Shut up. You're welcome." She looked out the window beside us and took a sip of her drink through the straw. "My parents will be totally pissed if they know I helped you guys with all of this. Let's forget about it for now, please."

"We can't." I put out my hand and stopped Alice mid-stir. She finally put the spoon down beside her cup.

I lowered my voice and leaned over the table. "We can't forget. There's just too much..."

Our waitress came back with a tray of food.

A burger and fries. Waffles and scrambled eggs. Chicken salad. Finally, something besides coffee saturated my nostrils. My mouth watered.

"Anyway," I continued, almost whispering. "We're taking too many risks being out in public. Even now, really." I plucked a French fry from my plate and dunked it into a pile of ketchup. I shoved the fry into my mouth and sighed. Salty. Hot. Deliciously greasy. "I think I speak for all of us when I say today has officially been the worst day ever."

"Yeah," added Kareena, rolling a cherry tomato around

on top of her salad with a fork. "You're right, but my parents are not going to let me ditch law school. They'd drop dead of heart attacks if I even suggested it."

"Can I have the syrup, please?" Alice pointed toward the far end of the table.

Kareena reached for the glass syrup carafe and passed it to her.

The bell on the diner door jingled and I glanced over, paranoid, expecting to see Jane... or the police stroll through.

A middle-aged man dressed in a dark grey suit and tie came stumbling in off the street. He toppled into the jukebox by the door and started heaving out ear-splitting, stomach-sickening coughs, while holding his chest in pain. Each inhale made a gut wrenching whooping sound. My appetite instantly waned.

He came tumbling down onto his knees and the hostess dashed to his side. "Someone call 9-1-1!" she shouted. The three of us veered around in our booth to watch the commotion.

"Holy shit!" Kareena leapt from her seat and held a hand over her mouth.

"What? What is it?" I stood, too. "What do you see?"

"He's... infected. But... it's all weird and shit. Like, ugh. I don't know. I can't... Oh my God." She scowled with disgust.

"Can I help him?" I slid out of the booth toward the huddled mass of restaurant staff surrounding the man. He gasped for breath and stared up at the ceiling, his pupils engorging, gleaming with fear.

"I don't know..." Kareena started.

I knelt onto the cold tile floor.

"Do you know him?" the manager asked hysterically.

"I... uh... no. But I can help."

"EMTs will be here soon. Are you trained to handle this?"

"Yes," I lied. "Sort of. Just give me a little space, please." I reached out a hand and clasped the man's wrist. The heat inside me built and my arm grew warm. A hint of blue light began to surface and I hunched over, resituating myself to obscure the views of the staff.

A sudden sharp jolt of pain shot through me and I let go of the man with a yelp, bounding backwards, slamming into the front counter. The breath had been knocked out of me.

I pulled my arm back. Sharp, riveting pain tore through me like molten lava coursing in my veins.

"Come on!" Alice helped me to my feet. "We can't be here if the police come," she added in a hushed tone, pulling me toward the door. The man on the floor started to convulse, his body arching and writhing around as the other customers watched in terror.

"What did you do?" the manager asked, frantically snagging the cuff of my jeans as I passed.

"I didn't do anything!" I yanked my leg away from her. "I was trying to help." I caught another glimpse of the man's face just before we bolted out the door. His color gone, he'd taken on a dead, robotic expression.

The doors of Kareena's car unlocked with a beep and we jumped in. Ambulance sirens wailed in the distance.

What had I done?

Chapter 27

"That was some scary shit back there!" Kareena gripped the steering wheel and glanced at me in the rearview mirror. "What happened to you, Brian?"

"I don't know," I replied, holding my aching arm. "I touched him, the fluorescence started to glow, and then a jolt of energy ripped through me. Like a charge or something. I don't even know how to describe it. It happened so fast. Next thing I knew, I had my back against the counter and the wind knocked out of me."

"Well, that guy had some freaky shit swirling around inside him so no wonder. His infection was seriously screwed up. Like, the white light was being snuffed out by brown and black spots. Weirdest thing I've ever seen, and I've seen some pretty weird shit, you know?" She glanced back at us.

"Yeah."

"Had he been started?" Alice asked, leaning forward, grasping onto the back of the passenger seat.

Kareena shook her head. "I don't think so. He was too dark inside."

"They're hiding so much information from us," I said, massaging my forearm. "Damn Saviors. There was something very wrong with that guy."

Kareena pulled into the parking lot of a hotel and turned off the engine. We got out and walked behind the car.

"Hey... um..." Kareena looked off at nothing, shifting her weight apprehensively. "Do you... Never mind." She reached into her pocket and pulled out a closed fist. "Here." She held it out toward me. I lifted an open hand beneath hers and she dropped something papery into my palm.

I thumbed through the bills. A hundred dollars—all twenties.

"Just in case, you know?" She cracked a nervous smile. "In case we can't get in touch for a bit. Or whatever."

"Thanks." I closed my hand around the money and tucked it into my pocket. I'd been under the impression that money itself meant very little to her, but the act of *giving* it to us meant a lot to me.

"Be careful, guys," Kareena added beneath her breath.

"You, too."

Alice and I headed up the outdoor stairwell to the third floor. We followed the brass number panels until we located the room Kareena had booked for us. A keycard reader perched above the door handle flashed with red light. I swiped our card down and a click sounded, the light changing to green. I pushed down the handle and opened the door.

A short, narrow hallway lit with soft yellow light took us from the entrance past the bathroom, and then opened up to the main room with a small sofa, bed and television.

"This feels weird," Alice said, peering out the huge bay window at the very end of the room, watching Kareena's red sports car peel out of the parking lot.

She slid the blackout curtains closed and turned.

"Yeah." I locked the deadbolt and the chain lock above the door, then walked over to the bed and set my wallet and cell phone down on the end table. "It is kind of weird. I suppose it wouldn't be if the circumstances weren't so bad."

"I guess." She shrugged. "People probably think we're just dumb teenagers hiding out in a hotel."

"Well, we're not."

"Do you know how to work this?" Alice squinted at the thermostat and rubbed her arms. "It's cold in here."

"Yes." I chuckled. "You flip this to heat or cool and use the arrow buttons to adjust the temperature." I poked at them accordingly.

"Oh. Okay." She dropped her head down. "You must think I'm an idiot."

"No. I don't." I wrapped my arms around her waist and tugged her closer. "I would never think that about you." I touched my thumb to her chin. Alice had a lot to learn, but she wasn't an idiot.

"Thanks."

My embrace loosened and she wriggled away. She plopped down onto the bed and fell back on one of the pillows.

"I can't believe we did this," she groaned, staring blankly toward the ceiling. "I'm a horrible daughter."

I crawled up onto the other side of the bed and lay down beside her.

"I can't believe it either, but, we'll be okay." I reached for her hand. "Alice, you're not a horrible daughter. We just..." The words had barely slipped off my tongue, and already her eyes began to glisten with tears.

"I'm so stupid!" She yanked her hand away and rolled over, clutching her pillow tightly.

"You're not stupid, Alice. Believe me. You're not." I scooted closer and leaned over to kiss her shoulder.

"Yes, I am. Mom is going to ground me forever." She grumbled and buried her face into the pillow, letting out a hefty, muffled scream.

"Alice?"

"Leave me alone, Brian."

"What is it? Talk to me, please." I ran my fingers through her hair and she batted my hand away.

"Stop it. Just leave me alone, okay?" She huffed and rolled over to face the wall. "We shouldn't even be here. We should be home in our own, nice bed. Safe. Not scared."

"Alice?" I rested a hand on her shoulder and her nostrils

flared.

"Let me go to sleep, please," she growled. "I'm tired."

"Fine." I pulled back. "Go ahead." I sat up and crossed my arms. "But don't act like you're the only one who got screwed here."

Alice reached down to grab the folded blanket from the base of the bed and pulled it over her body, just to her nose.

I'd almost died today. Lost my job. Came within seconds of losing Alice to that nut job, David. And she had the nerve to suddenly shut me out as if she was the only one going through hell.

I held my face in my hands and rested my eyes.

I'd only done what I had thought was right. I'd never wanted to upset her. I only...

My phone buzzed, jittering toward the edge of the night-stand.

A text from Jane.

JANE: Be careful. Wherever you are. Come home soon.
JANE: Please...
JANE: I'm not mad at you.

I swiped the texts away and glanced at Alice curled up in her blanket—asleep already. Some days, it made me jealous how easily she could fall asleep.

.   .   .

A loud knock at the door jarred me awake.

"Housekeeping!" a woman's voice sounded from the hall.

She knocked again, banging harder this time. The thump-ing noise made my head pulse.

I leapt off the bed, carefully untangled a corner of the blan-ket from around my ankle, and stumbled over to the door.

"Hi." I opened it a crack and smiled awkwardly at the short little maid looking up at me. "Can I... help you?"

"I'm sorry. Did I wake you?" She cupped her hands together apologetically.

"No. It's fine. It's just... my, uh..." I looked back toward the bed. "Never mind." Alice remained asleep.

"I'm terribly sorry, sir," the woman apologized again. "I'll just leave these with you and if you need anything, you can call the front desk from your phone. Just dial 1-1-1."

She handed me a stack of towels and toiletries.

"Thank you." I shuffled back inside and pushed the door closed with my hip.

"Who was that?" Alice asked, her feet dangling over the side of the bed, her eyes only half open.

"Housekeeping. I forgot to put the stupid sign on the outside of the door last night. I'm sorry she woke you up."

"It's okay." Alice stretched her arms high above her head and yawned. "Ugh. Everything hurts." She rubbed the back of her neck.

The bed wasn't comfortable.

"Well, it's better than sleeping in an alleyway or—"

"I'm just talking, okay?" She narrowed her eyes at me and I shut my mouth.

She slid off the bed and dragged herself into the bathroom. The faucet squealed when she turned it on.

"Do you want to get breakfast soon? We can grab something downstairs or—"

Alice shut the bathroom door.

"Or not," I muttered, shaking my head. I flipped the TV on and hopped back onto the bed. My stomach grumbled.

A basket of teabags and instant coffees sat on the table by the nightstand. In a fridge near Alice's side of the bed were several bottled waters. I took out two and poured them into the coffee pot's reservoir. Water dripped through the empty filter, sizzling and steaming inside the glass carafe.

Nothing interesting on TV. Commercials. Soap operas. Talk shows. I located a news channel and stopped surfing.

Maybe they'd mention something about the man from last night. I wondered if he'd made it... if the infection had killed him or...

If *I* had killed him...

A weather reporter came on. Sports were after that. I'd have to wait until the next hour to learn anything.

I grabbed my phone off the nightstand.

Twenty percent battery remaining.

Damn.

I didn't have my charger. I'd have to conserve power until I could grab a new one. Assuming Jane didn't shut off our service... or use it to track us.

I sent Kareena a quick text to let her know what was up and then shut off my phone.

We'd make do without it for now. The hotel room had one anyway.

"Are you okay?" I called. Alice had been in the bathroom for quite a while.

She didn't reply.

"Alice?" I meandered over to the bathroom and knocked gently, pressing my ear to the door.

A faint moan. A heavy sniffle.

How long had she been crying?

"Can I come in?" I wrapped my fingers around the knob.

She sniffed again. I twisted the handle.

Alice sat on the edge of the bathtub, doubled over. Her face in her hands.

I took a step closer and knelt down in front of her, resting a hand on her knee. "Alice. Come on. We need to get something to eat."

"We shouldn't have run away," she said, congested. "Mom would have helped us." She balled up a length of toilet paper and blotted her cheeks. "She would have."

"And she still can, but not like this. She can't stop the Saviors from hurting us."

"What are we supposed to do now?" Her blue eyes glared at me with contempt. "Seriously, Brian. What now?" She tossed the wad of soggy paper into the garbage bin.

"I don't know yet, but you saw that guy last night! Something was wrong with him. What if those people at the diner think *we* had something to do with it? What then? We can't go back home until..."

Another knock at the door.

I sighed and pushed myself up off the floor. "Give me a sec, Alice." I marched out of the bathroom, impatiently unlocked the front door and jerked it open.

"Yeah? What did you... No!" I gasped.

A lump formed in my throat.

I was staring down the barrel of a silver handgun.

"How the hell did you find us?" My eyes met David's. The putrid scent of cigarettes had my lips wrinkling.

"I had a little help." He shot a glance toward the sky and grinned, his yellowing teeth just showing.

"Brian?" Alice crept out of the bathroom, screamed and moved back against the wall.

"Stay back, Alice!" I lifted an arm slightly.

David forced the door open with his free hand and shoved the muzzle of the gun against my forehead. Cold, hard metal against my temple. My knees trembled.

"Do they want us dead that badly?" I backed up a step, unintentionally allowing David across the threshold in the process. "That you have to resort to shooting us?"

Alice clambered to open the window in the back of the room, but it had been bolted shut.

David chuckled, amused by her sorry attempt.

"People are always flinging themselves out the damn things," he said with a smirk. "Can't be too careful nowadays."

"Don't hurt her, please. I'm the one they want. I'm the one who's been giving all the orders around here. Not her. Not Kareena."

"Aw, they don't want me to kill you. In fact, they told me I wasn't allowed to." He lowered the gun away from my forehead and I took a breath.

"Can you believe that shit?" He looked away for a split second. Too quickly for me to make a move. "But I don't care what they say anymore. They can't tell me what to do. They can't boss me around. I only work for myself now."

Himself? But before he'd seemed so willing to do the Saviors' bidding.

"David, listen to what you're saying." I took another step back and he lifted the gun toward me again. Toward my chest. I shuddered.

"I'm not going to let them turn everyone into freaks," he growled. "I'm not going to let her infect anyone else." He nodded toward Alice.

"No!"

I looked back. She had backed herself up against the wall in a panic. David aimed the gun past me. At her. Her eyes shimmered with fear.

"I was going to shoot your ass first because you've been a thorn in my side from the beginning," he said, sneering. "But I think I'll shoot your girlfriend instead. How does that sound? Not so tough when it's not your own blood on the line, huh?"

"You son-of-a-bitch! Leave her alone or I'll—"

"What?" He swung the gun toward me again. "Come at me? We all know how that ends. Besides, I'd like to see her squirm. After what she did to me." He wiped the back of his hand across his mouth and furrowed his eyebrows. "It hurt like hell."

"She was only trying to protect me!" I sidestepped to block him from targeting Alice. "David, please. She never chose to be a part of this! We don't deserve this."

"Yeah? Well I don't deserve everything those Saviors did to me, either. They told me they were gonna leave Lucy out of this. That if I followed orders, she'd be safe from this shit they put in us." Amber golden light sparked beneath his shirt.

Lucy? Had they lied to him, too?

"They lied to us all," I said, raising my hands in surrender. "Put the gun away, and we can talk this over. No one needs to get hurt."

David sucked a breath in through his teeth.

"When your other girl tried to blow my brains out with that pink venom of hers, I started seeing things. Everyone looked different." He dragged a hand through his short, slick black hair. "All I could see were the different lights inside us all. The sight stayed with me for a while even after I'd been sent home. Long enough for me to see what they'd done to Lucy. Long enough to see that the bastards had already infected her!" He rammed the butt of the handgun into the wall, cracking the plaster.

Alice yelped.

"We've all been hurt." I held out my empty, trembling hands. "If you give us a chance, we'll explain everything to you. Maybe we can even help your... Lucy."

"I don't want to be part of this anymore." He lowered the gun to his side and stared at the floor. "Hell. I never wanted to be part of this to begin with. They just..."

"Forced you to?"

"Yeah." He eased his head up. Tired, bloodshot eyes met mine for a moment and then he looked away. In that moment, I caught a brief glimpse of the truth. Of his weakness and uncertainty.

The fears he harbored were reflections of my own.

We weren't so different after all. We were fighting to do the same thing—to protect the ones we loved.

Chapter 28

David tucked the gun into the back of his belt and bent over to rest his hands on his knees.

I backed away. Just in case.

"Do you want to talk about it?" I asked, trying to stay calm. Still rattled by the vivid image of a gun pressed to my forehead. "I know we got off to a bad start, but we're more than willing to talk if..."

David looked me in the eye and I flinched.

"I guess." He pushed the door shut behind him and came down the narrow hallway toward me, past the bathroom door. "I feel like a dumbass." He shrugged, looking away sheepishly. "I thought I was doing the right thing, but..."

"We all did. We wanted to help the Saviors—even believed we were doing something good, at first. But then they started making it clear that they had no concern for our own safety or feelings." I straightened my shoulders and offered him my hand. "We can work together, David. You have a power we don't—the power to fight back."

"That's not how I saw it yesterday. Not after your girls almost took me out."

"They were protecting me," I said matter-of-factly. "I didn't know they were capable of all of that."

"I know. I know." He hesitated, staring at me—studying me for a moment—before finally reaching to grab my hand.

"You've got balls, kid," he said, his powerful handshake catching me off guard. I grunted. "Standing up to me like that, with a pistol pointed straight at your brain. It's no wonder you made it this far. You've been through some shit, haven't ya?"

"I've got a history. Don't we all?" I moved toward the writing desk beside the TV and pulled out the wooden chair. "Maybe I used to be a smartass when I was younger, but it's not who I am anymore. Not since..." I turned. "Go ahead and sit down, Alice. You'll be okay. Right?" I glanced at David. "She *will* be okay. Right, David?"

"Yeah. Yeah." He held up empty hands. Black, thick-lined tribal tattoos decorated the centers of his palms. I couldn't make out exactly what they were. "I put her away already." He'd meant the gun.

Alice sat on the edge of the bed and I sat on the chair in front of the desk.

"Your, uh... accent. Where you from?" I asked.

"Staten Island." David lingered in the hallway. He leaned back against the closet door and crossed his arms, propping a shoe against the door.

"New York? Wow. You're a long way from home."

"Uh-huh. The Saviors have the whole teleportation thing down. Slowing down time. White light. Mind-blowing shit, but effective. I'll give em' that."

"New... York?" Alice's grasp wavered. "Brian." She leaned toward my ear. "What if... he was one of the..."

"Alice, no." I raised my voice, craning my neck back. "Don't."

"What's she talking about?" David cocked an eyebrow.

"Nothing."

"No, tell me." He reached behind his back for his gun. "Tell me what the hell she was about to say."

"Okay. Okay!" I panicked. "Just don't point that thing at us again, please."

David rested his arm back down at his side.

"Alice and I were at the ball drop last year. We were sent there with the Seeker to start people. A lot of them. Nearly froze to death doing it, too, but we finished the job. Most of it."

David shifted his weight against the door. "Most of it?" he asked, squinting. He was difficult to read. Even his resting expression had a tinge of anger in it.

"The light in Lucy. What did it look like?" I asked.

"I don't know." David glared at me as if it was stupidest question in the world. "Like... white. Glowing. It wasn't anything like ours. It was—hell, I don't know how to describe it. I'm not a freaking poet."

"Was it... breathing?" Alice cut in, leaning toward him.

"Breathing? Shit, I don't know. How the hell does it breathe? It's just light, right?"

"We think it's more than light," I said. "I don't know how else it moves the way it does. Through us. Like it's alive."

"Damn." David's eyes widened. "All I know is it was bright as hell."

Then she'd been started. I shot a worried glance at Alice.

"Brian." Alice whimpered behind me. "What if..."

"Calm down," I replied. "David. Were you and Lucy there? That night?"

"No."

I heaved a sigh of relief. "So it wasn't us who started either of you then."

"Are you trying to tell me *I* infected her?" David moved away from the door and bent down, leering, his face inches from mine. "How do I know you're not lying—that you didn't put that stuff in her?"

"We don't infect people," I corrected, trying hard not to shift in my seat. "We only start those who are already infected. The ones with the dormant light inside them—sleepers. Look, we've told you so much already, why don't you answer some of our questions? Starting with Lucy. Who is she?"

He sunk back. Hesitant to answer at first.

"She's my sister. My little sister. That's all I'm gonna

say."

His sister?

"We never touched any kids," Alice said quietly from behind me. "Not before you came along and forced us to."

"Shiiit." David's eyes widened. His expression went straight. "That's why they sent me after you. To start... kids." He ran a hand through his hair and hissed through his teeth. "Damn it! How could I have been so stupid?"

"What?" I perked up.

"I thought you two had something to do with her infection. But if you guys didn't touch any kids before, well..."

"It wasn't us," Alice said firmly and stood up from the bed. "I remember every single child I've touched, and you were there for every one of them."

"So how the hell do you explain it then?"

"Someone else started her," I butted in. "The same way someone else started you, David. The Saviors want us to start as many people as possible who have dormant fluorescence, but apparently they have their own way of doing it that they've been keeping secret."

My stomach rumbled. "Look, I know we're all under a lot of pressure and stress right now, but can we talk about this more after we get something to eat?" I gestured toward the door. "We haven't eaten since yesterday afternoon."

"Then let's go." David untucked his button-up shirt from his dingy jeans and let the hem fall past his belt, concealing his handgun. "We can walk and talk."

I tipped my head to the side. "Do you... have to take the gun with you? You could leave it."

"Hell no!" He shook his head adamantly. "She goes where I go. *Period.*"

"Alright. Alright. Just, try not to draw attention, okay? We just want to be normal for a little while."

"Kid, we haven't been normal since they put this stuff in us," he added.

True. So true.

.　　.　　.

"So, are they going to get pissed at you for not doing your job?" I asked. We were walking along the sidewalk toward the convenience store at the end of the block. After what had happened last night, Alice and I didn't feel comfortable sitting down inside a restaurant.

"I don't know," David replied. "But I don't give a damn either way. They'll figure it out and they'll take me back when they're ready. That's what they told me, at least. Work things out. Move on."

"They probably want us to get along," Alice added.

"I'm sure they do." I hit the big silver button on the crosswalk post with my palm and waited for the light to change.

"They do now," David confirmed. "Seeing how you kids have a hell of a lot more fight in you than they thought you did. They told me to fix this—to get along with you—or they'd choose someone else to take my place."

The green WALK sign flashed and we darted across the street. David lagged behind, weaving in and out of the white guidelines on purpose like a kid lazily playing hopscotch. I was starting to think he was bipolar.

"I panicked when they threatened to take out my fluorescence. I...I," he stammered, stopping to kick a smashed soda can out of the crosswalk and beneath one of the stopped cars. "I had a meltdown, thinking Lucy would be in trouble. I thought as long as I had this power inside me I could change things. Protect her."

"Now you know why I did what I did, too." I looked back at him as I stepped up onto the curb. "Why I would do anything to protect her." I glanced at Alice.

We strolled up the parking lot toward the store. David stopped and looked around to see if anyone had been watching, then he readjusted his handgun. The sidewalks were relatively empty, but it would only be a matter of time before the lunch crowd came out.

"I hope they don't notice it," Alice murmured, tangling her arm around mine.

David sauntered through the sliding door and I followed behind, keeping some distance between us. Awkwardly forcing a zombie-like grin at the cashier.

Keep cool. Act normal.

A beep sounded as we passed beneath the motion sensor.

Knowing David was brandishing a gun beneath his belt had me on edge, but we were the only customers in the store, so I was hoping for the best. He seemed so confident no one would notice. That freaked me out. I could make out the small, wrinkled bulge in the back of his shirt and couldn't stop thinking about what it was concealing. Then my mind started to wander. What had he actually done with the thing? Had he killed anyone before?

"I'm going right over there." Alice pointed toward the next aisle.

"Okay." We split up. I kept a close eye on her, watching the top of her head drift down the neighboring aisle. David disappeared toward the back of the store, near the refrigerated section, while I sorted through a small end cap of cell chargers.

Alice came back a few moments later with an armful of snacks and ready-made sandwiches.

"Nice haul," I said with a laugh, though she barely cracked a smile before turning to head toward the cashier. I changed my mind on the charger cable and tossed it back onto the rack. No use. Our cells could be tracked.

"This, too," I said, snagging a cheap disposable cell phone from a nearby display and setting it on top of our stuff. Better than nothing. Anonymous.

The cashier packed everything into a few bags and handed

them over to Alice.

I sorted out the money and offered it up. The cash drawer popped out with a loud ding and then the cashier's eyes widened like he'd seen a ghost. His jaw dropped.

"Uh, sir?" I began, but suddenly a sick feeling washed over me. "Is everything..." I felt someone else's presence and swerved around.

David stood behind us, arm outstretched, pointing his gun straight at the man.

"Jesus!" I glared at him. "What are you—"

"Shut up, kid!" He pointed the gun at me, and then aimed at the cashier again. "Come on, you know the drill." David put out a hand and wiggled his fingers. "Come on, man, I don't have all day. Put the money in a bag and hand it over."

"What are you doing?" I muttered through clenched teeth.

"Do it, or I'll shoot the kid." David swung his arm toward me, targeting my face.

I sucked in a breath, unable to swallow.

Alice let out a whimper.

The cashier dug bills out of the money drawer and shoved them into a white plastic bag with "Thank You" ironically stamped across it. He tossed it over the counter to David.

"Thanks. I knew we'd come to an agreement." David snatched up the money and pulled the gun away from my head. Then he rushed out the door with a maniacal, satisfied grin on his face.

Freaking moron.

The cashier crouched down and reached under the counter to press something.

"You kids, uh, okay?" he asked, out of breath.

"Yeah." I heaved a sigh. "Yeah, we're okay. Shit." I drove a hand through my hair and slumped over. My chest ached from the tension.

Alice covered her mouth. "Oh my God, Brian. I thought..."

"It's okay." I looked up at the black orb protruding from

the ceiling. "Did you get his face on camera?"

"Probably," the man replied. "He was too dumb to cover it. He didn't sound like he was from around here either, so the police shouldn't have trouble finding him."

"Good. We need to step out and get some air." I relieved Alice of one of the bags of things we'd bought.

"The police are going to want to question you!" The cashier shouted after us. "Don't go too far."

"We won't. Don't worry!" We passed through the automatic doors and walked over toward the bike rack on the corner.

"David. What a freak." I started to sit.

"Hey! Psst," a voice called from the side of the store.

Alice shook her head and swallowed hard. "Don't."

"Brian!" Again. I recognized the accent.

"Da-David?" I crept around the corner of the store and into a narrow alleyway. David poked his head out from behind a huge metal garbage bin in the distance.

"Come here!" he whispered as loud as he could.

"Wait here." I gestured for Alice to stay where she was.

"Okay, but hurry up. The police are coming." She sat down cross-legged on the asphalt. I heard police sirens wailing in the distance.

"David?" I approached cautiously, my eyes darted toward the camera protruding from the side of the building. Sweat beaded on my forehead and my heart pounded in my chest. "What the hell was that back there?" I said, my voice cracking.

"I cut it off." David smirked, revealing a small butterfly knife from the back pocket of his jeans. "Don't worry, they won't see us."

I exhaled, relieved. "Jesus Christ, David. You're crazier than hell!"

"Maybe." He chuckled. "But you got to be a little crazy to survive nowadays."

Can't argue with that.

I stared at the bag tucked beneath his arm. "What are we supposed to do with the money?" I asked.

"Come back after you've finished talking with the cops." He reached into his side pocket and pulled out a narrow roll of duct tape, smashed almost flat. He stretched a length of it from the roll, bit the edge of it with his canine teeth and tore it off the roll. "It will be here. Waiting for you." He reached down beneath the giant metal trash bin and shoved the bag on the underside near the wheels, patting it flat against the base to make sure the tape stuck.

"But, it's... stolen. We can't... We shouldn't..." I was so angry, all I could do was stammer like an idiot.

David shot an anxious look over my shoulder. "I gotta cut before the cops come."

"But..."

"I'll find you later. They didn't make me your Tracker for nothing." He darted off down the alley, running faster than I ever could have.

Tracker?

I walked around to the front of the store.

"It's official. David's insane," I grumbled, lowering myself down beside Alice.

"But he's one of us now," she said, "right?"

"Yeah. Unfortunately."

.   .   .

"Holy shit! He robbed a place?" Kareena's eyes widened and a huge grin spread across her face. We sat on the hotel bed in a circle around a sizeable pile of money. She, creepily, seemed quite in her element. I, on the other hand, felt horrible.

"It is illegal, you know," I said. "Why are you so thrilled about this?"

"Because it's freaking badass," she replied, picking several hundred dollar bills out of the stack. "Damn. He really knows what he's doing, doesn't he?"

"But now we're thieves," Alice cut in. "We should return the money. It's not right."

"Neither is what the Saviors did to us." I ran a hand through the pile, filtering some bills through my fingers. It was surreal. "Neither is having to run from that store before the cops showed up so they wouldn't call Jane on us. That was too close. No doubt they're looking for us now, too."

"What happened to him?" Kareena asked, now starting a third pile for all of the tens.

"I don't know. He ran off. He didn't seem worried about the cops at all. My guess is, he knew the Saviors were going to send him home any second and used that as an opportunity."

"Smart." Kareena nodded. "That's smart." She patted the sides of a wad of ones to straighten it and then placed them neatly beside the other bills.

"You're not bothered by this at all, are you?" Alice narrowed her eyes at Kareena, who shrugged and didn't answer. "What now? We're going to resort to stealing? This is stupid! It's not who we are. Brian?" Alice looked up at me, her blue eyes desperate. "Please? Tell her it's not who we are."

"I don't know what to say, Alice. Maybe, as much as I hate to admit it, David is on to something. We need money if we're going to survive on our own. I'm sorry."

Alice looked down, disappointed.

"Maybe what David did was extreme, but... until we figure out what we're doing, we have to take some chances. We can't go back home. Not now. Not yet."

"I miss my mom," Alice whined. "I really do. We shouldn't have cut her off like that."

Kareena bit her lip and glanced at the clock on the nightstand. "Um, Alice?"

"What?" Alice huffed, crossing her arms. "Now you want to talk?"

"Your mom... Jane... I... kind of told her you guys were here."

"What!?" Alice and I echoed.

"Why?" I slammed my feet on the floor and stood. "Why would you—"

"Shut up, Brian." She shot off the bed and made fists with both hands. "Just stop being a little bitch and listen to me! We need her on our side."

"But... she can't find out about..."

"She called me a couple of times and I felt like shit ignoring her. So I told her you two were okay and... the next thing I knew, she said she was coming. I'm sorry, okay? Jesus! I thought I was doing the right thing! How was I supposed to know you and that crazy ass David were gonna rob someone!?"

How was *I* supposed to know we were going to rob someone?

Chapter 29

The hotel room phone rang and I clammed up.

Should I answer? What if...

It rang again. Alice cringed.

A third time.

She wouldn't stop twiddling her fingers. Nibbling her bottom lip. Shooting me anxious glances.

I lifted the receiver slowly to my ear.

"Hello?"

Silence. The caller took a breath.

"Hello?"

"It's Jane. Please don't hang up."

"I won't." I cut a glance at Alice.

"Mom?" she mouthed and I nodded.

"Brian, I know you don't want to see me right now. I know you're scared and worried for Alice and yourself. But I want to help. I need to help you in any way I can."

"We've been through this before, Jane. How are you supposed to help us with—"

"I've left something for you just outside. There's a note in there that explains everything. Please, go get it."

I veered toward the door.

"She left something for us," I said, gesturing for Alice to retrieve it.

A moment later, Alice lumbered back inside carrying a stuffed pack in her arms, our leather riding coats draped over her shoulder.

"My backpack?"

Alice set it onto the bed beside me and unzipped the top to peer inside.

"There are some things in it I thought you could use and some extra clothes. Please, Brian, don't be angry with me for what happened." She started to breathe more audibly into the speaker, like she was fighting back tears. I thought I should say something comforting, but nothing came out.

"I really do care about you as if you were my own. Be careful out there. Take care of my daughter and take of yourself. That's all I ask of you. Goodbye, Brian."

"Jane, wait!"

CLICK

The line went dead.

"Mom!?" Alice shrieked, scrambling to snag the receiver from my hand. "Mom?"

"She hung up," I said. "I'm sorry."

Alice groaned and pulled her knees up to her chest.

I slid my hand into the top of my backpack and lifted out a folded up piece of paper.

I unfolded the handwritten note and quickly scanned over her writing.

"Oh no." I shook my head and passed the note to Alice.

"We're... wanted by the police?" She dropped the note onto the bed like it had been laced with poison. "But we didn't do anything!"

"I know that and you know that, but no one else knows the truth."

According to Jane, the man from the diner had died in the hospital this morning and the police were searching for us in connection both with his death and with the robbery of the convenience store.

I squeezed my eyes shut and dropped my head back. "We're screwed. We're so screwed right now."

The bag contained several other things. A stack of money we'd need eventually. Extra clothes. A water bottle. Protein bars. A first aid kit. A map of the entire state and at the very bottom... something soft and leathery—my art journal.

It made me crack a brief smile. To think she'd known what my art meant to me, even in desperate times...

She'd thought of everything. More than I would have, at least. I had stormed out with nothing but the clothes on my back and a useless, battery-sucking cell phone.

"Get out of the city," Jane instructed in her note.

But, where would we go?

What would we do once we got there?

.   .   .

The phone rang again and Alice nearly jumped off the bed in fear.

I didn't wait so long to pick up this time.

"Hello?"

"Hey. I'm outside in the parking lot," Kareena said. *"I've got something for you guys."*

"Such as?"

"Look, I know this chick... she's made me fake IDs in the past so I could buy drinks and, well, if you're going to do anything on your own, you need these. You won't be able to do shit without them. You're not eighteen. At least now you'll be able to... Oh no!"

I heard the car engine revving up.

"Kareena?"

"Shit! The cops are out here. They're talking to the hotel manager and... damn it. I think they're looking up at your room. Yeah. They totally are. Shit! I gotta go. Get out of there! Meet me behind the strip mall down the street. I'll wait as long as I can."

"Where? What do we do!? Kareena!"

Alice panicked.

"What's going on?" She hopped off the bed. "Brian?"

"Grab the money. Get our jackets." I pointed. "Give me the backpack."

Alice yanked the drawer out of the dresser and took out the bag of money.

"Kareena? You still there? Kareena?"

"Yes! Christ, Brian, just get the hell out of there before they—" She gasped. *"I have to go."*

The phone disconnected.

I peeked through the blackout shades. Two police cars with lights flashing. A handful of cops walking around.

I shrugged on the backpack and grasped Alice's hand tightly.

"Come on. We have to get out of here." I pulled, but she pulled back, refusing to move. "Alice? Come on!"

"I'm... I'm..." She squeezed my hand harder.

"This is no time to let fear get the best of you. We have to be strong. We have to!"

"But..." She craned her neck to look over her shoulder. Green light skittered up her back.

"There's nothing we can do. Put on your coat and let's go. Now."

She shrugged on her jacket and I took her hand once more.

"You'll be okay, Alice," I said, looking into her terrified, pale blue eyes. "I promise."

We ducked out of the room as fast as we could and darted around the corner, down the wraparound hallway and to the stairwell at the back of the hotel. From the ground floor, we crossed the street and jogged toward the strip mall in the distance.

We spotted Kareena's car parked out back and broke into a sprint. She saw us coming, peeled out of the driveway and met us at the corner with a screeching halt of her brakes.

She rolled down the passenger window and unlocked all the doors.

"Get in!"

Alice hopped in the front seat. I tossed the backpack onto the backseat and jumped in beside it.

"Thanks," I said, short of breath. "That... was too close." I buckled my seatbelt and tossed my head back against the seat.

"What do we do now?" Alice asked, turning around in her seat to face me. She hadn't put on a seatbelt.

"I don't know." I looked out the window. "I really don't know."

Chapter 30

My legs were starting to cramp. We'd been in the car for over an hour, driving God knew where. I couldn't keep myself from checking our tail every five minutes for flashing red and blue lights.

A headache pulsed in my temples and my stomach churned. *Deep breaths.*

"How much farther?" I asked, leaning forward against the back of Alice's seat. She'd been silent the entire ride.

Kareena pulled out her phone and swiped it on. She thumbed some text into a map application and then shot her attention back up at the road. I guessed the odds of us getting into an accident because Kareena was on her phone were slimmer than being snatched up by the Saviors. At least I hoped so.

"There's a major bus station up ahead. Somewhere downtown. I'll drop you off there."

"Alright then. It's as good a plan as any." I fell back against my seat and cupped my hands in my lap.

She parked on the forth tier of a huge parking garage set aglow with flickering, off-white fluorescent lights. The three of us wandered down the moldy grey concrete stairwell and into the street, where we crossed and entered the bus station.

"Wait here, okay?" Kareena said. "I'll get your tickets."

"You don't have to—"

"Shut up. I'm trying to help."

"Okay." I shrugged. "Th-thanks."

Kareena headed into the office.

"It's nice of her to do this," Alice murmured, looking off into the distance at the busy streets of downtown wherever.

"Yeah. Though you and I both know a couple of bucks isn't shit to her."

Alice scowled at me.

"I'm sorry I say stupid stuff when I'm anxious. I can't help it."

"Yes. I know. I'm pretty freaked out, too. You really need to calm down sometimes. Be thankful she's helping us at all."

She was right. Without Kareena's help, we'd probably have been arrested already.

"I'll try," I replied.

"Thanks."

We walked over to a metal bench along the wall just outside the station and sat down. I dropped the backpack by my feet and shoved one of my legs through a strap so it wouldn't walk away if I took my eyes off it. The station was fairly empty now, but with dusk looming on the horizon, shadier people might come lurking.

"I can't believe this is really happening," Alice said, looking down at her lap. "It feels like I'm going to wake up any minute now and be back home in my safe, comfortable house, with a steaming cup of tea waiting for me in the living room."

"I think we're a long way from a hot cup of tea right now."

"Probably." She heaved a sigh and looked back toward the office. Kareena stood in line, thumbing through her wallet. "What do you think is going to happen now?"

"I... really don't know, Alice. I'm sorry. All I know is, we need to get out of this city. This state. Find a way to breathe on our own for a few days. To think about what's happening and how we're going to fight back."

Alice stared blankly ahead, nodding ever so slightly at my reply.

Kareena came out through the large sliding glass doors behind us and walked around to where we sat. Her hands were full. I reached up to help her with the two bottles of soda and bag of chips she had sandwiched between them in her arms.

"You're allowed to have food on the bus, so... Yeah. Anyway, I don't know what you like to drink and all they had were these."

"They're fine. Don't worry." I hadn't expected her to get us anything.

"Thank you," Alice said as Kareena gave her one of the sodas.

"Here." She handed us two printed tickets. "There's, like, three transfers or something, so pay attention. They're on there, though. On the sides there." She pointed to the list of transfer times and locations. "You'll get into town sometime in the middle of the night. I thought that would be better because there wouldn't be as many people out, maybe."

She was smarter than I'd thought.

"Thanks." I took the tickets, separated them and handed one to Alice. "So where are we headed?"

Kareena unfolded a map she'd gotten inside the office and hovered her finger over an area I'd never heard of. "I asked and they said this town is pretty rural. You should be safe there for a little while, at least. Maybe the Saviors won't be able to find you with all of the cows out there?" She let out a nervous chuckle and then went silent.

"Are you going to be okay on your own?" I asked, looking up at her from the bench.

Her eyes narrowed. "Seriously, Brian? Like I need you two to survive? I've been fine for this long without you."

"Sorry. I'm just... I worry about us all, you know?"

"Me, too," Alice chimed in. "I don't want anything to happen to you, either."

The expression on Kareena's face softened. "Yeah. I-I

know. Just don't start thinking I'm helpless, okay?"

I glanced at Alice and then back at Kareena. "What's with you two and making these assumptions? I *never* said anything about either of you being helpless or useless or whatever. Besides, Kareena, we would have been kind of screwed without you tonight."

"Oh, I know." She smirked, perking up. *How humble.*

Bright yellowish lights glimmered in the distance, casting huge shadows behind us. We turned our heads. I grasped onto my backpack and lifted it up into my lap. A dark blue and silver bus came toward the station, halting with a loud hiss of the breaks.

"Is that it?" I tried to make out the name of the city on the LED screen in the front window, but it had stopped quite a ways down the sidewalk.

"Yes," Kareena confirmed, squinting. "Yeah. That's it."

I stood up and shouldered my backpack. "Are you sure you're going to be alright?"

Kareena jerked her head toward me. "What? Yeah. I'll be fine." She bit her lip. "Just text me or something when you can, please? So... so I know you're okay."

"We'll do what we can," I tried to reassure her.

Alice and I started off toward the boarding line.

"Brian!" Kareena trotted after me, her heels clicking against the pavement. She grabbed my free hand and stopped me in my tracks. Her fingers were cold and clammy.

"Be careful," she whispered, squeezing tighter. "Please?" Her worried eyes glistened in the fading light.

"Kareena, I..." She had caught me off guard. I struggled to find the right words.

"Brian?" Alice tugged my arm. "We need to go. We can't miss this bus." She pulled me along with her and Kareena's fingers slipped from mine.

I approached the bus doors, put one foot onto the metal steps, and then the other. I took a few more steps up and then turned around. The anxious, sullen look on Kareena's usually confident face made my heart sink into my stomach.

"Bye, Kareena," I mouthed the words, as the glass doors closed in front of me.

Leaving her behind felt... wrong.

·   ·   ·

Alice had fallen asleep on my shoulder. I wanted to sleep, too, but couldn't yet. I'd sleep once we got where we were going. Once I felt safe.

Safer, at least.

I leaned against the window and looked out, watching the city pass us by. Then long stretches of open field zipped past. Barbed wire fences and wide open pastures as far as the eye could see. The clear deep-blue sky sparkled with stars, and the lights of the city faded more and more with every mile traveled.

We arrived at our final destination at just past three in the morning. I gently nudged Alice awake. She stretched her arms out high over her head and yawned. I reached under the seat and took up my backpack.

We shuffled our way down the aisle, carefully avoiding sleeping passengers who had their legs sprawled out into the aisle. I quietly thanked the driver and stepped off the bus.

"Where do we go from here?" Alice asked, looking around at the dismal town square. Obscure, private restaurants and shops lined the sidewalk across from us. An old-fashioned diner. A thrift store. A bakery. All closed up tight for the night. The streets were narrow and quiet, and the bus station was much smaller than the previous ones.

A man sauntered out of the tiny office building behind us.

"A little late for you kids to be out here all by yourselves, ain't it?" he said, looking us both up and down quickly. His dark blue lapelled jacket and slacks appeared black in the dim light of the station overhang, but I could tell he was a bus driver.

"We're visiting family," I replied.

"I take it you kids ain't from around here, then? You look like you're from the coast."

"Yeah. Maybe," I stammered.

"Whatchya so afraid of, young man?" The driver took a step closer and squinted at me. I held my breath. "You'd think ya had ants crawling in your jeans."

"We're tired, that's all," Alice said, coming up to my side. "We've been riding on that bus most of the night and we're exhausted."

"That'll do that to ya." He nodded. "Long bus drives. I've had my share of those for sure, but in this town, you gotta take whatcha can to make a living." He sniffed hard and wiped his upper lip with the back of his hand. "Pardon me." He pulled a tissue out of his jacket pocket and blew his nose. "This night air always stirs up my allergies."

"Do you know where we can get a room for the night?" I asked. "We don't know our way around this town yet."

"Sure." He shoved the balled-up tissue back into his pocket. "There's a little motel just a few blocks down the road. I can call ya a cab if you'd like."

"That'd be great. Thanks, sir."

"No problem, son." The driver tipped his head and walked back into his office.

"You don't think he's calling the police, do you?" Alice whispered.

"No." I shook my head. "He seemed honest. And besides, we're in the middle of nowhere. I doubt anyone here's even heard about what happened back home."

"True." She tucked her hands into her coat pockets and looked away.

Fifteen minutes later, a bright green cab pulled up in front of us. I glanced at Alice and smiled. "See? Honest, right? I think I like this town already."

．　　　．　　　．

A bell clanged loudly against the glass door as we entered the motel office. A musty smell irritated my nose the moment we walked in.

The man at the front desk turned toward us and cocked his head to the side, raising an eyebrow. He wore a tired old sweater vest and had a shiny bald head that reflected the light of the nearby desk lamp.

"Can I... help you?" He had a thick southern accent.

"We need a room, please," I replied, adjusting the backpack strap on my shoulder.

"I don't deal with minors," he said, gruffly. "Go home to your parents."

"We're not minors." I slapped our fake IDs onto the counter.

He squinted at them and shook his head.

"Don't mess with me, kid."

"Do I really look like a kid to you?"

"Well, I don't know about you." He shrugged. "But she sure as hell does." He pointed a boney finger at Alice. "What are you, girl? Thirteen?"

"She's not. Trust me." I was trying hard to not let him see how impatient I was becoming.

"I don't trust kids," he sneered, sucking his teeth.

"Okay. Then... let's try this another way." I shoved my hand into my pocket and pulled out some cash. I counted out the correct amount and then laid an extra hundred-dollar bill on top. "We pay cash. We don't cause trouble and we'll be out of your hair before you know it."

The man glanced suspiciously at the bills, at me, and then

back at the money. He cupped a hand on top of the pile and slid it off the counter. After a quick shuffle through it, he shoved it into the pocket of his corduroys. Then he turned, plucked a brass key from the hanging-rack behind him, and dangled it in front of me.

"Enjoy your stay, sir," he said, with a crooked smile.

Chapter 31

I pulled the door shut behind me and the hinges let out an ear-piercing squeal.

"Are you going to be okay, Alice?" I asked, peeking through the grimy peephole as I locked the deadbolt. It was so dark outside, I could barely see a thing.

Alice sat on the edge of the bed kicking her heels against the frame. The ugly paisley decor surrounding her looked like something from the '70s.

"I didn't like the way that guy looked at me," she said.

I walked over to the window, separated the grungy beige curtains with my fingers, and peered out at the empty parking lot. The motel was only one floor and it backed up to a dairy farm. Nice and quiet. Almost too quiet.

"I'm sorry I couldn't defend you better. We kind of needed this room for tonight and we couldn't have risked him throwing us out." I sat beside her on the bed.

"It wasn't about that," she continued, fidgeting with the hem of her shirt and wrinkling it in her hands. "It was how he argued with you about me. Like I couldn't even hear him! I'm not a thirteen-year-old kid! I'm sixteen and I been through a hell of a lot more than—"

"I know that, Alice." I cupped a hand over her knee. "Don't get so upset. I'm not the one questioning you." I leaned down to press a kiss to her cheek. "You're definitely not a child anymore. Don't worry about what he said." My lips gravitated toward her jaw line and I could taste the salt on her skin. "Don't worry about anything else tonight." I kissed the base of her neck, inhaling a deep breath of her scent, while my fingers caressed her leg.

"Stop it, Brian." She jerked away. "I'm tired." She rubbed her neck where my lips had touched it and scowled. "And you need to shave."

"I'm sorry. I just... We've been through a lot lately, and... I miss *us*. You know?"

She rolled her eyes. "Have you even noticed what time it is?" I shot a glance at the clock—4:32 AM. "I think you're being a little selfish, actually. Just leave me alone tonight, okay?"

"Alice, I'm sorry."

"I said I was tired. Now move, please." I got up the instant she nudged me in the side with her elbow.

I helped her fold down the sheets.

"This place was so not worth that extra money," she grumbled, fluffing up a pillow and tossing it back onto the bed. "But, whatever." She crawled up under the sheets, laid her head down, and tugged the fleece blanket up to her shoulders.

"Goodnight, Brian," she said and reached to switch off the lamp on the end table.

Now the room was lit only by the bright white fluorescent bulb buzzing in the bathroom.

I sulked over to sink and twisted on the faucet. Cool water felt good against my face, washing away a day's worth of hell. I rubbed the prickly stubble on my chin and sneered. Two-day-old shadow. I hated it.

A flimsy disposable razor rested on the counter, wrapped in frosted plastic. I picked it up, peeled open the wrapping and then craned back around to look at her.

What had I done wrong? She didn't want anything to do with me.

We were tired, I knew, but all I had wanted was her support. A "thank you," or a kiss goodnight. That was all.

But no. Nothing.

Screw it.

I dropped the razor on the counter, flipped off the light and crept over to the side of the bed opposite Alice. I carefully lifted up the covers and squeezed under them, trying not to disturb her.

My eyes shut tight. I took a deep breath.

Sleep.

I needed sleep.

But there was so much adrenaline still pumping through my veins. Throbbing in my head.

A chill shot up my spine and an image flashed through my mind.

Kareena's icy fingers latching on to mine. I could feel it—her hand. Even in the darkness.

What the hell?

I rolled over to face Alice, who was sound asleep, her hands clutching onto her pillow like they always did, her breathing quiet and slow. The light from the streetlamps shone through the curtains and outlined her face, highlighting the soft curves of her cheeks.

For a moment, her dark brown hair reminded me of Kareena's. Glossy waves of black framing cinnamon skin and falling down past a tiny waist. Vibrant green eyes that begged me not to go even when she knew I had no choice. So unlike her to show such compassion.

I closed my eyes again.

"Be careful," she'd said. And her words kept playing through my head. That frightened voice. The glisten of tears building in her eyes. Everything she'd done for us—for me.

The way she'd grabbed my hand. How tightly she'd held on. Her pulse racing through her fingertips, thumping against my skin.

I opened my eyes to Alice.

Damn it, Brian, go to sleep.

Go to sleep...

.　　.　　.

Out of breath. Panting.

We ran as fast as we could through the building. Trying to find the door—the portal—whatever they called it. Wherever it was.

We dodged rubble and ash—fiberglass insulation and drywall crumbling all around us. The entire building was caving in, trying to swallow us whole.

"We can't leave her!" Alice screamed, grabbing on to my arm and digging her heels into the ground.

"We don't have a choice!" I tugged back, overpowering her easily enough, and she stumbled into me.

"How could you!?" She shoved me away. "We need her!" Hatred flashed in her gaze. "You're selfish, Brian! You can't do this. You're not in charge!"

She broke free and darted off down the hall into oblivion.

"Alice!" I went after her. White flakes floated down from above, clouding the air. Making it difficult to breathe. I coughed hard and pulled my shirt collar up to cover my nose and mouth.

"Alice!" I called out again, but heard nothing.

The electricity shorted out and the halls went pitch black. I staggered forward in the direction she'd headed, calling out for her again and again. No answer. No footsteps.

"Alice!"

Nothing.

I blindly took another step and heard a crack beneath my foot.

The ground gave way and I fell.

"Brian!"

I opened my eyes to the dingy motel room.

"Brian!" Alice shook me violently.

"What?" I sat up. Blood rushed to my head and the room swirled. "What is it?"

Burning white light stung my eyes.

My stomach tightened and... I fell.

Again.

We hit the ground hard. Alice landed beside me. I looked up. Everything was white.

No.

I veered my head around.

"You!"

Saviors surrounded us. The translator stepped closer and looked down his nose at me.

"Hello, Brian," he said, tilting his head to the side. "We are pleased you and the Tracker have made amends. We hope you have learned to control your anger."

"Hardly!" I hissed, coming to my feet and making fists. "You bastards better tell us the truth. What happened to that man who died? The one who was infected?" I rolled my shoulders back. "Tell me."

The translator focused over my shoulder.

"I'm talking to you," I growled. "Why aren't you..." Then, I heard sobbing. Loud, congested sobbing. I turned.

"Kareena?"

She sat cross-legged on the floor behind us, her face buried in her hands.

"Kareena!" I rushed over and knelt at her side. "Are you okay? What's wrong?"

She slowly looked up from her hands. Her face was wet with tears. Black smudges of mascara bled down her reddened cheeks.

"Brian?" she wheezed, sucking in a strained breath. "They found out. They... found out."

"What do you mean they found out? Who?" I bent down farther to look her in the eye. "What are you talking about?"

"They won't let me go home." She shuddered, gasping for breath. "They've been holding me at the station for hours. I don't want to go back there. They'll put me away... They'll..."

I wiped her cheeks with my thumbs and cupped her face.

"Kareena? Look at me."

She eased her gaze up to my face.

"Who?"

"Th-the," she stammered. "The police."

"No. But... how? I thought you'd be safe if we..."

"They found the charges. On my credit card. The hotel. The bus tickets. They traced the last few calls I made." Her lip quivered and her darkened, nearly black eyes pierced me to the core. "I'm screwed, Brian. I'm so screwed!"

"We can fix this, Kareena. We'll make things right." I tried to hold on to her, but she pulled away and wrapped her arms around her body so tightly I couldn't pry them off. She rocked back and forth. Tears dropped into her lap.

"They're going to put me in jail, Brian! Daddy can't help me this time. I'm screwed. I'm just—"

"Shh." I embraced her and brought her close to my chest, cradling the back of her head. "I'll make sure nothing happens to you. I promise I'll keep you safe." My fingers ran through her hair.

"Brian?" Alice came down beside us. "Is she... okay?"

"No. And she won't be okay, either. Not anymore," I replied, gritting my teeth. "I'll fix this, Kareena. I swear I'll fix this."

"Thank you." She sniffled and wiped her eyes with the backs of her hands, leaving smears of black makeup across her temples.

"You!" I stood and confronted the translator again. "You did this! You fix this! Now! Unless you want us all to end up in prison. Experimented on or worse. Killed. Who the hell knows what our government will do to us once they find out we're freaks?"

"We cannot interfere with the operation of your government."

"Bullshit. You've probably already infected half of the damn politicians. You even infected David's sister after you promised not to. You can't just go around playing God to save your own asses."

"We promised nothing," he said, filtering the thought a moment. "You do not comprehend the importance of our mission."

"And you don't comprehend what's happening to us! She needs your help." I pointed behind me. Alice sat beside Kareena, holding her hand. "Look at her!" I veered back around. "Fix this, damn it. Or we'll put an end to this ridiculous game. Or I'll do whatever it takes to make sure you and your kind are destroyed."

The translator's eyes narrowed and he stared at me, silently.

Studying me.

The blank, unreadable face sent a chill up my spine.

My heart thumped faster.

I regretted the threat.

Grey eyes. Dusty-white skin. Emotionless. Cold.

He waited for me to crack.

I felt warmth flushing through my fingers. Up my arm. My fluorescence sparking to life.

"Why aren't you saying anything?" I growled. "Why are you just... Ahh!" I doubled over and held my arm. Blue raced toward my fingers, going in the opposite direction it usually flowed.

"Do not question our methods," he said, reaching an arm out toward me.

Sharp pain shot through me like lightning. Tightness choked the air from my lungs.

I fell and hit the floor hard. I couldn't breathe. My ribs were aching.

"We put the fluorescence inside you," the translator said, looking down at me with his hand outstretched. His eyes reflected a glimmer of hot blue and his fingertips sparked with blazing azure light. "We can remove it."

I strained, reaching toward nothing. My skin turned a sick greyish-purple.

"But," he continued, "your imperfection will flourish."

No!

No. I wouldn't take it back. Not the arrhythmia. Not for anything.

The translator rippled and warped out of focus. I closed my eyes against the sudden weakness. My energy draining. Oxygen being sucked out of me. The air so thin...

"Brian!?"

Someone called my name. I gasped and rolled over on the floor, grabbing at my throat. Wheezing.

No words came out.

My eyes burned. I squeezed them shut against a sudden glow of light.

The floor vanished from beneath me.

My back slammed against the ground.

A musty scent filled my nostrils.

"Brian!"

Alice helped me sit up. My hands brushed against carpet.

The hotel room?

I looked around. Things slowly came into focus. Ugly brown wallpaper. Paisley patterns everywhere. We were back.

I took another breath, realizing how close I'd come, yet again, to death. Because of *them.*

"Shit," I huffed.

Alice took my arm.

Kareena? She crawled over on her hands and knees.

"You're here?" I said as our eyes met.

Kareena's lips curled into a small, thankful smile and she nodded. "Yeah," she replied, taking my hand. "I'm here."

Chapter 32

"We can't fight back," Alice said, unwrapping the brightly colored foil from one of the protein bars Jane had given us. "They almost killed you." She took a bite, crunching on the nutty center.

I plopped down in the chair across from her. "The Saviors won't kill me. I think they need me. I've put up enough of a fight already and they haven't killed me yet. They want me alive, obviously."

"Mmm. These aren't bad," Alice said, munching on the bar.

I needed real food. Soon.

"Your big mouth is what's going to get you killed," Kareena snapped, crossing her arms and screwing up her face. She was leaning against the TV stand. "Keep your damn mouth shut and maybe—"

"I'm not going to help them hurt people!" I shot up from the chair. "Do you want to be responsible for someone's death? And seriously, Kareena, do you want to live like this forever?"

"Well, no." She shrugged. "But we don't have a choice. We're not shit compared to them. In case you've forgotten, they're freaking aliens. They can snap their ugly fingers and zap us anywhere they want. Jesus, when was the last time you watched a sci-fi movie?"

"You think this is some kind of joke, don't you?"

"No." She rolled her eyes. "Do you really think I'm enjoying this? I'm not. I just want to go back to the way things were before Alice shocked me. Before I hit my head and you—"

"Saved your life?"

Her lips thinned. She averted her eyes.

"That's what I thought."

"Forget it," she muttered. "You can stay in here and keep wallowing in your broody shit. I'm going to take a walk."

She stormed out of the room and slammed the door behind her.

.   .   .

My mind raced—swirling with thoughts of vengeance. Bustling with worries and fears about what we would do next. Where we would go. How we could get there. What would happen if the police found us again? How could we possibly explain everything to them?

I dropped my head back. Hot water drizzled down my face. Almost too hot to bear, but my tired muscles needed to be soothed.

Steam clouded the glass walls of the walk-in shower, thickening the air with warm, silky mist. It felt good to breathe in the steam. Relaxing. Clean. The quietest few minutes I'd had in days.

The Saviors always toyed with us. Used us as pawns in some game they refused to explain.

Now, they were threatening *me*?

Threatening to remove the one thing keeping my heart stable.

How could they?

I twisted the rusty faucet and the shower shut off. I squeezed the excess water from my hair and reached for a towel.

People fear death, but feeling it—actually tasting it—is a whole different story. Too many times already. Too much pain within the past few weeks.

And after all of it, Alice had the nerve to turn cold. Pushing me away as if I were a stranger.

After everything I'd done. Everything I'd been through.

Helping her.

Protecting her.

Sacrificing anything I could for her.

At least Kareena seemed grateful—if only marginally. She had thanked me, and that was what mattered.

.   .   .

The next morning, I found Kareena leaning on a wooden fencepost behind the motel, staring off at a fresh, green pasture that stretched for miles. Tall stalks of grass swayed in the wind. A cool, pleasant breeze tickled my nose and I took a deep breath of clean country air.

Black and brown cows moseyed along in the distance. Some sprawled out on the ground, sunbathing. Others mindlessly chomped away at the grass. A few little calves—about the size of German Shepherds—bounded playfully in circles around their mothers.

I smiled.

"Hey." Kareena turned toward me.

"Hey. So, did everything go okay with the manager?" I asked.

"Yeah," she replied, wrinkling her lips to the side. "It went okay. I mean... I didn't have any trouble getting a room or whatever but the guy's a total perve."

"Oh?" I ran my finger over a smooth section of the barbed wire fence and gently prodded at one of the barbed knots down the line.

"He freaking tried to hit on me." She scoffed. "He tried to hit on me and he wouldn't stop staring at my boobs. I mean, seriously. Back off, Grandpa."

"I'm sorry to hear that." I returned my focus to her. "He was a little creepy."

She was wearing the same skimpy black-lace skirt and burgundy tank top from yesterday—not that she had any other alternatives—so no wonder the manager had gotten the wrong idea.

"You might have to start dressing down a little around here. Maybe a bit more conservatively even?"

"Damn." She shook her head. "It's bad enough we're in the boonies out here. I have to dress like a hick, too?"

"Well, no, but..."

"Yeah. I get it. Get off my ass, Brian. I'm in no mood for this."

"Sorry." I brushed some crumpled dead leaves from the top of a nearby tree stump and sat down. "I'm a little on edge, too."

Kareena took a step closer. "So... you and Alice. You guys okay?"

"Yeah. Why?" I squinted. "It's not really your business."

"I know. I'm just asking. You've been under a lot of pressure and she doesn't seem like she's taking it very well."

"We're fine. Don't worry about us."

"Okay. Whatever. Sorry I asked." She turned back toward the pasture.

I watched some calves prancing back and forth, bucking and jumping at each other. Oblivious to the outside world.

It's ironic how in movies, cows so often get abducted and dissected by aliens.

In movies.

But not in real life. Not in our lives. We were the ones being picked apart.

"Hey, Kareena?" I shuffled toward the edge of the tree stump and picked at a piece of loose bark peeling up on the edge.

"What is it?"

"About Alice... have you noticed anything different about her since you got here? I know it's only been a few hours, but still."

"If by different you mean she's not glued to you, then yeah."

"You noticed that, too?"

"I noticed she's not hanging all over you like she usually is, if that's what you're trying to ask me. It's probably stress. Maybe she can't handle it like you can. Or, maybe she just..." Her voice trailed off.

"Just... what?"

"Maybe she doesn't want to be here. You ever thought about that?"

Didn't... want to be where? With me? Is that what Kareena was hinting at?

The idea crushed me.

Sure, we had marched out on Jane abruptly, but I thought Alice had trusted my decision. I'd done it for both of our sakes. We'd needed to get out of there. We'd needed to move on.

I didn't do this for myself. I did it for us.

"Brian?" Kareena bent down and looked me in the eye. "You asked me what I thought, and I told you. But don't let it get to you. I can't do this without you, you know. You have to stay strong for me, too."

．　　．　　．

"Alice? We need to talk." I slammed the motel door shut behind me and locked the deadbolt. Alice jerked her face up from a brochure she'd been reading while sitting on the bed.

"Brian? What's wrong?"

"Don't bother getting up."

She plopped her feet onto the floor and stood. "What is it? Tell me what's wrong."

"So now you care?" I reached toward her shoulders and she staggered back, frightened. "Look! You're doing it again.

Pulling away from me."

"Brian, what are you talking about? I don't understand."

"Kareena was right. Do you even want to be here? With me?"

"Of course I do, Brian. But I'm just—"

"Exactly. There's always a 'but.' You can't just admit that what I did was the right thing, can you? You can't even thank me for putting my own ass on the line for you. You haven't shown me a sliver of gratitude for any of it." I grasped her forearms. "You can't keep pushing me away." Her legs bumped against the edge of the mattress and then she tumbled onto the wrinkled up sheets.

"You don't get it, do you?" I bounded onto the bed and crawled up over her. She tried to scramble out from under me, but I straddled her legs and wrapped my fingers around her wrists, forcing her arms back by the sides of her head.

"Brian? What are you doing?!" Her eyes glistened. "I don't understand. Why—"

"You've been acting like a goddamn child for far too long." I squeezed her wrists a little tighter. She flinched and sucked in a shuddering breath. "You're repulsed by me. Like I'm a horrible mistake you can't stand to admit." I took a breath and broke eye contact with her for a moment. "I've been trying to tell myself that you just need some space and that I should let it go, but I can't." I looked down at her again. "I won't let you treat me like this. We're in this together. You're not the only one having a hard time."

I pulled her left hand up so she had to face the ring I'd given her. "Do you even remember why you accepted this? Because you used to... want me."

"Brian," she muttered, her lip quivering. "Stop this."

"Do you remember back when you texted me because you couldn't stand another second without me? When you wanted me so much you almost gave in and we... But, no. You were so worried about what your mom thought of you that you couldn't make your own decisions. You couldn't decide what *you* wanted. What *you* needed." I put her arm down and pressed it into the bed, crouching down even closer over her.

"Stop, please. You're hurting me." She squirmed and tried to wriggle her arms out of my grasp.

I wouldn't let go.

She trembled beneath me. Something she once did passionately... not fearfully.

Never fearfully.

I brought my lips to the side of her neck and exhaled.

"You used to need me, Alice." I breathed the words against her skin. "What changed?"

She squeezed her eyes shut and turned her face away. "This isn't you. Please don't..."

I scoffed.

Seriously?

"I would never *ever* force you to do anything!" I pushed her arms deeper into the mattress and then released her abruptly. "The fact that you even thought for one second that I would, disgusts me." I hopped off the bed and marched toward the door. "Stop being so goddamn selfish and think about me once in a while. What I've given up to be here. And what we've been through together. Think about that."

I left, slamming the door behind me.

I needed air.

Space.

Anything to clear my head of that fearful look in her eyes.

I walked to the edge of the parking lot and sat down on an old prickly wood pallet. It creaked and bowed a little beneath my weight but held up.

Alice actually thought I would force something on her?

How could she even think that? I love her.

Damn it, Alice. Damn it!

I heard movement and lifted my face, hoping it was her

but...

Kareena knelt beside me.

"Is everything okay?" She bit her lip.

"Yeah. Sure. I... Never mind." I drove my hands through my hair and groaned.

She sat down, her hip pressing against mine, and rested a hand on my knee.

"Do you want to talk about it?" she asked, walking her fingers up my leg. Bright red nails lightly scratched against my jeans.

"No." I exhaled loudly.

She rested her head against my shoulder.

"I know how you feel," she whispered, so close to my neck, I felt her warm breath on my skin. "I know *exactly* how you feel."

"Do you really?" I stared off into the distance, focused on nothing. I doubted she could ever understand how I actually...

"Brian?"

I turned and looked her in the eye, our noses almost touching. She gazed up at me through ebony lashes and cracked a smile.

"I'm here for you... if you need me. If you need *anything*, I mean." She pressed her fingertips deeper, sliding them up toward my thigh. Her eyebrows rose.

I swallowed hard and a lump caught in my throat.

She had this *look* in her eyes. This I'll-sleep-with-you-and-we-don't-have-to-tell-anyone look.

But I'd seen it before. More times than I had wished to.

And in a way, I couldn't blame her. With the fluorescence threatening to burst her head every time she flirted with a regular guy, it had to be hard for someone like her—someone who made a hobby out of sleeping around.

"I know you care about me, Kareena," I said. She glanced at my lips. "I've seen it in your eyes. But..."

She brushed a hand across my jaw line. Warm fingertips

sliding over my face. My eyelids drew closed against my will and I exhaled.

Maybe it wasn't so bad—her wanting me.

At least someone did.

But all she wanted from me was...

Fingernails tickled the back of my neck and I opened my eyes. Her woodsy green irises glimmered with longing. Her hand crawled toward my waist. She tangled two fingers around my belt and tugged gently, inching closer. Her shallow breaths rising and falling in her chest. So near, I could feel the heat of her body—the intense craving she had for me.

And for one goddamn second, I thought about it.

I almost considered her blatant offer. Considered saying to hell with the rest of the world and humoring Kareena. Knowing how desperately she wanted to please me with her twisted little fantasy, it probably would have been freaking amazing.

But it would have ended right there.

It wouldn't change things. It wouldn't extinguish the fire building inside—the need to have Alice back. My Alice.

I didn't love Kareena. Maybe I'd grown to care about her, but I didn't *want* her.

I couldn't. Not the way I wanted—needed—Alice.

"This is just a game to you." I pushed her hand away. "I'm not that desperate, Kareena."

It wasn't about sex. It was about having the girl I loved with me the way she had been before—back when she wasn't filled with so much fear. Before every minute threatened our very existence. Back when I'd embrace her and she'd melt into me, trusting me completely.

Back when I knew she needed me in her life.

Now she recoiled. Annoyed by my every word and action.

"You can't win this one," I said. "So save your energy and drop it. I'm with Alice. Only Alice." I pushed up off the pallet and headed back toward the motel.

"Have fun with your little girl!" Kareena called after me, snarkily.

I clenched my teeth and turned. "Have fun being alone."

Her jaw dropped and she huffed, crossing her arms and looking away. She let out a loud, frustrated groan as I walked away.

Chapter 33

From outside, I heard sobbing beyond the door. I shoved the key into the knob, turned it until it clicked and released the lock, then eased the door open.

At that moment I couldn't have hated myself any more.

Alice lay curled up in the fetal position, quaking, crying her eyes out on the bed. A mountain of tissues balled up on the floor. I approached slowly and climbed onto the bed. My weight sunk into the mattress and she let out a muffled whimper.

"Alice?" I scooted up behind her, resting my fingers onto her bare shoulder. I kissed her arm and she cringed.

What have I done?

"I'm sorry, Alice." I kissed her cheek, tasting salty tears. "I am so damn sorry." Her skin trembled beneath my fingers and my chest tightened. "I shouldn't have done that to you. There was no excuse for it." I shuddered and strained to keep my composure. Every stitch of my being was unraveling. "I did all of this for you. I can't... I don't want to be here without you. I'd rather be dead right now, than go this alone. Please, Alice." I rested my forehead against her shoulder and a tear streamed down my cheek.

My face grew hot. "We have an entire lifetime ahead of us, but I feel like we're drifting apart already. In just a few days. And that scares the crap out of me, Alice. Every moment I breathe is only because of you—because I want to be here with you. I need you in my life."

She sniffled, then rolled over to face me, wiping her cheeks with the backs of her hands. "I want a life with you in it, too, Brian," she said, quivering. "But I never wanted a life like this. Always afraid. Uncertain. Like oddities in a traveling freak show. I'm tired of it."

I scooted closer and rested my arm on her waist. "So am I."

Her breaths softened.

"Brian, I can't find the strength to love you when I don't even love myself right now. I wake up every morning and contemplate how I could die that same day. How I might lose you. How we'll get by. How to end the day without hurting more people. These aren't the kinds of things a girl my age should be worrying about."

"I love you, Alice. I'll love you no matter what. But you can't let this nightmare the Saviors created change who we are." I took her hand into mine and pressed a kiss to her knuckles.

"I understand," she replied. "But I need you to believe in me, too. Respect me for being who I am. For being strong. Responsible. I can do it, if you let me. If you believe in me."

I propped myself up onto my elbow and brushed her hair behind her ear. The fluorescence ignited in my arm and the blue cast a soft tint on our surroundings. I couldn't hide how much passion I had for her.

"It never should have gone this way, Alice. I shouldn't have pushed you. I'll try to let up more from now on and give you space to grow. I'll try."

"Thank you, Brian." She combed her fingers through my hair. I closed my eyes and exhaled a slow, contented breath. Warm fingertips gliding across my scalp. Slender fingers lovingly coiled a length of my hair.

If she could forgive me, maybe I could forgive myself.

Maybe...

"I love you, Brian," she said, cupping my face with both hands, her voice breaking. Her eyes gazed into mine. "Don't ever... *ever* doubt that." She leaned in to kiss me briefly, then came onto her knees and pushed me off my elbows and onto my back.

"I won't doubt you anymore. I promise. I'm sorry for what I did to you earlier. I—"

"Shh." She pressed a finger to my lips and moved forward, on top of me. "You've been dealing with so much anger and pain. Bottling it all up inside. We all have. What you did was a mistake, but I forgive you for it. It's in the past now."

I slid my hands to her waist and wrapped my fingers around the supple, smooth skin peeking out above the waistband of her jeans, my thumbs flitting over her hipbones. The warmth of her body made me shudder. Goose bumps rose across my arms, and the hairs on the back of my neck perked up. She came down to kiss my lips first and then the sensitive flesh of my throat.

The light of my fluorescence tinted her skin a gorgeous soft blue. The green glow of her shoulder sparked to life dimly at first and then grew brighter, taking on a faint teal hue.

Alice?

"We're meant to be together," she said, exhaling a hot breath near my ear and then kissing me there. Her wandering hands wrinkled up my shirt. "Together we'll get through this."

My Alice.

•   •   •

I put my feet onto the knobby carpet and craned back to look at her. Even tangled up in ugly beige sheets, Alice was breathtaking. Wavy dark brown tresses complimented a porcelain white complexion.

Warm, afternoon light seeped in between the curtains, making the soft blue of her eyes sparkle. A subtle pink flush of color on her skin made her glow with new life.

I didn't want to leave her, even for a short while. But she

could take care of herself. She needed me to believe that—to trust her.

From now on, I would.

I bent down to scoop my clothes up off the floor and pulled the t-shirt over my head. Alice reached across the bed and twisted her fingers around the hem of it.

"Don't go," she said, looking up at me with a frown.

I chuckled. It was the first time I'd smiled in nearly two days.

"I'm just going to take a quick walk down the street and see if I can grab us something other than protein bars to eat."

"Be careful," she added, withdrawing her hand as I stood. I tugged my jeans up both legs and weaved my belt through the loops.

"I will. Don't worry, beautiful."

Alice smiled.

"I'll be back soon." I quietly closed the door behind me and locked it.

The manager had mentioned a gas station and some drug-stores not far from where we were.

I set out to cross the parking lot toward the main road.

After only a few steps, I froze.

Voices.

I heard someone talking. Worried it could be the cops, I held my breath and listened.

Kareena?

Who was she talking to?

David?

No. It couldn't have been. At least I hoped it wasn't. I wasn't prepared to deal with the havoc he brought along with him. Not today.

I listened intently to her voice and followed the sound around to the back of the motel.

"Kareena?" I asked, rounding the corner that led to the pasture.

There she stood, alone in the distance, staring straight out at nothing. Fixated on something—or someone—I couldn't see.

"Kareena?" I called quietly, trying not to startle her.

She ignored me so I tried again. "Kar—"

"What... are you?" she asked no one.

My eyes widened and my jaw eased open.

Had she lost it?

There was nothing there but grass, going on for miles in front of her. Nothing.

Then her brow furrowed and she nodded, still watching the invisible thing intently.

"You can help us?" she said, anxiously cupping her hands together near her heart. "But... how?"

BOOK III

FALLOUT

Chapter 1

While sitting back on my heels beside him on the bed, I drove my hands through his hair and watched the blue light burning inside him as it always had. Alive. Skittering through his bloodstream. Brightest in his left arm. A glimmer of azure surged through his heart, outlining the organ in slivers of throbbing white fire.

His eyes wandered, his gaze flitting from wall to wall before finally returning to meet mine. I glanced into his weary eyes and cracked a small, sympathetic smile. Even in his darkest moment, the vivid greens and soft golden browns drew me in. Only now there was fear and uncertainty in them. Fatigue.

He was tired of running. Tired of feeling like he was fighting this battle alone.

"Kareena, I—"

"No." I pressed a finger to his lips and shook my head. "Don't over think it."

He lowered his head in submission.

"Hey," I whispered, tipping his face up. "You deserve better. You know that, don't you, Brian?" I reached for his hands. "She doesn't deserve you."

It wouldn't take long for me to alter his world. I'd make him forget her—even if only for a moment. I'd leave a mark on his soul. Leave him spellbound, wanting more. Wondering why he hadn't chosen me instead of *her* from the beginning.

I straddled his legs and leaned in, exhaling a breath near his throat that made him shudder—his chest swelling with sheltered desires. His smooth, musky scent made my heart pump faster, the beat thumping into my fingertips.

My hands drifted up to his collar, where they worked to begin unbuttoning his shirt. His eyes locked on to mine and an anxious breath escaped his lips as I set the second button free. And then the third. And fourth. Blue light licked at the surface of his skin, forking and reeling through him, the soft color tinting me with its wintry glow.

I continued until I could peel apart the sides of his shirt and run my fingertips across his bare chest. I traced his collarbone with a bright red fingernail and grinned, caressing flawless curves of ivory skin.

A stroke of my tongue against the sensitive flesh on the side of his throat made him drop his head back against the wall with a muted thud. The sexual tension quickened his pulse, making his breaths hasten. His face came back down and our gazes met, a new kind of need glistening in his hazel eyes.

Damn it! Why can't I have him?

I could hardly stop slipping in and out of the daydream whenever he was near me.

"I know you care about me, Kareena," Brian said, looking off into the distance.

The sun glistened off his light brown hair. His soft, beautiful hair. So perfect, bristling against my palms. I inched closer to him until our hips touched and took a breath near his collar. My fingernails gravitated toward the back of his neck where I scratched him playfully. Imagining us together in my motel room, intertwined, made my heart race.

I wanted to be in his arms. I wanted to snuff out whatever glimmer of *her* remained. With my experience, I could fill his head with things he'd never thought about before. Things he wouldn't soon forget. Things that would bring him crawling back, wanting more. Moaning in the ecstasy *I* could give him. Calling out *my* name.

If I could take him now in his moment of weakness...

If I could...

"This is just a game to you," Brian said, swatting my hand away. "I'm not *that* desperate, Kareena. You can't win this, so save your energy and drop it. I'm with Alice. Only Alice. Stop lying to yourself." He stood up and turned to head toward the motel.

He had no idea what he was missing. Alice was nothing but a child.

How dare he treat me like such a...

"Have fun with your little girl!" I shouted after him.

He swerved back around and sneered. "Have fun being alone." Then he turned his back on me again and marched off.

Bastard.

I clenched my teeth.

He'll regret that.

Alice wouldn't be able to satisfy his needs. Not like I could. Not for long.

He'd get tired of her sooner or later.

Then I'd have him.

Chapter 2

I hate turquoise. A hideous blend of blue and green.

Brian and I could make something amazing—a rocking, fiery purple. If I could only get to him. If I could just see the look on her face when his arm shimmered a different hue.

But it wouldn't happen today. Not as long as he and Alice were still together mixing their own disgusting shade of color while I sat on my lonely ass in the motel parking lot staring at the pavement.

I'd throw up if I saw it again—*their* color. That damn vivid turquoise I'd seen coiling through their bodies the last time they'd slept together. They can't hide it from me. I can see right through them. Literally. The way it bleeds into their veins, the fragments of mixed light staining their auras. Taunting me.

I pushed up off the pallet and looked around. The Saviors had ripped me out of the police department and almost everything I owned was still back at my house. Extra clothes. Makeup. Jewelry. Aside from the diamond stud still piercing my left nostril, all I had on me was my wallet and a couple of bucks.

My clothes smelled like sweat. I felt like shit, and I probably looked like it, too. No wonder Brian had turned me down.

The creepy old man at the front desk found me appetizing, though.

Perv.

•　　•　　•

I had been wandering around the hick town for a while and all I'd gotten was flack from strangers. Nosey old women. Lumberjacks. Pastors. Conservative bastards just wouldn't keep their judgmental eyes off me.

No, I wasn't lost. And no, I wasn't a hooker. But in this little town overrun by churches, I apparently needed to be saved by the Lord Savior Jesus Christ. And fast.

Inside, I was laughing. Laughing at how we had coincidentally been getting the complete opposite treatment from the ones *we* called *Saviors*—meddling aliens who didn't seem to give a damn about our wellbeing.

I found my way back to the motel and sat in the grass near the fence line out back. There was wide-open pasture for as far as I could see. The cows that had been there earlier must have moved on because I couldn't see them anymore. The silence was soothing and considering how crappy the motel A/C was, the cool grass was comforting in the sweltering summer heat.

A sudden sharp pain shot through my head. I flinched, grunting as my stomach tightened and my eyelids squeezed shut involuntarily. Colored light flushed through my eyes and I blinked uncontrollably as silver sparks flickered in and out of my vision, fading and pulsing. Distorting my line of sight.

A second wave jolted me and I doubled over, clutching my face in my hands. I sucked in a breath and gritted my teeth hard against the ache. I gasped for breath and tumbled forward onto my knees, thick blades of grass slicing into the tender skin of my palms.

I dropped my head and moaned. Tears welled. My cheeks flared with heat. Then I heard a buzz—a high-pitched humming in the back of my head—a ringing in my ears that blocked out everything else. A million colors blinded me. I shielded my eyes with the back of my hand and looked up to see the colors swirling and rippling. Wild, like lightning.

They came together into a shape I couldn't define. Tall. Rounded. A multitude of hues dancing inside an oblong form, bouncing and ricocheting through themselves in tiny explosions of color. A silhouette created only by light.

The painful noise in my brain dampened just enough for me to gather my thoughts. I came to my feet and brushed the grass from my knees.

"Kareena," a subtle, echoing voice sounded from the light. Ghostly and muffled as if it had manifested from some distant place. From what I could tell, the being had no mouth and no eyes. The sound simply resonated from waves of intense cascading light.

I gasped and stepped back. A rush of cold air swept over me and I shivered.

"Who..." I coughed, my mouth dry as paper. I cleared my throat and tried again. "*What* are you? And... how do you know my name?"

"We are what is inside you," it replied, the voice tainted heavily by reverb. I squinted, straining to listen.

"What do you mean?" Pink fluorescence invaded my vision and it revealed to me a beaming spark of white thumping inside the thing like a heartbeat. Slow. Rhythmic.

"Fluorescence," it replied, the fiery light of its silhouette stinging my eyes. Its core was so bright, I had to look upon it with soft focus.

"Fluorescence? You mean you're..." My heart raced.

"Yes." The shape flickered. "We are the origin of that which you now carry in your blood—fluorescence in its ancient, purest form."

The brightness dimmed and I could almost focus on the wavering shape filled with sparkling arcs of color. *Almost.*

"I don't want to be a part of this anymore," I said, still shielding my eyes with my hand. "We've been through enough hell. I don't want anything to do with you or the Saviors."

"We are not part of what the Saviors have done, nor do

we condone their negligence," it continued, inflecting its words carefully. "We are very much aware of your plight and how they have used you against your will. The Saviors, in jeopardizing your race, have put many species at risk. By infecting you, they have created vulnerabilities and have allowed the disease to grow and mutate into something stronger—something that may poison the futures of *many* worlds."

"Then why are you here?" I asked. "What do you want from me?"

"It is against our nature to interfere with other worlds, but a small number of our kind have grown very concerned." The saturation of its colors grew deeper and more vibrant.

I swallowed hard.

"We have taken it upon ourselves to reach out. To... help you."

"You can help us?" I stammered, stepping closer to the being. The phantom cold dissipated and the warmth of its energy suddenly overwhelmed me. It was a creepy, yet comforting type of warmth—like an unfamiliar embrace. Static made the tiny hairs on my body stand on end. "But how?"

"Stay away from the Saviors and you may have a chance for survival."

Survival? Is this a matter of life and death now?

At the time, I had known what was going on around us was all sorts of wrong, but that it might *kill* us? No!

"But what can we do?" I replied, unable to focus on any one part of the being. "We can't stop them from taking us." Light kept moving around, sparking from edge to edge, causing the entire form to change color over and over.

"You are correct. You cannot stop them from interfering, but there are indirect ways in which you and the others can protect yourselves. We will do what we can to assist, but—" The being dissolved partially into nothingness and then faded briefly back into focus before fading out again. "There is very little time. This atmosphere is not ideal and we must go."

God, I wanted to believe it, whatever it was. I wanted to believe it could help us somehow, but...

"How do I know we can trust you?" I asked. "That you're telling the truth and not—"

"We are the reason you live," it replied, its iridescent light softening to a comfortable glow, as its voice became a soothing, ethereal whisper. "We came before you. Before *them*. We are the foundation of that which your people call the soul. What moves you. What makes you alive. We are the Prism."

I should have been scared, but I wasn't. I knew in my gut it spoke the truth. I knew it because I felt no fear. No sickening tangle of knots in my stomach. No nagging conscience telling me to fight or flee. And—especially—no hatred building inside me.

Not like it was with the Saviors. They terrified me. Cold, corpse-like and grey. Like death incarnate.

But this, Prism, burned with something else. Something familiar and sacred.

Life.

"Kareena, you and the others must leave. Find shelter elsewhere."

"Where do we go from here? How do we get there?" I took another step toward it, my skin prickling from the heat. "There has to be more you can do! Please!?"

"Not yet. We apologize." Its voice faded out and the light shrank away, sucked into the center until it collapsed upon itself and disappeared into nothing but a vanishing white sparkle.

I blinked a few times, trying to focus on my surroundings again. Everything looked washed out. Tinted pink. I closed my eyes and took a deep breath, waiting for the myriad of tiny black particles to fade from my vision. My headache returned, subtler than before.

"Kareena?"

I veered around and gasped. "Brian? How long have you been watching me?"

"Long enough to know you were talking to someone. Who?" He came closer and tilted his head. "Who was that?"

"You saw it, didn't you? The colors. The light. It was right there in front of me. It was—"

"No. I didn't see anyone. I saw you staring off toward the pasture like some crazy person. Talking to yourself. Or—"

"Someone who can help us escape from the Saviors!" I blurted.

"What?" He narrowed his eyes suspiciously at me. "What are you talking about? Kareena, if you're screwing with me, I'll—"

"I'm not lying, Brian. I swear to God, I'm not." I reached out for his arm, but he jerked away.

"Stop it. Just stop." He shook his head and scowled.

"Brian! Listen to me." My voice cracked.

"No. This is about me and Alice, isn't it?"

"No." True, the color inside him had become a muddled green-blue, but this wasn't about them right now. It was about us. *All* of us. "I'd show you, but it's gone. Brian, there are others out there. Others who want to help us."

"Really?" He stifled a chuckle of doubt. "Why should I believe you? How do I know you're not putting on a show because of this jealously shit you've been pulling lately?"

"Because you have to, Brian. If you want to get out of this alive, if you want to save Alice and yourself from whatever killed that man back at the diner, you're going to have to believe me."

Brian's eyes widened. "You... you're not screwing with me, are you?" he asked in a low, wavering voice.

"No." I shook my head and reached out to touch his

hand. He didn't pull back this time. "No, I'm not."

Chapter 3

All I wanted was for Brian to trust me, but that was apparently asking for too much.

I set my hands onto the edge of the sink and lifted my face toward the mirror. *Dark circles? Already?* It had been less than a week since we'd left the hick town.

After a drawn out argument with Brian about our safety, I'd finally convinced him that we needed to trust the Prism. No one had put him in charge, and yet, it made him so damn upset just to agree with me, for once. He was so stubborn. Sometimes, I really wanted to knock some sense into him, but it wasn't worth busting a nail over. We'd been butting heads since I was teleported to their motel in the first place.

I shook my head and heaved a sigh.

Crap motel.

Splotches of black and brown mold dotted the grout along the sink. The mirror had become permanently clouded and unreflective in some places, and the metal fixtures had spots of brass showing through where the chrome finish had dissolved.

I popped open a stick of red drugstore brand lipstick and brought it up to my lips. Lack of sleep made my hands unsteady.

There was a knock on my door and I jumped, smearing red wax on my chin.

Damn it.

"Just a minute," I called, sticking my head out of the bathroom. I twisted down the lipstick, snapped the lid on, and then used a tissue to wipe the red mark off my face.

The Saviors hadn't taken us recently, but we also hadn't found what seemed to be a stable, safe place to stay, either. Most big hotels (hell, most self-respecting places in general) require a credit card or bank account on file in case things get damaged. Credit cards weren't an option. Not while people were looking for us.

"Hey." I opened the door to Brian and Alice. Brian had his backpack slung over one shoulder and Alice had a small duffle bag hanging from her hands—both filled with supplies we'd been gathering along the way.

"Ready to leave?" Brian asked without taking a step into my room.

"Yeah." I grabbed a canvas bag from the coat closet door-knob and threaded my arm through the handle. "Let's go."

Because of the whole financial situation, we'd been confined to mostly dumps and dives that didn't care much about our identities; places that just wanted cash in their hands. *That* we could give them. We had a good amount of money leftover from David's escapade, so we just kept moving, farther and farther away from home. No particular goal in sight, but staying on the move simply felt like the right thing to do.

"So, I saw something interesting on the local news this morning," Brian started, adjusting the shoulder strap of his pack.

"Yeah?"

"There's an abandoned hospital not far from here that was shut down a while back because of some electrical issues—fire hazards with the wiring or something like that. According to the news, it will be demolished next year and a shopping mall will be erected in its place."

We approached the front desk and slid our room keys over to the receptionist, who leisurely reached an arm out to retrieve them while focusing only on the screen of her cell phone. She was scrolling some social media site.

"Anything else we need to do?" I asked.

"Nope," she replied, without looking up from her phone. "I'll take care of it. Have a nice day."

Her words sounded pre-recorded. She hadn't made eye contact with any of us, but whatever.

I wandered across the lobby and picked through a large cascading shelf of brochures, grabbing a local bus schedule and an ad for a taxi service.

"So, do you think this hospital would be a good place to," I lowered my voice, "lay low for a while?"

Brian nodded. "That's kind of what I had in mind." He stepped in front of us and propped open the exit for Alice and me.

"Great. We're gonna be squatters," I cheered sarcastically. I knew we didn't have many choices anymore, but still... squatters? I could pawn my diamond nose stud for enough cash to get us a stay at a hotel in Times Square on New Year's Eve.

Well, I *could*. But...

"Kareena, you know we don't have a lot of options," Brian continued. "Not as long as... *they*... are still out to do whatever with us. We could be grabbed up any second now." He followed us out and let the door swing closed behind us. "We need to keep moving. We need to stay out of the public eye."

I pushed the slipping strap of my bag back up over my shoulder and crossed my arms.

Stop telling me what I already know.

Chapter 4

An intense, chemical odor made me dry heave. I cupped a hand over my mouth. A layer of soot lingered on the walls of the hallway and the heavy scent of smoke and must saturated the air.

We'd found a broken window and made our way inside the abandoned hospital without much trouble. The place was in utter disarray. People had rummaged through everything and stolen pretty much anything that might have been useful. Windows had been shattered. Cabinets ransacked. Broken glass was scattered in piles all over the floor. It wasn't just a fire hazard, it was a health hazard.

"Be careful," Brian cautioned, tapping me on the arm with his hand.

"I know," I replied. "I'm trying to be."

"I don't like this at all," Alice said, peering nervously down the long hallway. There were a few gurneys staggered about, blocking the path, and a broken wheelchair flipped over on its side near the wall. "This place is way too much like the place we saw in our dreams. You know, the one where we—"

"Don't remind me," I interrupted. This place was scary enough.

Against my will, an onslaught of flashbacks struck and a sick feeling came over me. It was a long time ago, back before my fluorescence had become active, but I could remember it like it was yesterday—the nightmare. The fear. Something or someone was chasing us, and then... something horrible happened and I got separated from the group. It was painful, recalling the way I had felt when I woke from a dead sleep in a panic. Sweat dripping off my forehead. My hands trembling.

That goddamn dream.

"It was only a dream," I said, puffing my chest out and regaining my composure. "It doesn't mean shit, you know?"

"But..." Alice tipped her head to the side. "We *all* had it."

"It's been, like, two years," I said, looking back at her. "Let's just forget about it, okay?" Not that I could. I just wanted them to drop the subject before I felt any more nauseated.

"That's probably a good idea," Brian added. "Now let's take a look around and see if we can scrounge up some things for the night. Blankets. Pillows. Anything that looks clean. Then let's find a decent room somewhere on one of the upper floors to stay."

I walked around the long half-circle-shaped receptionist counter and moved a few stacks of papers aside. Next to an outdated calendar was an emergency evacuation map.

"This place has a basement," I said, tugging the map off the thumbtacks and then lifting it up over the counter to show the others. "There could be some supplies there we can use. It looks like there are two sets of stairs leading down. One on this side and one on the opposite end of the hospital." I slid my bag off my shoulder and unzipped it, reaching inside to grab an LED flashlight. "I'll go take a look around down there if you guys want to stay up here and search."

"Sure," Alice replied.

"Be careful," Brian added. "We may not be the only ones here."

"I know." I reached into my bag again and took out a compact can of pepper spray. "I'm sure as hell not going to let anyone touch me."

The sun was setting and the place was becoming darker by the minute. A few timed emergency lamps kicked on, but they were so dim, they hardly made a difference. I clicked my flashlight and followed the map toward the entrance of the basement. The smell of mold hit me and I grimaced, trying hard to stifle a violent cough before I even opened the door to the stairwell.

It was surreal—the dank walls and eerily quiet surroundings were like something out of a cheap horror movie. I held tightly to the guardrail as I made my way down the concrete steps one at a time. A sudden temperature drop made me shudder and a growing stench turned my stomach. I descended twenty, thirty steps or more. The odor became nearly unbearable just as I reached a massive metal storm door. I pushed down on the cold metal lever, but it wouldn't budge.

I gagged and covered my nose and mouth against the putrid scent wafting out of the room. I took a step back and my shoe came down with a splash.

I swerved, pointing my flashlight at the ground.

Water.

Everywhere.

Damn it. It must have gotten flooded after the power had been shut off. That would explain the horrible smell. I heaved a sigh and turned to head back up the stairwell. Halfway up, the ground rumbled beneath me.

"Shit!" I froze in place, clutching the guardrail as if the floor was going to drop out from under me. I waited a few moments, bracing myself for another tremor before jogging back up to the main lobby.

"Brian! Alice!"

It was even darker now that the sun had slipped completely below the horizon.

"Brian!" I called out again, straining my voice. I pointed my flashlight down the main hall. Two dim colored lights moved among the distant shadows—green and blue fluorescence heading my way.

"Kareena!" Brian called back to me. "Are you okay?"

"We need to leave. Now!" I shouted.

"Did you feel the earthqu—"

The earth shook again, and I clamped onto a nearby countertop with my fingers. "Guys!?" I yelped, my heart jumping into my throat.

"Get out of the building!" Brian yelled. "Go out the front! We'll meet you outside!"

The entire room quaked and a thunderous crack rippled overhead. I looked up. A line of black split open the ceiling and crumbling drywall dust rained down.

"Brian! Wait!" I called out to him, but the falling debris cloaked the room in plumes of white. I inhaled a mouthful by accident and started to choke. I tried to call out again but instead coughed hard, gagging on another breath of white.

Dust stung my eyes and I shielded my face with my hand as I made my way blindly through the lobby. I bumped into a waiting room chair and then a small table. I stepped carefully. Everything felt the same beneath my shoes.

The earth trembled a third time and a loud crack boomed overhead. I darted forward. Too slow. Falling ceiling tiles struck me in the back, and I lost what little breath I had left in my lungs as I was pushed onto the floor.

A whirring sound buzzed in my ears and my entire body felt the impact of the blow. The adrenaline had me kicking and pushing—struggling to get out from beneath whatever the hell was holding me down. I wriggled a hand up through the rubble and something sharp tore into my flesh.

Help! I opened my mouth, but nothing escaped. A grunt. A strained attempt to breathe.

Don't leave me!

"Help!" The word came out this time, muffled, but it came out. I felt something digging into my back leg but couldn't contort myself enough to see what it was. Something heavy kept pushing into me, keeping me down. I used every ounce of strength to push back—to ignore the pain—but I couldn't get out.

"Please! Help me!" I choked on the words as I swallowed a mouthful of what felt like sand. I moved my hand and a sharp pain stabbed through it. Then a tingling. Then I couldn't move my fingers anymore, or at least I couldn't tell if I could. They were numb, like the rest of me. Cold.

I pushed back once more against the debris, but it only weakened me.

Oh, God. Why the hell did we have to do this? Why the hell did I suggest we split up? The dream. That damn dream!

I suddenly felt very small. Alone. Helpless. I wanted my parents, my friends, my family—anyone.

Someone, please. Help.

Brian?

Alice?

I coughed again, unable to swallow as grit scratched my throat. I'd lost feeling in my legs and stopped fighting back. All I could do was wheeze. High-pitched, short, aching breaths. Straining to fill my lungs with air, I lay there, letting myself drift off. Letting the darkness, dust, and dirt consume me.

Little by little, the weight lifted off me and my body felt less heavy. Someone took my hand and dragged me out of the rubble.

"Do you think you can walk?" he asked.

I grunted in confirmation. He pulled me up to my feet and draped my arm over his shoulders, wrapping an arm around my waist to stabilize me.

I tried to say Brian's name, but my dry lips wouldn't separate.

"Can you see?" he asked.

I shook my head, struggling to pry my sore eyes open. They kept snapping shut against the particles of dust caught inside.

"Shit! You're bleeding everywhere," he said. "We have to move. This place is coming down."

The next several moments were a blur. He guided me out of the building and we stumbled a safe distance away. The ground shook another time and the jarring sounds of glass, metal, and concrete mashing together made my head hurt.

"Too bad you can't see this," he said, his voice suddenly sounding much less like Brian's. "It's some epic shit."

"Who—" I coughed so hard I almost threw up.

"Take it easy," he said, helping me down so I could sit on the ground. "Just take it easy for a minute."

My eyes watered nonstop and I had to keep wiping my cheeks with the backs of my hands. All of the dust and dirt that had gotten into them kept me flinching uncontrollably.

Eventually, I was able to take a normal breath; one where my lungs didn't seize up because of all the crap caught in them.

"Who are you?" I muttered, trying to open my eyes.

"David," he replied, his outline still a blur. He sat down on the ground next to me and reached for my arm.

"Damn, your arm got mangled up back there," he said, sucking in a breath through his teeth. He carefully moved my arm to the side and glanced over it. "For a girl, you're taking it well."

I scowled at the sexist remark and he went straight back to looking over my other arm. David reached into his pocket and pulled out a pocketknife. He snapped it open, jabbed the knife into the lining of his hoodie and tore a piece of fabric off. "Do you think you'll be alright here by yourself for a few?" he asked, tying the strip of fleece around my arm like a tourniquet. I winced when the knot came forcefully down onto my skin.

"Uh, yeah. Why?" I pulled my arm in close to my body

and rested my hand in my lap. Leftover blood drizzled down onto my jeans. "Where are you going?"

"To get you help."

He probably meant Brian. Yes. Brian could fix me. *Hopefully*.

"Just stay here," David said as he stood. "I think you'll be safe for a little while. It's getting late and the way everything went down, the cops and the media shouldn't be here for a while. The roads look trashed." He looked around and nodded. "I won't be long."

He took off toward one of the other buildings.

I coughed again and the movement made everything sting. All I could do was slouch over and rest my aching, bleeding arm in my lap. All I could do was hope and pray that the last of the tremors had passed and that I'd be safe until the others returned for me.

David came back in much less time than I had expected. Brian and Alice were jogging close behind him.

"Kareena!?" Alice shrieked.

I looked up at them weakly, my eyes growing heavier as blood loss took its toll.

Brian's eyes widened. "Crap!" He dropped to his knees in front of me. "What happened in there?"

I looked into his eyes and sighed heavily, too fatigued and frustrated to reply. I didn't feel like explaining how angry I felt that Brian hadn't come back to save me once the ceiling collapsed.

I shrugged and it hurt.

"It doesn't matter," Brian replied with a shake of his head. "Let me help you." He reached out his hands and gently clasped onto my arm. Blue light radiated from his fingertips, the warmth making the hairs on my neck perk up and a feeling of comfort drift through my bones.

Within seconds, the skin of my arm regenerated over

the open wound. Brian carefully untied the tourniquet.

"Good thinking," he said, glancing at David and then looking back at me. He tossed the bloodied fabric off to the side.

"Hey!" David snagged the material before it hit the ground. "You don't want to leave that lying around. Cops might find it and—"

"I already got blood on everything else," I said.

His anxious expression softened. "I-I guess. You're right. Hopefully, it won't stir too much up."

"These things take forever to run anyway," I added. "My dad's a lawyer and I've heard enough horror stories about DNA evidence to know it shouldn't be a big deal right now. Besides, *if and when* they run any tests and start asking questions, we'll be long gone, right?" I glanced at Brian.

"Hopefully, yes." He nodded.

David eased up a little and took a step back as Brian continued checking me for wounds.

"Is there anything else?" he asked, gently sliding his fingers down my shoulder. "You've got a lot of blood on you."

"Yeah," I said, looking down. "My... leg." I had felt the pain of something stabbing into me while I was still buried beneath the rubble, but I never stopped to assess the damage.

I twisted my left leg outward, revealing a soggy patch of red on the back of my thigh. I couldn't tell how deep the wound was through my jeans, but something had definitely gouged into me earlier. Shreds of denim curled up around the area.

Brian rested his flattened hands on my outer thigh and I swallowed hard as a flush of heat shot through me, numbing the pain.

He wiped his bloodstained hands on his jeans, and then stood and reached toward me.

"Thank you, Brian," I said as he helped pull me to my feet.

"You're welcome."

I stood there staring into his hazel eyes for a moment, and then a look of discomfort came across his face. He cleared his throat and looked away.

"We need to get out of here," he said.

"Yeah," David agreed. "Before the cops show up."

"You would be worried about the cops, wouldn't you?" Brian raised an eyebrow.

"Aren't you?" David sneered in response.

Brian's snarky expression instantly vanished.

"Come on, guys," I said, pressing my fingers into Brian's forearm. "Cut the crap. We have to go."

Just as they turned away from me, Brian shot David a nasty glare and then started walking off ahead with Alice. David responded with a "kiss my ass" kind of smirk and then hung back to wait for me to catch up to him.

"How did you find us?" I asked.

"I've been following you guys for a couple of days, actually. I'm a Tracker," he replied. "It's what I do. You might not realize it, but you three leave a hell of a trail behind."

"What kind of trail?"

"Wherever you go, you leave a trace of fluorescent energy. Like a fingerprint. It's an aura of color that lingers and then fades after a while. It usually gives me enough time to see where you've been and where you're headed."

"Wow. That's crazy."

"Maybe. You see fluorescence inside. I see it outside. We're not so different. Right?"

"No. I suppose we're not. Hmm." I looked down at my feet as we walked.

No wonder he'd been able to spot us so quickly all those times before when he had been *hunting* us.

"What are you thinking?" he asked.

"What?" I looked up. "Nothing. Sorry."

He shrugged.

"About your injuries," he said, glancing at me. "I'm, uh, sorry I couldn't do more."

"It's okay," I replied with a partial smile. "You're not a Healer, but you have your own skills."

"True." His sharply curved eyebrows rose and he grinned. "Having this shit inside me has definitely changed the way I see things," he said.

"It's changed the way I see things, too." *Literally.*

"I've experienced your powers once before, back when you tried to kill me with them." David let out a nervous laugh. "No thanks. I don't know how you get through a day seeing things like that. Doesn't it drive you crazy?"

I wanted to tell him the truth—yes. The fluorescence makes me crazy. I see everything. Every. Effing. Thing. I see infected people. Started people. Sleepers. I see if Brian and Alice have... screwed around.

I see David's yellow glow illuminating his chest like a radioactive heart, throbbing to a quickened, inhuman pulse.

I rarely see people for people anymore.

"Sometimes," I replied, pretending to be unaffected.

"Only sometimes?" He cocked his head to the side. "Alright then."

I think he could tell I was lying.

Chapter 5

We managed to clear the scene before authorities came snooping around. David showed us a shortcut under an overpass—a maintenance tunnel—that spit us out right into the heart of the downtown district in front of a strip of decent-looking businesses and hotels. We probably didn't have a chance, but David seemed to think we could get a room at one of the nicer ones, despite our lack of credit.

"If they're not a chain hotel," he'd told me, "you can usually convince them to take a risk if you hand over enough deposit upfront."

That's what we had been doing up until now, but all of those places were hardly adequate. I'd like to sleep in a room that didn't smell like mold or beer for one night.

"So, where's *he* going to stay?" Brian asked me in a presumptuous tone. The four of us had stopped outside the entrance to one of the hotels.

"He can stay with me," I replied. "Getting two hotel rooms is hard enough. Three?" I shook my head. "It's not worth the risk."

"Are you sure that's a good idea?" Brian added, wrinkling his brow.

"Yes, Brian. We're adults. We can handle it."

"If you say so." He rolled his eyes.

"Shut up, Brian." I shoved him in the shoulder. "I don't sleep with everyone. Quit acting like you're so damn right-eous."

"Alright. Whatever!" He threw up his hands. "I'm going

to go talk to someone and see what they can do for us. Alice, wait here, okay?" She nodded in response, and then he jogged up ahead toward the sliding glass doors of the hotel.

I leaned against the side of the building near the lobby windows and turned toward David, who was looking at me with a raised eyebrow.

"Don't get any ideas," I growled, narrowing my eyes at him. "Brian's just trying to start shit."

"Sorry." He averted his gaze. "I... wasn't."

Alice took a few steps away so she could sit down on a bench near the curb.

"So, have you talked to the Saviors at all since we last saw each other?" I asked David.

"No. You?" He tucked his hands into his pockets.

"No." I glanced over at Alice, who didn't seem to be listening to us, and then back at him. I kind of wanted to tell David about the Prism. In fact, it was right there on the tip of my tongue, but it didn't seem right. He'd just rejoined our messed-up party and I hardly felt like I could trust him. Maybe telling him wasn't the right thing to do. Yet.

"How's... your sister?" I couldn't remember her name, but I knew he was taking care of her.

"She'll be alright. I called in a few favors to make sure she's in good hands until all of this shit blows over. I can't risk disappearing on her again, and I need to know she's taken care of."

David didn't seem like a trusting kind of guy, so I couldn't help but wonder who he'd gotten to take care of his sister. It wasn't my business, though.

Suddenly Brian came marching out of the hotel lobby with a scowl on his face. Alice leapt up from the bench to rush to meet him.

"What happened?" I asked, pushing up away from the wall.

"This place isn't going to work out," he said and started

walking off in the opposite direction.

"Hey!" David went after him.

"What?" Brain veered around.

"Let me handle this, okay?"

Brian stiffened. "No." His eyes widened. "You can't just—"

"No. No. Not like that." David shook his head. "Jesus, man. I don't need a Glock to get a hotel room."

Brian took a breath. "Fine," he said, looking away. "Do whatever the hell you need to. Just don't get us in trouble or I'll—"

"Leave him alone, Brian," I butted in. "I'm tired of all the ghetto places we've been stuck in lately. Maybe he can help us. Let him do his thing and we'll see what happens."

"Thanks." David flashed a smile at me. I wasn't trying to stick up for him. I only wanted Brian to shut it.

David looked down at the tear in his hoodie and grimaced. "Damn. This won't do." He rolled his shoulders back, slipped the garment off, and then handed it to me. "Would you mind holding on to this? I don't want them to see it."

I took the torn hoodie from him.

"Hey, kid," he said to Brian. "You got that leather jacket with you? The one you had..." He stopped himself. "Anyway, do you have it?"

Brian hesitantly pulled his black riding jacket from his pack and unfolded it.

"Don't get it wrecked," he sneered, handing it out to him.

"Damn, man. You've got a hell of a complex. It's a coat, not a car." David shrugged on Brian's coat. The fit was off—snug in the shoulders and too short overall—but he pulled it off well enough to get by. He perked up the collar. "Stay where I can see you guys," he said and then headed into the hotel.

From the outside, it looked like a much nicer place than

any of the previous ones we'd stayed at. No wonder they had turned Brian down. A young guy like him with a handful of cash. That's not suspicious, *said no one ever*.

"What do you think he's telling them?" asked Alice, peering at the lobby through one of the windows along the sidewalk. We couldn't see David very well. He was speaking with the receptionist. She had a very concerned look on her face as he spoke and she kept nodding at everything he said. I barely noticed him pointing at something and then tucking it away into his jeans, but I couldn't see what it was.

"Who cares? As long as we get a room, right?" I shrugged.

"I do," said Brian, wrinkling his lips to the side. "If that creep screws us over and..." He glanced across the street at a police car parked near the sidewalk. "If he screws us and we get caught..."

I crossed my arms and glared. "You need to calm down, Brian."

"She's right," Alice murmured. "Let's just see what happens, okay?"

Brian heaved a sigh and looked away from me. "Okay."

He'd been a nervous wreck ever since he'd run away with Alice. It was wearing me thin, too. I had my own fears to worry about. It wasn't just about him and his little golden child.

"Guys!"

We all turned our heads. David was standing between the sliding hotel doors, gesturing for us to come join him.

"Come on! Hurry up," he called out. I was the first to start walking. Brian and Alice trailed behind me.

We went inside and followed David across the room. I felt someone's eyes on me and glanced at the receptionist as we headed toward the elevator door. She immediately looked away, as if embarrassed to have been caught gawking, and pretended to search for something on her desk.

In passing, I saw she was a sleeper, but not an ordinary

one. She had a dark brown aura resonating from her outline, along with murky, dirty color swirling inside her, reminiscent of the man we'd seen at the diner not long ago. The one who... dropped dead in front of us. It was different from the stuff inside sleepers Brian *could* heal. This... was almost completely discolored—polluted with vile darkness.

I shook it off for the moment, without saying a word to the others, and followed them into the elevator. Once we were inside, David smacked one of the numbered buttons and the elevator door closed.

"What did you tell her?" I asked, standing between David and Brian to help keep them separated. David didn't scare me anymore, not since I had discovered I could hurt him with my powers.

"I saw the cop car across the street and used it to our advantage. I told the receptionist and her manager that you were under protection of the state and that I was your bodyguard."

"And she believed that load of crap?" Brian scoffed.

"People will believe *anything* if you say it with enough confidence." He pointed at me. "Then I pointed out the blood on your clothes and she caved in real quick. As long as you guys are here, you're going to have to keep your heads low, alright? Try not to wander around too much. I don't want people asking you too many questions."

The elevator stopped and a ding sounded just before the doors slid open.

David exited first. He handed a keycard to Brian. "1532. Attached to room 1534, which is our room."

The disgruntled look on Brian's face convinced me he was angry that he hadn't somehow managed to execute this type of plan earlier. David must have been one smooth talker to really pull it off the way he had. Either that, or the receptionist was gullible as hell. It was so far-fetched, maybe it sounded legit. Or maybe cops would come snooping around later on. David seemed fairly confident that they wouldn't. Then again, I did see him tuck something away after talking with the people at the front desk.

David reached into his pocket and took out another hotel keycard.

"Here." He handed it to me. Then he shrugged off Brian's jacket and gave it back to him. "Thanks."

Brian didn't even reply. He could have at least thanked him for everything. *Stubborn ass.*

I slid the card through the card reader on the door and waited for it to click before turning the knob. The lights came on as soon as we entered and the smell of bleach, wood cabinetry, and clean sheets filled my nostrils.

"We haven't been in a place this nice before," I said, poking my head into the bathroom and looking at the large garden tub. "Thanks for hooking us up with these rooms."

"Don't mention it." He slid his gun out from behind his back and flopped onto one of the two queen beds in the room. The sight of the gun made me uncomfortable, but I snuffed out my fears and reminded myself how he'd just put his ass on the line to help us.

He tucked the gun beneath one of the pillows on his bed and then shot me an offensive glare. "I... don't think I have to tell you this, but—"

"I won't touch your gun," I replied. "I'm not stupid."

"Good. Though I'm not gonna lie; it wouldn't hurt for you to learn how to use one."

"Maybe later." I shrugged. I didn't want anything to do with it.

He sat up and rubbed his face with both hands. "Ugh. You feel as shitty as I do right now?" He glanced up at me while I fiddled with the A/C console. It was ice-cold in the room.

"Uh, I was sort of the one who almost got buried alive today, remember?"

"Ah, yeah. Almost forgot about that." He stifled an awkward chuckle. "How's your arm doing?"

"Better," I replied as I walked into the bathroom and turned on the hot water to wash my hands in the sink. I needed to take a shower, too. My jeans had stiffened from the dried blood and I felt disgusting. "How long can we stay here?" I asked, pressing a hot washcloth against my face and taking a deep breath of the steam.

I didn't hear a reply.

"Da—" I turned my head.

He was in the bathroom doorway now, looking down at me.

"Jesus. Don't sneak up on me like that!" I huffed and squeezed the muddy reddish water back into the sink.

"A few days if we need to," he said, leaning against the doorframe.

"David?" I set the washcloth down. "What did you show the receptionist downstairs?"

His eyes widened briefly in surprise. "Uh. Why?"

"Because. I want to know," I said, turning to face him. "You didn't tell the others, but you can tell me. Really. I won't say anything."

He stared at me for a few moments, as if he were contemplating how to reply, or whether or not to tell the truth.

"It's okay," I added, reassuringly. "I won't tell them. I swear. I just want to know because we're—"

"This." He pulled a wallet out of his jean pocket and flipped it open to a fake ID and goldtone badge. He pulled it back before I could make out what the ID said. "Now don't go saying anything to the kid."

"I won't. I promise." I took up the washcloth again and ran it under the faucet. There was absolutely no doubt that Brian would let David have it if he found out he was brandishing a fake detective's badge. I didn't really trust him, either, but I had to. *We* had to.

I squeezed hot water from the cloth and started scrubbing the rest of the dried blood from my arms.

"How do you stand those two?" David blurted, coming up from the doorframe and taking a step closer. Our gazes met in the mirror. "Really? How do you do it? That Brian kid is such a hard-ass. And his girlfriend—"

"There aren't a lot of people I can trust." I hung the wet rag on the nearby towel rack and leaned back on the edge of the bathroom counter. "We're kind of stuck together."

"But you don't *have* to be with *them*, you know. No one can force you guys to stay together."

I glared at him. "You don't get it do you, David?"

His brow furrowed. "Get what?"

"Those things up there can force us to do whatever they want. The Saviors almost killed Brian when he tried to stand up to them. I'm not ready to take that risk."

I didn't want any more pain. I didn't have someone to worry about like Brian did. I didn't have someone worth fighting for or worth dying for.

My throat tightened. I had to muster up every ounce of strength I had left to keep my eyes from watering in front of David.

Chapter 6

After my shower, I threw on a terrycloth hotel robe and tied the belt snugly at my waist, hoping David wouldn't get any stupid ideas. I didn't feel that comfortable half-dressed around him, but I also didn't have any other choice. My only set of clothes was covered in blood and I'd lost my bag (and with it, my change of clothes) in the earthquake.

I filled the bathtub with a few inches of warm water and a drop of shampoo and tossed in my shirt and blood-soaked jeans. As I swished them around in the tub, swirls of brown mucked up the water. I wrung them out as best I could and then flung them over the shower curtain rod. Hopefully, they'd be dry by morning.

Back in the spacious hotel room, David lay flat on the bed closest to the window, his eyes closed as if he were asleep. Dark cinnamon skin showed through webbed tears in his denim and the laces on his black sneakers were frayed, like the hem of his jeans.

I sat on the edge of what was apparently my bed for the night and cupped my hands in my lap.

I glanced at my arm—the one that had been wounded earlier. Hidden beneath the fluffy white facade was fresh, pristine skin. It was as though nothing had ever happened to me. I hadn't been cut up. I hadn't almost been crushed to death and suffocated because of an earthquake. I hadn't been rescued by a man I knew little about, and I wasn't about to spend the night in a room with him.

"What the hell am I doing here?" I murmured. It had

barely been a week since the Saviors had teleported me out of the police station. My entire world had been turned upside down just as school ended and college loomed on the horizon.

I didn't want to be stuck with the group like dead weight. Alice and Brian had each other. David had himself and that was obviously all he needed.

Me? I was just... there. Useless while we weren't actively searching for sleepers.

"Can I sit with you?" The voice made me jolt. I glanced up at David, who was now standing beside me with a concerned look on his face.

"Uh. Yeah. S-Sure." I scooted toward the corner of the bed to make room for him and he sat down, his weight sinking in beside me.

He spent a moment studying me, searching my face for something. Then he leaned closer and reached toward my face. His fingers drifted past my ear and as he drew back his hand, a metallic shimmer blurred by the corner of my eye.

"How long have you been hiding that there?" He smirked, playfully investigating the coin that had appeared in his hand.

"Wait. How did you?"

"Some sleight of hand, that's all." He tipped his head to the side and grinned, holding his open hand out, palm up.

The coin was large. I didn't recognize it. *1 Onza... something*. And an image of an angel.

"It's from Mexico. A silver Libertad," he said with a nod. "It used to be my mother's. They found it in my father's hand just after..."

He stopped himself and averted his gaze.

"Just after what?" I asked, having a gut feeling the answer wasn't something I really wanted to know.

"Well, let's just say after he passed away. Anyway." He shook his head and adjusted his grasp on the coin. "She found it the year I was born and truly believed with all her sweet little Catholic heart that it was some kind of sign from God—a good luck charm dropped for her by an angel. See, she and my dad wanted kids real bad, but because of a health defect, my mother couldn't get pregnant. Or, at least, that's what a bunch of doctors had told her."

I squinted to try to see the year on the coin, but he flipped it over too quickly. The back showed an eagle with a snake in its beak mounted atop a cactus.

"This is the Mexican national seal, by the way," he added.

"What does it mean?"

"Hell if I know. I didn't grow up in Mexico. I'm American. Grew up in a few different states until..." He stopped himself. "I didn't take this out to give you a history lesson on myself."

He flipped over the coin again and held it up to my eye level, pinching the rim between his thumb and index finger.

"Do you see the two mountains behind the angel? One on each side in the background?"

I nodded.

"They represent two lovers from an Aztec legend. Supposedly, there was this warrior who wanted to marry a princess, but her father—the king—said he couldn't have her unless he won a battle against a rival tribe. So, long story short, the rival tribe spread a rumor that the guy was killed in battle and the princess ended up dying of a broken heart. The warrior returned, buried her on top of this hill, and knelt beside her to watch over her. Over the years, snow covered them both and they eventually became the two volcanoes you see there."

He shifted in place, tilting the coin in his hand while pointing to the mountain on the left side. "This one looks like a sleeping woman—the princess."

I couldn't see it, but I took his word for it.

"And what does all of this have to do with me?" I narrowed my eyes, struggling to see any kind of people-like shapes in the mountains on the coin stamping.

"I told you the story because I wanted to make a point. Sometimes two people care for each other so much, their feelings evolve into something bigger. And, for better or worse, unchangeable."

David reached out and pressed the coin into my open hand.

"W-what are you doing?"

"Take it," he said, smiling kindly at me.

"But... No. It must be important to you. Right? I-I couldn't." I tried to give it back to him, but he gently refused, pushing my hand away and forcing my fingers to close around the coin.

"Keep it," he said softly. "It's kept me safe all these years. Hell, it may have even saved my ass from a bullet or two. But right now, you need the luck more than I do. Look, I know I haven't been with you guys for very long, but I can already see what's going on."

"What do you mean? What do you *think* is going on?" I squeezed the heavy coin in my fingers.

"You've got an eye for Brian. I'd have to be blind not to notice the way you look at him and the way he avoids you. You try to hide it behind your angst, but it's obvious. The thing is, you've got to come clean about what's really happening. Life that can't or won't adapt to change will struggle to survive, and as long as you're holding on to something you can't really have, you're only hurting yourself. You can't keep trying to do the impossible. You can't move mountains."

"M-mountains?"

He motioned toward my closed hand. "Think about it for a minute."

I did.

Brian and Alice were the mountains...

Chapter 7

I spent the next few moments trying to think of smart ways I could retort to David's "advice." Stupid things like "yeah, well, water can erode anything" and "earthquakes destroy shit, too."

Really, I was trying to avoid the painful truth.

I couldn't move mountains.

I couldn't stop Brian and Alice from loving each other. Thinking about it constantly was doing nothing but causing *me* pain and reminding me over and over again how very alone *I* was.

I miss my family... I miss being safe... I just want a stable life again.

"Thank you for finding me and for pulling me out of that hellhole," I said, looking at David. "To be honest, I thought that gun of yours was some kind of front, and that you were only acting tough because of your powers, but you're a lot braver than I thought you were. Thank you for saving my life."

He looked off to the side, fixating on something I couldn't see and licked his lips. "You're brave too, you know?" He turned to look me in the eye. "To stand up to Brian like that. To really hold your ground even when it means putting aside your feelings."

"He acts like a jerk, but he's a good guy at heart." I shrugged. "I've learned a lot hanging around him and Alice. I didn't know shit before they came along."

"People change," he said quietly. "I'm not sure what they *really* think of you, but I know you're a whole lot smarter than you let on."

I sighed. "Maybe." I took a deep breath and squeezed my fingers around the coin, wondering if it might bring me any luck at all—not that I believed in that kind of shit. "I was a lot happier before those bastards put this stuff inside me." I brushed my thumb over the angel's image and then tucked the Libertad into the pocket of my robe.

"We all were," David said.

"Yes, but the Saviors put some kind of curse or something on me and, unlike Brian and Alice, it's impossible for me to even try to be happy. I can't get close to someone because I get these damn migraines. They're so painful that they—"

His hand rose toward my face and I gasped.

"Don't!" I squeezed my eyes shut and cringed. "Please. No!"

"No?" he echoed, his palm cupping the side of my neck. "Why not?" His fingers slid up to my jaw and he traced my lower lip with his thumb.

"Because..." My eyes eased open. His face was only inches from mine.

No debilitating pain. No migraine.

"Because it usually..." I stopped again and glared at him. "Wait. After everything I just said to you, why the hell would you do that!? How did you know it wouldn't—"

He shrugged. "I didn't." A small smile curled on his lips. "But I had to find out." His fingers slipped from my chin.

Ass.

I crossed my arms and scoffed, trying to ignore the audacity of his actions. But then I felt a twinge in my stomach—a flurry of emotions took wing—and I felt compelled to look David in the eye.

Butterflies. Maybe?

Over... *him?*

It was a sickness so good, it made my heart flutter. I couldn't remember the last time I'd felt it.

Challenging the anxious thoughts bubbling inside, I brought a hand up to David's face and let the backs of my fingers drift over his strong jaw line, contemplating his carefully chosen words.

"I had to find out," he'd said.

The dark stubble on his chin bristled against my knuckles. His intense eye contact held me captive while I traced my thumb from his trimmed black mustache down to his goatee. Dark brown eyes watched my expression change. The golden amber light brightened in his chest, flecks of yellow-gold leaching through his grey t-shirt. His gaze locked onto my lips and he leaned in to kiss me.

The deep kiss made my head swirl with dirty thoughts— twisted, erotic visions of the pleasure I'd been forced to abstain from for too long. A hand inched up my bare knee and slid beneath the robe, lingering on my thigh. I pressed my palm against his chest and felt his heart pounding, the golden light growing brighter with each beat. The heat and energy drew me in, every pulse pulling me closer and closer toward his body as we kissed.

Our lips parted and he held my face, staring at me, studying me again as if he were waiting for some kind of response.

"I'm sorry," he said with a loud exhale. He lowered his hand. "I didn't mean to assume that you—"

"Don't be," I said, as I stopped his fingers from sliding off my leg. "I mean, it's fine." My voice trembled with more urgency than I had wanted him to hear. "It's like I said earlier. We're both adults, right?" I leaned in closer, surrendering with a consensual smirk and an innocent nibble of my lip.

Men like that.

David scanned up my body, making my heart thump even more eagerly in my chest as his eyes slowly made their way back up to lock with mine. Then he forked a hand through my hair and pulled me into another kiss. More passionate than the first, the second kiss tore away apprehensions, exposing my long-overdue desires. Every inch of my body flushed with waves of carnal need and I exhaled a groan.

Breathing in the fiery scent of his skin. Tasting his lips against mine. His tongue in my mouth.

Jesus...

His t-shirt clung to his chest, sticking already to sweat. I wrinkled it up to his underarms, provoking him to peel it over his head and toss it off to the side. On his left pec was a tattoo of a lion's head with an intricate mane weaved into the coils of a geometric design. The swirling tribal patterns spread up over his shoulder and down his arm like a short sleeve.

I bit my lip again. Tasteful, well-done tattoos on a firm, maintained body were one of my fetishes—an addiction I couldn't cure. I slipped off the bed for a moment and turned to face him. His hands stayed fixated on my waist as I straddled his legs. Rough denim tickled my inner thighs and the friction made me quake as he forced my hips closer.

High school boys didn't know how to touch me. They didn't know how to make me cave in with a well-paced kiss, or how a stroke of the tongue to my décolletage could render me breathless.

David did, and it made me writhe.

No stupid games. No clumsy questions. Just pure instinct driving us together.

I kissed his collar bone, tasting salt on his skin, and he dropped his head back, sucking in a breath through his teeth. He shuddered and I squeezed my legs tighter, needing him inside me.

Hot embers of golden light flickered across his chest, bringing the tattoo on his shoulder to life with hypnotic bolts of color.

Just when I had started to believe that my life could only get worse, David—a man I didn't trust ten minutes ago—reached out, took me into his arms, and blew my mind.

• • •

I collapsed beside him on the bed, panting, and wiped my forehead with the back of my hand. Sweat glimmered on my skin and my muscles burned. My hair was damp—tangled all over me. I combed my fingers through it, but they caught on a knot. *Ouch.*

David reached for a pillow and tucked it beneath his head. I curled up against him and rested my face on his chest. His scent was musky—peppery, almost—and tainted by the pungency of cigarettes.

The glow inside him had toned down and the color had changed into a more blood-orange now. I assumed mine was the same as I could just make out a faded orange halo in my vision. My knees ached. My wrists hurt. But the satisfaction rippling through me felt so damn good. I don't know if it was my need or his skill, but it was crazy perfect.

Laying my head against him felt strange, though. Like it was *too* intimate. I'd barely gotten to know him and yet we had sex. Mindless, primitive sex. And yes, it felt great. And yes, I'd do it with him again in a heartbeat.

But maybe it'd have been better if we'd...

"So, what did you want to do with your life before all of this?" he asked, in a voice much softer and more soothing than I'd ever heard come out of his mouth. "Before the Saviors came and screwed it all up?"

"I don't know." I grabbed another pillow and moved over, sliding the bed sheet up to my shoulders. The room had gotten stuffy and warm since I'd turned down the A/C. "My parents wanted me to be a lawyer. It wasn't my thing. They wanted me to make shit-loads of money and marry a 'nice Indian boy.' *Also* not really my thing."

He smirked and raised an eyebrow—the smart-ass—clearly touting his conquest of me. I liked the cockiness. It made me think he had nothing to hide, that he'd made every decision confidently and without regret. Something I wish I could do.

I rolled onto my side and looked into his endless brown eyes. His nose had a nice slope to it, but the shape of his face seemed different than what I'd become familiar with in Hispanic guys. I couldn't tell exactly what his ethnicity was, and that bothered me. "Speaking of Indians, what are *you* exactly? If that's not too forward to ask after sex?"

He laughed. "My mother was Hispanic-American and my father was a pure-blooded Samoan. I was born in Hawaii, but we moved to Chicago when I was six."

"Ah." That explained a lot. I had to admit, it was an attractive combination. All the toned muscle without all the bulk, and a unique face that really set him apart—in a good way. Maybe I wasn't into him much at first, but now I liked the way he stood out. The clean, sharp lines of his face and goatee made him look fierce and intense but also... beautiful, in a badass sort of way.

"So... Indian, huh?" he asked.

"Yeah."

"Can't say I know much about your culture. Aside from a handful of Bollywood movies where they're always singing and dancing and... wow, I sound like a jackass right now."

I grinned. "No. Don't worry about it. I've heard worse. 'Jai Ho' and all that Americanized crap. I'm not Hindu like my parents anyway. I don't practice anything. I just want to live for myself." I laid my hand on his chest and brushed my fingertips over the soft little curls of hair. It quieted my fervent thoughts. I felt raised lines on his skin—scars—and it made me wonder where he'd gotten them all.

"I... like you," he said, his voice a broken whisper.

"I kind of like you, too, David." I scooted closer and rested my head on his outstretched arm.

"Maybe... we should get to know each other a bit more before we—"

"Yeah. Maybe."

He had a point. For the first time in my life, I did feel awkward about what we'd done. It wasn't regret. It felt more like something was missing. I was used to casual sex, but this... didn't feel so casual anymore.

He wrapped his arm around me and pulled me in toward his side. His body felt good against mine. I draped a naked leg across his and wriggled closer, feeling more comfortable and safe than I had in a long, long time.

Something inside urged me to keep David near—to make our tryst more than a fling. But that wasn't what *I* wanted.

"David, I..." I knew what I had to say but didn't know how to say it.

"What is it?"

"We've got a lot going on and... I-I don't want things to get messy between us."

"Messy?" His chest shook lightly as he stifled a laugh. "What are we, high-schoolers? Things are only going to get as messy as you let them." He stroked a line down my arm with his warm fingers. "This won't involve any broken hearts unless you let it."

It won't.

I won't let that happen.

Chapter 8

David told me later that night that he couldn't remember my name.

Awkward.

It's not like we were ever formally introduced. Well, it wasn't the worst thing I'd heard after sleeping with someone. Still, it was awkward.

Sunlight filtered through the window curtains. I stayed in bed, rolling over beneath the sheets to stare at David, as he lay asleep in the bed across from mine. There was a look of discontent on his face, as though something was bothering him.

After securing the belt on my bathrobe, I sat up and placed my bare feet on the carpet. I could see fluorescence living inside David's chest, swirling and moving of its own accord. Each inhalation made its flow quicken; each exhalation caused it to briefly become sluggish. Then I saw something else—a dark, sinister color creeping through his veins.

"Why are you watching me?" he asked, opening his eyes.

I gasped. "I'm sorry. I-I didn't mean to wake you."

He sat up and slid his bed sheet off to the side. "I don't care," he said with a grin, putting his feet on the floor. The sight of his tattooed chest reminded me of last night and I felt heat flush through me.

"Did you sleep in your robe?" he asked, tugging on his pants, zipping them up, and then weaving his belt through the loops.

"Yeah."

He chuckled as he reached under his pillow for his gun and tucked it into the back of his jeans.

"What?"

"Nothing. Women are strange. You take it all off and then put it right back on as if nothing ever happened." A grin twisted his lips before he pulled his t-shirt on over his head. "Are the others awake?"

I shrugged. "I don't know."

"Hungry?"

"Yes," I replied. My stomach had already started to grumble.

"There's some stuff in the fridge and beside the desk. Help yourself." He walked over to the door connecting the two rooms and unlocked it. Then he knocked. "Wake-up time, kids."

The fridge? When did he...

The door unlocked from the other side and opened. Brian stood there with a horribly bitter look on his face.

"Stop calling us kids, jackass," he growled.

"Nice to see you bright-eyed this morning," David replied with a chuckle.

I was certain Brian was going to punch him in the face right then and there.

But he didn't.

While they talked, I went over to the refrigerator, opened it, and took out a small carton of milk. Then I checked the desk drawer beside it and pulled out a box of breakfast snack bars.

I headed back to the bed and sat on the edge. Just as I took a bite of a granola bar, David closed the door between our rooms and turned toward me.

"Those okay?" he asked.

"Sure." I'd barely finished chewing my first bite. I took a sip of milk and set the carton down beside me. "When did you have time to get this stuff?"

"I don't sleep much," he said matter-of-factly as he walked over to the desk and flipped on the coffee pot. "I went out for a smoke and figured I should grab something for us."

"What about Brian and Alice?"

"I'm sure the kid's got it covered. He thinks he can take care of himself, so I'll let him keep thinking that."

It kind of frightened me, how incredible stealthy David was. He snuck out in the middle of the night, took a walk, and got a smoke, and I didn't even hear him come back in. If he wanted to hurt us, he could easily have done it by now. But who was I to judge? I'd barely known him for day and already we'd had—

A sick feeling washed over me and I held my breath. The room closed in. Spots of light invaded my vision and I felt weightless. A burst of hot white light blinded me and I opened my mouth to scream, silently choked of all oxygen by the swift change in atmosphere.

Ugh! I hit the ground hard and shook my head as my vision returned to normal.

"What do you think you are doing?" a terrifyingly familiar voice asked.

God, no. Not again.

I lifted my face to look upon the snow-white translator— the one Savior who spoke to us.

I looked back down at the cold, glossy floor and swallowed.

"What do you want?" I asked in a weak voice. My vocal cords suffered because of the thin air.

"We have not granted you permission to bond with the Tracker," he replied. "Such behavior is unacceptable."

"What?" I almost laughed but couldn't find the strength. "Who the hell are you to tell me that?" I came to my knees. "First, you make it so I can't be with any other men. Now that I've found one I can be with, you're going to try to stop me?"

"There will be consequences if you do not meet our demands. The Seeker and the Tracker must be separate. You cannot choose him as your mate."

My mate?

"I didn't." I scoffed and gritted my teeth. "For an advanced race, you guys don't know shit about our kind." I stood. "People can hook up without choosing 'mates,' or whatever the hell you want to call it. Having sex doesn't mean we're bonded for life."

The translator's eyes narrowed and he tipped his head to the side, staring into my eyes as if he were searching my soul.

"This is your only warning," he said, in an unaffected tone.

"Hey," I started. "Why are you only telling *me* this? You can't just—"

The room flashed white and I was blinded once more.

"Kareena?"

Someone's fingers pressed into my arm.

"Kareena?"

I blinked several times until my focus returned.

"David?" He stared at me, concerned, and cupped his hands around my shoulders.

"Are you okay?" he asked. "Where'd you go? You tripped out."

"Uh... Yeah. I'm fine."

The coffee pot hissed and steamed as water began dripping into the carafe.

Chapter 9

I didn't want to tell him the Saviors had snatched me from the hotel that morning. Crucial information, maybe, but I didn't want him to know what they had told me about *us*. Besides, David and I weren't a *thing*. We were only using each other because we could. He was an opportunist and I was, well, okay with that. That was all it was, and I wasn't about to let the Saviors screw me over again.

I stepped out onto the balcony and slid the glass doors closed behind me. David was leaning on the balcony fence looking out over the street below.

"Hey. You okay?" I asked.

He turned. "I guess."

I set my forearms onto the warm metal banister and clasped my hands together. David brought a pack of cigarettes out from behind his back. He flipped open the lid and drew one out of the box.

I bit my lip as I watched him tuck the pack away into the pocket of his jeans. Then he plunged a hand into another pocket and took out his lighter.

"You... want one?" he asked, once he'd noticed me staring.

"Sure," I replied. He brought the pack out again and popped open the lid with his thumb so I could pluck one out.

"I didn't know you smoked." He closed the pack and put them away.

"I don't, really." I let him light it for me and allowed the paper to burn a moment.

I inhaled. Hot smoke swirled in my mouth and my eyelids eased closed. I took a deep breath, dropped my head back, and released the smoke from my lips. "I used to do it once in a while with friends. And to piss off my parents." I chuckled, then brought the cigarette back up to my lips and sucked in another mouthful of smoke. The subtle, but not-soon-forgotten nicotine buzz quickly began its seductive dance.

I couldn't ignore the real reason I had come outside. I had to warn him about...

"It's not good for you," I blurted, the words escaping my mouth with plumes of smoke. "Or Lucy, for that matter."

He raised an eyebrow at me and then looked off at nothing.

"I think it's making you or your fluorescence sick," I said, trying to get him to look me in the eye. "Seriously, Davi—"

"How the hell do you know? And who are you to talk?" He motioned toward my hand—the one holding the cigarette. He was right. I was being hypocritical.

I thinned my lips, letting smoke drift out my nostrils and fade into the air. I didn't want to tell him the truth— what I was really seeing inside him: jagged black lines coiling around his lungs like parasites, wriggling through the arteries in his heart. Fluorescence being choked out by illness— cancer or whatever it was forming inside him. I'd been seeing it for the past two days.

"I can see it. Your fluorescence, it's screwed up. I'm not really sure why, but maybe because of how much you smo—"

"Hey! Wait a minute." He veered toward me and tossed his cigarette over the banister. "So we sleep together and now you think you can tell me how to live my life? I never opted into this kinda shit. I thought we had an understanding about our relationship? I thought we settled this last—"

"Damn it, David." I snuffed out my cigarette on the banister railing and tossed it over. "Why can't you just listen?

This has nothing to do our relationship. It's about you and what's..." I gritted my teeth. "And what might be killing you."

He sneered. "Stay out of my business, alright? I can take care of myself."

"Sorry." I turned away. "I'm only trying to help." I went back inside, walked into the bathroom, and shut the door.

I turned on the faucet and looked up at myself in the mirror.

What the hell am I doing here?

For a passing moment, I actually believed David could be the answer to my problems. At least, for the time being. That being with him could mask the feelings of loneliness and uselessness growing stronger every day. And the jealousy and anger I harbored because of Brian and Alice.

David wasn't exactly my type. Nor was he the kind of guy I imagined myself being with for more than a one-night stand, but last night—as lame as it sounds—the rest of the world disappeared. All of the darkness, fear, and hate trying to swallow me up went away. That meant something to me, even if it meant nothing to David. We had agreed to keep our relationship simple and—

A high-pitched buzzing noise filled the room. I doubled over in front of the sink and pressed my palms over my ears, but pain still rippled through my brain.

"Kareena," a familiar ethereal voice sounded.

I slowly opened my eyes and lifted my face toward the mirror. There, in the reflection, was the Prism. Out of instinct, I turned, but there was nothing behind me but the bathtub. I returned my focus to the mirror and shielded my eyes with the back of my hand. My headache diminished slightly.

"You're back," I began. "The Saviors, they—"

"We are aware," it said, interrupting me. "We are aware they have threatened to chastise you for your interactions with the Tracker."

"Yes. They did." I could barely hear my own voice. "Can

you help us yet?"

"We are in the process of studying the disease as well as mutations the Saviors have incited; however, it will take some time. We also bring unfortunate news."

I perked up, my eyes widening unconsciously until I felt the burn of the Prism's iridescent light and had to shy away, squinting to regain focus.

"They have created an abomination—a hybrid form of fluorescence that did not exist before. It is dangerous and volatile. You and the others must be vigilant as it is unnatural and, therefore, we cannot predict its effect on any of you."

"Will we know this hybrid stuff when we see it?" I asked, noticing how the thing was already flickering in and out of focus. "Can you tell me more? Please?"

"I'm sorry," it echoed, its voice quieter and more distant now. "We are working quickly to develop a stable solution. Please tell the others what we have told you."

"I-I will. Please, don't go!"

The light dimmed, swirled, and shrank away into a tiny black spot which faded into nothing.

I heard a loud bang on the bathroom door.

"Kareena!"

David! I jerked my head toward the sound.

"Are you okay!?" he shouted, his voice rising with fear.

"Yes!" I replied, opening the door.

"What was that all about?" he asked, glaring at me for an answer. "Who the hell were you talking to?"

"David, there's something I need to tell you." I left the bathroom and walked over to the edge of my bed to sit down. He followed and sat beside me.

"What is it?" he asked, his eyes narrowing.

I shook off the sick feeling creeping through my stomach and looked David in the eye. "The Saviors, they aren't the only aliens involved in all of this," I replied, looking down at my trembling hands in my lap. "There are others—a different race—called the Prism."

"What?" His eyes widened. "Who the hell are the Prism?"

"I don't know exactly, but I do know that they want to help us. They want to protect us from the Saviors."

"When did you find this out? I wasn't gone that long."

"About a week ago. I... didn't tell you at first because—"

"You didn't trust me," David interrupted. "It's understandable. But I'm part of this, too, so I need to know what the hell is going on. I can't see things like you can."

"One of them told me the Saviors are endangering more than just us humans—that their manipulation of us and fluorescence could be devastating to other worlds, too. It basically said that if we stayed away from the Saviors, we might survive."

"Stay away from them?" David raised an eyebrow. "How?"

"Can we take a walk?" I asked, brushing my fingers against his. "Please? I *really* need some air."

Chapter 10

A few shots of amaretto went down easy. And then a couple more. The smooth liquor calmed my nerves, leaving a subtle sweetness in my mouth.

Our walk ended up evolving from a brief conversation about what the Prism had told me into a long discussion about how messed up our lives had suddenly become. One thing led to another and the next thing I knew, David and I were drowning away our sorrows the only way we knew how.

Afterward, we staggered back up to our hotel room. Both of us were still a bit buzzed, but that helped blur our cruel reality for a few moments. Screw the Saviors. This was about me and what I needed to be happy, to have a normal life. They couldn't tell me what to do. They couldn't tell me who to—

David leaned down to kiss me, the scent of vanilla rum lingering on his breath and the essence of the tequila on his tongue making mine tingle.

While I fumbled to unbuckle his belt, his arms snaked around me so he could swipe his keycard through the lock and open the door to our room. We stumbled past the threshold and the door clicked closed behind us.

He took my wrists and pushed me back against the door, bringing my hands up over my head and holding them there once his lips found my throat. My knees trembled as his mouth explored my neck, the sensation stealing my breath away. Then his tongue licked a path toward my ear, where a heated whisper about what he intended to do next and a gentle nibble to my earlobe made me surrender completely.

Bright yellow light radiated from his chest and the potent warmth overwhelmed my body. He released my hands and inched down my side, wrinkling up my shirt so he could plant a line of kisses on my ribs. Then, my abdomen. With a quiet snap, my jeans came unbuttoned and David came down onto one knee in front of me.

I forked my fingers through his hair, sucking in an anxious, shuddering breath as he lowered my jeans just enough to kiss the hypersensitive skin of my outer thigh. Jesus, he knew how to control my body with his mouth.

But even while my mind raced with voracious wants and needs, I had to conjure up enough sobriety to pull one hand away from his head and keep it away. My hands were dangerously close to his temples, and I couldn't risk hurting him with my fluorescence.

Without warning, white light blinded me and a breath caught in my throat. I opened my eyes to darkness and blurry shapes swooping in and out of sight. A sharp pain tore through my upper arm and I cried out, losing my balance and falling against David.

"Kareena?"

I cringed and crumpled over, holding my arm close as the searing ache intensified and warm liquid seeped down off my fingers. My vision slowly began to return to normal.

"Kareena!" David stood up and grabbed me by shoulders.

I screamed, recoiling from his grasp. A quick glance at my arm revealed that the skin had been ripped open and blood was drizzling out of me. I covered it with my hand and pressed my fingers tightly over the wound.

"What happened?" David asked, putting a hand on my face to get me to look him in the eye.

"I need Brian," I said, shaking with pain. The alcohol made my head heavy. "Please. Get him. Now!"

David hurried out of the room.

I looked at my inner bicep again and trembled. The freaking aliens had torn out my implant and left an open gash. *Damn it!* So their first line of action against my sexual freedom was taking away my birth control?

Brian showed up at our door, in what seemed like seconds, and rushed over to me. "What did they do to you?" he asked.

I lifted my arm and turned so he could see the gaping hole in my bicep. It was deep. Deeper than it needed to be—to make a point, no less—and I was bleeding. A steady stream of red dripped off my fingertips. David snatched a towel from the bathroom to put beneath my elbow to help keep some of it off me and the carpet.

"What the hell?" Brian grimaced, reaching his glowing hand up toward the wound. He cupped his fingers over the frayed skin, and my blood oozed out from between them. Our eyes met briefly.

I flinched as his hot blue light did its work, stinging at first and then soothing the pain with gentle warmth. I felt the skin stitching itself back together beneath his touch.

A moment later, Alice came jogging into the room.

"Oh my God! What happened!?" She came up behind David and looked at me with widened eyes.

"It's nothing," I replied, straightening up and clumsily buttoning my jeans. My head was still swirling from all the alcohol. "I'll be fine."

"What?" Brian grabbed me by the wrist and pulled me back, forcing me to face him. "What happened to you, Kareena?"

"I don't want to talk about it," I said, scowling at him. "Really, Brian. Butt out. Okay?" I jerked free of his grasp and pushed past David and Alice so I could get to the door. I darted off down the hall as quickly as my tipsy body could carry me.

"Kareena!" David came sprinting around the corner. I looked off to the side to avoid eye contact with him just as the elevator doors closed in front of me, separating us.

The elevator chimed and I wiped some of the blood on my jeans just before the doors opened. The main lobby was relatively deserted and, luckily, so was the bathroom.

I bent over and contorted myself enough to get most of my arm beneath the faucet and douse it with warm water. The blood rinsed away down the drain. Then I scrubbed some subtle red splashes off the porcelain sink with a paper towel.

I lumbered out of the bathroom and looked around the empty lobby. I'd had too much alcohol. Swallowing made me taste the bitterness of indigestion. I really needed to sleep it off, but I didn't feel like dealing with the others again.

There was one receptionist at the front desk and no one else in the room except a bellhop sorting through someone's dry cleaning order. I glanced over at the elevator, expecting David to pop out at any moment.

He didn't.

Then I felt a hand on my shoulder.

"Are you okay?"

"What!?" I jerked my head around and my heart almost stopped. The man looking into my eyes looked... like Brian; too much like Brian. He was a little older but had the same hazel eyes, fair skin, and nose shape. His shorter hair was more blonde than brown, and more kept up, but their similarities were... uncanny.

"Miss, I asked if you were okay." He squeezed my shoulder lightly and I snapped back into reality.

"Uh. Yes. I'm fine, thanks," I replied, panicked, still trying to shake off the weird feeling I got looking into his familiar yet unfamiliar eyes. He could have been Brian's doppelganger.

"You've got blood all over you and you..." He leaned closer and grimaced. "You smell like alcohol. I think you need to see a doctor. Did someone hurt you? Should I call the pol—"

"No!" I said, so loudly the receptionist glanced over at us. "I mean, no. Please, don't. I'll be fine. It was an accident and it looks worse than it really is."

The man brushed a lock of hair out of my face and looked me in the eye.

"Please, just tell me what happened to you," he said, narrowing his eyes. "I'll do whatever I can to help."

"Is everything okay?" The receptionist had overheard our brief dispute and was taking a step out from behind her counter.

"We're fine, thanks," the man replied, raising his voice so she could hear him. He returned his focus to me. "You *really* don't look well," he said. "You should come with me. I'm here on the first floor and you can sit down for a few moments and maybe get your bearings." He placed a hand on my cheek and a rush of warmth went through my body. I felt dizzy—weak all of a sudden. Maybe I'd lost too much blood. Or...

"Uh..." I tried to take another step, but I staggered, my knees trembling. "O-okay." The walls shifted and phased in and out of focus.

"I'll help you," he said, and then he wrapped an arm around my waist to stabilize me. We started walking.

He sat me down on the edge of the bed in his room and took a bottle of water from off his desk. He unscrewed the lid and handed the water bottle to me. I took a sip. The room started coming back into focus again.

"Thank you," I murmured, wiping a stray drop of water from my chin. "I don't normally drink so much but... I don't know. Never mind." I couldn't seem to put my words together.

The man knelt down in front of me and set a hand on my knee. "Name's Taylor. Do you mind if I ask for yours?" He offered his other hand out to me and smiled.

"Kareena," I replied, keeping my hands in my lap. "So, what are you staying here for?" I looked around his room and didn't see anything that gave away his occupation.

"Business," he answered. "Not pleasure, unfortunately." He grinned. His smile was much warmer than Brian's had ever been. "Kareena." He sat beside me on the bed and pressed his hand over mine. "I can't say I'm an expert on giving advice or anything, but it seems like you're going through something really bad right now. Is there anything at all a stranger like me can do to help you with whatever it is you're facing?"

I closed my eyes involuntarily at his gentle touch and a flush of heat went through me again.

"Do you have someone you can talk to about it?" he asked as his warm palm cupped my fingers.

"Thank you, but no. There's nothing you can do for me." I lowered my head. "And yes, I have people here I can talk to. I mean, the group I'm staying here with. They're my friends—sort of.

"Sort of?" He got up and slid the desk chair out so he could sit across from me.

"I didn't exactly choose them as friends, but we get along. One of the guys is kind of a jerk sometimes. He doesn't take what I say seriously even though I think he should."

"I'm really sorry to hear that, Kareena."

He kept using my name as if he liked the way it sounded when it rolled off his tongue. I kind of liked the way he said it, too. It made my heart beat faster. Either that, or it was the alcohol affecting me.

"I should be getting back," I said, standing on wobbly legs. "They'll be worrying about me."

"Oh, alright." He stood up. "I'll be here for a few more days. If you want to... um... hang out or talk or anything." He took a slip of paper from his desk and scribbled something on it. "Here's my cell number if you want to call. Anytime is fine."

I chuckled. *Hang out?* He was hitting on me, in a sweet kind of way.

"Sorry. I'll probably be busy," I replied, "but thank you."

"No problem."

He walked me to the elevator and pressed the up button for me. The elevator dinged and I stepped inside.

"I'm here if you need a friend," he whispered just as the elevator doors closed.

"Thanks," I raised my voice as he was shut out of view.

I looked down at my feet as the elevator ascended.

Taylor seemed nice. David was okay and all, but Taylor was definitely more my type. Too bad we couldn't see each other somehow. So much drama going on around us and then there were my—

Shit!

I slammed the stop button.

Migraines! But my head wasn't hurting. Nor had it hurt at all when Taylor had touched me.

I looked at my arm again and brushed a hand over where the open gash had been earlier. David was the only man I'd been able to be with since I'd become a Fluorescent One.

Had things changed? Or... were they, maybe, done punishing me?

I waited for the doors to open and then pushed the first floor button at least a half dozen times until it started to descend. After the ding, I rushed out through the open doors and down the hall toward Taylor's room.

"Taylor!" I shouted after him. His back was turned. He swerved around to face me and my heart plummeted.

Violet light glimmered in his veins, glowing and flickering through his right hand and up his arm like purple lightning.

"Are you okay?" he asked, jogging over to me. "Kareena?" He took my hand and looked into my eyes. "Kareena, talk to me." His fingers anxiously squeezed mine.

I closed my gaping mouth and licked my chapped lips. "I-I..."

"What? What is it? You look like you've seen a ghost."

"No. Not a ghost," I said, shaking my head. His hazel eyes stared fearfully back at me. "Something... worse."

Chapter 11

I closed the door behind me as gently as I could, pressing a hand up against the lock to dampen the click.

"Where have you been?" David asked just as I turned around.

I couldn't really see him with the lights off, but I could see his amber glow glittering from the other side of the room. He flipped on the lamp by his bed and got up to walk closer.

"Well?" He looked down at me. "The others are worried about you."

"I met someone and we started talking. I lost track of time, that's all." I crossed my arms and glared at him. "Why? Why do you care anyway?"

"You found him, didn't you?"

My jaw dropped. *Him?*

"The purple one?" he added.

"You know about him?"

"Yeah." He turned away and heaved a sigh. "He's been here for as long as we have."

"So you've met him already? You've met Tay—"

"No. I saw his aura when I went walking the other night. But I didn't want to say anything yet because I was hoping I could learn something about him first. You know, find out if he's on our side or not."

"Why wouldn't he be?" I scoffed.

"I wasn't, at first." He lifted a hand and brushed his fingers over my ear. "Or have you already put that behind you?"

"Seriously, David." I turned my face, pulling away from

his hand. "Is everyone out to get you?" I walked over to the window and pried open the curtains a few inches so I could see the busy streets down below.

"That's not it." He came up beside me and tugged the curtains closed. "We can't trust anyone."

"No. We can't. I'm aware." I shook my head. "Damn it, David, don't you start trying to control me. Brian thinks he can tell me what to do, but he can't, and neither can you."

"That's not what I'm trying to do." David's eyes narrowed. "Kareena, listen to me for a minute."

I turned and pointed a stiff index finger at him. "You didn't want to listen to me when I tried to tell you what I saw inside you."

He bit his lip and looked down. "I'm sorry about that, but I'm not used to getting help from anyone. I don't trust people. How do you think I've made it as far as I have? How do you think I've survived all of the shit I've had to deal with in my life?"

I shrugged.

"You've seen my scars, Kareena."

Yes...

"Well, they each have a story—pretty shitty ones at that." He looked into my eyes again. "I've spent the last few years trying to right my wrongs, but you know what? Karma's a bitch, and things like to come back to bite you in the ass. I'm the way I am because I have to be. Because I want to make it out of this damn world alive."

Hearing all of that made my stomach uneasy. I knew David was independent, but I didn't know he held such a grudge against society.

"I'm sorry," I whispered, my voice raspy from my throat tightening up. "Can you help me figure out what to do about the new one then? About telling the others?"

"Yeah." He put a hand on my shoulder. "Why don't you get some sleep first?" His fingers drifted down my arm to where my implant once was. He caressed his thumb across my bicep. "You've been through a lot of hell yourself. You could use the rest. Clear your mind."

"I-I guess," I whispered beneath my breath. "I'm... still shaken from earlier, though. I mean...what the hell, you know? What the hell were the Saviors thinking tearing my... my damn implant out? What the—"

"Kareena, that's enough." His grasp on my arm tightened unintentionally and I winced. He immediately let up. "Sorry. That's enough for tonight. Get some rest, please. We'll worry about it in the morning."

.　　.　　.

"Hey! You've got to... Stop... together."

The words were mostly inaudible.

My eyes eased open and I rolled over in bed, straining to hear the muffled angry voices coming from the hall.

"Don't... what to do... You can't..."

The voices kept fading in and out. I couldn't make out who was speaking. Brian and...?

I sat up in bed. *Oh, my head.* There was a pounding in my temples. *A hangover?* I didn't remember drinking *that* much last night.

"You can't... Someone's going to... Stop... an idiot!" More arguing in the hall. David. His accent was a dead giveaway.

I slipped my feet out from under the covers and onto the floor. It was freezing in the room. I shivered and wrapped my arms around myself as I crept over to grab a robe from off the nearby sofa and throw it on over my clothes. The thermostat had been set low. Maybe David had changed it in the middle of the night.

I walked over to the front door and listened for a moment, pressing my ear against it. It was definitely Brian and David bickering about something. I opened the door a crack and squinted, struggling to focus on the shapes in the hall. My head still ached and their raised, angry voices only made the pain intensify.

"You can't go wherever you want!" David said.

Brian stood across from him, both hands curled into fists. "And you can't tell me what to do! You can't make us stay here forever. How long are we gonna be safe here?"

I opened the door a little more, my fluttering eyelids still fighting the fatigue of a restless night.

"Guys?" It came out slurred. I cleared my throat and tried again. "Guys! What's going on?"

Brian shot a glare at me and threw up his hands. "This idiot wants us to stay here for a few more days or something, but I said we should keep moving. We're not safe in one place."

"We're safe here right now," David hissed in a lower tone. "Keep your damn voice down, too," he added through gritted teeth. "Do you want people to start asking questions?"

Brian narrowed his eyes. "Shut up." He sneered. "I don't care what you say, David. Alice and I are leaving and you and Kareena can—"

"There's another one!" I blurted out, opening the door wider.

"What?" Brian's gaze met mine.

David's eyes widened and he shook his head at me, trying to silently tell me not say anything else.

But I had to. Brian and Alice needed to know.

"There's another Fluorescent One here in the hotel."

David sighed and looked at me, disappointed.

"Another one?" Brian's jaw dropped and he unclenched his fists. "Wait. Did you know about this, David?"

David looked away and Brian took a step closer to me. "You knew about this person and you didn't even bother to tell us?" he asked. The dark shadows under his eyes were more prominent than ever.

I folded my arms and lowered my head as I replied. "Yes,

but we were going to tell you. We just wanted to learn more about him first."

"Him? Well, where is he?"

Alice had already poked her head out of the room and she was now standing in the hall behind Brian, listening to us.

"I don't think it's a good idea," David said. "We don't know anything about him yet."

"You're one to talk," Brian added. "You're the one who tried to kill me before asking any questions. You're the one they sent to punish us for disobeying."

"Exactly," David snapped. "All the more reason to wait before running downstairs to make friends with the new guy who could be exactly like I was... or worse."

"He's not," I butted in. All eyes were on me. "I talked to him last night for a while. He seems okay. Friendly. Hell, he didn't try to choke me right away." I shot a glance at David and then looked away. I'd already forgiven him for that.

Alice stepped out from behind Brian. "What does he do?" she asked. "What color is he?"

"Purple," David and I said together.

Brian's eyebrows twitched as he mouthed the word to himself.

"I don't know what he can do, though," I said, shrugging. "Not yet, at least. I don't even know if he's figured that out yet, either. He said he was here for business."

Brian took Alice's hand. "We're going downstairs to find him."

"Brian. Come on." David lowered his voice. "I don't think it's a good idea. We need to keep our heads down."

Brian's lips wrinkled. "You're not the leader of this group."

"Neither are you," I said, without looking him in the eye.

"We'll be quiet," he replied. "We'll play it safe. Does that make you feel better?"

David shrugged and then nodded reluctantly. *"Really*

safe. Okay?"

"I'll go with you," I said. "But give me a minute to wash my damn face. I just woke up, for God's sake."

"Yeah." Brian rolled his eyes. "Hurry up, please."

I rushed back inside my room and went into the bathroom to throw warm water onto my face. My dark circles were apparent, too. Not enough sleep and too much shit going on. A few days into this whole mess and I already looked like hell.

The room door clicked open and then closed.

"Make sure Brian doesn't do or say anything stupid, okay?" David said, poking his head into the bathroom just as I was patting my face dry.

"I can't guarantee he won't *say* anything stupid," I replied, "but I'll try to keep him from *doing* it."

"Thanks. Let me know how it goes. I'll wait here. Three's already a crowd anyway."

I heard the TV power on.

Chapter 12

"Let me handle it, okay?" I said, putting a flattened hand up to stop Brian from following me any farther. "He's already talked to me. I don't want to freak him out or something. So just let me speak to him first, please."

Brian's lips crinkled to the side. "Yeah. Alright." He backed up and leaned against the wall adjacent to the elevator. Alice did the same beside him.

I took a deep breath and continued down the hall toward Taylor's room. Last night, I had told him a little about the others and myself, but I didn't tell him I'd be back with them first thing in the morning.

I knocked gently on the door with the back of my hand and waited. I heard steps and then the door unlocking.

"Nice to see you again," Taylor said, smiling with his eyes. He had a pretty smile. It made me feel somewhat bad because I hadn't come to see him for, well, fun.

"Hi. Can we talk?" I asked.

"Of course. Come in." He opened the door wider and stepped back, gesturing for me to enter.

"Well, I can't. I'm actually here for another reason."

"Oh?" His eyes narrowed and he took a step out in front of his door. "Is... something wrong? Do you want to go somewhere else to talk about it or—"

"The others want to meet you. Now."

"Oh." His eyebrows lifted.

"I wasn't going to say anything about you to the others until we had more time to talk amongst ourselves, but...

Brian wanted to leave the hotel and I had to say something to get him to stop."

"I see." Taylor looked down. "It's okay. What else could you have done? Really?" A small, understanding grin curled his lips.

"Thanks for understanding. They're just down the hall." I pointed behind me. "Do you want me to bring them here?"

"I'll go with you," Taylor suggested, turning to pop back into his room to grab a black blazer from the nearby closet. He shrugged it on and then closed the door to his room behind him.

"Don't be nervous, okay?" I said, brushing my fingers against the back of his hand as we walked. "They might be intimidating at first, but we're all in this together."

"Whatever *this* is," he added, lifting his right hand—the one where I could still see the purple color inside.

Brian came meandering around the corner as we approached, then suddenly froze in place, his eyes widening. "Oh, shit." He locked eyes with Taylor and I watched them both tense up.

"Guys?" I said, noticing Brian make a fist. "Guys, what the hell?"

Brian scowled and bared his teeth a little as he sneered. "You son-of-a-bitch," Brian growled, his nostrils flaring. He shot a quick glance at me and then went back to staring at Taylor like a wolf about to attack.

Taylor chuckled softly and raised both of his hands as if he were surrendering. "Hey. Come on, man. Chill, alright? I'm not here to—"

"Shut up, Taylor."

I hadn't told the others his name yet...

"Taylor?" I pulled on the cuff of his blazer to get him to back off.

"I've got this, Kareena," he said, turning to me and grinning confidently. "Trust me."

"Okay." I released his sleeve. "I hope so."

"Well," he started, looking Brian over briefly, "you're certainly not the little brother I—"

"Left behind?" Brian interrupted with an angry huff. I could hear his breaths growing heavier.

Shit. I didn't know he was Brian's...

"If you want to call it that," Taylor replied, shaking his head. "But I call it saving my ass. I got the hell out of there before—"

"You could have taken me with you," Brian said. "You didn't have to leave me alone with those... bastards."

"Who? Mom and Dad? How are they anyway?"

"Dad's dead. Mom's not doing much better. She lost her damn mind and tried to kill herself."

"Damn." Taylor's eyes widened. "Well, I'm sorry to hear that, Brother."

"Don't call me that," Brian hissed. "Kareena, go tell David we're leaving right now."

"But..."

"Or we're leaving without you both." Brian grabbed Alice's hand and stepped backward toward the elevator, not breaking eye contact with his brother.

"Brian, please." Taylor walked after them, but Brian took a defensive stance and coiled both hands into fists again.

"Don't come any closer," Brian growled. "I swear to God I'll—"

"Stop." I came between them and took Taylor's hand. "Just let him go, okay?" I said, looking him in the eye. His fingers were cold and clammy.

The elevator dinged and Brian and Alice disappeared behind the metal doors.

Taylor took a deep breath and exhaled loudly.

"What happened between you two?" I asked, squeezing his hand gently.

"It's a long story. To make it quick, our parents were

horrible, and when I turned eighteen, I got out of that house as fast as I could and never looked back. Maybe I should have done something for Brian, but I couldn't. I just couldn't take him with me. He would have been a liability since he was so young at the time."

"Your mom went crazy last year. Tried to kill herself and everything. It was scary shit for Brian to go through all by himself, you know? He's got a lot of problems and a lot of weight on his shoulders now, not even counting those nut jobs up there who..." I lowered my voice. "Who put this stuff in us."

"They haven't said much to me yet," he said. "I don't really know what's going on or what this stuff is doing to me."

I could see light flickering in his right side and all the way down into his fingertips in arcs of white and violet energy. Same overall look of Brian's, but light fluorescent purple, and in his right arm instead of his left.

"Do you want to go sit at the café?" I motioned toward the lobby. "We can talk there for a while."

"Sure."

"Brian will cool off eventually," I said, trying to sound optimistic. "He's... hotheaded."

"Same old Brian." Taylor laughed quietly to himself. "He hasn't changed at all, apparently."

I smiled. Brian wasn't known for making the best choices, but I knew he had good intentions.

The two of us exited the main hall and passed the receptionist desk where I caught a glimpse of the lady with the weird darkness crawling inside her. I stopped walking and looked her over briefly.

"What is it?" Taylor asked.

"Uh... nothing. Sorry."

"You're looking at her like there's something wrong with her. Can you see something I can't?"

"Yes. Well..." I turned toward him and looked up into

his eyes. "Um, Taylor. Can I..." I looked down at my hands and then back at him. "Would you forgive me if I did something to you that might cause some slight pain, but... well, it will help you see what I'm seeing. It will be temporary and the pain won't last. I promise."

"Uh, I guess." His eyes wandered. The lobby was fairly deserted for the time being, so I wasn't worried about people seeing us. That didn't mean he wasn't concerned, though. "What are you going to do to me?"

My hands were already level with his temples. "I can touch you and let you see what I'm seeing for a few moments. It will be quick. I promise."

He just stared at me like I was crazy, clearly unable to process my peculiar request. Even though he was still uneasy, he nodded in agreement. I pressed my fingertips against the sides of his face and he squeezed his eyes shut, wrinkles of pain crinkling his brow as pink fluorescence invaded his body through my fingers.

I removed my hands and he grunted, shaking his head.

He opened his eyes. "Oh my God," he said, staring at the receptionist. Magenta glinted across his pupils. "What is that inside her?"

"That's what we're trying to figure out," I said, pulling him past the desk so we wouldn't draw any more attention. "Let's keep moving. I'll explain more after we sit down."

He shook his head and cupped his forehead with his hand. "Ugh... my head." He grimaced and blinked several times. "I feel like I've got a migraine."

"I'm sorry. I had to do it to let you see what I was seeing."

"I'll be fine. It's only a headache, right?" He squinted. The pink light quickly faded from his eyes.

"Yeah. It's only a headache."

•   •   •

"The Saviors told me there were others out there, but I had no idea one of them would be my brother." Taylor lifted a cup to his lips and took a sip of black coffee.

"It must be because you have similar genetic makeup," I said. "They told us they needed us because we were compatible with them."

"That makes sense, I guess." He set the cup down and it clinked against the glass table.

We'd been talking for nearly an hour. I'd quietly told him about what had been happening to us over the past year and a half. I didn't tell him about Alice's pregnancy, but I did tell him about David's early attempts to overpower us. I told him about the man at the diner who had dropped dead mysteriously and how the receptionist at this hotel looked as though she had the same messed up light inside her.

I stirred my cherry cola with a straw to blend the grenadine and soda together. The café had been quiet and nearly all of the patrons had taken their drinks to go. I wasn't concerned about being overheard, though. How many people would have thought we were telling the truth if they actually had been listening to our outrageous conversation about aliens and glowing super powers?

"So, do you have any idea what your fluorescence does?" I asked.

Taylor used a napkin to wipe a smudge of fingerprints off the clear glass table. "No." He shrugged. "I just got it a few months ago and I've been so busy flying back and forth between business trips, I've hardly thought anything about it. From what you told me, I don't think mine flares up like everyone else's. I've hardly seen it since the beginning."

When he ran away from his crazy parents, he went to Canada of all places. Taylor was now a public relations consultant for a printing company in Calgary.

"Do you think you should go check on my brother and the others?" he asked, adjusting the cuffs of his blazer. "They haven't come back down yet."

"No. He's probably starting shit with David—the one I've been staying with. David won't take any crap from Brian, that's for sure."

"Ah." Taylor nodded. "It would take a lot of guts to do that. Even as a kid, Brian would get riled up about little stuff."

"Now more than ever," I chuckled. "Especially since his girlfriend is with him constantly."

I had also told Taylor how the two of them had run away from home. I told him almost everything, but I didn't tell him about the earthquake or that the Saviors had ripped out my implant. I made up a lie about the injury, and I kept my knowledge of the Prism out of the conversation.

"That's one thing I'll give Brian credit for—he's determined," Taylor said. "I try to stick with something, too, when I commit to it, but learning all of this really changes the game. I can't go back to work and pretend none of you are out here fighting for your lives and that my own brother isn't in danger. I need to do whatever I can to help out with the mess we're all in now."

We? I perked up. "Oh?"

"You're in trouble, too, aren't you?" he asked, cocking his head to the side. "I mean, technically we both are. It seems those aliens haven't been very nice to you four in general. I'm probably next on their list, so we should start working together before it's too late. Before... something really bad happens."

I was surprised by how quickly Taylor seemed willing to join us in our fight against the Saviors, but we could use another ally and I didn't want to question his motives. Taylor may not have taken part in everything we had thus far, but he had been infected for a reason. It wouldn't be long before the Saviors started pulling his strings, too.

Chapter 13

"So you're the new one?" David asked. He'd just wandered into the café and had come over to our table. "Name's David."

"Nice to meet you," Taylor replied, offering out a hand.

David half-grinned and shrugged. "Not to be an ass, but I don't know what your fluorescence does just yet and... well, I don't want to find out the hard way, if you know what I mean." He tucked his hands into the pockets of his jeans. "Anyway, I didn't come down here with any news. I was going out for a smoke and a walk. I'll be back later."

"Alright." I wanted to wave goodbye, but it seemed childish, so I didn't. "See you, David."

"Isn't he worried about the others leaving without him?" Taylor asked, leaning over the table so I could hear his hushed voice.

"No. He's a Tracker. He could probably find us with his eyes closed."

"That sounds like a useful talent."

"I wouldn't call it a talent."

"True. Well, a useful ability then." He folded his hands together on top of the table. "It's better than whatever I have, apparently."

"Or more obvious. Don't worry so much about what you can do. The important thing is we're together, and together we'll be much stronger. All of us—the Fluorescent Ones."

"Fluorescent Ones?"

"That's what we've been calling ourselves. Maybe it's lame, but..."

"No. I like it." His lips separated into a toothy grin.

"He's not one of us," someone said in a husky voice from behind me.

I swiveled my chair around.

"Brian!?" I groaned, disgusted with the bitter look on his face. "Jesus, don't start this again."

"Don't butt into things you don't know shit about, Kareena," Brian said, rolling his shoulders back as he approached. "You don't know him like I do. You don't know who he really is."

"And you do?" I glared back at him and scoffed. "He left when you were, like, what? Eleven? And you think that after all these years, you still know who he is?"

"I asked you to stay out of this, Kareena." Brian made a fist. "I ought to rearrange your face for what you did to me back then, Taylor."

"Brian, come on." Taylor got up from his seat. "Let's talk about this, please."

"Talk about what? How you abandoned me because you were a coward? About how you left me as the only target for our freak parents to pick on? You knew I had a heart problem and you knew how much it disappointed them. But you... you had to run off and save your own ass. You had to leave me there to rot in that nightmare other people thought was a normal family. Mom and Dad didn't give a shit about either of us, but at least when you and I were together, I felt like we had a chance."

The hostess at the café podium looked over at us and I tensed up.

"Guys. Stop," I hissed through clenched teeth. "You're making a scene. People are looking."

"I'm sorry, man, really," Taylor said, keeping his cool. "I didn't mean to leave you there like that. I just—I just had to get away." He shrugged. "You know Dad, always going on about how we'd have to enlist and then Mom always freaking out about everything. What was I supposed to do? Stay there and let them take me down with the ship?"

"You could have gotten me help. You could have done something for your own brother, damn it!"

"It's too late for that," I interjected. "Brian, please. You can't change the past, and even if you could, it wouldn't change the fact that he *is* one of us right now."

"I don't care what he is, I—"

"Excuse me?" It was the woman from the podium. "Could you take this outside, please? This isn't the time or place." She crossed her arms. "Don't make me call security on what's obviously some kind of... family matter."

"Ma'am, we're sorry for the trouble," Taylor said, lowering his head. "I was just leaving anyway."

"I thought so." Brian sneered, scoffing at the sight of Taylor turning away.

"Shut up, Brian," I growled. "You're only making things worse. Go back upstairs and pack your shit or whatever." I glanced at the hostess. "I apologize, Ma'am. We'll settle this elsewhere."

"Let's go, Kareena." Brian gestured for me to follow him. I glanced at Taylor, who was already walking off, and then back at Brian.

"I'll meet up with you guys in a little while."

Brian rolled his eyes and sighed. "Fine." He walked off toward the elevators and I waited for him to get out of sight before bolting off after his brother.

"Taylor, wait!"

He was already unlocking the door to his room.

"Yes?" He propped open the door with his shoe.

"They want to leave, but I want to say goodbye first. I couldn't really do that in front of your brother. I mean, he's really not himself at all right now. I'm sorry. I tried. I really—"

"Kareena?" He paused and looked around nervously, letting his foot slip from the doorway and the door click closed.

"Yes?"

He bit his lip and then ran a hand through his short hair. It was a classic Brian-like thing to do, actually, and it made me laugh to myself.

"This is going to sound crazy," he started, looking me in the eye, "but just hear me out, please."

"I'm listening."

"Do you feel like you fit in with the others?"

The question caught me off guard. "Uh... Well, obviously we all have the same stuff in us, but I don't know if I *fit in*. They have their own drama going on most of the time."

"Brian has his girlfriend, right?"

I nodded.

"And David?"

"He can take care of himself," I added with a shrug.

"Then I'll be honest with you here. I can't promise to do any better than they have, but if you want, you can come with me and I'll try to put you up someplace a lot nicer than this. Somewhere you can get some fresh air. A place to clear your head, even if only for a little while."

I stood there, silently staring at him. "Are you serious about this?" I asked, narrowing my eyes.

"Yes. Yes, I am."

Run away with Taylor?

I hardly knew him, and yet his offer made more sense to me than anything the others had said in the past forty-eight hours. This guy had a real life—a real job and a plan to keep on living. As long as I was with the others, my future had been stunted. It wasn't about me anymore. It was about them. Always about *them*. Hell, I was old enough to make my own decisions. I could do whatever I wanted.

If only I knew what that was...

"I don't know, Taylor. It's kind of ridiculous, isn't it? I mean, the Saviors pick us up and move us whenever they want, and who can say when they'll tear me out of whatever place you put me up in and drop me right back in the middle of these three again? Really?"

He took my hands into his and our eyes locked.

"I don't want to leave you with them," he said. "I'm worried about you."

I gasped. A warm stream of purple light leached through his fingers and into mine, making my hands tingle.

"Why do you care about me so much?" I asked, trying not to lose myself in the oddly pleasant sensation of his fluorescent touch. "We barely know each other."

"I don't know," he replied. "I just feel like I need to help you. But like I said, I can't promise you anything better, even though I'll try. I know you want something better than this, and you deserve it. They're not really pulling for you right now. If all you guys do is fight, what good is it doing for you to even be with them at all?"

David and I didn't fight. Well, okay, maybe we did. He had something wrong with him and didn't want to admit it. Brian was glued to Alice and couldn't think about anything else because of it. Alice was... ugh, Alice.

"Okay, let's say—hypothetically—I agree," I started. "How am I going to go back with you to Canada? I don't have a passport and..."

"I've got friends, too, you know? We'll stay near the border if we have to. I know it's a crazy idea and... ah, forget it. It was stupid of me to even—" He released my hands.

"No."

"I'm sorry. I—"

"No. I mean it's not a stupid idea. If I get teleported back here, then, oh well. I'll deal with it. But, I have a suspicion you'll be coming with us next time anyway. There's no way this whole meeting was coincidental. We were all drawn to this place because of what we are."

"I was drawn here all the way from Canada?" He chuckled lightly.

I crossed my arms. "And that purple light inside you is a hallucination, right?"

"No." He fell silent. "Okay, well, what do you want to do? You don't have to—"

"I'll go with you."

"Y-you will?"

"Yeah. I'm kind of screwed right now anyway. Maybe I can enjoy a few minutes of life in between all of the drama. I don't own shit anymore, so what have I got to lose?"

.   .   .

Taylor offered to buy me a few things to help get me back on my feet once we got to the new city, so I decided not to return to my room. I had David's coin in my pocket still, and if I had gone back to say goodbye, I'd probably have ended up being confronted by Brian. It didn't matter what *he* thought about Taylor. I had a good feeling about him and that was all that mattered.

I mean, yeah, maybe he looked a lot like Brian and that might have influenced my decision. Hell, I wanted Brian and couldn't have him. Maybe... just maybe, Taylor might want me. Or maybe I could get out of the way of Alice's and Brian's emotional rampages. David and I almost had a thing going but... I didn't really want him. We agreed—no broken hearts; no hard feelings.

Taylor finished packing his carry-on bag and double-checked all of his dresser drawers for leftover items.

"I already checked," I said, trying to smile even as a twinge of nausea roiled my stomach.

"Thanks."

We headed to the door and then down the hall to the front desk to check out.

That's when I started to second-guess myself.

What the hell am I doing? What kind of idiot girl runs off with a guy she met only a day ago—regardless of whether or not he happened to have the same kind of alien DNA surging through his bloodstream as she did?

Who would tell the others where I'd gone?

Oh, screw it. The others don't care about me.

I sat down on a burgundy leather couch in the lobby and watched Taylor from a distance. The receptionist with the weird dark jagged lines going through her light was there, checking him out of his room.

I couldn't hear what they were saying very well, but she was pointing at some paperwork and he was looking it over. Then he folded the papers and tucked them into the pocket of his coat.

He thanked her and handed her his keycard. Their fingers touched briefly and I saw his color flash.

I covered my mouth to stifle a yelp of surprise as my heart almost leapt from my chest.

As Taylor turned to walk toward me, the brown ridges of the receptionist's infection softened and faded away. Then the dull grey light inside her burst to life, glowing like an orb of white energy.

"What the hell?" I whispered beneath my breath.

Taylor approached me and bent over at the waist to look me in the eye. "Hey. Everything okay?" He waved a hand in front of my face, but my eyes remained locked on the woman.

"Having second thoughts?" he asked. "You don't have to come with me if you don't—"

"Shh!" I silenced him with a flattened hand toward his face.

The sickening darkness inside the receptionist had changed.

Holy shit.

She'd been started...

Chapter 14

Should I tell him?

Should I tell the others?

"Is something wrong?" Taylor propped his carry-on back on its feet and took a seat beside me on the couch. "Do you need a few minutes or something?"

"You're a goddamn Starter," I muttered.

"What?"

"A-a... Starter. Like Alice. The Saviors must have made another one because they knew she didn't want to do it anymore. Oh, Jesus Christ." I folded over and dropped my face into my hands. "Shit. Shit. Shit!"

"Kareena, keep your voice down. What does that mean? Starter?"

I hadn't explained to him in much detail what Alice could do.

"I can't talk about it right now. Can we just get the hell out of here, please?" I bounded up off the couch.

"Are you sure you're okay, Kar—"

"Yes!" I'd already started toward the exit. Taylor had to dart after me to keep up.

We left through the rotating glass doors, rushed across the crosswalk, and then turned a corner at the end of the block, finding ourselves on a sparsely populated stretch of sidewalk.

"Okay, what now?" he asked, leaning over to investigate the heavy scuff marks on the wheels of his roller bag. "Crap. This was kind of expensive and not really meant for—"

"Damn it! They screwed us."

"Who?" Taylor tipped his head to the side. "I have no clue what you're going on about."

"We have to go somewhere safe. Somewhere there aren't many people. It's only going to be a matter of time before those things start pushing you around—making you do things you don't want to do."

"Does this have something to do with the Saviors?" he asked.

"Yes! They've..." My head started pounding again. "Oh, no." I doubled over as a massive headache flooded my skull. "Oh, God." I held my face in my hands and blindly reached out for Taylor as my surroundings closed in on me. The pain in my temples increased.

"Kareena!" A familiar voice called to me from the distance.

"David?" I could barely see him through warping spirals of light flickering in and out of my vision. I cupped my forehead and squinted, trying to see where he was coming from.

"Kareena, are you okay?" he asked, jogging up to us. "Taylor, what's going on? What's happening to her?"

"I-I don't know, man. We were just leaving and—"

"Leaving!? What the hell do you mean? Leaving?"

Warm, strong fingers wrapped around my wrist—definitely David's.

"It's okay. It was my idea," I muttered through clenched teeth. "Back off." The light brightened even more until I could see nothing but—the Prism.

"You cannot go with him," it said, its voice wavering while rainbow flashes of color sparkled all around it. "His fluorescence is tainted."

"What?" I shook my head and grunted against the pounding headache just beginning to taper off. "What do you mean?"

"His fluorescence is unnatural. What the Saviors have done to him may put us all at further risk of infection. For your own safety, stay with the others. The other Fluorescent

Ones need you."

"What? Wh—" My head felt heavy and I tumbled backward. David caught me in his arms and helped lift me back onto my feet. I pushed his hands off me. The radiant lights faded into nothing and my peripheral vision came back into focus.

"Are you okay?" He placed his hand on my shoulder and looked me in the eye. "What just happened to you?"

"Leave me alone," I sneered, forcing his hand away. "I'm not made of porcelain!"

"Where are you going?" David asked, crossing his arms. "Why didn't you tell any of us? Or me, at least?"

Taylor took a step back from us.

I propped my hands on my hips and scoffed. "David, you're the one who told me I didn't have to stay with the others. You told me that it was pointless to go on without growing or changing. Well, I thought about it, and I've made a decision. I'm leaving *all* of you guys. Brian doesn't need me and Alice doesn't give a damn. You..." I looked at him and shrugged. "Well, you can take care of yourself," I carried on in a softer voice. "What the hell do you need me for?"

"I know what I said earlier but, Kareena, you need to rethink this." He reached out to me.

"Why? You said things weren't going to get messy unless I let them. Are you changing your mind now?"

"No." His hand dropped back to his side. "That's not the point I'm trying to make. We need to stick together and I'm not going to hang around with those two brats if you leave. I-I can't do it."

"Then don't." I shrugged. "Leave. Go back to your sister. Go back to living your life the best you can while you've got the chance. If the Saviors want us back together, they'll make that happen. There's no point suffering in the meantime. Putting up with each other has made our lives crap and you know it."

"Even so." David shot a sudden, threatening glare at Taylor. "What did you say to her?" he asked, confronting him with a step closer. "What the hell did you say to get her to leave with you?"

"I said back off!" I shoved David in the chest with both hands, but he hardly budged. His jaw hung open in disgust.

"Fine. Do whatever the hell you want," he said, scowling. "But just know that the minute you leave this city, I'm out." He raised his hands up and backed away from us. "I'm not staying here with those kids. Not alone, I'm sure as hell not. Not if you want me to keep your boy Brian alive."

Taylor's eyes widened.

"Y-you're not going to kill him, are you?" he whispered, his voice cracking. "My brother?"

"No," I interrupted. "He's talking shit again. He thinks just because he's got a shiny gun—"

"A gun!?" Taylor staggered back.

"Yeah. A gun." I veered around. "He won't use it on *you* so stop freaking out." I turned back around toward David. "You're such a dick, thinking you can push people around because you've got bullets in your back pocket. You're no better than anyone else. I'm going to make my own decisions and you're going to have to make yours. Sorry if that means going on without you, but that's how things go. Life sucks and then you die." I turned around. "Let's get out of here, Taylor."

I waved without looking back.

"Goodbye, David."

Chapter 15

"Don't feel bad about David. He's got more issues than Brian, I think." I sat beside Taylor on the trolley. His carry-on was wedged between us on the floor so it wouldn't slide into the aisle. It kept bumping me in the knee every so often as the car swayed gently over hilly roads and around curves. "He acts cool, but he's not. Sorry he confronted you like that."

Taylor glanced at me and then looked away. "Were the two of you...?"

I shook my head. "Hell, no." I rolled my eyes. "He didn't mean anything to me."

"Oh." Our eyes met again. "He seemed awfully worried about you, though."

"Yeah. He's got his nose in everyone's business. I can take care of myself. Besides, you're going to help me, too, right?"

"Sure." The trolley hit a bump and Taylor lunged to stop his suitcase from rolling away. "As best I can. I mean, I don't really know much about what's going on either."

Damn. I liked Taylor a lot, at first. Now, I was having second thoughts.

Maybe the company I was forced to keep wasn't the best, but both Brian and David had guts—boldness and bravery in their blood. Unpredictability sometimes, even. A man with some fire inside was a turn-on.

Taylor, on the other hand... The way he freaked when he'd heard David had a gun. He might have been Brian's brother, but the similarities stopped at their faces.

"So, do you think David and the others will come looking for us?"

"No. Why would they?"

Taylor shrugged.

. . .

"You've got a nice place here," I said, plopping onto the suede couch in Taylor's living room and stretching my arms up high over my head. He told me it was one of the many temporary apartments he stayed at in places he frequented on business trips. All paid for by his company, too. If he wasn't staying in a hotel, he was living it up in a beautiful flat perched high above whatever city where he had his next appointment. *Nice.*

I examined the sleek, silver crown molding and the pin-striped wallpaper. All stainless steel appliances. Large glass windows surrounded us, offering breathtaking views of the sparkling cityscape below.

He had good taste, or at least his company did.

"Would you like something to drink?" he asked, poking his head up from behind the open refrigerator door.

"Sure." I rested back against the supple leather couch cushions and closed my eyes. I took a deep breath and exhaled slowly, taking in the most peace and quiet I'd had in days.

Taylor rummaged around in the fridge and then I heard the clink of glasses. I opened my eyes to him setting a bottle of wine on the black granite countertop. He pushed the refrigerator door closed and reached a hand into a nearby drawer for a corkscrew.

Wine? I wasn't a fan, but I had to be polite. It was difficult to tell if he was trying to impress me or if this was a normal thing for him. He acted so natural and at ease.

"What am I, your girlfriend?" I asked, batting my lashes

jokingly as he handed me a glass flute.

"You could be," he replied with a smirk. "Right?"

"Maybe." I tried to hide my nervous smile.

Is this guy for real?

"We hardly know each other, but here we are," he said, with a look of admiration in his eyes. "Two people implanted with some crazy glowing alien DNA, who just happened to find each other in this huge world full of millions of people. I think that means something. Don't you?"

"Maybe."

"You like that word, don't you?" He cocked an eyebrow. "*Maybe?*"

Maybe...

"Oops." I smiled and he smiled back. "I'm a little out of my element here. Honestly, you're too nice, I think."

"Too nice?" He scoffed lightly. "Oh, great. I know where this road's going to take me." He rolled his eyes and sat back against the couch, bringing his glass to his lips to take a sip of blush colored wine. "Next thing out of your mouth is going to be something about us just being friends. Right?"

"No. That's not it. Sorry. Things—"

He gasped and the grin vanished from his face. "Something's wrong," he whispered, his eyes widening.

I felt it, too—the air around us growing thinner. My muscles tensed.

"No!" I stood, grabbed Taylor's hand, and pulled him up from the couch. Then I closed my eyes tightly. His hand squeezed mine as the floor disappeared out from under us.

We touched down on pavement. Taylor lost his grip and slipped. I grabbed him by the arm to keep him from falling.

"Thanks," he said, out of breath.

I flashed a small grin in response.

"Where are we?" He looked around.

"I don't know." It was dark, but I could make out faint auras of infected people as shapes around us materialized.

Instinctively, I opened my mouth to call out to the others—Brian, Alice and maybe even David—but then I stopped myself. Even if they were there, the farther they were from us, the better. I wouldn't have to worry about Brian tearing Taylor apart, or me having to point out any sleepers to Alice. If they wanted us together, the Saviors knew damn well how to do it.

It was still difficult to see our surroundings, but there were hoards of people everywhere. I took a step back, scuffing my shoes against what I then realized was dirt, not concrete. I squinted. Thousands of people in rows of raked seating all around. There was a white line on the ground and I followed it to a point where it met grass. A stadium?

A... baseball field.

What in the hell?

A tremendous boom shook the ground and I ducked, shrieking in fear. Taylor looked up, unmoved, and chuckled.

"Fireworks," he said nonchalantly.

"What?" My gaze shot up. A splash of cascading colored lights sprinkled down from the black sky, sizzling and crackling and then vanishing into subtle plumes of smoke.

"That scared the crap out me!" I straightened up, clutching onto Taylor's arm for balance since my unnerved, shaky legs made it difficult to stand. "You're afraid of guns you haven't even seen, but a random explosion doesn't faze you? Jesus, Taylor." I shook my head.

Maybe I was wrong about him.

A second round of whirring and popping sounds reverberated through the air and a scoreboard up in the distance flashed names I didn't recognize.

"They just had to find some party for us to crash, didn't they?"

"What do you mean?" Taylor raised his voice over the sounds of exploding fireworks.

"They're always sending us some place where there are

lots of people. Last time, it was freaking Times Square. Well, not *last time*. Anyway, let's go find a place to sit a while until everyone clears out." I took Taylor's hand and started walking toward the bleachers. "Be careful not to touch anyone, okay?"

I felt resistance as I pulled him to follow.

"No, Kareena," he said in a quieter voice.

I veered around. "What?"

"We *can't* wait this out," he replied flatly.

"What's... going on?" I released his hand. "Taylor?"

"Look around. There are a lot of people here. Do some of them have tainted light inside? Are they what you might call... sick? Compromised is probably a better word."

I hesitated. There were more sleepers here than I'd seen in any other city I'd been to so far.

"Compromised?" I narrowed my eyes. "You mean..." I glanced around at the mass of pulsing lights. Many of them had black and brown bolts of darkness smothering their glowing cores, forking through the white light like glass fractures. I could see it in them even from a distance. It was the same messed up pattern the guy at the diner had inside—before he died.

"That's why they put us here," Taylor said. "To make things right."

"No," I snapped. "They put us here to start people. That's how it's always been with them."

"Start," Taylor repeated. "Make things right. It's all the same now."

I cocked my head to the side. "A day ago you had no clue what was happening and now, all of a sudden, you're some kind of martyr sent here to *make things right?* Do you have any idea what you're talking about?"

"You saw what I did to the receptionist at the hotel. That's what I'm meant to do. That's what they made me for."

"*Made* you?" I tried hard not to laugh. "You're delusional, Taylor, if you think those idiots up there made you into something special. They're sick, twisted creatures who don't give a damn about our wellbeing." I crossed my arms and turned away just as streaks of red, white, and blue sparks twinkled overhead. "No. I'm not doing this," I said. "I'm not going to be the one who puts these people in danger. I won't help you. This is why we've been running."

"You've been running to get away from the life you used to have," he retorted, raising his voice. "The one you can't have anymore. You ran away to keep people from finding out about you and the others because you were too afraid to accept it."

"Afraid?" I glared at him. "Is that what you think I am? No. It's not that at all. This is crazy!" I backed up. "I don't want to do this. I never did. They never gave us a choice!" I was yelling amidst the booming cheers of the crowd.

"We're here to help people!" He took a step closer.

"What do you mean, *help* people? Do you even know what this stuff does to us?"

"Yes, I do." He lowered his head and looked away from me. "In fact, I know a lot more than you do about this outbreak."

Outbreak!?

"What!?" My stomach felt sick all of a sudden.

"I know the truth about the man you guys saw a while back at that diner. He died of the same thing the receptionist at the hotel had inside her."

"How do you know that?"

"They... told me," he said, looking up at me. "The Saviors."

"But you said they only spoke with you once. How did you—"

"Maybe it was more than once. Okay, I lied, but would you have gone with me if I had told you the truth?"

A burst of yellow sparkles came down in the distance and the crowd cheered again. I hunched down, covering my ears for a moment.

"How could you!?" I shouted, coming to my feet and flexing my hands angrily. All I had to do was grab his face and force my fluorescence into him. It would hurt like hell. It would snap him out of his shit faster than anything. "I'm not helpless, you know. I'll hurt you if you can't give me one good reason why I shouldn't." I growled beneath my breath.

"The Saviors put something in me, a different kind of fluorescence. Something that can combat the side effects it's been having on some humans. I can extract the infected light from them and then... I can start them."

I grimaced. "Ugh. So you're like Brian and Alice shoved together. Jesus. This was all just a freaking ploy to get me to go with you so we could carry on this homicidal mission of theirs."

"No. That's not it, Kareena." Taylor made an attempt to grab my hand, but I yanked it out of his reach. "I can help people," he added. "I can save them while the Saviors search for the cure. If I start people, I can keep them from dying. People who haven't yet been started are the most susceptible to it, and if they don't get cured quickly, who knows how long it will be before it starts harming the uninfected? It's up to us to help them."

"Help them!?" I stomped a foot, kicking up a small cloud of dirt. "Stop trying to call it that! We wouldn't even be in this mess if those things up there knew what the hell they were doing in the first place. They came down here looking for a cure, and now they're killing *us* instead! They're going to take us down with them, and you want to be responsible for that?"

"Kareena, please... listen to me." He reached for my hand again.

"No!" I jerked it away a second time. "I won't!"

"This is your last chance," he sneered in a huskier voice, tipping his head down.

"Last chance? What are you doing? Threatening me? Screw you, Taylor!" I turned and started walking.

"Agh!" Like a firework exploding in my face, an immense flare of purple light blinded me and I doubled over.

"I said please, Kareena," Taylor hissed, coming up from behind. "I asked politely, didn't I?"

I was frozen in place, my legs so heavy, I couldn't move. I tried to speak, but nothing came out.

"You didn't really think that us meeting at that hotel was all just a magical little coincidence, did you?" he asked. "That being the brother of one of their very first chosen ones didn't somehow affect their decision to choose me, too."

Molten heat poured through me and I gasped for breath, my entire body trembling uncontrollably from the unbearable pain scorching my veins.

"I thought you were a lot smarter than this, Kareena," he whispered, his airy breath right behind my ear. "We could do great things together. It's still early in the game. You should reconsider which side you're playing on."

Purples and pinks flushed across my eyes, blurring my vision while fiery waves of energy rushed through my face. Then Taylor wrapped his arms around me and all went black.

· · ·

I awoke in a darkened room, my face nestled against a balled-up shirt that wasn't my own.

"Taylor?" I sat up and a gush of nausea made me hold my stomach. My head swelled with dizziness and I lay back down. My arms were weak. My head... so heavy. Pain blanketed every inch of me.

I rolled onto my side and forced my eyes to stay open long enough to adjust to the darkness. The window blinds had been drawn. I couldn't recognize the empty place.

All I could remember was being with Taylor last night. I remembered him touching me, and his hungry eyes tearing into my soul, poisonous violet light choking the strength from me.

I remembered that much...

"Taylor?" I called to him again, but words were difficult to get out of my mouth. My lips and throat were so dry.

No reply.

Cold, empty air swelled in my lungs and I coughed on nothing.

Then my eyelids clamped down and I...

Chapter 16

Daytime in the city. Street vendors, business people, and everyday Joes and Janes bustled past us, oblivious as always. My feet hurt from hours of walking in shoes totally not suited for it. I hugged the storefronts closely to avoid as many people as I could. Taylor stepped down off the curb to walk precariously near unyielding traffic. He was so absorbed in his own abilities he didn't care about anything else.

I wanted to strike the conniving grin off his face, but I couldn't. He was even more powerful than David. He could start people. He could suck diseased fluorescence out of them, and he could drain me, too.

He could draw the pink light straight from my body and use it to see sleepers if he wanted to. That's what he had done to me at the baseball park, and it hurt like hell. It was like someone shooting alcohol straight into my bloodstream. It burned. Every hair on my body stood and the overwhelming pain made my stomach spasm.

"Keep pointing," he commanded, glaring at me. His face looked much less like Brian's now that I despised him.

A little girl *and* her mother. An elderly man. A businessman with a briefcase in one hand and a smartphone in the other. Some kids—twins. They couldn't have been more than nine or ten. So many freaking people. It was like the Saviors infected every other person they saw, and Taylor didn't think twice before going after any one of them.

To protect myself, I had to do what he asked. At least until I could find a way out of his grasp. I hadn't seen the

Prism in two days. No sign of the others, either. It was just Taylor and me being shuttled to different cities every few hours, forced to start hundreds of people. A quick, careless press of his fingers to their shoulders was all it took for Taylor to start someone.

I kept my head down as we walked, carefully dodging people and avoiding their faces. I didn't want to remember any of them. I didn't want to remember the people I helped to damn.

"Don't be so angry with me," Taylor said, coming up beside me to reach for my wrist. He pulled me off to the side near a bike rack. "You're bad company while you're in this mood."

"How can I *not* be angry with you?" I looked over his shoulder, praying now more than ever to see another familiar face. Brian. David. Alice, even. Wishful thinking. "You're hurting innocent people. You could be destroying all of us."

"Not all of us," he said, brushing the backs of his fingers across my cheek. I turned my face away and scowled. "We're the chosen ones. We'll survive this. You of all people know we have something the sleepers don't—*colored* light. It gives us power. It separates us from them. We're immune to this evolution of the virus. That's why it's so important for us to go forward with the Saviors' plans."

One thing I hadn't told Taylor was how David, too, had the twisted dark light crawling inside him. Now I knew what it meant. It meant we were all susceptible to the deadly infection going around. Considering how quickly that man from the diner had dropped dead, I could only assume that if I couldn't get Taylor to remove the infection from David, he'd suffer the same fate.

"What makes you think it won't come for us someday? How can you possibly know this disease won't evolve again to take down all the humans and the Saviors? They've done it before, you know!"

He squinted suspiciously. "How do you know that? Who told you this?"

I gasped. "Uh. They did." I couldn't let him know about the Prism.

"The Saviors?"

"Y-Yes. The Saviors. They told us when we first met them about their unsuccessful attempts to find a cure. They've destroyed other planets and other species. You need to know the kind of evil you're working for."

"Evil?" He laughed. "There's no such thing as evil. To believe in evil, you have to believe in good, and *that* I don't."

"What? But there are good people out there. People who help others and people who—"

"Don't give a shit," he finished my sentence. "Do you really think I went into public relations because I liked people?" He scoffed and leaned his weight against one of the curved steel pipes of the bike rack. "Well, I didn't. I went into PR so I could use the skills I had to make a damn living. I manipulate people. I make them believe what I want them to believe because that's what people pay me for. Just like I convinced you to like me when we first met."

"Shut up," I growled.

He laughed in my face. "You wanted to believe so badly that I was the sweet, hardworking brother of Brian you could wrap around your finger, when in fact, I was leading you to make exactly the decisions I required."

My jaw started to hurt from being clenched. "I was making my own decisions. You didn't—"

"You left with me, didn't you? The guy you hardly knew—the poor coward you couldn't help but find yourself attracted to." He cocked an eyebrow. "Well?"

"Stop!" My fingernails dug into my palms as I squeezed my fists.

"The Saviors told me it would work. They told me you were a—how do I put it nicely—promiscuous girl." He smirked.

"They told me you pretty much threw yourself at Brian and the other guy you left at the hotel. It's kind of a shame you won't share that side of yourself with me."

"Never!" I stepped back. "You've screwed yourself out of having a chance with me. I thought I could like you, Taylor, but I was wrong. You're a—"

"Shut up and get back to work!" he snapped, pointing at a passing crowd. The purple light in his right arm flared up, flickering brightly beneath his skin.

I was so damn angry, I wanted to grab him by the head right then and there and blow his damn brains out with my light. But I'd learned the hard way what his fluorescence could do to me in return and I didn't want to feel that again. That helplessness. That out-of-body-like drifting feeling I got when it burned through my veins. Excruciatingly slow, like poison, eating away at my insides.

I heaved a sigh and started walking, lifting a finger to point out the next sleeper I saw.

"Now, that's a good girl," Taylor said, reaching out to pat me on the shoulder.

Bastard.

·   ·   ·

A hand caressed my cheek and I opened my eyes.

"Brian?" I rolled over onto my back and looked wearily up into his eyes. "Brian, how did you find me?" He sat on the edge of the bed, near my side.

"Don't worry about that," he whispered, his voice warm and serene. It immediately made my heart less heavy. "What's important is that you're alive... and safe."

An attempt to sit up made me lightheaded, so I stayed where I was. "I wouldn't call being with Tay—"

"Don't say it," he interrupted, scooting closer. "You're safe with me. I'll protect you."

"Thank you." I peered around the room but couldn't sharply focus on any one thing. It was dim and I was fatigued. "Where's Alice?"

"Alice?" Brian repeated, wrinkling his brow and shaking his head as if he were put off by the thought. "Why are you worrying about *her* right now? This is about you, Kareena." His fingers sifted through my hair. I really tried hard to stifle a smile but couldn't stop the edges of my lips from curling.

I wanted Brian so much, it hurt. Every time I looked into his hazel eyes, I lost myself. The scent of his skin made me feel at peace. Protected. The thought of actually having him seemed like the only thing keeping me going anymore. Maybe I was part of the group, but I didn't want to be. I only tolerated it because of him.

Being separated for only a few days felt like an eternity. He may have been Alice's, but it wouldn't stop me from trying. Or, from dreaming. He could change his mind any day. He could be mine eventually...

Maybe.

"I'm glad you're okay," he continued. "I... missed you. A lot." He massaged the back of my neck and leaned even closer. "I was worried I'd lost you."

Lost me?

"Brian? Wh—"

"It's okay," he continued in his soothing voice. His reassuring smile made my heart flutter. Those eyes tearing into me, reaching into the depths of my soul with an unfamiliar sense of longing in them.

Why was he staring into my eyes like that? As if... he wanted me? I'd seen it enough times to know what it looked like in a man's gaze. That carnal look of desire. Hunger.

But it couldn't be.

It wasn't possible. Was it?

"I missed you, too," I muttered and tried once again to sit up. He stopped me with a kiss.

A wonderful, lovesick dizzy spell came over me and I exhaled a groan. I forked a hand through his soft hair and tugged him down on top of me.

The heat of his breaths mixing with mine invigorated me—filling me with a new sense of reason. I had so much to live for and so much to gain by fighting back against the Saviors.

I had *him*.

I had Brian.

His lips slid across my jaw line and down to my neck.

That was when I saw his fluorescence ignite to life, tinting me with a cool glow as the sparks of color emanated from his arm.

His... *right* arm...

Chapter 17

We were at a mall in some other city. The sixth or seventh place we'd been thrown into during the last few days. I'd lost count because my memories were a blur. I don't know if it was Taylor manipulating me with his fluorescence every night, or just me trying to block out all of the faces of the people we were putting in danger. Maybe it was both.

I walked ahead of Taylor, pointing out sleepers and trying hard to pretend the entire thing was a dream. I'd wake up soon from the nightmare.

I would. *Right?*

At least, that's what I kept telling myself.

I pointed out another sleeper and Taylor jogged after her— a middle-aged woman with golden skin like mine. Indian. Hispanic, perhaps. When the Saviors made us invisible, it was difficult to see much detail in people who hadn't yet been started.

My gaze swept from side to side as I searched for more infected people. Then I heard a feminine scream and turned around. Taylor was bent over, looking at his hands in disbelief. The dark-skinned woman was laid out on the tile floor in the walkway and a crowd was quickly gathering around her.

"What happened?" I asked, frantically making my way over to the victim. Her white light was swirling with black and brown streaks. "Why haven't you started her!? Taylor!"

He jerked his face up toward me. "I did! At least, I tried. I don't know what happened! She just screamed and fell over. I don't know what the hell I did wrong."

The crowd of people started pushing back and forth against one another, snapping photos with their smartphones, and fighting to get a better look at the suffering woman.

"Can you try it again?" I asked, my breaths quickening. My heart was thumping in my chest.

Taylor reached down to touch her hand and then snapped back with fear. "Ah!" He pulled his hand in close to his chest and shielded it with his other arm.

"What happened?" I shouted over the rising voices of the growing mob.

"She... shocked me."

Oh, God. I took a second look at her light, which was now small and barely visible.

"It's too late for her," I said, my voice breaking. Adrenaline made my hands shake. "She's... fading. She's going to die! Because of you, Taylor."

"No!" Taylor shook off the discomfort of the shock and reached for the woman again.

"Taylor!"

Nothing happened.

The light inside her vanished.

She was dead.

"Just get away from her!" I started moving back from the crowd as quickly as I could so I wouldn't get trapped.

Taylor straightened up and backed away as a mall security guard rushed to the woman's side. He stood there, watching the guard check the victim's pulse. For a second, Taylor's attention wasn't on me, so I did the only thing could think of.

I ran.

I knew I wouldn't get very far, but I turned and hauled ass out of there. I ran as fast as I could through the mall, dodging anything and anyone that came between me and the exit doors.

"Kareena!"

I heard Taylor roaring my name, but I didn't look back.

I just kept running.

Through the food court.

Down the escalator.

My shins and even my chest started to hurt, but I didn't slow down. Not while I had a chance to get away.

"Kareena!" I heard my name again, but this time it wasn't Taylor's voice; it was Brian's. I stopped dead in my tracks and listened.

"Brian?" I called back, unable to see him anywhere. Then I heard my name again. Now it was Alice calling for me.

"Guys! Where are you?" I darted off in the direction of the voices, calling for them and pausing between spurts to listen.

Then I heard *him* again, too. "Where are you going!?" Taylor was gaining on me and his voice was angrier than I'd ever heard.

"Brian!" I screamed at the top of my lungs as I shot through the crowded mall, pushing past people, knocking a few people over. Anything to get where the others were. I had to make distance. I stopped for a split second and checked behind me again. Taylor had gotten caught up in a crowd pouring out of some store. His purple light was glinting and I saw him mouthing words at me I couldn't make out. Whatever they were, they were vile.

"Where are you guys?" I called out again.

Suddenly, I heard a high-pitched humming noise and turned my head. A flash of white blinded me and then it was as though the air had been cut open to reveal a swirling gouge of white light. I could barely see it at first as it faded in and out of view. I swallowed hard and froze in place, uncertain of what to do next.

"Kareena!" both Brian and Alice called. Their voices resonated from the light as if they were only inches away.

Another quick look behind me. Taylor was closing the distance between us, his anger making the violet in his arm outrageously bright.

I went closer to the thing that appeared to be some kind of portal and watched as rings of vivid white spun through one another, making the large oval shape pulsate.

"Go, Kareena!" an ethereal voice echoed in my head. I recognized it.

A quick swallow and then I held my breath, closed my eyes, and passed through the light.

A whirlwind tossed my hair all across my face and I felt a whoosh of cool, crisp air surround me. A second later, I was vomited back out onto solid ground.

Brian and Alice came rushing over to me, their eyes darting around as they searched for the thing that had dropped me there. I turned and saw nothing. The portal had vanished.

"You're back!" Alice said, as if she were happy to see me. "Are you okay?"

"I'm fine." I looked into her worried blue eyes and felt relieved. Then I looked into Brian's and my heart plummeted again.

"Are you alright, Kareena?" he asked, quickly looking me over. "Are you hurt?" His arm was already glistening with soft blue light.

"No," I replied. "Thank you for helping me get out of there."

"Helping you?" Alice cocked an eyebrow. "We were just here and suddenly heard you calling for us. The next thing we knew, you came falling out of nowhere."

"What? But I-I heard you two calling my name. I know I did."

Brian shook his head. "We weren't the ones calling you, Kareena."

"Prism," I whispered. "It must have been the Prism. It said it would try to help us. Maybe it found a way. Neither of you could see that thing at all?"

"No," replied Alice. "We couldn't see anything until you appeared."

"It was as big as me. A swirling line of light just floating in front of me like someone cut a hole in the air and the sun was shining through it."

"We definitely didn't see that," Brian said. "Let's get out of here in case anything or anyone else tries to come through that thing."

•   •   •

I sat down on a bench near the hotel parking lot. It was a different hotel than the one we were at before. Rundown, but safe enough for now.

Brian sat beside me. His troubled expression put my stomach in knots.

"Now that you're back and settled down a bit," he started, "I have to ask you something." His jaw tightened and he narrowed his eyes at me. "Why would you abandon us like that? Why did you leave without even saying a damn word about it?"

"I... I'm sorry." I entwined my fingers together in my lap. "I just—"

"Didn't think about anyone but yourself," Brian cut me off. "You only thought about poor Kareena and what she wanted, right?"

"Well, I—"

"You thought that if you couldn't have me, you'd have my brother." His judgmental gaze made me feel so small. I looked down and hunched over. "Right?"

"I'm sorry," I murmured beneath my breath. "I'm... sorry, Brian," I whispered, my voice breaking.

Brian took a deep breath and exhaled slowly. The drawn-out silence made my chest tighten.

He leaned closer to me. "Don't be," he said, his voice much softer than usual.

"What?" His swift change of tone caught my attention. I lifted my head and looked him in the eye. "Aren't you pissed at me?"

"Yeah," he answered, scoffing. "Of course I am. But by the looks of it, you've been through more than enough hell already." He touched my shoulder gently. "You don't need to be instigated by us, too."

I felt like shit, but I forced a little smile in reply. "Thank you, Brian." His forgiveness was all I could ask for.

"So... did Taylor try to hurt you?" he asked.

In more ways than one.

He pressed his lips thin. "Well?"

"Yes."

"I tried to warn you about him, you know. But..." He sighed. "Never mind. Like I said, I won't rub it in." He patted me on the back and tried to grin. "At least you're back."

"I don't know for how long," I replied.

His brow furrowed. "What do you mean? Do you think they'll take you again soon?"

"They need me."

"They needed Alice, too."

"Not anymore."

"What?" Brian drew back, surprised. "What do you mean? Are they... done with us?"

"I don't know." I shrugged. "Probably not, but now that they have Taylor, they only need the two of us to do their dirty work. He's... even more powerful than David."

Brian's eyes widened. "What? But how can that be? What the hell does he have that's *more* powerful than David's fluorescence? What can Taylor do with his?"

"He can steal mine."

Brian gasped. "Shit," he muttered beneath his breath.

"He can steal my powers as a Seeker, and... he can start

people."

"No!" Brian's jaw dropped. "No. No." He ran his hands through his hair. "This... can't be happening."

"It is. And we have to stop him. We have to put an end to this before he finds us. Where the hell is David, anyway?"

Brian stared at me. "He left," he said. "He told us he didn't have a reason to stay. What did you expect him to do?"

"I don't know." I crossed my arms and leaned back against the bench. "I thought he was overreacting. I didn't think he'd *actually* leave you guys."

"We're getting on fine without him," Brian huffed.

"Still, it's us against the world. And David's one of us, even if you two didn't get along."

"That's what you said about Taylor, too." Brian tipped his head to the side.

I nibbled my lip. "That was before I learned he was a psychopath bent on infecting everyone. He doesn't care if it means killing people or not."

"How many people have you two started since all of this began?" he asked.

"Hundreds. Thousands. I don't know. Taylor does something to me at night. I can't even remember what the hell I'm doing, where I am half the time, or what happened the night before. I wake up fatigued and blurry eyed. Then I black out again until morning. It's happened almost every night since I left."

Brian's eyebrows crinkled. "Taylor and I never got along well," he started, "but I never would have known he could be so vicious. A liar and a jerk, yeah, but a killer? That's just twisted."

"Yes. Yes, it is."

I hadn't even told him about the second infected person I had to watch die.

Chapter 18

"I hope you can get some rest now that you're back with us," Brian said, ushering me to my room. This hotel was nicer than some we'd stayed in before. Maybe he'd learned a thing or two from David in the short time we were with him.

"I'll try." I sat down on the crisp beige duvet and lifted a bleach-scented pillow to my face to nestle my cheek against it. It wasn't home, but it was clean and comfortable enough.

Brian headed for the door.

"Brian, don't leave," I said, just as he wrapped his fingers around the handle. "Please."

"I have to go back to Alice. I can't stay with you. You know that, Kareena."

I did, but... I didn't care.

"Please? Just for a few minutes? I'm..." I hesitated. "I'm worried they'll take me again." My voice was shaky. "I'm... scared, okay?" My throat tightened and tears started to well in my eyes. I didn't want to cry in front of him. Brian didn't like it when I complained. He'd probably hate it if I started whimpering like a child.

Still, my heart was so tangled up in everything that had happened, with all of the fear and anger closing in on me. I wanted to believe I was safe now, but... I couldn't.

Brian paused and turned away from the door to come back over toward the bed. He sat on the edge beside me and cupped a hand over mine. An eager breath caught in my lungs and I tried not to seem overzealous.

"I'm sorry you've been through so much, but we're all

living in hell right now," he said. "We have to keep fighting back any way we can. Okay?" He reached for a tissue from the nearby dresser and handed it to me.

I nodded and took the tissue.

"What you did back there—running away with Taylor—was stupid. But... we all make mistakes. We've *all* screwed up."

I sniffled. "He's nothing like us. He's... evil."

"The powers the Saviors gave him are messing with his head, probably," he replied. "You said it yourself, he's more powerful than any of us, and it sounds like he can do a lot of damage. I'll do what I can for you. I'll try, but I have Alice to think about, too."

Sometimes I wish you didn't...

"Thank you," was all I said.

Brian looked down at me, a frown weighing on his lips. "I'm sorry for whatever he did to you."

Then he left the room.

I kept my eyes closed and tried as hard as I could to sleep, but every few minutes they were wide open again. Staring at the clock beside the bed. Counting dots in the spackled ceiling. Listening intently to muffled, indistinct conversations of people outside.

My heart was racing. I was exhausted, but I was also terri-fied the Saviors would grab me at any moment. Closing my eyes for a second made me vividly recall Taylor's breath close to my neck. I whined in fear and finally sat up in the bed, pull-ing my knees close to my chest, then dragging the blankets up over them toward my neck.

"Damn it, Kareena!" I groaned. "Why the hell aren't you able to sleep!?"

Brian was just next-door... but he couldn't stop Taylor by himself.

What if me being back with the others would put them in danger of being abducted?

"Ugh!"

All I wanted was one single decent night of rest. I'd been on a full-blown adrenaline rush for days. At least while I was conscious. At night, whatever Taylor was doing to me that was causing spontaneous blackouts kept me sleeping until midday. He'd wake me abruptly, just moments before we were tele-ported somewhere.

I clicked on the lamp on the side table and dropped my head back, staring blankly at the ceiling. I stayed like that until I started seeing odd shapes in the spackling. Stars. Birds. Squiggly arms and legs without bodies. Twisted little creatures missing heads and limbs. Some of the simpler patches re-minded me of scars—David's scars. I remembered one that I could have sworn was from a bullet. I couldn't guess anything about the rest, but that one in particular gave me chills. To think of all the shit he'd been through, and there I was fighting just to get myself to go to sleep.

I lowered my head, stared at my hands in my lap, and then I looked at the clock again—1:37 AM.

My eyes closed and I rested my head against the wall, taking slow, deep breaths to try to calm my nervous pulse. Warmth swept over me and my eyes opened.

An intense flash of light lit up the room. The swirling blur of hot white at the end of my bed grew brighter and brighter until I could make out subtle veins of color flitting through it.

The Prism.

The warmth increased as the glowing energy neared me, and a small, less painful than usual headache swelled in my forehead.

"That portal that opened up for me... was that your doing?" I asked, sitting up straighter on the bed.

"Yes," it replied, its light fading slightly in and out. "You may rest now without fear of the Saviors taking you again for approximately one earth day. We cannot stop them indefinitely, but the energy inside the portals is so potent, it masks your own fluorescence and distorts their ability to locate you for a short time."

"What about the others? What about Brian and Alice?"

"We will do our best to watch you all and try to intervene if we detect activity on their part. We believe the Saviors have shifted their focus to the new one, however—the fluorescent abomination."

"Taylor." The name was barely audible coming from my mouth.

"Yes. As you have experienced firsthand, his power is corrupt and dangerous. Fluorescence is not meant to be modified into such a misshapen genetic pattern that it infests one's mind with darkness and rage. He is unstable and his genetic code is not completely compatible with the light, unlike his brother."

I huffed, disgusted by the news. So the Saviors had only picked Taylor because he was *close enough* to what they needed. They probably knew damn well he'd start shit with us, too.

Damn them.

"As you have already witnessed, we are diligently working to improve the door of light—the portal between dimensions, which we used to tear a hole between the stasis realm and the natural realm."

"What?" I shook my head. "You're getting too sci-fi on me. What's a stasis realm?"

"When you are sent places by the Saviors, you are placed within a layer between the natural and spectral realms—it is called the stasis realm, and while you are trapped within it, no one can see or hear you. It is a discreet layer in the fabric of time that allows you to interact nearly unnoticed while you continue to exist in real time."

The rainbow light started to dim, signaling our chat was about to end.

"What else can I do to fight back?" I came onto my knees and crawled a few inches closer toward it. "What can I do about Taylor?"

"We do not know how to deal with him yet. Please tell the others what we have told you. You and the Tracker are the only ones with the sight and ability to see the doors of light. Therefore, you cannot separate from the group or the Starter and Healer will be lost."

"But David's already gone."

"Then you must find him and tell him what you have learned. There is no other way. He will not survive without this information. The group must stay together."

The light flickered again and then the entire mass of fiery colors vanished into nothingness.

I knew it. The Prism had opened that portal for me.

I vaguely remembered something about it in the vivid dream I'd had a few years back. The dream that had brought the three of us together—the one we experienced simultaneously. In it, we were searching for some way to escape. Some kind of "door."

I scooted back over to my pillow and reached into a pocket in my jeans. I pressed David's coin into my palm and brushed my thumb across the surface, rubbing away a subtle layer of residue.

The dream finally made sense. Pieces were falling into place after almost two years of ignorance. What now? The last thing I remembered happening in my dream was the ceiling crashing down on me. In real life, David had already rescued me from the debris after the earthquake. Now he was gone.

I didn't *miss him*, but I'd be lying if I said I didn't feel safer with him around.

"What now, David?" I whispered to myself, squeezing the Libertad tightly with my fingers. "What now?"

Chapter 19

"What should we do if they take you again?" Brian asked, pouring boiling hot water from a glass carafe into a foam cup with a teabag in it. He dunked the teabag in his cup a few times until the water turned copper brown.

"I don't know," I replied. "The Prism are trying to help us and I think they're getting closer to a long-term solution. Until then, we have to keep our heads down, I guess. I saw some pretty serious shit when I was with Taylor. The Saviors are screwing around with things they shouldn't and... more people are..." I stopped.

"Are what, Kareena?" Brian asked, leaning closer.

"Dying."

Alice gasped.

"What?" I continued. "You didn't really think that guy at the diner was going to be the only one, did you?"

I wrapped my fingers around the cap of my cola bottle and tried to twist it off, but I couldn't grip it right. I tried again, grunting because the stupid thing seemed ridiculously hard to turn.

"Damn it." I sighed. Why was I so weak?

"Here. Let me get that," Brian said, setting down his tea and then offering out a hand to me. I passed him the bottle; he unscrewed the lid and then passed it back to me.

"Thanks."

"You're welcome." He grinned slightly and then his expression became solemn again. "Kareena, I don't want anyone else to suffer or die as a result of their experiments."

"Neither do I." I wedged the soda bottle between my thighs and held it there as I tried to decide what to do with it now that my stomach was suddenly feeling sick.

"Would you like to try some tea, maybe?" Alice asked, offering me her cup, which she hadn't taken a sip from yet. Steam wafted up over the lip as she held it out toward me. I glanced at it for a moment—black tea with cream and a single packet of sugar.

"You can have mine," she added. "It might be better for you than... pop." She motioned toward my bottle "This early in the morning, at least." She shrugged and smiled an honest, caring smile.

My parents drank tea religiously, but I wasn't much of a fan. We brewed homemade chai for holidays and family get-togethers. I used to really love it when I was little. Chai is basically the Indian word for tea, but it's a lot more than that. Chai is rich and creamy. Sweet and spicy. Aromatic and hearty any time of day. Soothing to the stomach... and the mind.

What Alice was offering me was anything but my mother's delicious family chai, but it was something that (sort of, kind of) reminded me of home. I reached out to carefully take it from her. The cup was super hot.

"Thank you," I said quietly, meeting Alice's gaze for only a moment. Her young, innocent blue eyes were starting to show signs of fatigue. It was unflattering, especially on a cute sixteen-year-old girl. Hell, it was unflattering on us all.

·   ·   ·

The Prism had told me it would be about a day before the effects of the door would wear off, so with the evening of my third day back just hours away, I couldn't relax.

I felt like a ticking time bomb waiting to explode and take everyone with me. Waiting for Taylor to suck my seeking ability from me and poison another thousand or more people with this damn curse of ours.

I found a few sleepers at our hotel, too, but kept my mouth shut so Alice wouldn't feel obliged to start them for any reason. We couldn't risk activating any more people.

There was a knock on my hotel door. I got up from the bed, clicked off the television and went to check the peephole. It was exactly who I thought it was, so I opened the door.

"We need to leave," Brian said, slinging his backpack over one shoulder. Alice stood beside him with a smaller pack hanging from her hands. "Are you ready?"

"Yes. I'm ready." I grabbed the small travel bag they'd given me off the floor and closed the hotel door behind me.

It seemed three days was the most we could do without overstaying our welcome at these places. Three days was a safe number, Brian had told me, and fewer days were even better.

We didn't have any idea where our next place would be, but we had to keep moving. Funds were getting low, so we had to budget every dollar we had left. It made me think about the diamond stud still in my nose. I wasn't about to give it up before, but... things were getting tough and we weren't exactly in any city long enough to get part-time jobs.

But... funds were *low*, not gone.

I'd pull my own weight, somehow.

"I got us some bus tickets to the next city," Brian said, holding one out to me. "Grabbed them last night."

"Where are we headed?" I asked, flipping the ticket over to read the destination and answering my own question. "Oh." A city in Minnesota, apparently. It was as good as any other.

We'd arrive in the morning.

.　　.　　.

"Kareena, wake up." Brian nudged me in the arm and I jolted awake, kicking the seat ahead of me accidentally. He stood in the aisle of the bus looking down at me. "We're here. We have to get off."

I groaned beneath my breath and grabbed hold of the headrest in front of me for balance as I lifted my groggy ass up off the chair. Brian handed me my bag and I followed him off the bus.

The motel was only a block from the bus station. Thanks to our remarkably on-schedule bus, we'd arrived just after six in the morning. It was a nice place. Ten floors and very clean from what I could tell. I was going to ask how he'd managed the reservations, but it wasn't my business. If David did it, so could Brian. And so could I, if I needed to.

Alice went ahead and took their things to their room while Brian followed me to mine. It was a few doors down. He slid the keycard through the lock and pushed down the handle.

"Thanks, Brian. I appreciate everything you've done for me," I said as he came in behind me and started looking around the room to make sure everything was in order. For some reason, I thought back at how stupid I must have seemed to him when this had all started. At that first hotel we were in, I was hitting on him so hard, I must have looked really desperate. "I'm sorry," I said just as he headed toward the door.

"What? What for?" He turned back around and took a step closer to me.

"For being a bitch earlier—when all of this started. I shouldn't have tried so hard to get your attention. You're with Alice and... that's your choice. I shouldn't—"

"It's fine," he replied as his hand came up toward my face and then jerked away suddenly.

My brow furrowed. "Brian? Is everything okay?"

"I'm sorry." He shook his head and backed up. "It's...

never mind." He forked a hand through his hair and heaved a sigh. "It's just that... Alice hasn't been herself lately. She's... distant. I don't know what's wrong with her."

"She seems to do that sometimes," I said quietly, reaching for his hand. "It will be okay. You love her, don't you?"

He looked into my eyes and tried to smile. It was so forced, it was unsettling.

"Don't you, Brian?" I repeated.

He looked away. "Yeah."

I squeezed his fingers a little more tightly and cupped my other hand over his.

"Brian?"

He looked back at me.

"It will be okay," I said, trying to console him. I didn't like Alice much, but I didn't want to see him upset, either. "You're strong. Things will be okay. Like I said, stay strong for me. Okay?"

He nodded and a tiny grin curled his lips. "Okay."

"Thank you, Brian," I said and then leaned in to kiss him on the cheek. Before I could withdraw completely, he turned his face and our eyes locked. I tried to pull away, but his hand held tightly to mine.

"Brian?" I whispered, looking him in the eye.

His eyes widened and he immediately released my hand.

Without another word, he left my room.

Chapter 20

After getting settled, the three of us went to breakfast at a café down the street. We should have gotten the food to go to avoid being recognized, but we put our best interests aside in an effort to actually sit down to a decent meal. But after what Brian had done last night, I was apprehensive.

Alice and Brian got water to drink and I ordered a hot tea—for once.

"You guys don't want tea this morning?" I asked, laughing a bit at the irony as I reached across the table for a couple of sugar packets.

"I don't know. Guess I don't have a taste for it this morning," Alice replied, shooting Brian a brief but judgmental look.

Brian's eyes narrowed angrily at her and he mouthed something I couldn't hear.

"Are... you guys okay?" I asked.

"Yes," they both replied, clearly annoyed that I had even asked.

"We're fine," Brian added, putting his menu down so he could fold his arms.

"You don't look fine," I continued, knowing it wasn't my business but still... Weird shit was going on, and if Brian and Alice were breaking up, the world was surely ending or something.

"Stay out of this, Kareena," Alice snapped. "What do you know, anyway? You haven't known Brian for as long as I have."

Actually, I *had* known him for nearly as long. Not... intimately, but as an acquaintance and then a friend.

"Okay. Fine." I rolled my eyes and scoffed. "Chill. Jesus."

"Could you watch your language, young lady?" The patron behind us swerved around and glared at me. Her two toddlers were bobbing around in the bench across from her, dueling each other with drinking straw swords.

"Sorry," I dropped my head down.

The server came back to our table with our food and started sliding the plates across to each of us. I didn't say anything to the others, but our server was infected, too. Not just a sleeper, but one of those with the corrupted darkness inside. I shook it off and returned my attention to my plate. French toast and scrambled eggs with a sprinkle of cheddar cheese on top. Normally I'd hold the cheese. And the eggs. And the French part of the toast, for that matter. But I was freaking hungry and I had a killer craving for fat, sugar, and salt.

"Wow." Alice gawked at me. "Are you eating for two over there?"

I dropped my fork on the table. "Ex-*cuse* me?"

"You're not going to keep your figure if you stuff your face with all of that," she continued.

My jaw had dropped so far open, I probably looked like a gargoyle water spout. "What in the hell are you talking about, Alice? Worry about your damn self, okay?" My stomach was tangling up already. I wanted to eat in peace.

What the hell, Alice!?

"Sorry. Just saying." She shrugged and went back to moving a pile of hash browns around on her plate with a fork.

I looked at Brian and shook my head. He shrugged, too, and then reached for the syrup to pour on his pancakes.

Alice's comments had me ruffled, but I needed to eat so I forced the uncomfortable feelings aside and took a bite of my food. The French toast was amazing. Perfectly cooked with just the right amount of sweetness and the perfect texture. I cut another square off the slice with my knife and fork and shoved it into my mouth. A sip of tea. A bite of the deliciously cheesy scrambled eggs.

Why don't I eat real food more often? Dieting sucks.

"I'm going to take the rest to go," Alice said, standing up and ushering Brian out of his seat so she could scoot past.

I looked at her food, which had been nearly untouched, and tipped my head to the side. "Alice? What's going on?"

"Nothing. I just don't have an appetite right now," she replied, carrying her plate over to the front counter.

"She knows they'll *bring* her the box, right?" I watched her march over to the bakery case and wave down a server.

"Let her go," Brian said. "She's in a bad mood today."

"I can tell."

Alice took the to-go box from the waitress and came back over to us.

"I'm going back to our room to watch something. I'm tired anyway," she said, then turned and left the café.

I could hardly believe Brian didn't bolt out of his seat to go after her. Things between them must have gotten *really* bad while I was away.

"Wow, and I thought I was the hormonal bitch in this party," I said, chuckling, trying to get Brian to perk up. He didn't, and I quickly cleared my throat and straightened my smile. "Sorry."

"It's okay. She's just... I don't even know anymore." He sighed and then picked up his fork and knife and went back to eating his pancakes.

"Brian?"

"Yeah?" He looked up from his food. "What is it?"

"There's something I need to tell you."

He set his fork down beside his plate and I leaned over mine.

"Our server," I whispered, "is infected with the same stuff

as that guy we saw at the other diner. The stuff that's," I lowered my voice so it was hardly audible, "killing them," I finished.

"Really?"

"Yes." I ate another fork-full of scrambled eggs. "There are a lot more of them now than there were before. It's ridiculous."

"Hmm." He looked for our waitress and flagged her down as she came out of the kitchen. She walked over to us with a friendly smile on her face and asked if we needed anything.

"We don't need anything," Brian said with a slightly exaggerated smile. "I just wanted to say that we're new here in town and we really appreciate your hospitality. People like you make this kind of town a great place to visit." He reached a hand out to her.

"Oh, you're welcome, dear," she said, just about blushing, offering her hand to him.

He took it and cupped it between his hands. "Thank you." He glanced quickly at her nametag. "Rachel."

I gasped, just about choking on my scrambled eggs.

"Brian!" I stood up from my seat and pointed. The corrupted ball of fading white light inside her had cleared and brightened.

"Yes, Kareena?" He turned his head toward me while simultaneously releasing Rachel's hand. She walked off without saying a word.

"What the hell is going on here!? Does Alice know about this?"

"We don't need Alice, do we?" he said with a smirk. "You and I make a much better team."

He stretched out his arm toward me, blue light sparking from his fingertips as if it were leaking out of him like liquid electricity. I'd never seen it do that before. *Ever.* Not even David could manifest external bolts of fluorescence.

"Brian? What's happening to you?" I tried to back away

but felt my body grow heavier, causing me to thump right back down into my seat.

"Don't worry about it, Kareena," he replied. "Just rest. You'll feel better in the morning." Tiny crackling lines of fluorescence skittered across the table toward me, and a pulse of hot energy blasted into my chest, knocking me back.

The room blurred and my head hit the table.

.   .   .

I awoke in a musty room. The blinds had been drawn.

I glanced at the clock. Noon.

No. Not again.

"Nice to have you back," a voice said from the hall near the bathroom. I turned my head and huffed with disgust.

"Taylor! How did you find me!?"

"I didn't find you just now," he replied, grinning from ear to ear. "I've been with you for a while; manipulating your thoughts so you'd believe you were still with the others."

"What? How? How long have I been here? Where are the others?"

"Does it matter? They can't get to you now. Not while I'm with you. Why are you so worried about them?" He sat on the edge of my bed and inched closer to me. I squirmed to get away, but he reached out and grabbed my arm. "You have me now. Aren't I enough?"

"No, Taylor! You have to stop this sick game of yours. I'm not yours to do whatever you want with!" I fought to get my hand free of his, but his grip tightened and his fluorescence started to burn my wrist.

"That's not what the Saviors told me," he said, almost breathing on me now.

"You're full of crap and delusional."

"No. I clearly recall them telling me I could do whatever I wanted with the Seeker as long as I did what they asked of me."

"And you think you can use me because of that?"

"At first, I thought that was pretty messed up, but then I met you and I saw how important you were to your friends, not to mention how incredibly powerful your fluorescence is." He sucked his lip. "It's already been too long. I need you." Violet light started glowing and flickering through his skin, creeping its way across mine. A hundred tiny shocks of electricity stung my body and I winced.

"Taylor, please. No." I pushed away from him but trapped myself against the headboard of the bed.

His eyes glinted with pink light and I clenched my teeth as he siphoned more and more fluorescence from me.

"No!" I pushed him with my aching arms, but he didn't budge. Then the air suddenly became thin and even he flinched as we both realized what was about to happen.

A blast of white light filled the room, the floor disappeared, and we fell into nothingness.

I looked up and met the translator's stern gaze. There was a small number of other Saviors behind him. Five. No. Seven. The number was much smaller than it had been in the past. We usually had quite an audience. I struggled to come to my feet, but the feeling of being sedated stopped me.

The translator turned to address Taylor. "What are you doing with her?" he asked him.

"What do you mean?" Taylor replied, cocking an eyebrow as if he were so innocent and he couldn't understand the translator's intention. "Nothing. I'm not doing anything with her. I'm doing what you asked me to."

"We never instructed you to deliberately exploit the Seeker."

"No." He scoffed. "But you said I could use her power if I needed to. That's what I'm doing."

"She has offered to comply, has she not?" He looked at me and I nodded in confirmation. Then he focused on Taylor again. "Why do you continue to take unnecessary action?"

Taylor lifted his chin and narrowed his eyes at the translator. "It makes me stronger, okay? And that makes it easier for me to take care of everything you asked me to. I don't need her help to do this."

"But you *do* need her abilities. Yet you choose to take them from her forcefully?"

"Yes," he replied nonchalantly.

My jaw tightened. I couldn't just stand there and let him talk shit.

"I don't want him to," I interjected, taking a step closer to the Savior. "I'll help you if you make him stop draining me. Please."

The translator tilted his head to the side. "We will consider it; however, there is another concern we must discuss with you, Seeker."

I swallowed hard, already knowing what he was about to ask.

"Who is responsible for the portal that sent you back to the others?"

Wait. They didn't know?

"I-I don't know," I lied. "It just appeared and I thought I heard the others calling for me, so I went through it. I don't know who created it. I thought it was you."

"We had nothing to do with it. If you should see one again, you must choose to ignore it. It is dangerous."

"Dangerous? How?" I was finally able to come to my feet. "It took me back to Brian and Alice. Ever since I left them, Taylor's been doing nothing but hurting me. I'm not strong enough to deal with this every day. If you want my help, you need to protect me. You need to help me!"

"What is it you want us to do?" the translator asked.

"I want to be safe." I shot a quick glance at Taylor, who was fuming. "From *him*. I don't want him taking my powers anymore. I don't want to black out. I'm sick of waking up places and not remembering what the hell happened before I fell asleep. Help me, please!"

The Savior considered my words momentarily before speaking again. "Will you continue to resist our instruction? Because of the disobedience of you and the other three Fluorescent Ones, we were forced to resort to another option— a Variant." He gestured toward Taylor. "The fluorescence inside him differs greatly from your own. It was of our own creation. Without viable offspring from the Healer and Starter, we had to find another way."

I curled a hand into a fist and my nails pricked my skin. "Can't you see this isn't working!?"

"To judge what is or is not working is not your job," the translator snidely replied.

"People are dying! You're going to kill us if you keep doing this. Is that what you want?"

"We *will* find a cure," he answered sternly, "at any cost." The tone of his voice was more unaffected than ever.

My jaw dropped and then I closed my mouth and swallowed hard. They didn't give a damn. They didn't care if they took the whole damn world down with them.

The Prism were right.

We were screwed.

Chapter 21

"How dare you lie to the Saviors about me," Taylor hissed, the bitterness on his face sending my heart into panic mode. "Why did you do that?"

"You're being an ass. And I didn't lie, either! They said it themselves; you don't have to keep hurting me if I'm willing to help you!"

"But you're not!" he snarled through bared teeth, his sloping eyebrows accentuating his vile expression. "You say you are, but you're not."

"Taylor, why are you so obsessed with starting people? Why can't you admit that what you're doing is wrong? That—"

"You don't get it, do you, Kareena?" he continued in a raspier voice. "This is about more than what the Saviors want. When they first put fluorescence inside me, I thought I was in trouble. I thought what they did to me was outrageous and it made me furious. But as time went on, I started to realize that my ability to start people was a gift. When I absorb someone's energy, it does something to me. It makes me feel alive. Then I learned that there's energy in everything. Whether I take it from you or not, I'll thrive. It's around us constantly. In the air. In the ground. We breathe it in. We consume it. We are made of it." Subtle bursts of neon purple light emanated from his fingertips. Witnessing the external manifestation of his power sent chills up my spine. I took a step back.

"If you can feel all of that energy," I started, "then why do you keep wanting to take mine, too?"

"That pretty pink light flowing through your veins is

more potent than any of the rest," he said, making a fist. The light danced across his knuckles, encircling his hand. "Starting people is a quick fix, but pure fluorescence is the real deal."

"What!?" I scowled in disgust. "So you're getting high on fluorescence? Is that it? You're using me like a drug to foster this sick craving of yours?"

He put his open hands out to the sides and a ripple of purple light bubbled up through the floorboards, arcing and darting toward his palms as if he were channeling it like a receptor.

The lights in the room shuttered on and off until Taylor made closed fists again and the bolts of light faded into his skin.

"The Saviors gave me a gift they don't have," he said, raising his hands toward his chest. "One you don't have, either. I can move energy—bend it to my will." Purple sparks crackled between his hands and flickering color coursed through his entire body, no longer isolated to his right arm. "The Saviors can't do that, but I can because I'm... different. And you, Kareena, you're filled with the very basic form of this energy."

"It's toxic, Taylor," I huffed. "This shit is going to kill us all if we don't do something about it."

"How do you know?" he asked, showing his teeth in a wicked grin. "How do you know it's going to kill *us*... and not just, say, *you*?"

The way the words rolled off his tongue made me cringe. A death threat? *What the hell?*

He came closer and I staggered back, trying to keep my distance even though the room was quite small.

"Do you know why we're all different colors?"

"No."

"Because they want diversity. They tried to match their genetic code to ours and it bonded with each of us differently. But they called me the Variant—the one they created by mixing different strains and colors."

"You're a DNA cesspool!" I snapped. "That's all you are!"

"Maybe so, but what would happen if I were able to drain abilities from the others and not just you? How much fluorescence could I absorb if I chose not to stop even after you went unconscious?"

My eyes widened at the thought. "You're sick. They created you because they couldn't control us. We were strong enough to fight back and you're too weak!"

"No!" He bolted toward me and caught me by the throat with both hands. I strained to breathe as he squeezed my airway.

"Tay—lor." I fought to pry his hands from my neck, but he squeezed harder. Fluorescence seeped out of him, threatening to poison me into submission.

"I own you," he sneered, bringing his face close to mine. "I don't care what the Saviors say. As long as you're with me, I own you." His grasp tightened and I wriggled in resistance. Tiny flashes of light distorted my vision and I reached both hands up to grab his face.

Immediately, he let up.

I didn't.

I sucked a labored breath into my recovering windpipe. "Don't you touch me, Taylor," I wheezed through gritted teeth, my throat still tight. "Don't you ever touch me like that again!" Hot pink light streamed down my arms and into my fingertips, pulsing into his head and invading his bloodstream, illuminating the outline of his skull from the inside out. His eye sockets blazed with colored light as he grimaced and gasped in agony. "How do you like it?" I bent down to stay locked onto him as he slipped onto his knees. "It doesn't feel so good, does it?"

Oh, but it felt good to me. Revenge for all the things I knew he'd done—and the things he may have done while I was unconscious.

He clawed feebly at my hands and I tolerated the discomfort to watch him squirm. I wanted to break him. I wanted him to know just what it felt like to be helpless.

"Kareena!" he howled in a wavering voice.

I kept my fingers firmly planted around his head.

What if I didn't stop? What then?

Vigorous heat radiated from my body. I'd never taken it so far before. So far that a line of sweat beaded up on my forehead and my skin tingled.

Brilliant white light flashed beside me and a humming noise caught my attention. Another portal appeared, shards of white sparkles spinning around in a circle.

"Kareena," a soft, transcendent voice echoed through my head.

Taylor was on all fours now, grunting while the pink light infiltrated the rest of his body, veins of color seeping down his shoulders and spine.

"Kareena, you must not kill him," the voice requested. It was the Prism.

Jesus, I wanted to kill him! I really did. I didn't even know if I could or not, but it might have been worth a shot to get him out of my life. He'd been nothing but hell since the Saviors forced me to stay with him. Then he grabbed me and...

No one puts their hands on me like that.

No one.

The sparkling portal flashed brighter and the swirling rings spun faster.

"Kareena, go! Leave him!" The Prism's voice grew more thunderous in my head.

Taylor was hunched over on the ground near my feet. I released his head and he fell forward onto my ankles. I shoved him away, turned, and dashed toward the portal. A rush of cold air hit me as I passed through.

Weightlessness engulfed me and I screamed. There was

no ground beneath my feet, and my first reaction was to kick my legs and flail my arms in a poor attempt to keep myself from falling.

But as I levitated in the darkness, my body unmoving, I quickly realized the resistance did me no good. I hadn't moved an inch—that I could tell—through the inky blue-blackness.

Like the night sky long after dusk, tiny flecks of glittering dust came to life around me, fading in and out—glowing like pure white candlelight. The stars cast a dim ambience on my skin and reiterated the fact that I was still hanging in midair, my body suspended by an unseen force.

I let my arms sink down to my sides. My hair drifted in a ghostly manner near my face as if moved by a gentle current. I took a deep breath and exhaled comfortably. The air was natural. Easy on my lungs. The temperature around me was tepid and mild. Surreal. I felt like a constellation suspended in the night sky—otherworldly.

I lifted my hand and reached toward one of the sparkling lights, but my fingers passed straight through it. It was fixated and unmoving in its place as if hanging from invisible wire. The glow warmed and illuminated my skin.

"Kareena," a voice sounded from everywhere. I turned my head and saw nothing but more tiny stars glimmering for as far as I could see. Hundreds of sparkles began moving toward each other until they came together to form a single massive light. Branches of color bolted through the shape and I instantly recognized it.

"Where am I?" I asked the Prism, resisting the innate urge to wriggle my dangling feet. I tried not to move my arms so much, but it felt necessary—as if "swimming" in the ethereal atmosphere was the only way to stay afloat within it.

"We have brought you to our world in an effort to speak to you at greater length about your fight with the Saviors. Our atmosphere is better suited for this than your own."

"But I thought your kind didn't want to get involved with

us? I thought only a few of you—"

"You are correct, Kareena," the voice echoed, interrupting me. "It has, however, taken on much greater significance than we had originally believed and we had no choice but to inform the rest of our kind about your struggle. What the Saviors have done to the Variant is an unthinkable horror, which has endangered us all."

"I almost killed him," I whispered, dropping my head. "Didn't I?"

"As a Seeker, you are capable of many things," it replied, not fully answering my question. "We will attempt to find another way to solve the issue with the Variant. One that will allow him to live on without the infection corrupting his judgment."

"What if the Saviors start abducting us all again?" I asked. "Can you help the others, too, please?"

"That is why we have brought you here," it continued. "We have been able to create a token which can protect each of you from being taken again. You must distribute them to the others, however."

"Can't you give them to them yourself? What if I touched them all and let them actually see you? They already think I'm crazy and—"

"They cannot see us," it said, glowing slightly brighter and then softening again as if emphasizing the words. "Even if you were to give them your sight temporarily, they are not bonded to the genetic code. Their eyes are incapable of viewing Prism essence. The consequences would be dire and irreversible. Blindness or worse. Do not ever subject the others to your touch while we are present."

Blindness? Worse?

"Lift your hand," it requested.

I stretched my arm out in front of me, palm up.

A flow of white trickled out of the Prism and a stream of twinkling smoke wandered through the air, curling toward me. I flinched as the icy aura touched my skin and coiled around my wrist. It solidified and came together in the shape of a thick bangle, which I instinctively brought my other hand across to touch. Smooth, supple snakeskin beneath my fingertips. Cool to touch, but soft and weightless against my skin.

Inside the clear resin-like casing was a spiral of prismatic energy. I rotated my wrist and watched rainbow sparkles arc and ripple through the bracelet, bending and darting off the edges like wild, multi-colored fire.

"The portals protect you for a day," the Prism said. "But these will protect you indefinitely."

As if moved by invisible touch, my hand turned back over. Three small pearl-sized orbs appeared within my palm.

"You must give them to the others so that they will be safe, as well."

"How do they use them?" I asked, closing my fingers around what felt like feathers in my palm.

"Distribute them between the other Fluorescent Ones and the orbs will take liberty with the rest," it replied. "We will send you back to the others now."

"Wait!" I kicked my feet but didn't move at all in the air. "What are you going to do about Taylor? How are we going to stop him from starting more people?"

"He is much too volatile at this time to confront. We will search for a way to contain his powers. Please do what you can to avoid him. In the meanwhile, you should attempt to relocate the Tracker. He may be in danger if the Saviors decide to search for him once they lose sight of you."

David? I felt a tinge of guilt for leaving him at the hotel, but how was I supposed to know everything would go south so quickly?

"I'll try. We don't know anything about where he went, though."

"We will speak again soon." The large mass of light burst

into pieces, breaking off into hundreds of tiny stars that redistributed themselves all around. Then a line of white cracked in the air before me, and a shining portal split open. I was pulled through and a gush of cool air swept over me.

Chapter 22

I landed on concrete—more gently than I thought possible—and the portal sucked itself closed behind me. A cold breeze licked at my skin and I shivered, rubbing my bare arms briskly as I glanced around. The huge empty place appeared to be a parking garage aglow with sputtering fluorescent lights.

"Hello?" I said in a barely audible tone. Thick columns of concrete held up the floor overhead. I staggered toward the edge of the lot where the floors separated and poked my head out over the side of the overhang to look down. The garage towered several stories over the empty darkened streets below.

I turned around and stared at the hundreds of vacant parking spots marked with white lines. Graffiti paintings decorated the walls in loud colors that the flickering lamps brought to life in flashes of dying light. Some of them art, others slurs of hate and anger. All of them making me feel out of place—frightened.

I heard a door hinge squealing and veered my head toward the sound. There was a small concrete room in the distance with lights on inside. An electrical room, or something like it. I could just see a cutout of a window and a door from where I was. I wanted to call out to whoever it was, but I couldn't. My lips parted and nothing came out. Fear paralyzed me.

I swallowed hard and made my way toward the room. A lamp crackled above me and I gasped, ducking. Then I heard the door again. This time, I was close enough to see it crack open. Soft blue light radiated from inside and my heart began to race.

"Brian!" I called out to him. A silhouette came out of the room and the blue light got brighter, followed by a green aura behind it. "Alice!"

I picked up speed and jogged over to meet them. Brian raised a flashlight toward me and I saw his eyes widen with surprise.

"Kareena? You're back!" He lowered the flashlight down to his side and clicked it off. "We were worried. Where did you go? What happened to you?"

Alice poked her head out from behind him. "Are you okay?" she asked.

"I'm fine. Your freak-of-a-brother, Taylor, tried to choke me." I clenched my fists at the violent memory and felt the cool marble-like Prism orbs press into my palm. "Oh, but the Prism saved me and gave me these." I put out my hand and unfolded my fingers.

Brian's and Alice's eyes lit up with curiosity as they leaned in closer to watch the mesmerizing glow of the sparkling balls.

"Oh, thank God you can see them," I said, heaving a sigh of relief.

"What the hell are those?" Brian asked, his eyebrows wrinkling together.

"I don't know, really, but they wanted me to give them to you." I glanced at the iridescent band of light twirling around my own wrist. "They're bracelets. I have one, too. Can you see it?"

They both shook their heads.

"The Prism told me they will keep the Saviors from abducting us. Just like the portal helped cloak me for a day when I first went through it. These are made of the same stuff, I guess."

"So, we free ourselves from the Saviors," Brian started, cocking an eyebrow, "only to become prisoners of the Prism instead?"

"No." I scoffed. "We protect our asses from the Saviors

now before they kill us all, and then we worry about the Prism."

"Good point." He took a deep breath and nodded. "Alright. I get it."

"Here." I plucked one of the balls up between my thumb and index finger and handed it to Brian. "Take it."

He was hesitant to put out his hand but finally did.

I dropped the ball into his open fingers and it combusted upon impact into a plume of metallic dust. Brian's jaw dropped as he lost sight of the thing.

"Where did it go!?" he asked, turning his hand over frantically.

"It's fine. It's fine," I assured him, taking hold of his hand while I watched the mist of light swirl around his wrist and solidify into the same kind of colorful bangle I, too, had. "It's there. It's on you, now."

"It... is?" He turned his hand over again and squinted. Then he reached his other hand across to touch his wrist. "I don't... feel anything."

"I can see it on you. You can hardly feel them. Trust me, it's there."

"If you say so." He shrugged and continued to stare at his hand.

"Here, Alice," I said, turning toward her and holding out one of the orbs. She lifted her cupped hands up to meet mine and I released it into them. Like the first, this one also erupted into a cloud of colorful, metallic dust. It coiled around and took its shape on her petite wrist.

"Is it... on me?" Alice asked, lifting her hand to eye level.

"Yes. Do you want to see it?" I replied. Alice was the only person I hadn't shared my vision with yet, and considering how mildly Taylor reacted to the brief spell of it I had first given him, I was convinced I could lend it gently to Alice, as well.

"No, Alice," Brian advised, raising his voice a little. "It...

hurts."

"She'll be fine," I said reassuringly. "I'll be gentle, I swear."

Brian looked uneasy even as Alice seemed to perk up.

"Can you show me?" she asked in an awed, child-like voice.

"Yes." I tucked the last orb away into a pocket in my jeans and then lifted both of my open hands out toward the sides of Alice's head. I noticed Brian tense up as I briefly pressed my fingertips against Alice's temples. She closed her eyes and sucked in a breath as light penetrated her skin, making her hairline glow momentarily with a subtle pink hue.

"Look." I took my hands away from her head.

"Oh my God!" Her eyes grew wide. "Oh my God!" She lifted her wrist up and turned it over, staring wide-eyed at the colorful light dancing around her skin. "It's... it's beautiful!" She swerved around. "Brian, you have to see this! It's so beautiful. It's like... fairy dust or... magic or... Oh. Ow." She cringed and cupped her hand against her forehead. "Ugh."

The headache had started already.

"Yeah," Brian interrupted, putting his hand on Alice's shoulder. "That's the not so beautiful part." Then he lifted his glowing blue hand toward her face and brushed his fingertips across her forehead.

"Oh my God, wow, though!" Alice continued, grinning from ear to ear now as she looked up into Brian's eyes and then mine. "Is that what you see all the time?"

"Kind of. I mean, the stuff in you guys isn't the same, but that's sort of what the Prism look like to me."

"I'd love to see them, too, someday," she added, sighing. "They must be so... breathtaking."

"Yeah. You can't, though." I shrugged. "They told me it would cause irreversible damage of some kind if one of you guys tried to look at them."

"Oh..."

"Let's scratch charades with the Prism off our to-do list

then, shall we?" Brian said with a smirk.

His upbeat, slightly sarcastic tone made me smile.

Chapter 23

I propped my back up against the frigid concrete wall and pulled Brian's jacket over my knees. He'd lent it to me to help stave off the cold that kept creeping up through the floors of the garage. It was nastier outside in the open though, and the bitterly cold wind gust whistled through the floors, taunting us even while we stayed huddled up in the safety of an enclosed maintenance room.

"I... wonder if my mom's okay," Alice murmured, leaning her head on Brian's shoulder. The two of them sat with their backs pressed to the wall across from me. He reached for one of her hands and pulled it into his lap.

"I don't know," he replied. "I've been thinking about Peter and everyone else who may be in danger."

"And my parents, too," I added, almost whispering.

We all sat there with our heads hung low, like little lost animals, forced to stay wherever we could find shelter. Brian had told me money was getting tight, and that they were trying to stretch it as far as they could, even if that meant staying in less conventional places for a night or two.

"I miss Sam," Alice uttered in a mousey voice. Brian wrapped his arm around her and pulled her in close. I watched them cuddle and felt my heart sink.

I didn't know Sam very well. She was Alice's best friend and the first person to know about her fluorescence.

"We all miss someone," I said, folding my hands together under Brian's jacket to keep warm and looking away from them.

"What about David?" Alice asked.

"What?" I looked up. "What do you mean?"

"Do you... miss him?"

I twiddled my fingers. "Why would I miss him?" The question made me uncomfortable.

"I dunno," she said, shrugging and looking off to the side. "He seemed really worried about you when you got hurt in that building. I thought maybe you liked him."

"No." I shook my head. "Just because we stayed in the same room for a couple of days doesn't mean we hooked up." I narrowed my eyes at her to make the lie seem more legit. The truth was none of her business.

"I didn't mean that." She grumbled. "I just thought maybe you two might have gotten along. Sorry. Forget I said anything. Geeze."

Brian glared at me judgmentally and I rolled my eyes.

"We have more important things to worry about right now," I said. "Like all of the damn people the Saviors are trying to infect. It started off as a few every dozen, but now it's like fifty percent or something crazy. Everywhere I turn, there's a sleeper. It's... insane. And Taylor, well, he's totally lost his mind. At first, he was like you, Alice, and he could start people. He sucked diseased fluorescence right out of people like some kind of anti-venom magnet, but then he started getting high on it or something. I don't even know how to describe it. First, it was a quick fix, but now, he wants to come after both of you."

"What?" Brian straightened up. "What do you mean, come after us? Like, kill us?"

"I don't know." I shook my head. "I don't know what he's capable of. He just said he wanted to see what would happen if he could drain fluorescence from you... without stopping."

Brian forked a hand through his hair and sighed in disbelief. "You said you blacked out after he drained you, right?"

"Yes."

"What the hell would happen if he didn't let up after that?" he asked.

"I don't want to know, Brian." I hugged myself and shivered.

"Me neither," Alice said with a faint whimper, nuzzling against him.

We didn't have a lot of options, but we had to think of something.

"I know this isn't what you want to hear, Brian," I began, "but maybe if we could find David, we could use him to negotiate with Taylor. He's powerful and maybe he can—"

"David's unpredictable," Brian snapped. "We don't need him to survive."

"I-I didn't mean that," I stuttered. "I just—"

"If you want him back so badly, *you* go look for him. I'm not going to risk getting one of us hurt or exposed going on some wild hunt for a guy who obviously doesn't want shit to do with us."

"He helped us a lot," I added with a huff.

"Yeah, before you ditched us and took off with Taylor," Brian growled beneath his breath.

"You're just pissed you didn't think of everything he did," I added, raising my voice. "Stop being such a stubborn ass."

"I thought you didn't like him," he sneered.

"Shut the hell up, Brian!" Under the cloak of his jacket on my lap, I made fists he couldn't see. "Shut up." His eyes widened and Alice cowered slightly. "In the last week, I have been through more shit than you can imagine. I don't care how rough you and Alice think you have it, you have no idea what the hell I've been through or what your damn brother did to me. What if it was *her*, instead?" I took my hand out from under the warm jacket just long enough to point at Alice. "What if your precious little Alice was the one being tormented by him? What then?"

Brian snapped his mouth shut and kept it that way for the next several moments. Then Alice tipped her face up toward his ear and whispered something.

His eyes met mine briefly. He nodded and muttered something quietly back to her.

"I'm sorry," he said, looking me in the eye again. "I've been acting like a jerk this whole time because I'm angry, stressed out, and... scared. I didn't ask for any of this... but neither did you." He bit his lip and dropped his head back against the wall, exhaling loudly. "Sorry," he mumbled, again.

·　·　·

I lay there on the floor staring up at the ceiling, my head nestled into Brian's crumpled-up leather coat. The subtle scent of him lingered on it, taunting me and comforting me at the same time. I watched him and Alice sleeping together on the floor a few feet away. She laid her head on his backpack and he lay behind her, his arm draped over her waist and his head sharing a small portion of the pack as if it were a pillow.

Even after dealing with all of this hell—sleeping on the floor of some parking garage in the ghetto—Alice's expression was a peaceful one.

Maybe it was because she felt safe with Brian. The same way I did.

Damn it. I don't know why I couldn't get over him. I just... couldn't.

And when Taylor appeared, I thought maybe I had a chance—that my instincts to pursue Brian weren't in fact mistaken, they were simply misplaced. But Taylor had nothing in common with Brian. Other than the fact that they looked a lot alike, I wasn't attracted to anything else about him.

I closed my eyes and tried to sleep, squeezing my eyelids shut while they twitched anxiously. A train passed by outside, making the ground rumble beneath us. It reminded me of the tremor just before the earthquake that nearly took my life. I rolled over, readjusted the balled-up coat, and laid my head back down on it. My eyes shut and I tried to let my mind drift off.

Bright light hit my face and I lifted a hand to shield myself from the glare. I squinted and peeked through my separated fingers at the swirling light. A quick glance at Brian and Alice confirmed they were still asleep—unaware of the portal—so I pushed myself up off the floor and stood.

A queasy feeling roiled in my gut, but before I could step away, a hand reached out from the spinning light and grabbed me by the arm. I called out for help just as I was jerked through the portal.

The ground came at me fast and I scuffed my elbow against the gravel floor. I groaned in pain and pulled back against the hand that held me tightly.

"Where did you think you were going?" Taylor said, squeezing my arm so hard it was unbearable.

"You son-of-a—"

"Hey! You abandoned me. Your friends—the ones who made that portal for you—came and got you and you didn't even say goodbye. But you know what? When you tried to fry my brain earlier, you gave me your sight for a few minutes. With it, I saw that portal spinning in the air just seconds after you went through it." He smirked wickedly. "There was incredible energy radiating from it—calling for me. So I put out my hand, touched it, and... absorbed it."

"How did you find me!?" I resisted again, but he dug his fingers into my wrist and I grimaced.

The swirling white door disappeared behind me.

"Funny you should ask. All I had to do was think about it—the portal—and the energy dripped right back out of my hands. I could barely see it without your sight, but I saw the other side just well enough to reach through... and take you back."

A jolt of purple sparks shot into my body and I clenched my teeth.

"Wh-what do you want from me?" I stumbled onto all fours and coughed hard, my lungs straining to bring in air.

"I wanted you to help me find the others," he said. "That's all I wanted originally. Now it seems like I'm going to have to do that alone. And for that, I'll need the rest of your power."

Branches of vibrant violet light sprouted and rose up from the ground, surrounding me like broken pieces of a chain-link fence. I tried to move forward, but a spark bit me and I withdrew, yelping in pain.

"Let me go, Taylor! You've completely lost your mind."

"Maybe." He shrugged and lifted his hands up over my head, closing the coils of electricity over me—caging me like an animal.

"What the hell are you!?" I shifted and bumped an arm against the sparking wall. Current ripped through, leaving a black, cauterized scar across my bicep.

"I really don't know, Kareena," he replied, leaning down toward me. "But I'm more powerful than you are. That's a fact. One you made the mistake of ignoring."

A purple bolt licked at my face, stinging my cheek. I veered away and flinched. A whirring sound buzzed in my ears. Then out of the corner of my eye, I saw another portal rip open in the air. I turned my head carefully inside the flickering cage to try to watch.

A yellow light appeared inside it and then David suddenly came bursting through.

"David!" I called out to him, bumping my shoulder on another line of purple fire and burning a hole in the cap of my sleeve. The pain made me wince.

"What's happening? Where are we?" David asked, looking

around.

"Nice," Taylor said with a scoff, watching David approach. "If it isn't your Mexican boyfriend coming to join the fiesta."

"Shut up, Taylor," David sneered, taking an offensive stance. "You don't know shit about me!" He glanced at me and his brow wrinkled. "Kareena!" He took a step closer.

"Hey! She's mine now," Taylor shouted, coming between us. "You'll be next if you don't back off."

"I don't know what you think you're doing," David said, "but it's wrong." The amber glow sparked to life in his chest and I couldn't stop my breaths from shuddering. I knew what Taylor could do, but David didn't.

The electric wires surrounding me sputtered and popped and I hunched down lower to the ground to avoid the loose particles that flitted dangerously close to me.

David coiled his hands into fists and sneered. "Let her go," he said, the fiery yellow fluorescence growing brighter. "Let her go, Taylor."

"I don't think so," Taylor hissed. Then he stretched out his hands and a flash of purple burst from them, hitting David in the chest and sending him staggering back.

He'd caught him off guard.

David shot a confused glance at me and I shook my head.

"Be careful," I mouthed through the bars of arcing fluorescence.

"Being one of us is one thing," David said, "but using your powers against us, makes you one of them. Leave her alone. Let her go and we'll forget any of this ever happened. We can just go our own separate ways."

Taylor laughed callously. "Is he for real?" he asked, glancing at me. "What do you think you are? A hero? You're just like the rest of them. You're weak. They made *me* powerful for a reason."

"I knew there was something wrong with you when I met you at the hotel," David continued. "Your fluorescent aura is corrupted. It's purple and then it's black and grey and purple again. It's out of control. I could hardly track you at all even when you were right there in front of me. Now I know it's clearly done something to your head. The Saviors screwed all of our lives up. You don't have to do this. You can just stop following them. It's what I did."

"This doesn't have shit to do with the Saviors anymore!" Taylor yelled. "Not a single damn thing. This is about *me* now."

David tipped his face down, narrowing his eyes. He pushed a hand out and yellow color skittered down toward his wrists. Taylor doubled over as David's invisible pulse of energy choked the breath out of him.

"They sent me to control the others, you know," David added, forcing more color through his body, which sent Taylor crumbling to his knees in pain. "They made me powerful, too."

Taylor groaned and gasped for breath, pawing at the dirt and gravel beneath him and then cupping his head in his hands.

The cage holding me split open and disintegrated. I shot up and ran to David's side.

"Are you okay?" he asked, looking me over swiftly.

"Yes." I swallowed hard. "Be careful, please. Taylor's really—"

"Resilient?" Taylor said beneath his breath, panting. His face came back up and a streak of crimson shimmered on his lips. He swiped it from his face with the back of his hand and came to his knees.

"David? What's going on?" I asked, panicking. David's fluorescence was still aglow in his chest, but Taylor was able to stand.

"I don't know!" He held out both hands and amber fire lit up his veins again.

Taylor straightened up and brushed the dirt from his

pants. "You can't stop me," he slurred, taking a wobbly step closer toward us. "You can't. I'll take out every one of you if I have to. Starting with you." He gave me a nasty stare. "And then I'll drain you, too." He looked at David. "And when I'm done..." He lumbered closer, spat blood on the ground, and wiped his mouth again. "I'll come for Brian and his little girlfriend."

David reached an arm out and gestured for me to get behind him.

"David, do something, please!" I said as I moved back. He flexed his hands and tried again. Bolts of yellow crackled beneath his skin toward his fingertips.

Taylor didn't flinch.

A wave of searing violet lighting burst up from the ground and latched on to David's body, tangling around his arms and legs and bringing him down to the ground. He grunted and squirmed as purple sparks nipped at his face and hands, leaving charred black dashes on his flesh.

"David!" I moved closer. A fleck of color ricocheted off him and hit my arm. I snapped back as it burned me like hot oil.

Taylor held out his hands and the cage started shrinking around David, burning him more and more until he finally cried out from the pain.

"Stop it!" I sucked up my courage and took a step closer. "Leave him alone, Taylor!"

"What are you going to do?" Taylor smirked and then closed a glowing fist, causing David to let out another stifled moan. The burning fluorescent cage had gaps in it in various places around David's body. I hunched down behind him, held my breath, and reached through one, biting down to resist the urge to cry out as flickering sparks sizzled a band around the circumference of my wrist.

I jerked my hand back from his belt and out of the cage. Then I straightened my arm out toward Taylor, braced myself, and squeezed the trigger as hard as I could.

A piercing bang rang out and a loud buzzing sound made my head twinge.

The electric cage holding David collapsed and... so did its maker.

Chapter 24

I dropped the gun.

David coughed violently and struggled to sit up, slipping once until I reached over to help him up to his knees. His clothes were shredded and burned—his jeans covered in holes with singed edges still smoldering. He brought his face up. A dark brown line of burnt skin marred his left cheek.

I looked across from us at the body lying stretched out on the ground in a puddle of blood and my stomach turned. The fluorescent light inside him had gone completely dark and I knew in my gut what that meant.

"Holy shit!" I slipped down to my knees and covered my face with both hands. The adrenaline screeching through my body wasn't enough to stop my eyes from welling with tears. I gasped for breath as my heart pounded against my ribcage. "Oh my God." I wheezed, tears rolling down my face. "Oh my God. I fucking killed someone!" I pulled my arms in close to my chest and took short, whooping breaths through my mouth while rocking back and forth. My wrist ached from the fresh burn.

"Kareena?" David shuffled closer, cupped my face, and forced me to face him. I halfheartedly tried to push him away. "Kareena! Look at me."

I did, and my heart skipped a beat.

His endless brown eyes begged me to listen.

"Do you want to live!?" he asked, his breaths still labored.

"Yes! Yes, I do!" Salty tears kept drizzling onto my lips. I coughed again.

His fingers spread out and he caressed them toward my hairline. "Then you did the right thing, Kareena," he said softly.

"But..." I wheezed again, fighting weakly to get out of his grasp. "I-I killed him!"

"You're not a killer" He slid his hands down to my shoulders and grasped me tighter. "I am."

"What?" I stopped squirming. "What do you mean, David?"

He looked down and closed his eyes. "I've had blood on my hands since I was seventeen." He opened them and continued, speaking slowly. "It was *my* gun you used. Those were *my* bullets and that makes it *my* responsibility. You're not a killer, Kareena. You were fighting for your life and it was going to be either you or him. You did the right thing."

"Then why do I feel like shit?" I whimpered, my chin dripping with tears. "Why do I feel like I'm the most horrible, disgusting thing alive?"

"Because you're human. Because you *are* alive. You care about things. You value life." He glanced quickly back at Taylor's body and then at me. "Him. That *thing* he became... it wasn't human. All he lived for was himself and that's not living. I know this, Kareena, because I used to be like that, too. I never gave a shit about anyone or anything. Then things changed and I started to realize the world didn't revolve around me."

He was probably talking about his sister, but his words still made me feel better.

"What do I have to live for?" I replied. "I have nothing. Brian has Alice and you... you don't seem to need or want anyone. What am I supposed to do if I can't find purpose? I can't go back to school. I can't have a real job or even a damn boyfriend. I'm just trapped in this hell with this stuff inside my body that makes me see terrible things inside others. Disease. Death."

He reached down, picked up his gun, and tucked it into the back of his belt. "Come on. Stand up." He grunted and tried to hide his pain as he stood and helped me to my feet. "This isn't what you want to hear right now, but the others care about you," he said, wiping a stream of tears from my cheek with his thumb. "Brian. Alice. Even if they don't seem like it, they *do* care. They probably missed you when you left them." He looked off to the side and swallowed hard. "Like I did."

I think it hurt him to tell me that. I could see the discomfort twisting his face. The way his eyebrows wrinkled and his frowning lips fought back a quiver. I didn't think he liked me all that much. I thought we were only using each other, but maybe there was more to it than that. More than he wanted to admit.

"We're better off without Taylor," David added. "He wasn't one of us. Brian was actually right about that."

Brian...

"He's not right about everything, you know." I tried to cross my arms, but I scuffed my burnt wrist against my shirt and grimaced.

David brought his arms up around me and coaxed me into a careful embrace. I closed my eyes and rested my face against his chest, noticing the rapid pitter-patter of my heart finally softening.

For a sliver of time I felt... safe again. His warmth pressed against me—his arms holding me earnestly. Then he shifted slightly and I heard a quick gasp from his mouth.

"Kareena!?" He pulled back, his hand came up toward my neck and he delicately inspected my throat. "What happened to you?" His fingertips barely touched my skin. "What did he do to you?"

I moved away and covered my neck with both hands. "It's nothing. It's over with."

"Your neck, it's... Oh, shit, did he try to... choke you?"

I broke eye contact with him and didn't reply.

"Jesus, Kareena, I'm sorry." He carefully pried my fingers away from my throat and then cupped my face in his hands so I would look up at him. "I'm sorry that happened to you. Taylor was... evil. A misogynistic jackass. He preyed on you because he thought it would be easy, but you were stronger than he thought you'd be. You shouldn't have had to go through what you did. I wish I could have helped you before any of this. Before—"

"You did." I looked into his eyes and smiled. "You did help me, David. Thank you."

He stroked his fingers through my hair, took a deep breath, and then backed off, dropping his hands down to his sides.

"So how did you find me?" I asked.

"That doorway thing showed up out of nowhere and I heard you calling for me from it—whatever it was."

The portal. That wasn't me he'd heard, but I didn't have the courage to tell him that. It must have been the Prism impersonating me like it had with the others once before. It worked, though. For once, I was grateful for the deception.

"You could see it, then? The door of light the Prism sent?"

"I saw what looked like smoke. It was a faded halo of smoke. That's all I could see, but I heard your voice and knew it was coming from within it. You sounded like you were in trouble, so I went through."

"I can see the entire portal, myself," I added. "It's a swirl of white light just spinning and sparkling like—"

"Like a Stargate?" He cocked his head.

"A-a what?"

"A wormhole that kind of looks like glowing water swirling around a drain. It was alien technology from a book and a movie and—"

"I don't get nerd references."

"So now I'm a nerd?" He raised an eyebrow.

"Geek. Nerd. I don't know." I shrugged. "And, well, no. I didn't mean that. I just... never mind." I would have chuckled, but the fleeting opportunity passed quickly and reality sunk back in.

We both sighed and looked back at the swirling portal and then briefly at Taylor's body.

"What are we going to do about him?" The sickness was waning, but I still felt like I might throw up if I dwelled on the sight of the blood for too long.

"There's nothing we can do," David replied.

"You're right. Do we just... leave him?"

"It's probably our only option. I know it's bad, but—"

"He would have left us," I said flatly.

David nodded. "Alright then. You'd better get back to the others," he said, pressing his hand against the small of my back to nudge me gently ahead of him.

"Me? What about you? You're not coming?"

"There's no place for me." He shrugged. "Brian and Alice have each other and you—"

"I'm just here," I interrupted, frowning. "Seriously, David, I don't really belong, either, but we each have a purpose. We're all here for a reason—whatever the hell that may be. And as much as I hate to admit it, we're stronger when we're together. All of us. And... I'd..." My throat tightened and I strained to clear my throat. "I'd kind of like you to come back with me. Please?"

He looked into my eyes and studied me for a moment. It made me uncomfortable, waiting for him to decide what to do and how to respond, but I meant what I said. I *wanted* him to come back with me.

"Okay," he finally answered.

"Thank you," I replied, relieved. "Thank you, David."

We approached the glowing white light and he glanced at me just before passing through. I stepped in after him and a cool rush of air filled my nostrils.

Chapter 25

Within seconds, we were back in the parking garage. The portal that had brought David to where I was had taken us both back to the others.

"Are they here?" David asked, looking around. "Oh, wait." He squinted. "I see traces of their fluorescence. There." He pointed.

"Yes. They're in that maintenance room on the other side," I confirmed. "I was with them before Taylor grabbed me." We started walking toward the room when David slowed down and stopped.

"What is it?" I asked, turning toward him.

"Are you sure about this?"

"Yes." I smiled reassuringly and took his hand. The black lines of burnt skin on his knuckles made my heart sink. Hopefully it wasn't too late for Brian to heal him. "I'm sure. You'll be fine. Brian's... changed. Trust me, please?"

"Okay." He squeezed my hand and a nervous grin flashed on his lips. "I'll try."

"Thanks."

We walked across the parking garage and just before we got too close to the maintenance room, I let go of David's hand. He shot me an understanding smile and I walked up ahead of him to see if the others were inside still.

"Brian? Alice?" I called to them. A few seconds later, the knob on the door jiggled and the door swung open.

"You're back!?" Brian came out first and jogged toward me. "Are you... wait..." He froze. "Is that...?"

"It's me," David said, moving out from behind the shadows.

"Oh. I never thought I'd be happy to see you, but I am." Brian's brow wrinkled. "What happened to you?" He walked up to David and stared in shock at the burn marks all over his body. "Shit. What caused all of this?"

"Your brother," I said. "Can you heal David?" I looked into Brian's eyes. "Please?"

"Yeah. Of course." Brian quickly lifted up his hand. Vivid blue was lighting up his veins and wafting up through his skin already. "Can I?" he asked, holding out his glowing azure hand toward David.

"Sure," David consented and looked off to the side.

Brian wrapped his fingers around David's wrist and concentrated. Blue veins of light crept through his hand and onto David's skin, making its way across his arm, healing the burns one by one. A streak of blue flitted across his cheek, fading the line of seared skin. David looked down at his hands and then craned his neck to look at his shoulder and down his arm.

"Thanks," he said with a small, grateful smile at Brian. "Her, too," he added, motioning toward me.

I tucked the arm with the band of burnt skin on it behind my back and pushed my other shoulder forward, turning so he could see the thick dash marking my bicep. Brian looked me in the eye and I nodded in consent. A quick brush of his hand across my arm sent a warm trickle of blue fluorescence darting over the mark, instantly healing the burn. I smiled and Brian tipped his head in understanding.

"So," he said, stepping back. "What are we going to do about Taylor? What if he comes looking for us?'

"He's not a threat to us anymore," David replied, tilting his head down and looking Brian straight in the eye.

Brian's eyebrows came together and his lips separated in a breath of surprise. "Wh-what... happened to him?" he stammered.

"Does it matter?" David replied, still looking Brian fiercely in the eye.

"N-no." He shrugged. "I-I guess not. I just—"

"Then don't worry about it," David interjected. "I've taken care of it and all you need to know is that he won't be getting in our way again."

Brian fell silent. It seemed like the true meaning behind David's words had sunk in. He swallowed hard. Alice came up behind him and wrapped her hands around his arm.

"We need rest," she whispered. "Let's go back to the room and let them talk."

Brian acknowledged her request with a nod. He glanced at me and then David.

"You guys be careful, okay? Come join us whenever you're ready." He looked at David and swallowed hard, thinning his lips for a moment as he mustered up the nerve to say what he said next. "I mean you too, David. You're... one of us now."

I watched David's unchanging expression, expecting him to smile, but he didn't.

"Thank you," he replied.

Brian and Alice turned and headed back toward the maintenance room.

Once they closed the door, I turned to David and took a step closer to him, looking up into his eyes.

"Thank you for taking the heat back there for what happened to Taylor. Thanks for not telling them the truth."

"You don't need to thank me," he muttered, shaking his head. "Really. Now you tell me why you didn't let Brian heal your other burn." He gestured to the thick ridge of jagged black skin decorating my right wrist.

"We all have our scars, right?" I answered, repeating the very same words he had said to me not too long ago. "Now I have my own. And it has a story, too. One I'll never forget."

His brow wrinkled at first and then he nodded in

understanding.

"Look, David." I unconsciously reached for his hand and grasped it tightly in mine. "I know I treated you like shit back there at the hotel, and for that, I'm sorry. Forgive me, please. I'll do whatever it takes to prove myself to you and—"

"You don't have to prove yourself to anyone, Kareena. Not Brian. Not Taylor. Not even me. But now that Taylor's gone, we have to keep moving. We have to keep doing what we know is right. Whatever the Prism needs us to do."

I suddenly remembered what the Prism had given me and released David's hand so I could reach into my pocket and rummage around for the small energy pearl. I bumped David's Libertad at the same time and scooped them both up into my grasp.

"Give me your hand, please," I said, separating the pearl and coin into different palms and only revealing the tiny glowing orb to him.

"What is it?" he asked, lifting his wrist.

"It will protect you from the Saviors." I dropped the ball onto his skin and it shattered into prismatic dust. Within seconds, it curled around his wrist and took the shape of a sparkling bangle full of chaotic light and color.

"I can't really see it anymore," he said, "but I can see a faint aura of light there around my wrist."

"That's all you need to see," I said. "It's the same energy they used in the portals. It somehow keeps the Saviors from abducting us. And I know what you're thinking—that we're just becoming slaves to another race of aliens instead, but—"

"I trust you," he said.

"Y-you do?"

He nodded.

I didn't think he trusted me that much. Especially not after how I betrayed him so quickly and... abandoned him.

I squeezed my fingers and felt the cool touch of his silver coin.

"Oh. That reminds me." I unfolded my fingers and lifted the coin up for him to see. "You should have this back."

"No. Keep it." David replied, crossing his arms.

"But, I did something horrible and I don't think it's right to let something so important to you be blackened with... murder."

"It wouldn't be the first time it's seen blood," he said, uncrossing his arms. "And, besides, you're safe, right? So... maybe it did you some good."

"Maybe." I shrugged. "So are you and Brian going to be okay? I mean, get along? I know he's been grinding your nerves a lot lately, and I just want us to try to be friends. Until all of this is over with."

"Kareena?"

"Yes?"

"You said it yourself, you have nothing here. You're alone and you feel like you don't belong. Well, so do I. And I'm not going to stand here and ask you to give up who you are or commit to something you're not comfortable with, but I am going to tell you what I think the truth is."

He locked eyes with me as he continued. "I believe that you think you've got your entire life in the palm of your hand—that you've got everything under control and the entire world bows down to every one of your whims."

"What? That's ridiculous." I scoffed, rolling my eyes. "I—"

"But really," he interrupted, "you're afraid of being abandoned because the world doesn't revolve around you and you can't do everything on your own. You're afraid to admit it. Not only your fear of being alone, but of being hurt. That's why you can't make up your mind about what you want. Brian. Me. Taylor. Someone else tomorrow, no doubt. But the truth of the matter is, you're lost and confused and you don't know how to live your life without other people in it who want nothing more than to worship you and carry you wherever you want to go."

"That's not true..." The words barely came out of my mouth.

"It is." He put his hands on my shoulders and leaned closer to me. "It's the truth and you know it. I said I'd come back with you and the others, but I'm not going to be part of a lie. I know I said things didn't have to get messy between us when all of this began, and I stand by my words. But what we started back there—what you keep pretending we didn't— that was the start of something else. Something bigger.

You can keep denying it, or you can tell me what you really think. I'm more than willing to stay here and fight this fight until the end, regardless of how you feel about me or whether we *ever* even look at each other again. But I won't risk my life in ignorance. I need to know the truth. We need to set things straight."

His fingers slid down my arms and he awaited a response.

"The truth?" I started and then swallowed hard. "The truth is I don't need a man to make me feel valuable or to give me a reason to live. I don't, and no woman should. I've always tried to be independent and although, yeah, I like having guys around, I don't need one to survive. I don't need anyone. But, at the same time, I was so blinded by my infatuation with Brian, I couldn't see what it was doing to me."

David listened intently.

"But today, shit hit the fan and I realized I did need some- one," I added. "I... needed you."

"That's the truth, then?" he asked.

"Yes."

"Then that's all I needed to hear," he replied softly, a small beam of admiration coiling the corner of his lips.

A weight suddenly lifted from my heart.

But the satisfaction couldn't last.

I looked upon the dark brown and black lines crackling through the light inside David's chest. "David." I took a deep breath. "There's... something else."

"Oh? What is it?"

"Remember back when I told you about the darkness I saw discoloring your fluorescence?"

"Yeah." He nodded. "What about it?"

"Well, I can't pretend not to see it anymore... and I won't let you pretend it's not there."

"I knew something wasn't right," he whispered.

"Y-you did?"

"Yes," he continued. "I know what it means, too. Things haven't been right for a while and I had a feeling something was... wrong. Whatever it is, it's killing me. I have no idea how much time I have and you know I'm not one to ask for help, but I'd be a fool to think I didn't need yours now."

BOOK IV

LOST SOULS

Chapter 1

The ghoulish ash-colored thing watched me intently, sizing me up with its shallow grey eyes. Sleek white hair fell past its bony shoulders, and although its small, sloped nose and familiar facial features made it look human, it was anything but.

I reached for my gun, grasping the grip feebly, but relinquished the idea because my limbs were weak and heavy.

"What do you want from me?" I asked, trying to raise my voice. It was nearly impossible. I coughed, my lungs straining to take in air.

"Well?" I asked again, wheezing. "What do you—"

"We have an assignment for you," it said, its intonation robotic and stale. The thing approached me and reached out a hand.

I took a step back. "Don't come near me!" My hands were fists. The thing sure as hell wasn't going to touch me. "Whatever you are, I want you to put me back where I was. I don't want any part of whatever it is you're doing. Leave me alone!"

"Your kind refer to us as the Saviors," it continued, cutting into me with its stiff, judgmental gaze. "We are searching for a cure for a virus that is destroying our species. Humans have genetically compatible DNA, which we can bind with our own in an effort to develop such a cure."

Saviors?

"This is crazy," I said, scanning over more of the things standing behind the speaking one. "I'm not letting you do anything to me." I took another step back and grunted. Something stopped me—a wall I couldn't see.

"It is too late for that," the thing continued, approaching.

I was ready to take a swing at it, but something inside warned me to stay cool. I didn't need an alien pissed off at me.

"We have an offer for you," it added. "We are aware of the one you call Lucy. Your—"

"Don't you lay a goddamn hand on her!" I lunged at the thing, but an invisible blow to the chest propelled me backward. I hit the ground. Hard. Lost my breath. I struggled to come to my feet.

"You cannot tell us who to choose," it said coldly.

I coughed hard and wiped my lips with the back of my hand. A splash of blood colored my knuckles. *What the hell?* "What did you do to me?"

It forced a flattened hand out and a burst of fiery heat welled in my chest. I looked down and saw sparks of yellow light radiating from my sternum up to my collarbone.

"Shit," I said, the word caught in a labored breath. I lifted my shaking hands and watched golden vines of riveting color flicker in my veins, leaching through the surface of my skin. I gasped and rubbed my arm frantically with my other hand in a futile attempt to wipe the alien light away. Heat forked through my body, making me sick. Nauseated. "What have you done to me?"

"You now carry a compatible strain of our genetic material," it replied.

"No!" I staggered back, slamming into the invisible wall and getting the wind knocked out of me. I doubled over, holding out trembling hands, watching streaks of vibrant yellow-gold light pulsate down through my fingertips, fueled by a burning core of energy erupting inside me. "You... can't do this to me. You can't..." My heart pumped so fast, it made my chest ache.

"Do not fight it, or the pain will increase."

"What..." I could hardly speak. "What... do you want from me?" Every breath stung.

"There are others out there who must be punished for disobeying our commands. We have granted you the ability to find and reprimand them."

"Who are these people and what have they done?" I straightened up and tried to slow my breathing. The bright yellow light and heat were dissipating from my skin and the sharp prickling faded.

The thing took a few steps closer and I swallowed hard, lifting my chin and rolling my shoulders back. The alien towered a few inches over me. One of its grey hands reached toward my head and I flinched as cold fingers pressed to my temple.

Everything went black.

A group of teens walked together through a darkened city street. A boy, a short, skinny young girl tangled on his arm, and a slightly older, more mature-looking girl dragging behind them. Each of them glowed with intense neon light. Blue. Green. Pink.

The pink one kept pointing and the green one ran ahead to each of the targets.

She was touching people—*starting* them? *Is that what they call it?*

The green one pressed her hand against another person and a ball of white light ignited inside them. The blue one followed, guarding them vigilantly, his left arm ablaze with azure light.

Next, they were standing in a small circle, their arms crossed. Silent. Angry? They weren't going to do anything else the Saviors had asked of them. They didn't want to be part of it anymore.

Neither did I.

The bright white room came into focus again and I squinted,

grimacing from the sting of the instant lighting change.

"They are no longer following our commands," the Savior said, stiffly. "You must control them—force them back into submission."

"If you're so powerful, why don't you do it yourself?" I groaned and rubbed my eyes with my palms.

"No. We have chosen you to carry out this task."

I looked up at the thing. Its empty grey eyes were fixated on me.

"Why should I do this for you?" I asked, gritting my teeth. "Why do I have to do anything for you?"

"The one you call Lucy," it started, and I tensed up, "she is important to you. Correct?"

I didn't even know how to answer that. If I said yes, it would know the truth, but if I didn't say anything at all, it was just as bad.

"Yes. Yes, she is. She's just a little girl. Keep your hands off her."

"We have decided not to start her if you do as we ask," it replied.

"And... if I don't help you with these kids?" My voice was trembling now as I fought back rising fears.

"We will subject her to the light, as well. She is a close genetic match to your DNA, and that is highly sought after by those working to find the cure. We could use her for our studies, but will sacrifice the option if it makes you compliant."

I wanted to say no. I wanted to lunge at the creature again, drive a fist into its sickeningly grey head and find out just how resilient it really was.

Pull the trigger.

Put an end to it—whatever *it* was.

But something inside me knew it wasn't possible. The whole thing was a nightmare I couldn't wake up from.

My eyes reeled opened and I gasped.

The room eased into focus; the light of dawn filtered in through the concrete pillars of the parking garage.

Kareena was asleep, curled up close to me, the curves of her warm body fitting against mine and my nose buried in wild lengths of her silky, ebony hair. I had one arm bent somewhat uncomfortably beneath my head—tingling now—and the other draped over her waist. Our fingers were loosely entwined.

Heat radiated from her. The rugged scent of dirty skin and sweat. A deep breath brought me back to reality and tamed my anxiety. Kareena had only begun to taste the true dangers in life, and yet, she'd already shown grit in the line of fire. That was something I appreciated about her. Admired.

Although I liked feeling her close, and I was fairly certain the feeling was mutual, I think the need ended there. Last night, she had reluctantly requested I stay with her while she slept—her pride getting in the way of her attempts to sooth her distress.

She was afraid the Saviors would take her again, even though the Prism assured her they couldn't. She also feared Taylor would somehow rise from the grave and force her back into the torture of constant confusion and memory loss. Regardless, I offered to do what I could to bring her any kind of peace. After what she had done for me, I felt like I owed her. Yes, I'd put my own neck on the line for her, too, but for her to do the same for me was... unexpected.

I carefully slipped my fingers out from between hers and dragged a gentle stroke up her arm, avoiding the dark line of burnt skin circling her wrist—the scar she'd acquired when she saved my life. Having declined Brian's healing touch, it was beginning to mend on its own now.

She stirred, a faint sigh escaping her lips as she pushed back into me, nuzzling her face against the bunched-up coat beneath her head. I withdrew my other arm and shook it to relieve the numbness. Then I got up from the floor and walked over to the door.

Outside of the maintenance room, I lit a cigarette and watched it burn, the subtle yellow-orange embers vaguely mirroring my own vivid color. I still couldn't believe the Saviors had infected Lucy, and how if it weren't for Kareena trying to melt my brain a while back, I probably never would have found out.

Then again, I couldn't believe it was happening at all—that aliens were screwing with us, threatening our existence, and that I, three others like me, and a new race of aliens I knew damn near nothing about, were the only ones who could do anything to try to stop our complete annihilation.

Chapter 2

"You're worried about your sister, aren't you?" Kareena asked, coming up behind me. She rested her forearms on the concrete overhang and looked out at the empty streets below.

"Yeah." I released a puff of smoke with my reply. "Sorry if I woke you."

"Don't worry about it," she replied. "I just wanted to say... I get it. I'm worried, too—about my parents. You know, Brian and Alice may have each other, but it doesn't make them immune. We're all missing someone, I think."

"I know." I inhaled through my cigarette. "But I think I need to go back to her. I need to make sure she's safe."

"Safe?" Kareena turned to look me in the eye. "I thought she was with someone you trusted?"

"She is." I shrugged. "But I don't trust anyone more than I trust myself when it comes to Lucy's safety. I just... have a feeling shit's about to hit the fan, and I need to know I can protect her."

"You can protect her by keeping her out of this, David."

Her words rubbed me the wrong way.

"What is that supposed to mean?" I snuffed out my cigarette on the concrete guardrail and flicked it over the side. "That I can't take care of my goddamn—"

"That's not what I meant and you know it!"

"Then what *did* you mean?" I rested my hands on my belt. "And keep it down before you wake the others."

"I'm just saying the Saviors are probably going to try to find a way to circumvent what the Prism did for us, and

Lucy is likely going to be better off out of the line of fire."

"But you don't understand," I said, shaking my head. "They've been using her as leverage from the beginning. If they can't get to me directly, she may be their next target. I can't let anything happen to her."

Her brow crinkled. "Oh, shit. Are you saying they're going to go after our families next?"

"No. Only the ones they want."

"Like Peter," Brian said, appearing from around the corner of the maintenance room, walking toward us.

I shot Kareena an angry glance. I *really* didn't need Brian on my ass this early in the morning.

"Who's Peter?" I asked, trying to stay composed. Brian had calmed down since our last confrontation, so I had to give him the benefit of the doubt.

"The son of the people who were taking care of me while we were working through the custody case so I could stay with Alice and her mom. He was infected, too, but we never started him. At least, Alice never did."

"They've already proven they don't need her for all of them," I added. "They didn't need her to start me or Taylor, apparently."

"True." Brian cleared his throat. "So, where to?" he asked.

"What?" I cocked my head. Was he asking *me* for advice?

He shrugged and looked off to the side. "You're the oldest one here. What do you think we should do now?"

Kareena cracked a smile.

The kid's attitude had changed since I had last offered him a suggestion. Not that I minded, but Brian needed to be strong. I couldn't have him breaking down in the middle of all of this.

"Are you... okay?" I asked. His gaze met mine and he nodded.

"Yeah. I'm fine. I just know we're kind of screwed right

now and I, um. I—"

"I get it," I interrupted. He was uncomfortable enough. "I understand, Brian, and I appreciate you asking for my thoughts."

"He wants to go get his sister," Kareena interjected. I shot her a bitter glance. "What?" she replied with a shrug. "They need to know. We're in this together, remember?"

I didn't want her telling them about my business, at least not until I had a plan—which I didn't.

"Is she in danger?" Brian asked, perking up, his voice seeming as though he really was concerned.

"Maybe. I don't know for sure, but... I told you guys a while back that the Saviors were using her as leverage to get me to hurt you. I don't know what they might do to her if they think I've gone rogue. I need to go find her."

Brian mulled over the idea for several moments. "Well, where is she right now?" he asked.

"Back home. New York."

"We can all go with you," Kareena suggested, nudging me gently in the elbow. "That way, we'll be safer. Right, Brian?"

Brian looked back toward the maintenance room—where Alice must have still been asleep. "I... guess." He chewed his lip.

"I'll go alone," I said, grabbing Kareena's hand.

"What? Why?" She squeezed back, surprised. "David, seriously, what the hell are you thinking? Going without us... I mean..."

"David?" Brian came a little closer. "We'll go with you if you want us to. There's no point in us splitting up right now. Not until we know what's going on."

"It will be easier if I go by myself, Kareena," I said, trying to reassure her. "Really." I looked back at Brian. "I can be back in two or three days probably."

"How are we going to keep this up without you?" she asked. "We're... kind of broke, and this place isn't going to be safe forever."

"I'll make sure you're set for a few days before I go. Alright?"

"Are you sure, man?" Brian continued, fidgeting, clearly uncomfortable. "I mean... we *can* go with you. It's okay. I won't—"

"No. No," I stopped him. "I'll be fine. Been on my own for this long, after all."

"Alright then. I'm going to wake up Alice and tell her what's going on, okay? Don't leave yet."

"I won't. Gotta get my shit together. Mentally, at least."

Brian went back to the maintenance room.

Kareena squeezed my hand even harder.

"What is it?" I asked.

"Why are you going alone?" She furrowed her brow at me. "Seriously?"

"Because it will be safer for us all," I answered, wriggling my hand free of her uncomfortably tight grasp. "Seriously."

She scoffed and crossed her arms. "You're a real dick, too, sometimes. You know that?"

"And it's only bothering you now?" I raised an eyebrow at her and she rolled her eyes.

"Shut up."

"Sorry. Anyway, I'll try to set something up for all of you before I go so you'll be safe for the time being. We can work out a place to meet if something happens. As far as money goes, though, I... don't really know what we're going to do—"

"I can handle it," she said beneath her breath.

"What?" It caught me off guard. She wasn't the type to offer to take responsibility. At least, she never came across that way to me.

"I can help take care of the others for a few days," she clarified, bringing a hand up to her face and brushing a fingertip briefly over the diamond stud in her left nostril. "I-I can sell this."

I didn't know it was a real diamond. Imagining Kareena without the prismatic sparkle on her nose seemed hard. It was pretty on her. But times were tough and unless I robbed another convenience store—probably not going to happen—we *were* going to need money.

"It's worth a lot," she continued. "I know it is, but... I don't know shit about pawning stuff."

"I do." I put my hand on her shoulder and looked into her bright, leafy-green eyes. The color was unusual—otherworldly. "I'll make sure no one screws you over and that you get a fair price for it. Okay?"

"Thanks," she whispered. She clasped her hands together and heaved a breath.

"You gonna be alright?" I brushed my thumb across her chin and tipped her face up toward mine. "You seem... I don't know. Worried."

"You just came back," she replied, looking me in the eye. "I don't want anything to happen to you. I'm the only one who can see the Prism, and what if we need to contact you or—"

"I'll only be a few days. I'll be fine, Kareena. And so will you. Trust me."

She tried to fake a confiding smile but couldn't even crack a semi-believable one for me. It didn't seem like her to be clinging to anyone other than Brian, and it made me wonder.

Was Kareena actually going to miss me?

Chapter 3

By bus, the trip home would take me at least a day and a half. So, maybe I was off on my estimate by a day or two, but the teens could do okay without me. Kareena was smarter than they thought she was. She told me she'd take care of them, and I believed her. Not that Brian and Alice needed a babysitter, but the three of them were stronger together.

Earlier in the day, Kareena had said goodbye to me. It was an awkward goodbye—one that seemed out of place and harder than it should have been. We didn't have a "thing" going as far as I could tell. She had made it clear she didn't want an actual relationship, and I was cool with that.

No attachment. No pain. Right?

Shit.

Then why was I feeling so... low? Maybe because I'd almost died trying to help her. Or maybe it was because she had asked me to sleep beside her last night—in the same room with Brian and Alice—even though she acted like it wouldn't change things between us. Or... it could have been the way she'd said goodbye to me. There was a subdued nature to the way she looked up into my eyes with worry. Or maybe I was reading between the lines like a sentimental ass.

I'd barely been back with Lucy for a few hours before the portal showed up and I was whisked away again—not that I regretted being there just in time to help save Kareena's life—but I didn't even have a chance to say goodbye.

I missed Lucy so much. Poor girl. She was probably starting to wonder why I kept popping into her life and then back out. Like I was a bad guy, when all I really wanted was to spend time with her.

She was all I had left. She was the only person who loved me for me. I needed to be there for her whenever I could—guide her through growing up and dealing with shit before the wrong people got to her the way they had gotten to me.

Or maybe *I* was the wrong person, the bad influence she didn't need in her life.

No. I was going to make something of myself. Or try to, at least. I wanted to be more than a petty criminal. But then, alien drama took over my life and things went to hell fast.

We needed a more permanent place to call home...

.   .   .

In a small, middle-class suburb on the South Shore of Staten Island was a strip of un-eclectic, beige, two-story homes lined up as far as I could see. Tidy green lawns diligently cut to the maximum height required of the subdivision. Matching plain, black mailboxes perched on a post at the end of every driveway. The street wasn't unique or charming in any way, but it was a safe neighborhood for her. Safer than the places I had to take her to some days.

Not too far on the outskirts of the middle-class street was a slum. I'd passed it on the way over. The people there used to be my kind of people, but I'd since moved away from the bad influences in my life and toward the good. Or at least *closer* to the good.

I approached the front door of one of the clone houses and knocked with the back of my hand. A moment later, I heard a man and a woman bickering just on the other side. Something about me being unreliable and a bad influence on their kids. Then the woman shouted something about "forgetting it" and "you'll see" and both voices went silent after that. I tried to shake off the awkwardness of what I'd just overheard. I knew exactly what was going down.

The lock clicked and the door opened.

Eli, a good friend of mine since I'd come clean, was standing in the doorway, one hand keeping the door from opening too far. There was a tired look of doubt on his face, one eyebrow raised higher than the other, while he looked me over.

"Where've you been?" he said in a hushed voice. He slipped through the crack in the doorway and quietly closed the door behind him. "Really, bro. You can't keep pulling this kind of crap on us. Ellie's getting pissed. She's threatening to call CPS, even, but I keep trying to tell her—"

"I know. I know," I interrupted.

Eli's wife, Ellie—their names similar by coincidence alone—hated my freaking guts. She had ever since the day they'd gotten married. It was like she'd taken the reins and something clicked once they'd tied the knot. She was done with me before she'd given me a chance. After they had their first kid, we got into a scuffle over the ethics of the way I was living with Lucy, but in the end, Eli came through for me.

"I didn't mean to disappear. I swear," I replied. "I swear I didn't. Please, Eli. You've gotta believe me."

"I get it, bro. I do." He took a deep breath and reached an open hand toward me. I took it and he pulled me closer and wrapped his other arm around my shoulders in a brief, but tight, embrace. "Jesus, I missed your ass. I thought something had happened to you after you vanished the other day. We thought we were gonna be stuck with... well, not that we don't care about her, but..."

"How is Lucy? Is she... okay?"

"Yeah." He shrugged. "I mean, she's pretty upset and she really lost it when you left without warning. Ellie did, too. She thought... well, she thought it meant, you know? Trouble."

"Yeah." I shook my head. "I never meant to leave her here for this long."

Eli had three other kids—two-year-old twins and a four-year-old—whom Lucy played with often. Leaving her with his kids helped keep CPS at bay, and the one extra kid every now and then didn't look suspicious to neighbors, either.

"We can't keep doing this, David," he said, looking away anxiously. He scratched the back of his neck. "I mean... people are going to start asking questions sooner or later. She's getting older and—"

"I know. Okay? I'm working on it." I grumbled beneath my breath. "I'm thankful you've gotten us this far. I really am. I just don't know what to do with her now and... I can't lose her, Eli. I just can't." I grabbed him by the shoulders and looked him in the eye. "But you know what? Good news. I'm here to take her from you. Permanently."

"What?" His jaw dropped. "No shit, man? Did you get things straightened out?"

"I wish." I couldn't lie to him. We'd been friends for too long and I owed it to him to tell the truth. Though I couldn't tell him all of it.

"Things are going to change soon, and I want her to be with me when that happens so I can protect her."

"What do you mean?"

"Weird shit's been going down lately. I don't have time to explain. Look, just let me in, okay? Let me get Lucy and get the hell out of here. Out of Ellie's way for good." I took a step closer to the door and Eli swung his arm out to stop me.

"No, David." His arm was trembling and he avoided eye contact. "I-I can't." His breathing became heavier and I felt tension building in his voice.

"What? What the hell do you mean *you can't*?" I tipped my head down and clenched my teeth. "Let. Me. In."

"It's not me, David. It's... Ellie. I mean, I think you're doing what you can, but she—"

"Don't make me do this, Eli." I reached behind my back and wrapped my fingers around the grip of my gun. "Please. Don't."

"No!" His eyes widened. He knew what I was reaching for. "Come on, David. You know you can't take care of this little girl anymore. She needs a real family. Someone who loves her and—"

"I do love her! Jesus Christ, Eli, don't start this kind of crap." I took a step closer, glaring. "I am *not* going to let you try to take her away from me. Not now. Not ever. I'm not going to let anyone touch her."

"She needs to grow up with kids her age. Go to school and—"

"Move, Eli!" I drew my gun out from behind my belt and he swiftly shifted his weight from the door. "I don't want to hurt you or anyone else. But I'm not going to let you do this to me. Move!" I barged past, into the house. His wife was on her cell speaking frantically with someone.

"Yes. He's still here," she said. "Oh my God! He's got a gun! He's got a gun and—"

"Ellie, no!" I yanked the phone out of her hand and disconnected the call. "Don't do this to me. Where's Lucy!?"

"Stop it, David!" Ellie screamed. "Just stop! You can't keep living this way—expecting us to take her in every time you get wrapped up in some kind of mess you can't get out of. You can't keep doing this to her!"

"Lucy!" I yelled, my eyes darting toward the second floor stairwell. "Where the hell is she?"

"David, calm down." Ellie's voice shook. "Please. Put the gun away and let's talk about this."

"Give her back to me and I'll leave. She needs to be with *me*." I looked at the stairwell again. "Lucy! Come down here, now!"

"How are you going to keep this up?" Eli came up behind me. "Really, bro? Drugs? Stealing cars? You can't expose her to that kind of stuff."

I swerved around and lowered my gun. "That's over with, Eli! I don't shoot-up anymore or strip cars. I stopped years ago and I haven't looked back. I want a better life."

"So you're just going to keep toting the girl around every time you earn a buck to live somewhere for a month and then drop her off here again like we run some kind of deadbeat daycare? We can't do this any longer. She's five years old, and she needs to go to school. She needs a *real* home."

"I'm trying to give that to her! I just—"

"You don't even have legal custody of her!" Eli put a quivering hand onto my shoulder, pressed firmly, and looked me straight in the eye. "David, you're gonna lose her someday and there's nothing either of us can do about it."

A muffled police siren blared in the distance outside and I sucked in a breath. *Shit.* I cut a glance at Ellie, who was shaking her head at me, and then I grabbed Eli's collar and yanked him toward my face. "Tell me where she is, damn it!" Heat radiated from within me and a warm golden glow reflected off Eli's terrified gaze.

"What's happening to you!?" he shouted. "What the hell is that?"

Fluorescence flickered to life in my chest and sparking yellow veins crept down my arms toward my hands—toward Eli's face. He wriggled violently until he was free of my grasp and then backed away in a panic.

"I said weird shit was happening, Eli. I meant it."

Chapter 4

Lucy dashed down the stairs as fast as her little legs could carry her, arms flailing in the air as a smile lit up her face. I tucked my gun away and knelt at the foot of the steps, arms open to catch her just before her purple sneakers hit the last stair. I scooped her into my arms and stood, hoisting her up to my chest. She flung her arms around my neck and held on tightly. My fluorescence faded away before she had a chance to notice.

"David, no!" Ellie tried to stop me. "Think about what you're doing!"

"I'm done thinking about it," I growled. "Eli, thank you for everything you've done to help me and Lucy. You saved my ass more than a few times and I'm grateful for it, but I have to go." I headed toward the door. Lucy sobbed on my shoulder, but I couldn't tell if they were tears of joy or fear with all of the commotion.

"It's okay, Lucy," I said quietly, flinging the front door open while adjusting my grasp on her. "I'm getting you out of here."

Things were going to be okay. Somehow. I had gotten her back and—

Police sirens blared—sounding much closer than they had minutes ago.

Flickering red and blue lights became visible not too far down the street.

"Shit," I hissed.

Lucy hugged me tighter still, and I barely heard the

squeaky whisper, "I'm scared."

"I know you are." I cupped the back of her head with my other hand. "Just be strong for me, please. I'm gonna get you out of here, but things are going to get scarier first. You have to be a big girl, okay?"

She sniffled loudly and lifted her face from my damp shoulder. Her brown eyes glistened with fear and she rubbed a hand across her face to wipe away the tears.

"Okay," she murmured, her voice breaking. "I'll try."

"That's a good girl," I replied with a smile. "Be strong, like me. We'll be safe."

Before I could get past the front gate of the lawn, one of the police cars swerved to a stop at the end of the driveway, the brakes squealing against the asphalt. The cop flung open the car door and hopped out, his hand hovered above a holster on his hip. Taser or gun, I couldn't tell.

Lucy shrieked in fear and buried her face against my shoulder once more.

"It's okay." I looked frantically around for an escape route. The damn yard, while not entirely fenced in, was flanked on both sides by other houses and a line of thick hedges. I could run, but how far would I get with the police on my tail? By myself, maybe, but with Lucy... No way I'd make it half way across the street before someone tackled me.

"Put the child down!" the officer barked from the edge of the lawn.

I shook my head. "You don't understand. She's with me. She's—"

"This is your second warning," he shouted. "Put the girl down and back away from her. I want to see your hands in the air!"

"What the hell are you gonna do!? Shoot her?"

Lucy let out a high-pitched whimper.

The officer gave me a nasty look and adjusted his stance, his hand nearing the weapon. Another police car pulled up behind him.

Damn it!

"Put the girl down. We know you're armed, but we're not letting you leave with that child."

"She's mine," I replied, out of breath as my heart beat faster. "Those people don't know what the hell they're talking about. They're just trying to protect their kids. I'm not here to hurt anyone."

"Sir," the cop at the edge of the lawn started, "if she is yours, then put her down and let's talk this over. There's no need to get hostile."

"Hostile? You're threatening *me* right now!"

Lucy yelped.

"Shh. It's okay, Lucy," I whispered near her ear. "I'm not gonna let them hurt you."

"We're not going to use force unless we have to," he added. "Now, please, for the safety of the little girl, put her down so we can talk about this."

The second officer got out of his car and drew a weapon from his side—a gun.

"Please, don't do this to us," I said. "You don't understand what we've been through. You don't know what's happening out there right now."

"What's happening right now is you're committing a crime. If you don't release that child, you will be arrested for kidnapping. Kidnapping in the first degree is a class A felony."

"I'm not kidnapping her," I replied, raising my voice. "She's been with me her entire life!"

Warmth came over me and I felt the light flaring to life inside my chest again. Lucy gasped and pulled her face away from my shoulder.

"Crap! What is that!?" The officer closest to me stumbled back a step and jerked his gun from his holster.

Every hair on my body straightened and a wave of cold air hit me out of nowhere. I flinched, but didn't let go of Lucy.

I turned my head and saw a faint ripple of smoke swirling in a circle just inches from where I stood. It looked exactly the same as it had when I heard Kareena calling for help a few days ago. I could see through the shape—barely—but everything was distorted, as if heat waves emanated from it. I looked back at the cop, who was now pointing his gun straight at us, and then back at the coiling plume of energy.

It was a portal. It had to be!

As soon as the two police offers took another step forward, I swerved and dashed into the smoke—shielding Lucy the best I could in case a shot was taken.

A cloud of grey surrounded me and we descended into emptiness. An ocean of the deepest, darkest blue swallowed us whole, and seconds later, dropped me flat on my back on a carpet of soft grass. The thud didn't knock the wind out of me, surprisingly, and Lucy was safe and unharmed.

I was sure they were going to shoot me on the way through, but they hadn't. Thank God.

"Where are we?" Lucy asked, getting up off me and staring out at the empty street ahead. We had been dropped in what appeared to be a small park in the center of a downtown city strip.

My fluorescence faded instantly and she didn't so much as mention it. She'd find out sooner or later, but right now, I was glad she was staying calm.

I lifted myself up from the grass and looked around. None of the buildings or even the street name looked familiar to me, but that didn't matter. We needed to be safe—it didn't matter where or how at this point.

I knew the others were nearby...

In the distance, traces of neon pink, blue, and green light marked a trail of where they had gone. The wispy remains of fluorescence essence became more vibrant just up ahead—a sign that they were close.

"Lucy, come here." She had wandered off a few feet.

Lucy jaunted back over to me, her arms flung out to the side, closing in as she approached. I knelt down, a willing victim to her embrace, and she let out a happy squeal. "I missed you sooooo much!" she said.

"I know," I replied. "I'm here now." I held her close as she nuzzled her face against my shoulder, her soft brown hair tickling my neck and the gentle warmth of her hug reminding me how precious life really was.

Her grasp loosened and she looked up at me and grinned, her beautiful eyes narrowing with joy. I smiled and pressed my thumb playfully to her chin. She was taking this so well; it made me very proud of her.

"I missed you, too. I'm going to take you to meet some friends of mine, okay?" I said, reaching down for her hand. "They're nice kids and I think they'll like you, so don't be scared, alright?"

"Can I play with them?" she asked, looking up at me with an innocent, inquisitive grin. It made my heart skip a beat.

I chuckled. "No, Lucy. I'm sorry. They're a little too old for that, but we'll find some new friends for you. I promise." I took a deep breath and sighed, her smile bringing me to my knees again. "I'll do everything I can to make you happy." I embraced her a second time and she hugged me back—harder than before. "I love you, Lucy."

"I love you, too, Daddy."

My throat tightened.

Chapter 5

Five years ago...

The door hung open and lamplight filtered out through the crack. The television had been left on and late-night info-mercials resonated from inside.

I didn't want to go in, but I had to confront her. I had to cut it off once and for all. She was poison, now more than ever, and being near her would only make the habit creep back into my bloodstream.

Things had gotten out of hand, and if she wanted to pry child support money out of me, she'd have to prove the damn kid was mine to begin with—something I *seriously* doubted, knowing she'd do anything (or anyone) to support her filthy addiction.

"Angie?" I nudged the door open with my shoe and wrinkled my lips at the smell of mold and piss that drifted out. I walked past the kitchen and into the living room where the TV was.

"Angie? Where the hell—"

Then I saw her on the couch. Her head was dropped back against the cushions and she was staring up at the ceiling with a sickly, glazed look in her eyes.

"Christ, Angie." I inched over to her, side stepping piles of crap she'd left everywhere, immediately noticing the line of cocaine on the end table beside her limp arm.

"Shit." I grimaced. She'd been on it for so long, the highs had tapered off—a side effect of long-term snorting. Back when we'd first hooked up, she was the most social person in the world.

Confident.

Invincible.

Just like anyone else who gets high on cocaine.

At first.

Then it hits you—the low. The need to get more and more because the highs aren't cutting it and reality is bleeding back into focus. You start thinking your life is shit. You're shit (by then you are). And that you're not worth a damn thing to anyone. Depression. Darkness. It eats at you, closing in until you've lost touch.

I backed out of the game just before I crashed. But not without help... Eli's help.

"I-I came to tell you I'm out," I said, hoping she was coherent enough to comprehend.

"I don't care," she slurred, twisting her neck to look at me while the rest of her body remained dead still. "Go. I don't give a shit what you do." She dropped her head back and stared at the ceiling again.

"Good. Then we're clean. Don't come begging me for money anymore, Angie," I added, backing away. "And don't even think of pinning that—"

That's when I heard it. The painful cry of a baby screaming at the top of its lungs from another room. I took another look at Angie—her eyes rolled back in her head—and then I shot a glance at the room across from us. "That damn thing," she groaned. "All it ever does is cry. All it ever does is keep me up because it needs shit. Milk. Changing. What-the-hell ever."

The baby kept wailing and I waited for Angie to budge, but she didn't. Not that I had expected her to. She was crashing so hard that nothing else mattered to her. I'd seen others go through it. You could put a gun to their forehead and they'd likely dare you to pull the trigger. No fear. No connection with reality.

"Damn it, Angie," I hissed beneath my breath. "Damn it." I walked behind the couch toward the sound of the cries and crept into the room where the baby was. A nasty smell saturated the room and I choked, covering my nose and mouth with my arm as I stepped over the threshold.

I switched on a light. Only one bulb came on out of the three screwed into the rickety ceiling fan overhead. It was enough light to see the large black plastic bin in the center of the room with a blanket hanging over the side. A sickness came over me and my jaw tightened in anger.

That bitch had no idea what she was doing. This was no way to raise a kid.

The feeling worsened as I leaned over the container to look inside. There was the baby, wrapped in an old towel, nestled atop a pile of damp, soiled newspapers and paper towels.

I slid a clean corner of the blanket out of the bin and bent down to take the crying baby up into my arms. I cradled her head as carefully as I could with one hand and tried to hold my arm like a sling. It was difficult at first—especially for a man who'd never touched an infant in his life. I got it after a few careful shifts of my hand position.

The baby must have felt secure because she stopped crying and looked up at me. Her dark, sparkling eyes gazed into mine and we stared at each other for a few moments. She had fair, golden skin and dark hair sprouting from her chubby round head.

The baby was in poor shape. Dirty and malnourished. I could hardly believe she had survived this long in these conditions, probably damn near starving. No wonder she'd been howling for attention.

I knew for a fact that Angie slept around—one of the many reasons why we'd split—and for the longest time, I had convinced myself that her baby couldn't have been mine.

But as I looked down into the baby's dark eyes and they peered up into mine, I realized something.

Through all of the hell, drugs, and alcohol she'd been exposed to, the baby looked... okay. Maybe there were underlying things going on, but as far as I could tell, she had five fingers on each hand, five toes on each foot, a nose, a happy curl to her thin lips, and two pretty brown eyes that were now locked intently onto my face. She looked perfect, unlike her mother, who was sprawled out on the couch high on snow and as sallow-skinned as a zombie.

This baby was strong. She'd barely been alive a few months and, already, she was a survivor.

Just like her father.

Just like... me.

Chapter 6

I located the group resting in an alley behind a shopping strip. Alice was the first to greet us. Brian followed behind her and Kareena hung back. She looked unsure, or... uncomfortable. I caught her glaring at Lucy.

No way she could have figured it out that quickly, right?

No. She was smart, but so was I.

Guilty conscience.

"Hi," Alice said in a gentle voice, bending down to eye level with Lucy, who was now grabbing my hand and huddling near me. "My name's Alice."

Lucy tilted her head to the side and her grasp on me loosened.

"My name's Lucy," she said, raising her hand up and waving shyly.

"Your sister's adorable," Alice said, looking up at me. "She definitely looks a lot like you."

I shrugged. "But she's the prettier one."

Alice laughed.

Lucy was remarkably intelligent for a five-year-old. I'd coached her early on about the importance of hiding her true relationship to me from new people. Eli knew the truth, but I wasn't ready to come clean with the Fluorescent Ones. For a lot of reasons...

Okay.

Mainly Kareena.

I couldn't imagine Brian and Alice freaking out about the difference between her being either my daughter or my sister, but Kareena—definitely. Even now, she was straggling several feet behind the others, leaning up against a brick wall, pretending not to watch us.

Brian approached Lucy next and knelt down to greet her—a small gesture that made me grin. He was a few inches taller than Alice, but his coming down to Lucy's level made him much less intimidating.

"Hey," he said, offering her a hand. "Nice to meet you, Lucy. I'm Brian."

She looked down at her feet and shuffled in place bashfully.

"It's okay, Lucy," I assured her, setting a hand on her shoulder. "He's a friend."

"I know," she muttered. "Hi, B-Brian." She tangled her hands together, wrinkled her lips to the side, and continued to look away from him.

Brian glanced at me, confused, and I shrugged again.

"Well, uh... Lucy," Brian added. "I'll try to get Kareena to come over and say hi." He came to his feet. "Alright?"

I nodded. "Thanks."

Brian walked off. Alice followed, waving sweetly at Lucy again before turning away. She seemed to really like her for some reason. Or maybe she just liked kids in general. I couldn't tell.

I looked down at my little girl and grinned. "You like him, don't you?" I asked, once Brian was out of earshot.

"I don't know..." Lucy lied, twiddling her fingers.

I knew meeting Brian had made her a little nervous, but there were obviously some other budding emotions swirling around in her head at the time. It made me chuckle. Maybe Brian and I didn't hit it off so well at first, but Lucy clearly had a fondness for him already.

Why on Earth the kid was so freaking popular with girls was beyond me.

Finally, Kareena came over. It was strange seeing her

without the glittering diamond stud on her nose. She crossed her arms and scrunched her lips, making no effort to hide her discontent.

"Hi," she said, glancing at Lucy and looking away. "I'm Kareena. Um..." Her gaze met mine briefly. "I don't like to be bothered, so try not to get in my way, okay?"

I narrowed my eyes at her and mouthed "what the hell?" at her through clenched teeth.

"What?" she said, raising her voice. "I don't like kids, okay? Quit judging. I just... don't. I know she's part of your family, but she's not part of mine. I'm being honest."

Lucy whimpered and reached up for my hand.

"It's okay," I said, running my fingers through Lucy's hair. "She's joking. I promise. Why don't you go talk to Brian and Alice for a minute? They want to be your friends."

She squeezed my hand harder but then worked up the nerve to let go and jaunted over to where the others were standing.

"Now that was a dumbass thing to say." I sneered at Kareena. "Really."

"Sorry." Kareena scoffed. "I'm not going to pretend I like kids when I don't and I'm not obligated to. I didn't like that boy Brian had to stay with when he was being fostered either, and he was, like, ten or something. What's she? Like, three?"

"Five," I corrected. "And old enough to do a hell of a lot on her own. Don't judge *her*, either."

"Okay. Whatever." She huffed beneath her breath. "God."

I almost wanted to call her out on her idiotic behavior— at how irrationally uncomfortable she was around a child. She was overreacting.

"You got back fast," she said, interrupting my chain of thought.

"Uh, yeah. With some help."

"Oh, shit." Kareena's eyes widened.

"No. Not the Saviors," I replied. "The Prism, I think. I

couldn't tell, but I think it was one of their portals."

"Oh, good." She heaved a sigh of relief. "I was... sort of wondering if they'd step in to help. They said they were watching us and..." She looked down at my wrist. I'd have forgotten about the alien bracelet already if it weren't for the subtle plume of white I could always see curling around my wrist. "With the bracelets and everything... I was sure they'd do something for us if we needed them to."

"Yeah, but... not without reason," I said, taking a deep breath. "Don't tell Brian yet, but people saw me. They... saw my light."

"Oh, no! How could you let them!? How the hell did you—"

"I didn't do it on purpose! Quiet down!" I shot a look at the others who were now sitting on the ground beside Lucy, talking. "I was trying to get Lucy back and some cops showed up, some shit went down, and my fluorescence started glowing right while I was standing in the middle of the damn yard."

Kareena groaned. "Oh, crap. Now what? What if they start to think something's going on? What if people start looking for us? Or... fluorescence?"

"I don't know right now."

"Did you notice anyone taking pictures?"

"Not that I saw. It was just for a minute or two. That's all! The cops were going to try to take Lucy away. I panicked, and it just happened."

"We need to be more careful," she interrupted. "The other day, I saw on the news something about a mystery disease that's killing random people around the states. I mean, if they start to actually *see* weird shit happening, we're going to be really, really screwed."

"I know. I know." I closed my eyes and took in a deep breath. Then I exhaled and opened them. "It's hard enough to find a safe place to sleep at night. If people start asking too many questions, we could all be in trouble. But I'm not going to let anything happen to us. I'll make sure we're safe. We're going to have to stay alert for any information we can find on how much people know about us and the disease going around."

"Sounds like a good idea." Kareena fell silent and looked back at the others. "Is *she* going to be okay? With us, I mean?"

"You mean with *you*?" I replied, with a trace of "back-off" in my voice.

"She's just a little kid. We can barely get by as it is."

"I've been taking care of her for this long, Kareena. Leave her to me and don't worry about her." I took a step closer and looked into her tired eyes. I wanted to be angry with her for being so rude to Lucy, but I knew Kareena was only using her attitude to mask her fear.

She was scared. She needed support and she desperately wanted someone to care about her, even when she pretended not to. Brian cared, but not in the way she hoped he would. Not the way I had begun to...

A stroke of my fingers through her hair provoked a fleeting smile in her eyes.

"I'll try not to worry so much, David," she whispered.

My fingers drifted down her arm and I smiled. "Thanks."

I wanted her to trust that I had at least a *few* things under control, even if I didn't...

Chapter 7

"The death toll has risen from 216 to approximately 587 statewide, due to what many are calling the Ghost Plague. In less than one week, the number of deaths has nearly tripled, leaving scientists baffled and the public outraged. The increase in sudden deaths by the phantom killer doctors and scientists are still struggling to decode has government officials warning people to stay vigilant but stay calm. Officials report there is no evidence that the infection is transmitted through the air or by physical contact.

Doctor Matthew Hannigan, a senior microbiologist with the CDC, claimed at a recent panel that doctors have been unable to find any information on exactly how this disease chooses its victims. We attempted to contact Dr. Hannigan for questioning, but he has not returned our calls. A spokesperson for the CDC has assured the public that they are doing everything they can to find a cause and cure for what some believe could be the next SARS pandemic."

"No shit, it's not SARS," Kareena said, clicking off the television and tossing the remote onto the end table. She lay down on the hotel bed and kicked off her shoes. "Good luck finding a cure for something you can't see," she added and glanced back at me. Her expression turned solemn. "Sorry, David."

Whatever was killing people was inside me, too. Kareena was the only person who could actually see it, but that didn't mean I could ignore the gut feeling creeping through me that something was wrong with my body—even before she had pointed it out. It could end me in an instant. Without warning.

Kareena once told me it was probably from smoking, but we both knew that wasn't the truth. That, and she was a hypocrite for assuming I would be the only one dying if that were the case. She harbored the habit, too. Albeit, intermittently.

I stood in front of the window, peering out at the quiet, near-empty driveway. Fireflies flashed against a colorful backdrop. Dusk rolled in, cloaking the sky in rich, dark colors.

Now that we were migrating closer to my home state where people might recognize me, I held off waving around my fake detective's badge. Without it, a couple of sweet, carefully baked lies helped us grab two rooms at a small Ma and Pa style motel just on the outskirts of the city.

"So, I take it we're not going to be alone again any time soon," Kareena said, crossing her arms and looking over her shoulder at me.

Lucy lay on her stomach, propped up on her elbows, busying herself with an activity book Brian had purchased for her from a nearby gas station. I was grateful he accepted her presence with such grace, unlike...

"She's not deaf," I said, turning to face Kareena.

I walked past the bed where Lucy was coloring and ran my fingers playfully over the top of her head. She craned her neck up at me, squinted and grinned, and then went back to work on her connect-the-dots page. Crude, unsteady lines were a sign of fatigue.

"Yes. I know," Kareena answered.

"You really think you're entitled to everything, don't you?" I added, sitting down on the corner of Kareena's bed.

She huffed angrily. "Your loss."

"What? What does that mean?" I touched her arm.

She looked me up and down quickly and her lips thinned. "If you don't know, I'm not going to spell it out for you."

"You have got to be kidding me." I laughed. "All this shit goes down, people are dying—*I* might be dying—and all you're thinking about is—" I lowered my voice to a whisper, "...sex?"

"I don't know what you're talking about." She looked away.

"I don't even know how to respond to that, Kareena." I stood and walked back over to Lucy, who was now stretching her arms out over her head and yawning.

"So where's she sleeping?" Kareena asked, raising her voice. "On the couch or..."

"We have two beds. She can sleep with me," I replied.

She cocked an eyebrow. "Aren't you a little old to be sleeping with your sister?"

"Aren't you a little old to have your nose in everyone else's shit?"

She sneered and flipped me off. All I could do was shake my head and wonder why in the hell I was attracted to such a coldhearted bitch that flaunted her dislike of children like a gold medal. In her defense, a beautiful coldhearted bitch who had recently saved both of our asses from that psychopathic brother of Brian's, Taylor.

"Lucy," I said, and bent down to draw her attention away from her activity book. "You should be getting to bed. Come on." I slid the book away from her and reached out my hand to take her marker. She relinquished it without a fight, yawned again, and rubbed her drowsy eyes with her palms.

I tucked Lucy into bed and pulled the blanket up to her chin. As I came down to kiss her forehead, she curled her delicate fingers around the hem and closed her eyes. "Goodnight," I whispered. She smiled and rolled onto her side, nuzzling her pillow.

"Night," she muttered and wriggled further down beneath the covers.

I clicked off the lamp on her side of the bed and walked over to the bathroom tucked in the back of the room. Kareena was sitting on the edge of the counter with her arms crossed and her head down.

"What's wrong?" I stepped in and closed the door behind me so the light wouldn't keep Lucy awake.

Kareena looked up and sighed, fatigued.

"Kareena?" I reached for her shoulder. "What is it?" My fingers cupped the side of her arm and I resisted the urge to try to bring her closer to me. "Tell me, please." I shifted my touch from her arm to her chin, gently lifting her face.

Her pleasing green irises looked back at me and my heart swelled with emotion. Even without a smudge of makeup on it, Kareena's face was beautiful. The rich warm color of her skin and the subtle natural rose tint on her lips accented the perfection.

"What do we do now?" Her eyes pleaded for an honest answer.

There wasn't much we could do.

"I don't know," I replied. "But I'm going to do what I can to protect the two of you. I may not have a chance in hell at surviving whatever it is that's infecting me, but I'll do anything and everything to fight back." I forked my fingers through her hair and tried to smile reassuringly. "Believe me, I will."

I leaned in to kiss her, but she turned her face away before I could.

"I need sleep," she said.

Her frigid reaction left me at a loss for words.

Then I remembered what she had said to me the first time we'd gotten together. She didn't want things getting "messy."

Was I complicating things?

"Sorry," I muttered, really only half apologizing for my actions.

"It's alright," she added, still looking away from me. "I'm going to go to sleep. Goodnight, David."

She cracked open the door and I flipped off the bathroom

light as we exited.

•　　•　　•

I heard a voice in my sleep.

A small, mousey voice.

Words I couldn't put together in my dreams until I realized whose voice it was.

Lucy?

I was sure of it.

My eyes opened. I rolled over in bed and a wave of fear and dread washed over me, prickling my skin with goose bumps and gnarling my stomach into knots.

Lucy was sitting up beside me, legs crossed, her hands in her lap. Her eyes were fixated on a slightly smaller shape across from her.

A soft white glow resonated from the shape. I tried to speak, but words wouldn't come out.

"Lu-Lucy." It was barely audible. Fear choked the breath from me.

"He's one of the friends you promised," she said cheerfully.

My gaze darted toward her tiny wrist where a faint tail of smoke swirled.

A bracelet? From the Prism?

Another lamp clicked on.

"Holy shit!" Kareena threw her covers off to the side and crawled across her bed toward us.

The white light faded. The thing sitting with Lucy was a child. A tiny, naked little boy with a pillowcase draped over his back and shoulders like a cape.

"Who are you?" I inched closer. He couldn't have been more than three or four years old. His hair looked brown in the dim light and his skin was extremely fair.

The child glanced up at me and I flinched when our gazes

met.

His eyes were different colors. I couldn't tell which colors, exactly, in the poor lighting, but one was darker than the other. I could see that much.

"Solus is shy," Lucy replied, grinning. "But he showed me pictures."

Solus?

I was confused by what she had just said, and then I was even more confused by how calm she was acting, despite his nakedness. She'd always been very intelligent and composed for her age, though.

"Showed you?" I leaned closer to her but kept my eyes locked on the frail little boy. "How? How did he show you?"

Kareena stood beside us, watching from the edge of the bed.

The boy brought a hand toward my face and I drew back. He froze, hand hovering midair, and stared at me. His expression was gentle. Inquisitive. I was more confused than frightened. Unnerved by the soft white glow that radiated from the boy before Kareena had switched on the lamp.

I didn't feel threatened by him now that I could see that he was, presumably, human.

Still...

"It's okay," Lucy said, taking me by the hand to coax me closer. "Don't be scared."

I held my breath and leaned closer to the boy, permitting his fingers to rise toward my brow again. Three fingertips pressed against my temple and everything around me vanished.

Chapter 8

*T*he *Solus Child.*

That's what the Saviors had been calling him.

Solus' fingers lifted away from my temple and the room came back into view.

"David?" Kareena came up beside me and set her hand on my shoulder. "There's something I need to tell you. Right now."

"I think I already know," I whispered.

Solus had showed me everything.

He was the only one of his kind, the only true hybrid—the authentic offspring of two Fluorescent Ones. He also showed me what should have been his twin sister, the one who died early on in development upon exposure to the virus.

"This is wrong!" Kareena exclaimed, her fingernails starting to dig into my skin. "I don't know how the hell they did it, but I can see it in him. In his face. His color. Holy shit." She threaded her fingers through her hair and tangled them together at the back of her head. "This is so damn wrong. Brian and Alice are going to—"

"Calm down, Kareena," I grabbed her by the wrist when she paced past me.

"Don't you get it!?" She pointed toward the wall separating our room from Brian and Alice's. "This kid is theirs!"

"Shh." I gently tugged her closer. "I know. Now stop freaking out or you're going to scare the crap outta the poor kid."

Solus watched us with widened eyes until Lucy reached over to cup her hands around one of his. His face veered

627

toward her.

"It's okay," she said softly. "Don't be afraid."

Somehow, I didn't think he was afraid. Confused like the rest of us, maybe.

"How did you survive?" Kareena asked, her voice wavering. "We thought you were dead—that the Saviors exposed you to the disease and you..."

Solus lifted his free hand up toward Kareena's face and she gasped, staggering back. "What does he want from me?" Her wrist wriggled and worked its way out of my grasp. "David?"

"It's okay, Kareena," I said, adjusting my hold on her so I could try to bring her nearer to the bedside, toward Solus. "He only wants to show you what he knows. He already showed me and I'm fine. Just let him touch you for a moment."

Kareena glared at me like I was crazy, and the judgmental crinkle in her brow made me feel like she didn't trust me as much as I had hoped. But she conjured up some courage, swallowed hard, and approached Solus. She bent slightly at the waist and let him move his hand up until his pale fingertips made contact with her left temple.

I watched closely, expecting some kind of light or aura to be emitted from the point of contact, but nothing changed—that I could see. Seconds later, Kareena pulled away.

"Jesus!" Her jaw dropped and she backed up and flopped down onto the edge of her bed. "What the hell kind of freaks would do something like this!? What the hell were they thinking?" Then her gaze shot toward me. "Did he show you everything?" she asked, exasperated. "Did he show you what those sick bastards did to Alice and Brian?"

I shook my head. "The only things I saw in the visions were of Solus, his twin, and the Saviors." I saw enough to put two and two together, but nothing more. "Why? What happened?"

"About a year ago," Kareena started, "I saw a new color

inside of Alice—bright turquoise. Which meant...”

Mixed colors. That made sense to me. Like the flame-red our own fluorescence made when we...

“So they slept together,” I replied with a shrug. “So?”

“Actually, they hadn’t... at the time. The Saviors wanted Alice and Brian to, well, hook up and make some kind of GMO baby. And when they didn’t, the Saviors stepped in and...”

“Impregnated her?” My stomach started to feel uneasy.

“Yes. But things changed. The Saviors kept screwing with us and they ended up taking the fetus out of her after a few months. It was exposed to the disease and...”

“That’s insane.” I glanced at Solus, who was now being introduced to a coloring book by Lucy. The tilt of his head as she tried to explain her connect-the-dot work to him convinced me the kid had never touched a marker in his life.

“I mean, they kind of thought they were actually going to have a baby together,” Kareena added, looking down at her lap. “Then shit happened. She was pretty messed up for a while after that.”

Brian, too, no doubt. I know how it feels to have a child snatched away from you.

“Who wouldn’t be?” I replied.

I flexed my fingers, made a fist, and knocked lightly on the hotel door.

I heard movement, then a slow turn of the deadbolt lock. My heart jumped into my throat and the pounding in my chest made my breath shudder.

The door opened.

“David?” Brian’s half-open eyes looked up at me. “Wh-what is it?”

“We need you to come to our room. There’s something we need to talk to you about.” Thinking of Solus put my stomach in knots. I didn’t know Brian nearly as well as the others, but I knew him well enough to predict how much this was

---

going to tear his heart open. "Bring Alice, too," I added. "Please."

Like it had happened yesterday, I recalled exactly how I felt the moment I realized Lucy was my baby girl. She filled a place in my heart I never even knew was empty, and I learned to love her with all of my heart and soul. Then I remembered how pissed off, scared, confused, and hurt I was, too. How, at the time, I couldn't begin to imagine what life with a kid might be like for a guy like me.

"Oh, okay," Brian muttered, cocking an eyebrow.

"Alice," he turned and called to her. She came shuffling up beside him and he opened the door wider so she could see me.

"Come with me, please," I said softly to her. "Just... try to stay calm."

At this point, I noticed Brian's adrenaline beginning to kick in as his expression became more alert. His eyes opened wider. His posture straightened.

"Calm?" Brian repeated.

"You'll understand soon," I added, then turned and headed back to the others.

Solus was sitting with Lucy at the far end of the room, looking out the window at the night sky. As I approached, he turned toward me and blinked a few times.

"Come with me," I said.

I offered him my hand and he studied it for a moment. His grasp was feathery soft, like a baby's. Gentle. Warm. I led him to the other side of the room where Brian and Alice stood. Kareena remained tucked off to the side, watching in silence.

"Who is that?" Alice asked, taking a few steps in front of Brian.

Solus let go of my hand and walked up to her, his colorful irises sparkling with awe. He tipped his head and blinked some more, narrowing his eyes in deep study. Then a look of surprise erupted across his face and he gasped.

The sight made my heart skip a beat.

Alice knelt down in front of him and lifted her fingers toward his cheek, sweeping a lock of his unkempt light-brown hair away from his eyes and over his ear. The two stared at each other for several moments. Silent. Unmoving. I held my breath in anticipation of her next words. I think Brian did, too.

Solus raised a hand toward her brow and pressed three fingertips against her unflinching temple.

Alice snapped her eyes closed and grunted, then her eyes opened and she took in a deep, trembling breath.

She turned. Tears glistened in her eyes. The reaction sent Brian dashing to her side.

"Alice?" He came down onto his knees and looked at the boy. "What is it?" He glanced at Alice and then at Solus. Alice covered her mouth with her hands and started weeping more heavily, hunching over, burying her face behind a curtain of her hair as she sobbed.

"Alice?" Brian tried again, but she only kept crying into her hands, ignoring him. "Tell me what's going on. Please!"

Alice turned her head and muttered something to Brian. I could barely read her lips as she said it.

"Oh my God." Brian sat back on his heels. "How? How the hell? I thought…" His breaths hastened.

The pain on his face got to me, making my eyes burn with sympathy. I knew exactly what he was feeling right then and there. My own heart pulsed with memories of the day I found Lucy.

I glanced at Kareena, who was looking off to the side, uncomfortable, and upset, too. Her short, fleeting breaths were a sign that she fighting back her own emotions.

Solus reached out to take Brian's head into his hands, his slender fingers weaving into Brian's hair. He pulled him into an embrace, wrapping his arms around Brian's neck.

Brian softened into the hug and embraced him back, bringing his arms around Solus. Alice shuffled closer and threw her arms around the two of them, tears still pouring from her eyes.

This time, I heard the muffled words come from her mouth.

"He's ours," she murmured, and sucked in another labored breath.

"I... know," Brian replied, his voice breaking.

I knew the Saviors were keeping secrets from us, but for them to hide something so important—so incredibly personal and monumental—from these two was beyond comprehension. I could only begin to imagine the anger and confusion welling up inside Brian and Alice as they discovered the truth about what the Saviors had done.

Solus: the son they didn't know they had.

Chapter 9

Alice wiped tears from her cheeks. "I don't understand. If he's ours—which we both know he is," she said, glancing at Brian, "why is he so big already? He's more than a year old, right?" She looked at me for an answer.

"Oh, yeah," I replied with a nod. "He's definitely at least three. Maybe four. I can't tell."

"It's the time difference," Brian said. "I don't know what it is, exactly, but I remember back when I was with the Jamesons." He looked at me. "They were a temporary foster family I was with while Alice's mom, Jane, tried to get custody of me after my mom, well, tried to kill herself."

I grimaced. "Christ. I didn't know you'd been through something like that, too." Kareena shot me a curious look. "I mean... Nothing. Sorry. Go on."

I didn't feel like sharing.

My father died from a mid-life crisis—he committed suicide.

Makes you feel like absolute shit, that's for sure—when you lose someone that way. Especially when it happens a few days before you're able to introduce them to their new grandchild.

"When I was with them at breakfast one morning," Brian continued, "the Saviors abducted me and then threw me back down minutes later, but it had literally only been about a second. The Jamesons didn't even notice I had disappeared. So... if they can do that, maybe time passes differently there. So much that if Solus were raised with them, it would explain why he's a lot older than he would be if had remained down here with us."

"I second that theory, actually," Kareena interjected. I focused my attention on her as she continued. "That happened to me back at the hotel." She looked sheepishly toward me. "That, uh, morning... after... um, the earthquake. We were talking and I spaced out. You know what I'm talking about, David. Right?"

"Oh? That was them?" I remembered that morning vividly, because it was the morning after we'd hooked up. When we were talking, she froze for a second or two and then came back. I thought she was just lost in thought, but apparently not.

"Whatever the reason," Brian interrupted, "we both know who he is."

"Yeah." I turned around. Lucy and Solus were on the other side of the room on the bed. Lucy had fallen back to sleep on my pillow and Solus was sitting up beside her, forking his fingers through her long black hair as if he were stroking a kitten's fur. I couldn't understand how the kid had grown fond of my little girl so quickly. He seemed very gentle for a boy his age. Typically, they're running around, day or night, looking for trouble as soon as they are old enough to walk.

Solus had an almost angelic calmness to his demeanor. The way his hand drifted over Lucy's hair and he cocked his head curiously as he watched her sleep.

"Solus?" Alice called to him tenderly.

The boy turned, as if he'd already accepted the word as his name.

"Come here, please," she asked.

Solus scooted to the edge of the bed and dropped off the side. Then he walked over to Alice and stood attentively, staring up at her.

"Can you speak?" she asked.

Solus blinked a few times and then his lips parted. He

took a breath, closed his mouth, and looked away as if the attempt made him uneasy.

"It's okay." Brian knelt in front of him. "You don't have to talk if you're not ready or able. We just need to know that you understand what we're saying to you."

Solus nodded.

"Stay close to us. Okay?" Brian continued. "We'll protect you. I promise."

I saw the beginning of a grin curl Solus' lips. It vanished in a second, though, as he fought back what must have been an unfamiliar urge. If the Saviors raised him, it was no wonder he didn't understand how to smile. Still, he seemed content—pleased to be with his real parents, even if he wasn't showing it.

"Do you think you can go to sleep for a little while tonight?" Brian asked. Solus tipped his head to the side. "Do you... even know what sleep is?"

Solus stared blankly and blinked again. The kid did a lot of blinking.

Brian looked back at Alice and shrugged.

It was only two in the morning and we were all exhausted.

"Like her." I pointed at Lucy. "Sleep."

Solus squinted and then his eyes widened like he'd had a revelation. He hoisted himself onto the bed, crawled up beside Lucy, and clumsily attempted to make himself comfortable on the pillow across from her. He kneaded the pillow and nestled his head into it, analyzing Lucy as if he were checking to see that he'd done it correctly. Then he curled up into a fetal position and squeezed his eyes shut, his face crinkling from the pitiful, forced attempt.

The poor kid recognized what sleep was, but it didn't look as if he'd ever been naturally induced into it.

"Uh, we can switch rooms, or whatever you guys want," I said to Brian and Alice. "But you guys have to look after Lucy for the rest of the night, too, please. I don't know if taking her away would be a good idea right now. He seems to be acclimating with her around."

"Yeah. I see that," Brian said softly. "Hmm."

"I'll grab him some clothes first thing in the morning." I rummaged around in my pocket. "I've got enough money to take care of it for you."

"Thanks." A tired smile curved Brian's lips. "We'd appreciate that. A lot. Yes. We'll keep an eye on Lucy for you. I won't let anything happen to her."

Alice sat on the edge of the bed beside Solus and pulled a blanket up to his neck. She rested her hand on his bony little shoulder and the strain on his face melted away. He murmured a small, contented sigh.

"It's okay," she whispered. "We'll protect you from them now."

"You guys need sleep. You can stay in our room," Brian said. "Get some rest."

Kareena shrugged and slinked away from her corner toward the door.

I glanced back at Lucy—who was sound asleep across from Solus—and assured myself she was in good hands.

Brian meant what he said. I knew he did.

Surprisingly, closing that door behind me on my way out was less difficult than it had been in the past.

She'll be fine.

Chapter 10

"We're completely screwed!" Kareena's words woke me abruptly. "I'm not the only one who knows this, right?"

"Wh-what?" I rolled over to face her, still half asleep. She was sitting on the edge of the bed, bent over, with her feet on the floor and her face in her hands.

"We're screwed. The Saviors must be totally pissed off about this whole Solus Child thing. I mean, really. The Prism seemed helpful at first, but to just drop this bomb on us. Seriously!? What kind of shit is this!?"

"What do you mean?" I sat up and rubbed my eyes with my palms, then dropped my head back and to the sides to work a cramp out of my neck. I glanced at the clock beside the bed. 7:45AM.

"You *do* know how the Prism got Solus, right?"

I shook my head. *Nope.* I slid my gun out from beneath my pillow and tucked it into the back of my jeans.

"They kidnapped him from the Saviors. And for a race of aliens who don't show a lot of emotion, they're pissed."

"How do you know all of this?" I stretched my arms up over my head.

"They told me this morning," Kareena replied with a growl, crossing her arms. "God damn them. I thought they were our friends. I thought they were helping us. Now this? Like we need the damn Saviors at our throats any more than they already have been."

I didn't like the sound of anything she was saying. We didn't need the Saviors on our asses. They were powerful.

And we... we were pawns in their game. Weak. Disposable. *Human.*

"This isn't good," I replied, trying to shake off the frustration and fear pulsing through my veins. "We can't be held accountable for something the Prism did. The Saviors might kill us for it! They might kill..." I shot off the bed and hustled toward the door. "I'm going to wake the others."

"Wait! Wait!" Kareena raised her voice. She rushed over to me before I could open the door. "Can't you wait a damn second?"

"What?" I was itching to check on Lucy.

"The Prism told me something else."

"Yeah? Spit it out."

"Since Solus survived full-on exposure to the disease, they thought he could help us. Or... *you.*"

I could still feel it—the corrupted light shooting through my bloodstream. The unnerving tightness in my chest at night while I tried to force myself to sleep.

"Maybe." I shrugged. "But we don't know that for certain."

"No, but that's why they want us to protect him."

"Protect him!? We can't even protect ourselves, damn it!" I felt a lump in my throat all of a sudden and my heart started pounding against my ribcage. "But we don't even know if he's safe to be around."

"Solus is human, after all. I can see the light in him— Brian and Alice's. And you'd have to be pretty damn blind to not see the resemblance, too. He's not a threat. The Prism know that much, but they also know he's better suited for our atmosphere than their own."

Kareena had told me briefly about the dark, starry sky-like world of the Prism. From what I remember, it was a scattershot of sparkling lights in a sea of dark blue emptiness. That's all I could take from her story. The description reminded me of swimming in the ocean at night. Weightlessness. Twilight twinkling beneath the bright white halo of the moon. But that may have been my own nostalgia. The serene Hawaiian shores after dark.

I missed my childhood home...

Maybe, I just missed having a home.

.　　　.　　　.

Solus made me nervous. I needed to keep Lucy safe at all costs. The Prism were helpful enough to arm her with one of their anti-abduction bracelets, and for that I was grateful. But that wouldn't keep us out of the line of fire. If the Saviors were pissed about losing their hybrid, we'd be facing their wrath soon, for sure.

How long did we have? How would we deal with them?

I had a plan.

I *always* had a plan.

Until today.

Lucy trotted past me, down the hall, leaving Solus behind her. He was bewildered and unsure if he should follow. He also kept stopping to fidget with his shirt and tug at the collar.

His new set of clothes, while they required some getting used to, made him look *normal*. A green shirt screen-printed with the image of a dinosaur, khaki pants, and a pair of white sneakers. It all fit him well enough. For now.

"Be careful, Lucy!" I called. "Quit running around and get back here, please."

Kareena and Brian had gone to check out of our rooms. I waited with Alice and the children.

Lucy frowned and sulked back toward us. Solus didn't seem to want to stray more than a few feet from his mother.

Now that morning light was shining through the waiting room windows, I could see Solus had vibrant light skin with a subtle pink undertone, unlike the Saviors' ghostly white flesh. The child was small and fragile, with medium-length, straight, unkempt brown hair.

I leaned down and smiled at him. "You've got very pretty eyes."

He didn't know how to respond.

He had one fair blue eye and one deep green eye. The first thing to mind was the irony of the colors, but before I could carry the assumption for long...

"They're heterochromatic," Alice said.

"Hetero-what?" I raised an eyebrow.

"It's a genetic thing. Brian has it," she continued. "I don't know if you've noticed, but he has a dark brown spot in one of his eyes."

I nodded. I had noticed, actually.

"That's from a genetic trait called heterochromia. It causes people's irises to be different colors or to have splotches of different colors in them."

"And they teach you this stuff in high school nowadays?"

"No." She looked away sheepishly. "I sorta looked it up back when we were first going out. I didn't know what it was and felt like an idiot having to ask him. Didn't want to make him self-conscious."

"Ah. So, you think that's why Solus has two different colored eyes?"

"Yeah. Yay for the Internet, huh?" She let out an awkward chuckle and then cleared her throat. "Anyway."

"So we're calling him Solus, then?"

"Yes," Alice replied. "Brian and I talked about it last night and, well, it fits. I guess. We don't really know what else to call him and after we heard Lucy using it..." She fell silent.

"I like it," I said. Alice immediately looked me in the eye.

"You do? It's not stupid or weird, is it?"

"Nah. I think it fits. He's one of a kind, after all."

"Yeah. He is." Alice smiled with her eyes.

She didn't smile much. Not around me, at least. I couldn't blame her for her sadness. She was at that age where she should have been out growing up, having fun with girlfriends, and

640

doing whatever the hell she wanted to with her boyfriend. But they were being forced to act like adults and play house with a child they didn't even know they had.

I'll give Brian credit. He sure as hell didn't miss a beat when he found out about Solus. He took on the responsibility like he was meant for it. Just accepted it without question.

If only I could have been that brave.

"David?" Alice whispered my name.

"Yeah?"

She looked down nervously. "I... we—Brian and I—were wondering about something." She looked over at Lucy.

My heart started beating faster.

"Yes?"

"Please, don't be offended by this, but I didn't want to ask you in front of Kareena because, well, I'm pretty sure I understand why you wouldn't want her to know. But I kind of want to know the truth. Just so I can stop wondering about it. Is... Lucy your sister, or is she actually your—"

"Daughter."

"That's what I thought, but, you kept telling us she was your sister, and... I don't know. It seemed wrong to assume otherwise. But when we saw her, I had a feeling that she was even more precious to you than that. She looks so much like you, David."

"Don't tell Kareena," I said quietly. "Please. Not yet."

"I won't, but you *need* to. Before she finds out. She's not stupid."

"I never said she was." I looked away.

"I think Lucy's a beautiful little girl," she added.

"Yeah."

I didn't know how else to respond. I was too busy thinking about how I could break the news to Kareena without her freaking out on me. She didn't like kids *at all*. Obvious by the way she treated them.

I had to come up with some way to tell her. I had to stop

keeping secrets if I wanted a chance at having a real relationship with her.

She needed to be able to trust me.

I heard footsteps and turned. Brian and Kareena came walking toward us. Kareena's head was down and Brian had a discontented sneer on his lips.

"What is it?" I asked.

Kareena glanced up at me for a split second and shook her head, pressing her lips thin. I recognized that look.

"We have to fix this," Brian grumbled. "This is a nightmare. So many people are infected."

"Let me guess," I said, clasping Lucy's hand. "The man at the front desk?"

"The man at the front desk," Brian confirmed.

Chapter 11

My skin tingled. It was the familiar, stomach-twisting, skin-prickling feeling that came just before being abducted. I crouched down, shielded Lucy with my embrace, and held my breath.

The others felt it, too.

Worried, Alice knelt beside Solus. He appeared unaffected by what was going on.

"No!" Brian clenched his fists. "I thought the Prism said—"

Lucy coughed. "Daddy, I feel weird," she whimpered. I tried to calm her with a stroke of my fingers down the back of her head.

"It's okay. I think." I glanced at Kareena. An angry sneer crinkled her lips. She must have heard what Lucy had called me.

Shit.

The feeling intensified until my entire body itched from the overwhelming sensation of static electricity swallowing me up. Then my lungs tightened. The air was getting thinner.

"What's happening?" I looked at Kareena again, believing that, somehow, she knew what the hell was actually happening. She was fuming with anger and trying to fight back fear at the same time.

Then our surroundings blurred and a pale glow engulfed us.

This time, we didn't fall.

I squinted against the searing light and tried to focus on the approaching shape. My body tensed.

643

Tall. Grey. *Savior?*

I mean, I was pretty damn sure it was a Savior, but its face was partially covered with a silver mask. The metallic thing covering its nose and mouth was about the size of a compact respirator, with notches on the sides and a row of translucent blue rivets running along the top. The rivets faded in and out as if an energy source were pumping through them. Sensors? LEDs? I couldn't tell what they were, and the mask definitely didn't make the thing any more approachable.

Lucy grabbed on to me and yelped.

"What do you want?" Brian growled. He was the first to confront the Savior.

I looked at the blurry shapes surrounding us. We were inside a cylindrical space, separated from the outside world by a transparent wall of distortions. I wondered if we could somehow step outside the barrier, but with Lucy holding tightly to me, I wasn't about to take a chance.

"We need the Solus Child back," the Savior said, his voice barely altered by the mouthpiece.

I assumed it was the translator, as the others had never spoken to us.

"You're never getting Solus back," Brian snapped. "Damn you for keeping him from us to begin with!"

"You did not want him in the beginning," the translator said, matter-of-factly.

"Shut up! You've got a lot of damn nerve coming down here to face us."

"The child is a vital part of the future of our species," the translator added.

"And now he's a vital part of *ours!*" Brian looked at Alice and his son, then back at the Savior.

Kareena came up beside him.

"Leave us alone," she said, raising a hand to flaunt her Prism bracelet. "You can't abduct us right now and you know it. Just go away. Go back to wherever the hell you're from and leave us alone. We've got enough on our plates trying to save our own asses from this shit you did to us."

Damn, she could be brave when she wanted to be. *Or... maybe it was because Brian was involved.*

"You're not taking the kid," I said protectively, lifting my chin, inching closer but not letting go of Lucy.

The Saviors were taller than us all, but that didn't intimidate me. Height didn't equal power, and if they had the power to take Solus from us with force, they'd have done so already.

The translator stared at me and I glared back, unable to keep my eyes from wandering toward the bottom half of his face. The constantly twinkling blue beads of light on his mask distracted me.

"I see," he replied flatly. "You are willing to sacrifice an entire world to protect a single child?"

"Don't play mind games with me," Brian said. "Our own world is in trouble now, too. You went behind our backs and kept our child a secret from us this entire time. You can suffer the consequences of your own actions."

"The Solus Child is a danger to your race. His genetic material will be a threat to others—started or not."

"You're lying," Alice said. "You're lying because you're scared."

"He is ours." The Savior took a step closer and reached toward Solus.

"No!" Alice lunged at the translator and shoved his arm to the side, then she gasped, frightened by her own actions.

The Savior tipped his head and stared down at her. Brian immediately rushed to her aid. Kareena backed off a little after that, but I took it as my cue to step in.

Golden light warmed my chest and a subtle yellow glow crept down through the veins in my arms.

"Leave the kid alone," I said, squeezing my fists as amber energy pulsed beneath my skin.

The Savior backed away.

I'd heard that Brian had tried to stand up to them at one time, too, but that he was injured in the process. This time, the Savior didn't resist our revolt. Maybe they were getting weaker. Maybe it was because he was alone. Either way, we had the upper hand. Clearly.

"You will regret this act of defiance," he said, narrowing his eyes.

A cloud of white blinded me and everything around us came back into focus. I blinked a few times to adjust my blurred vision.

Damn. That face it made at us.

The translator almost never emoted, but even a forced sneer of anger from the creature made my heart jump into my throat. The words he said were flat and monotone, but... those grey eyes and the frail white brow line leering at me from just above the flashing lights on his silver facemask... That made me feel sick. Lightheaded, almost. And that's not something that's *ever* happened to me before.

"So that was creepy as hell," Kareena said. "Well, I guess these work." She lifted her wrist.

I looked down at the white band of smoke swirling around my own. "Yeah."

"What was that thing on his face?" she asked.

"I don't know." Brian shrugged. "But it's always hard for us to breathe up there, so maybe it's hard for them to breathe down here."

"Solus seems to be doing okay," Alice added, ruffling his hair. He peered up at her.

"He is. But he's human, too," Brian added with a subdued grin.

"You know, the low oxygen up there probably made him a little stronger," I said.

Brian's brow wrinkled. "Why do you say that?"

"There's a type of mask that simulates high altitudes.

Some guys train with them to hold up better in MMA fights. It constricts airflow so your lungs work harder, and you have to train your body and mind to function better under those stressors."

Brian cocked an eyebrow.

"It's crazy, I'll give you that," I continued, "but I've seen guys win fights even after having an opponent block their breathing. Scary shit, but some guys swear by it."

He stared at me and grimaced. "That's messed up."

"Whatever works, right?" I wasn't about to delve into the reason I knew so much about them. "We should get moving. Lucy?" I turned. She was standing beside Solus with an arm draped across his bony shoulders. Lucy's protective nature—probably inherited from me—really shined around him. It was heartwarming, while worrying. How long would Solus be with us? Could he really survive here on Earth? What would Lucy do if he was suddenly ripped away from us?

But all of that wasn't what I needed to focus on right then and there.

"What's the plan?" I asked Brian.

I liked being in charge, but so did he. We agreed to split decisions between us in order to keep things quiet. If Alice and Kareena had something to suggest, we listened. If Brian had a better idea, I listened.

The kid was smart, even though I hated to admit it. There were moments he made me feel like an idiot. If only I'd had my own head screwed on as tightly when I was his age—things might be—

"Whoa!" My wrist felt hot. I looked down. The band of smoky essence radiated with brightly colored light.

I heard a voice.

"There are things we need to show you."

The words echoed not through my ears but through my head. Somehow. It wasn't sound I could hear coming from anywhere around me. The words resonated from a strange place inside my head—my skull. It was only inside me. Inside my brain.

Kareena heard something, too. Her fingertips were pressed to her temples, but I couldn't tell why. She shut her eyes.

Alice and Brian froze in place.

Solus was looking up, unmoved and unafraid, listening intently to a ghost I could not see. Lucy didn't appear to be fazed at all.

"Who?" I opened my mouth to say the word, but before it left my lips, I got a reply.

"*The Prism.*"

The fluttery, subtle voice seethed through my brain and I sucked a breath in through my teeth from the eerie, sickening sensation. Hearing something without my ears.

I looked back at Kareena, who was clenching her jaw and groaning in pain. "Y-you said we were safe!" she bellowed, doubling over to clutch her head in her hands.

Was she getting a migraine from the voice?

"*You are,*" it replied. "*The Saviors are hiding information from you. We want to show you the truth, but we must ask for your permission. We must bring you here and, therefore, require your consent.*"

"What about Lucy? And Solus?" The question drifted through my mind.

"*They will accompany you to the neutral atmosphere we have prepared. We will protect them as we have already.*"

They were right. They rescued Solus from the Saviors and they gave Lucy a bracelet as I slept.

"And, if I agree, will you bring us back here after?" Again, I didn't have time to speak the words before I got my reply.

"*Yes.*"

I couldn't tell if the others were hearing the same thing I was or not. I couldn't tell if they were hearing my voice—

thoughts—whatever they were, or if they were having their own private conversation with the Prism.

"I don't know what it means to you in your language," I started, still only thinking the words I wanted to say, "but promise me you will protect my daughter from harm if we go with you. Please."

"We will. She is important to you and you are important to your people and your world. We promise sanctuary while you are with us."

Before I could verbally agree, a large plume of sparkling silver burst before me. The portal of glistening light spun like a vortex, beams of white intersecting and then splitting through each other to spin around the circumference again.

I took a deep breath and looked at Lucy. She stared up at me with beautiful, trusting brown eyes. I took her hand, stepped into the doorway of endless white, and pulled her through.

The familiar rush of cool air hit me, my surroundings blurred, and my body was propelled into nothingness. We were transported to a vast white room not unlike the glossy interrogation chamber the Saviors brought us to when they wanted to talk. But the air here was different and the temperature mild.

I took in a breath. The air felt no different in my lungs than what I was used to on Earth. The room was tepid. Comfortable.

"Where are we?" Lucy asked, tugging my arm.

Then a flare of white light sparkled beside me and I stepped back. Brian, Alice, and Solus instantly appeared, their gazes quickly taking in the surroundings.

For a split second, I thought Kareena had said no—that she'd had enough.

But then a final blast of white proved me wrong and she arrived, agitated, with a look of immense pain twisting her expression.

"Are you alright?" I turned to her, still clinging to Lucy's hand. "Kareena?"

"No," she muttered, and cupped her forehead with her hand.

"Can I do something?" Brian's arm sparkled with a hint of blue.

"No," she grumbled, turning from him. "It will go away soon. Probably."

"Do the Prism make the headaches worse?" Alice asked.

"Kind of," Kareena replied, shaking her head. "But, whatever. Just don't worry about it." She cringed.

I reached out for her hand.

"Kareena," I whispered, trying to get her to look me in the eye. "Kareena, it's okay to ask for help."

"You think I don't know that?" Her face shot up and her narrowed eyes met mine. "Just leave me the hell alone right now. I don't want your help."

"Okay. Okay." I backed off. "I'm sorry."

I caught her glare at Lucy just before wincing and rubbing her temples again.

Lucy's fingers squeezed mine.

"I don't know where we are, but Solus is here." I motioned toward him. "And he's being good. I don't think you need to be scared."

Solus stood between Alice and Brian, looking off into the empty white distance in anticipation.

"What is it?" Alice set a hand on his shoulder. He turned toward her and then lifted up his arm and pointed forward. "I don't see anything."

We all looked off in the direction he was pointing and waited. The room was completely silent. So quiet, I could hear everyone breathing, including myself. I swear my heartbeat was louder than anything though, and I felt it throbbing in my chest.

Then Solus' eyes grew wide and he marched off after

something.

Without a sound, a massive hole opened in front of us, as if a curtain was being drawn to reveal a movie-theater-sized window so tall and wide, it nearly devoured us.

I cleared my throat and gawked at the monstrous opening. It encompassed almost half of the room, surrounding us in a semi-circle of glass—like a snow globe. But we weren't looking into a ball of plastic glitter. We were looking out... at the Earth.

A ball of greens and blues, browns and whites, hanging before a backdrop of star-studded black. Tiny white lights flickered subtly in the ocean of space.

"Is... that..." Brian cautiously walked a few steps closer so he could reach his son. Solus took a seat very close to the window and stared out. He turned his head and gestured with his hand for Lucy to come join him. She let go of me and darted off.

"L-Lucy!" I called out, but she ignored me and plopped down beside Solus, cross-legged. Together, they peered intently out at the stars.

Somehow, I think she trusted Solus more than she trusted me. Then again, I was starting to wonder if he knew things we didn't.

I approached the window slowly, half of me wondering if we might fall right out of the place if we got too close. We knew nothing about their technological limits.

It was straight off one of those satellite images often seen in magazines—the Earth floated in a sea of blackness, so close, yet so far away. Clear enough to make out the silhouettes of the continents. The vivid blue and aqua oceans saturated with radiant color. Misty clouds wafted across the surface in a circular motion, like fluffy puffs of snow blowing in the wind. But the motion was subtle, more like a 3D photograph than anything else.

The colors and crispness were unreal. Golden edges along

the shores, framed by beautiful teal outlines where the water must have been shallow. All encompassed within a globe with a fading blue aura. I could reach right through the window and touch Hawaii—if the Earth rotated slightly and the clouds moved out of the way.

"Are we really this far from Earth?" Alice asked.

"I think so," Brian replied.

We were captivated by the majestic ball of color we called home.

Chapter 12

"Thank you for coming," the voice spoke. This time, I heard it with my ears.

A basketball-sized orb of wild silver energy floated in the distance. It drifted up and down, slowly, tiny bolts of white light arcing across its surface as it hovered a few feet in the air.

Solus was the first to approach it, his hand already reaching up high to touch it.

"Solus!" Brian lunged to stop him, but Solus looked back with a calm and assuring expression, as if he'd done this before.

His fingers barely made contact with the bottom of the sparkling ball, and the white began to cycle through thousands of colors. Red. Pink. Orange. Yellow. Green. Blue. Purple. Everything in between. White again, and then the cycle continued—every hue of the spectrum being displayed in split seconds of time.

"Hello, Solus," the light spoke. Solus bowed his head slightly, acknowledging the greeting.

Kareena squinted and shuffled closer. We were all surrounding the thing now. Even Lucy looked up at it curiously.

"Prism," Kareena said.

"I know," I replied, putting out an arm to pull Lucy back a few inches so the light wouldn't damage her eyes. She didn't have colored fluorescence like we did.

"She will be safe," the Prism said. "We promised."

I hesitated and then withdrew my arm from in front of

Lucy.

Solus lowered his hand and the colors faded instantly back to white.

"Kareena, please raise your hand up to the sphere. We must show you the truth."

The pink light in her face ignited to life, casting a soft fuchsia glow on us all. She lifted her hand just above the orb. Hot pink flushed half of her face and then the ball blazed with bright magenta fire.

"Look back at Earth," the Prism requested.

We turned to the window and watched faint glimmers of white reflect back at us.

"Are those... infected people?" Alice asked.

"Yes. You are seeing what the Seeker sees."

"There are so many," I said through clenched teeth, while my eyes flitted over the scene, darting between flickers of white spawning all across the globe.

"There are more," the Prism added.

The planet began to gradually spin, but the room didn't feel like it was moving at all.

We inched past North America and then across South America toward the shadowed side where Africa and Europe were cloaked in night. Golden veins of electricity must have been cities. White sparkles outshined them though, shimmering in and out of view beneath wispy clouds swirling overhead.

Antarctica, then Asia and Australia spun into view. A small ball of yellow fire peeked out from behind the Earth and then slipped from sight. The sun.

Then even more flashes of white in the darkness.

"Shit." Brian forked a hand through his hair.

"They're everywhere!" Kareena shouted, accidentally withdrawing her hand from the light. The markings faded briefly and then came back into view once she put her hand above the orb again. "They're freaking EVERYWHERE!"

"The Saviors did not tell you how many people they have

infected with the disease."

"What can we do?" I asked, my voice shaking, as I feared for Lucy's future.

"There is nothing you can do at this moment," the Prism replied. "What the Saviors released is more volatile than they realize. It is unstoppable in this form."

"What do you mean 'this form'?" Brian asked.

"The Saviors have been to Earth before. Many, many years ago. The infection then was mild—isolated to only a few—but the damage was done, and the Saviors refused to acknowledge their error. They left in search of a more suitable environment for their DNA, but were unable to find a species more compatible with it than the humans of Earth."

"What happened to all of the people they infected back then?" Kareena dropped her hand down to her side. "Did it kill them?"

"No." The ball of light turned white once her hand parted from it. "It changed them. It destroyed their humanity and turned them against one another."

I sucked in a sharp breath. *Turned them against each other?*

There was no way in hell I would hurt my little girl. Or the others.

"Solus survived exposure because he is strong," the Prism continued. "He carries an evolved form of the Healer's genetic material. We do not yet know how to protect the rest of you, but there is something we can do to help the young one since she is still healthy."

"Lucy?" I asked, my voice trembling.

"Yes."

The room fell silent. I watched Solus listening to a voice I couldn't hear. He looked down at his open hands and tipped his head to the side, confused.

Solus turned toward Lucy and reached his hands out for hers. Just as she offered hers back, I panicked.

"Don't!"

But before the words could get out, their fingers touched and a glimmer of rich blue light ricocheted through her. It faded instantly, but a faint cyan essence drifted around her now.

"What did you do to her!?" I shoved Solus away and knelt in front of Lucy.

"Shit!" Kareena yelped. "He's a Starter, too! But—"

"Do not worry," the Prism echoed, its voice louder. "Please."

"Are you kidding me?" My heart raced. "You infected her? How can I *not* be upset right now!? What the hell were you thinking? Are you trying to kill—"

"She was already infected and started. You were aware of this previously. Colored fluorescence will make her stronger—resistant to the disease. Just as the Hybrid is. This is why he shared a fraction of his light with her."

"How can it make *her* resistant when it's killing me!?" I tried to catch my breath. My adrenaline was raging.

"What?" Brian reached for my shoulder. "What does that mean, David? Since when were you—"

"There's something wrong with me. With my fluorescence." I pulled away from Brian's grasp. "It's been there for a while now. Kareena's seen it. Why don't *you* tell them?" I looked at her and she looked away from me.

"I see darkness in him," she murmured beneath her breath. "Like all the other poor bastards who died. The ones you couldn't heal, Brian." She glanced at him and frowned.

"Why do this to Lucy, then?" Alice asked. "Aren't you putting her at risk?"

"Yeah! Why!?" I clenched my fists. "We trusted you!"

"Sleepers started by Alice have higher chances of survival," it replied. "Lucy carries your DNA, Tracker, and is therefore receptive to becoming a host for colored fluorescence as well as falling prey to the mutation that attacks you now. The Solus

Child's immunity, combined with her preexisting condition, will lower the mortality rate."

"Wh-what?" Some of the heat diminished from my face. "It will?"

"Each time you were ordered to start others, the Saviors had you taint the DNA of those infected with a small portion of your own colored DNA. This made the light inside them stronger—more resilient. But it does not make them immune to the evolution of the disease. The time between when the Starter, Healer, and Seeker were first activated was enough for several more mutations to occur before the Tracking DNA had even been bonded to you, David. What the Saviors experimented with centuries ago was a much weaker strain. It moved slowly and had little ability to transfer between hosts. What is killing your people and the Saviors today changes rapidly—almost instantly upon attacking a host."

"So starting people is really like vaccinating them?" Alice asked. "It didn't actually do anything? Oh my God. All this time, I thought—"

"It slows the infection—a start of what the Saviors were trying to accomplish," Prism went on. "But the true cure could only come from the correct combination of genes and fluorescence."

"Solus," I said.

Chapter 13

Dusk encroached upon the city. We set up a makeshift camp in a quiet alley to rest for the night. I sat with my back against the brick wall of an abandoned Chinese restaurant. Lucy lay curled beside me with her head on my leg. Kareena sat opposite me, several feet away, her knees pulled up to her chest, her arms crossed, and her elbows on her knees. She turned her face away from me and rested her head on her arms.

She'd been ignoring me since the Prism had put us back down on Earth. I wanted to talk things over with her, but she wouldn't let me.

Brian tore thick strips from an old newspaper to toss onto a meager fire we'd made. Alice sat on the other side with Solus huddled up close to her and Brian's jacket draped over her shoulders. She was sitting on a towel we'd swiped from the hotel this week.

The sky overhead was navy blue, flecked with stars. No sign of rain, but it was getting colder. Winter was just around the corner and the farther East we moved, the faster temperatures dropped. We didn't have a clue where we were going, but as long the nights were clear, we saved a few bucks by enduring the company of abandoned city backstreets.

Having my gun made me feel safer. Safe enough to take the risk so we could eat the next morning. We needed help and we needed it soon. Money was drying up and my clip had fourteen bullets left.

To most people, that sounds like a lot.

It's not. Not when I had no way of refilling my clip if the

need arose.

Brian tossed a few wood scraps onto the fire and poked it with a stick of rebar.

"Why don't you get some sleep and I'll keep watch," I suggested.

"Are you sure? I'll be okay. I—"

"Shut up and get some rest, Brian." I smirked when I said it so he'd know I was kidding. "But, seriously, you've been wearing yourself thin since Solus showed up. Get some rest. I promise I'll wake you if something goes down."

"Thanks," Brian said with a small but grateful smile. He dug around in his backpack and pulled out a thin fleece blanket. He tossed it to me and I caught it.

"Thanks," I said with a nod.

He shuffled over to Alice and, from the corner of my eye, I saw him embrace her and Solus. Solus still hadn't shown much emotion in the form of facial expressions, but every time his parents looked at him, you could see a glimmer of excitement light up his eyes. Light up, as in figuratively, not literally, thank God. But the sensitive blue and green irises did show some affection. The Saviors hadn't made him into a total robot child, at least.

I stopped watching them and shifted my attention back to Lucy, who was still awake in my lap. "Lucy? Are you okay?" I nudged her gently. She looked up at me.

"I can't sleep," she said, sitting up. "I want to sleep in a bed. The ground is hard."

"I know and I'm sorry. But you're going to have to try tonight, okay? I'm gonna keep you safe, and you've got Brian and Solus right over there, too." I pointed. "Solus is going to sleep." At least, he looked like he was trying. He and his parents were curled up together on the other side of the fire.

"Here." I got to my knees and un-crumpled the blanket Brian had thrown to me. I shook it out and laid it down flat on the ground. Then I slid off my hoodie and rolled it into a ball. "Lie down," I said, patting it with my hand.

Lucy sighed and reluctantly lowered herself onto the ground, nestling her head against my hoodie. "I don't want to sleep right now," she whined.

"You need to," I said firmly, but caringly. "Everyone else is and I need sleep, too, but I won't go to sleep until you do. So the longer you stay awake, the more tired you're going to make me."

"Oh. Sorry, Daddy," she whispered.

I brushed my hand over her forehead and leaned down to kiss her there. She squinted and grinned.

"I love you, Lucy," I said, tucking a lock of her long dark hair behind her ear.

"Love you, too."

She rolled onto her side and exhaled loudly.

I sat there for a while, watching her until sleep finally came and whisked her off to dreamland. Part of me wondered what kind of dreams she'd be having following everything she'd seen recently. The Prism. A Savior. Our fluorescence. They were the kinds of things you'd expect your kid to see on TV, not in real life. And the kinds of things you'd wait until they were older to expose them to.

I glanced at the others. Brian and Alice looked like they were asleep, too. The alley was vacant as far as I could tell, but that didn't mean I felt comfortable letting my guard down with our lives in the balance, especially since we had two incredibly important children with us.

A brisk gust of air whistled through the alleyway and I shuddered. "Ugh." I shivered and rubbed my arms. Damn, it was getting cold. And now the fire was dying down and I had to take a piss.

I made sure Lucy was still asleep before getting up from the ground to look for scraps of wood. Behind the restaurant, there was a busted-up pallet we'd started dismantling earlier. I cracked a few more pieces off it and tucked them into the fire. Then I headed off to find a corner not far from sight, but not close enough that everyone would have to watch me do my business.

When I was done, I zipped up my jeans and rummaged around in my back pocket for a cigarette. I had a few left, but I was trying to hold off as long as I could between them so nicotine withdrawal didn't turn me into an asshole. The lighter cast a warm glow around my fingers as I singed the tip of my cigarette with the flame.

I took a puff.

By the third inhale, my nerves began to settle. The idea of having to go cold turkey wasn't one I was fond of, but if it came between tending to Lucy or to my addiction, I'd suffer. Besides, cigarettes weren't the first addiction I ever had to overcome.

With my cigarette partially burned down, I turned to head back toward the group and the dancing reddish glow of the fire. There was a faint shuffling sound. I reached for my gun.

"David?" Kareena crept out from around the corner.

"Jesus," I huffed. "Don't sneak around. I could have shot your ass."

She crossed her arms and scoffed. "Yeah. Okay."

I glanced over her shoulder. Brian, Alice, and the kids were still asleep.

Kareena's judgmental gaze met mine and firelight illuminated the curves of her face—an enticing sight, had a lump not formed in my throat from her piercing anger.

"Why didn't you tell me she was your daughter?"

The fire crackled.

I hesitated.

"David?"

I cleared my throat and tucked my gun back into my belt. "I didn't know if I could trust you."

"Bullshit. You didn't tell me because you knew I wouldn't

sleep with a guy with baggage."

"What!? Hey, shut the hell up, Kareena. You know damn well that had nothing to do with it. And don't talk about her like that. Besides, we both know you've got a shitload of baggage, yourself, and you don't even have a damn kid."

"Really? You're going to try this with me?" Her nose flared. She tipped her head down.

"If you gave a damn about anyone other than yourself, it wouldn't matter to you whether Lucy was my daughter or my sister. But everything has to be about you all of the time. If you're so upset about my kid, why don't you drop Brian, too, while you're at it?"

Her eyes widened and she scoffed. "Don't you even—"

"You and your twisted fetish. All you do is pine over a guy you can't have. Like he's some kind of goddamn angel or some shit. I don't get it."

"David!" she shrieked.

"Keep it down. Others are trying to sleep." I pushed past her and walked back over to the fire. I crouched and tossed in another chunk of wood.

Then a hand reached in front of me and yanked the cigarette from my between lips.

Kareena took a puff from it, exhaled, and tossed it behind me.

"You shouldn't smoke around your kid," she hissed.

Chapter 14

"I'm sorry Kareena's pissed about Lucy." Brian tossed me a bottle of water. "I'm sure you know she's one of those people who wants what she wants. She doesn't care much for anyone else's feelings. She pretends to, but—"

"She cares, damn it!"

Brian jerked his head back in surprise.

"I-I know she does," I continued. "She needs time to adjust."

"Sorry." Brian's tone softened. "I didn't mean to... I mean... I knew you two had something going, but I didn't think it was—"

"Real?" I glared at him. "You thought only you and your perfect little godsend, Alice, could have a *real* relationship. Is that it?"

"No! That's not what I meant!" He backed away. "Jesus Christ, man."

A wave of heat flushed through my chest. "Then stay out of this, Brian."

"I'm sorry I said anything. I just don't want your daughter getting hurt. I've known Kareena longer than you have." He turned his back and walked away, shaking his head. "But you apparently know her better than I do," he muttered.

I wanted to argue with him, but—damn it—he was right. I didn't know her that well. Just because she and I slept together didn't mean I knew shit about who she was. Hell, I didn't know much of anything about her. What I did know was that she had a lawyer for a father and she came from a wealthy Indian family on the West Coast. She liked fast cars and had a thing for white guys. And that she was a Seeker— a Seeker who got migraines whenever she tried to hook up with anyone other than a Fluorescent One.

Basically, with a guy other than Brian or... *me.*

I had thick skin, but there were moments when I needed a shoulder to rest my head on. I didn't have one and I hadn't in almost a decade.

"I don't want things to get messy between us," Kareena had told me the very first night we'd hooked up. And then I made the ignorant decision to tell her that it would only get messy if *she* let it.

I lied.

It burned inside me—more fervent than the amber-yellow fluorescence in my chest. I'd started feeling the one thing I'd basically told her I wouldn't. I mean, yes, I valued Lucy above all things, but that didn't mean there wasn't some part of me that wanted to be happy—that *needed* to feel *wanted* by another.

Aside from being beautiful, Kareena wasn't self-sacrificing, kind, or much else I had imagined a good woman might be. She didn't seem to have a sliver of motherly instinct in her body, and she had issues with strings and long-term commitment.

Brian seemed like an exception, though, as she always had this admiration for him in her eyes, no matter what he said or did. No matter how many times he turned her advances down.

I didn't have a chance in hell at having a meaningful relationship with a woman like Kareena, but I had to put my cards on the table. Maybe, just maybe, she could find the courage to love someone who couldn't give her everything. Someone who didn't have the world at his fingertips.

. . .

We left early in the morning, not knowing exactly where we were headed. Moving for the sake of it now. Maybe if we kept going, we'd find someone who could help us. Or maybe the Prism could figure out why Solus was the key and how to stop people from dying.

And, they were still dying. We hadn't been able to watch the news for a day, but I skimmed a headline on a local paper. More dead. Over a hundred in the past forty-eight hours. No common denominator doctors could use to predict new targets. Teens. Adults. Different races and different cities. There was no correlation whatsoever, and that put people on high alert. This whole thing planted fear in everyone's hearts. Including my own. How long did I have? What if I died tomorrow? Or worse—today? Who would take care of Lucy?

The Prism showed us infected sleepers all across the globe. It was only going to be a matter of time before people in other countries started to die and the United States put two and two together. We were the epicenter.

Why were we getting the brunt of it? Shouldn't it have been moving more slowly here since we had the Starter? Or did the few started people not make a visible impact?

"Where should we go from here?" Brian asked, turning to face me. "There's an overpass that leads north, and a tunnel below it we could follow, I think, but I'm not sure. I saw a sign a little ways back." He pointed toward the huge concrete tunnel ahead of us with signs and yellow "do not enter" tape stretched across the entrance. "I can see some light coming in on the other side, so I don't think it's closed off completely. It is pretty early in the day to stop, so we should keep going. Which way?"

I found it gratifying that Brian finally respected my opinion enough to ask me for advice. Ever since Lucy came along, he'd pulled back from being so ornery. It was a nice change.

"If we take the tunnel, we can avoid some of the elements," I suggested. "It could rain later today and we aren't pre—"

A humming sound filled the air, dull and low, but just the right pitch to get under my skin. My chest tightened and I strained to take in my next breath.

What the...

Things in the distance became blurry. I shot a glance at the bridge overhead. The rumbling of passing cars softened to a muffled whir. I spun around to see that a wall of rippling distortions had boxed us in—just like it had when...

White light loomed over me and I grabbed Lucy by the hand.

Not again.

From the blurred distance came a figure—a Savior—walking toward us from a fading mist of white. The lighted silver mask still covered the bottom half of his face and shimmered in the light as he approached.

"You, again!?" Brian straightened up. "We asked you to leave us alone."

"Yes. You did," the translator replied. "Things have changed. We must ask you again for..." He paused and his head jerked. A twitch? "We must ask you again for the child."

"No," Brian growled.

Alice crouched beside Solus.

"We do not have much time," the Savior continued.

"*You* don't have much time? Neither do we!" Brian said. "You lied to us. You didn't tell us this shit was global!"

"We did not feel the need to disclose that information to you."

"You don't feel much of anything, do you?"

"If you had known, what would you have done differently?" The Savior's eyes met mine and then he glanced down at Lucy. "What can you do now?" He looked at Brian.

"Walk away. That's what we should have done and it's all we can do right now." Brian signaled us to follow. He reached down and scooped Solus up into his arms. He approached the boundary of the enclosure—the distorted wall—and studied it.

"Can we go through?" Alice asked.

"Maybe," Brian replied, passing Solus off to her. "I'm going to try."

"No," said the Savior, raising his voice more than usual. "You cannot pass through."

"Really? Or are you just trying to keep us here? I'll take my chances." Brian shoved his hand into the distortion and I held my breath.

"Brian!" Kareena screamed.

We could barely see Brian's hand and wrist emerging from the other side of the wall, but it was there, still in one piece.

"Does it hurt?" Alice asked, adjusting her grip on Solus so he could hook an arm around her neck for balance.

"No," Brian said, shaking his head. "But..." He rotated his arm as if he were turning his hand over. As his arm twisted, the hand on the other side didn't rotate along with it.

"Oh my God. What's happening?" Kareena's eyes widened and she looked back at the Savior. "What's going on!?"

"Time passes differently outside of the projection. More slowly in your world than in ours."

"I'm going through," Brian said, turning his arm back to the starting position. He thrust himself into the field and we watched as he came out on the other side. Still whole. Still alive, as far as we could tell. We stood there watching, but he wasn't moving. He was frozen or... No. Wait! He *was* moving. His other foot was slowly coming down toward the ground. So slowly, I could barely tell he was moving at all.

"Do you think it's safe?" Alice asked.

"Maybe." I shrugged.

Solus reached up a hand and pointed at the blurry vision of Brian.

"Okay," Alice said to him. "Let's follow your dad." Then she took a deep breath, closed her eyes, and rushed through the barrier.

She, too, popped out the other side, Solus still in her arms, but her pace slowed to a crawl. Frame by frame. Nearly indiscernible movement.

Kareena swallowed hard and shook out her arms. "Damn it." She scowled and darted after her.

I took one last look back at the translator, grabbed Lucy up into my arms, and shot through behind them.

I came out, unscathed, and veered around to look back through. The sounds of passing cars overhead filled my head and I could breathe normally again. I had to squint to see him, but the translator was still standing inside the enclosed area, looking at us.

A single blink and he was suddenly right there, face to face with me. Only the thin blur of energy separated us. Alice gasped and Kareena let out a frightened yelp.

"Get away from the wall!" Brian commanded.

A split-second blink and the translator was now outside the barrier, his grey eyes staring straight down into mine, barely an inch of space between us. I almost dropped Lucy out of surprise, but adjusted my grip and backed away. He followed, and the heat of my fluorescence began to warm my chest in anticipation of a fight.

"Don't come any closer!" I held Lucy tightly. Yellow light flitted beneath the surface of my skin. Lucy roped an arm around my shoulders and I had her balanced well enough that I could stretch a free hand out toward the Savior. Fluorescence crackled through my fingertips.

"No." The translator lifted both hands and took a step back, nearly in contact with the blurry wall.

Was he afraid of me, for once?

"Please," he said, his head jerking slightly again. "Do not use the light."

A painful wheezing sound came from his mask and he lifted a hand to press a finger against one of the blue lights. Its flashing rhythm slowed and the Savior shook his head as he seemed to be adjusting to our air.

"We need that child," he said, his voice softer now. "Do not leave with it."

"First of all, it's *he*, not it," Brian corrected with a snarl. "And the answer is still no. Our own people are dying because of what you did to us."

"So are—" The translator twitched. "We." He took a step closer and I took one back.

"Leave him," Brian said. "We need to get out of here before someone sees us. Or... sees... *him*." He motioned toward the translator.

I didn't want to turn my back on the thing, but we needed to get the hell out of there before people started noticing and taking pictures of the big cylinder of blurred atmosphere plopped down in the middle of nowhere under a major overpass.

Just as I began to turn, the apparition behind the translator started to flicker.

He twisted his neck to watch and I heard one quiet word leak out from beneath his mask: "*No.*"

"What's happening?" I asked, moving farther away.

The energy field wavered and everything on the other side of it sharpened into focus. Then the entire thing dissipated.

The translator lifted a hand up and spread out his fingers so they were at his eye level. A flicker of green light beamed through his hand and faded.

"Uh, what just happened?" Brian asked.

The translator turned. "I have been away for too long," he replied. "They have... closed the connection. I believe it was to preserve resources."

"Wait. Wait. Wait! What!?" Brian came up beside me. "Are you trying to tell us that they deserted you? No. Just no."

The Savior looked down at Brian and then off into the distance at nothing.

"I do not believe I am able to leave at this time," he said.

The blue lights in his mask continued to pulse, but he said nothing else.

Chapter 15

"Stop following us!" Brian shook with anger.

The translator took slow, unsteady steps behind us as we walked through the tunnel below the overpass. His long, twiggy legs didn't look as if they were suitable for extensive walking.

"Please. Wait," the Savior said. He'd been attempting to get Brian to reason with him for what seemed like half an hour. Or maybe all his monotone groveling was grinding on my nerves.

I didn't know what to do. I had Lucy. They had Solus. Kareena, well, she was hanging beside me, reluctantly, just to get away from the Savior. I was the one with the gun, after all, and the yellow light he seemed apprehensive about.

"Brian!" I called out and jogged after him. Lucy tagged alongside me.

"What?" He swerved around and tried to avoid making eye contact with the translator, who was maybe twenty feet or so behind. "What, David?" he lowered his voice.

"We need to do something with him. We can't... I mean, as much as I know we should, we really can't leave him wandering around out here alone."

"What do you want me to do? Buy him breakfast?" Brian scoffed. "That thing is trying to take my son away. He infected your daughter with something that's apparently killing you and God knows how much of our planet now, and you want me to feel sorry for him? To help him? No. I can't. I-I just can't!"

"Brian, look, I'm not saying we need to feel sorry for the son-of-a-bitch, but if someone finds out about him, what do you think will happen to us? I mean, what if he gets nabbed by some psychos down here, experimented on, killed—whatever—and then the other Saviors decide to come back and annihilate the shit out of the rest of us!? What then? We can't fight back if we're all dead. Think about it, Brian."

Brian's jaw tightened. "I *am*. I'm trying." He grumbled.

"You're doing all of this to protect the people you care about—Alice, Solus... maybe even Kareena. But what good is it if it all leads to the same end? What if avoiding our enemy now could be more dangerous than facing him?"

He heaved a sigh and shrugged. "I don't know. David, I'm tired. I'm tired of fighting something I can't even see. Tired of running from something we can't escape. What do we do, Alice?"

"I don't know," she replied quietly. "I'm scared, too, but I think David has a point. Leaving the translator to wander around on his own can't be the solution."

By now, the Savior had closed the gap between us and was only a few feet away. He staggered nearer, having difficulty keeping his balance on the gravel pathway of the tunnel as he walked in his footed, white scuba-like jumpsuit. He didn't have shoes of any kind on that I could tell, and I didn't know how durable the material was. Or even what it was.

Alice gasped and her attention shot to Solus, who had pulled out of her hand and was jaunting toward the translator.

"Solus!" Brian lunged for him.

Solus paused when Brian's hand touched his shoulder. He pointed up at the Savior's face.

"Why is he pointing?" Kareena asked from behind me.

"Your mask," Brian said. "I think he's pointing at your mask."

The Savior barely nodded. "Yes. He has not seen it before."

"What does it do?" Alice asked, coming up beside Solus

and Brian.

"It assists my breathing in your heavily oxygenated atmosphere," he responded. "We cannot tolerate high levels of oxygen."

"So if you took it off, would you die?" Brian asked with a tinge of coldness in his voice.

"I would rather not theorize about that at this time," the Savior replied. "May I follow you? Until the others return for me?" He looked down at Brian. "You. You are the leader, are you not?"

Brian looked at me and I shrugged.

"We work together," he replied.

Good answer. I may have grinned.

"Then whose permission do I require?" The Savior tilted his head to the side and scanned over all of our faces swiftly.

"How do we know you're not going to try to kill us?" Kareena asked, crossing her arms. "You jerks have been lying to us from the beginning about everything. How do we know you don't have ulterior motives?"

"We have not harmed any of you."

Brian scoffed. "I can think of at least one time when you have. You tried to rip my fluorescence out of me when I stood up to you and—"

"If we removed the light, your heart defect would have returned," he interrupted. "It is a matter of principle and anatomy that you would exhibit distress, not an act of abuse."

"You treated me like shit and lied to me, too, remember?" I said.

"Not to mention what you did to my arm," Kareena added.

"Being a Fluorescent One has side effects," he replied. "You were being reprimanded with purpose. We do not revel in your pain."

I rolled my eyes. "Well, this is getting us nowhere."

"So if we agree and allow you to follow us around for a

while," Brian started, "how can we keep people from seeing you? You don't exactly look... normal."

He was right. The Savior's platinum white hair and ashy grey skin tone were more plastic and mannequin-looking than human. He was also several inches taller than me, and I'm a hair over six feet, myself. There wouldn't be much camouflage for someone so obviously out of place.

The translator lifted his left hand, palm out, and fanned his fingers. A subtle emerald glow rippled out from beneath the cuff of his suit sleeve, up his wrist, and through his palm toward his fingertips.

"Whoa! What's he doing?" Brian shouted.

Hot lime-green light lit the Savior's fingers. Tiny bolts of electricity forked through his hand and he went out of focus, fading into a transparent ghostly-white silhouette.

"Where did he go!?" Brian barked, looking around in a panic.

"It's okay! Chill! I see him," Kareena said. "He's still here."

"I see a shape," I said, watching the smoky essence.

"You sure?" Brian asked, still freaking out. "Y-you guys can still see him?"

"Yes, Brian." Kareena lifted her hands. "I can show you if you want."

"Uh... Y-yeah," he stuttered. "Yeah, go ahead."

"It's gonna hurt, you know," Kareena whispered apologetically as her fingers came up to make contact with Brian's temples. "Sorry." A sparkle of pink light illuminated her fingertips and his attention shot toward the Savior.

"I *can* see him," he said and swallowed hard. "How did you do that?" Then he grimaced and clenched his teeth. "Agh. Damn it," he hissed. He cupped his left hand across his forehead and bent over. "I'm alright," he said to Alice, who was wrapping an arm around his. He came back up and nodded at Kareena. "I'm fine."

"It's just like it was when we were sent places to start

people," Alice said. "We could see them, but they couldn't see us."

"You are correct," the Savior replied.

"Shit!" I jolted, not expecting to hear him in his current state.

"I am invisible to those without the sight the Tracker and Seeker have," he continued.

"So you're in the stasis realm?" Kareena asked.

"Yes."

Brian bit his lip and grumbled beneath his breath. "Then, I guess he's staying... for now." He looked me straight in the eye. "You and Kareena need to watch him. Be careful, but don't hesitate to use whatever force is necessary to keep him in line."

•   •   •

"What are we supposed to call you, anyway?" Brian asked begrudgingly. "Or is it just going to be 'Translator' from now on?"

"Why must you name all things?" the Savior asked.

"Because that's the way humans work," Brian replied. "We use names. We use words in our conversations. We can't just look at each other or touch people like you and Solus can. We can't make each other see things like that."

"I am the only one who is able to speak," the translator continued. He glanced down at Solus. "We do not use titles unless we have no other way of describing the thing."

Alice sneered. "He's not a *thing*."

Then Kareena chuckled. "We *should* call him Judas," she said, looking pleased with herself over the idea.

"Why?" I shook my head at the ridiculous suggestion. "Because you like the song?"

"No, dumbass." She scoffed. "Because of what he did. Betrayed Jesus and whatever. That's damn near what they've done to us, isn't it? Pretended to be nice and then—I mean, think about it. Isn't Solus *kind* of like Jesus, anyway?" She propped a hand on her hip and waited for me to agree.

Alice looked embarrassed and confused, and even I was put off by the comparison. But, as bizarre as the analogy was, it *kind* of made sense. In a warped, Kareena-humor kind of way.

Judas was the apostle said to have betrayed Jesus for a handful of silver. The betrayal basically led to the Last Supper and eventually to Jesus being crucified. He was supposed to have been his friend, ironically, but there are a lot of different variations of what people think really happened and why.

"Ju-das." The translator muttered the name to himself. "Why?" he asked. "It has a negative connotation, does it not?"

"Because you lied to us," Kareena added. "And you're basically sending all of us to our deaths now if we can't find a solution to stop this from killing more people."

"It is kinda macabre," I said, cocking an eyebrow. "Don't you think?" The translator wasn't the only Savior at fault.

"Is it really?" She shrugged. "They took some of us with them, remember?"

Brian and Alice had nothing to say about it. They also couldn't see Judas anymore.

"Judas," the translator said the word again, this time, loud enough for us all to hear his dull, monotone voice. "It will do." He seemed unaffected by the name one way or another.

Brian shook his head. "Now that that's settled... teach us how to do whatever it is you're doing right now—shifting planes or however you're becoming invisible. We need to stay out of sight. We're too conspicuous wandering around together all of the time. Especially with the kids."

We waited but got no response.

"Well?" Brian prodded further. "David, I can't see him, but I need an answer."

"Answer him," I looked at the soft white shape across

from me.

"I cannot teach you," Judas finally responded. "May I become visible again?"

We looked around. The tunnel was empty, but overhead traffic rumbled constantly beneath our feet.

"For a minute, I guess," Brian said, glancing around nervously. "What is it?"

Judas flashed into focus from the white blur and became opaque.

"I cannot show you how to shift between realms, but..." He looked down at Solus. "I can show the child."

"His name is Solus," Brian stated. "Call him that."

The Savior tipped his head in understanding and bent over at the waist to reach out to Solus. "Solus," he said. "Come."

"Don't hurt him," I growled, threatening him with a raised hand glimmering with golden light.

"I will not harm the child," he responded. He thought for a moment. "I will not harm Solus."

Solus let go of Alice and approached the Savior. Judas reached a hand toward him and spread out his fingers. They emanated silver and green bolts of light. Then he reached out his other hand toward Solus' temple and touched him.

Solus mimicked the gesture, his hand shining with teal light, and then they both faded into white smoke.

Alice shrieked.

"They're still here," I said, trying to calm them quickly. "I can see their silhouettes. You can, too. Right, Kareena?"

Kareena nodded. "I can see them both."

The soft shapes drifted past me toward Alice. She looked down at her hand and flexed her fingers.

"I... feel something touching me," she said.

"It's—" Kareena started.

Alice vanished, becoming part of the white blur.

"Alice!" Brian called out. "Alice! Where are you?"

"I'm here," she replied, her voice distorted but recognizable.

"Are you okay?" Brian asked. "Is Solus okay?"

"Yes. He's with me," she answered.

The entire white shape floated past me again and then stopped. The three of them reappeared and I saw Solus lower his glowing hand down to his side. His other hand was firmly wrapped around his mother's.

"Holy crap." Brian shot over to them and forked his fingers through Solus' hair, ruffling it up. "You did that?"

Solus looked up at him and nodded.

"That's amazing!"

"I think Judas helped," I added.

"Yes," Judas confirmed. "I have explained the process to him."

"Good boy, Solus," Brian said, smiling at his son. "And Alice? Was it okay? Did it feel any different than when we were in it before?"

"No. Just like Times Square, Vegas, and all the rest," she answered. "But I felt safer since Solus was controlling it."

"Will you trust me now?" Judas asked.

"Trust is a big word," Brian said with a doubtful shake of his head. "You have to earn it."

Judas twitched and jerked his head again.

"Why the hell do you keep doing that?" Brian cocked an eyebrow.

"I do not believe you can understand," he said.

"Try me."

"Saviors are connected. This is most obvious when we communicate. You have never seen us speak to one another."

"So you're like a hivemind?" I asked.

"What is that?" Judas looked at me.

"It's when many things or minds are connected to a point where they think collectively, not independently," I clarified.

"This exists here? On Earth?"

"Not with humans, but some creatures do it, yes."

"Then, yes. That is how we communicate."

"So... then what's with the tick? I mean, the twitching thing you keep doing?" Brian reiterated.

"Unlike humans, there has always been an unchanging number of our kind. We do not reproduce. We evolve. Each has core energy of a single color and provides a shared resource of energy needed to continue our evolutionary process. Until recently, we have never had access to less than the minimum required. But when one Savior fades, we all experience the loss of light."

Were they immortals before?

"So your kind have never had to deal with death?" I asked.

"Death was nonexistent in our society before we chose you as carriers of fluorescent strains. It is strange and difficult to tolerate the loss of our kind after so many years. Unexpectedly, we have become subject to common mortality."

"Now you know how it feels," Brian said.

Chapter 16

Brian exited the tunnel first to scout out the area. "I think it's an old construction site," he said, turning to face us. "I can't really tell, but there's a lot of old masonry stuff lying around." He scanned his surroundings, bringing a hand to his brow to shield his eyes from the afternoon sun. "There may be a street on the other side of the containment fence." He pointed, squinting. "I can't really tell from here. If not, we'll just have to go back the way we came and try another route."

"What are you searching for?" Judas asked.

"A place to stay," I answered. "Mostly."

"Do you not have a permanent place of shelter?"

"Not anymore. Not since you Saviors screwed up our lives."

He stared at me blankly.

"I'm in trouble with the law and so is Brian, technically," I elaborated. "You don't understand how this works, but because he left with Alice, it's considered kidnapping. That's a crime here, among other things. I robbed a place to get them some money to stay in hotels, and then Kareena disappeared from the police department, thanks to you."

"So you wander? Every day?"

"Yes."

I left the tunnel next with Lucy trailing behind. Alice and Solus followed, and then Judas' misty shadow and Kareena.

"If we're going to have to put up with you, you should at least be able to pull your own weight," Brian said, trying to figure out where to look since he couldn't see the translator. I pointed to where Judas was standing and he adjusted his line of sight. "Can you do anything to help us?"

"Help you with what?" Judas replied.

"Help us find a safe place to stay. Someplace we won't be in danger and where there aren't a lot of people. You've got to have a better sense of direction than we do. Right? Don't you have anything other than that breathing mask with you?"

Judas materialized and Alice gasped, caught off guard by his sudden reappearance.

Judas paused, still as a statue, and gazed off into the distance. I couldn't even hear him breathing.

"Judas?" I broke the silence.

"Yes," he responded, moving again. "I have thought of a solution. I can alter the Prism's creation to help you move more easily between locations."

"How?"

"Let me see your wrist."

"No way." Brian shook his head. "I don't trust you. The Prism gave us these to protect us from *you*."

Brian was right, but what if Judas could help us? He was kind of screwed at the moment, too. If it were so easy to grab Solus and run, he would have already.

Right?

I lifted my arm. "Go ahead."

"David?" Brian looked at me, disgusted. "What the hell are you thinking?"

"We need help, and if he can do something to make it easier for us to get around, I'd like to know what it is and how to use it. Don't worry about me. I'm the one who has a shot at fighting back, remember?"

"I-I guess," Brian replied. "I still don't think it's a good idea."

Judas bent over and investigated my bangle closely. He raised his left arm, turned it over so the forearm and palm

faced up, and used his other hand to pull open an incon-
spicuous flap on his jumpsuit sleeve. He withdrew a set of
delicate silver tools and sorted through them in his hands.

With a tool that looked a lot like a sanding burr, he poked
at my bangle. Heat flushed through my wrist at the site and
I flinched.

"What are you doing to it?" I asked.

"Minor adjustments," Judas replied. "Please wait until I
finish before asking questions."

Okay then.

He tucked the first tool back into the pocket on his sleeve
and used a second one—a long, cotton-swab-like stylus with
a glowing white tip—to resume prodding at the thing on my
wrist. The heat continued to rise until I grunted from discomfort and pulled back.

"It's getting too hot," I said.

"I am nearly finished." He blinked and waited for me to
relinquish the bracelet again.

"Can you hurry up, please?" The others' gazes were fixated on my wrist.

An electrical shock jolted through me. "Ah!" I jerked my
hand away. "What was that!?"

"I am finished." Judas slid the glow-tipped rod back into
its slot and folded the cover closed on the pocket. The outline of the pocket faded into obscurity against the rest of his
suit.

"What was that shock from?"

"It was your fluorescence linking to the band. It will act
as an additional power source to support the adjustments I
have made."

"Which were?"

"It can condense fluorescence, amplifying what you already have."

"How?"

"You control it, as you always have. Direct the light toward the band."

I imagined yellow light skittering through me, warming me from the core. Golden amber bolts of wild, dangerous electricity rocketing through my veins. I concentrated on sending fluorescence through my chest and down my arm, but the heat wouldn't rise and the light wouldn't spark to life.

Nothing.

"I can't call on it whenever I want," I replied. "What am I supposed to do?"

"The process will be simplified after it has been activated for the first time," Judas said. "Could you do it if your daughter's life were at risk?"

"What?" Warmth flushed through me and my hand started to tremble. "Don't bring her into this again!"

My arm jerked forward involuntarily. An arc of white blasted from my wrist into the air and tore open a swirling whirlpool of gleaming light.

"A portal?" I stared in disbelief. It was close to what I had pictured it to be, but with a vivid, pulsating glow more brilliant and mystical than anything I could have put together in my head. Streaks of white-hot light zipped around the circumference, weaving between continuous streams of soft blue and pale copper. "And... I can actually see it."

"Yes," Judas confirmed. "Because it has merged with your fluorescence."

"I see it, too," Kareena added.

Brian and Alice appeared mesmerized by it. They hadn't been able to see portals before.

"Where does it lead?" I asked.

"That is decided by you," Judas replied. "You must choose a location and clearly understand where it is before you make that choice. If you do not visualize correctly, you could become stranded in a dangerous or unfamiliar place."

Another sharp zing of electricity buzzed through me and I brought my arm in close to my chest, reeling from the heat of the sting. The spinning white portal sucked closed and disappeared into nothingness.

"Shit! It burns, damn it!" I shook out my wrist. "Why does it burn so much?"

Brian tried to take a look at the subtle reddish mark left on my wrist, but I declined his healing.

"You must learn to channel your light more effectively to minimize physical injury," Judas said.

"Are the portals safe?" Kareena asked. "Are they exactly the same as the ones we used before? The same ones the Prism created for us?"

"They have been altered slightly. The variation allows you to power the doorway with your own energy instead of the external source previously required."

Alice looked down at her wrist. "Judas, can you program all of our bands to do this?"

"If you want." Judas looked at her. "Is this something you want me to do?" He glanced at Brian and Kareena. "You two, as well?"

"I don't know," Brian said, his lips wrinkling with cynicism. "I don't know if I trust you that much. I don't know if I trust you enough to let you screw with whatever it is the Prism gave us to keep us safe from you. If it hurt me, I could heal, probably. But we haven't tested one of the portals. How do we know they work?"

"Maybe we should test one," Alice spoke up. "I'd... like to see my mom again."

"Jane?" Brian faced her. "We can't go back there. You know that, Alice. We ran away for a reason. If we go back, I could get arrested. Who knows what they'll do to Kareena. We might both end up in jail."

"I'm not going to jail!" Kareena yelped. "No freaking way." She took a step in front of me and walked toward Brian. "Brian! I'm not going back there! Because I know you'll get your ass arrested and mine, too! We don't need this right now. We've been safe ever since we left our homes. We should just keep moving. It's been working."

"And do what?" Alice raised her voice. "Be homeless forever!?" She rolled her hands into fists—something I'd *never* seen her do before. "No! I don't want to live like this. I want to go home. I want to see my mom and my best friend. I want to know that they're okay! That they aren't sick or... worse. Don't you, Kareena? Don't you want to see your family? Or do you not care about them anymore?"

Kareena pressed her lips thin and frowned. "Of course I care, damn it. Why in the hell wouldn't I care about my own family? Jesus, Alice. What do you think I am? A robot? I-I just don't want our asses to get into trouble. We're all the world has right now. Us and that kid of yours. We're the only people who have a chance in hell at saving everyone from this shit. If we die—"

"We need to know if they work," I interrupted. "We need to know if they can get us where we want to go, regardless of where that is. I'll try it if you two don't want to. I'll test it out first."

"Are you sure about this, David?" Brian asked. "You don't have to do this. You've got—"

"Just watch Lucy for me. Okay? If... by some chance I can't get back or... something happens to me, please—"

"Of course," Brian cut me off. "We'll take care of her either way, but you'll be fine, so... don't say shit like that."

Immediately, I regretted my decision and started to ruminate on the risks.

But I wasn't a man who'd go against my word, so I had to suck it up and hope for the best. The ability to teleport anywhere we needed to could be a lifesaver.

I closed my eyes and tried to visualize a place. Details were fuzzy at first and then they eased into view, becoming crystal clear, complete with color and sound. Vivid imagery set free from the depths of my memory.

It was the perfect place and a perfect opportunity to test the bracelet.

"Okay. I've got a location in mind now," I announced, lifting my arm. It was difficult to keep the picture in focus while I tried to simultaneously conjure up the anger and emotion necessary to make my skin glow.

Positive and negative emotions whirled inside. I wanted the portal to work, but I wanted to keep my daughter safe even more. If I could do both, maybe... just maybe we had a chance.

I can't lose Lucy. I can't get hurt doing this. I just can't.

Heat filled my chest and I felt light emerging. I opened my eyes and watched flecks and dashes of yellow shooting down through my veins toward my hands. Then a burst of white light boomed from my wrist like a firework and ripped open a gash of radiant, swirling white light in front of me.

I glanced back at Lucy and smiled. She smiled back with confidence and I stepped into the glowing whirlpool. It blinded me momentarily, as a whoosh of cool air pushed me through nothingness. Weightlessness engulfed me, but it didn't feel like falling. Not like being propelled or pulled. I was floating and I couldn't tell which way was up.

The illumination dissipated and there was ground beneath my feet. I moved my foot and soft ground moved with it. A breeze licked past my cheeks and I took in a deep breath of warm, salty air. A low rumbling noise filled my ears, tainted by the shrill squawks of seabirds.

I didn't have to open my eyes to know where I was, so I waited a moment to do so.

I waited until a gentle wave rolled in, splashing against my ankles before retreating back from where it came. Then I opened my eyes and looked down at the sand around my feet. I scanned up to see patches of sea foam dusting across the ocean surface and the beautiful, majestic blue-green water of the Hawaiian shores. I sighed. My heart filled with peace.

My shoes were soaked, my feet wet, but it didn't matter. For a single, frozen moment in time, nothing mattered.

All I could do was smile, close my eyes, and take in a slow breath of the deeply missed, salty sea air.

It had been so long since I'd been back to the one and only place I'd ever truly called... home.

Chapter 17

It took time for me to channel the negative energy required to create a portal back to the others, but it finally happened, and I reluctantly stepped through. If my little girl hadn't been waiting for me on the other side, I may not have.

"We thought you'd gotten lost," Brian said.

"I did. But not because of the portal."

"Oh?"

"It took me back to one of the beaches I used to play at when I was a kid. A stretch of shoreline just behind a rock formation most people didn't know about."

"Did anyone see you?"

"Apparently nobody knows about it still." I chuckled. "Lucy, I want to take you there someday. It's beautiful in Hawaii. The air tastes clean and the ocean is so blue it's..." I drifted off in thought.

"Your shoes." Alice pointed. "They're soaked. Are you going to be okay like that?"

I shrugged. "It's only water. I'll leave them out overnight by the fire and they'll dry." The damn things had enough holes to drain most of the water already. I think some sand had even gotten in.

"So I take it they work, then? The portals?" Brian looked at me.

"Uh huh."

"Did it feel any different than the ones we used before?" Kareena asked.

"No."

"Good. Maybe they're right. Maybe these are useful."

"Mine, too," Alice spoke up, lifting her arm toward Judas. "This is the wrist with it on there, right, Kareena?"

"Alice!?" Brian's eyes widened. "No!"

"I want to protect our son as much as you do," Alice said. "But we can't keep doing what we're doing. We have to change something. We have to learn new things. Any new ability we can get, we should, because we don't know where we'll be tomorrow, or what the world will be like." She cupped his cheek in her palm and stared up into his eyes. "We *need* this, Brian."

"So you trust it, then? That... thing?" He motioned at Judas and scowled. "Really? And the rest of you think this is a good idea, too?" His eyes scanned Kareena's and then mine. "Well?"

"I think," I started, "we need any technology we can get. Anything that might help us."

"Ugh!" Brian clenched his teeth and huffed angrily. "Shit! You guys, I don't like this at all."

"Just think of it as if we're using the Saviors like they used us, alright?" I suggested, trying to smooth the tension. "They took some things from us. We'll take some things from them."

"What do you think the Prism will think about this?" Kareena asked, intently watching Judas remove his tiny, lighted tools from the inside of his sleeve.

"I don't know," I replied. "Hopefully they'll understand the circumstances. If they were concerned, shouldn't they have been here by now to warn us? We haven't seen them since he showed up."

"Guys!" Alice called out. Judas had already finished and was tucking the instruments back into his hidden pocket. "I'm going to try it." She held her hand out and closed her eyes tightly. "What do I do, David?"

"Uh. Well," I stammered. "I don't know how your

fluorescence works, actually. I mean, what makes it glow?"

"Getting pissed off seems to work." Kareena smirked.

"I'm not mad at anyone right now," Alice replied. "Judas, what do I do?"

"Ask the child to help," he replied, looking down at Solus.

"Solus? Can you..."

He was already lifting a hand toward his mother's. He cupped his fingers over her wrist and teal light radiated from his hand. A subtle glimmer of neon green fire lit her shoulder, emanating through the back of her shirt. Pencil-thin lines of hot green light crackled down her skin, racing toward her hand.

She grunted in pain and a ball of energy shot from her wrist into the air, transforming into a spinning oval of white light.

"I did it!" She opened her eyes. "Thank you, Solus."

Solus forced a toothy smile in response and Alice laughed.

"It's nice to see you smile," she said.

We could all tell he was forcing it, but the fact that he even tried meant he was beginning to understand how we worked. He didn't seem dead to the world by any means, but the kid needed to learn to not stifle his emotions.

"Are you absolutely sure about this, Alice?" Brian asked, taking her hand.

"Yes." She smiled. "Absolutely."

"And what about Judas?"

"Mom will understand, Brian. You know that."

"It's still a lot to take in." He looked at the translator. "Can you go into the other realm until we're able to introduce you properly?"

Judas acknowledged the request with a partial nod and then lifted his hand and spread out his fingers. Green fluorescence saturated his hand and he faded into soft white smoke.

"I'll go through first with Lucy," I suggested. "Then Kareena can send Judas through and she can follow. Then you two and Solus, just to be certain the portal stays open long enough for us all."

"Okay," Alice agreed.

I reached for Lucy's hand and, together, we passed through the swirling white light.

After the initial blindness, blurred surroundings, and cool rush of air, we arrived in a darkened room. Light from the portal cast a soft, TV-like glow to us, making our shadows bounce from wall to wall. The floor was soft. Carpeted. I stepped forward slowly, Lucy's hand still tight in mine, and raised my fingers in front of me. I felt the wall. Textured paint of some kind. Warm, not cold. We were indoors, at least.

Kareena and Judas popped out behind me. She moved out of the way just as Alice, Brian, and Solus came through.

The portal collapsed into itself and vanished, leaving us all in pitch darkness.

"Where are we?" I asked.

With a click, the lights came on. Alice had flicked on a switch beside me.

"We're in Jane—Alice's mom's—basement," Brian announced, looking around. "I lived with her for a little while after my mom overdosed. Well, her mom actually had legal custody of me at the time."

"Nice," I said quietly. "At least someone cared enough about you to go through all of that."

"It wasn't a nice time for me, regardless." Brian walked over to the dresser beside the bed and picked up the digital clock. "This thing right?"

"Time zone difference, remember?" I reminded.

"Oh. I forgot about that. Do you think she's even home yet?"

"I can go up and check," Alice replied. "I just don't want to give my mom a heart attack. It's been a while, you know? I'm sure she's not expecting us all to just pop out of the basement like nothing happened."

"And with our kid," Brian added.

"Yeah." She tangled her hands together. "What do I do?"

"Let's go upstairs and see if she's home."

"Hey, wait!" I said, blocking Brian from walking past. "What if Judas *and* Solus are in the other realm while you're talking to your mom and introducing us? That way, you can explain to her about him before she has to actually see him and the translator. Wouldn't that be better? Or... easier, at least, for her to take in?"

"That's a good idea." Brian bent down to look Solus in the eye. "Can you do that for us, Solus? Can you stay in the other realm while the rest of us talk to Alice's mom? We'll tell her about you and then you can say hello. Okay?"

Solus tipped his head to the side and narrowed his eyes. He nodded and walked toward the blurry white shape that was Judas. He lifted his hand and parted his fingers. Streaks of blue and green light swirled through his skin, up his wrist, and toward his fingertips. Then he faded into a transparent white shadow.

Alice walked by and started up the carpeted staircase on the other side of the room. "I'll come back for you in a bit."

Brian jogged after her and followed her up the steps. The basement door opened with a soft click; they waited at the top of the stairs, and then ventured into the house. I heard their footsteps on the basement ceiling as they walked across the room. I glanced at Kareena. Her eyes were firmly set on Solus and the Savior.

Lucy squeezed my hand. "How long do we have to wait here?" she whispered.

"Not too long, I hope." I brushed a hand over her hair. "Let's just try to be patient, okay?"

"Okay..." she mumbled.

I heard heavier footsteps overhead pounding swiftly across from one end of the room to the other and then going silent.

"I bet that's her," I murmured.

We waited about fifteen minutes before I got antsy and needed to check things out myself. "I want to go up and make sure everything is alright. They've been quiet for awhile."

"Hurry up," Kareena said, crossing her arms. "I don't want to be left alone with this guy for too long. I don't know if I can do much if he decides to try anything."

"I'll just be a sec. Lucy, stay behind me." We crept up the stairs and I stopped every few steps to listen for movement. I heard voices. Brian. Alice. Another muffled female voice.

It had to be Alice's mother.

I turned to Lucy and brought my index finger to my lips. "Shh." She pretended to zip her lips closed with her hand. I turned back toward the door at the top of the stairs, turned the knob slowly, and pushed open the door a crack. The voices became clearer.

"Brian?" I called quietly. "Alice?"

The rumble of footsteps across hardwood floor had me pulling the door closed again.

"It's okay, David," Brian said, opening the door. "You guys can come up now. I was just about to get you."

"Thanks."

He held open the door and I guided Lucy out with me.

"Kareena!" Brian shouted through the doorway. "Bring the others up with you."

"Others?" I heard the female voice repeat in the room just around the corner.

Lucy broke free of my grasp and darted back down the basement steps.

"Lucy!"

"It's alright!" Kareena shouted back. "She was waiting on Solus. I'm coming up now."

"Come with me," I heard Lucy squeal excitedly. "We're going to meet Alice's mommy."

Lucy came out of the basement with her hand curled as if she were grasping something. Or someone. The subtle, faded outline beside her was Solus, holding her hand like a ghost. It was a little unnerving.

Brian directed us into the next room—a dining room—where Alice's mother stood waiting.

"Jane, this is David and Lucy," Brian said. "And, of course, Kareena."

The poor woman wasn't all that old, maybe a handful of years older than me, but she looked like she'd been through hell. Her brunette hair was a tousled mess tucked back behind her ears and the dark shadows beneath her eyes made her look restless and worn.

She approached and looked me over. "Is this the other one?" she asked. There was a judgmental air to the way she analyzed me. "Isn't he... the one who hurt you, Brian?"

"Yes," Brian confirmed. "But it was only because he was protecting his daughter." He gestured at Lucy, who was standing between Kareena and me, her hand still cupping the phantom, Solus.

"She's adorable," Jane said, bending down to smile at Lucy. "Nice to meet you, Lucy."

Lucy looked up at me with widened eyes and pointed at her pressed lips with her free hand.

"What's she doing?" Jane cocked her head.

"You can talk now," I said, laughing.

Lucy "unzipped" her mouth. "Nice to meet you, too," she replied with a big, warm grin. "This is—"

"Wait!" I cut her off as she started to point at Solus. "Not yet, Lucy."

"Sorry."

"Mom." Alice fidgeted. "There's something we need to tell you."

Jane's smile faded and a look of worry wrinkled her brow.

"You remember how the Saviors let what was going to

be our baby die?"

Jane gasped and covered her mouth.

"Well, it turns out there were actually two. Twins. One boy and one girl."

I heard Jane's breath quiver as a muffled whimper escaped her mouth.

"And the boy survived. Somehow. But since he was with them, he grew up faster and... Oh, Mom. I don't know how to tell you this, but—"

"Is he here!?" Jane blurted through her cupped hands.

"Yes," Brian said. He turned toward Lucy. "Solus, show yourself, please."

Lucy shifted eagerly and flexed her hand.

Solus materialized and dropped his glowing fingers to his side.

"Oh my God!" Jane stumbled back. "You have a son!" She propped herself against the dining table. I pulled out a chair for her and prompted her to take a seat. "How long have you known?"

Judas remained invisible, and I hoped he'd stay so a while longer. Jane could collapse from shock if she had to face everything in one blow. It was too much.

"Not very long," Alice replied. "Only a few days."

"And he can turn himself invisible!?" She hunched over in the chair and cupped her hands over her face again. "Oh my God. How? Why? Why didn't they tell you about him sooner? And how did you even get here? How did he—"

"There are other aliens out there, Jane," Brian said. "They rescued Solus from the Saviors and brought him back to us so we could protect him. He's the key to whatever it is that's killing people. That Ghost Plague everyone's talking about."

Jane's eyes darted toward Alice and then away with a horribly sharp, shuddering gasp.

"Mom!?" Alice dashed to her and knelt beside her chair, pressing her hands onto her mother's knees. "Mom!? What's wrong!? What happened?"

Jane shook her head and muffled the word "no."

"No, what, Mom? What happened?"

"Jane, please," Brian added. "You don't have to be afraid of Solus, he's ours. He really is—"

"That's not it!" Jane cried, bringing her face up. Tears ravaged her cheeks and her skin flushed red. "It's not that, it's... it's Sam."

"Mom?" Alice yelped. "What do you mean? What happened to her? Mom! Tell me." She grabbed Jane's hands. "Please!"

"I'm so sorry, baby. I'm... so sorry..."

"Mom!" Alice shrieked. "No! Don't tell me Sam... No!" Alice moaned beneath her breath and her mother reached down to hug her tightly.

Brian stood there in shock.

I didn't know who Sam was, but she must have meant a lot to Alice and her mother. I glanced at Kareena, uncomfortable myself because I didn't know what to say.

Kareena frowned. "I'm sorry, Alice," she said. "I'm really sorry."

Chapter 18

"We're too late!?" Brian sneered, clenching his teeth. "Shit! We can't be too late! Too late to save... Sam?" He brought both hands up to rub his face and let out a loud, frustrated grumble. "Damn it! Why did this all happen so quickly?"

I looked away and tried to come up with something to say, but the truth was, I didn't know shit about Alice or her friend. She was just lucky she didn't have to watch her die— that she wasn't there when it happened.

I've seen people die. A horrifying chill creeps through your blood stream, taunting you with the inescapable truth about your own frail mortality. It's not something you forget. Ever.

But there's a weird quirk about being told about someone's death and not actually seeing it happen. There's an emptiness in you that believes they're still here. You don't see them go and you want nothing more than to believe in the possibility that they never really passed away to begin with.

"Who's Sam?" Lucy asked, tugging on the hem of my shirt. "Daddy?"

"Shh," I whispered. "She was Alice's friend. I'm sure she'll tell you more about her later on, but right now, she needs us to be quiet."

"When, Mom?" Alice asked. "Did she say anything about me? What happened?"

"A few weeks after you two left, actually," Jane replied, her voice trembling. "Her parents said she didn't even act like she was sick. They didn't know anything was wrong with her until she went to school one day and..." Jane heaved a breath. "And... it happened in the middle of class. The school closed for the rest of the day. Doctors couldn't figure out what it was, but they're blaming it on that thing that's going around. Whatever it is."

"So this is our fault?" Brian muttered. "We did this? We killed Sam?"

Alice lifted her face from her mother's lap. "No. We didn't do this." She narrowed her eyes and scanned the room. "*They* did!"

She staggered to her feet, seething. "Where are you?" she roared, a vile expression creasing her brow. "Damn it! Where are you!?" She lunged past me, pressed a hand to the wall, and started dragging her fingers across as she walked the length of the room. "Coward!"

"Alice!" Jane stood.

"Come out of hiding!" Alice waved her arms around the empty space between us. "Judas! Show yourself!" she hissed. "This is your fault!" Alice wrapped her fingers around the back of a dining chair and hurled it across the room. A leg cracked off and the decorative back split open. I shielded Lucy from wood shards that spit toward us.

"Calm down, Alice!" Brian grabbed her from behind and tried to pull her arms in close to her body to restrain her. "Alice! Calm down! Please! There's nothing we can do!"

"He's here! He's the one who did this to her! He killed my best friend!" Alice screamed at the top of her lungs and kicked her feet like a wild animal, thrashing and pushing to try to get out of Brian's arms. He held on tightly.

"Alice! Stop! Damn it!" Brian grunted and fought to keep her arms down as he backed away from the table. "Please!"

"I... He..." She wheezed. "This is all their fault. Brian... you know that, don't you?" Her voice broke. "Brian?" She gasped for breath.

"I know!" Brian strained to reply as he held her back from the furniture. "Alice, it is their fault."

She quit flailing and collapsed into his arms. Brian stumbled back and adjusted his grasp on her to help her catch her balance. Then he turned her around and put his hands on her face, cupping her cheeks.

"Alice, it's too late. We can't change things now. We can't change what's already happened."

"But... that *thing*. He..." She searched the room with weary eyes.

"I know. But we can't change that now. We have Solus to take care of and I can't have you breaking down on me." He brushed his hand through her hair and lifted her chin with his fingers. "Alice, we'll get through this, somehow. Please calm down. I feel like shit, too, but taking it out on Judas isn't going to change things."

"Judas?" Jane repeated. "Who's—"

I lifted a flattened hand toward her and she paused.

Solus inched his way over to his mother and stared up at her. When she didn't acknowledge him, he tapped her on her leg. She looked down at him and sighed.

"What is it, Solus?" she said weakly.

Solus gestured for her to come down to his level. When she did, he stretched both arms out to the sides and closed them as tightly as he could around her.

She let out a painful cry and burst into tears. Solus rested his head against her as she wept.

Her heavy sobbing made my stomach twist into an anxious mess. Every shuddering inhalation made my heart ache. She didn't deserve this. She didn't deserve any of this.

Maybe if we had all said no to begin with and I hadn't forced her and the others to play their parts... Maybe then—

"I-I think I should go see my family, too," Kareena said. "Just in case something happened to them."

Brian turned. "It's probably not the best idea, you know?

With everything going on and, well, you were already arrested once. What if someone finds you and you end up getting arrested again?"

"Yeah," I agreed. "And not to mention, who the hell is going to watch Judas? You and I are the only ones who can and I'm not doing it on my own."

"Well, then, come with me!" Kareena groaned. "Please!? I really, really want to check on my parents. I mean, if Sam died, how do I know my parents are safe? What if something happened to them, too? Or... what if it reaches them soon and I never even said goodbye? Guys, please."

Shit. There she goes again. Feeling things.

Brian wasn't budging and Alice was a blubbering mess on the floor with Solus. Judas stood in the far corner of the room, still only a faded halo of light, and Kareena was about to start crying her eyes out, begging us to let her see her family.

I didn't think it was a good idea, but if I had been given the chance to see my dad before he died, even if it meant going to jail because of it, I'd have taken that risk in a heartbeat. Because living the rest of your life having never said goodbye to someone you love is worse than jail any day. And I would know. I've lived through both.

"I'll go with her."

Everyone's eyes were on me.

"Y-you will?" Gratitude curled Kareena's lips. "Thank you, David. Thank you so much."

Alice wiped her arm across her eyes and sniffled. "Be careful."

"I will," Kareena replied. "Jane. Do you have a cell we can borrow? In case something comes up?"

"Oh, sure." Jane cleared her throat and stumbled off into the kitchen. She returned a moment later with a cell phone in hand and passed it to Kareena. "Call if anything happens, please. It's the home number in the address book."

"Will do. We'll be fine. Just a quick visit."

"Judas, Lucy." I turned. "You're coming with us."

Lucy jogged over to me and I began to follow Kareena toward the front door.

"Lucy!" a tiny, unfamiliar voice cried.

I jerked my head around and a breath caught in my throat.

Solus ran toward us, flailing.

"Lucy!" he repeated, eyes wide and a glint of fear on his face.

My heart dropped like a stone. The one word Solus finally spoke was my daughter's name.

He thought I was about to take her away from him...

Chapter 19

Dusk closed in. We had to get moving. After some firm convincing, I agreed it would be okay to leave Lucy with Alice and Brian. Solus didn't want to see her go and it hurt to hear him call out to her in his tiny, underdeveloped voice.

Kareena's parents lived a few streets down. Having not even introduced him to Jane, we brought Judas along. We decided it was for the best. Seeing how Alice had almost attacked him, we didn't need Jane losing it, too.

We kept to ourselves for most of the walk, trying to avoid attention, but then we turned a corner and Kareena stopped abruptly. I tripped into her and nearly fell.

"Hey!" I composed myself. "What is it?"

She was staring off at someone's lawn across the street.

"That's *my* goddamn car!"

"What?"

"Oh my freaking God! They sold my car! What the hell!?"

"Kareena, keep your voice down!" The tiny, sickeningly wealthy-looking suburb looked like the type that would call 911 any time some kid fell off a bike. I didn't like the look of the neighborhood at all. Nice, maybe, but not my kind of subdivision. Extravagant two- and three-story brick houses all around. Tiny mansions a guy like me couldn't afford in a million damn years. And here, privileged Kareena was yelling at a red sports car parked in someone's driveway.

"But... but... it was, like, the only thing I ever loved!" She frowned, over exaggerating beyond belief. "My baby! How the hell could they sell her!? That son-of-a-bitch. He had his eye on her from day one. Damn it."

"What are you going on about, Kareena? Really? Right now? We have some seriously important sh—"

She pointed. "My neighbor's son, Brad, was jealous of my car from the day I got it. He didn't take long to creep up after I'd disappeared and make a deal with my parents for it. Sneaky little bastard."

"Look, Kareena, it was your parents who sold it to him, so stop freaking out."

"Well, they shouldn't have," she growled.

What I would give for the slick ride she once had. Custom platinum rims with matching red spinners. Black accents. Racing stripes. Tri-coat finish. Shit. The car must have cost more than sixty grand. Easily.

I could have stripped that beauty and made back a quick ten or twenty thousand overnight. However, I couldn't help but think Kareena wouldn't have appreciated me cutting up her "baby." Even if we *did* need the money.

Besides, I wouldn't try it in a neighborhood like this. And definitely not in plain sight. Cars weren't as easy to hot-wire as they used to be.

Kareena bent over and scooped a rock up from the edge of sidewalk. "I should go over there and bust a window." She exhaled loudly. "Would serve him right."

"Kareena, we're not here to settle grudges over stupid shit. Come on. Let's get going before people start thinking something's up. I don't want to be caught staring at a car like that for too long in a place like this." I looked at some windows on the houses and then scanned a few overhangs in peoples' driveways. No doubt there were security cameras everywhere. This subdivision was rich. Filthy. Rich. Perfect for the little princess tagging alongside me.

"Fine." Kareena huffed. "My house is, like, three houses down. On this side of the road." She tromped off ahead and I sprinted to catch up with her, checking behind to make sure

Judas was keeping up. The fuzzy white blur followed us like a ghost.

She stopped in front of a large, bright white, two-story brick mansion set right at the end of the cul-de-sac, and turned to head up the driveway.

"Wow," I accidentally said out loud.

She turned. "What?"

"Oh, nothing." I wasn't going to say anything else about how small I felt right then in front of her parents' million-dollar house. If only I could give something like that to Lucy. Gleaming stone pillars on both sides of the archway leading to the hardwood and stained glass front door.

We didn't need that kind of extravagance. Really. Money buys a lot of things, but this... this kind of paid-for happiness didn't jive with my definition of necessity.

I dragged behind her a few feet to keep an eye on Judas as she marched up the concrete steps and knocked on the door with her knuckles.

"Mom!" she yelled, impatiently tapping her shoe on the ground.

I held my breath as she waited.

"Mom! Damn it. Where are you?" She knocked again, harder, and then pushed the off-white button beside the door-frame, setting off the doorbell. "It's me. Come get the door, please!"

"Maybe they're not home," I whispered.

"They're home." She veered back to look at me. "They're home, okay? I'm sure they are. The upstairs light is on in Mom's office. They have to be here." She turned and lifted her fist to bang on the door one more time.

The door clicked and she lowered her hand.

"See. I told you," she said, glancing at me and then eagerly looking back at the door, biting her lip as a smile lit up her face. Something I hadn't seen before.

"Kareena?" a male voice said.

"Jordan!? What the hell are you doing here?"

I perked up, but stayed where I was, listening from the driveway.

"I-I was gonna ask you the same thing. We all thought you'd been kidnapped and murdered or something."

"No. I'm fine, as you can see. It's a long story, okay? Right now, tell me where my parents are, please. It's important."

"Kareena," I called. "Is everything okay?"

"Yes." She turned. "This is my cousin, Jordan. Get over here, David."

I hesitantly neared the front porch and walked up the steps toward the ornate glass and dark wood front door the young man was propping open. He looked to be in his early twenties and had dark tan skin, a short buzz cut of black hair, and wore thin-rimmed glasses. His dark blue button-up collared shirt made me think he was in some kind of technology field. Or maybe I was just assuming since he fit the stereotype.

"Who is he?" Jordan asked suspiciously.

"The guy who kidnapped me," she replied without an ounce of sarcasm. "Just kidding. He's a friend. He's been helping me out since I left."

"You *left*? So you're saying this whole mess was voluntary?" Jordan looked disgusted. "Kareena, I know you've done some weird-ass crap in the past, but this... this is just—"

"Let us in, damn it!" Kareena roared. "This is my house!"

"Okay! Okay!" Jordan flinched and stepped away from the door. "Sorry."

She barged in and swung the door wider open behind her for Judas and me to follow.

I didn't spend much time looking at the ornate stairwell just off to the side of the entrance, or the elegant white trim outlining the mahogany floorboards below my tattered shoes. I didn't dwell on the cathedral ceilings above or the sparkling crystal chandelier twinkling through the doorframe of the next room.

I didn't have time to feel like a nobody.

"So where are my parents?" Kareena asked again, poking her head into the kitchen, then returning to stand beside me.

"Your dad's in the hospital and your mom's staying in a nearby hotel. They're paying me to watch the house for them while they're gone."

"What!?" Kareena's eyes widened. "What does he have? Is he okay? Is my mom okay? Jesus. You know she has anxiety attacks." She jerked her head toward me. "Did you hear that, David!?"

How could I not when she had just screamed it in my face?

I nodded.

She returned her attention to Jordan.

"What does he have, Jordan!?"

"They, uh, don't know." He shrugged.

"What do you mean they don't know? How can they not know what he's got? It's not like we don't have enough money to pay a specialist. What are they thinking it is? How long has he been in there? How long have you been—"

"Kareena." I took her hand. "Calm down."

"How am I supposed to calm down," she shrieked, jerking her hand away from me, "when my parents are in trouble?"

"Kareena, please." I gave Jordan a look implying he should give us some space and he got the message and backed away.

"I'm just going to go upstairs for a minute," Jordan said, his voice shaking. "Try to relax and I'll tell you more when you've calmed down."

He darted up the staircase and I heard a door close on the second floor.

"Kareena," I took her gently by the forearms. "Let's sit down and think about this for a minute. Okay?"

"What's there to think about, David?" She shoved me

away again, but I held tight enough that she couldn't escape.

"Your dad's in the hospital and your mom's with him. They're in good hands."

Kareena's brilliant green eyes judged me for a fool.

"I need to go see my dad," she said. "What if he has this shit the Saviors caused?" She shot an angry glance at Judas and made a fist. "I need to go see him now!"

"And do what!?" My fingers pressed into her arms to make the point and keep her attention.

"David. Let me go!"

"Do what, Kareena?"

"I-I don't know," she muttered, quieting down. "I don't... know." She stopped resisting me and I released her.

"Exactly. And we don't know what we can do—if anything at all, at this point."

"But, what if he dies? What if my dad dies thinking I never came back? And what if my mom loses it after that and then... Oh, shit. I have to go see them, David. I just..." She lifted her wrist and turned to Judas. "Can you alter mine, too?" A flicker of pink light shot through the white of her right eye.

I grabbed her and pulled her away from Judas before she could channel any more energy.

"Kareena, no!"

The door upstairs clicked open. Footsteps thumped down the staircase.

"What's going on?" Jordan asked frantically. "Is he hurting you? Should I call the cops?"

"Stay out of this," I yelled back at him. "You have no idea what you're getting yourself into."

Jordan backed up and clutched the guardrail so tightly, his knuckles turned white.

"I'm... I'm just going to go back upstairs and—"

"No!" Kareena looked up at him. "Jordan! You don't understand. Get back down here, please. I'll explain everything to you."

"No," I whispered. "No, you won't."

"Would you rather he call the police?"

I gritted my teeth. "No," I hissed. "But..." I glanced at the drifting white silhouette behind her.

"We can trust him," she said, pushing away from me to meet Jordan at the base of the stairs. "Jordan, we *can* trust you, right?"

He nodded nervously. "Yes."

"Good." She rolled her shoulders back, lifted her chin, and looked down her nose at him. "Because if you screw us, you'll be sorry. I'm sure as hell not afraid of hitting a guy with glasses, even if you are related to me."

We sat and talked for a few minutes. Jordan thought we were both crazy, and against my better judgment, I asked Judas to reveal himself momentarily in an effort to convince him we were telling the truth. All it took was a brief flash of the pale thing and Jordan was damn near clinging to the ceiling.

But when he finally calmed down, he listened, and listening made him understand. We weren't out to hurt anyone. We didn't ask for this.

"I'm going upstairs to grab few of my things and a change of clothes."

"Uh... y-you can't do that," Jordan stammered.

"And why not? Have you been playing dress-up?"

"No! Kareena, you don't get it, do you? Everyone really does think you're dead."

"What? I thought they were still looking for me? Why would they—"

"They found your blood all over the place after that huge earthquake in—"

"I didn't die there! I got hurt, yes, but they didn't find my body, right?"

"Well, no, but it was enough for them to make a case that you'd gotten buried beneath the rubble somewhere. I'm sorry, Kareena, but that's what happened. How long did you expect your parents to keep looking for you after they got the news?"

She dropped her head down. "Longer than this..."

"We need to get back to the others," I said, trying not to sound inconsiderate. We couldn't stay out for too long and I was worrying about Lucy already.

"I don't want to go."

"We have to," I reminded, touching her hand.

"Can I just take one last look at my room before I go? Just... look out the window, so I can remember what it felt like before everything went to hell? Please? I may never get the chance to come back."

I hesitated.

Those rich leaf-green eyes pleaded for me to let her go.

So I did.

"Okay. But please don't be long. We *really* need to go."

Kareena tried to smile, but her quivering lip wouldn't comply. Then she got up from the couch and walked toward the staircase. She made her way up, each step coming down so softly, I couldn't hear it, but I watched her get to the top and turn to walk across to the door on the other end of the upstairs railing. She twisted the knob and walked inside.

I waited as patiently as I could while Jordan seemed to study me.

"So, uh, your accent. Where are you from? Boston?"

"New York."

"Ah." Jordan swallowed and looked down at his lap.

"So, are you, uh, her boyfriend?"

"No." My leg started to twitch. *Damn nicotine withdrawal.*

"Oh. Okay. What kind of work do you do in... New York?"

"Look, kid." I glared at him. "I don't feel like making small talk right now, alright?"

"Sorry." He clasped his hands together while we sat in silence for a few more minutes.

"I hope her dad is okay," Jordan uttered.

"Me, too."

I know Kareena's more fragile than she pretends to be. Sure, she'd been through a lot of hell with Brian's brother, Taylor, but it left a mark on her—one people couldn't see on the outside.

It was there, and it had changed her.

"Come on, Kareena! We gotta go!" I stood. "Kareena!"

We waited a few more minutes until I heard the muffled blare of police sirens. I shot up from my seat.

Damn it.

"Now!" I yelled one more time.

Kareena popped out of the room upstairs and hurried down the stairs.

The sirens grew louder. Closer. My palms were sweating already. I snagged Jordan by the collar and sneered. "You called the police didn't you, you little pr—"

"No!" Kareena grabbed my arm and started prying me off him. "He didn't!"

"Then who—"

"I-I did." She looked away.

"What!?"

"I'm... I'm sorry, David."

"Why would you do something so stupid? We can't let the police find us."

"We need help, David! We need a hell-of-a-lot more help than we're going to get hanging around with a couple of teenagers. We have Solus and he's supposed to be the key, right? Maybe we can get some doctors or scientists to help us—"

"Are you out of your mind!?" I released Jordan and he nearly toppled over trying to catch his balance. "They can't find me! I can't let the cops find me. Some of them back home already saw my light and—"

"So I'll show them mine, too, and we'll be okay. My dad's a big name in this town. We'll be okay, David."

"No. No, we won't." I marched toward the front door and saw lights flashing. Police sirens whirred from the driveway. "Shiiit!"

"David, please! Listen to me!" Kareena grabbed my shoulder.

"No!" I veered around and yanked my arm out of her grasp. "You listen to *me*, you ignorant... little... bitch."

She gasped and covered her mouth.

"Sure, I'm wanted for robbing that damn convenience store to get you guys some cash, but I'm on the records for a shitload more than that. If they run my prints, I'm screwed. They'll lock me away for good."

"Holy shit! I didn't know—"

"You didn't need to know. I didn't tell you because you didn't need to know!"

"Well, what am I supposed to do now?" she whined.

The police were already in the driveway. I heard them outside the window via a loudspeaker.

"We have the house surrounded," one said.

"Wait," Kareena asked, her brow furrowing. "What are they doing out there?"

"What did you tell 911 was going on?"

"Uh. I may have told them my house was being invaded and that I needed help ASAP." She grinned sheepishly.

"What!? Why would you make up shit like that?"

"Well, how else would I have gotten them here before you decided to up and leave? Don't worry, okay? I'm going to go talk to them. I'll fix things."

"Stay here!" I grabbed her by the wrist and pulled her to my side. "No. You've done enough for tonight. We have to get out of here. Where's—"

I hadn't seen Jordan for several minutes.

"Where did he go?" My heart was about to bust out my chest. I couldn't get arrested. I couldn't get taken away from my Lucy. "No!" That's when I heard another door open from the other side of the room.

"He's in there," Jordan's distorted voice said from the other room.

Heavy footsteps.

There were cops in the kitchen. Armed cops.

"Step back from the woman," one of them shouted. He clutched a taser in his hands. "Step away from her and this will all go down easy. Okay?" He took a step closer and I let go of Kareena's wrist. She let out a scared, high-pitched whimper and stepped back.

"Don't hurt him, please!" she cried out.

"You don't know what you're messing with," I growled.

"Is that a threat?" the cop asked. Two more police officers came up beside him and the front door crashed open.

"You don't have anything on me," I said. "I didn't do anything. Kareena! Tell them you were bullshitting them on the phone."

"Shut up and put your hands up by your head!" the officer yelled. As soon as I lifted my hands, two more cops rushed in behind and tackled me, grabbing my arms and bending them behind my back. One of them pulled my gun from my belt and slid it across the hardwood floor to an officer on the other side of the room. They quickly patted me down even as I tried to fight my way free. A pair of cuffs snapped around my wrists and I couldn't pull my hands out from behind my back.

"Let me go! You don't understand. Please!" I grunted and wriggled violently, trying to break away. "Let me go!"

"If you keep fighting... we will use the necessary force to incapacitate you."

"Kareena!" Heat filled my chest as I summoned my fluorescence—golden light sparking to life inside me like a match being struck. My wrist felt warm. I channeled the light toward my fingertips. Just a little bit more and a portal would—

I lost control of my body. Hit the ground hard.

The room shook. Spinning.

I couldn't think.

Every muscle in me was having a spasm. I didn't know if I'd created a portal or not.

All I knew was that two metal barbs had pierced my flesh and were pumping thousands of volts of electricity straight into my system.

Chapter 20

Blurry surroundings. The cops scooped me off the floor and hauled me across the room. My shoes dragged over the brick walkway. Everything ached. Flashing police lights blinded me. My head was spinning. My body tingly and weak.

Someone pushed my head down and I slipped into the backseat of a car. My hands were still cuffed behind me. I wriggled around, trying to right myself until I could sit up and look through the wire divider at the police officer in front of me.

"Hey. I have to get back to my daughter. This is a mistake. That girl lied about everything."

"You have the right to remain silent," he said stiffly. "I told you your rights already, but if you need to hear them again—"

"No. No," I replied. "I got it." I'd heard them before.

I looked out the side window at the street. Nosey people were lined up on both sides, gawking at us like we were some kind of parade float driving by.

And I was the goddamn President.

What the hell was I going to do? Where did Kareena and Judas go? When did Jordan skip out on us?

Questions zipped through my brain. Mostly about what the hell I was going to do now and how I could get back to Lucy.

As soon as I set foot in that police station, I was gonna be hammered with felonies. Larceny. *Murder.* Prison for life, probably, even if they *didn't* connect me to a scrap I'd gotten into with a dealer way back. It was self-defense at the time, but now—six years later and still running from it—it looked a lot worse on my record. They'd find something to pin on me. Some reason to take my little girl away.

Damn it! They had my gun, too, and with my hands cuffed behind my back, I couldn't even try to make another portal. Not that I had the energy to. Every muscle ached from the induced seizure I'd had from being tased.

"I'm not going to lie," the cop in the passenger seat started, "those were some damn good special effects you put on back there at that girl's house. What are you? A pyrotechnic?"

I didn't reply.

"Hey. I'm talking to *you* back there."

"I thought I had the right to remain silent," I grumbled.

The driving officer laughed. "He's right."

.   .   .

They pushed me down into a chair and one of the cops sat behind the desk in front of it. He slid a flat electronic device out from behind his keyboard and handed it to the cop standing beside me. He flipped a switch on the side and it beeped faintly.

"I'm gonna need a finger for this," he said, reaching behind me for my wrist.

So I gave him one.

"Smartass." He popped me in the back of the head with his elbow and I grunted. "Don't screw with me."

"I don't belong here," I snarled.

"That's what they all say." He pried one of my fingers from my fist and pressed the tip against something cool and glass-like. Another shrill chirp came from the thing.

A fingerprint scanner? Not one I'd ever seen before.

"Looks like they've got you pinned for larceny here and that you're a suspect in a homicide case in New York," the

715

cop behind the desk read. "And those are just the things we do have you for. This isn't even counting the kidnapping in NYC. We heard a story about some guy there trying to steal someone's child and all three witnesses swore he had yellow light coming from his chest. Sound familiar? We thought that precinct was trying to get attention, but I guess it wasn't a load of crap, after all." He took the scanner from the other cop and pushed a button that released a USB adaptor. He plugged it into his computer and started typing something on his keyboard.

"You must enjoy being in jail. You have a lot on your record," he said, leaning closer to his monitor and scrolling down the page. "David—"

"I know my name, damn it." I shifted in the uncomfortable metal chair. "So what are you going to do with me?"

"That depends."

"On what?"

"On what else we find out when we run that shiny, limited-run gun of yours."

Shit...

.　　.　　.

I did not have time for this.

They set my bail at thirty grand. *Thirty. Freakin'. Grand.* I can't remember a time I had more than a couple hundred bucks on me, let alone thousands of dollars in loose cash. A lot of people don't even make that much in a year. I sure as hell didn't.

I scuffed my feet against the concrete floor of my claustrophobic temp jail cell and shuddered. It was cold and nasty, but it wasn't supposed to be comfortable. The odor of B.O. and vomit kept wafting through the air.

"Where did you say you were from again, José?" a man in the cell across from me asked, slurring his words together.

"It's David," I snapped. "Shut the hell up and leave me alone. Unless you want the crap beat out of you when I get out of here."

It didn't help that there was some drunk-ass guy in another cell wallowing in his vomit-soaked shirt and pants who had been asking me questions since I'd arrived. That, and I must have had a name change every ten minutes. Pedro. Mario. Javier.

Jesus. I've gotten wasted and said and done some stupid stuff in my time, but this guy was so far gone, it wasn't even funny. At some point, though, he muttered something about his wife kicking him out, and for a moment, I felt a little sorry for him.

A little...

The cops said they'd move me to another jail in the morning, but that wasn't soon enough for me.

A wanted man in three states. One allegedly, but only because they couldn't actually prove they saw me glowing back at Kareena's house, which meant they couldn't pin me 100% for the kidnapping either.

I couldn't believe Kareena thought it would actually be okay to call the cops and make up a fake story. She was smart most of the time, but this afternoon, I lost all respect for her.

What kind of idiot was I to develop feelings for a brat like that? She didn't care what happened to me. If she did, she'd have asked before cooking up a half-ass-baked plan.

I'd overheard one of the other cops verifying that they couldn't find the girl at the scene. One of them even went so far as to claim he saw her disappear into thin air.

Either my portal worked or Judas got her out of there. Either way, she was safe, hopefully. I really shouldn't have even been thinking about her.

I should have been worrying more about Lucy than the woman who betrayed me.

. . .

Someone rapped on the bars of my cell.

"Hey, Pyro." It was one of the cops who had brought me in. Officer Kenneth, I think. I didn't look up when he walked over. I'd just woken up and was sitting on the edge of my bunk, irritated and antsy from the crappy sleep I'd endured.

"Hey. I'm talking to you," he said, raising his voice.

"Name's not Pyro."

"Yeah, okay, smartass. There's someone here to see you."

I lifted my face. A middle-aged woman in a dark pantsuit came in behind him with a small black briefcase dangling from her hands.

"Are you a lawyer?" I asked, raising an eyebrow at the stuffy-looking woman. She had short, layered, and highlighted brown hair and a pair of glasses tucked into her shirt collar.

"I'm afraid I'm not," she replied, approaching the bars. "I'm Doctor Sasha Cortez. I'm a biologist working with the city forensics department."

"And you want...?"

"I'm here for some samples I can take back to the lab for analysis. I was told by the department that you were seen glowing at the scene yesterday. Is that right?"

I shrugged. "Does that sound normal to you, Doc?"

"Well, no, but..."

"They didn't see shit."

"Regardless of what they think they saw, we've had two different accounts from over six witnesses who say they've seen you glow with some kind of yellow light. Whether it was a trick or not, that's what I'm here to investigate." She crouched down in front of the cell so she was slightly lower than eye level with me. "David. Can I call you David?"

I nodded.

"David, I'm not the bad guy here. I'm a biologist trying to do my job. Can you cooperate with me, please?"

Sasha sounded like she'd done this before and was just going through the motions like she would with any suspect.

But at the same time, she was right—she wasn't the bad guy.

I was.

"Yeah. Alright."

Officer Kenneth unlocked the door and slid it open to let Sasha in. "Don't try anything stupid," he warned.

I laughed to myself. I could have grabbed the doctor by the throat and have broken her neck if I had wanted to. *If.*

She opened her box and laid it beside me on the bunk.

"I need your arm," she said as she rummaged through her things for a pair of gloves, a rubber tourniquet, and a syringe. She slid the gloves on.

Better yet, I could use the syringe to pierce her throat. Take out an eye and then relieve the cop of his gun. *Could.*

This precinct wasn't used to guys of my caliber, apparently. It made me feel sorry for the doctor. Officer Kenneth was putting the doctor's life in danger by allowing her to get close to me without making sure I was properly restrained first.

I laid my arm out on my thigh with the sensitive inner flesh facing up and she tied the rubbery strip around my bicep. She wiped the insertion spot with an alcohol pad.

"Relax your arm, please," she said, tapping the spot she was about to aim for.

I grimaced as the needle pierced the thick scar tissue of my inner arm.

The blood collection tube began to fill. "I see you're no stranger to needles." She looked me in the eye briefly and then untied the tourniquet.

My jaw tightened. I had scars from my days of shooting up. They weren't something to be proud of, but they were obvious if you knew what you were looking at.

"I've been clean for a while," I replied. "I've got a daughter to worry about now."

"Oh?" Sasha withdrew the needle and capped it. She tucked a piece of gauze over the mark. "Bend your arm, please. Hold it there."

I shook my hand to drive off the tingling sensation.

"How old is she?" she asked, swiping a piece of bandage tape over the mark.

"Five."

"Just at the age when you can actually start taking them places, huh?" She smiled. It seemed genuine and I cracked a small one myself, chuckling at the irony of her words.

"Yeah. You have no idea," I replied.

Chapter 21

Sasha packed the syringe carefully back into her case and took out a plastic bag with a label on it.

Officer Kenneth tossed a plain white t-shirt at me through the doorway. "Change your shirt."

I caught it. "What? Why?"

"I was getting to that," Sasha said, wrinkling her lips to the side and shooting him a dirty look. "You could have given me two more seconds." She looked at me again. "We need your shirt to test for flammables or chemical residue from whatever it was you did back there that made you glow."

I reached behind my neck for my collar and began pulling my shirt over my head. "I seriously doubt you're gonna find anything on here," I said. "But if your police friend wants to see the goods that badly." I flashed a smirk at the officer and his nostrils flared.

"Shut up!" he barked.

"Please stop!" Sasha tucked my shirt into the plastic bag and zipped it closed. "Christ, you two." She walked over to the cell doorway and turned. "You're from New York, right, David?"

I nodded.

"Then let me put this into words you'll understand. Behave if you want a chance in hell at making it to court in once piece. They're sending you to Pembrook Detention Center later today. That place is a shit hole compared to this slice of heaven. It will do you some good to make friends while you're there. If I were you, I'd start appreciating the last few hours you've got here."

Officer Kenneth slammed the metal cell door closed behind her and scowled at me as the doctor walked past him.

"Damn it!" I slammed a fist against the metal bars and recoiled from the shooting pain ripping through my bones. A glimmer of gold beamed from beneath my shirt and I quickly turned away from the hall and brought my arms in close to my chest to shield the light from view.

My bracelet...

The heat of my light made the bangle warm around my wrist. Maybe, just maybe I could use it to escape.

I scooted over to the bars and looked out. No one was in the hall and the guard at the front wasn't close enough to see what I was doing from his post. I returned to my bunk and shook out my hands.

"Okay. Come on," I whispered. "You can do this again. You want to see Lucy, right?" I clenched my fists and tried to summon my light, using the pain from a moment ago as a catalyst to aggravate the fluorescence. My hand came up and I parted my fingers just as I'd seen Judas and Solus do. The light in me grew brighter. Hotter. It sparked and crackled beneath my veins and skittered down my wrist until it crashed into the bangle and...

"Ah! Shit!" I jolted and slammed my back into the concrete wall. A line of black raised skin sizzled across my wrist. "Shit!" I tried to shake it off, but the searing pain wouldn't fade. Damn. The energy burned the hell out of me.

It had worked earlier though. Maybe the taser had shorted the thing out.

So that option was off the table.

For now.

I flopped onto my bunk and dropped my head back against the cell wall. Would I be in for the long haul this time?

Once ballistic reports came back on my gun... I was screwed. Guns and cars were a passion. I got my hands on a rare gun because I wanted something uniquely mine, but being cocky like that only makes it easier to trace the bullet striations when you end up having to use it.

Striations—rifling impressions—are tiny, scratches inside the barrel of the gun that get imprinted on the bullet casing when it's fired. Think of it as a kind of fingerprint. Every gun is unique due to manufacturing variations.

"Knock knock."

I looked up. A new police officer was at the door of my cell, along with Officer Kenneth.

"Let's go, Pyro."

"Quit calling me that," I muttered through gritted teeth.

"Hey, I know what I saw, and until Cortez or someone else at the lab finds out why you lit up like a damn firework, that's what I'm calling you. Besides, the boys at Pembrook will come up with something else soon enough."

They unlocked my cell door and entered with two pairs of cuffs. One for my hands and the other for my ankles.

"Where the hell is this Pembrook place anyway?" I asked, putting my arms behind my back before they could force me to.

"All you need to know right now is that it's where guys like you belong. You'll be right at home with the others there."

The last time I was in jail was when I was a teen. Got caught stripping a car and had to do three months behind bars in juvie and another nine of community service. It sucked, but it didn't change who I was or keep me out of trouble for long.

They snapped the second pair of cuffs onto my ankles and walked me to the back exit where a police van waited. They opened a door, gestured for me to get in the back, and then attached another chain to my cuffs, securing me to the seat so I couldn't get away even if I had the chance. Not that I would have tried. I was no good to Lucy dead. As long as I was alive, I had a chance at getting out in one piece.

The ride to Pembrook was a bumpy one.

Once inside the jail, they made me change into ugly jail garb—a conventional orange short-sleeve jumpsuit with buttons up the shirt.

"Orange, my favorite color," I said sarcastically.

"Keep moving." One of the guards pushed me in the back with a baton and I took a breath of warm, stuffy air.

Damn it. This is really happening.

·   ·   ·

The cell was small, as expected. No more than about eight feet by eight feet. Ugly white brick walls. Two metal bunks with sad excuses for bed linens draped over top. Steel toilet. A tiny writing desk in the corner and an even tinier TV perched on the wall above that. My cellmate, Herman, was a tall, hefty guy with a shiny bald head and a spider web tattoo up his neck and throat. He was slow in the head, a little punch drunk, maybe, and quiet. That was okay with me.

You know how, stereotypically, the guy people end up bunking with in jail is an asshole? Well, that wasn't the case.

The guy in the cell across from me was.

They called him Splitter. He was in for, allegedly, cracking some guy's skull clean open after he found the guy messing around with his wife. Then he did the same thing to her.

Technically, he belonged in a high-security prison, but someone slipped up on his paperwork and he ended up here, with guys like me who weren't out for blood.

He was still awaiting his sentence, and from what I'd overheard, it was going to be a while before that day came. Splitter had been behind bars for a year and a half, but the courts were taking their sweet time getting to his case.

When were they going to get to mine?

Why hadn't the Prism made any attempts to free me? They

were quick to coerce me into saving Kareena when Taylor attacked, but now that I needed help—nothing.

"Hey, pretty boy!" *Splitter*. His voice was an awkwardly higher pitch than I'd suspect to hear coming from such a husky guy.

I ignored him.

"You got a girl back home?" he asked, pressing his face between the bars. "I'm talking to you, Mexico."

"No. I don't." I looked up at him and sneered. "Leave me alone." I turned away and went back to shuffling a worn deck of playing cards Herman had lent me. There were "water stains" on the edges, but those were the least of my worries.

"You might think you're smart, Mexico, but I run the show here!"

I laid a card down face up and six more in a row face down, setting up a game of solitaire.

"You're in jail. You don't run shit," I replied, not looking up from the cards.

Herman grimaced. "Careful, bro," he mumbled. "You don't wanna get Splitter pissed."

I smirked. "He already is, isn't he?"

I knew guys like Splitter. They were all talk and when that didn't work, they were all jabs and punches. Ignore them— you're a dead man. Confront them—you're a dead man. I wasn't about to end up on the bottom of the pecking order.

Once you hit bottom, you're everyone's bitch.

And I am nobody's bitch.

Chapter 22

5:30AM. "Chow time" they called it.

I rolled over on my bunk and groaned. A headache pounded in my forehead. My shoulders ached and there was a tightness in my chest from tossing all night. Sleeping on the ground would have been more comfortable.

I sat up and put my feet on the floor.

Herman poked his head out over the side of his bunk above me. "If I were you, I'd go back to sleep," he said.

"Why?" My stomach grumbled. "I'm really hungry."

"One thing you'll learn here, David, is sleep is more valuable than food."

I thought on it a moment. "Hmm." It made sense. Sort of. I rubbed my tired eyes with my palms and blinked a few times to bring everything back into focus. Splitter was shuffling his way out of his cell and heading off to breakfast. With him gone, maybe I could get some rest. He was a noisy night owl and the place didn't have a lights out policy.

"Thanks, Herman."

He lay back down and I did the same.

About an hour and a half later, I awoke to a hand waving something around in front of my face.

"Hey! What!?" I sat up and snatched the thing from Herman.

A croissant? A quick sniff and a gentle squeeze. It was fresh.

"It ain't poisoned, I swear," he said, smiling, though he had few teeth to do so with.

"I believe you, actually." I chuckled. "Thanks. What do I owe you for this?"

"Complimentary. Today only." He laughed and tore his teeth into another croissant he was holding. "When you get your job, you can pay me back," he said, crumbs escaping his mouth.

I was supposed to be given a job to do soon. A whopping $0.36 an hour, but meals—aside from specialties from the commissary (like the croissant)—were provided.

"You alright?" Herman asked, motioning to my knee while I chewed the last bite of breakfast.

I couldn't stop twitching. Nicotine withdrawal.

"Yeah. I'll be fine."

"So what do they got you for?" Herman hopped down from his bunk and bent over to touch his toes in a stretch.

"Everything and nothing at the same time."

"Oh?" He lifted both arms over his head and bent to one side and then came back and bent to the other.

"They think I kidnapped my own daughter and six witnesses are claiming they saw yellow light coming out of my chest during a police confrontation."

"Well, damn, and I thought having a glowing reputation was only an expression."

Herman made me laugh. I liked that.

After a friendly game of poker, we watched the news from the tiny television in our cell and talked about nothing for a while. Turns out Herman had a daughter, too, but she had graduated from college and moved to another state a long time ago. He hadn't seen her since he and his wife separated seven years back. I didn't ask him what he was in for. I didn't want to know. He was the only ally I had at the moment and I didn't need a reason to question that.

Pembrook had open door hours during the day, which allowed select inmates (including Herman and me) to leave the confines of their tiny cells and access designated areas of the facility.

I got up to stretch my legs and took a walk out into the main courtyard. It was about the size of a little league baseball field, and there was a concrete wall wrapping around the entire yard that stood about ten feet tall. There were guard outposts on both ends and electrified, barbed wire strung across the top like Christmas lights.

Some jails had gyms, but this place... all it had was a flat of concrete with some benches and a small basketball court set up on the other side. Guys on the benches were smoking and talking. Seeing puffs of cigarette smoke made me antsy.

Ripped guys were playing basketball at the court and a few dozen others were jogging around the perimeter. They had the right idea.

If there was something I learned on the streets, it was to maintain your body. Work hard. Fight harder. Staying in good shape was the only way to stay alive on the streets. And in a place like this.

I found a quiet corner near the wall, rolled up my sleeves and flexed my hands a few times, cracking my knuckles. Then I dropped down and started doing pushups. Fifteen. Twenty-five. I rested a minute and then finished with a second set. My hands ached from grains of concrete pressing into them, so I stood and brushed them off.

Exercise would help with the nicotine cravings, too. I'd kept myself in decent condition over the years—sometimes by choice, other times by necessity. You don't need to throw a strong punch to put someone in their place, you just need to throw a good one. One that makes contact, and to do that, you have to be quick.

To survive, I had to be faster. Stronger. I had to keep myself on the tip of my toes and at the top of my game. These guys were thieves and cutthroats. And if I didn't give them a reason not to mess with me, I could be dead before trial day—whenever that was gonna be. I hadn't gotten a date set yet. It had barely been forty-eight hours since I'd been taken in.

I wiped sweat from my forehead with the back of my sleeve and began jogging along with the rest of the group already doing laps.

What were the others doing without me? Were they trying to find me?

Of course, I—the Tracker—had to get my ass thrown in jail. A whole lot of good I was doing tracking myself.

I passed a few inmates and sped up, pushing the air from my lungs and sucking it in as my feet pounded against the ground.

I used to jog every morning back home. Gave me time to think.

I was tired of running from the law. I just wanted to settle down somewhere and—

"You!" Someone grabbed a hold of the back of my shirt as I passed. They jerked me back and I lost my balance and slammed into the ground.

I shook my head, disoriented.

"This is a no passing zone," Splitter said, leaning over me with a crooked grin on his face.

Crap.

"I'm not bothering you," I grumbled, pushing back onto my elbows and scrambling to get back on my feet.

He shoved me in the chest with a massive elbow and knocked me back down before I could stand. "I didn't say you could get up!"

Two other heavily-built men surrounded me and my adrenaline went into overdrive. I rolled over and pushed myself up off the ground as fast as I could and made a few feet of space between us.

"I don't want trouble," I said, bringing clenched fists up to my chin. "I don't want to fight any of you guys, but I will if

I have to." I adjusted my stance so I was steadier on my feet.

Splitter laughed and his two henchmen boxed me in.

Damn it.

"Why are you harassing me?" I hissed. "I don't want anything to do with you."

"I'm just putting you in your place, Mexico," Splitter sneered. "You disrespect me, you pay the price."

I glanced over his muscular shoulders at the guard post in the distance. They weren't watching us. Herman was still inside somewhere and the other inmates couldn't have given a shit less about me. They were all going about their business, some of the other joggers even passing us by like we were having a friendly conversation.

I glanced at the guys surrounding me. One was blind in one eye. The other one looked like he could skin a deer with his bare hands.

Stay calm.

Be faster.

Be smarter.

Splitter made brief eye contact with the guy behind me and nodded. I ducked and spun around, raising my arm to deflect a fist aiming for my ribs. A swift kick to the knee sent the half-blind guy down with a crack and a moan of pain.

"Look, man," I said to Splitter and his pal. "I've been through some shit you can't even begin to imagine in that tiny brain of yours. I have no idea where the hell my daughter is right now, the girl I thought I had feelings for just sold me out, and I haven't had a goddamn cigarette in two days. Don't get on my ass, because I'm not afraid to put you in your place if I need to."

"Randy, get up," Splitter yelled at the guy rolling around on the ground holding his knee. He shoved him in the back with his foot.

"I think he shattered his kneecap," the other guy said with a grimace.

"I was gonna spend the rest of my day picking flowers." Splitter laughed. "But if you insist on getting your ass kicked, I guess I must oblige."

I planted my feet again and Splitter came at me like a raging bull. A fist swung at my head and I ducked. A second one at my ribs and I dodged backward.

Splitter roared in frustration. "Quit moving around!"

Faster.

He came at me again and I darted out of the way, leaving him free to bash his hand into the perimeter wall. He howled in pain and shook out his hand. Blood flecks splashed onto his uniform.

I backed away.

"My name's David," I said, making distance between us. "And I don't want shit to do with you."

I veered around and picked up speed to head back inside.

My guard was down for a split second as I ran and someone blindsided me with a punch from the side. I went hurling to the ground. I shook my head and opened and closed my jaw. It cracked and popped back into place. Hurt like hell, too.

I came onto my elbows and someone's arm swung around my neck and put me into a chokehold from behind. I had no strength or balance with concrete in my face, and I couldn't get away from the arm squeezing my windpipe.

Dark spots flickered in and out of sight, and I writhed and jerked to try to get away. Whoever was holding me flipped me over onto my back, forcing me to watch Splitter throw a punch that landed against my cheek. The impact vibrated through my skull, blurring my vision for an instant.

He straddled my legs and wound up for another swing. Dizzy, I kept fighting, trying to wriggle my way out of their grasp before I blacked out.

"What the hell?" His jaw dropped. "What the hell is that!?" Splitter shot off me and backed away.

"Woah! My arm's burning!" The guy who had me in the chokehold let up, dropping me onto my back.

I coughed hard, wheezing to get air in as I sat up.

There was a sensation of heat welling inside my chest and I looked down to see my fluorescence licking up through the top button of my orange shirt.

"What is that?" Splitter's cohort asked, shaking.

"It's nothing," I said, slurring the words as I struggled to peel myself up from the ground. My jaw hurt. I swiped the back of my hand across my cheek and wiped the blood on my pants. A single step sent a jolt of pain through me. I cringed and pressed a hand over my lower abdomen where a sharper pain mounted.

"What the hell are you?" Splitter asked, making space between us as I stumbled past him and his friend.

I spat blood onto the concrete. "You don't want to know."

Chapter 23

Aw, damn it! I was bleeding.

In the sanctity of my cell, I unbuttoned my shirt and peeled soggy fabric away from my skin. A jagged gash split the flesh open just below my rib cage. They'd stabbed me with something during the struggle. Through all the adrenaline, I hadn't even noticed.

I wasn't gushing blood, but it was an unsightly wound. Muscle tissue looked nicked, but the rest was superficial. It would heal alright on its own. I didn't feel like crying for help. I wasn't the only guy there with a blood stain.

I lay back on my bunk and lifted my arms up to tuck them behind my head. It hurt to do that; the skin stretched over my ribcage as my arms rose. I changed my mind and dropped my arms to my sides.

Day one. Already got my ass handed to me.

•   •   •

This morning, Splitter walked past and didn't even blink in my direction. Seeing my light earlier had scared him, and that was okay with me. I spent the remainder of the morning resting. Mentally and physically fatigued. I wanted Lucy back. I wanted to know everyone was safe. Even... Kareena.

Damn it, I was pissed off at her for stabbing me in the back, but why couldn't I keep hating her? Why did I have to lie there on my bunk in my empty cell and start remembering what it was like to spend a night with her? Even if it was only that one time.

She was beautiful. The scent of her skin. Her stunning green eyes. The silky long hair that shimmered in the sunlight. Gorgeous full lips, too often slathered with bright red lipstick. It wasn't like I hadn't been with other girls like her. I had.

But... they weren't *her*.

Around noon, a guard alerted me that I was to be escorted to the onsite medical facility.

"What for?" I asked, my heartbeat racing as he clapped cuffs on my ankles again.

"Something about gathering more test samples," the guard replied.

More?

I was walked halfway across the facility, wrists and ankles cuffed. Down a long white hallway and then past a series of what appeared to be empty classrooms. At another desk, the guard took me by the arm and tugged me over to the receptionist, who proceeded to sift through a stack of folders.

She passed one over the top of the desk to me and the guard had me sit on one of the chairs in the waiting room.

The room was surprisingly empty. And quiet.

I glanced over at my escort and looked back down at my hands.

Less than ten minutes later, the receptionist called for me and directed both of us into a tiny room with glass and metal cabinets all along the walls. Each had some kind of electronic lock and keypad attached to its door. A large microscope was set up on one side and a wall of tiny vials and colored Petri dishes were stacked up beside it. There wasn't a blood pressure monitor anywhere to be seen. No stethoscope. No tongue depressors in little jars on the table. It looked more like a lab than a doctor's office.

"The doctor will be here in a moment," the receptionist said, then stepped out and closed the door behind her.

Through the frosted glass window in the door, I saw the doctor approach. She knocked and entered.

"Hello, David," Dr. Cortez said with a small, friendly smile. "Can you sit down, please?" She pointed to the padded examination table in the center of the room. The guard walked me closer to it and I sat on the edge.

"Why am I here?"

"You can wait outside," she said to the guard. He acknowledged her request and let himself out. He didn't go far, though. I could see the side of his head while he waited just outside the door.

"I need to ask you a few questions," she said.

"I thought you worked in forensics, not as a medical doctor."

"I do, but that's also part of why I requested you here. Some of your test results were skewed. It may have been a bad sample. I'm not sure, but we need to run them again." She looked me over quickly and her brow furrowed with concern. "Speaking of blood, where's all of that coming from?" She pointed at my side. "Your ribs? What happened to you?"

"A scuffle. Nothing to worry about."

"In my line of work, blood is always something to worry about."

A forensics joke? I *almost* laughed. Almost.

"Let me take a look at it while you're here." She tugged a pair of plastic gloves from a nearby box and put them on.

"It's nothing."

"David, please. I'm trying to help. This place is crawling with bacteria. You might have walked in, but with an untreated wound oozing blood like that, you'll be lucky if you crawl out."

I huffed a breath, defeated by her nagging. At the same time, she was right about the living conditions.

I unbuttoned my shirt and parted it just below my ribs. With my cuffs still on, I couldn't actually remove my arm from my sleeve, but at least she could see the gash in my side.

"Wow." She squinted, peeling the flap of my shirt to the side. "This is some dirty handiwork. Any idea what the weapon was?"

"I didn't see." I shrugged and it hurt. "Probably paper-clips and a plastic knife or something. Who knows."

"When was the last time you had a tetanus booster?"

"A what?"

"I'll take that as never. I'll leave a note to make sure they give you one." She turned to her desk and scribbled something down on a sheet of yellow paper in my folder.

"Again, *forensics*?"

"Yes, but before I got this job, I worked part-time for the city health department giving vaccines. Shingles. Influenza. That type of stuff. But when you work in a place like this, you learn a little of everything. You start making yourself useful. I don't like the daily grind. Get samples. Test samples. Compare samples. Fill out paperwork." She paused. "Mostly fill out paperwork. It might be riskier, but I like working with the inmates when I can. You wouldn't believe the number of guys put in here for weird crap that turns out to be someone else's doing, and then they get pinned for something they hadn't even been arrested for. And then there are the few ones I've gotten out. The wrongly accused."

"Like... me?"

"Oh, no, David. I don't think you've been wrongly accused of anything. I think you did whatever they've got you in here for, it's just why you did it that's getting to me."

She grabbed a bottle of something from an unlocked cabinet on the desk and rummaged through a drawer beneath it.

"I know they've got one in here," she said, shuffling things around in the drawer. "Ah. There you are." She pulled out a small blue plastic box. Inside it was a suturing kit.

I chuckled and shook my head. "You know how to stitch things up, too? Jesus, what can't you do?"

"When I was a teenager, I used to hike a lot. Slid down the side of a steep cliff once, bashed into a protruding rock, and split my forearm open. You learn things fast when you have to. And that was just a regular sewing kit, too."

"Sorry you had to go through that," I said, looking her in the eye.

She had kind eyes. Weathered, but kind. Like she had good intentions but life had thrown her a share of curveballs along the way.

"We learn from our experiences, right?" She laughed it off and then pressed her lips thin. "Anyway, where was I?" She threaded the short, curved needle. "That's, uh, an interesting tattoo you've got. Any particular meaning?"

"I'm half Samoan. It reflects who I am and who I'm trying to become. Too much to explain but, yes, it means a lot to me."

"I see. Well, it's better than most of the crappy ball-point pen, self-inflicted trash I see coming out of here." She patted the skin around the wound with a gauze pad and some liquid that stung like hell. "I know this isn't your first battle scar, but hopefully it will heal better than the rest of these," she said, gesturing to a line of scar tissue near the center of my chest.

"I'm used to it."

"Bleeding?" she asked.

"Fighting."

"You really shouldn't be proud of that." The needle pierced my flesh and I flinched. "Do... you want me to use an anesthetic?"

"No. And who said I was proud of that?"

"Well, I just assumed by the way you brushed it off."

"These scars are the reason I am who I am today. Every single one of them shaped me."

"Even the bullet wound?" She stopped abruptly and lifted her face up.

"Even the bullet wound."

She shrugged and went back to work, gently tugging the thread before sticking it back through and tugging it down again several more times.

"Look, David, I'm not supposed to be getting involved with your case, but I did some asking around and it seems like they have some fairly hard evidence pinning you to a handful of crimes. The ballistic report hasn't even come back yet."

"Then why are you telling me this? I thought you just wanted another sample."

She pulled the thread through and tied it around itself somehow before snipping off the end with a tiny pair of scissors. She tossed the remnants in the trash and peeled off her gloves.

"I've been at this game long enough to know that there are normal samples and there are abnormal samples," she said, typing a code into the keypad on one of the cupboard doors. She pressed her thumb into it and it beeped, clicking open. "Yours were neither. They were messed up. I'm going to need another sample of your blood to run them again." She removed a syringe and rubber tourniquet, along with a new pair of gloves.

"What makes you think the abnormalities you found weren't real?" I shrugged my shirt back up over my shoulders and buttoned it.

"Because if they were, you'd be in the hospital right now. Or dead. There's no way someone in your condition could have a blood count so low." She rolled up my sleeve.

I pulled back.

"There's nothing wrong with the sample you have now."

"What? You don't know that."

"I do," I said, clenching a fist.

She tensed and held her breath.

I narrowed my eyes at her. "Those witnesses weren't lying when they said they'd seen me glowing."

"David, I think you may have taken one too many knocks to the head out there in the streets." She reached for my arm again, but I resisted. "David!"

My escort overheard the commotion and rapped on the door. I heard an intercom switch on. "Do you need help?" His voice came through the speaker on the door.

I panicked and did the first thing I could think of. I thrust my weight into the wall beside me, sending a shockwave of pain through my system.

Dr. Cortez gasped.

I lifted my head and stared at her, my ears ringing and my shoulder pulsing with pain. The burning sensation in my chest assured me I'd done the right thing and the wide-eyed look of disbelief on her face, confirmed it.

She staggered toward her desk and pressed a red button next to the microscope. "I-I'm fine," she replied to the guard in a shaky voice and cleared her throat. "Everything's fine," she reiterated and lifted her finger off the button. The intercom clicked off.

Chapter 24

The throbbing pain persisted. I cupped my forehead and dropped my face down. I'd bashed myself hard against a concrete—not drywall—wall.

"Are you okay!?" Dr. Cortez pried my hand away from my face and swiped her fingers across my brow. "No broken skin. David, look at me, please? Oh my God, you're burning up."

I lifted my face, squinting in pain. Fluorescence flickered through me but quickly began to fade as the heat cooled.

"Is your vision blurry?" she asked.

I nudged her hands off me and blinked a few times until she came into focus. The pulsing ache softened. I rolled my shoulders back and stretched my neck to the side.

"You saw it, didn't you?" I asked.

She broke eye contact with me and chewed her lip. "I-I don't know what I saw."

"I *know* you saw it—the light. The... fluorescence."

Her brow furrowed and she looked me in the eye. "Is that what it's called?"

"Yes."

"Wh-what is it? This... *fluorescence?*" She bit her lip again and cautiously reached toward me. "How did you get it? What does it do?"

"It's a long story." I motioned toward the door. The guard was getting restless and moving around a lot. "One I don't think we have time for today."

"I need to know. Please!" She wrapped her fingers around

my arm and pleaded with her eyes. "This is what I live for, David! Anomalies like this. Something new and—"

"I'm not an anomaly," I said, jerking my arm away. "Don't ever call me that again."

"I'm sorry, David. It just came out. I didn't mean you, I meant... Oh, I don't know what I'm saying. I'm sorry, but I need to know what's going on inside you. Maybe if I can figure out what causes that light to glow, I can help get you out of here."

I sneered. "What? Why would a biologist want to risk her job to get a thief and accused kidnapper out of jail? Why don't you stop with the bullshit and tell me the real reason you want to help me. What's in it for you?"

She heaved a sigh. "Why do you think I took this job? Because I enjoy getting people put in jail? No, because I like seeing justice served. I want guilty people to be punished and innocent people to be set free. And no, I don't think you're innocent. Not by a long shot. But I think you deserve a second chance. I don't know what kind of situation you were in back when all of this happened to you, or who put you up to any of it, but people change."

"What makes you believe that?"

"Those scars on the inside of your arm." She pointed. "It's not common for people to get clean without major intervention. And I think that story about your daughter is true. She's the reason you aren't shooting up anymore or dead in some back alley right now."

She sat on the edge of the counter across from me and clasped her hands together in her lap. "Is there anything at all you can tell me about this? Something I can look for in your blood? Anything?"

"Do you really want the truth?"

"Yes. Of course I do!"

"Two words: Ghost Plague."

The color drained from her face. "What?" Her lip quivered.

"Do you... have it?"

My jaw tightened.

"David? Tell me!?"

I didn't reply.

"David! This could be the difference between life and death! We can't stop this if we don't know what we're dealing with or how you acquired it. You have to tell me what—"

"*I* don't even know what I have!" My gaze shot to the cutout in the door. The guard heard me shout and veered around to try to peer in. "I don't even know what the hell is going on," I whispered through gritted teeth. "But I do know that if I don't get out of here soon, I'll be next on the list of victims. I have to get back to my daughter. I don't have much time."

There was a knock on the door. The intercom came on.

"Doctor?"

She pressed the button to reply. "Everything is fine. I'll be finished in just a moment." She turned toward me. "David? Why don't you trust me?"

"I don't trust anyone. I can't. How do you think I ended up in this mess to begin with?"

Dr. Cortez frowned. "I'm sorry for whatever happened to you. I wish I could help. And... I wish you believed me." She pressed the intercom button again. "I'm finished here."

•   •   •

Un-cuffed back in my cell, I was restless, but too precautious to try to burn it off. I wanted to take another jog around the field, but it would likely tear open the stitches. So I sat on the edge of my bunk and stared at the blank white wall opposite me.

Did the doctor really want to help me? Or was she talking shit like everyone else? I couldn't trust her. I couldn't trust anyone. Not anymore. Brian and Alice were the only people left I could trust. They were the only ones who seemed to remotely understand—

I saw movement in the corner of my eye and jerked my head to look.

A ghostly white blur sifted through the air, wafting closer. I backed into the corner of my bunk and held my breath, petrified. The thing flickered and danced for a few seconds and then a shape manifested in its place—a small, fair-skinned child with one blue and one green eye.

"Solus!" I hopped off my bunk and bent down toward him. He looked to the side and up, and a second shape burst into focus. Alice.

My heart started thumping in my chest and I quickly ushered them behind me, toward the back of the cell where others wouldn't see them immediately.

"How did you guys find me?" I whispered.

"It was Solus," she answered quietly. "He found you. Kareena said the Prism told him where you were."

"Thanks, kid." I patted him on the shoulder.

A small grin spread across his lips and he lifted a hand toward my temple. One touch and a flash of commotion warped through my brain—visions of the police standoff, Judas and Kareena disappearing into a portal behind me, and a blinding white light. Then a flicker of Solus helping Alice conjure a portal.

"Where are the others?" I looked at Alice.

"They're in a safe place for now. Solus will take us back to them." She looked down and offered him her hand. "Solus? Let's leave."

He nodded and reached up to clasp his fingers around hers.

That's when Splitter started shouting at the top of his lungs. "Jail break! Jail break!"

Damn it.

The three of us swerved around. He was standing just

outside my cell flailing his arms.

"Shut up!" I yelled back at him, but he carried on.

"Come on, Alice! We gotta get out of here right now. Solus, you need to help us. Fast."

"Lockdown in cellblock D," someone announced over the intercom.

My cell door slid closed with a clang and locked. An alarm wailed in the building, prompting Alice to crouch down and cover her ears.

I swallowed hard, panting from the fear building inside me.

"Alice!"

"I know. I know!" She mustered up the strength to withstand the jarring noise and took Solus' hand. "Solus, please, we have to go *now*."

"How'd you get in here!?" someone shouted. A group of guards rushed to my cell. One already had a taser drawn and pointed toward us.

"Don't! She's not armed!" I shouted. Solus was tucked safely behind us both, so they hadn't noticed him yet.

A glint of green drew my attention. Alice's shoulder sparked with neon light and a bolt of it snaked down her arm toward her bracelet.

"What is she doing?" the guard asked, quaking at the sight of her chemical green glow. "Stop what you're doing! I am authorized to use force."

"I can't!" Her voice quaked. "I... can't stop it."

A flash of white energy burst from her wrist and flashed against the wall of my cell, creating a pool of swirling light.

The guard's hand shook; he pointed the taser at Alice. I stepped in front of her to take the brunt of the shot, but he didn't shoot.

"Whose kid is this?" he asked, drawing back his taser.

The entire group of guards stumbled over each other trying to withdraw from the gate. Solus was standing right up against the cell door, looking curiously up at the guards.

"Solus!" Alice screamed.

The portal spun rapidly beside us. I wanted to grab them both and go, but a sudden move could get her son hurt.

"How did he get in here?" The guard approached the bars and looked down at Solus. "Your eyes... they're..."

Solus lifted a hand toward him.

"What?" The guard's voice broke. "What does he want from me?"

"He wants to show you something," Alice said, glancing at her son and then at me and then the portal again. "Please let him! He's just a little boy. He won't hurt you!"

"Show me what?"

He was hesitant at first, but with little Solus just standing there with a hand raised up as high as he could reach and a look on his face that couldn't possibly be misjudged as deceptive, the guard soon gave in. He bent cautiously at the waist and let Solus stick his tiny hand through the bars just far enough to press a few fingers to the guard's temple.

There was a gasp, and the guard swung an arm out to the side, motioning for the rest of the group to back away.

"What was that?" another guard asked.

"I-I don't know. But we have to let the kid go. Just... back up. Go! Give them space!"

Alice called to Solus and he rushed past me to rejoin her. She scooped him up into her arms and gestured for me to go first.

I took a deep breath and dashed headfirst into the whirlwind of light.

Chapter 25

"You're back!" Kareena barreled into me, throwing her arms around my neck, nearly pulling me down with her frenzied embrace. I froze, confused.

"I... uh... Kareena?" I clutched her by her arms and gently pried her from my neck. "Since when are you happy to see me?"

"I'm sorry for what I did. I was a dumbass, and I didn't know it was going to get you arrested." She grimaced. "Oh, shit. What happened to your face?" She brought her fingers toward my bruised, inflamed cheek.

"It's nothing." I brushed her hand away.

She looked down. "My heart almost stopped when they tased you, and the way your fluorescence reacted, well, I thought it was going to kill you! I'm so sorry, David. Please forgive me for being such an idiot."

I didn't want to forgive her. I wasn't ready to.

As much as her embrace should have been appreciated, it wasn't.

"David?" She swallowed hard and bit her lip. "David, say something? Please?" Her warm fingers took up mine.

"I can't." I exhaled. "Sorry." I shoved past her.

Out of the corner of my eye, Brian looked surprised.

"Wh-what? Why?" Kareena approached me again. "I told you I was sorry. I screwed up. I didn't mean to."

"I don't want to hear it right now," I muttered, turning away. "I need some time."

"Daddy!" Lucy came at me like a wild animal. I smiled

and lowered myself down to give her a hug. "I missed you!"

"I missed you, too," I replied, hugging her tightly. She squeezed back and I clenched my teeth to stifle a grunt of pain. My jaw ached. Everything did.

Kareena heaved a breath and walked off somewhere, muttering.

"Solus told me you'd be okay," Lucy said, grinning from ear to ear. "We're best friends now!"

I chuckled. "That's good."

Brian and Alice were both smiling.

"So, what now?" I stood and looked around. We were still in Alice's mom's house. Jane was at work.

Judas materialized nearby, startling me.

"You're still here?" I asked. "I didn't even notice you."

"The others have not yet returned for me."

"But he's been, um, twitching a lot," Alice said, frowning. "You know... because..."

"More of them are dying?" I completed her sentence.

"Yeah."

"So what happened to you?" Brian asked, looking me over. His gaze snagged on the bloodstain below my ribs.

"You don't want to know. Whatever you do, Brian, don't get your ass put in jail."

"Uh, I'm not planning on it."

"Neither was I." I puffed out my cheeks as I exhaled.

"Do you need my help?" His hand radiated with a blue aura.

"I'm fine, thanks." I folded my arms to hide the distracting injury from view. I'd survived many fights without Brian's healing touch. "So, does anyone have something else I can wear? This is not exactly incognito swagger."

"Orange isn't your color, either." Brian grinned, trying to make me smile. "Jane still has some of my stuff down in the basement," he said. "Think any of it will fit you?"

A few inches taller and slightly more built than Brian, I

probably couldn't wear his clothes. If they were my only option for now, I'd take a shot at seeing if they fit. Luckily, Brian was in damn good shape for a guy his age. There was a chance they'd work out well enough.

There was something unnerving about popping out of the basement wearing Brian's clothes. A belt helped adjust the fit of the pants, and the shirt—although more snug than I'd prefer—was alright for the time being. The sleeves of one of his hoodies were too short, as were the pants, but at least I had a pair of shoes that fit. Albeit, plain white jail sneakers.

Alice cocked an eyebrow at me. "That's so weird," she said. "I've actually seen Brian wear that exact set before."

"Sorry." I shrugged. "It's weird for me, too. Don't normally go around wearing other dudes' clothes."

I glanced at Kareena. She was leaning against the wall on the other side of the room, arms crossed.

"Judas." I sat on the edge of the coffee table in the living room. "Since everything's going to shit right now and you're stuck here with us, I want to ask you something. Assuming the others haven't already."

"Yes?"

"What is fluorescence? The way you explained it to me initially, I thought of it like it was living inside us—like a virus or parasite."

"Fluorescence is not parasitic in any way. It is energy," he replied.

"Like the soul," Kareena said, pushing up from the wall. "The Prism said it was like the soul. That the energy is a life force."

"We were once part of the Prism," Judas said.

Everyone's eyes were on him.

"The Prism are made of all variations of color. We are made of one. As are each of you, aside from the child. We parted from their kind centuries ago, evolving to host only one variation. In order to do this, we had to forgo the spectral form and succumb to a physical one."

"So, if each of you are one single color and the Prism are all... doesn't that mean Solus is closer, biologically, to the Prism than you?"

"That is why we need him back," Judas said. "Blue fluorescence is the rarest of them all. It is both the most difficult to cultivate and the most tedious to bind to a host."

"That's why it had to be our child," Alice said.

"Yes. But because fluorescence is energy, it is volatile and can be transferred between individual carriers. This is why you cannot be with others." He looked at Kareena. "Your light cannot blend with the energy of others or it will corrupt the strain."

"Well, it's too late for that." She scowled. "I'm still here, so it can't be that bad."

"Your simple human mind cannot understand the consequences of this complex process," Judas replied, almost sneering. That surprised me. Then he twitched again and the expression went straight.

Another death? How many were left?

"We did not know it was possible with your technology, but the Seeker and I witnessed the crude piece of equipment utilized against you earlier. It disrupted your fluorescence."

"You didn't know this could happen?" Brian asked.

"We were unaware primitive technology could interrupt the fluorescent bond."

"What about the portals?" I looked at Brian. "Do you—"

"I declined. I didn't want Judas messing with what the Prism gave me."

"And you?" I looked at Kareena.

She pulled her wrist in close to her chest and shook her head.

"Come on, guys! This thing saved my ass! We may need portals later on when things get... worse."

"I don't want it," Brian said, gruffly. "I don't want anything from them, especially not their help—if that's what he wants to pretend it is. We've been screwed over enough by the Saviors already."

"But it worked, Brian." I stood. "Well... it *did* work." I lifted my wrist and showed the line of burnt skin to the others. "Mine shorted out when I tried to use it in jail. The fluorescence went haywire and did this."

"A malfunction?" Judas came closer. He lifted my wrist and rotated it slowly, staring at what was only a wisp of white smoke to me. "This should not have been possible. How did this happen?" Judas looked me in the eye.

"I don't know. Maybe it was the shock from the taser that did it. You saw what it did to me, Kareena. It took me down fast."

"It did," she said in agreement.

"But for your light to attack you... that is not typical behavior." Judas turned my hand over and prodded at the bracelet I could barely see. "I will attempt to repair it," he said, dropping my hand so he could reach into his sleeve compartment for his tools.

.   .   .

The first ten minutes of the evening newscast was a report on the death toll from the Ghost Plague and how it was spreading across North America like wildfire. Cases were popping up in other countries, too, and scientists were baffled by the lack of comparable symptoms. The second report was about me—and how I had disappeared from the county corrections facility. They mentioned one of the guards had been relieved of duty after a sudden onset of hysteria.

Who wouldn't be hysterical after seeing all of that crazy shit? On top of whatever Solus showed him.

"Can I... talk to you?" It was Kareena. She'd lightly crept

down the basement stairs into the guest room and was hanging back on the last step, leaning on the railing. Lucy was upstairs with Solus and the others.

I got up from the bed.

"Uh, yeah," I replied, though I wasn't thrilled to see her. I wanted to be left alone, which is why they let me rest in the basement to begin with. "Shouldn't you be up there keeping an eye on Judas?"

"Solus can see him just fine. I came down to check on *you*. Are you... okay?" she asked, chewing her lip as she cautiously approached.

"I don't know if *okay* works in this situation, but I'm alive and Lucy's safe so..."

"You've been a little, um, different since you got back. What happened to you in there? In jail?" She closed some distance between us.

"I think I need some time to myself, Kareena."

Those damn bewitching green eyes of hers were drawing me in already.

"I need... to get my mind off other things so I can focus on what matters. I need to clear my head."

She took another step closer until we were only inches apart, her heat making me tense. "I can help with that, you know?" she whispered as her hands came up to my chest. Her warm, golden skin reflected the diffused light of the nearby lamp.

I tried to reply, but nothing came out and my mouth hung open.

"I can get your mind off everything else," she said, a coy smile curling her auburn lips. Fingers slid beneath the hem of my tight-fitting shirt and fingernails crawled up my side. I tried swallowing but couldn't. A lump in my throat. Yellow light started up in my chest, burning and flickering—making her shadow dance upon the wall beside us. Heartbeat racing. I could barely breathe.

"You know, I can make you forget about it all, even if only for a few minutes." She backed me up against the wall and pressed her nails into my skin as she leaned closer, electrifying me even as I wanted to hate her for it.

I wanted her, but... I wanted what Brian and Alice had even more. Something stable. *Real.*

"Say you'll forgive me, David." Her wispy words caressed my throat. "I said I was sorry."

"Kareena..." Every inch of my skin ignited from her touch. Everything inside me yearned to cave in—to satiate the incessant thirst I still had for her.

When I was younger, I'd have screwed any girl who'd have me, but today, I had responsibilities. I just—

Pain sparked through me and I recoiled.

"What is it?" She gasped and lunged for me as I slipped away. "What did I do?"

I peeled up my shirt and showed her the swollen, stitched-up wound below my ribs. A splotch of rusty old blood framed it in color.

"Holy shit. Did someone stab you?" She reached a hand toward my face. Fingertips sliding across my jaw line felt nice. The tenderness made our eyes meet again. "David, I'll ask Brian to heal it for you."

"No!" I pulled away and scoffed. "No, damn it! I don't need Brian's help." It hurt to move that quickly, but I bit my tongue and sucked it up because I was angry. "I already told him no."

Brian wasn't the answer to everything and I wished she could spend one damn second *not* thinking about him.

Then I remembered... I was even wearing his clothes.

Chapter 26

Platinum metal shimmered in the low light. Stars of bright blue twinkled on and off in a line below his eyes. I locked gazes with Judas and didn't let him out of my sight while the others slept. Brian and Alice were upstairs in Alice's bedroom, Solus and Lucy were in the basement with Judas and me, and Kareena was asleep on the couch in the living room.

Maybe I should have let her stay with me because she was in pain, too, knowing her father's life was in danger. But no amount of sympathy could prepare me for another night beside her.

Sweat beaded on my forehead and I wiped the back of my hand across my brow. My stitches ached. Sitting hunched over on the edge of the bed aggravated the wound. I never did get that tetanus shot the doctor recommended. I didn't know shit about that kind of stuff. I just wanted to live—to be a good father for Lucy. Somehow.

"You are in distress," Judas said, staring at me. He stood near the staircase, refusing to sit because he claimed it was unnatural for him.

"I'm fine." I looked behind me. Lucy was fast asleep beside Solus, her hand clutching one of his.

"You are in pain, as well," Judas added. "But your pain is beyond the flesh wound you hide."

"Thanks to you," I grumbled through clenched teeth. "I've got whatever is killing everyone else. My fluorescence is killing me because of you."

"Experiments carry risks," he said flatly. "You are a powerful Tracker, nonetheless."

"Is there anything I can do about this?" I said, shaking from an onset of chills. "I don't want to ask the others. I don't want to ask Brian."

Judas lurched closer.

"Your wound will soon be infected." He lifted a hand toward me. "It will take you before your light fades if you do not get help."

"I don't want help." My voice broke.

"But you need it," he said.

The bed quaked.

"Daddy?" Lucy came up behind me. "Are you okay, Daddy?" She wrapped her arms around my neck and leaned against my back, hugging me. I reached up to grasp her arms and smiled.

"Yeah, baby, I'm fine."

Judas retreated back to his spot by the wall and looked off at the other side of the room.

"You're tired. Why don't you go to bed?" She nuzzled me with her nose.

"Daddy needs to stay awake to make sure Judas doesn't get into trouble."

"Oh..." She released me and dropped down into a cross-legged position on the bed. "Solus said the Prism are watching us. That they're going to protect us from whatever it is that's making people sick."

I didn't even know she knew about the pandemic. I wanted to keep it secret from her.

"Are the Prism coming back?" I asked, scooting over and turning toward Lucy.

"I don't know," she replied with a shrug.

There was a gentle tapping on my knee and I jerked my head.

It was Solus.

How the hell?

"You were just sleeping. How did you..." The kid was a ninja. I couldn't hold back a nervous laugh. "Lucy, could you turn on that light over there, please? What is it, Solus?"

He stared up at me and blinked.

"The child knows you are ill," Judas announced.

"How?"

"He can sense the corrupted light in you because he carries Healer DNA."

"Does that mean he can—"

"No. He does not have the ability to stop the corruption from taking you. This is why we must study him further. He can assist you with your other infection, however."

Solus cupped his hands and lifted them toward me.

"What is it? What do you want me to do?" I asked.

He used one hand to motion that he wanted me to give him mine.

I put out my hand and he carefully took it into his tiny, pale fingers and turned it over, palm up. Then he clasped his hands around it and closed his eyes. A teal glow emitted from his chest and tiny flecks of blue, green, and icy white light rose from his fingertips, prickling me with jolts of what felt like cold air licking my skin.

A rush of warmth shot through me and I grimaced as the heat became nearly unbearable. I doubled over on the edge of the bed and clutched my side. Fire rippled across my ribs and I peeled up my shirt to watch as a spark of wild blue color knitted through my wound, sealing the skin closed and soothing the inflammation.

"I didn't know you could—" I rolled my shirt down. "Th-thank you."

My entire body cooled and the sweat on my forehead dissipated. A serene calmness flushed through every muscle and tiredness swept over me. My eyelids became heavy.

Everything around me softened out of focus. I wanted to

panic in fear, but there was no fear within me.

"Solus," the name barely came out of my mouth. I fell backward onto the bed and tried to fight back the heaviness in my bones.

Every thought zipping through my brain vanished and I was sucked into a deep, dark sleep.

I awoke, unable to recall when I'd fallen asleep. Lucy sat beside me on the bed, combing her fingers through my hair lovingly.

"Morning, Daddy." She smiled. My heart melted.

"Hey." I pushed up from the bed and looked around. "Where's Solus?"

"He's upstairs with his mommy and daddy."

"Oh." Then I gasped. "Where's Judas!?"

"Solus said he had to go home."

"What? Do the others know?"

"He went to tell them, but he said I should let you sleep because you needed it."

I assumed when Lucy said Solus *told* her things, she meant he *showed* her, because I still hadn't heard another word from his mouth since he had called her name.

I went upstairs with Lucy. The others were eating breakfast at the kitchen table. Alice's mother sat on one end and Kareena on the other. Brian and Alice sat beside each other and Solus sat in a chair across from them with a bowl, pushing cereal hoops around with a spoon. Getting Solus to eat was almost as much trouble as getting him to sleep.

I pulled out the chair beside Solus and gestured for Lucy to sit there. Immediately, Kareena pushed her chair out and stood. She scooped up the plate and fork from her place and stormed off into the living room.

I sat in the chair she had relinquished.

"Would you like me to make you something?" Jane asked.

Brian and Alice had eggs and toast. Nicest breakfast we'd

had in a long time. Lucy took the empty bowl at her place setting and dumped cereal into it. She reached for the half-gallon of milk and I scrambled to grab it before she could.

"I'll get that," I said, twisting off the cap and pouring just a little milk into the bowl on top of her cereal.

"Thanks." She flashed a toothy grin and then started eating. Solus suddenly took a greater interest in his own cereal.

Jane got up and went over to the stove. She grabbed a pan from the sink and started cleaning it with a sponge and soap.

"Hey, it's okay." I waved at her. "I'm fine. Don't worry about me right now. I'll just have cereal."

"You sure?" Brian looked up from his plate. "I can make you something." He twisted in his chair to look back. "Jane, you should sit down and relax."

She scuttled back over to the table and sat in her seat. "Is, uh, she going to be okay?" Her eyes darted toward Kareena.

"Yeah," I replied, taking a clean bowl from Jane. I poured some cereal and drowned it in milk. I glanced behind me into the living room. Kareena sat on the couch, leaning over her plate, picking at her food with a fork. "I think she'll be okay. Things have been rough for us all lately."

"I of all people know that," Jane replied with a nod. "Things haven't been the same since you two left. The police asked a lot of questions." She gestured at Brian and Alice. "Part of me wanted to tell them the truth—that some crazy alien race had implanted in you all glowing DNA and that you ran away from home to get away from other people. But then I realized how ridiculous that sounded. I didn't need to be put away with your mother, Brian."

"How is she? Do you know?" Brian stacked his fork and crumpled paper towels on top of his plate and pushed all of it aside. "Have you heard anything at all about her?"

"No, Brian. I'm sorry, I haven't. Since I'm not family,

they don't send updates. I don't think she liked me much anyway."

"She didn't," Brian said. "I don't know why, but she didn't. I'm sorry, Jane."

"We aren't obligated to like everyone," Alice muttered, chewing the last piece of her toast.

"No, we're not," I agreed and ate the last scoop of cereal from my bowl. "Excuse me." I pushed out my chair and walked into the living room. "Kareena?"

"I don't want to talk to you." She crossed her arms.

"Kareena, come on."

"No." She looked up and then away. Then up again. Her jaw dropped. "Your light!"

"What about it?"

"The corrupted light—it's gone!"

Solus.

"What?" she asked.

"Solus touched me last night and his light started glowing. I don't know what he did, but it knocked me out cold."

"Did he heal you?" She set her plate on the coffee table and stood. "Do you feel—wait—it's still there. I can see it. It's just smaller. Maybe it's in remission?"

"Judas told me Solus carries Healer DNA, but he also said Solus couldn't stop the corruption from... *taking me.*"

"Anything that buys us more time is better than nothing, right?"

"I guess, but we can't go around letting Solus touch every person in the world. That's too risky for us all."

"My dad. Can he touch my dad? Maybe it will slow the progression of the disease until we can find a cure."

"Maybe. I don't know if that's the safest idea right now, though."

"Why not? You know damn well you'd do anything for Lucy, but now that I'm asking for one tiny little favor, you're gonna shut me down just like that?"

"It's not that simple."

"I think it is, David. I think you just don't want to—" She sucked in a breath and her eyes widened. "What do you want!?" she shrieked, squeezing her eyes closed.

Everyone came rushing in from the kitchen. My bangle grew warm and emitted iridescent, colored light.

"Bring the child," an ethereal voice reverberated through my head. *"We will help you."*

Prism.

A dazzling portal of light appeared before us.

The decision was instant. "I'm going," I said, turning to Brian and Alice. "Kareena?"

She was holding her head in her hands.

"Kareena?" I pressed a hand onto her shoulder. "Let's go."

She looked up at me, squinting. "My head... Ugh." She groaned.

"I know. I'm sorry, but we need to hurry. The Prism may be able to help your dad."

My words seemed to give her strength. She straightened up and wiped a fresh tear from the corner of her eye.

Brian and Alice went through first, Solus' hands in theirs. Then I ushered Kareena through and turned to Jane, who was staring toward the portal with huge eyes.

"Can you see it?" I asked.

"No... Where did they all go?"

"All you need to know is we'll be in good hands, Jane. Thank you for what you've done for us."

She smiled for half a second before her expression curved back into one of worry.

I took Lucy by the hand and pulled her through with me.

Chapter 27

We were transported to the white room—the one with the enormous window looking out over Earth and the glowing white orb floating in the center.

"The Saviors, though few remain, are coming for you," the Prism announced in their fluttery, echo-like voice. "They want the Solus Child."

"We know," Brian said. "Judas—I mean the translator— went back to them in the middle of the night. He said he wouldn't hurt Solus while he was with us, but I don't know what he told the others when he got back."

"Your bracelets have been altered to harness the ability to create portals," the Prism added. "This is a valuable asset."

"Only two of us can do it, though," I said. "Does that mean we'll always be the only two with the ability?"

"Yes. We are unable to manipulate energy in such ways. The Saviors have always been creators. They thrive on experiments and the study of energy use and binding. This is how they created a Variant and this is how they changed all of you."

Out of the corner of my eye, I saw Lucy walk over to Solus and sit in front of the huge window to watch Earth.

"So the Saviors are scientists?" I approached the glowing orb. "Judas said something about separating from you—the Prism—but having to take physical bodies in order to do that. Why?"

"The Saviors believe their fluorescence is more viable than ours and less vulnerable to discrepancies and weakness.

However, the onset of the virus proved them wrong, and that we were stronger as a single entity. When you separate a life force into various parts of its whole, it is easier to understand how the dissection could cause vulnerability."

"What do they want to do with Solus?" Brian asked. "Take him apart or..."

"They will study his inherited immunity in an attempt to create a vaccine which can be distributed among the remaining Saviors. But time is short and they have become desperate now with very few survivors left. It is not like their race to understand death. This desperation has made them reckless and dangerous, and we believe they may have hastily infected more humans with the light after the virus mutated."

"What!?" I looked back at the others. "Doesn't that mean more people will die?"

"Unfortunately, yes."

"They're not getting Solus," Alice snapped. "No way. We'll fight back... somehow. They're going to have to go through me first."

"They're going to have to go through *all* of us," I added.

"We know Solus slowed the progression of your infection, David," the Prism said. "His Healer light combined with his mother's Starter DNA made it possible to share a small portion of his energy with you. This is not enough to stop the virus from spreading or from taking others."

"Could you help us?" Alice asked. "If we stayed here, would you be able to use Solus to find a cure?"

"We have been watching him closely since the moment we retrieved him from the Saviors," the Prism started, "but we have been unable to formulate a solution that will resist evolutions of the virus on your planet. His genetic makeup defies logic. He is the child of two humans who have fluorescence intertwined with their DNA, and yet he has partially acquired Savior abilities. We cannot explain this, nor comprehend how he has been able to resist the outbreak altogether."

"If we can't stop it," Kareena spoke up, "will we all... die?"

"That is likely."

She tried to resist frowning and turned away. I didn't need to see her face to hear her angst manifest as shuddering breaths.

"We'll find a way to help your dad," I said, trying to be optimistic. I reached out to put a hand on her shoulder, but she pulled away. I didn't want to see her in pain, and if I could have done something to help her dad, I would have, but I was dying, too. Maybe Solus had slowed down the progression of the corrupted light, but in reality—I didn't have much time left. I didn't know how much time I had to be with Lucy or how she'd cope when—

The floor quaked and I teetered, fighting to catch my balance.

Kareena shrieked and stumbled into me.

"What was that!?" Brian shouted, taking Alice and Solus by the hand.

I lunged for Lucy and scooped her into my arms just as the floor rumbled again.

"The Saviors," the Prism echoed.

A thunderous boom pierced my ears and a blast of white light flashed against the window. A fiery wave of yellow-orange sparks tore through it, fracturing the material into a mosaic of flaming red cracks.

"Guys!" Kareena darted toward me and grabbed onto my arm. "Make a portal and get us the hell out of here, David! Hurry!"

"I...I can't!"

"What do you mean, you can't? Why not?" Her eyes kept darting between the fracturing window and me. "You have the bracelet!"

"Yeah, I know! But I haven't tested it since Judas fixed

it. I don't even know if it's safe—"

"We're about to die!"

Ripples of light the color of molten lava skittered across the window, leaving behind a trail of jagged, singed, smoldering lines.

If that window shattered, we'd all die. Instantly.

Alice attempted to conjure a portal, but her light kept flickering in and out. Solus reached up to help her channel her power.

Something ripped Lucy out of my grasp. I lunged forward, flailing and reaching for her. The ground disappeared from beneath my feet and blinding white light swallowed me up.

I fell, tumbling, drifting through nothingness. Unable to breathe. Suffocating as my body spun, freefalling. I couldn't tell which way was up. Which way I was—

I hit the ground hard and let out a gruff moan of pain. My jaw and ribs ached from impact and my head spun from the disorientating fall. I opened my eyes and groaned, blinking several times to try to bring the room into focus.

"Where...?" I came onto my forearms and pushed myself up off the ground. Standing hurt. My stomach throbbed with sickness. Every time I took a breath, I strained to bring in enough air. Like breathing through a straw...

Where am I?

I heard someone struggling and turned.

Alice! She was face down on the ground with her hair fanned out around her.

"Alice!" I bent down and touched her.

"No!" she yelped, cringing.

"It's me, David!" I could hardly speak as my vocal cords tightened.

She craned her neck up to look at me and relief washed over her face.

"Oh. Thank God." She lifted her arm toward me and I helped pull her to her feet. "Th-Thank you," she whispered.

"Save your breath." I wheezed.

She nodded.

We were in a giant white auditorium of some kind. Exactly like the room where we'd met the Saviors before, except there were no Saviors there to greet us with their ugly faces.

Not yet...

"Solus!" Alice strained to get the name out of her mouth.

My chest hurt. We weren't going to last long in this atmosphere. Too little oxygen. Every breath stung like needles sticking my insides.

"Cowards!" Alice cried, toppling to her knees. All of her weight against me made me stumble.

I knelt beside her and wrapped an arm around her shoulders.

"Please... Alice," I said, my voice raspy. "Save your breath. We'll... find him."

She whimpered and looked up at me with dismay on her face. Frightened, deep black pupils shimmered in her sky-blue eyes.

"We will," I mouthed and squeezed her reassuringly.

She was too scared to respond, but nodded a little, and I saw gratitude in her watery eyes.

I had to protect her. For Brian's and for Solus' sake. Alice was an innocent bystander—a necessary soldier in a war she'd never chosen to fight. The very same war I, too, had never chosen to be a part of.

She came to her feet and we walked together through endless white. Nothing in front or behind. Nothing to the sides. Just white and more white. It was disorienting after a few minutes.

Bright light.

Hard floor beneath our feet.

White in every direction.

Everything looked the same and we couldn't tell if we were covering any distance or walking in circles.

She stayed close to me, too weak and afraid to let go. The place was making me drowsy, though I tried to hide it from her. Every step was like walking through three feet of mud. Every breath was like my lungs taking in water. I kept calm, willing myself to stay quiet and move slowly so my heartbeat wouldn't quicken, causing more oxygen to be used.

We kept walking.

And walking.

And walking...

Endless white. More endless white.

Alice's fingers loosened around my arm and she slid down my side to the ground, collapsing onto her hands and knees.

"Alice," I whispered hoarsely. "You have to... stay strong... for Solus." Every word pierced my ribs with sharp pain.

"I... can't."

The weight got to me, and I gave in, dropping down to sit beside her on the glossy white floor. I put my hands in my lap and hung my head down.

"I'm... sorry," I said, glancing over at her as she resituated herself and pulled her knees up to her chest. Tears drizzled down her face.

She turned her face toward me. Her damp cheeks were red and her eyes were barely able to stay open.

"I'm... so..." She sighed. "Tired."

I was, too.

We were suffocating...

I wanted to close my eyes and lay myself down on the ice-cold floor right then and there.

And go to sleep.

And never wake up.

Chapter 28

"I'm... sorry I was such an asshole in the beginning," I wheezed.

"It's okay," Alice whispered. "You were protecting... your daughter. Brian would have done the same."

I swallowed. My mouth was so dry.

All I could think about was how Alice had attacked me back when we had first met and I was fighting with Brian. She latched onto my neck and wouldn't let go. Her fluorescence burned into me like wild lightning, bringing me to my knees even though she was just a petite young girl. I never would have thought that a tiny frame could pack such a punch.

They had taught me a lot of things. Like how two people can love each other even while their entire world crumbles around them. How when things aren't going your way and you feel powerless, you can still find the strength to care for someone other than yourself.

I stared off into the endless white.

Were all of the Saviors dead or had they isolated us as punishment?

A deep sense of dread sunk in. We were going to die.

The reality crept through my bones, a riveting, painful revelation that my next few breaths would be my last.

Alice leaned on my arm and exhaled slowly, her body-weight pressing into me as she let go.

"Alice." I caught her as she fell against me. Her eyes closed. "Alice." I shook her gently, but she didn't respond. Panic set in and my heart began to race. The thumping in my chest made me gasp for air, but each inhalation did nothing to satisfy the need for oxygen. An invisible force pushed against me, making my body heavy and difficult to move. Just supporting Alice in my lap was laborious.

No.

Lucy...

I dropped my head back and sucked in a breath, staring up into the infinite white. Breathing didn't soothe the pain in my lungs. Invisible hands choked the air from me and I couldn't stop them.

I exhaled and fell. My mind drifted into the abyss.

.   .   .

"David. David, wake up!" Someone's hands were on my shoulders.

I opened my eyes and squinted. Soft blue light radiated from nearby.

"David. Are you okay?" Brian leaned over me. "Come on, man. Get up."

"Ugh." My stomach churned. I rolled onto my side and tried to swallow, but couldn't. So much acid burned my throat. Spots in my vision.

Lightheadedness. Things spinning in and out of focus.

A stomach spasm and...

I threw up.

Pain shot through me as I retched.

Oddly enough, I was thankful. Throwing up was better than being dead.

Brian kept me from toppling over as I regained my composure and scooted away from the vomit.

"You're alright now," he comforted, patting my back. "You'll be okay." He spoke in a much friendlier voice than I had grown accustomed to.

I coughed a few times. Hard. And then took in some deep

breaths. My face was on fire. Sweat dripped into my eyes and I wiped my brow with the back of my hand.

"Thanks." I looked around. Alice was sitting, too, cheeks flush and an uneasy look on her face like she'd start heaving any second now. "Is... she okay?" I asked.

"Yeah. She should be."

"What happened?" I came to my feet beside Brian and rubbed my neck. A headache throbbed in the back of my skull.

"Judas screwed with your bracelet—altered it so it couldn't block out an abduction attempt."

"Shit."

Why hadn't I thought about that?

"But we got you two back." He reached into the small backpack slung over his shoulder, dug out a bottle of water, and handed it to me. "The Prism had to create an even more powerful portal so we could go through and rescue you. They couldn't disable the changes made to your bracelets, but by crossing back through the light, we were able to cloak ourselves again temporarily. Now, if the Saviors want to start something, they're going to have to do it on our turf."

I dumped water onto my palm and splashed it at my face first, and then I opened my mouth toward the sky and poured some in.

My face came back down. "Solus?"

"He's with me," Kareena said, her voice coming from behind. I craned my neck to look at her. "The Prism got him back."

"And Lu—"

"Yes. I have her, too."

I caught a glimpse of Lucy standing beside Solus.

I heaved a breath of relief and swallowed again, still tasting acid and remnants of an upset stomach. I grimaced and took another swig of water to wash it down.

"Thanks," I said, capping the half-empty bottle before

handing it back. "Where are we?"

"I don't know," Brian replied. "We haven't had time to look around."

We were on a rooftop—the highest one in the area, by the look of it. I staggered toward the edge, where a large satellite dish stood erect, and gazed out over the unfamiliar city.

"Be careful," Kareena warned. "Lucy!"

I jerked my head toward the sound of tiny feet nearing and flung out my arms to catch my daughter before she passed, nearly falling to her death. She barreled into me and I lifted her off her feet and into my arms.

"Be careful, Lucy," I scolded. "You could fall." I took a step away and watched the horizon. Brilliant hues of dusk stretched upward, tainting the sky with shades of violet, magenta, and fiery orange.

"Where are we?" she asked.

"I don't know." There were no discerning landmarks in the distance and the buildings surrounding us looked like any other skyscrapers. California? Chicago, maybe? From way up high, everything looked the same. Cars. People.

People...

But the streets below were empty. In big cities, especially, evenings were typically plagued by rush hour at the very least. Let alone early bar-hoppers and dinner dates out in force. Something was too peaceful about the place. Deserted. Silent. Only whispers of the breeze and muffled coos of pigeons filtered by.

"Don't let Solus out of sight," I warned. The hairs on my skin perked and a wave of static energy flitted over me. "Heads up!" The sky above us split open and a scorching white light shone down. A hazy, warped barrier manifested around the perimeter of the rooftop, boxing us in so we couldn't escape.

Not that we had that choice to begin with.

I lifted a hand to my brow to shield my eyes from the light. A figure appeared in the distance.

Judas?

"Give us back the child," he said, the lights on his mask flickering fervently. "It is for your own good that we confiscate him."

"You screwed us!" I growled. "You messed with our bracelets so you could abduct us again, you bastard."

"It was necessary," he replied flatly. "We did not harm you."

"We almost died! Alice and I were going to die up there and you were going to let us!" I adjusted my grasp on Lucy.

Judas tipped his head to the side. "A minor casualty."

"Minor?" Brian pushed past me. "You call murdering the mother of your last chance at survival *minor?*"

"We had the child in our possession at the time."

"Was that your plan all along then? To get back Solus once you found out what he could do and then exterminate the rest of us?"

"It was not... *my* plan," Judas said.

"Now that's a load of crap," I interrupted, releasing Lucy to the ground so she could stand beside me. I took up her hand instead. "You already told us about how you all think as one. That's why when one of your kind passes, you all feel it. Or was that all bullshit, too?"

"I am only the communicator," Judas defended. "I do as I am told to do and speak what is requested of me."

"So you're a drone." I sneered. "A mindless, insignificant drone."

"I suggest you give the child over now," Judas pressed, his voice stern and his gaze piercing. "We will not tolerate hesitation."

"There has to be another way!" Alice cut in, bringing Solus close to her side. "You can't just take our child away from us. Not again! Isn't there some way we can work together? Some kind of compromise? Please?"

Brian stepped up. "Alice, no! There's no compromising with them. They don't care about us. They only care about themselves."

"But they're dying, too, Brian. If we can help them—"

"They infected your mom, for God's sake, Alice! They kept our child a secret and then nearly got you and David killed. Why would you want to do anything to help them?"

"Because we're not like them," she said. "Right?"

"He's right, Alice," I said, glancing down at Lucy and then across at Solus. "They don't care about us. They don't even understand what it is to be alive. The Prism tried to help, but they could only do so much and now... this is our fight. I'll do whatever it takes to protect my daughter and your son." I looked at Judas and took in a deep breath. "Judas, you're not taking that kid."

Yellow light heated my chest and I let Lucy's fingers slip from mine so I could clench my fists and focus.

"You cannot resist," Judas said. "We created you. The light cannot be turned against us."

"We'll see about that." I flexed my fingers and willed golden forks of energy through my body, down my arms. My hands. My fingers. Powerful sparks leached up through my skin, radiating warmth.

Judas robotically raised a hand and fanned out his fingers. "You are strong, Tracker," he said. "But only as strong as your Healer keeps you."

A wisp of chemical green light pulsed beneath his skin.

My body began to shake and my arm raised involuntarily. My fingers pried apart against my will, fanning out in front of me. "No! No! No!"

Amber light exuded from every pore and fluorescence consumed me, enveloping me in a blast of heat and color.

"David, stop!" Kareena screeched.

"I can't! Shit! Something's wrong! It's... burning. I can't control it! Get away from me! All of you! Hurry!"

I gritted my teeth and arched back, convulsing as tiny threads of light painfully ripped across my flesh. Wild lightning arced around me and an explosion of vivid yellow fireworks stung my retinas.

Chapter 29

The searing sensation ebbed. I regained control of my body and doubled over to rest my hands on my knees and let out an exhausted breath.

"Guys?"

I looked up. Things came into focus and my eyes grazed over a dark blur down in front of me. I blinked a few more times.

It was Brian, sprawled out on the ground, face down. Motionless.

"Brian?" I took a step closer. "Brian!"

Not even his fingers twitched.

"Lucy! Where are you?" I swerved around. She was behind me, standing close to Solus.

"Brian!" Alice screamed at the sight of Brian's body. She ran to his side and fell to her knees beside him. I followed and helped her lift him and turn him over onto his back. His face was dashed with black lines of charred skin.

"Brian?" Alice's breath shuddered.

I bent down close to his face, turning my head so my ear was just above his lips.

Silence.

I pressed my fingers against his wrist. No pulse.

"David! What happened to him!?" Alice looked at me with terrified, widened eyes. "David!"

"I... I think he's... dead."

She gasped so hard, she choked and started to cough. "What? No." She clasped his face in her hands. "Brian, wake up!" Her fingers combed through his hair. "This can't be happening!"

Kareena came up behind me.

"Alice…" Kareena squeaked, her quaking fingers pressing into my shoulder. "Alice, he's… right. Brian's—"

"Shut up!" Alice glared at her. "You don't know that!"

"Yes. Yes, I do," she replied, her voice breaking. Lip trembling. She lowered herself to his side and took his other hand into hers, grasping it fondly. "His light… it's gone. I can't see it in him anymore. Oh, God."

"No. You don't know what you're taking about, Kareena." Alice sniffed loudly, congestion getting to her as tears rained down her face.

She was right. I couldn't see a trace of his essence around him. All of his blue light had… vanished.

"David, please move." Kareena nudged me. I shuffled out of the way and let the girls have their space.

"Get away from him," Alice growled, glaring at Kareena.

"No!" Kareena brought his hand closer to her chest. "I have just as much right to be with him as you!"

"You didn't even care about him," Alice muttered. "You just wanted something you couldn't have."

"That's not true!" Kareena scoffed. "That's not true at all!"

"Girls, come on!" I tried to pry in.

"You've always been his perfect little plaything," Kareena sneered. "I didn't have a goddamn chance because of you. And now, you have him!" She pointed a stiff, trembling finger at Solus. "And I don't have shit! I have nothing and I can never have anything because of this god… damn… curse. You're just a lucky little bitch who got what she wanted. I've got news for you, Alice. It wasn't bullshit. I loved Brian, and I would have given him anything if he would have just…" She paused to catch her breath and wipe a stream of tears from her cheeks. "If he would have just given me a chance."

So that was the truth? I meant nothing to her?
Nothing at all?

Alice bared her teeth. "You're so full of it, Kareena. Do you hear yourself? I didn't get what I wanted. If I had, Brian wouldn't be dead, we'd be safe at home, and my best friend wouldn't have become the victim of this disease we're carrying. You say you'd have done anything for him, but that's a lie. I didn't ask for Solus, but he's here now and I love him with everything I am. Brian did, too. Could you love that child like I do? No. Because the only person you've ever loved was yourself!"

Kareena's eyes widened, a spark of pink fire dashed up her face and she lunged at Alice.

"No!" I grabbed Kareena by her shoulders and pulled her back. "No. This isn't about either of you." She wriggled and jerked around, flailing at my face while trying to get free. I pulled her to her feet and turned her to face Judas. "Right now, it's about them—the Saviors—and what they did to us. It's *his* fault Brian's dead. This isn't about your feelings for Brian." Kareena stopped struggling and went limp in my arms, panting hard. Choppy gasps for breath made her body shake. "Brian would want us to protect each other—to protect Solus. We need to rescue our own asses from this shit or there will be no world left to save."

Alice sniffed and wiped her face on her arm. "He's right," she said, panting. "It's all *their* fault."

Now that everyone's attention was back on him, Judas spoke again. "This is your final opportunity to do as we have asked without punishment." His head twitched and a subtle, fleeting look of discomfort swept over his face.

"Without punishment?" I repeated, still holding Kareena's shaking body close. "You killed Brian, you asshole!"

"You are the one who disposed of your own Healer," Judas remarked.

My jaw tightened. The bastard was playing mind games.

"No. It wasn't you," Alice said in a strained voice. "He made you do it, David."

"They are growing impatient," Judas added. "Give us the child. Now." He reached a hand out toward Solus, who ducked down behind me, beside Lucy.

What do I do?

What would Brian have done? Probably rushed in, guns blazing.

That reminded me. I didn't have my gun, and I didn't even know how to take down a Savior.

Damn it!

I couldn't let them take Solus. He was my only chance at survival.

Judas took a step closer.

"You tricked us!" Alice roared. The uncharacteristically sharp pitch sent a jolt of fear up my spine.

She flashed a bloodthirsty glare and bolted, bowling into him with all of her weight and sending him crashing to the ground. He made a feeble attempt to push her off while her fingers clamped onto the edges of his blinking silver mask. She grunted and strained, working her fingertips beneath the edges to pry it from his face. The shimmering metal mask tumbled across the ground, clinking softly against the concrete.

Judas began to wheeze.

Alice locked onto his lanky arms and neon green light glinted through her veins. It raced down toward her fingertips like a lit fuse, sparking and crackling through her bloodstream. It made contact with the Savior's skintight suit and he jerked uncontrollably as if a seizure spell had awakened his body. His spine arched and his brow rose and furrowed with twisted, restrained agony.

"Alice, no!" Kareena pulled away from me. "Alice!" She ran over and grabbed Alice by the shoulders to pull her off Judas. "Stop!"

"Let go of me!" Alice screeched, forcing Kareena's hands from her shoulders and readjusting her grip on the convulsing Savior.

"You don't want to kill him!" Kareena screamed. The panic in her voice made my throat tighten.

"How do you know?" Alice replied hoarsely. "Why shouldn't I kill him for what he did to us? For what he did to Brian!?" Radioactive bursts of color emanated through his clothing, illuminating his bones with sickening flashes of green light.

"You can't!" Kareena insisted, reaching out toward Alice, but hesitating in fear of being lashed out at again. "You don't want to have his blood on your hands!"

"He needs to pay," Alice replied.

The Savior squirmed beneath her weight. Forks of blazing fluorescence invaded his face and his grey eyes changed color as they opened wide.

"I killed Taylor!" Kareena cried.

"What?" Alice instantly released the Savior and turned her head. "What do you mean? I thought..." She glanced at me. "I thought David killed him."

We'd never told the others exactly what had happened. I took the heat when Brian had asked. "Yes. Kareena... killed Taylor." The lump in my throat made it difficult to swallow. "But she had to." I approached Alice. "He was going to kill us both otherwise and he had me... trapped. I couldn't do anything to fight back so she did what she had to do and... she shot him."

"And I *still* feel like shit because of it," Kareena said. "Let him go, Alice. You'll feel better without his blood on your hands. I mean it."

"It's true," I added. "You don't need someone's death haunting you forever."

"But... he... they..." She looked around, inhaling short, sharp breaths.

"I know, Alice." I reached down and helped bring her to her feet.

Judas rolled onto his stomach, came to his knees, and scrambled to scoop up his mask from the ground. He coughed violently as he frantically worked to reattach it over his mouth and nose. It clicked into place with a small strap over his ears. He sat back on his heels and closed his eyes, coughing still, wheezing, and struggling to take in his next breath. The mask may have muffled the painful heaving sounds, but they still made my skin crawl.

Alice dashed away to go sit beside Brian and began sobbing again.

"Leave us alone," I said to Judas. My hands were sweating. I wasn't one to beg for anything, but grief over Brian's death had worn me thin. "Please, leave us alone."

There was a tug at my shirt and I glanced down.

Solus.

"What is it?"

He looked solemnly back at his parents and then gestured for me to let him go to the Savior.

"No! You can't go with him!" I shouted after him as he jaunted toward Judas regardless. My muscles were too burned out for me to catch him before he was out of reach.

My breath caught in my lungs.

When he got to the Savior, he paused and tilted his head to the side, watching Judas' facial expression change as their gazes met.

"So-Solus," Alice called out in a tired, mousey voice, stretching a shaking arm out toward him. "No."

Solus approached Judas and lifted his tiny pale hands until they made contact with Judas' temples.

An outburst of anger and then agony distorted Judas' expression. He gasped and his eyes grew wide and fearful. "Agh!" The Savior bent over and clutched his head, choking on shallow breaths.

Solus lowered his hands to his sides and quietly watched as the alien started to shake.

Judas strained to breathe, panting harder now and heaving in breaths even though his mask was reattached and blinking. His brow wrinkled. His head twitched and he let out a loud groan of pain, lifting his face toward the sky.

His face came back down and he glanced at Brian's body. "No. No," he muttered, wrapping his arms around himself and rocking back and forth in place. He uttered something I couldn't understand, whined, and cupped his face in his hands again. Long locks of tangled, platinum white hair draped over his shoulders.

"What's happening?" I asked.

Solus turned his head and frowned. His pale cheeks were turning pink and his eyes glimmered with tears.

Judas shook his head and gasped for air, stretching his bony fingers feebly out toward Solus. "What have you done to me?" he asked, the expression on his face mirroring the boy's.

Solus sternly pointed a finger at his father's body.

Judas cleared his throat. "I'm... sorry," he strained, his ashen lips curving downward. Then he hung his head low and hunched over, still shaking uncontrollably. "We... are sorry."

The hairs on the back of my neck stood and I froze in anticipation. The warped field of light around us faded and Judas disappeared in a flash of white.

"Oh, shit." I wiped sweat from my forehead with the back of my hand and breathed a sigh of relief.

"Are they gone?" Kareena asked, circling around to search the perimeter of the rooftop.

"I... think they are," I replied.

"Just like that?"

"Just like that," I repeated. "Alice?" I looked back. She and Solus were huddled together near Brian.

"Jesus, I'm sorry, Alice," I said. My chest tightened at

the sight of his lifeless body. "I never thought... I didn't mean... I mean—"

"It's okay," she said softly, lifting him up to rest his head in her lap. "Oh, Brian..." She bent over to hug him and started to moan uncontrollably. The sounds of her fervent tears made my face tighten.

Maybe I didn't know him like she did, but I didn't want him to die. The kid was brave as hell. The world could use more people like him. More guys as responsible as him at his age.

I sat beside her and put a hand on her shoulder. "We're here for you, Alice," I said. "I know I can't change things, but I'm here."

"Thank you." She sniffled without looking up.

Lucy peeked over our heads and let out a whimper.

"You'd think if he were the Healer, he could have survived anything," Kareena said. "But... he couldn't."

"Yeah."

A weird expression swept over Solus' face and he inhaled sharply. He came to his feet and nudged me anxiously.

"What? What is it?"

He reached for my hand, so I gave it to him.

Then he looked up at Kareena and stretched out an arm toward her, waving his hand impatiently.

"Give him your hand," I said.

She did. "What does he want?" she asked as Solus tugged her to come down onto her knees beside him. We knelt there next to Brian for a few moments, watching Solus intently as he squeezed his eyes shut tightly and grasped our fingers tighter.

"I don't—" I started.

Blue-green fluorescence glimmered in his chest. Yellow energy skittered down my arm and pink down Kareena's, rushing toward Solus' hands. A ray of effervescent light grew within him, shifting colors from blue to white, then pink to yellow, green, and teal. Then back to white.

He released our fingers at the same time and a flare of rainbow fire manifested in his hands. He lowered the light down and let it filter through his hands over Brian's chest. Rainbow sparkles flashed and zipped across Brian's body, lighting his outline in an array of colors. A subtle crackle of energy sounded and the colors sunk into him, disappearing beneath clothing and skin.

Brian jolted up and coughed.

"Brian!" Alice hugged him and he choked again, still trying to catch his breath. "I'm sorry." She released him and helped support his weight as he gasped. The charred markings on his face faded away.

"Holy shit!" he said, swallowing hard. Panting. "Holy... freaking shit."

"You died!" The words came out of my mouth before I could stop them.

Brian looked me in the eye. "I know," he said, a bone chilling darkness in his pupils. "I know." He brought a knee up toward his body and rested his arm on it. "What happened?"

"Take deep breaths, man," I said, patting him on the back. "It's gonna be okay now."

"How the hell?" He looked up at Kareena and then at Alice and Solus. "How? Oh, God, my head." He leaned over and groaned. "Ugh. My head. It hurts so—"

"Can't you heal it?" Alice asked, taking his hand into hers. "Brian?"

"Uh, I don't know. I haven't gotten a headache since—"

"No," Kareena interrupted.

I looked up at her. Her eyes were full of dread.

"He-he doesn't have it anymore," she said, her voice breaking.

"What!?" Alice shrieked.

"It's gone," Kareena repeated. "It's... not inside him."

"Then... how did he..." Alice's mouth hung open.

"My heart!" Brian raised his voice. "Oh, shit. My heart—"

"Prism," a tiny voice announced.

We all looked at Solus.

"What?" Brian asked, bringing him closer. "What do you mean?"

Solus pressed a flattened hand onto the center of Brian's chest.

"Prism. Here," he said, smiling.

Brian's brow furrowed. "My... heart?"

Solus nodded, his lips parting into an excited, toothy grin.

"I have the... Prism... in my heart?"

Solus shook his head in disagreement and pressed his hand again. "Prism. Life."

Brian cracked an appreciative smile. Solus' reply took his breath away.

Hell, it took all of our breaths away.

So the Prism really were like souls. Just like Kareena had told us. A life force. Energy in its purest form.

"So, is his fluorescence gone for good?" I asked Solus.

He nodded.

"Guess I'm going to have to be more careful from now on, huh?" Brian said with a little chuckle.

"Shit, man." I scoffed and jokingly punched him in the shoulder. "Don't go getting yourself killed now that I've started liking your crazy ass." Then I brushed my other hand across my face to sweep away the tear of joy that had nearly escaped. "Lucky bastard."

Brian grinned.

Chapter 30

"David!" Kareena yelped and I swerved to face her. She stared off into the distance at something I couldn't see.

"What is it?"

"The Prism," she said, pointing. "They're here."

Solus was already looking up at something I couldn't see.

The familiar prismatic orb of light appeared nearby, hovering a few feet above the ground.

"They said they can help us now," Kareena interpreted. "But they need Solus."

Solus walked toward the sparkling orb.

"No." Brian blocked him with his arm. "Wait. How do we know this won't hurt him?"

"What do they want Solus to do?" Alice asked, coming up beside Brian.

Kareena listened for a moment. "They're asking if you remember how they used the orb to magnify my abilities so you guys could see how the rest of the people on Earth were infected."

Brian and Alice nodded.

"Well…" Kareena paused. "They said they want to use Solus' newly developed light to cast a projection of his DNA. Like a cloud or dusting of his fluorescent, um, genetic pattern." She looked at me. "They said it should cure you, too."

"Did you hear that, Solus?" Lucy said, excitedly. "You're going to help people!"

Solus smiled, then turned toward his parents and blinked a few times.

"Help people," he said softly, an eager look in his eyes.

I held my breath as the tiny words came out of his tiny mouth. I didn't know if Lucy had been teaching him to speak behind my back, or if he had picked things up from listening to all of us, but hearing him talk filled me with joy.

Alice toppled down to her knees and clutched his face between her hands.

"Oh, he's perfect, Brian! Solus is going to save the world. Just like he saved you." Her lip quivered and she strained to smile amidst the tears welling in her eyes. "Promise me he'll be safe, please?" She looked up at the radiant ball of energy.

"They said they'll protect the children," Kareena announced. "That they already promised once before and want to assure you everyone will still be safe."

"Okay. Then I think he should do it, Brian." She looked up at him for approval. "If it could help the Earth in any way, he should try."

Brian hesitated at first, mulling over the idea in his head before replying. "Yeah. Alright. I guess that's probably the best thing we can do right now." Brian nudged Solus gently. "Go ahead, Solus. Let's help people."

Solus walked toward the glowing orb and lifted his hand. A pulse of bluish-green energy bolted through his arm, igniting the ball with teal light. Glints of blue, green, teal, and white light sparkled around him and a mist of metallic dust shot up to the sky, raining down as colorful sparkles of energy. Glittering colors spiraled out of the Prism orb and Solus watched, mystified by the bright light escaping his fingers.

With a subtle nod, as if someone were speaking to him, he lowered his hand from the orb and turned to us. He stepped away and peered up at his parents for approval.

Alice knelt down to brush her dainty fingers across his cheek. "You're a very good boy, Solus," she said, smiling with her eyes.

"Did it work?" I asked.

Kareena's gaze shot toward me and she squinted at my chest.

"Well? Did it work or not?"

"Yes. It did," she said.

I took a breath.

"I can't see the corruption anymore," she added. "Only pure yellow light. Like it was in the very beginning."

"Then it worked!" A huge weight lifted from my shoulders and relief rushed through me.

"Does that mean *everyone* is cured?" Kareena asked the glowing ball of rainbow light. The light pulsed a few times and then faded away.

She bit her lip and burst into a smile. Then a frown. She lowered her face and covered it with her hands.

"Is everything okay?" I brushed my hand against hers. "Kareena? Is your dad—"

Her hands parted from her face and her shimmering, teary eyes blinked at me. A sniffle. Then a bittersweet grin and short, shuddering breaths. "Yes," she said, coughing on her tears. "They said he'd be okay."

"Good. That's really good news," I replied and then turned away, my happiness for her overshadowed by the darker truth. "I suppose if everything is okay now, we don't really need to stick together anymore. Right?"

"What!?" she yelped. "What do you mean? Where are you going?"

"I don't know yet, but you don't want me here. I knew this day would come and it has."

"David, don't talk like that, please." She caressed my arm. "We've been through so much together."

"I heard what you said earlier. Your true feelings for Brian."

"Oh." She exhaled. "Um, I'm sorry about that, David. I don't know what came over me. I just lost my mind and, I mean, I did like Brian before, but you don't have to worry about that anymore."

"That quickly? You were literally professing your love for him five minutes ago and then, poof, you're done? You expect me to believe that? I saw the look on your face. The tone of your voice. You were shaking, Kareena. Shaking with fear, hate, pain. You were shaking because your heart had been broken. You lost your shit for a little while and you and Alice were about to—"

"Look, I know, okay! I don't know what the hell happened to me, but I'm okay now. He's back, and I'm glad he is, but... I've realized that we just aren't right for each other."

"Is it because his fluorescence is gone?" I asked. "Is it because you're worried that without it, you'll get your migraines back if you get close to him? You were willing to fight for him every second of the day, even attack the mother of his child over his dead body, but now you're done? Just like that." I snapped my fingers. "Instant change of heart."

"No. That's not it." She shrugged and rubbed her arms with her hands. "I don't feel right. I feel... empty. Alice is right, I wouldn't want Solus."

"But you want Lucy?"

Her lip quivered.

"The one guy you've been in love with for years suddenly drops dead, you're crushed and brought to tears by it, and then he suddenly comes back to life and you decide to relinquish him in the blink of an eye."

She looked away, trembling like a frightened animal.

Part of me wanted to feel sorry for her, but the other part of me knew the reality behind her feelings.

"You're confused, Kareena. I get it. And you have the right to live your own life the way you want to, but regardless of your feelings for Brian then or now, you didn't have to treat me like shit all this time." I gestured toward Lucy. "You—you didn't have to treat *her* like shit. You act like you hate kids, but you're nothing but a child yourself. You want everyone to do everything for you. You think you're entitled to something the rest of us aren't. Well, you're not, and you never will be."

Kareena took my hand and pressed it between hers. "No, that's not it. I've changed... I swear, something's changed. *Really.*"

"Yeah. Your mind."

She gasped and staggered back, glancing at Lucy, then the others, embarrassed.

"I mean it, Kareena. You're no good for me—for us. We need someone we can trust. Someone who can love *us* and not just themselves."

Her cheeks turned red.

"Fine," she murmured. "Then..." She stamped a foot on the ground. "Then send me home!"

My heart crashed. She'd pissed me off, yes, but... if she went home, I'd... never see her again.

I didn't need to see her again.

Did I?

I shook my head, fighting back the irrational feelings brewing inside.

"Okay." I turned to Brian and Alice. "She's going home. Alright?"

"Oh... um..." Brian started, confused. "Okay. I guess. Kareena?"

"Well?" She gestured for me to get on with it. "I'll figure something out and I'll be fine. Hurry up."

"Okay. Okay." I closed my eyes and tried to invoke a mental picture of Kareena's house. The vivid image had been branded in my memories since it was the last thing I saw before being tased.

Elegant white columns on both sides of the glass and wood front door. A huge stairwell peeking into the foyer. Beautiful hardwood floors beneath my feet.

A burst of yellow light bolted down my arm and shot into

the air, splitting a hole open in front of us. The spinning streaks of white light whipped wildly around in a circle.

"Goodbye, Brian." Kareena swallowed hard. "Goodbye, Alice." Her eyes met mine for a fleeting moment before she sprinted through the light and disappeared.

I waited. Somehow thinking she'd pop back through to say something to me, but she didn't.

So, I closed the portal.

"What are you guys gonna do?"

"We don't really know," Brian replied with a shrug. "Whatever it takes to have a normal life, I guess."

Alice entwined her fingers with his. "We have Solus. And we're not going to let anyone take him away from us."

"You know, it's worth it," I said, motioning toward their son. His mystical, different-colored irises looked back at me. "Took me too long to realize it, but my little girl's the only one who keeps me going some days. She's my world, and if I hadn't been such a dumbass when I was younger, I'd have learned that a lot sooner. You guys are good together. You'll be good for him, too. Just take care of yourselves, Brian, Alice. It's going to get rough, but you have to stick together through it." I smiled at Solus. "Be good, okay? And don't worry. I'll look after Lucy for you."

I ruffled his hair. He smiled with his eyes.

"Are you going home?" Brian asked.

"Something like that," I said with a smirk. "Lucy. Come here." She romped over and I grabbed her hand.

I concentrated on my light and conjured a new portal to the only other place I could visualize with all of my heart and soul. Flashing sparks danced before us and I flexed my fingers in anticipation.

Lucy and I stepped through and were carried by a vortex of crisp, cool air. Flying. Falling. Drifting through light. Our hands parted just as we touched down on solid ground. Soft, damp earth beneath my shoes.

Lucy let out a squeal of happiness and kicked at the lush wave rolling toward her feet. She ran around in a little circle, flailing her arms in the air while splashing at the water's edge.

She was a perfect little girl in every way. Happy. Loving. Kind. Full of joy. Something I hadn't been for a very, very long time.

I closed my eyes and took in a deep breath of salty sea air. Crisp. Warm. The sun shone down on my skin and I dropped my head back, savoring warm, golden light. Maybe I hadn't spent my entire childhood in Hawaii, but I'd wanted nothing more than to go back to my birthplace—to taste the sweet island air that teased me in my dreams. I belonged here and Lucy would feel at home here, too.

White light ripped open behind me and I covered my eyes.

All by himself, Solus popped through the portal.

"Solus?" Lucy grinned from ear to ear. "Are you coming, too?"

He smiled sweetly but shook his head.

"Oh. I'll miss you," she said.

He reached up to give her a hug. She threw her arms around him and held him tightly. They stayed that way for a few moments, little Solus' face fighting back sadness. A tiny whimper escaped him.

"Bye, Lucy," he squeaked, his arms slipping from around her.

"Bye, Solus." She embraced him again briefly. "You'll always be my best friend in the whoooole world."

That made him smile big.

"You need to get back to your parents," I said, not wanting to interrupt, but knowing Brian and Alice would be scared if they found him missing for even a second.

He acknowledged me and sighed.

Lucy patted him lovingly on the head, fluffing his light brown hair with her fingers.

He turned and disappeared into the portal. It closed

behind him.

Lucy sloshed over to my side and took my hand. "Will we see him again, Daddy?"

The kid could make his own portals at will to any place he wanted. He had transported himself to Hawaii in the blink of an eye without any adult help.

"I think so, Lucy."

"Yay!" Her other hand shot up over her head. I reached down to scoop her up.

"I love you, Lucy. You know that?"

"I love you, too, Daddy." She wrapped her arms around my neck and hugged me.

Lucy may not have been a Fluorescent One, but to Solus—the child who saved the world barely saying a word—she was something very special. They shared a bond I couldn't explain. They understood each other at a deeper level than I could comprehend.

Maybe, finally, I would be there in my little girl's life to learn everything about her—to watch her grow. Laugh. Cry. I'd be there for her and we'd finally be a family. We could start fresh. Have a new life. A new home.

I'd find a way.

I always found a way.

Kareena

Brian died.

It cut me deep. Real deep.

And so did Alice's words.

Then, just like that, I was free. My heart was released from whatever net had ensnared it. I thought I loved Brian, and maybe I did at one time, but after his fluorescence faded, so did my feelings for him...

Then there was David—the only light left in the darkness. And he turned me down. How? How could he be so damn cold? We've all been through shit. We've all suffered and paid the price for this sin called fluorescence. Maybe we could have been something together. I know I told him that I didn't want things getting messy, but I wanted him now. He was powerful, and together, we burned brighter.

Then his kid had to become part of all of this. Lucy. If he'd have just told me about her from the beginning, maybe things would have been different.

Hell. I didn't want kids. I didn't have time to be held back.

But now, what was I supposed to do with myself?

After Solus released the cure, I went home to check on my parents. Dad was released from the hospital—recovered. They were happy to see me, but the happiness was short-lived.

People were going to ask questions. Lots of questions.

How can I be safe?

How can I ever have a normal life again?

Friends?

A lover?

What do I have to do to be free of this curse?

Would I have to die?

Brian

What does it feel like to die?

Well, I can't really tell you because I was never actually dead. Okay, maybe I was for a few minutes, at least by legal and medical definitions. But to me, death is the end of life, and what happened to me was anything but the end. My soul lived. Untethered from my earthly body, but alive in every sense of the word.

I felt emotions—I felt hope. Hope for a future that would be much brighter thanks to us and the sacrifices we made for the people we loved. Hope for a world recovering from the brink of extinction. And I felt love—love for my son, Solus, and love for the beautiful, selfless woman I gave up everything for. Alice. My Alice.

After Solus revived me, I began to understand how very limited and fragile our mortal bodies were. I was human again—and I'd lost the ability to heal. Life is a gift, and we only have so much time to live it.

My heart is fixed, but there's another hole in me now because I know what it's like to be invincible. How powerful and endless the soul really is. Alice was wrong to think I had left her, because even in death, I was going to stay by her side. My energy and hers, always together, even if she couldn't see me. She'd feel me—guarding her while I waited for my chance for our colorful souls to reunite.

Now that I had heard the true nature of Kareena's feelings, it was harder for me to look away. But I had to.

Day one of school, she'd been there. Even before Alice had touched me. But I thought she was just trying to sample the new menu. A superficial fetish. I never knew she actually had genuine feelings for me. That she... *loved* me.

But David had a point. Kareena didn't have to be a bitch

about everything. No matter what feelings she had for me, she didn't have to treat *everyone* like crap.

I wonder if I'll ever see David again.

We hit a rough patch in the beginning, but I grew to like him. He held some small admiration for me in his heart over my relationship with Alice, I think. I sometimes noticed it in the way he looked at us. It wasn't jealously. Just... awe.

He wanted to be loved, and he was—by his beautiful daughter, Lucy.

Even the strongest man needs love to keep him going. I know this better than anyone.

Alice

People say children are our future. That they will lead the way to a better tomorrow. That the things we teach them—the lives we show them how to live—will shape the destiny of mankind for centuries to come.

It's never been truer than it is today.

Our son, Solus, changed the world. He wasn't just a child of circumstance, he was a child of love.

I've been thinking about what Kareena said to David—about not wanting Brian anymore—and it got me thinking about how our love had changed over the years.

I fell in love with Brian early on.

Earlier than I should have, maybe.

Before he opened up his notebooks and showed me his sacred drawings.

Before the dance that changed him. That changed *us*.

Before the night his light made my skin tingle and my heart flutter, and the kiss that left me dizzy and sick with happiness.

We didn't expect or want a child so soon, but it happened, and we didn't let it tear us apart. We grew closer. Stronger.

I don't know how long it will be before we can make a new life for ourselves, but we'll figure something out. It's going to be hard—probably the hardest time we'll ever face in our entire life.

But nothing will stand in our way. Together, we stopped our world from dying. We did something amazing. We saved David's life and we saved his daughter years of sorrow from not having a father to love her.

Our son changed the future.

Some people believe teens can't fall in love. Not for real,

at least. But Brian and I have a child—one who needs us to stay together. A beautiful, radiant child with glistening green and blue eyes. With light brown hair that mirrors his father's and a chubby, round face like an angel.

A fluorescent angel.

Now there's a little part of him in all of us.

And in *you*.

A NOVEL
DARK DIARY
P. ANASTASIA

Worlds collide when a young woman with a dark past encounters a young man with an even darker one. More human than vampire, *Dark Diary* is a quaint, sophisticated romance detailing the accounts of two lovers who have paid **the *ultimate price...***

A forbidden romance in the vein of classics like *Wuthering Heights*, frosted with the seductive allure of the original *Dark Shadows*, Dark Diary documents a pair torn apart by time. The story is told by a 400-year-old immortal and a 21-year-old modern-day artist.

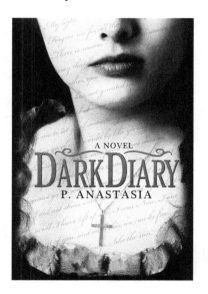

He's trapped in a never-ending circle of guilt over the loss of a friend and lover—the daughter of an English Baron in 17th century Ireland.

She's haunted nightly by visions of her own untimely death.

Together, they find solace by sharing secrets beneath the light of the moon.

WWW.DARKDIARYNOVEL.COM
VISIT THE WEBSITE FOR A FREE PREVIEW!

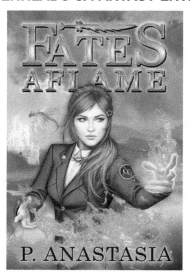
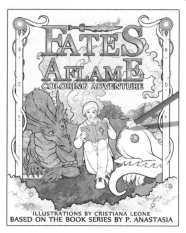